The Glister Journals

Book 2

B B Shepherd

China Blue Publishing

Paperback ISBN   978-0-9828936-8-5
Ebook   ISBN   978-0-9828936-9-2

Contents

Chapter One

Summer vacation, 2009
Los Angeles, California

I'm sure it takes a person of considerable character to wear a layer of ketchup with poise and good humor, so it's a good thing my aunt Audrey wore it and not me.

Weeks before, when I'd found out about my parents' summer trip, I was unhappy. Not because I wasn't going with them, but because I'd have to leave my relatively new home in Douglas and everything I loved there. At least, I'd been unhappy until I learned my two best friends wouldn't be staying either.

Robin was staying with an aunt, something she apparently did every summer. She'd avoided telling me more, but she didn't seem happy about going away either. I assumed it was because she had to leave her horse, Galahad, as well as her grandmother. All I knew was that she'd be staying somewhere south of Los Angeles, where I'd be. I hoped we could meet up somehow.

The Calderas, Dave's family, apparently took long vacations most summers visiting extended family. This year they were staying at his uncle's ranch on Oahu. I was sure he, and probably his little brother Henry and their dad, too, were in heaven being able to surf whenever they wanted. It made me smile to think of that. It was so easy to picture Dave soaking wet, hair windswept—dark and wavy from water—brown eyes shining, lips curved in a smile. Not the ice-meltingly charming one, or the crooked one, or the dangerous one that always made me weak in the knees. No, the gentle smile that seemed reserved for me. Well, me and his littlest brother, Stevey.

And that right there had been my biggest problem all last year. I knew Dave loved his little brother, but that didn't mean he loved me. Not the way I wished he did. He was fond of me, I was sure of it, and that was supposed to be enough but—things change.

Me, for instance. I thought I'd changed a lot on the inside last year, but I'd be starting my sophomore year looking different too. I thought it was a good thing. I hoped it was.

I hadn't grown any taller, which was a huge relief, but I wasn't as skinny as I'd been at the beginning of freshman year. I'd gained some weight when I started riding regularly and actually had some muscle now. I guess I'd eaten better too, though I hadn't been aware of it. Eating isn't something I think about much. My clothes definitely didn't fit the same way. Some didn't really fit at all anymore, and it wasn't because of muscle. I was especially thrilled that there was a more distinct difference between my hips and waist. I still didn't have the more developed figure of my friend Melanie—my standard for beauty—or of my friend here in Los Angeles, Brenda. But I thought the change in mine was noticeable.

Grandma noticed. "She's filled out a bit," she said to Aunt Kate as if I weren't in the room. "Boys will find her much more interesting now."

Grandma was very conscious of my lack of a real boyfriend, but I'm not sure why. I wasn't even fifteen and a half yet, and it seemed to be her primary concern for me. But I'd never been very interested in *boys*. There was only one boy's opinion I cared about.

Another big—no *enormous*—change was my eyesight. The first week in Los Angeles, before my parents left on their trip, I had eye surgery to correct my astigmatism. Dad's company could now afford better medical benefits, so I could have corrective surgery for at least a part of my vision challenges. It had been a major decision on my part. I hate any medical places, and just the thought of the surgery and someone messing around with my eyes gave me panic attacks. But I wanted to do it anyway. Between that and some post-traumatic shock symptoms leftover from my recent riding accident, the first couple of weeks in Los Angeles weren't fun at all and I barely slept.

Dave had called the day after we got to Los Angeles to tell me that Remmy, the horse he'd given me on my birthday, was safe and sound at Bar 8 Guest Ranch and happily flirting with the girl wranglers. That made me laugh. His call gave me the courage to call him back the next day. I thought maybe I should tell him about the surgery.

"Not satisfied with breaking your ribs, huh? Looking for new ways to be the center of attention?"

"It's hardly the same," I said, not sure if he was serious, "and I don't want to be the center of anything. Besides, my eyes are supposed to heal quickly. And my side already feels a lot better."

He laughed. "I'm kidding. Just giving you a hard time."

That made me happy. I'd been a little envious of Robin when I'd first met them. They'd been friends for so long, were obviously comfortable together, and teased and bantered with each other all the time. Maybe this was how that felt.

"So, do you still have to wear glasses?"

"The surgery will correct a specific problem," I said. "I'll still need glasses for reading."

"Hnh," he said, but I couldn't tell whether he thought that was good or bad.

He had called again right after the surgery to see how I was, and we talked a little. Phone calls with Dave are never long. Considering how much he seems to love being surrounded by people, he's not overly talkative most of the time, which is fine with me. Neither am I. But it was comforting to know he was thinking of me, at least at that moment.

I'm still so nervous talking to him, especially over the phone. I have a hard time knowing when it's my turn to speak, and sometimes it's difficult to process what I hear. And it's hard to talk to someone like Dave if you can't see their face or read their eyes. It's challenging for me to look at people's eyes, but not his. Not usually. I've never known anyone with such expressive eyes. Well, maybe my horse friends, Gold and Remmy. And, I guess, his older brother, Cris. Of course, talking to Dave face-to-face is also difficult. My heart feels like it beats harder when I'm close to him, probably because I have an unfortunate tendency to hold my breath. I just forget to breathe. I worry that he can hear or even *feel* how hard my heart is beating.

His last call had been two days before his family left for Hawaii, just before I stayed with Audrey. I tried calling him a couple of times after that, but the calls didn't go through. I couldn't even leave a message. I still didn't know if Cris had come home or if he'd at least called his family. He had disappeared right before I'd left Douglas, not telling his family where he was going, and I was angry about that. But I felt bad that I hadn't thought to ask about him before. Dave had sounded happy enough, though. Nothing too drastic could have happened.

I talked to Robin before she left, too, but couldn't get in touch with her after that. It felt like when she'd avoided talking to me around Christmas, but I was pretty sure I hadn't made her mad again. Maybe she'd just forgotten her charger.

Melanie was the one I talked to the most, and we spoke briefly about once a week while I was gone. She seemed very busy with shows and training. I told her about the mostly mundane things I was doing, but she always sounded interested.

We stayed the whole first week with my grandparents while my eyes healed. My old glasses didn't work for me anymore, and things were still a little blurry, so I couldn't do much at first. But after a few days, my middle vision became clear and focused. Amazing! I wouldn't get my new glasses for a couple of weeks, but we chose the frames before my parents left. I got two pairs, just for reading: a light pink wire pair and a much thicker, black-framed pair.

"Why do you want those?" Mom objected. "You should get another pair of wire ones. They look so pretty. Maybe a different color?"

But I could picture Dave's eyes alight with laughter when I'd worn my old dorky glasses. "No, I want these," I said, studying my face in a mirror and smiling. "They'll be better around horses."

Mom seemed to accept that. The ophthalmologist suggested I get contacts for the first time, too, and Mom agreed, but I wasn't sure how I felt about putting things in my eyes.

So my eyesight was the change that affected me the most. I still needed glasses sometimes but not for just walking around. It was so liberating! And I could finally *clearly* see what I looked like without glasses. I thought I looked all right, at *least* all right, but I wasn't a good judge.

The best thing was that I wouldn't even have to wear contacts when riding. I tend to be accident-prone, so not having to worry about falling off a horse with glasses on would let us all breathe a little easier. My parents were still uneasy about my sudden proclivity for all things equine, but there were no horses handy in West LA, and I wasn't allowed to ride again yet anyway. I was on restricted activity while my ribs healed from the accident in early June.

My distance vision was still questionable, and I still had problems with spatial awareness—not in an artistic sense, but relational to my own body. But I could live with that. I always had. My ophthalmologist said that my eyes weren't the problem anyway. It had something to do with the way my brain communicated to my body. He said it might cause problems when I learned to drive. That didn't make much of an impression on me. I felt no need to drive.

If nothing else, there was one thing I was sure everyone would notice immediately: my hair. It had always been long. Not for any religious or cultural reasons. It had just always been that way, and I'd never had a desire to change. It had been one of my defining physical features. I'd always been "the tall, skinny girl with glasses and *really* long hair." I usually wore it in one long braid, but when I began riding, it became a nuisance at best and at worst seemed out to kill me.

Now it was gone. Not all of it, of course. I hadn't shaved my head or anything. But that's what we'd been doing the day of the ketchup explosion.

After my parents left on their trip, I went to stay the second week with Mom's older sister, Katharine, and her family. I always felt especially awkward around her. She wanted me to babysit while I was there—a task that caused me more than usual anxiety. Added to everything else, it wasn't an enjoyable stay, and I slept very little.

During the third week, I stayed with Audrey, my mother's younger sister and my favorite aunt. She has two small children that reminded me a lot of my riding coach's kids, who I love. Audrey's kids are a little older than Cheryl's, and more rambunctious and quarrelsome with each other, but they're comfortable around me and I wasn't expected to babysit. We got along just fine.

The first day at Audrey's, we relaxed around their pool. I love to swim but wasn't supposed to open my eyes underwater so soon after the surgery, so I floated on my back or played in the shallow end with the kids.

The next day we went to the beach. When it comes to watery places, I much prefer the beach. In fact, when it comes to almost *any* place, I much prefer the beach. The smell of the surf; the relaxing sound of waves; breezes by turn tickling and caressing my skin; the feeling of hot sand between my toes as I dig them in deep. Sitting on the beach, I imagined a cosmic connection all the way to Hawaii to the most important person in my universe, though I knew he wouldn't be doing the same. He rarely sat still long enough, and I highly doubted he thought of me much.

After a couple more days at home, Aunt Audrey said, "We should go out. Let's get our nails done and have lunch. We can go shopping." She bent her head conspiratorially closer to mine, though no one else was there but the children, and whispered, "Your mom left some money for school clothes. I'm thinking, 'new wardrobe.'"

She made it sound like fun and I readily agreed.

We dropped the kids off at Grandma's and headed to Audrey's favorite salon. I usually don't take any special care of my nails. I try to keep them short—when I think about them at all—as they tend to break while grooming, saddling, and doing other things around horses. It's rare that they're completely clean either, which sounds kind of gross but is just the reality of my new lifestyle. But during the past couple of weeks—horseless—my nails had not only stayed clean but had a chance to grow. Getting my nails done didn't seem like a complete waste of time.

It had been a very long time since I'd been anywhere near a salon, and I'd forgotten how much the smells bothered me. When I was little, my grandmother took care of me while my parents both worked and she'd taken me with her for her weekly hair appointments. I'd hated it. The aerosols, perfumes, and other chemical smells were overwhelming, making my nose burn, my eyes water, my throat constrict. I'd always ended up very cranky with a headache, even nauseated, but could never communicate the reason to her.

Today I was determined to muscle through for Audrey's sake and the pursuit of girliness—the latter also being something I'd previously rarely thought about. Now, I'd take all the help I could get.

Audrey and I sat at neighboring manicure stations. I had a hard time relaxing and not flinching and squirming every time the lady took one of my hands. I really can't stand to be touched by strangers.

"Your hair is so long!" my manicurist observed. "How long have you been growing it?"

I thought she meant the actual length of my hair, so I didn't answer right away. Wasn't it obvious?

Audrey said, "Most of your life. Right, Allison?"

I nodded.

"You've *never* cut it?" asked the woman. She seemed horrified, which made me feel guilty. Had I been depriving people of employment all this time?

"Just a little, once in a while."

But Audrey smiled. "Have you ever thought about getting it cut? *Really* cut?"

Somewhere in the back of my mind, yes, I had thought of it, especially in the past year for various reasons. But apart from my aversion to salons, not liking strangers touching me, and not liking change in general, an easy opportunity had never presented itself. "Maybe," I said.

"It would look so cute shorter. Wouldn't it be easier to take care of, too?"

"Probably."

"What do you think?" she said. "Do you want to? We could do it today!" She said to my manicurist, "Do you think someone could squeeze her in this morning?"

I started to feel nervous and railroaded, but it also did seem like the perfect opportunity. While the woman went to speak to the receptionist about the availability of stylists, I wrestled with whether I was ready to make such a big change in my appearance. *Will it look all right? What will my parents think?* Mom probably wouldn't mind. *What will my friends think?* I couldn't imagine Robin or Melanie caring. They'd probably like it, or at least say they did. *What will—*

The manicurist returned, now all smiles. Maybe she hadn't been angry before. "They can slip you in as soon as we're done here. Would you like to?"

Banishing thoughts of Dave and what he would or wouldn't like, I said, "Yes. Yes, I would."

So, as my final coat of light pearly blue dried, I was led to a hairdresser's station. Two more stylists came over, and everyone exclaimed and commented on the length of my hair as it was unbraided.

"How much are we cutting off?" the stylist asked.

"Not *too* short," I said, wondering if I was doing the right thing and watching Audrey's reflection in the mirror. She was now unhelpfully reticent but seemed to be enjoying herself.

The stylist scissored her fingers on my hair just below my right ear. "About here?"

I tried to imagine my hair that short and started to panic.

"How about here?" she said, sliding her fingers down a couple of inches.

I shook my head. I thought of Melanie and how beautiful her hair was. Mine would never have the vibrant color or luxurious waves of hers, but I liked the length.

"Maybe just below my shoulders?" I said, almost a whisper.

The stylist let more hair glide through her fingers. I could see Audrey's reflection smiling and nodding. The other stylists were nodding too.

"Yes," I said, trying to feel as sure as I sounded. I closed my eyes.

My hair was rebraided, banded, and held firmly for a moment, and then a length of it, about two feet, lay forlornly on the counter in front of me. I had a sudden vision, a memory, of sitting on my bed, long strands of my hair clinging to Dave as he held me. My eyes stung for a moment until I got a grip on myself.

It's just hair!

Aunt Audrey said we could donate it to Locks of Love, which made me feel much better, and she kept the braid. My hair was now just below my shoulders—a little longer than Robin's had been the last time I'd seen her and a little shorter than Melanie kept hers. I wasn't expecting the highlights, though.

I usually wore my hair pulled straight back from my brow, and I suppose the top of my head got more sun, especially in the past few months. But now that my hair was shorter and loose, the lighter parts were very noticeable: ashy, almost-blond streaks framing my face. It looked like I'd had it lightened. In fact, my hair looked a little lighter all over. By the time I walked out of the salon, I didn't recognize myself at all and felt very strange, as if I'd forgotten something important. Like clothes. And I felt like I was floating. Not that my hair had been that heavy, but it had been such a part of me. Now it was gone.

Shorter hair. No glasses. Long blue nails. I didn't look like me.

"You look adorable," said Audrey. I almost blushed but successfully redirected my thoughts. She was my aunt. She was supposed to say things like that, right? "Let's go get lunch. Are you hungry?"

I really was. We went to a restaurant I'd been to many times when we lived in Los Angeles, which made me feel slightly more at ease. But it was disorienting every time I caught my reflection in anything.

A waiter with a name tag that said "Guy" came and took our order. We both ordered burgers and fries. The waiter smiled widely and assured us he'd be right back.

"He's cute," said Audrey. "He thinks you're cute, too."

"What?" I said, startled.

"Really!" she said, her eyes laughing.

"No, he doesn't. He probably thinks *you're* cute," I countered. Aunt Audrey was pretty and young-looking.

"Come on, don't tell me you don't think he's cute," she teased.

I could feel tingling in my cheeks. *No, I'm not blushing!*

I tried to shrug it off. Then I saw him talking to another waiter. Both were probably in their early twenties—too old for me and probably too young for Audrey even if she weren't married with children—and both were looking our way. Guy had brown wavy hair and a charming smile. He reminded me a little of Dave except much taller. And older. And paler. And *not* Dave. I looked back at Audrey and tried to keep track of what she was saying.

"Here you go, ladies," said the guy named Guy, placing our orders before us carefully and looking at me a little too long. "Let me know if you need anything. Anything at all," he added earnestly.

"Oh dear," said Audrey, after he'd gone. "I'm afraid you do look older than you did before. We'll be beating the boys off now. We'll have to carry a stick."

Not listening . . . blah, blah, blah, blah . . .

I was so tired of stupid blushes.

I picked up the ketchup bottle and shook it over the side of my plate, but it was almost empty and what was left seemed to be stuck in the neck. Almost immediately, Guy was back.

"Here, let me get you a new one," he said, taking the bottle from me and disappearing again.

"Mmhmm," murmured Audrey, a sly grin on her face.

"Stop," I said, frowning but trying not to smile. He did seem very attentive.

Guy came back and offered a full bottle to me. "Here you go."

"Thank you very much," I said, trying to appear very polite and mature for some idiotic reason.

He beamed back at both of us and retreated again. I took the lid off the new bottle and shook it over my plate with no success. The ketchup wasn't budging.

"Sometimes it helps to tap it really hard first," said Audrey.

I replaced the lid and pounded it against my palm a few times then tried it again. It still didn't move, so I hit the bottom of the bottle.

And that's how Audrey ended up wearing ketchup.

"Oh!" I exclaimed.

"Ah!" she shouted at the same time, her mouth and eyes wide in shock.

"I'm so sorry!" I said, suddenly shaky and trying not to get upset.

But Audrey's wide-eyed shock immediately turned into a laugh so contagious that I couldn't help laughing too. Then Guy and people at several nearby tables were laughing as well. Audrey laughed so hard she was wiping tears from her eyes.

"I've always wanted some of your artwork," she said, still laughing and crying. "This isn't exactly what I had in mind. But now I have an Allison original!"

"Early abstract period," I said.

She laughed even harder and so did I. Guy had been laughing with us but now disappeared.

"Well, now we *have* to go shopping," she said, trying to stop laughing. "I can't imagine why I thought I'd need it, but it's a good thing I brought a sweater."

She excused herself and headed toward the restroom. Guy returned with wet and dry cloths and wiped the table and the back of the booth where Audrey had been sitting.

"I'm sorry I made a mess," I said, feeling awkward.

"No problem," Guy smiled back. "You're lucky that your sister has such a good sense of humor. Mine would have murdered me."

"Oh," I said, feeling confused and even more awkward. "She's not my sister. She's my aunt."

"Really? You look a lot like each other."

I'd never been compared to Audrey before. I looked at him closely, trying to tell if he was being serious or just flattering me. He appeared to be sincere.

"Thank you," I said, and meant it.

He gazed back at me and paused as if he would say more. As Audrey returned, he looked around quickly as if remembering where he was, smiled again, and left with the ketchup covered cloths. Audrey was now wearing her twin-set cardigan buttoned up. I thought she looked even younger and prettier.

"Guy thought you were my sister," I teased her.

"Yes, I saw you flirting again," she teased right back.

"What? No I wasn't!"

"Why not?"

"He's too . . . I'm not . . ."

"Oh, I see," she said. "There's someone already. Poor Guy."

"No," I denied. "Not really." This was still a subject of great confusion for me—why I felt so fiercely loyal and attached to Dave when he didn't seem to feel the same way. I brooded over my French fries and Audrey changed the subject.

"Have a nice day, ladies," said Guy when he gave us the check. "Maybe I'll . . . see you around?"

I pictured the places I expected to go while in Los Angeles and wondered if it was likely. I highly doubted it. But Audrey smiled brightly and said, "You never know. . . ." which seemed to make him happy. I tried to smile and we left.

The afternoon was fun, Audrey having an eye for a bargain as well as great taste in clothes. She also had a good sense of what I liked—comfortable and feminine without being too frou-frou or revealing—so I didn't waste time trying on things I wouldn't like. Between the money my parents had given Audrey and some things she insisted on paying for herself, by mid-afternoon I had two bathing suits—which even I thought I looked cute in—and most of my back-to-school clothes. Audrey tried on some things too, but I think it was mainly so I wouldn't think she was bored. I had money of my own but was trying not to spend it. It was going to be a long summer.

After dinner that night I retreated to the guest bedroom and tried to call Robin and then Dave again with no luck.

For most of the fourth week, I stayed with Brenda. She had been my only close, longtime friend growing up, and we'd kept in touch after I moved away. But we'd both changed so much—or at least I had. It was sometimes difficult to remember exactly *why* we were friends as we were so different. But when other kids had made fun of me, tried to get me in trouble, or physically bullied me, she had stood up for me for some reason. That hadn't made her exactly popular, which I'd always felt bad about. She made fun of me too, a *lot*, but I didn't mind most of the time. She was never *really* mean.

I was up early at Grandma's the day they picked me up. Some of my new clothes were packed along with everything else I thought I'd need for a week at Brenda's house. The important things—the *most* important things I owned besides Remmy—were put away and safe in my backpack:

The frilly pink and gold scrunchy that Robin had given me for Christmas along with the rose-colored and scented candle. I didn't plan on using the candle while I was away, but the two items reminded me of her, and the scent of the candle reminded me of my room at home. It was comforting.

The picture of me riding Corona de Oro, my dear Andalusian friend who I'd called Gold. Cris had taken a video of me riding him bareback and then printed and framed a still for my birthday. If not for that proof, I could have thought I'd imagined it all. It had been a very thoughtful thing for him to do. He really surprised me sometimes.

The pictures that Estephanie, Gold's new owner, had sent of them both.

The leather-bound journal Aunt Audrey had given me two Christmases ago. Inside was a silly list I had started making when I was first getting to know—and falling hopelessly in love with—Dave. I was recording the past year's experiences in the journal. It helped keep everything fresh in my memory. And in perspective. I needed to remember the things that *hadn't* happened, too.

My yearbook helped me feel connected to all my friends, especially since I seemed to have temporarily lost contact with the two most important of them. Being back in Los Angeles made the past year, the good *and* the bad,

Copper

seem like a dream. The pictures and comments in the book were proof of my friends and life in Douglas.

Robin, her head tilted slightly, almost haughtily, but her eyes and lips smiling mischievously. It was a great picture and made me smile to look at it. Dave had prompted that expression.

Melanie, her beautiful features strangely diminished by the black and white photograph. She didn't look entirely well.

Matthew. I liked him because he didn't make me feel awkward and never pointed it out. In fact, he often glossed over it. He had a good sense of humor, too. I appreciated that.

I also had color photos of these three in my wallet.

Tanner, Kyle, Stacie, and Jessie had all written friendly comments with a personal touch, more than just, *"Have a nice summer."*

Dave, of course; the most important of all. There were several pictures of him scattered throughout the book: soccer team, track team, action shots at specific games and meets, and Best Smile. That last one was shared with Hannah Liu and they were entirely too close, which made it a little harder to like. He'd defaced his freshman photo with facial hair and spectacles. I could have killed him—but not really. It made me smile too. If anyone had a right to think highly of himself, it was Dave, but he wasn't arrogant like that. At least, not *too* much.

Cris was the only one of our group who hadn't signed my yearbook, though I hadn't specifically asked him to, and we weren't exactly friends. I was never sure what we were. It seemed to change according to the situation. Unlike our freshman photos, his junior picture was in color—his features a deep golden tan and his light brown hair tipped almost white by the previous summer's sun. He stared at the camera unsmiling, a neutral, cold expression that seemed unnatural. I was much more used to his frown if not deep scowl. *And yet*—I'd seen old photos of him smiling, his face bright and happy.

Later in the morning, Brenda and her stylish, celebrity-obsessed mother, Nicole, came to pick me up. They both exclaimed excitedly over my hair and the fact that I wasn't wearing glasses. Nicole wears me out pretty quickly, but Grandma loves her. While they had a cup of coffee and caught up with each other, Brenda and I escaped to the back yard.

"Wow," said Brenda, now looking at me very critically. "I can't believe I only saw you a few weeks ago. You look so different."

I searched her face, trying to tell if she approved or not. It shouldn't have mattered—I thought I'd gone beyond caring too much what she thought of me—but it *did* matter. She was the first of my friends to see my external changes. I was still feeling odd about them myself.

"Different good or different bad?"

"Oh, good. Definitely. You don't look like such a nerd. I could almost be jealous, especially with that cute guy you've got."

"*Brenda*," I said warningly.

Earlier in the summer, she had given me a hard time about Dave, even before she had seen him. After she'd met him, she even acted a little jealous. Of course, there was no reason for that.

"I know, I know . . . *'We're just friends.'* " she said in a mocking tone. "Still no action after I left? Not even a kiss goodbye?"

I refused to react to this. The last days and moments I'd spent with Dave were precious to me: the perfect day at the beach; the day he came over seeking *me* when he was worried about his brother; saying goodbye to him the day I left.

"Okay," she said, relenting. "I won't tease you about him. I'd like to see the look on his face when he sees you again, though. Have you talked to him? Did you tell him you cut your hair?"

Of course, I hadn't talked to him recently, but I wouldn't have told him anyway. It would have felt silly, like I expected him to care whether I'd cut my hair or not. *Which I don't. No.*

"I told him about my surgery," I said, feeling the need to establish that we *had* been communicating, even if it hadn't been in the past week or so.

I almost wanted to ask her about Trevor, her on-again, off-again boyfriend of the past year, but I didn't want to bring up a potentially painful topic. Brenda looked at me hard as if reading my mind. She changed the subject and we left soon after.

I hadn't been to Brenda's new house before. Her dad was a financial planner and had apparently built up quite an impressive clientele. The family had moved to a more affluent west side neighborhood about the same time my family had moved to Douglas. I think Brenda might have held this over me as a difference in status if she hadn't known my dad could have chosen to do the same as hers. Instead, my dad had always poured most of his share of profit back into his company and decided to move us away from Los Angeles. The company itself was still in transition but had mostly moved to an area outside Sacramento. We lived even further northeast in the foothills of the Sierra Nevadas.

I was *so* thankful. Nothing appealed to me here in the Los Angeles area. The only thing I missed was going to the beach: the tang of salt, soft breezes, the soothing sound of the waves. We lived so far from it now that I rarely got to go. But the rest—the smog, traffic, billboards, neon and building and street lights, the crowds of people, and especially the constant noise—I was happy to live without them. I *loved* my new home in Douglas.

Brenda's house wasn't a huge mansion, unlike some of the homes we'd passed, but it was large and in a well-maintained neighborhood in the hills near Brentwood. A heavy iron gate opened by remote, and we parked just in front of the house, a white, two-story, old Spanish stucco secluded from the street and next-door neighbors by thick trees and shrubs.

Brenda took my bag and led me inside and then straight up a staircase against the right wall. A large crystal chandelier hung from the open ceiling over the entryway, and large, garish paintings ornamented every wall. Brenda led me down a short hallway to a room on the left, one of the guest rooms.

"My room's right there," she said, indicating an open door across the hall.

I could see a large four-post bed with a flounced canopy and bedclothes that were covered with articles of clothing. Clothes littered what I could see of the floor, too. Same old Brenda.

My room was comfortably and, I was relieved to see, modestly decorated. No frilly bed coverings, no fancy wallpaper, no breakable knick-knacks. Compared to those I'd already seen, the paintings were small, delicately colored, and probably worth far less, if anything at all. I liked them much better.

"Put your stuff down. You can unpack later," said Brenda. "Come on."

I followed her back down the short hallway and along a longer hallway to the right. The first door was a bathroom.

"Guest bathroom, but you can use mine if you want." She paused and amended, "Unless it's the middle of the night. Or if we want to shower at the same time. Or . . ." Obviously thinking through other exceptions, she said, "Maybe you should just use this one."

I tried not to laugh. "Sure. That's fine." She had been the first guest in my new home. It looked like I was first in hers.

"This is Mom's sewing and crafts room," she said, showing me a very tidy room that didn't look used at all. "Those are more guest rooms," she said, waving toward more doors to either side. Then she stopped at a set of double doors. She knocked but there was no answer. "This is my mom's . . . my *parent's* room," she said, opening the doors wide.

The room was bigger than my family's living room and occupied most of the upper back of the house. Large windows on the back wall had filmy chiffon sheers that let in plenty of light. French doors stood open to the outside, their matching translucent coverings floating around in a soft breeze like something from an air freshener commercial. Everything was white—pretty, but somewhat antiseptic.

"Wow," I said. "It's really . . . big."

"Yeah," said Brenda, almost skipping to the open back doors. "I *love* this room. And look . . ." She led the way outside onto a huge, partially covered balcony. "It's great for sunbathing out here!"

Most of it was open, occupied by padded chairs, chaise lounges, and an umbrellaed table, making a perfect sundeck. The edge of the balcony was bounded by an ornate but aging cement balustrade that continued down a stairway. Leo, Brenda's old German Shepherd, got up stiffly from a spot in the sun and came to greet me. I gave him a hug and he licked my face.

The back yard area was less impressive. A swimming pool occupied about half of it but, as the rest of the yard was overgrown and wild, there was a lot of debris floating in it and material lurked at the bottom.

"We can swim after lunch if you want," she said.

"Sure," I said, but I felt a little uneasy. I had a problem with things floating in pools. Maybe it was because of my eyesight. I couldn't always tell if it was plant material or things with legs. Either of those things creeped me out anyway. Just thinking about it made me shudder.

The first couple of days with Brenda went by uneventfully. I never sleep well the first night anywhere away from home, but my room was quiet and the bed was comfortable, so I slept pretty well after that. We walked a lot and swam in the afternoons, though I felt it necessary to use the net first to clean as much flotsam from the pool as possible. Brenda just laughed and let me do it.

Her dad was there most evenings for dinner, but we didn't see him otherwise. I'd forgotten how uncomfortable he'd always made me feel, not for creepy reasons but because he was such a loud person. His voice, especially his laugh, boomed, which kept me pretty jumpy. It seemed like he was always shouting. But he was never around in the mornings, and I assumed he left early for work.

Both he and Nicole talked a lot at dinner. Perhaps I just misunderstood the situations, but neither seemed at all interested in what the other had to say. I didn't look forward to dinner times. Brenda seemed unconcerned, so I tried not to read too much into it. But it made me remember something else about them. I hoped for Brenda's sake that things had changed.

On the third evening, Brenda got a call from her friend, Lauren. They talked for at least an hour and it was decided that we—Lauren, Brenda, me, and three of their other friends—would go out together the next day. Brenda had told them about me and they were curious.

"I can't wait for you to meet them," she said. She proceeded to tell me about them—apparently all rich girls with "important" parents.

By morning, Brenda's excitement about my meeting her friends seemed to have been replaced by stress. The housekeeper, who cleaned for them three times a week, had tidied Brenda's room and hung up all her clothes while we'd been swimming the day before. But Brenda had tried on so many outfits this morning that it was a disaster again already. Wanting to make a good impression for Brenda's sake, I wore what I thought was the cutest outfit I had: a pastel plaid skirt and a soft blue short-sleeved sweater that Aunt Audrey had insisted on buying for me.

"You're going to wear *that?*" asked Brenda.

I started to second-guess my choice, but there wasn't much point in considering anything else. "Yes," I said, as confidently as possible.

"Well, try not to say anything weird. And for God's sake, don't talk about horses."

I understood this to mean to not dominate conversations with topics her friends wouldn't be interested in. But I had been much better about that since early middle school. "You look nice," I said to distract her.

She frowned at herself in her mirror. "Ugh. Well, maybe I can find something cuter today."

And that's pretty much how the next few days went. Brenda stressed over my meeting and being with her other friends, and I tried to downplay everything.

That first day we met at the Beverly Center. I had assumed, from what Brenda had told me both recently and in the past, that her friends would be well dressed and attractive. And they certainly were. The white girl with short, curly brown hair was Lauren, apparently the acknowledged leader and last-word-haver. The Black girl's name was Jahzara and she was taller than me. I liked that. She seemed to be on equal footing with Lauren as far as confidence. Another girl with deep brown skin and shiny, long black hair, almost as long as mine used to be, spoke with a slight accent. The last girl was also white, very pale with chemically-helped blond hair. These other two girls were Madison and Madelyn, the latter going by Maddie. And though they looked and sounded nothing alike, I had great trouble in keeping their names straight. Luckily, the others did most of the talking and I hoped they wouldn't know.

They all scrutinized us unabashedly, quickly losing interest in Brenda and focusing, to my discomfort, on me.

I had no desire to *ooh* and *ah* over or disparage things as the others did as we wandered around, and I found the activity extremely tedious. Just watching their interactions was much more interesting. I had learned a thing or two about social order by the time I finished middle school, but I had never really thought about it until I observed pecking order in the horses at Bar 8. Just like a new horse introduced into a herd, I was an unknown entity in this group and was afforded reserved judgment. My opinion was even solicited at times, everyone's eyes riveted to me until I'd given it—not my favorite situation, though I found it humorous. In this group, Brenda was clearly at the bottom, swept along with the others but never deferred to. I honestly didn't care what they thought of me and wasn't intimidated by any of them, but I was there for Brenda and tried to behave the way I thought she wanted me to.

This included taking part in a department store make-up makeover and even getting my ears pierced. I'd never worn make-up before and was curious and willing, but the ear-piercing took some convincing. When I finally agreed, I couldn't help laughing the whole time, though I tried not to. The others seemed to find that contagious and giggled, too, which made it even harder not to laugh.

The next two days were spent mostly at the beach with the other girls. Jahzara kindly came and picked us up—in a chauffeured Cadillac SUV—and we met the other girls on a Malibu beach. I'd never been to Malibu before.

I was content to just lie in the sun, soft breezes tempering the heat. Or to sit digging my toes in the sand, closing my eyes and emptying my mind of everything else to imagine Dave on a similar beach—minus other girls—connecting to me somehow. *Is he thinking of me at all? Have I even crossed his mind?*

The only disruptions to my serenity were the occasional arguments the other girls got into and the contempt they sometimes seemed to treat each other with, especially Brenda. Goodness knew Brenda could be demanding and needy, but most of these girls were far worse than her and didn't conceal their impatience well. I caught several interactions between the other four after things Brenda had said, rolling their eyes or shaking their heads when she wasn't looking. I knew what it was like to be the cause of such disdain and felt bad for her.

They were curious about me, though.

"You used to live around here?" asked Jahzara.

"Not around here," I said, not sure if she was talking about Malibu. "We lived in Santa Monica."

This, apparently, was an acceptable answer. It preserved at least the *possibility* of us having money and status.

"What do your parents do?" asked the pale girl.

This question surprised me. No one in Douglas had ever asked it. "My dad is partner in a company . . . robotic systems and programming."

They seemed impressed. I didn't enlighten them that it was nowhere near *Fortune 500* listed, nor that my mom was a lifeguard at the local pool.

"Cool!" said the darker girl. "So, do you have all kinds of computers and robots?"

"Um . . . no," I answered, wondering what on earth she was thinking. "There aren't any actual, you know, humanoid robots involved."

She looked disappointed.

"Do you have a boyfriend?" asked Lauren.

Of course, the answer to this was a simple no. But I sensed this might be a loaded question, the answer weighing for or against their final verdict of me. I didn't care; I wasn't likely to see them again after this summer. But

Brenda would. I glanced at her. Her eyes widened slightly, meaningfully. I wished I knew what it meant.

"I have guy *friends*," I said, not sure if this was acceptable. At least it was true.

They seemed to approve so far.

"Nobody special?" asked Jahzara.

"Yes," I said. "There's a boy I like." This seemed safe, though it was an absurd understatement.

"But he's dating someone else?"

"Oh . . . no. Nothing like that." But I suddenly realized I didn't know if that were still true. Vaguely imagined girls in Hawaii were some of the things I was trying *not* to think about.

The girls looked expectant.

"So what's stopping you?" asked Lauren.

He hasn't asked me. Something told me this would not be an acceptable answer. These were the kind of girls that went after what they wanted—whatever it was. The kind of girls that did seem to have Dave's attention a lot of the time. Disheartened, I cast about for a suitable reply.

"His brother's *fine*," Brenda said, perhaps to buy me time. The other girls all looked at her.

"You've met them?" asked the darker girl.

"Yeah. Her *friend*," she couldn't resist saying this with emphasis and a droll expression, "is definitely hot. But his *brother*. . . ." She didn't finish the sentence but I assumed she was intimating that Cris was even hotter. I didn't think so, but that wasn't the point. She certainly had the other girls' attention now.

"What does he look like?" asked Lauren.

Brenda described him accurately enough, I suppose, though I would have had trouble picturing Cris from her description alone. I guess I just didn't see him the same way. "He's eighteen," she added.

"He won't be eighteen until August," I said, surprised I remembered when his birthday was. His age probably didn't matter, but I couldn't help saying it.

"You should try to go out with *him*," said the pale girl.

That was the silliest thing I'd heard anybody say all summer, including Aunt Audrey's remarks about Guy and ketchup art. But they seemed to

be expecting me to respond, so I said, "My dad won't let me date until I'm sixteen. That won't be until January." That was true too.

This also seemed to be a satisfactory answer. Brenda looked grateful but I had no idea why. That conversation started a new one about all the "hot" boys at *their* school, who was or wasn't boyfriend material, and who was dating who or who *wanted* to date who. I couldn't tell if any or all of these boys were actual friends of theirs or not—it didn't seem like they cared about them or even really knew them—but I had mostly checked out of the discussion anyway. My eyes were on the horizon, toes rooted in the sand, seeking connection.

Then Lauren said, "Oh! You'll never guess who I saw on Monday." They all tried to guess, unsuccessfully. "Trevor Adams. He was with that Benedict witch, Victoria."

"Witch" wasn't what she really called her, and I had no idea what "Benedict" signified. Her last name? A school? I recognized the boy's name, though. I looked at Brenda. She looked a little sick. Didn't they know? That was answered a moment later.

"Oh, Brenda," said Lauren. "I'm sorry. I completely forgot you went out with him for a while last year."

Brenda rallied and managed a smile. "Yeah. But that was *last* year."

The other girls seemed to approve of her answer for some reason, but I was really proud of her. Whether Lauren had actually forgotten or not, the comment had hurt her, but she obviously wasn't going to let them know. I was really starting to question her friendship with these girls, though.

Back at her house, I tried to ask her about it; did she have any other friends? She laughed off her friends' attitudes and comments and said she didn't really care. She just liked hanging out with them. "Besides, if they didn't like me, they wouldn't bother with me at all. Right?"

I wasn't so sure. I couldn't understand their behavior on any level.

My remaining time in Los Angeles, all but the last few days before my parents came back, I spent with my grandparents. I was having difficulty sleeping again, sometimes waking with a start, my heart beating uncomfortably fast. Even the smells of the different houses I stayed in kept me awake. I missed the smell of my own home, the smell of grass and trees—warm and fragrant in the hot months, crisp and tingling in the cold—and the fresh smell of the stream that ran along the back of our property. I missed the smell of horses and hay.

I missed Dave—everything about him.

Grandma sometimes gave me little chores to do for her, which I didn't mind, but she didn't actually talk with me much. I didn't doubt her love, but she'd never seemed interested in who I really was. Grandpa always smiled kindly at me but seemed to have even less to say. This made me sad. It hadn't always been that way.

My grandfather and I had been very close when I was little. I had talked even less back then. I'd learned to read very early, and he had worked on language and played word games with me. He'd helped me understand similes and metaphors and the odd words and phrases people sometimes used that made no sense to me. He used a lot of them himself. And he'd taught me about butterflies from his extensive collection. I suppose it was understandable that my earliest remembered interest was butterflies. But I don't have the same interests now—I'd lost my fascination with butterflies after an incident in middle school—and we don't seem to have much to talk about now. He prefers it when my younger cousins come over as he can play more boisterous games with them. And Grandma still doesn't think I understand much, in spite of my vocabulary.

So staying alone at my grandparents' wasn't exactly fun or emotionally comfortable. But it left me a lot of time to draw and listen to music and think and record my past year's experiences in the leather journal. The biggest problem with all the spare thinking time was that one subject, one person, dominated it. Along with remembering every glance, every word, every gesture, it was so easy to imagine how things *could* be if I only knew the right way to respond to Dave. If I only knew the right words to say.

Grandma left me to myself most of the time, though I tried to help her around the house. One day I came out of the shower to find her in my room, my journal open in her hands, flipping through the parchment pages. I was flustered that she would pry in that way, though not terribly surprised. I guess it was my fault for leaving it where she could find it.

"I came to see if you have any laundry that needs to be done. What is this?"

"It's a journal, Grandma."

"Whose journal? Someone gave you their journal?"

This seemed a nonsensical question. Then I realized it hadn't even occurred to her that it could be mine. I felt like snatching it away. I didn't want her or anyone reading what I had written, reading my deepest thoughts and longings. But I stood with my hand out and tried to stay calm. I hardly ever lied for any reason, but it just seemed the safest thing to do right now.

"Yes. It's . . . my friend's. She let me read it over the summer."

I felt horrible lying to her, but she probably would be much too interested if I told the truth. She might not believe me anyway. I sometimes think she doesn't consider me capable of much at all.

The last weekend in Los Angeles I spent with Brenda. School had already started again for her, but she had Friday afternoon off. I'd planned to stay the whole weekend at her house, but something I'd almost forgotten interrupted.

My opinion of Brenda's friends changed a little, though. On that Friday afternoon, we went to the beach again. The other girls went off for food and drinks and left Jahzara and me to watch our stuff. She was lying back on the sand with her sunglasses on. I was sitting up, watching surfers and imagining one of them was Dave.

Out of the blue, she said, "I think Brenda still likes Trevor. Do you think so?"

I thought she was right but wasn't sure if it was okay to say so. "I don't know," I said.

"He's no good for her. He's a real jerk. We've tried to tell her, but she doesn't listen."

That sounded about right.

"You've been friends a long time. Maybe you can convince her."

I was surprised. Perhaps they hadn't meant to hurt Brenda before, but to warn her. "I'll keep it in mind," I said. "She doesn't really listen to me, either."

Jahzara just nodded her head slightly.

We stayed late at the beach, watching the sun go down and the stars come out. I was going to miss this, being at the beach, when we went back home. But the closer the end of my stay in Los Angeles got, the more excited I grew. I couldn't wait to get home and to see Remmy. I'd be able to ride again now! I couldn't wait to see *everybody*.

Very early Saturday, soon after Brenda and I had finally gone to bed, war broke out downstairs. The yelling and screaming woke me up, my heart pounding, my nerves straining. Harsh, ugly words, the kind my own parents never used, the kind that felt like physical blows, were hurled back and forth. I was getting used to what Grandpa called "colorful language" from the boys at school and even Robin and other girls sometimes. But it wasn't the language that provoked my anxiety now. It was the anger behind it. Brenda's dad's voice was the loudest, but her mom fully retaliated.

This is what I had forgotten about them—her parents fought. Viciously. I sat up in the dark, listening to them verbally rip each other to shreds. After a few minutes, my door slowly opened.

"Allie? Are you awake?" Brenda whispered.

"Yes," I whispered back.

"Can I come in?"

"Of course."

She came in and closed the door, then climbed into the big bed with me as if we were little kids again. She pressed something into my hand; soft earplugs. I hate wearing earplugs. My ear canals are small and plugs are very uncomfortable, but I fitted them in as best as I could. She fell asleep way before I did.

In the morning, I called Aunt Audrey and asked if Brenda and I could come and stay the weekend with her. She seemed pleased and said yes. Brenda was subdued, but I think she had a nice time. I did.

When we dropped Brenda off at her house on Sunday evening, she said, "I'm going to miss you."

I was surprised. And touched. She'd never said anything remotely sentimental to me before.

"Call me, okay? And get that cowboy to ask you out." She smiled slightly and closed the car door, not waiting for a response.

My parents flew in on Tuesday, and we stayed at my grandparents' house until Friday morning. On Thursday night, my parents and I, both aunts and uncles, and all the kids, drove south down the coast for a barbecue. The adults sat around talking while the kids chased each other, ran away from the waves, dug in the sand, or threw Nerf footballs. Later, the men and kids gathered driftwood and started a small bonfire as the sun went down.

I sat a little distance away by myself most of the time, listening to the surf and thinking. Except for a few days at my grandparents' house, it seemed like I'd had no time entirely to myself all summer. I tried to imagine what it was going to be like back in Douglas. Back at school. *Sophomore year.* I yearned for the quiet and space of home. And my friends and Remmy, of course.

And I felt like I had changed even more, inside *and* out, than before summer. Would Dave notice? Would it make a difference in how he saw me? *Enough* of a difference? I was sure I was more confident. Except for specific causes—my eye surgery, lingering aftereffects of my accident, and the fight at Brenda's house—I hadn't felt overwhelmingly anxious about anything. And I seemed to be getting a handle on the blush. These were good things. Last year had ended up being fantastic—mostly. I was determined that if it were within my power, things would be even better this year.

Chapter Two

August, 2009
Douglas, California

We left Los Angeles early on Friday, Mom promising to call my grand-parents as soon as we got home and saying that we would see them at Thanksgiving. When we'd driven south in June, there were still hints of green everywhere. But now the countryside was brown as far as the eye could see and continuing all the way home, even though vast stretches were apparently farmland.

Unlike the long drive there, the miles now seemed to slip by quickly, and the closer to home we got, the greater my anticipation. As we drew closer and closer to Douglas, the smallest landmarks were a thrill to see, every familiar swell and dip in the landscape a comfort. I was *so* relieved to be coming home.

I would have been happiest if Dad had driven straight to Bar 8 Ranch and just left me there while he and Mom went home to relax. I wanted to see Remmy so badly. I also wanted a solid connection. Though I had many dear memories of Dave at my house, Bar 8 held safer, more neutral associations. That was all I needed right now.

But Dad insisted I unpack and eat—as if I cared about that—and then he would drive me over to see Remmy and make arrangements to bring him home.

"Besides, the stable is done. Don't you want to see it?"

I did. I just wanted to see Remmy more.

Tom Reid from Bar 8 had a fencing business but also did some light farm and ranch construction. Dad had hired him to build the stable. Tom had begun leveling a site for it behind our house early in the summer and Dave had helped, at least until he'd left for Hawaii. Yes, I *was* curious to see it.

My room was deliciously dark and cool. I put my bags down and fell face first onto my bed. The comforter was cool, too, and smelled like home. *Wonderful!* I lay motionless, absorbing the stillness and quiet and familiarity. It was so good to be here.

After a few minutes, I got up to look out my back window to the yard and property below. A beautiful stable now occupied a leveled area about fifty yards from the edge of the neglected back lawn. It was bigger than I had imagined but otherwise looked exactly like the pictures Tom had shown us. I went quickly downstairs and out through the kitchen.

There were originally only going to be two stalls: one for Remmy and the other we'd keep feed and tack in. But Dad had decided that, for the difference in price, the three stall model looked better and he viewed it as property improvement. The original pipe corral that Dave and Cris had brought over was now a paddock attached to the farthest stall. Remmy would be able to wander in and out whenever he pleased unless I closed the rear door, much like his home at Bar 8. Eventually, Dad said, they would put in permanent stall runs and a fenced area for me to ride in. But for now, I felt very spoiled and couldn't imagine needing anything else. I hoped Remmy would like it.

I sat through a light dinner trying to be patient but unable to eat much. I was ready to leave as soon as Dad was. Mom came along with us to say hello to the Reids.

Remmy was in his old stall paddock and seemed to recognize the car or at least the sound of the engine. My heart leaped when he nickered softly and walked to the fence to wait for me. I stopped at the fence and breathed a soft greeting to him, nose to nose, enjoying his sweet hay-breath. Then I slipped through the rails to stroke and hug him. It felt so good to lay my face against his neck.

We didn't stay long as Dad was tired, but we made arrangements for me to have a lesson in the morning while Remmy was still there, and then Tom would trailer him home.

"Have you seen Robin . . . or Dave?" I asked Cheryl.

"No, I haven't, hun. But I know the Calderas are back. Miguel let us know and Phyllis had Tom take over a welcome home meal." She looked at me closely as if just noticing the changes. "Hey, I like the new look."

"Thank you," I said, but I mostly hoped Dave would like it, too.

When we got home, I tried calling him, deciding to use the house number. I figured I had a good excuse, too; I could tell him how wonderful I thought the stable was. I wasn't sure if I *needed* an excuse, but I always felt better when I had one, especially since it had been so long since I'd talked to him. Angel answered the phone.

"Allison! How are you? Did you have a nice summer in *Los Angeles?*" She used the Spanish pronunciation. "Did your parents enjoy their trip?"

I was immediately comforted by the warmth of her greeting, the tone of her voice, the familiar inflection of her accent. She and Dave's dad both pronounced my name *"Al-lee-sohn."*

"I'm fine. Actually, I'm really well. It was nice in Los Angeles, but I'm glad to be home. And my parents enjoyed their trip a lot. Of course, Dad had to work, but it was good that they could get away together." Having answered all her questions as accurately as I could, I had two for her. "Did you enjoy Hawaii?"

"Oh, yes!" she said and launched into a brief description of their time there. "I took many photographs. When I have them developed, I will show you. The next time you come to the house, perhaps."

I agreed that would be nice and was excited by the implied invitation. "Is Dave there?" I asked.

"No, no, they are all out. There has been much to do since we got home. Do you want me to ask him to call you?"

It made me feel funny, anxious, imagining her telling Dave I had called and that I wanted him to call me back. It wasn't unreasonable, but it felt like it was.

"No . . . no, that's okay. I'll see him at school."

I guess I assumed she would tell him that I had called and that, being Dave, he would call me back anyway. I was nervous all evening half expecting a call that never came. I called Robin's house, though, and was relieved to finally talk to her again.

"We're home!" I said. "I tried to call you this summer."

"I . . . lost my phone . . . right after I got there."

Something in her voice didn't sound right. It *did* occur to me that losing her phone shouldn't have stopped her from calling me, but maybe she didn't have my number memorized. I didn't want to make her feel bad so said nothing more about it.

"Did you have a good time? With your . . . aunt?" I asked.

She was quiet for a few moments, and I wondered if I had asked something wrong.

"No, not really," she said, her voice unusually low. "I hate it there." I was going to ask her why, but she continued, "What about you?"

"It was all right. I would rather have been here, though. Oh! And I got my hair cut!"

I thought this would be interesting news to her, but she sounded less than enthusiastic and replied, "Yeah . . . I cut mine, too."

"You did?" I tried to picture her with shorter hair.

"Mmm."

"Are you okay?" I asked. She sounded depressed.

That seemed to rouse her. "Oh, yeah. Sorry, I was just thinking about school on Monday."

That made sense. She probably wasn't looking forward to it as much as I was.

"Have you talked to Dave?" I asked.

"I tried calling him when I got home, but they weren't home yet, and he didn't answer his cell. I left him a message, but he hasn't called me back."

Well, at least I'm not the only one he hasn't talked to. If Robin hasn't heard from him either, I guess I don't need to worry.

We talked about classes, compared schedules, and agreed to meet up a little early Monday morning.

On Saturday morning I had my lesson with Cheryl. It felt *so* good to groom and saddle Remmy and felt even better to be riding again. I kept smiling, thinking about what Dave had written in my yearbook, *"Your butt's gonna be so sore in August!"* and knowing it would be too true. Tom trailered Remmy home that afternoon and the rest of the weekend passed too slowly. I spent most of it with Remmy, riding him around and keeping him company as he settled into his new home.

I also spent way too much time thinking about what Monday might be like—more precisely, what it would be like to see Dave again. I couldn't help fantasizing a little, imagining him waiting at the front of the school as he had on some days last year. With Robin, of course. But I wasn't expecting it. PE and English were both afternoon classes, so unless we had some other classes together that I wasn't aware of, I couldn't expect to see him until lunch.

I couldn't wait.

On Monday I was up by five. I just couldn't sleep and couldn't wait to get to school, to see Dave and reestablish our friendship. But I was nervous, too. *Very* nervous. The confrontation with my mirror took much longer than it should have, considering I had already decided the night before—*firmly* decided—what I would wear. I had worn my hair up in a ponytail for most of the summer but decided to wear it loose today. I put mascara on—but not *too* much—and took forever putting my contacts in, deciding I would wear them for at least the first day. But I took my pink wire-frames also, just in case. I still wasn't used to the contacts.

Last year Dave had said once that he thought I was cute. I'd never been sure what that meant to him. I didn't want to be vain, but I felt that now I looked reasonably attractive and more like the sixteen-year-old I'd be in January. I hoped I'd look more than just cute to him.

"Have a great first day," said my dad, dropping me off at the front of the school.

"I will," I said, sure that I would. How could I not? I'd be seeing my friends again. How I'd missed them! More to the point, I'd be seeing Dave. My existence hinged on that right now. I was convinced that just one glimpse of him, one smile, and my day, week, month, maybe my entire school year would be set on track. All would be right with my world.

I turned to face the front corridors of my school where I'd met with Robin and Dave many mornings last year, but I didn't recognize anyone. I already knew more or less where my first class was, and I was here earlier than I needed to be, so I began to walk.

Moving through the corridors felt like becoming reacquainted with someone I hadn't seen for a while. I hadn't always been happy here last year, but I had felt truly alive. I had *real* friends here. They and my experiences in Douglas had changed me. I knew I'd become much more receptive to and perceptive of not only the people and things around me but of myself as well. It was a continuing process that still had me feeling unbalanced and uncertain much of the time. Before today, I had felt a little anxious—both nervous and excited—about what would happen this year, but in these moments I couldn't think beyond this first day and the encounters I was so looking forward to.

Yes, I was happy to be back at school. I really liked Douglas High.

I was drawn first toward the tables near the lower field, our lunch site and where I had first been introduced to Dave. And Cris, of course. That memory stood out in my mind as one of the pivotal moments of my life so far. That had been a very strange day. There was no one there now though, just a few crows enjoying the morning sun and perhaps assessing the area's future dining potential. From there I walked toward the gym—not my favorite location but a place of interest to most of my friends.

Turning back toward the quad, I hesitated then decided to avoid it and the growing numbers of people there. Like last year, there were students everywhere obviously reconnecting after the long summer. But there was no sign of any I considered friends, even those I didn't know very well. A few people looked at me and stared. Some looked like they might wave or call out to me, but then they looked unsure and didn't. Most of them were boys, which seemed very strange, though *anyone* trying to get my attention would be highly unusual. Maybe they *did* recognize me from last year but weren't sure because I looked a little different. I often had difficulty recognizing people, and I didn't recognize any of them, so I pretended I didn't notice. It was just safer that way.

I walked back through the corridors and stood in front of my locker. I didn't need it yet, but that would change soon enough. Laying my hand flat against the cool metal door, I was thinking about trying the combination when Robin's voice made me look around.

"Allie! There you are! I was waiting at the front for you." Her head tilted slightly. "Wow, you look *really* different."

"I do?" I asked, hoping that was a good thing. "You look different too. Your hair is so short!"

Her hand came up to smooth the unevenly cut hair at the nape of her neck and she hunched her shoulders, an out of character gesture that seemed to indicate a lack of confidence. I'd never seen that in her before.

It wasn't the only thing that was different. She rarely wore skirts, but she was wearing one of the outfits I had helped get her for Christmas. And I doubted she'd ever been chubby, but she'd always appeared healthy in a scrappy, don't-mess-with-me kind of way. Looking at her now, she looked thinner, more frail somehow, pale with dark smudges under her eyes. It gave me a real shock. My usually vibrant friend didn't look the same. It reminded me again of when we'd had a misunderstanding, and she hadn't talked to me for days. She'd been obviously affected by it. This was even more pronounced.

"Have you been okay?" I asked.

She looked surprised, perhaps even offended by my question.

"Of course," she said. "Why wouldn't I?"

That's what I wanted to know, but I wasn't going to ask again. Not right away. I was too happy to see her and didn't want to start the school year with her annoyed with me already. I was sure that would happen sooner than later.

"You have Spanish first, right?" she asked, linking her arm in mine and pulling me along in the direction of my class. "I'll walk with you. The bell's going to ring in a couple of minutes. I wish we had our first class together again this year."

"Me too," I said, feeling happy and grateful for her. Even though I felt relatively at home at Douglas High and not as nervous as I'd been on the first day last year, Spanish was still a new class with a teacher I didn't know, and I was uneasy about it. Robin's thoughtful gesture meant a lot to me.

I couldn't help asking, "Have you talked to Dave yet?"

"No. I called and left a message again yesterday, but he never called me back. Shi . . . *Poop*head."

I'd never heard her call him *that* before and it made me want to laugh, but I didn't. I tried very hard to *not* visualize this literally and wondered exactly what she meant by it. But I was mostly just relieved that she didn't seem worried about the lack of contact.

She left me at my classroom door saying she'd see me later. The door was open and no one was there yet, so I entered and sat at a desk near the front, near a wall. I have tendencies to both go off into my own world *and*

to become distracted easily, so sitting toward the front seemed like a good idea, especially with a new subject that I wanted to do well in.

I knew very little Spanish; just what I'd been able to remember from a middle school class and whatever I'd picked up around Dave's family last year. In fact, though I probably should have taken it anyway, as it seemed the most useful second language to learn, I was really only taking it because of Dave.

There was so much I didn't know about him, but one of the things I knew for sure was that his family's culture was Spanish and they spoke the language fluently. Last year when my Andalusian friend was taken away by his new owner, a gentleman from Colombia, they had helped interpret for us. And Angel—I still wasn't sure of her exact connection to the family, but it seemed to be much more than just a trusted employee—frequently lapsed into Spanish, especially if she didn't really want to be understood. I had reasons, beyond just loving her, for wanting to understand her better.

And I confess, the thought that Dave would be the perfect Spanish tutor *had* crossed my mind. I'd even allowed myself to indulge in fantasies: Dave helping me with homework after school at the library, at the coffee shop, at Bar 8. At his house. *In my room.* Last year I would have shut those daydreams down at once, not letting myself dwell on what had seemed, if not impossible, then unlikely in the extreme.

But this year was different. *I* was different. And by the beginning of summer, I had felt that Dave and I were much closer. Closer to *what* exactly, I wasn't sure, but I didn't doubt our friendship and I couldn't help wanting more.

Yes, I had high hopes for this year. It was disconcerting that I hadn't heard from him yet, but not that unusual. He was always ridiculously busy; he'd get around to talking to me. Last year I had worried too much about it. I was determined to do better this year.

I absently watched the door as students entered, not consciously noticing them and trying not to stare as I have a tendency to do. But the last student, following close on the heels of the teacher, Mrs. Ochoa, caught my attention.

He was talking to her excitedly with broad gestures about a trip he had taken to Mexico. Mrs. Ochoa had a long-suffering expression on her face.

"Take a seat, Benjamin," she said patiently. "We'll have to talk another time."

He seemed about average height for a boy—probably about the same height as me—and very slender. His hair was mostly hidden under a cap but appeared to be straight, wispy at the ends, and dark auburn. His brows were even darker and very straight. His eyes were a medium color, maybe hazel, but interestingly shaped. There was an attractive but somehow otherworldly look about him.

"Okay," he said lightly and turned to find a seat. As he did so, he looked straight at me. His expression was open, his smile wide.

I'm aware that I don't always respond to people the way most people would or other people expect. It's always been that way and was probably one of the reasons I'd had trouble at school in the past. It wasn't until last year that I began to be more aware of my own feelings and reactions to others, or even care. At the same time, I had felt accepted and liked by my friends in spite of my differences. Even Dave's smile, which made the world go around as far as I was concerned, didn't always make me respond in kind.

Yet this boy's smile was so contagious, I could feel myself smiling too, though I didn't know why. *The first conscious smile of the day. I'd expected it to belong to Dave.* I felt a little annoyed, both with the boy and myself. I didn't think I'd even smiled at Robin this morning.

The boy found a seat somewhere in the middle of the room and, after hearing his name called, what sounded like Benjamin Newin, I didn't think of him again. The class itself seemed like it would be interesting, even fun, but I was mostly thinking about the potential for needing Dave's help and hoping that he'd want to give it.

My next class was chemistry and I was happy that Matthew was there. We weren't sitting close enough to talk, but he came over when the bell rang and we walked out together.

"So . . . you cut your hair."

I wasn't sure whether he liked it or what to say, so I just said, "Yes," then, "No. I mean, *I* didn't cut it." Now I felt flustered.

He seemed to sense my uncertainty but smiled again. "It looks great. I like it. And you don't need glasses anymore?"

As he'd always done before, he put me at ease. I was able to smile back. "I had eye surgery and have contacts now but mostly just for reading. I still have some trouble with distance."

"Well, you look really nice."

"Thank you," I said, feeling happy. Matthew's compliment was very welcome; I hoped it indicated what someone else's opinion would be. I was looking forward, more and more nervously, to finding that out.

I went directly to my next class, anxious to be with Robin again. We would have the following two classes together, Geometry and World History, though they would be on alternate days after today. Our friends Jessie and Kyle were in both classes too, and Matthew was also in History. We all sat near each other and the rest of the morning sped by.

There had still been no sign of Dave and no further mention of him since I'd asked Robin about him, but the minutes were ticking by closer and closer to lunchtime. I was feeling extremely nervous; butterflies in my stomach beating their little wings so hard I thought I might leave the ground and fly myself. I just couldn't wait to see him, to talk to him, and hopefully resume our friendship where we'd left it before summer vacation.

Robin and I left History together and made our way between the language arts building—the oldest and second largest building on campus—and the science and social studies buildings, moving toward the quad. The area was already swarming with other students making their way to the cafeteria, to the tables just outside it in the quad, to the caged vending machines against a wall near the library, to the bathrooms, or to their lockers—the latter probably freshmen trying to get into theirs for the first time.

It made me smile to remember how stubborn mine had been at the beginning of last year and how Dave had helped me. And Cris, too. Later in the year, it had worked fine. I never did find out if a custodian had finally fixed it or if it had just loosened up over time. And I still needed to find out if it would open for me this year, but that would wait until later. Right now there was just one place I wanted to be.

It seemed like people were reconnecting all around us: laughing, squealing, and talking loudly together. In fact, our progress across the quad was often impeded by people suddenly stopping right in front of us to greet each other, and on several occasions, we ourselves were stopped. It was always a friend or acquaintance of Robin's who wanted to say hi but nobody I knew well. They glanced at me, but not one of them said anything directly to me. I was okay with that.

I *did* seem to be getting attention from other people, though I wasn't sure why. I was aware of it whenever we stopped. While Robin talked to her friends, I would scan the area looking for anyone I knew and one person in particular. Of course there were kids everywhere who were *looking* everywhere, but at least three times it seemed like different kids were looking directly at me. I was already feeling self-conscious, smoothing my skirt down at the back and making sure the hem hadn't flipped up or something; twisting my arms in front, then behind my back—I never did know what to do with them; making sure I wasn't standing weirdly as I sometimes did; even pushing my non-existent glasses back up my nose, just out of habit. That probably looked really stupid. And all the waiting around was *killing* me. Was Dave wondering where I was? Was he looking forward to seeing me as much as I was him?

"Come *on!*" said Robin irritably, having extricated herself from the last group of people and pulling me after her. "We won't get there before the bell rings at this rate. And I see you're attracting attention already."

"Huh?" I said as if I weren't at all aware. Yes, I had noticed some attention, but I didn't know who she was specifically referring to and I didn't want to own up to it.

"Like that guy," she said.

She tipped her chin toward a boy who was crossing the quad some way ahead of us. He was walking toward the cafeteria but looking in our direction instead of where he was going. As soon as she finished speaking, he walked into the edge of one of the quad tables and fell over, hitting the ground pretty hard. She snorted.

I felt the blow, too, and felt sorry for him—it was exactly the kind of klutzy thing I was prone to do, and I knew just how it felt. But I thought that Robin must have been mistaken anyway. I thought it more likely he was looking at *her*. With her short hair and cute outfit, I thought she looked adorable in spite of looking tired. The boy could even have been looking at someone or something beyond us. Maybe he was just spacing out like I often did.

We were now within sight of the tables. *The* tables. *Our* tables; the ones Dave's and Cris' friends had made their own. I guess we kind of had squatter's rights over them by now as no one had ever challenged us for them. There were two of them down by the lower field, and Dave usually sat somewhere on the one parallel to the field, facing the quad. Cris usually sat behind him, facing away from the quad. At the beginning of last year, I had thought Cris sat that way to avoid me in particular. Later, I came to the conclusion that he sat that way to avoid *everybody*. He wasn't sitting there today though. Either was Dave. At first, I thought Dave wasn't there at all and my heart sank. Then I saw him, on the top of the other table, sitting sideways to us as we approached. And he wasn't alone.

I recognized her at once—Hannah Liu, the dark-haired girl who had been his dancing partner in gym last year. I didn't know her at all but thought she looked the same: athletically slim with beautiful straight, dark brown hair hanging to her waist. Much longer than mine was now. She stood right in front of Dave, both hands on his shoulders, playfully pushing him back slightly. Each time she did, he slowly leaned toward her only to be pushed back again. He wasn't touching her, yet the interaction seemed intimate some-how—much too familiar for my peace of mind. She was smiling and talking nonstop; his expression seemed neutral, but she definitely had his attention.

As we drew closer, a few people looked at us and said, "Hey." Some smiled. Some just stared at us blankly. Tanner, Kyle, Stacie, and Jessie were playing cards at the end of the other table.

Dave finally turned and looked our way but his expression didn't change. Nothing seemed to register on his face. Hannah said something and he turned back to her. It looked like he laughed slightly in response, but he didn't really smile.

I felt like I was watching a train wreck in slow motion. I could feel the blood draining out of my face, my heart thudding dully. This wasn't the way things were supposed to go.

Dave's supposed to see us coming and smile. He's supposed to be happy to see us—me—and ask how everything's going. He's supposed to—

Tanner, looking almost exactly the same as he had last year, bounded up to Robin. "Hey! You look like a boy!" he said, grinning mischievously.

"Gee . . . thanks," said Robin, very disgruntled and smoothing the hair at her neck again.

"I'm just kidding!" He looked worried and sounded surprised by her reaction. "Who's the new girl?"

It took a moment to realize he meant me. I probably stared at him blankly, trying to figure out if he was joking with me, too. Then it occurred to me that he had probably never seen me with my hair loose or without glasses. I wished that were true of Dave, but it wasn't. I was quite sure he recognized me.

"Hi, Tanner," I said quietly.

His eyes grew wide and he smiled broadly. "Allie! Wow, you look . . . different. But good!" he added, as if afraid of offending me as well.

I tried to smile in response but felt too odd to put much effort into it.

Hannah had turned her head to look at us, looking curious. She smiled. I was distracted by an argument breaking out among the remaining card players, and Tanner ran back to them, apparently repeating rules that had already been explained. Meanwhile, Hannah walked over.

"You look so cute!" she said, to Robin. "I *love* your hair like that! I wish I dared to cut mine that short!" She laughed lightly and turned her attention to me. "You've cut yours too, haven't you?"

I was a little flustered that she acknowledged me let alone noticed any changes. Her manner was open and friendly toward me, though. I knew I *should* have put all my effort into responding to her as positively as I could, but Dave had gotten up and now walked toward us, too. It was all I could do to just remember to breathe and try not to stare at him.

He hadn't changed at all. And he was completely different. At first he seemed taller, bigger somehow. Then I realized that, no, he had grown last year, making him just slightly taller than me, but he was about the same in height and build now as the last time I'd seen him. His skin was much darker, no doubt from all the time spent in the Hawaiian sun. His hair was longer than I'd ever seen it, too. It had been on the long side before summer vacation, but it didn't look like he'd cut it at all. It also appeared washed out and very light in places. He was dressed the same way as at the beginning of last school year—t-shirt, shorts, skate shoes—but there was still something different. I just couldn't pinpoint it.

"Hey," he said, looking from Robin to me. "Did you guys have a good summer?"

Robin shrugged then quickly punched out at him. "You never called me back . . ."

Dave shied away from the blow just fast enough to avoid the full force of it and smirked slightly. "I was busy," was all he said.

Then he looked directly at me. I looked back, searching for—I don't even know what; whatever had enraptured me last year. I expected to blush but felt nothing. There was no twinkle in his eye, no real smile. Something in his manner left me feeling—deflated. Dead inside.

The bell rang then—I guess it had taken us quite a while to cross the quad—but I felt relieved. And completely confused.

"Guess I'll see you later," said Dave and turned toward the gym. Hannah followed, playfully pushing him from behind before falling into step beside him.

"Who *is* that?" I asked. I hadn't meant to—I didn't want to appear curious at all, and I already knew her name—but I *had* to know.

"That's Hannah," said Robin, twisting her mouth slightly. "She's cool. We've known her forever. Her mom . . ." Robin stopped, still staring after them.

"What?" I wanted to know. *Anything* she could tell me might lessen the hollow feeling inside.

"Oh . . . nothing." She shrugged and seemed to dismiss the thought. She smiled crookedly at me. "I wish we had more classes together this year. I'll meet you at the library after school, though. Okay?"

"Yes, okay," I said, and we parted ways.

I felt very self-conscious following Dave and Hannah toward the gym. It had been reasonable to assume that Dave and I might have PE together again this year. Had he forgotten? I certainly hadn't. But I also hadn't reckoned on Hannah. Beyond noticing that Dave obviously enjoyed her as a partner during our dance unit, and her sharing a "Best Smile" picture with him in the yearbook, I hadn't been aware of her last year. I hadn't noticed her hanging out at the tables at all. Why was she around now? *And why do they seem so close all of a sudden?*

That was a question I really didn't want to contemplate too deeply right now. I was pathetically relieved to see the one other person that really mattered to me watching for me by the gym door.

Like everyone else so far, except maybe Tanner, Melanie looked slightly different. Not taller. Her hair wasn't noticeably longer or shorter than it had been. Her figure hadn't altered much—perhaps slightly fuller. But she looked older and more beautiful than ever, and I was sure it wasn't only because I was so glad to see her.

She smiled and said, "Allison! I love the way your hair looks!"

"Thank you!" At this moment the affirmation was deeply appreciated.

"Are you okay?" she asked, looking concerned and trying to read my face. She must have seen Dave walk in with Hannah before me and might be wondering the same things as me. I was sure she knew he was special to me.

"Yes, of course." I knew what the problem was, but I couldn't tell her. *What was there to say? Nothing really. Dave had been my friend; nothing more. Right?*

She smiled as we reached the lower bleachers, choosing to accept that I didn't want to voice my problems or worries, as she always had. "Are you glad to be home?" she asked.

"Yes," I said, though not as enthusiastically as I might have done yesterday. *Focus on the positive!* "It's great to have Remmy back and be able to ride again. I bet you rode a lot this summer, though."

"Yes, and I started a new horse, so now I have three that need exercising. It keeps me very busy. Plus lessons."

I would have liked to hear more, but the coaches came into the center of the gym and blew their whistles. They talked about the same things they had last year: PE kit starting tomorrow, early track tryouts, fitness testing starting next week, blah, blah, blah. Though I didn't feel as physically hopeless as I had at the beginning of last year, I didn't think my athleticism had improved enough to matter much in this class. I was more interested in looking around the gym at the other students gathered there.

On the far side of the bleachers were some freshmen looking bewildered. How well I remembered the feeling! I had sat by myself, knowing no one. Since PE was my worst subject, I had felt like an alien sitting among ordinary earthlings. Then I came to realize that Dave was in the class as well, which at first was horrible but then was—nice. I wasn't going to think about that right now though. And I had met Melanie, too, and then the class was bearable and not as intimidating. I was *so* comforted to be sitting next to her now, I could have hugged her. But of course, I didn't. *That would probably be too weird.*

A girl laughed behind us as if she had read my mind, startling me. Looking around to the top of the bleachers, where a large group was sitting together, I felt a sharp jolt of *déjà vu*. My movement had caused many pairs of eyes to turn my way, including Hannah's. And Dave's. He looked at me and grinned a little crookedly. *For me or at me?*

I looked away first, feeling insecure once more, and I didn't look that way again. I left the gym with Melanie the moment the bell rang.

I was extremely nervous while going to my next class. Dave would be there too. Miss Sanders, my English teacher, had "warned" me when inviting me to join it last year that Dave was in the AP class. I'd been looking forward to it immensely but now I wasn't sure. Would Dave sit nearby? Would he notice me a little more?

Pathetic already!

Melanie walked part of the way with me from the gym at the back of the school toward the front where the Language Arts building was. I really appreciated it; it would have been far worse walking the entire way alone, feeling the way I did.

There were still a lot of vacant seats when I entered the room, and I began to move toward the back. But Miss Sanders had other ideas.

"Allison! It's good to see you. And I'm glad you'll be joining us this year. I've saved this seat for you. I think you might do better toward the front?"

Although it sounded like a question, there was no inquiry in her manner as she pointed to a seat below one of the high windows, almost at the front of the class.

Feeling supremely embarrassed, I took the seat, thankful that only a few other students were in the room. *Especially* glad Dave wasn't there. The desk across from me was vacant though. Would he sit there?

My heart dropped a little further than it already had when Hannah entered the room. She went directly to the back, joining a couple of other kids already there that I didn't know. Dave walked in with Kyle a moment later. Part of me wanted to be invisible, but the other, still more substantial part clung to the hope that he would not only acknowledge me somehow but choose to sit in the empty seat to my right.

He never even looked in my direction but walked straight to the back also. I didn't turn to see where he sat but assumed it was near Hannah.

More people poured into the room right behind Dave in the minute before the bell rang, and the seats behind, beside, and the one in front of me had now been taken. Miss Sanders collected the essays we'd written over the summer and then took roll. My name was first; if Dave hadn't realized I was here before, he did now. I still didn't want to look behind me though.

Miss Sanders explained the class—what we'd be reading and what we'd be expected to do—but I couldn't concentrate. I was sure it was all on the handout; I'd have to read it carefully later. For now, I was too preoccupied with wondering what was going on behind me *and can this day get any worse?*

When the class ended, I gathered my things to try to leave as quickly as I could but found Dave standing next to my desk. It sounds corny, but I'm sure my heart stopped.

"So . . . you're in this class too." I couldn't tell how he felt about it.

"Yes. Miss Sanders invited me at the end of last year."

"Hnh. You never told me. It's good you're here," he said, but I didn't detect any enthusiasm. "Why are you sitting way up here by yourself?"

Well this is embarrassing. "You see, I have trouble . . ."

"It's because I . . ."

"Um . . ."

I couldn't say anything, so I guess I just stared at him.

His eyebrows went up slightly in question, but he still wasn't smiling. He wasn't even smirking. He wasn't acting like the Dave I knew and loved at all. I was crushingly confused.

"You should sit at the back with us," he said. Then he smiled slightly, but it seemed forced and his eyes looked wrong. It wasn't the soft expression I'd come to feel was for me, almost exclusively. That look was nowhere to be seen.

I didn't know how to respond but tried to smile back. I don't know if I was successful.

"Well," he said, the way people do when there's nothing more to say, "see you later." Then he turned and left.

I watched him leave the room, feeling something else was very wrong but not able to name it. I couldn't move.

"See you later."

Later—that word had always held promise in conjunction with Dave. Either he'd call me, he wanted me to call him, or we'd definitely be seeing each other soon. This time it sounded empty—just one of those throwaway phrases everybody uses that doesn't mean there will be a definite later at all. What could cause such a big change in him? Had I done something unknowingly? Did something happen over the summer? Something in Hawaii?

I couldn't afford to think about those possibilities right now. I still had the rest of the day to get through.

I walked slowly back to my Spanish classroom nearby, my homeroom, which meant it would be where I'd spend Study Hall. This would be very different than last year, too. Most importantly, Robin wouldn't be there. We could have worked on history and geometry homework together. I was going to really miss her help with math. But mostly I was just going to miss her.

Mrs. Ochoa was very different from Mr. Payne. Last year, even on the very first day when we didn't have much to do, he'd been extremely strict about talking. Mrs. Ochoa seemed to enjoy a more interactive class and spent the time getting to know us, as well as explaining how she wanted the class to function during study hall. She said she would make herself available to clarify assignments or answer reasonable questions, but that she wouldn't do our homework for us—Spanish or otherwise. That was fair enough. I was hoping I wouldn't need her help anyway, one way or another.

About halfway through the period, Mrs. Ochoa wanted us to take turns telling why we were taking Spanish. It was a simple question and should have had a simple answer, but I was panicking. I *couldn't* say why I was taking the class. It was too embarrassing, and I was sure it would mean total social annihilation for me. I had hoped that wouldn't happen this early in the year.

"My mom's family in Texas speaks mostly Spanish, and I want to be able to talk to them better on the phone and stuff," said a girl on the other side of the room. "We don't get to see them very often."

"That's a great reason," said Mrs. Ochoa, nodding.

"I love a boy who comes from a Spanish speaking family, so I want to speak it too." No, that wouldn't do.

"My grandparents still speak Spanish, but my dad only speaks a little, so he never taught us," said a boy in the middle of the room.

"So you want to learn because it's your heritage?" asked Mrs. Ochoa.

"Yeah," said the boy.

"I want to be able to understand when other people speak it." Especially Angel. *I'm sure I might learn more about Dave and his family if I only understood!* But that sounded weird, like I wanted to eavesdrop or something—which I suppose was true, but I didn't mean to be creepy about it.

"I like watching Japanese anime in Spanish," said a boy somewhere behind me. "But I don't understand it."

The class laughed.

"Can we watch it here?" he asked.

"Sorry to disappoint you, Benjamin," said Mrs. Ochoa, "but probably not."

"I need it to get into a good college," said a girl in the back.

I turned to see who had spoken and she turned her head to look back at me. Or rather, *glare* back. I'd read about people "looking down their noses" at others and never quite understood it. It made sense now. She'd been in my computer class last year. And *not* friendly.

"Yes, most universities require at least two years of a second language, it's true." Then Mrs. Ochoa looked at me. "What about you, Allison? Why do you want to learn Spanish?"

My scalp prickled. I thought I'd done amazingly well today, considering everything; no blush so far. But the combination of an embarrassing question I didn't want to answer, and the image conjured up of the *reason*, was proving too much for me.

"Um . . ."

I'm not going to say I had never lied before—obviously that would *be* a lie—but lying had never been easy for me. I had prevaricated a little last year, mostly in just withholding information, but to completely fabricate something didn't seem to be in my nature. And right now, I couldn't think of a thing to say.

"Um . . . I don't know," I whispered.

Somebody in the back coughed a few times, the last time sounding distinctly like "Caldera." There was some chuckling and snorting around the room, and I knew my face was now scarlet.

Mrs. Ochoa looked sideways at the people who'd laughed, then looked at me kindly and said, "It's okay if you don't have a specific reason. *Any* reason is a good reason to learn a second language."

She changed the subject then, but it was too late. I felt miserable. I had hoped that this would be a fun class, but apparently I was already on enemy radar.

When the bell rang, I was one of the first ones through the door. I had a feeling Mrs. Ochoa wanted to talk to me, but I didn't want to discuss anything. Last year Miss Sanders had told me that the teachers "were aware of a lot of things, both on and off campus"—intimating I'd been the topic of discussion—but I didn't want to know. Especially not now. It was the first day of school and self-preservation was kicking in already; I was going to avoid anything I wasn't forced to deal with.

I escaped to my last class, Art II, and the security of Melanie's companionship. As I took a seat next to her, her searching expression confirmed that she sensed my unhappiness. But she didn't say anything. That was *her* nature and I was very thankful for it right now.

When the last bell of the day rang, I just wanted to go home. But Robin would be waiting for me at the school library, and I would need at least a couple of my textbooks for tomorrow. I didn't have much choice, and Dad wasn't picking me up until four o'clock anyway.

Crossing the quad alone, I felt exposed and vulnerable. I kept my eyes on the ground ahead and tried to tune out the voices around me. It had been quite a long time since I'd felt like this. In fact, after last year I didn't think I'd ever feel this way again; yet here I was, blocking the world out. At least I didn't feel like crying. That had also been a new development last year—that and the despicable blushes. I hadn't really been put to the test over the summer, but I was determined to have more control over both.

Tanner cut into the library line to join us, and he and Robin kept up a lively chatter the whole time, including me to take sides when they disagreed or just trying to make me laugh. Robin appeared more her old self, which made me glad. There was color in her cheeks, and her bearing was more self-assured. It helped me feel more *my* old—no, my *newer* self. Their nonsense helped the time pass quickly, too. A half hour later we were heading toward our lockers to drop off all our books. Today might be the only day for a while that we didn't have homework.

I faced my old nemesis, half dreading and half hoping that it wouldn't open for me. I twirled the dial back and forth and tried to open it on the last number, but it didn't budge. I wiggled the handle slightly then heard a click, and the door popped open, just like it used to when Dave—or Cris—had banged on it. I put my books in sadly. I had initially hoped that it *would* open so I wouldn't have to bother Dave, but during the day I had started hoping that it *wouldn't* open, just so asking him was an option.

Stupid, uncooperative locker.

Tanner and Robin said goodbye to me and headed toward the north front side of the school together. Since I wasn't sure when I'd be done, Dad had said he'd wait in the parking lot, so I made my way there. Stupid thoughts—hopes and fears by turn—assailed me as I alternately scanned the parking lot then kept my eyes on the ground ahead. I was looking for one vehicle, Cris', and one person, Dave, both wanting and *not* wanting to see them.

I didn't see them.

Chapter Three

On the way home I tried to answer all Dad's questions concerning my day as positively as I could. Thankfully, he didn't ask about people.

Mom would be starting work again at the swimming pool in town next week. The lady she had taken the place of last year, Jasmine, had had her baby and returned full time, so they didn't need Mom as much. But they still wanted her to work, at least a few hours in the busy afternoons and sometimes on weekends or if they needed her to cover for someone else. She didn't really have to work but enjoyed getting out of the house and having people to talk to. She said she was going to save the money she earned for something special.

Today she was home and ready to pounce.

"How'd it go?"

"Fine," I answered, not wanting to elaborate.

"How's Robin?" she asked brightly.

How *was* Robin? I wasn't sure but didn't want to voice the doubt. "Fine. She got her hair cut short. It's really cute."

"And your other friend? You know, we still haven't met her." She was talking about Melanie, but her manner had changed slightly. I had a feeling she was *thinking* of someone else.

"Melanie's fine. We have PE and Art together again."

"That's great! And your other classes? Do you think they'll be all right? Do you have friends in them?" Now we were talking about something completely different; I was sure of it.

"Yes. Matthew's in Chemistry and History. And Jessie, Kyle, and Tanner are in a couple of our classes too." *Are you really going to make me say it, Mom?*

"And Dave?" She tried to say his name lightly, but the tone of her voice had definitely changed. "Did you see him today?"

There it is. . . .

"Yes. We have PE and English t— . . . at the same time." I was going to say "together," but it didn't feel right. We weren't "together." He and Hannah appeared to be "together." *Unsafe topic.*

Mom looked at me searchingly.

"I'm going to go change," I said, and escaped to my room.

When I'd changed, I went outside to Remmy. He seemed very glad to see me, nuzzling me and blowing gently in my face. I was incredibly happy to see him. He looked as pretty as ever, his light brown coat glossy and sleek, the strange, slightly pink patina glowing where the sun reflected off his hair just right. The Reids had taken excellent care of him, as I supposed they always had before Dave gave him to me—

Dave gave him to me.

Dave *gave* him to me.

Dave gave him—to *me!*

What was I worrying about? And what exactly was I expecting from Dave? Too much, obviously. I had done over the summer what I hadn't allowed myself to do all last year: fantasized that I meant more to him than I did. And this angst I was already feeling was the result. *Stupid me.*

Had Dave ignored me today? No, not at all. Twice he had approached me to say hi. Hadn't he even invited me to sit with him—okay, *them*—at the back of the English room? The fact that he hadn't said more was disappointing, to be sure, but hardly unusual. His manner? It had certainly seemed very cool, in the chilly sense, but maybe it wasn't that different than it had ever been. Perhaps I had romanticized our interactions of the past too much. And Hannah? I didn't know, but I wasn't going to think about her. Maybe tomorrow would be different.

Feeling much restored to my recent, more confident self again, I lunged Remmy in the corral down by the stream then rode him bareback up the dirt road and around the house for a while. It didn't take long before I was aching and I had to smile, remembering what Dave had written in my yearbook. How right he'd been!

The first week of school had been so strange last year. I had been very alone when school first started, as I'd always been in years past with the exception of Brenda's friendship. But by the end of that first week, I'd had at least *potential* friends. Those people were now indeed my friends. And yet this year I felt more and more lonely as the week progressed.

Dave was often in the company of Hannah, but even when he wasn't, he seemed so different to me. He wasn't cold, exactly, but very aloof. He asked if I was doing all right a couple of times, offhandedly, and I tried to smile and say yes, but I was actually starting to really hurt inside.

I had planned to continue my lunch pattern of the previous year: Tuesdays and Thursdays with Melanie in the cafeteria and the rest of the week at the tables with Robin and Dave. But I already felt so off-balance by Dave's behavior that I found myself at the tables on Tuesday, hoping I'd just been too sensitive on Monday and that things would be back to normal today.

Dave wasn't there. Either was Hannah.

I saw Hannah in PE, but not Dave. The coaches had split the class into two groups: one was running the track on the upper field while the other, the one Melanie and I were in, ran around the lower. Hannah passed us a couple of times. She even smiled directly at me once. Dave must have been up at the track.

I almost suspected that his group made up the athletic elite and we were the more physically challenged rank and file, except that quite a few of those running with us were obviously very fit and able, including Hannah. At least we weren't closely watched, and as long as we kept moving, the coaches didn't seem to care if we were actually running or not. I was surprised that I was able to run for quite a while without twisting my ankle, getting a stitch in my side, or becoming completely exhausted. Quite a change from last year. In fact, the reason I slowed to a walk was to remain with Melanie. She seemed to be having trouble catching her breath.

"Are you okay?" I asked.

"Yes . . . I'll be . . . fine."

Her breathing seemed strangely shallow, and she coughed a couple of times.

"Do you want to sit down?" I asked, concerned.

"No . . . I'm fine," she insisted. "Just . . . out of shape . . . I guess."

We walked without speaking for a while, she trying to act normally but reserving her breath, and me having plenty of breath but reluctant to talk. I can't talk unless my mind is entirely on the topic at hand and right now my mind was somewhere up at the track.

"This is boring, isn't it?" Hannah had caught up to us again and fell into step beside me.

I was a little startled by her joining us and just stared at her. She was so pretty! I suddenly felt utterly inconsequential—my beautiful friend Melanie on my right, Hannah on my left. I pictured myself walking between them looking like I'd felt last year—two beautiful girls with a dork who still looked twelve. *What a funny picture it would make.*

Hannah raised her eyebrows at me and smiled. "Your name is Allie, right?"

"Y . . . yes," I replied, my thoughts very scattered but pretty sure that was the correct answer.

Hannah looked over toward Melanie and smiled. "Hi, I'm Hannah. I've seen you around, too, but I don't know your name. I think we have Chemistry together. You didn't go to Foothill, did you?"

Melanie smiled back, not quite as openly, but I thought it was a real smile. That was probably more than could be said for mine, if I even had one.

"No, I went to Douglas," replied Melanie.

They were talking about middle schools. There were two that fed into Douglas High and I hadn't gone to either of them.

"I'm Melanie," she said. "It's nice to meet you."

Hannah smiled brightly. "It's nice to meet you, too. Well, I guess I'll run again. Bye."

Still smiling, she ran forward. Melanie and I continued to walk.

"New friend?" asked Melanie, looking curious and breathing more normally.

I didn't know what to say.

"Hardly! I think she might be too close to the person I love." No, I wasn't
going to admit to that.

"I don't know." Could I be friends with her?

"Maybe." Did I *want* to be friends with her?

"She's a friend of . . . a friend. I don't really know her." This was both
safe and true. "She seems nice though." I was surprised I thought this and
even more surprised that I said it out loud, but it was true too.

Study hall was a relief. I'd never been so happy to immerse myself in
math homework. The only thing distracting me for a moment was Benjamin
literally bouncing into the room just as the bell rang.

"Take your hat off, Benjamin," said the teacher.

"Yes, Mrs. Ochoa," he said politely with an enormous smile.

I went back to my geometry, wishing Robin were there and trying not
to think about Dave. I hadn't seen him all day.

Wednesday was much the same as Tuesday, but I got a surprise while
stopping at my locker before heading down to the tables at lunchtime.

"Is it working for you?"

The soft voice behind me caught me off guard, but it was nothing
compared to the jolt I felt on turning around. I recognized him at once, of
course; one look into his eyes confirmed who he was, and the indescribable
feelings as he returned my regard seemed strange yet all too familiar. Even
so, I was speechless. Cris looked so different! And he steadily looked *at*
me, not avoiding my eyes as he usually did. It was very disconcerting and I
broke eye contact first.

I couldn't tell if he was any taller—he'd always been several inches
taller than me—but he certainly wasn't as skinny as the last time I'd seen
him. In fact, he looked very healthy, his skin bronzed and the top, lighter
layer of his hair bleached out more than usual by the summer sun. And he
wasn't scowling. The only times I could remember him *not* scowling were
while involved in extreme sports and rodeo. And once I'd seen him asleep.
He didn't seem to frown in his sleep.

Like Dave, his hair was longer than I'd ever seen it, and I briefly wondered if they didn't have barbers or salons in Hawaii. That wasn't the only
change though. Light-colored hair lay above his upper lip and on his chin

and lower jaw, making his skin look very dark in comparison. It made him look much older.

He regarded me for a moment longer before he seemed to feel uncomfortable enough to look away himself. Or maybe he was just bored. "So, it opens?"

"Yes . . . yes, it opens just fine," I finally answered, feeling unaccountably awkward. My mind immediately went blank.

Cris nodded once then walked away.

Weird! I guess some things haven't changed.

I turned back to my locker, made necessary exchanges, and continued down to the tables, not quite as nervous as I'd been before seeing Cris.

Robin had saved a place for me, and everyone else appeared to be there, but again there was no sign of Dave or Hannah. It was difficult to keep my mind from exploring the possible—and what seemed more and more plausible—reasons for this. I tried to focus on what was happening around me.

Matthew, Tanner, and a few other boys were having a lively discussion about soccer, which normally wouldn't have interested me much except that Dave's name kept coming up. He would play varsity this year for sure, and while most of the other players were okay with that, some apparently weren't, on both the varsity and junior varsity teams.

Though small, Douglas High School had quite a reputation for high athletic standards. The school had held top positions in regional, state, and even national track events for as long as anyone could remember and had been in the regional playoffs for basketball for the last three years. The latter was credited in large part to Cris.

Dave didn't play basketball, but both he and Cris played soccer and were apparently very talented players. Last year had been the first time that both varsity and junior varsity soccer teams had made the playoffs. Everyone was hoping that at least the varsity team would actually win the final regional tournament this year and go to State. I'd been oblivious to most of this last year but was beginning to understand how seriously everyone else took it.

Robin and Jessie and some others were talking, too, but cards were in play again, and the subject kept shifting, making it difficult to keep track of. The only other thing I noticed, apart from Dave and Hannah's absence, was how close Stacie and Kyle seemed to be. Sitting side by side at the opposite end of our table, they paid little attention to anyone else, their heads close and talking quietly together with many gentle smiles.

I was trying very hard *not* to watch them, but I couldn't help wondering if Dave and Hannah were similarly engaged elsewhere. Perhaps somewhere more private. I knew how it made me feel to have Dave very close, focused solely on me. I had fantasized about it all summer. The thought of him being that close to Hannah, maybe closer, was horrible.

By the end of lunch I felt desolate. English was a trial. Compelled to sit in the seat Miss Sanders had assigned to me, I thought I detected reproach in Dave's expression as he entered the classroom. He was immediately followed by a brightly smiling Hannah. This bothered and distracted me almost completely for the whole period, wondering if Dave was annoyed or disappointed that I hadn't taken his "advice"—it hadn't been a *request*—to sit at the back of the room with them. And where had he been during lunch and with whom? And why did Hannah smile so darn much?

Miss Sanders asked me a direct question about the topic at hand, Shakespeare's background, and I gave what I thought was a reasonable answer based on the information I had actually processed. I was pretty sure they were talking about venues, but the only part of the question I'd really heard was, " . . . plays performed?"

"The Rose, The Curtain, Blackfriars, The Swan," I recited, trying to remember as many as I could from my summer reading. "The Globe is the most well known."

There was snickering from behind me somewhere, and I wondered what I'd said that was so funny.

"Well, that is true. It's not the answer to the question I asked though," said Miss Sanders.

As the bell rang and we gathered our things, she walked over to my desk. I couldn't help watching for Dave to walk by and saw him look my way again, but his face was blank. That seemed to be the only expression I inspired in him now.

"Is everything all right, Allison?" asked Miss Sanders.

I tore my eyes away from the now empty doorway to look at her. She seemed very concerned.

"Um . . . yes. I'm fine."

"Are you going to be able to concentrate?"

Don't blush!

"Yes, I think so." I was, in fact, beginning to doubt it highly, but I didn't want to say so. Not yet anyway. It was still just the first week!

She looked like my dad had on the first day of school, her mouth a tight line like she wanted to say more. Instead, she nodded and let me go.

Art was a complete relief, as study hall had been the day before. I was glad my last classes each day would provide some measure of escape for me, both from social interaction and my own thoughts. Melanie still looked searchingly at me as I took my seat next to her, but she asked nothing. It was just as well. I still didn't have a clue what was going on or if, in fact, anything was going on at all.

We spent the class time sketching. Several still-life groupings had been set up around the room: bowls of fruit, plastic flowers in vases, carpenter's tools, books and candles. We had ten minutes to make rough sketches and add as much detail as we could before moving on to the next set piece.

I *loved* it. For the whole period, I felt set free from my anxieties and concerns, free of the growing distress I was feeling, free of the gnawing in the pit of my stomach—or heart. I never was sure which it was. Once we'd started drawing, I didn't think of Dave at all. Not once.

I was amazed when the last bell rang; time had flown by so fast. Everyone chatted happily as we gathered our things and left the room. I felt somewhat restored in mind and spirit as I walked to the front of the school with Melanie. Nobody hailed us and I saw nobody of consequence to me.

We waved goodbye, and I turned to go farther up the street where my dad usually parked and waited for me. I was glad he was picking me up at the front of the school again. Mom always parked in the parking lot. I was relieved to avoid that area. Melanie crossed the street to where an older model blue Mercedes was parked, then she waited by the passenger door. I remembered seeing the car last year. I got in Dad's car and said, "Hi," but was still watching the Mercedes with interest as we passed it. Sure enough, Roger crossed the street behind us, unlocked and opened the door for Melanie, then got into the front driver's side. He hadn't been the one driving last year.

Roger looked much the same, possibly taller but otherwise as clean-cut and well-dressed as ever. I had always wondered what his relationship with Melanie was, but all I'd found out was that he was *not* her brother, as I had at first conjectured. She had said, "Just a friend," and *that* was open to all sorts of interpretation.

I should know.

Thursday was much the same as Wednesday, except for being an "A" instead of "B" day as far as my class schedule went.

I was enjoying Spanish but not letting my mind touch on why I was taking the class. I liked learning new vocabulary and I'd always been relatively good at memorizing words in general. I was also something of a list maker which helped. I thought I could do well in the class. It was already apparent that there was a potentially unfriendly element there, but I was determined to avoid and ignore it as much as possible.

There was one other issue which so far only caused me significant annoyance if the room was otherwise quiet, such as if we were reading or working on material independently. Today we were writing out and working on memorizing our first real vocabulary list. A constant clicking somewhere behind me got on my nerves so badly I couldn't concentrate at all.

Click, click, click, click . . .

I tried to ignore it. It probably wasn't bothering anyone else, but I'd always had trouble with this kind of distraction. I willed myself to concentrate, writing each word with care and saying the meaning over and over to myself.

La cuaderno

Notebook, notebook, notebook . . .

Click, click, click, click . . .

El pais

Country, country, country . . .

Click, click, click, click . . .

I finally turned around to see what was aggravating me and saw Benjamin, his cap on backward, clicking his pen in and out. I was immediately diverted, not just by his baseball cap—similar to the ones he'd worn on Monday and Tuesday only neon yellow—but because he wasn't clicking the pen absent-mindedly, as I would have supposed. He was watching it with great concentration as if it were the most interesting phenomenon he'd ever experienced. I found *his* fascination in itself fascinating and forgot about memorizing words to stare at him until he betrayed his awareness of me. He looked neither embarrassed nor surprised as his gaze slid slyly to me, and he grinned widely. The expression was far too familiar and in more than one way.

I turned away and tried to recapture my concentration, but now my mind was wrangling again with questions about Dave and, curiously, Cris too. I sighed and tried to focus on my list.

"Please stop clicking the pen, Benjamin," said Mrs. Ochoa, a little too late to do me any good. "And take your cap off."

"Yes, Mrs. Ochoa."

It seemed strange to look forward so much to math, my next class, but it was the only class besides World History and Art that I felt comfortable in. I didn't let myself dwell on the fact that I was *not* feeling comfortable in the two classes I shared with Dave. He and Hannah still didn't join us at the tables for lunch.

In PE, Dave was still in a different group up at the track. Hannah acknowledged me with a smile but otherwise stayed with a group of girls I assumed were her friends. A few of them had had a problem with me last year, including the girl from my Spanish class. I didn't pay much attention to them. Melanie seemed to be feeling much better and didn't get short of breath at all. We ran around the field together then partnered with each other during our fitness tests.

Though I still struggled to block out random noises around the classroom in study hall, I was able to get a good start on my geometry homework. Whether I was doing it right or not was another matter. It had been so much easier to concentrate when Robin had been in the class with me last year, not to mention having her help with math. I had reading to do for History and English, too, but that would have to wait for the relative quiet of home.

I was so happy to finally get there and spend time with Remmy. He was pleased to see me too.

At least someone is.

Just after dinner, the phone rang. Dad answered it, saying, "Oh, hi! Very well, thanks. How about you and your family?" He listened for a moment.

My heart had started beating just a little faster. I was trying not to get my hopes up.

"Yes, she's right here. Hold on . . ." Dad looked at me and held the phone up.

My heart sped up even more. *Please, please, please. . . .*

"Hello?"

"Hey hun, how're you doing?" The voice belonged to Cheryl Reid.

"Oh . . . hi! I'm fine, thank you." I was happy to hear her voice even though I felt a little disappointed.

"I was wondering if we could swap services on Saturday."

"Swap services?"

"Mmhmm. You do something for me, and I do something for you."

"Oh. Yes, I guess so."

"Tom and I have been invited to a special dinner Saturday night. Would you babysit for us? Then I could give you a lesson on Sunday whenever you like. We'd even come and pick you and Remmy up. Tom can pick you up and take you home on Saturday too. Gloria will be up at the guest house, of course, and there are a few wranglers around so you won't be alone. It would sure help us out."

Babysitting. . . . "Um . . . yes. I think so. Let me ask my mom if it's okay." I did and it was.

The plans were made, and I tried not to think too much more about it. I liked the Reids, and I was fond of Cody and Zoe, but I'd never babysat children that young. Watching them with Robin last year didn't count. I'd barely even been left entirely on my own with my cousins, and they were much older anyway. I guessed there was a first time for everything and I'd find out if I was any good at it.

Friday was picture day. I dressed with care—one of the skirts and tops Aunt Audrey had bought me over the summer—and remembered to put my brush in my backpack. I was still getting used to needing it more often now that my hair was shorter and not braided all the time. After some consideration, I put some mascara on as well, but I didn't want to appear to be trying too hard. I hadn't worn much make-up around my parents, and nothing since the first day of school. Mom just said she thought I looked nice and Dad didn't seem to notice at all.

Matthew was very attentive in Chemistry. I was happy he was in the class with me. Like Spanish, PE, and even English, there were definitely unfriendly vibes in the room and, as I didn't think I was going to be adept at the subject, I was thankful he'd elected himself my lab partner. He seemed to have a good grasp of the terminology and principles. He said that he'd been in Ag. Science the year before in order to stay with his friends, especially

Dave and Tanner. But as he didn't intend to go into agriculture or agricultural business, there didn't seem to be much point in staying in it. I was just glad I wasn't alone in the class.

There was still no sign of Dave or word from him at lunch. I wanted to question Robin about him, but she always seemed a little preoccupied, and I didn't know how to open the subject. I kept hoping she would say something or ask the question herself, but she didn't. I couldn't believe the week was ending and I'd barely seen or spoken to him at all. It was getting harder and harder to stay positive, but I was determined; unless he did or said something overtly negative to me, I would not despair. I wouldn't believe things had changed that much. I was probably just being too sensitive.

When the bell rang, I took my time going to my locker and then walked away from the Language Arts building to circle back in hopes of seeing, perhaps getting to exchange even one word with Dave. As I finally climbed the stairs toward English, I heard his voice. He sounded exasperated, speaking softly but very distinctly.

"Yes, I *was* aware of it. It's not like that though."

"Well . . . all right," Miss Sanders didn't sound convinced. "You're an excellent student, David, but I have to make sure *all* my students have the same opportunities to excel. Do we understand each other?"

I turned the corner of the stairwell and, as I walked up the remaining stairs, saw Dave and Miss Sanders standing just outside the classroom.

"Yeah, I understand. Believe me," Dave's voice sounded cold, "I understand completely."

They both turned and looked at me as I approached. Then the bell rang. Miss Sanders looked complacent enough and smiled, but Dave's expression made me feel like I'd been hit with a wrecking ball. Not that I actually knew how it felt to be hit with a wrecking ball, of course, but at that moment I could imagine it. His eyes looked hard as granite, his mouth grim, a deep scowl on his brow reminding me of his brother. I'd only ever seen him look that angry once before. He looked from me to the floor for a moment as if to compose himself, his expression becoming blank, the way I was getting used to seeing it. Then he entered the room. Miss Sanders greeted me and held the door open for me to pass through, then followed me in.

As I walked to my desk, Dave threw himself into his chair at the back of the room, puffing his cheeks out slightly, and then turned to look out the window, frowning again. The whole class had noticed our entrance into the room and were watching both of us.

"What's going on?" I heard Hannah ask him softly, voicing my thought exactly.

"Nothing," he replied. And that's all he said.

Miss Sanders had us open our books and take turns reading. She didn't call on me once, which was a good thing; my mind was a scattered mess. Dave was one of the first people out the door when the bell rang, and he didn't look back.

We were scheduled to have our pictures taken during our last elective, which for Melanie and me was Art. There had apparently been at least two cameras and backdrops set up, but one was in the process of being dismantled. We appeared to be the last class needing photographs, and I was glad there were no other students around. Yes, I was. There was no one there to distract me or make me blush. Last year's picture had actually turned out better than any I'd ever had, due to a certain someone. I hoped this year it would be even better without his influence.

I was in line but nowhere near the camera when an office aide ran in and gave a note to Miss Laski. The aide was a boy I didn't remember seeing before. But he seemed to know me, giving me a sly, slightly appraising look. Miss Laski said I was wanted immediately in the counselor's office.

"Tell them you're getting your picture taken and see if you can reschedule. Okay? I don't think they're going to be here much longer."

I nodded and gulped, suddenly very nervous. We'd been told that counselors would contact Sophomores sometime during the second week to talk about our classes, plans for the future, and any problems or concerns we might have. I had very few thoughts about the first two topics and too many to count of the third, though there was no way I was going to discuss *any* of them. And why was I being called in now instead of next week? I didn't know of anyone else being called in early.

I still hadn't recovered from the way Dave had looked and sounded before English. Feeling sick and very guilty for no reason I could name, I made my way from the gym at the back of the school to the office at the front as quickly as my legs—feeling rubbery and wobbly from nerves—would carry me.

The counselor's name was in a slotted holder next to the closed door: Ms. Woolton. It also said Student Counselor A-L. I'd never met her before. I had met semi-regularly with a counselor at my last school starting in sixth grade, but seeing a counselor had been voluntary last year unless you were called in for some reason. I hadn't even known about them. It had never occurred to me to talk to a counselor about anything, so I guess I'd never felt the need. I still didn't.

I had to wait a few minutes while she finished talking to another student, someone else I didn't recognize at all. When they'd left, Ms. Woolton stood in the doorway.

"Allison? Come in."

Feeling very uncomfortable, I entered her office. She closed the door.

"Sit down," she said in a friendly but businesslike manner.

I took a seat across the desk from her.

"How is your first week of sophomore year going?"

The question sounded casual, the way any adult would have asked it, but her direct stare was anything but casual. It was *intense.* She was expecting more than "fine" for an answer. I didn't have anything more I wanted to give.

I dropped my gaze, looking at the top of her desk, and said, "Fine."

"Are you happy with your classes?"

"Yes."

"Let's see," she said, and I looked back at her face. She was looking at something in the file before her. "You're taking . . ." She recited my class schedule. "Which are your favorites?"

A difficult question to answer at the moment. The ones I felt most at ease in were Art and study hall, though I *wanted* to like the others, too. "Art," was all I said.

"Do you think you'll be able to do well in all your classes?"

"Yes."

"Is there anything you wish you could change?"

Can Hannah be in a different English class? Maybe PE too? That's probably not the kind of change she meant.

Can I switch to Ag. Science? I knew the answer to that one. Last year the intro classes had been too full, and there were even fewer of Ag. Science 2. There was little chance of getting into it this year if you weren't in it last year, which I wasn't. *Oh well, at least Matthew's in Chemistry with me.*

"Allison?"

Oops. My eyes snapped back to hers, then quickly away again. There was something about Ms. Woolton that had me even more nervous than usual. Like she *knew* something; something that may or may not have been in that file in front of her.

Sometimes I stare at people without realizing it. It's gotten me into plenty of trouble in the past. It's usually because I'm thinking of something having nothing to do with them personally. Unless it's Dave, of course, and then it's *all* about him. I just get lost. Sometimes it's even happened with my other trusted friends, and even Cris, only that's different. Much weirder.

But most of the time I find it difficult to hold eye contact, especially if I don't know the person, and *especially* if I don't trust them. The more I try to make myself do it, the more strange and uncomfortable it feels, sometimes unbearably so. It's too intimate. Too invasive. It had gotten better last year after I'd met Dave and Robin and the rest, though I even avoided looking directly into the eyes of some of the people I now counted as real friends. I tended to avoid everyone else anyway. It wasn't something I could describe or explain, but it had been that way for as long as I could remember. I wondered if it was one of the things in the file open in front of Ms. Woolton.

Now I realized, sitting across from her, that it was as bad as it had ever been. I didn't want to look her in the eyes because I was afraid she would see something I didn't want her to, or she would read my mind, or have some kind of power over me—the power to make me say what was *really* on my mind. That, I felt sure, would prove disastrous.

Ms. Woolton sighed slightly, I think in resignation as I still couldn't think of how to safely answer her.

"There's been some concern from your teachers about whether you'll be able to focus on your work and not be too distracted by other things," she paused and then added, "or people."

What the heck? I could picture and hear Miss Sanders talking to Dave and I squirmed inside, a wave of guilt making me feel sick again.

"You enjoy art?"

I nodded.

"Miss Laski says you did well in her class last year."

Say something again, or she'll think you're stupid.

"Yes." *Ugh.*

"Have you thought much about what you want to do after high school?"

Yes . . . and no. Up until the start of last year, I'd sometimes thought, in a very vague sort of way, that I'd do something with books—maybe work in a bookstore or perhaps be a librarian. And then we moved to Douglas. And then I met Dave. And then there were horses, too. Since then, I'd only had one—no, *two*—real ambitions. One was to ride really well. The other—well, I most certainly wasn't going to share *that* with Ms.Woolton.

Formulate a whole sentence, or she's never going to leave you alone.

I mustered up my flagging courage, pushed down the guilt, and struggled to focus on an answer that would satisfy her. I remembered overheard conversations from the tables last year when this subject had come up.

"I'm not sure yet. I'll probably go to Lowell College and get general education classes out of the way. I might know by then."

Ms. Woolton smiled and looked a little surprised but pleased by my answer, and then wrote something down. Maybe she had been beginning to think I was less capable than I was. I get that a lot.

"And how do you feel you're doing socially here? Have you made friends?"

Nonsensically, tears sprang to my eyes, and I was both surprised and angry at myself because of it. My emotions on the subject were intense but also very confused right now. It was a button I wished she hadn't pushed. I clearly remembered the angst I'd gone through last year and, though previously not as sensitive, how easily my emotions had gotten the better of me. I was determined to do better this year. And I *had* been doing better.

Ms. Woolton was looking at me with obvious concern, and I struggled to think of the positive aspect of that question.

"Yes," I said firmly but a little huskily. "Yes, I have wonderful friends."

"That's good," she said gently, nodding her head. "High school can be difficult for a lot of people, for a lot of reasons, but the social aspect can be especially hard. Just let me know if you have difficulty with anything. Okay? Or if you just need someone to talk to."

I knew she was just doing her job, and I was sure she was a really nice person and genuinely wanted to help, but these kinds of discussions always had more of a quelling effect on me. Now I felt not only guilty but betrayed, as if someone had seen me unintentionally doing something wrong and tattled. Elementary school all over again. I just wanted to get away.

And then I remembered.

My pictures!

"Um . . . I'm supposed to be getting my picture taken right now . . ."

I looked at the clock. Only twenty minutes remained before the last bell would ring.

"Oh, certainly. You can go, Allison. Let's talk again soon. I'll schedule an appointment. All right?"

I couldn't help frowning, but I nodded, then got up and left her office. I headed down to the gym as quickly as I could without tripping or running, the latter being something I still didn't really like doing. When I got there, the photographers were packing up the last of their equipment. The gym was otherwise empty.

"I . . . I didn't get my picture taken," I said, feeling nervous and guilty again. I didn't want to bother them but wasn't sure what would happen if I didn't get it done now. I knew it wasn't my fault, exactly, but I *had* forgotten to tell the counselor right away. There had been too many other worries on my mind.

The man and two women looked over at me. The man looked rather stern, but one of the women smiled and beckoned me closer.

"What's your name?"

"Allison. Allison Anderson."

She found my name quickly. "There you are." She circled my name and wrote something next to it. "We'll be here again, probably in October. You can get them done then and still receive them when your classmates do. We'll let the school know and send you a reminder. Okay?"

I nodded, slightly relieved. When I rejoined my art class, there was only a few minutes left to work on my sketches, and I didn't get much done. I was too distracted anyway, thinking over everything that had happened today but trying not to. Melanie and I walked together again to the front of the school after class. Not needing to stop at my locker, I walked directly to where my dad waited. He smiled as I got in the car.

"So, you got through your first week. How'd it go?"

He had asked lightly, a typical Dad question, but I was *so* tired of being asked how I was doing.

"Fine," I said, more shortly than I had meant to. "It was . . . fine."

He looked at me, started the car, and then looked at me again. "You don't look like everything's 'fine.' What's going on?"

"Nothing, Dad. Really. I guess I'm just tired." Then, figuring this was as good a time as any, I said, "I missed getting my picture taken, so I'll have to get it done later."

He nodded his head as if this was an acceptable reason to not be fine. I didn't want to say anything about the counselor.

I spent the rest of the afternoon and most of the evening out with Remmy. Grabbing my pencil case and sketchbook, and putting his hay in a hay net, I walked him down to the corral to play. There was very little vegetation left; most of the corral was dry and quite dusty. The first thing Remmy did when I let him loose was roll—of course. I laughed and tried to sketch him on his back with his legs flailing in the air. Then he got up, leaping and bucking, and frolicked for a bit.

There was a small patch of grass near the stream in the shade of the trees and bushes on the west side of the corral. I tied the hay net closer to the front. While Remmy ate nearby, I sat in the shade and sketched, trying to capture his different poses and expressions. I wouldn't have thought of horses having expressions before, but I had discovered last year with Gold that they did. Subtle, perhaps, but they were there. Remmy's usual expression was one of bright-eyed interest, aware and curious about everything going on around him. If he'd been human, I would have said he looked ready to laugh at any moment; ready for fun. But instead of making me smile, it hurt.

Why doesn't Dave look like that anymore?

On Saturday I got up early, fed and groomed Remmy, and then rode him in the area just beyond the stable while the morning was still chilly. The ground was dry and hard, most of the vegetation either crisp and brown or already worn away from our recent exercise. I had cleared the biggest remaining weeds so that the area was starting to look like a small fenceless arena.

Around five o'clock, Mom drove me over to Bar 8. I watched a video with the kids while Cheryl finished getting ready. I'd never seen her wear a dress before; she looked even prettier and more petite than usual. Tom, also dressed up, had sneaked through the kitchen and out the back door as soon as I got there, I assumed so the children wouldn't notice him leaving.

"They've had their dinner, but there's i-c-e-c-r-e-a-m in the freezer. They can have a little later. There's a list on the table with bedtime and what to do. Oh, and if you need anything, there's a radio here. Gloria's got it on up at the guest house. Just push the button here to talk and then release it. She can answer any questions, and come and help if you really need it. We just don't like asking her to babysit as she already puts up with a lot!"

She smiled then sighed, and for the first time I wondered how often Cheryl got to do anything she wanted to do, just for fun. I felt delighted to help her get out for the evening. I hoped they had a good time.

"Mike, Rachel, and Vince are our wranglers this weekend. You're not alone. Okay?"

I nodded.

"Just remember to ask Cody if he needs to pee every once in a while," she said, her eyes laughing, "or you may have a surprise!"

I tried to smile back and nodded again, now wondering what I'd gotten myself into.

Cheryl managed to sneak out the back door like Tom had. A few moments later, Cody got up and looked around the corner into the kitchen.

"Where's Mama?" he asked.

"She'll be back in a little while," I said, hoping it was a good enough answer.

Apparently it was good enough for him, and he came to sit with me again. But now Zoe was aware that Cheryl was missing. She stood and tottered toward the kitchen too, then stopped and began to whimper, looking lost. I tried to interest her again in the video we were watching to no avail. I was terrified that she would have a meltdown before her mother had been gone five minutes.

Reaching for a large, colorful book laying nearby, I opened it and began to "Ooh" and "Ah" at the pictures. It was an old book of nursery rhymes and songs.

"Look at this, Cody," I said, and he obligingly scooted closer to me.

I began to play a naming game with him that I remembered using when my cousins were younger. Taking into account the kind of boy he was, I pointed to the things I thought he'd identify most with: horses, cows, dogs, spiders. Sure enough, within a few moments, Zoe had tottered back to us and peered upside down at the book laying in my lap. Soon she too was pointing to things for Cody to name, and they both started giggling when he began to make words up.

When they got tired of that, Cody wanted me to actually read the book to them. I had to move the large book onto the floor in front of me as Zoe wanted to climb into my lap. Feeling proud of myself for successfully distracting the children, and also very content and cozy with them, I began to read the pages Cody indicated.

One of the page spreads was predominantly light purple.

"Lavendar blue . . ."

There was a picture of a little boy and girl dressed in royal robes that were too big for them.

"Whilst you and I . . . keep ourselves warm . . ."

I pictured Dave holding me on a cold day when I was heartbroken. I continued reading, but my vision was blurry. I started sniffling.

"Who told you so?"

The little boy had brown hair. The girl had hair in a long braid that was a lighter color.

"'Twas my own heart that told me so."

Stupid heart.

Chapter Four

I spent as much of the day as I could at Bar 8 on Sunday. Tom had kindly picked Remmy and me up before he went out to a job. We had a long lesson with Cheryl, working mostly on the basics and making sure I hadn't forgotten anything over the summer. I didn't seem to have, and I already felt at home in the saddle again. After a little lunch and a rest, Remmy and I joined a group going out on the trail. It was hot and dusty, and I didn't know anyone in the group, but it was good for us. We didn't often get the chance to trail ride. Remmy loved it but seemed to prefer company, and I still wasn't supposed to go off on my own.

Riding wasn't the only reason I wanted to hang out there though. I was hoping against hope that Dave would appear. Tom hadn't said anything about him before leaving, but I knew Dave was still working for him sometimes. *Or he might just randomly stop by. It could happen.*

But it didn't. I stayed until Tom got home, then he took Remmy and me home.

Brenda called with the news that she and Trevor were back together. She was ecstatic. She was so caught up in telling me all about him that she didn't ask about Dave or anyone else. I was glad and tried to be happy for her, but I couldn't help remembering what her friend Jahzara had said.

"Where were you on Friday?"

The voice speaking unexpectedly behind me startled me, but not as much as the edge I detected in it. I was used to a much softer tone.

"Friday," I repeated and turned away from my locker to face Dave.

I thought he looked annoyed. "Yeah. We were hanging out. I thought you'd be there."

My heart started thumping, my thoughts thrown into confusion. "I . . . I . . . didn't know." I was sure I would have remembered if anyone had mentioned it.

And now I was sure he looked annoyed. "Yeah, I told you about it."

It felt like my color might have changed two or three times and I nonsensically wondered if I looked like a chameleon or one of those octopuses that change color according to their surroundings. My changes had nothing to do with the locker behind me.

Dave told me they were hanging out on Friday? There's no way I would have forgotten that, but I was too confused to disagree with him. Worried that I'd offended him or caused him to think I didn't care, I stumbled to find the right words without being defensive.

"I . . . I'm sorry . . . really! You didn't . . . I'm sure . . . I . . . just don't remember you telling me." I looked into his eyes, hoping he could read the truth in mine and trying to find that connection we'd had. But what I saw was different, distant, and after a moment he looked away, which was odd. He wasn't usually the first to break eye contact. Not with anyone. He looked like he was trying to remember.

"I'm sure I told you," he said, sounding less certain and still looking away. "I remember . . ." Now he frowned deeply. I couldn't tell if he was mad or just questioning his memory.

I was almost afraid to speak, to express what had been troubling me all last week, but it might be now or never. "You haven't really talked to me at all."

It sounded like an accusation, but I hadn't meant it to.

He looked back at me and, for just a moment, I felt he saw me again. Really *saw* me. The connection was still there, I was sure of it—I could feel it deep within me—whatever *it* was. His frown was now more one of concern, one I was familiar with, his eyes softening. Then he looked distracted, scratching his head and tousling his hair.

"Yeah, I know. I've been pretty busy."

For those few moments, he seemed himself again, like Dave. *My* Dave; the one that really cared about me. And just as quickly, he was gone.

"So, what's up with you?" That question could have been simply conversational, but the tone wasn't. He looked annoyed again, his eyes harder, colder. "You seem . . . different."

I felt hurt. Then angry.

"I'm not the one who's acting differently."

Did I just say that out loud? I couldn't believe it. I hadn't meant to, but his words stung. I didn't think he was being fair.

"I don't think I'm different," I said, trying to amend what I'd said, but now I just sounded sullen.

He looked uncertain again and I wished I could read his mind. *No, I wish he could read mine! Then any question of how I feel about him would be answered.*

"We're going again this Friday. You should come." After a moment he shrugged and said, "I gotta go," and abruptly turned. He turned back to look me in the eye once more, and said, "I'll see you later." Then he walked away.

I just nodded and waited; watching, feeling numb.

Benjamin distracted me a little in Spanish with tapping and his hat—today a red, fluffy Elmo face—but the rest of the time I struggled to concentrate anyway. We were still practicing pronunciation and learning numbers and more basic vocabulary. I had trouble trusting myself to say the words accurately, sometimes confusing the ones that looked or sounded similar. This caused some muffled laughter behind me.

Geometry was better; Robin's presence, Tanner's silliness, and Jessie's accepting smile provided comfort and minor distraction. But I couldn't help replaying the morning's scene with Dave over and over in my mind, cringing over what I thought my words must have sounded like, puzzling over his changeful demeanor, and very focused on his last words, "I'll see you later." It seemed like he kept saying it, but it held little promise anymore. Still, I was anxious to get to the tables at lunch.

He never came. Hannah was there though, so at least I knew he wasn't with her. I finally had to ask, sure that Robin must know.

"Dave hasn't been here at lunch since the first day of school. Do you know where he is?"

She looked around as if she hadn't noticed him missing, which surprised me. "I think he might be training?"

She obviously wasn't sure, but I took some comfort in the answer. This morning he'd said he'd been busy. I guess he really was. Matthew joined us then, and I tried to at least follow the conversation at our table but with little success. I was still very preoccupied.

PE was next. I hadn't exactly forgotten that this would be track week, but it hadn't been at the forefront of my mind. I'd lived through it last year, and I was fairly confident that I would survive it this year just as well, maybe even better. My legs and arms were stronger. That was thanks mostly to riding and taking care of horses in general, but also just from all the walking I did now. I didn't think my coordination had improved much though.

Deciding to get all the running out of the way first, I went up to the track, sure that's where Dave would be. I didn't know what his best event was, but I knew he could run. Melanie was going that way as well, so we walked together. When we got there, however, she said that Coach had told her to record the times of the runners. Nothing struck me as strange in that, and I left her, reluctantly, to line up for the first race.

My present situation seemed so similar to last year, at least emotionally. By the second week of school, I'd realized how strongly I felt about Dave but had made up my mind to avoid him. I'd felt sure that I could never be more to him than Robin's dorky friend. I now knew that to be untrue; he'd made it very clear on numerous occasions that he cared for me. I was at least *his* dorky friend too.

But now something was different. I just didn't know what. It left me feeling almost as forlorn as I'd felt back then.

Dave was on the other side of the track. My distance vision was slightly fuzzy, but I'd have known him anywhere. I was at the end of the group of girls lining up for the hundred-meter race so had plenty of time to watch him. And I did *watch* him. Unlike last year, I *wanted* him to look my way. I hoped that he would wonder where I was and look around for me. I desperately wanted that contact, however brief, that would make my world right again.

He was in the first group of boys to sprint down the track, easily pulling ahead of the others. Staying at the finish line, he seemed to look toward us, but his gaze didn't linger in any one spot, and he certainly didn't acknowledge me. I wondered if he was looking for Hannah. He took over one of the stopwatches then, and I didn't notice him looking our way again.

And in spite of his "see you later" that morning, I never did. At least, not in any way that mattered.

"It's a test tube. It won't attack you," Matthew whispered the next morning.

I guess I'd been glaring at the apparatus on the lab table. I was preoccupied, as usual, and had been since I woke up, but I certainly couldn't tell him why. So I said, "Glass makes me nervous," which was very true.

"This will be good practice for you then."

"As long as I don't have to use *that*."

"The Bunsen burner?"

"Yes."

"I'm sure you can handle it."

"I have accidental tendencies."

Matthew laughed. "Yeah, I guess you do. Still, I'm sure together we can keep everything under control."

"Well, you're not allowed to be absent on Chemistry days."

He laughed again. "I'll do my best."

I was afraid I wasn't going to do very well in this class. Even math seemed less abstract to me than the periodic table. But Matthew didn't appear intimidated in the slightest. I was really glad he was my lab partner.

After Chemistry we walked to History together. As we entered the classroom, he said, "See you at lunch?"

"Oh . . . um . . . I'm eating with a friend." Then, because I didn't want him to think I didn't consider *him* a friend, I amended, "A *different* friend . . . today."

Matthew regarded me steadily and sort of smiled, though I thought it looked a little wrong. "Well, then I'll see you later."

I didn't know whether he was talking about a specific *later* today or a general *later* sometime in the future, but it didn't seem to matter too much, so I just said, "Yes."

I was happy to join Robin and the others in History and was able to concentrate reasonably well. I was grateful for my "B" day mornings, getting to spend two classes with friends I felt relatively confident with, shielded from potentially unpleasant elements—there was evidence of some in both classes—and mostly free of angst-causing agents.

The same couldn't be said of my afternoon. Since Dave didn't seem to be around during lunch for whatever reason, it made sense to resume eating with Melanie again on Tuesdays and Thursdays. I enjoyed being with her, telling her about my summer, and I was pleased that I was able to make her laugh a little too. She especially appreciated the ketchup story. In turn, she fascinated me with her equine exploits of the summer, though picturing the things she told me about was based purely on videos I'd looked up: jumping, eventing, and dressage.

After lunch was English. My stomach twisted in knots as I walked to class. Participation in discussion was a significant part of our grade in the AP class, and it was going to prove the hardest aspect of the class for me, along with the fact that Dave was there. Even at the best of times I often stumbled over spoken words, preferring situations where I had time to thoroughly think things through or, even better, write them down without speaking at all.

The rest of the class apparently had no trouble speaking out, even interrupting and disagreeing with one another, sometimes quite loudly and energetically. At those times my intellect fled. I sometimes had a problem following the discussion and even more trouble *not* focusing exclusively on Dave. Turning around to face the speakers helped me track the discussion, but any help was diminished by Dave's presence.

That's what happened on this day, and I eventually turned back to face the front again, sighing deeply. Miss Sanders looked at me sternly for a moment. I'd have to be even more careful than I already was; she was far too watchful. I remembered the counselor's questions and briefly thought about changing this class for regular English, but I couldn't seriously consider it. I *wanted* to be here, and not just because of Dave. Or maybe in spite of him.

In Art, we continued working on our still life sketches. Miss Laski had us firming up our lines and adding shading and texture. We could spend the entire time working on one sketch or split the time between several or all as long as we were really working. Melanie and I stayed together and worked mostly on the books and candles, but we didn't talk. Once again I was able to lose myself in the task at hand, jumping when Miss Laski stood between us. She was looking at what we'd both done so far.

"Very nice work, girls," she said gently and smiled at us. She leaned a little further over me and pointed to a couple of areas on my piece. "Don't forget to leave the highlights as well as showing depth of hue and shadow. Remember the contrast work we did last year." She smiled again and moved away.

I looked over at Melanie's work. It always looked perfect to me. She had a light, exacting hand and her forms had a solid yet delicate appearance. Even her straight lines seemed graceful. I often thought her drawings looked better than the subjects themselves; softer, prettier. Mine looked more crudely drawn, my lines more irregular, angular, harsh in comparison, but I liked the way they looked. I drew things the way I saw them, and I think they looked a little more realistic. I still liked hers better though.

Spanish on Wednesday was a little nerve-wracking for me. We were practicing forms of address and simple greetings and, while I had no trouble learning the words themselves, I stressed over pronouncing them correctly. I was sure that as soon as I tried to say something, I'd verbally trip.

I wondered if that was why it had taken me so long to talk when I was little. My mother told me they'd been worried because I spoke very little until I was over four years old, but then I spoke in clear and complete sentences. Or not at all. Things hadn't really changed much. My love of words guaranteed I'd learn quickly, but my lack of confidence and difficulty articulating thoughts and emotions made it seem otherwise. A lot of the time my thoughts just weren't anything I wanted to communicate.

When it was Benjamin's turn, I was startled that he turned to me.

Rising from his chair, he sauntered over to my desk and said, "*Buenos dias, señorita,*" in a low, husky voice, as if he were trying to—I don't know—*seduce* me or something. "*Como esta?*"

The other kids laughed. I was so surprised I just gawked at him for a moment.

My surprise was for several reasons. First, that the unexpected and obviously intentionally flirtatious attention didn't trigger my blush response. That was highly satisfying. Second, that his accent was excellent—from his appearance and name, I doubted there was anything Latino in his background. Lastly, that it irritated me so much. Benjamin was a cute guy, albeit a little odd. In other, similar circumstances, I'd always felt at least a small measure of gratification; that anyone found me attractive was always a pleasant if disconcerting surprise. But all I felt now was annoyed, and I didn't want to think about why.

"*Buenos dias, señor*," was all I could manage in reply, but it didn't come out right; my "n" was wrong and my "r" wouldn't roll so it sounded like I said "snore."

Perhaps it was just as well that I was annoyed as it distracted me just enough to be able to leave my seat, approach a girl close by, and speak a simple greeting. She responded to me much better than I had to Benjamin and looked a little haughty as she did. I went back to my seat, still annoyed.

Geometry kept me engaged enough to recover. After class, Robin and I walked out to the tables together. I was glad to see Shane and a few of the other seniors there today, including the girls who had gone shopping with us during winter break. I'd begun to think that the seniors were too elite to hang out at the tables this year. I hadn't seen any there before now, though I couldn't remember seniors hanging out there last year either. There was no sign of Dave or Hannah.

Robin sat down next to me, and Matthew arrived soon after and sat on my other side. I was hoping someone would mention Dave and where he was or what he was doing, but no one seemed to question his absence. I assumed they must have information I didn't, as I couldn't believe they didn't care. *I* sure cared, and my imagination continued to torment me.

About halfway through lunch, Cris walked over from the direction of the gym. I felt unaccountably happy to see him and then realized that I hadn't seen him at all since about the same time last week. *Then* I remembered I was still mad at him. Even so, I hoped he would notice me, if only to validate my existence.

I watched him until he returned my gaze in a disconcertingly direct manner, then he turned his back and talked to Shane and the others, standing on the far side of the other table. Most of the sophomore girls present were already showing ominous signs of infatuation toward the older boys, but Shane still seemed to be with the dark-haired girl he'd been with last year. Cris seemed as aloof as ever. I decided that I didn't like his facial hair, but that could have just been because I was mad at him.

"You . . . swim . . . spring . . ."

"Hmm?"

Matthew had spoken to me, but I'd only caught about every third word. He wore an amused but longsuffering expression.

"I *said*, 'You should join the swim team this spring.' You swim really well, right?"

"Oh . . . yes. That is, I swim okay."

I wasn't sure I wanted to swim races, and the word "team" made me feel anxious. Historically, teams and I weren't compatible.

"You should think about it. I can put in a good word for you, and it'll be fun."

I tried to smile. Perhaps it *could* be fun. To feel capable of doing a sport in the spring like all my friends might be a wonderful thing.

"I'll think about it," I said, with the best intentions.

When the bell rang, I said goodbye to Robin and Matthew and walked toward the gym. I didn't look forward to PE, but so far this year I didn't dread it. Halfway there, Cris caught up and walked beside me.

"You still okay?" His voice was gruff as if he were compelled to ask and not because he cared.

I wondered why he was asking, and my heart leaped at the thought that Dave might be asking through his brother. But only for about two seconds. The brothers didn't seem to work that way. I didn't *expect* Cris to care, but his manner of asking brought my negative thoughts back to the surface again.

"Yes. I'm fine," I said shortly. Then I realized that he could probably answer my most urgent question. "Is everything all right . . . with you . . . and your family?"

That's not exactly what I wanted to ask, but it would have to do.

Cris looked sideways at me and didn't seem fooled. " 'Everything?' "

I *wasn't* going to blush!

"Yes. I've hardly seen you . . . or Dave . . . since school started." That was true and seemed relatively safe.

"We're both pretty busy. But if you need anything, let us know." Then, as if to clarify, "You know, for Remmy or anything."

The offer disarmed me. I answered meekly, "Oh . . . yes. Thank you."

"I gotta go." He stopped and abruptly began walking back the way he'd come, perhaps toward the parking lot.

"Cris!" I said, needing an answer and not wanting to lose this opportunity. "Is everything really all right . . . with Dave? He seems . . . different."

Cris observed me calmly for a moment, and I wondered what he was thinking. "He's fine. He probably just got too much attention this summer. Is he being a jerk?"

I was horrified that he would think I thought that, and even more horrified that he might tell Dave. "No! No, not at all! I . . . I just . . . wondered."

Cris watched me for a moment longer, then shrugged. "I'm sure he'll get over it. Eventually." He started to walk away again, then turned back long enough to say, "Probably."

If that's supposed to make me feel better, you failed! He could be so infuriating. And I *still* didn't know why he'd gone missing this summer.

I was conscious of tension in the locker room when I arrived, but I got changed and tried to ignore it. As I walked back toward the door, Hannah joined me.

"Hi, Allie," she said in a friendly voice.

I was a little startled—the fact that she seemed to be going out of her way to acknowledge me had me puzzled—but I was about to return her greeting when I was shoved roughly from behind. I barely caught my balance as a group of girls jostled both of us out of the way.

"Hey!" said Hannah, catching herself and frowning. "Be careful!"

I caught the haughty looks a couple of the girls cast at her and was surprised; they were girls I had assumed were her friends.

"Oh, sorry, Hannah," said another girl with a smug expression.

"Yeah, sorry," one of the first girls echoed, but her expression looked anything but sorry.

Then they laughed and continued out the door.

Hannah rubbed her arm where she had collided with the edge of the doorway and shook her head. "What was *that* about?"

She seemed to be asking me, but I wasn't sure if I was actually supposed to know the answer. Only one explanation appeared to answer this kind of question for me, but I didn't want to voice it. Besides, it couldn't possibly be the same for Hannah. She was pretty and sociable. I suspected she was smart, too. Maybe those girls weren't her particular friends, but I was sure I'd seen her hanging out with them. A couple of the girls were in my Spanish class, and one was in English, too. Her name was Roberta. She was also one of the girls that had been in my computer class last year. I knew she didn't like me. Was Hannah's friendliness toward me the reason for their behavior?

I shook my head and tried to smile, then followed Hannah outside.

Though I was relieved to finally get to study hall, I thought it would never end, and I barely got anything done. That meant I'd have to do all my homework later. Apart from the nagging uncertainties that made it hard enough to focus, there was an incessant tapping right behind me. The more I tried to ignore it, the more my ears and nerve endings screamed for relief. I finally looked behind me.

Benjamin.

His unusual eyes were bright and seemed to smile at me. They were a lighter color than I had thought; a very light brown. Then he grinned in a way I can only describe as impish. With his straight, dark brows and wispy, dark auburn hair, I thought he looked like a fantasy being. An elf perhaps— *Lord of the Rings* type, not the packaged-cookie kind. Except for that grin. Leprechaun maybe?

His grin broadened to reveal very white but slightly uneven teeth that made him no less attractive. Not that I cared. His smile continued to widen. Now I was in Lewis Carroll territory. I suddenly realized how long I'd been staring at him.

"Is everything all right, Allison?" asked Mrs. Ochoa.

"Yes!" I said, a little too loudly, and I almost got whiplash from turning to face her so quickly. "Yes," I repeated at a more reasonable volume.

"Well, turn this way and do your own work." She had spoken gently, but her expression was stern.

There was muffled laughter from the rest of the room. Mortified, I felt a tell-tale prickle all over my scalp. Then I got mad. *No blush! Not for this. Especially not because of him, for heaven's sake.*

Benjamin was starting to take on nemesis characteristics in my mind, in much the same way Robin had at the beginning of last year, though for different reasons. But they were similar in some ways too. Technically, they both had red hair, though Robin's was a brighter, coppery color. They both seemed very confident and comfortable with themselves, not concerned with what anyone thought of them. Though something was different with Robin this year, beyond her change of hairstyle. I just hadn't figured out what.

Pursuing this type of comparison distracted me for a while until the tapping started again. I pretended to ignore it as long as I could, then turned around once more.

This time I was *not* going to look at his face. Instead, I focused in what I hoped was a very pointed way on the pencil in his left hand. This was a mistake, for not only was I now distracted with the knowledge that he was left-handed—not that it was significant in any way other than I hadn't seen many people write with their left hand and had often tried to do it myself with laughable results—but his hat was next to his hand on the table. And it was also smiling at me. With teeth.

I'd seen Benjamin come in—it was hard not to as he usually drew attention to himself somehow—and he had swept his cap off in a grand manner to make sure Mrs. Ochoa saw him do it. But apart from the fact that it was blue, I hadn't seen any details. Now I could see that it was a Disney character, Stitch, and the brim was its gaping mouth. Then I noticed that Mrs. Ochoa was standing next to my desk.

"Allison?" Her voice was firm but not unkind. "If you and Benjamin are working on something together, you should sit next to each other."

Even though she'd kept her voice lowered, there was undisguised laughing in the room now, and I blushed furiously.

Unbelievable!

When the last bell rang for the day, I was ready to bolt. I jumped up and squeezed out the door with the others rushing to leave; something I never did. I made my way quickly toward the front of the school, but not quick enough.

"Hey!" a voice shouted behind me.

I ignored it.

"Hey!" The owner of the voice caught up with me. "Allison, right?"

I looked at him warily. "Yes."

He grinned widely, looking freakishly like his hat—except not blue—and rocking slightly on his toes. "I'm Ben," he said enthusiastically as if it were possible I hadn't caught his name yet.

"I know," I said, still wary.

"Well, hey . . . I'm sorry about that. I mean, I wasn't trying to get you in trouble or anything."

I frowned. I wondered if he meant it or was making fun of me. I could never tell. I nodded, turned, and continued toward the car. Dad was watching us.

"Okay," he called after me. "Well, see you tomorrow."

I suppose I should have made an effort to be polite, but I was too annoyed and wondered again what his game was. I was sure he had one. I kept walking and got in the car.

"New friend?" asked Dad.

I looked out the window in the direction he was looking and saw Ben still standing there, watching. He raised his hand slightly. I looked away.

"Not exactly," I said. I didn't know what else to say.

Thursday morning flew by quickly, even pleasantly. Matthew had a way of taking up the slack for me in Chemistry without my asking and without making me feel stupid and without anybody else seeming to notice, and I was very grateful. I didn't know how I'd fare in an exam, but I wasn't going to worry about it. History was easy enough, and I even volunteered to answer a question—not something I did often anymore, even when I knew the answers.

I enjoyed lunch with Melanie, but I was anxious, too, so I had a hard time participating in conversation. We were going to begin reading *A Midsummer Night's Dream* in English and everyone, sooner or later, would take a turn reading a character. Then we'd analyze the scenes and the language used. I hoped other people would volunteer first.

I went straight to class. There didn't seem to be any point in lingering outside, hoping to have some kind of interaction with Dave. And I didn't look his way when he came into the room, but I was aware when he did. Yes, very aware.

We finished up our still life sketches in Art. Before the bell rang, Miss Laski set us an assignment for the weekend. We were to assemble a still-life at home, somewhere with a source of light, and where it could be left set up indefinitely. We could use any stationary objects we wanted, but she'd award extra points for a distinct theme. Then we were to do a very loose sketch of it, just enough to show the objects' basic shapes, their spatial relationship, and the direction of the light source. We would have to do a short presentation describing the still life and our plans on how we would complete a drawing of it. The rest of the class and Miss Laski would then critique the project and give suggestions. The fully rendered drawing would be our first semester's project.

Everyone except Melanie and me groaned. I was excited and couldn't wait to get started. I was amazed when the bell rang and realized I hadn't thought of Dave for the whole period again.

Mom was picking me up, so I hurried to the parking lot and didn't look around at all.

"Allie!" my favorite voice called.

I looked up to see Dave and some other kids standing next to Cris' truck.

"You're coming tomorrow, right?" Matter-of-fact. A reminder of an appointment.

It had been on my mind all week. How could it not? He'd made such a point of it on Monday. But I'd been wrestling all week, too—whether to go or not. I'd had so little contact with him since Monday morning, I'd almost decided—yes, probably, for sure—that I *wouldn't* go.

I didn't like the way I was starting to feel. Not just missing him; something deeper and more disturbing. I didn't blame Dave for it, but he was definitely the catalyst if not the cause. I guess my own feelings for him were the cause, and that wasn't his fault. But I no longer felt important to him in any way and that hurt. I'd been trying to make up my mind, not to avoid him entirely like last year, but to distance myself from him as he seemed to have distanced himself from me.

And now he'd asked me pointedly about hanging out after school. I was still staring at him, and he tipped his head slightly, but there was no corresponding smile. Still, I couldn't help my answer.

"Yes," I called back as loudly as I dared.

He nodded once, and I turned to continue to the car. Mom had seen our exchange.

"How is Dave doing? I haven't seen him since before vacation."

I wasn't sure what to say. I had no idea how he was doing. "I don't see him much either. He was just wondering if I was going to hang out after school with everybody tomorrow. I said yes."

Mom looked at me, her eyebrows raised, and I looked back wondering what she'd say. Usually, I'd ask permission first to do things, but I didn't think I should have to about this. Oddly, I almost hoped she'd say no.

"That sounds nice," she said. "Do you want to call me when you want a ride home?"

I hadn't thought that far ahead and felt a little flustered. "Is that okay?"

"Yes, tomorrow it's fine, but don't forget that sometimes I'll be working, and Dad won't always be able to help either. Okay?"

I understood the gentle rebuke and nodded. I loved how my mother usually didn't make a big deal of things. I had a hard enough time carrying around the guilt I *didn't* understand. I hadn't meant to assume she was at my beck and call. We hadn't talked about my learning to drive yet, but I was starting to think that being able to drive might be an excellent thing.

We had just turned onto Main Street toward Old Town on our way home when I saw Ben coasting on his skateboard. He looked up and saw me, then waved. I looked away and pretended I hadn't noticed. But Mom had.

"Do you know that boy?"

"What boy?" I said, looking over on *her* side of the road.

"He was just back there. I'm sure he waved at you."

I looked behind us on my side. "I can't really see him." This would have been true if I hadn't already seen him. I shrugged and said no more about it.

On Friday there was only one thing on my mind. I didn't see Dave all day except briefly in the distance during PE, but I knew I'd at least see him after school. More than that, I didn't know. But I'd made up my mind to try to be as open and upbeat as I possibly could and happy with any attention from him, no matter how brief. One glance, one look the way he *used* to look at me, and I was sure I could be content.

I was conscious of Ben in both Spanish and study hall, but he didn't bug me, and I avoided looking at him.

Quite a large group assembled near the parking lot after school, which was where Robin told me to meet her. I'd gone to my locker before my last class to save time and make sure I didn't get left behind.

Most of our friends were there—Matthew, Tanner, and Jessie—and some not-exactly-friends to me such as Hannah and Roberta. Some of the other kids I'd seen around but didn't know. I noticed that Stacie and Kyle weren't there.

I wish I could say I enjoyed the time spent with my friends. Instead of heading down to the coffee shop as we'd always done before, we walked downtown to the park. It was a scorching hot day, but there was plenty of shade there, and if we stood close enough to the big fountain, the mist from it kept us cool. Some of the kids split off to go to a sandwich shop for drinks. Some were just playing around or lounging on the grass. Robin and I sat on the grass near the fountain for a while, then Robin decided to get on the children's merry-go-round. We took turns pushing each other and whatever children were on it, getting very dizzy and laughing a lot. I hadn't done anything like it in a very long time and had forgotten how much I loved spinning.

I couldn't help keeping track of where Dave was and was very aware of everyone else's proximity to him, especially Hannah's and Roberta's. In fact, I was surprised that Roberta seemed to get more of his attention than Hannah. She certainly was more demanding. Hannah didn't seem to mind, though I thought she looked a little sad at times.

Eventually, Dave and a few of the others came over to the merry-go-round too, and began to push it very fast. Luckily there were no tiny children on it, and the bigger ones that were there squealed with delight. Their mothers watched warily. Roberta made sure to be close to Dave at all times and fell against him whenever she could. He didn't seem to mind. I watched for any indication that he was particularly aware of me but saw none. None at all.

I began to feel a little sick—just from the spinning, I'm sure—and eventually got off to call my mom to pick me up. When she arrived, Robin said to say hi to her and that she'd walk home with Tanner. I tried to slip away without drawing attention to the fact that I was leaving, all the while hoping that Dave *would* notice and react somehow.

He didn't, and the weekend looked pretty bleak.

Chapter Five

I tried to keep myself occupied over the weekend, spending a lot of the time grooming and riding Remmy. I was feeling as confident on horseback as I had before summer vacation. That might not be saying a lot, but it was a lot for me. It was difficult to not think of Dave around Remmy, but I was trying.

The rest of my time was put into homework and especially my art assignment. I took it very seriously and wanted to do well on it. The moment Miss Laski had told us of it, I had known exactly what I wanted to do. After riding Remmy on Saturday morning, I cleaned the things I wanted as best I could and took them up to my room. Mom looked curious as I passed through the kitchen but didn't say anything.

Saddle blanket, bridle, body brush, and hoof pick; I placed them all in the middle of my bedroom floor and looked around. A corner near my dresser suited my purpose well, so I put my desk chair there. I arranged the blanket on the chair so that a couple of large folds were created against the back, then placed the bridle over the corner of the chair, the reins curving into what would be the foreground. I took my boots off and set them at the other side of the chair, then placed the body brush and hoof pick on the blanket. I wasn't happy with the composition and rearranged it many times, especially the boots and reins, until I felt the arrangement was attractive. But something was missing. I went back downstairs and took one of the now ever-present apples from the bowl on the kitchen table and a couple of big carrots from the refrigerator. Mom now looked curious.

"Art project," I informed her.

"Oh," she said, looking skeptical.

I added the carrots and apple to my arrangement and moved my work lamp off my desk to the floor nearby. I have no idea how long I experimented with the positioning of the items and the lamp, trying to get just the right composition and lighting, but Mom came looking for me when it was dinner time.

"So this is what you've been doing." She still looked curious and confused. "What, exactly, *are* you doing?"

"It's a project for art," I told her enthusiastically. "We have to do a rough sketch this weekend, then we'll work on fully rendering it."

Mom nodded slowly but looked worried. "Isn't it going to be difficult to keep arranging and rearranging everything?"

I looked at the items and back at her, not sure what she meant.

"Aren't you going to be using those things pretty regularly?"

"Oh." *Oh. Of course I am.*

My heart sank. It had seemed like the perfect idea for me, and I'd hoped to get extra credit for my theme. She was right, though. It *would* be difficult to use the items and then put them back in exactly the same spot every time; it would make drawing very frustrating if not downright impossible.

"Wait a minute . . . I have an idea." She left my room and ran downstairs. She was back in a moment with the camera. "We can at least take some pictures. It might help."

She took some pictures from different angles, and we spent some time after dinner downloading and printing them. I went to bed feeling like I had accomplished a lot, then realized that I hadn't thought of Dave the whole afternoon; at least not in any focused way. I felt a little sad, even slightly guilty that I could be so easily distracted, but relieved too. In spite of his lack of attention, I thought I was coping pretty well.

I spent a good part of Sunday sketching the objects and trying to give an indication of highlights and shadows, listening to music and trying not to think of anything else. When I'd done as much as I could, I took the bridle and hoof pick and spent the rest of the time with Remmy. I left the blanket in its place. I had a thick saddle pad that would work just fine without it for a while, and I had other brushes.

If anyone had asked, I would have said I'd had a good weekend.

Matthew saved me from blowing myself up in the middle of chemistry on Monday—testing reactions—and it seemed like we were laughing for the rest of the period.

"Are you doing better now?" he asked as we packed up before the bell.

"Doing what better? Science?"

He laughed and said, "No. You've seemed, I don't know, even quieter than I remember. I thought maybe something," here he paused, looked down for a moment, and his expression changed, "or some*body* had upset you."

I didn't know how to respond to that but didn't feel like laughing anymore.

"No," I said quietly. "No one has done anything. I'm fine."

He didn't speak again right away, but I could feel him watching me. I tried to keep my expression neutral, an old skill that wasn't as easy now as it used to be. It looked like I'd have to start practicing again.

He said quietly, "If you ever need . . . anything . . . I'm here." After another moment, he said, "You know, sometimes people aren't exactly what you think they are . . . or want them to be."

It seemed like such a random thing to say that it startled me into looking at his face. His expression was serious, and I thought he was trying to read my reaction. I also thought that it was a very Cris kind of thing to say, then fully realized what—or *who*—Matthew was alluding to. My heart felt a couple of pounds heavier. Was I that easy to read? And what exactly was Matthew trying to tell me?

I couldn't ask. "Thank you," was all I could say.

The bell rang, and he gave me a tight-lipped smile. We walked to History without saying anything more.

Dave wasn't at the tables at lunch, but Hannah and Roberta were. Robin and I had walked there together, but it wasn't until Tanner joined us, very boisterously, that I realized how quiet she'd been. We'd barely talked in History—not that we were allowed to speak much, but she'd seemed very subdued. Now that Tanner had arrived the noise level around us rose considerably, the other kids, even Kyle and Stacie, joking and laughing loudly about this and that. Some were trying to play cards again, but they kept arguing about the rules.

Robin seemed lost in her own thoughts. It occurred to me that what Matthew had said to me really applied to Robin as well. She definitely wasn't acting the same this year, and I wondered why. Was she missing Dave, too? I'd been so preoccupied guessing about other aspects of Dave's social life that I hadn't been able to get a handle on Robin's current relationship with him any more than I had at the beginning of last year. She rarely mentioned him unless prompted to, but she didn't seem to be avoiding him or upset with him in any way.

I existed through English, glad that I wasn't called on to actually do or say anything, and I gave my presentation on my proposed project in Art. Class feedback was mostly positive, and Miss Laski liked the theme but made some suggestions for light direction that might yield more depth and contrast. Melanie thought it was good and that meant more to me than anything.

In spite of my productive weekend and determination to be optimistic, Matthew's words from the morning had rattled me, especially added to what Cris had said before, and I thought about them all day. By the time I got home, I was fighting a losing battle with analysis. I'd only seen Dave in English, and we hadn't talked. He'd barely glanced my way when he came into the room. It was clear to me that either something had drastically changed, or I was a complete idiot who had not only romanticized a simple friendship but misunderstood the reciprocal value of that friendship, too. I honestly thought we were much closer than we apparently were.

And yet . . .

Other memories prodded me insistently, making it hard to concentrate on homework, even without other distractions.

I could clearly recall the way he'd looked the day Cris went missing. He'd called me—not Robin, not anyone else, but *me*—and even though I'd told him over the phone that I hadn't seen his brother, he still came over. He seemed to need to be with and talk to someone, and he'd chosen me! I'd felt helpless at the time, knowing there was nothing I could do or say to alleviate his concern, yet he *had* seemed comforted when he left. And there were so many times last year when he had sought me out, when my well-being seemed important, and my companionship seemed of some consequence to him. I had *not* imagined that; it had been too remarkable. Then there were the special events and outings I'd been invited to. He hadn't *had* to ask me. He had truly seemed to want me around.

And I would never, *never* forget the way his arms felt wrapped around me.

No, I definitely hadn't imagined everything. That only left change. Something must be different.

I was different, of course. I guess I did *look* quite different; my shorter, loose hair and lack of glasses being the most obvious changes. My shape had changed slightly. I still lacked the more voluptuous curves a lot of the girls at school had, including some of my friends, but I seemed less angular, even to myself. The contours of my body were softer, and my legs and arms didn't seem quite as out of proportion long. I couldn't imagine that any of these changes would matter to my best friends, though. Why would Dave *not* like me because of those things?

Then there were the changes on the inside—*significant* changes—but I doubted it was evident to most people. My parents had noticed. And Brenda had, too. But I didn't think Dave, Robin, or any of my other newer friends had either known me long enough to know how *much* I'd changed or would care even if they had. It certainly didn't affect how I felt about *them*. Isn't that all that mattered? What else could it be?

Hannah.

I'd barely been aware of her last year. I was sure she hadn't hung out at the tables—at least not enough for me to remember her. Had she and Dave connected over the summer somehow? He hadn't been around in Douglas much, though. Had she been in Hawaii? I felt suddenly sick when I considered that. The vague thoughts I'd had all summer and continuing as school started, of unknown numbers of girls vying for his attention, seemed to diminish in magnitude at the possibility of this one girl sharing the vacation with him. How many days away? *How many nights?*

That led to the remaining possibility, that Dave himself was different; that his feelings had changed toward me, or that place I held in his life— whatever it had been—had changed due to some cause having nothing to do with me at all.

This last thought was momentarily comforting. I hated the idea that something I'd done, or even more distressing, something I *was*, had alienated him somehow. But then I realized that if the change had nothing to do with me, it was actually far worse. If the problem was me, I could perhaps fix it. I could change, or change *back*. I could always grow my hair or wear my glasses. I could even lose weight if I had to. I still had trouble remembering to eat sometimes; I was sure I could get skinnier again.

As much as it hurt imagining having to change to regain his good opinion, it was nothing compared to the pain I felt every time I thought of how *he* might have changed. Had he just outgrown me; outgrown the friendship we'd had or the brotherly feelings he'd apparently felt toward me? Had he fallen in love over the summer? With Hannah? Someone else? Or was it a different kind of change? I could hear my mother saying, after she'd first met him, *"He's obviously a very physical boy."* She was right. He was.

Each time my mind arrived back at this point I felt overwhelmed, sick to my stomach, and immensely sad, though I never would have been able to express exactly why. I'd been unhappy last year when I first realized the depth of my feelings for Dave, sometimes *very* unhappy. But I would gladly have felt that way again instead of this—this nothing.

Less than nothing. . . .

Tuesday was an "A" day, which was becoming A for Avoidance. I avoided interacting with Ben in Spanish. I avoided, with varying degrees of success, being any kind of target in PE and trying to *not* let myself look around for Dave's whereabouts. I avoided contact with Ben again in Study Hall. I avoided all male acquaintances after school. Being Tuesday, I had eaten lunch with Melanie—effectively avoiding Dave, whether or not he was at the tables, *and why would I want to be there just because of him anyway?*

So far, every day since school started had been scorching hot, and my after-school activities had fallen into something of a routine: work on homework before dinner while it was still too hot to do much outside—usually whatever was the hardest for me or that I liked least; later, feed Remmy, eat dinner myself, then groom Remmy and work with him until dusk. I most often took him down to the hidden corral and rode him there, though occasionally I just lunged him. Sometimes I did both, especially if he was very frisky.

I was also riding him more in the relatively flat area just beyond the stable and paddock. My parents liked me to ride there as they could keep an eye on me. They had a tendency to worry and, considering what had happened the last time I'd ridden before going away for the summer, I couldn't really blame them.

Sometimes I just lingered around the stream with him—under the trees where I'd first met Gold and we'd played our games—and walked along and even through the water in my oldest and favorite Converse. This felt really good as the water was cold. Remmy loved just standing in it and sometimes pawed it, which made me laugh. I had avoided coming to this area for a long time, but now, with Remmy by my side, I felt I could enjoy it again and think of my time with Gold as a beautiful dream.

Though I was sorely tempted to, I didn't stray much farther than that. The dirt road that continued past the corral became more of a wide track and, beyond a fence, disappeared through the trees and around hillsides. I wasn't brave enough to explore there yet. I hadn't been riding anywhere near as long as my friends and, in the time before we'd left Douglas for the summer, I hadn't been allowed to ride because of my injury. I wanted to take my time and feel completely secure again before trusting my riding skills beyond known territory, at least by myself.

As for homework, there was already a lot of it, especially geometry which I thought I was going to like better than algebra. Something about visual representations was easier than formulaic equations for me; abstract but comprehensible. While I couldn't imagine how I'd ever use it in real life or what its practical application was, it made more sense to me than just numbers and letters. History and English had required mostly reading so far, which was not a problem but there was a lot of it.

And then there was Spanish. It wasn't particularly hard; I could understand the assignments just fine, and I didn't need anyone's help with it. But even that distracted me badly. I had to keep my mind detached from what I was actually doing, or I got nowhere.

El chico. *Dave*

La chica. *Me. Or maybe Hannah. Or maybe someone else . . .*

La conversación . . . *that we* don't *have.*

La problema. *I don't know!*

Lately, I'd chosen to do the bulk of my homework either in the kitchen before dinner or at the dining table after playing with Remmy. Under normal circumstances, trying to do it while Mom and Dad pottered about before dinner or watched television after would have been too distracting. Right now, doing it in my room was far worse.

My room held too many dear and tortuous associations. One in particular. My mind always ended up in the same place: on my bed, wrapped in Dave's arms. Throughout the summer I had let my mind dwell there whenever it wanted to. Now I tried to completely avoid it.

I thought I'd been holding up pretty well, considering. This time last year, before Dave had let me know that he *did* notice me and he *did* care, I'd been a basket case. The pain I'd felt was so real and raw that just thinking about him had brought tears to my eyes. What I felt now was a dull, constant ache. It weighed me down and oppressed me, but I could function through it. After all, everything was still conjecture at this point. I didn't *know* anything was wrong, I just *felt* it. I wasn't sure which was worse, and would I be happier knowing that, yes, there was something wrong? I doubted it.

By Wednesday morning I was determined to confront Dave. I quailed inside every time I thought about what I could actually say to him, so I tried not to think about it. Just finding him alone would probably be difficult enough, but maybe I could wait for him before English.

That didn't happen. Soon after Robin and I got to the tables, we saw Dave walking toward us from the quad with a new girl. I have a hard time recognizing people I don't know well, but there weren't many Black students at our school and very few in our grade. I was sure I hadn't seen her before. She and Dave were talking animatedly together in Spanish and I tried not to stare but couldn't help it. I think everyone was staring as it had gone suddenly quiet. Stacie elbowed Kyle and he abruptly shut his mouth.

The girl was several inches shorter than Dave, petite and curvy. She wore her hair pulled back from her forehead and held with a band, then loose in tight waves to her shoulders. Her skin was clear, smooth, and very deep brown.

"This is Paola," said Dave, looking around at everyone. "Her family just moved here from Cuba. She speaks English really well but is still learning, so help her out, okay?"

Paola looked around at all of us with happy-looking eyes. "Hello," she said, smiling broadly.

All the boys were quick to return the greeting, a couple almost falling off the benches in their haste to make space for her at the other table.

"What are you up to now?" said Robin as Dave sat down across from her.

He shook his head. "Not up to anything. Got called to the office and they asked me to watch out for her. You know, translate and stuff. Her dad's a friend of my dad."

"Mmhmm . . ." she returned, noncommittally.

Dave looked at me steadily for a moment, really the first time since that day outside English.

"Everything all right?" His eyes lingered on me a moment more, then he looked back at Robin.

"What do you care?" she asked with such attitude that I caught my breath. It was exactly what I'd been thinking. Then she grinned and said, "Just kidding," and kicked him hard under the table.

"Ow!" he scowled at her. "What was *that* for?"

"I just thought you needed a reminder that you're a human being, not Superman."

"What the hell?"

"You can't be everything to everybody," she said as if that clarified things at all.

Dave looked as baffled as I felt. He looked at me and I shook my head slightly. When he continued looking at me, raising his brows in a familiar query, I understood and gave my standard, "I'm fine," but I couldn't look him in the eyes.

He looked at me a moment longer without expression, then turned back to Robin and said, "I'd never be Superman anyway. Batman, maybe." He flashed a smile at her, the kind I hadn't seen since the start of summer, and his eyes glittered a little, a dangerous look that confirmed my heart was still reactive. *That* was the Dave I knew, or at least one aspect of him. Where were the others? The gentle, affectionate side? The considerate, comforting side?

After that, I found it difficult to look at him at all without staring and feeling short of breath, so I turned my attention back to the new girl, the activity at the other table, and the dynamics taking place there.

Most of the boys were very solicitous, obviously asking Paola questions, but I couldn't make out any specifics. She looked comfortable with and appreciative of the attention. Most of the girls sitting and standing close by seemed less inclined to talk but watched her closely too. Hannah wandered

over and stood with some of the others, listening and contributing to the conversation.

Roberta had looked Paola over critically, but now her attention was entirely on Dave. She had moved toward him when he sat down across from us, but there was no room next to him, so she stood behind—close enough to hear and to rest her hand on his shoulder. It seemed odd and I didn't like it. Dave didn't seem to notice.

I'd been too focused on other things to closely follow conversation at our table, though I knew it was mostly sports related: track try-outs and cross-country training, which quite a few of the kids were involved in, including Dave; girls' volleyball, which Stacie and Jessie were excited about; boys soccer, of course; and the start of football.

Kyle was the only one of our close group playing the latter, but a few of the girls were cheerleaders and were very excited about the upcoming season. There was some talk about the previous season and how well Kyle had played. Stacie, sitting next to him as she usually did these days, surprised me by leaning in and kissing him right on the mouth.

"Are you going to have time to play?" asked one boy.

"You know, you've got to conserve your strength. You're not supposed to . . . *you* know . . ."

Kyle looked uncomfortable. "Shut up," he said, but he was grinning.

"Yeah, now that he's going out with *Stacie*," teased another.

Now Kyle looked genuinely embarrassed, but Stacie smiled, obviously not concerned.

"The youngest guy here and the only one dating. Right?" said Matthew.

There was some laughter, but I noticed that almost everyone looked at Dave, as if for his affirmation. Roberta still had her hand on his shoulder.

"If you can call it *dating*," laughed Tanner. "Do you guys actually *go* anywhere? Kyle can't even drive."

The others were laughing again, and Kyle looked much more annoyed now. "Shut up. You're just jealous."

"I've got *my* license," said Stacie, smiling slyly. She pulled out a beaded keychain and jangled the keys.

There was more laughter, but I guess what I'd begun to suspect about them was confirmed. Robin didn't look surprised at all.

The conversation turned to soccer, and I listened more closely. There was mention of a tournament sometime in the future, but a scrimmage game was here at Douglas after school today.

"Are you going?" asked Dave, looking from Robin to me and back again.

"I'll hang out if I can get a ride after," she said.

"Yeah, sure," shrugged Dave.

"You can always walk home with me," said Tanner, grinning widely.

Robin gave me a longsuffering look.

"I'm going!" said Roberta, loudly.

Dave half turned as if to verify who was standing behind him. Roberta's hand lifted from his shoulder, and she looked slightly self-conscious but recovered quickly. He smiled at her and turned back to us. Her hand returned to his shoulder. The girl sitting next to him and a few of the others affirmed their intentions also.

Cris had wandered over while I was watching the other table. He stood nearby, facing us and talking to some juniors. He could probably hear everything being said, but he didn't move closer. He was the only senior around today. I remembered I still had things I wanted to say to him. I kept missing the opportunity and wondered if I should risk drawing attention to myself by going over to him now. *The last time I'd been seen talking to him—*

"Are you staying?"

I turned to see Dave looking at me.

"Hmm?" *Staying?* I thought maybe I'd missed the bell and looked around to see if anyone was leaving.

Dave returned my gaze impassively; I couldn't tell what he was thinking or feeling.

"After school. Are you staying for the game?"

"Oh . . . I didn't . . ." I looked toward Cris. He was still watching. "I didn't know about it," I mumbled. *Ugh. Déjà vu.*

"Hnh," Dave said, still impassive and still watching.

I felt like a complete jerk. This was important to him, and I should have known about it. Now he probably thought I didn't care—if he thought anything of it at all. He didn't seem mad but didn't look disappointed either. Then he frowned slightly.

"Where've you been at lunch anyway? You're never here."

I gaped at him now. What was this, some kind of cruel joke? Was he just messing with me?

Robin came to my defense. "She's been here."

Dave frowned again and shook his head, but also looked confused.

More *déjà vu*; different but very similar circumstances. I thought over the past days and weeks since school had started.

"I've been eating in the cafeteria on Tuesdays and Thursdays," I offered. "Like last year."

He looked like he was thinking, too, and his brow cleared. "Hmm . . . I guess those were the only days I was here, huh."

Robin nodded and rolled her eyes, then said to me, "Coach Barry's been making him train three times a week during lunch." Then she leaned closer to me and pretended to lower her voice, though Dave could hear her just fine. "It's obviously affecting his brain."

He grinned slightly. "Maybe," he acknowledged. "I don't seem to have time to even think lately."

Matthew spoke up, apparently thinking more explanation necessary. "Some of the guys aren't happy about Dave playing varsity this year. The older JV guys don't think it's fair, and the guys on the varsity team think he needs to prove himself more first. So Coach is making him train harder than them."

Dave nodded, ruefully. "Some sort of compromise, I guess."

"Coach is just trying to protect your fragile ego," said Matthew. I couldn't tell if he was joking, though he'd said it with a smile. I assumed he was just giving his friend a hard time. "He's scared your feelings will get hurt if the other guys dis you for being a sophomore."

"Whatever," said Dave, but his eyes looked cold.

Everyone else laughed, but Matthew had a similar expression to Dave. There seemed to be some tension between them, but the subject changed and the moment passed. They were soon acting and talking together as they usually did, but I was wrestling with the new information.

Logically, if Dave had been in training all this time during lunch, then he *wasn't* with Hannah or anyone else. Right? And he apparently *had* noticed, at least a little, that I wasn't here on the other days. I should have felt relieved, but my heart had been overpowering my logic for over a year now, and things still didn't feel right. Last year he would have noticed *sooner* that I wasn't around; maybe would have come looking for me. I certainly hadn't been expecting or even hoping that he would do that, but it sure would have been comforting.

I also wondered where Hannah had been on the days Dave had been missing. And what was up with Dave and Roberta all of a sudden? And what was going to happen now that the new girl, Paola, was here? I was already worried about the "watching out for," the "translating," and especially the "and stuff" Dave had been asked to provide. I was indignant too. Couldn't they have found a suitable *girl* to do those things?

The bell rang and I felt a little desperate. Dave got up, and Roberta remained by his side. There was no way I could talk to him with her near. Not only would it be embarrassing and annoying, but it would also be dangerous. I didn't trust Roberta any further than I could pick her up and throw her, and I doubted I could even pick her up.

Dave moved as if to go toward the other table, but Paola had seen him get up and ran to him. Hannah followed more serenely.

"So what's next?" Dave asked Paola.

"*¿Qué?*" She looked confused.

"*¿Qué clase tienes ahora?*"

"Oh!" She handed her schedule to him. "*¿Es historia, no?*"

"Yeah," confirmed Dave. "History."

"Heestory," repeated Paola.

He smiled at her. She beamed back at him. A thread that had already worked loose, somewhere in my heart, began to unravel.

"It's near English," said Hannah. "I'll take her."

Dave smiled at her, and the two girls began walking up the hill, talking and obviously getting to know one another as they went. Dave followed in the same direction with Roberta. She was talking nonstop, and Dave's head was bent slightly toward her, listening, but her conversation didn't appear to allow him much room to respond. I remained where I was, watching them and feeling useless, until I noticed Matthew had walked back.

"Are you planning on camping out here for the rest of the day?" he asked. He was smiling, but his eyes looked wrong again. "Come on. I'll walk part of the way with you."

I tried to smile in response and walked up the hill with him, still watching Dave and Roberta. Dave turned and looked over his shoulder once, then did a double-take. He continued walking but didn't seem as attentive to Roberta.

When Matthew and I reached the corner of one of the math buildings, we parted ways and I continued alone to English through the now almost empty corridors, ideas of confrontation abandoned, hope diminished even more.

As soon as school was over, I rushed to the parking lot to find Mom. This time I wasn't trying to avoid anyone, too intent on an answer to the day's most urgent question to notice anyone else.

"Can I stay for a while?" I asked, trying not to sound desperate but feeling it greatly. I hadn't been able to talk alone with Dave, and I probably wouldn't get a chance later, even if I stayed for the game. But it felt vitally important that he know I was there. "There's a game . . . soccer . . . here."

Mom frowned. "I don't think so, sweetheart. I have dinner planned and Dad will be home around seven. He's going away again soon, you know."

"Please?" I tried not to whine. "Robin will be here. I don't mind missing dinner, and you can pick me up at her house later—"

"No," said Mom, firmly. "I don't want to drive all the way back into town again today. Another time. Okay?"

I nodded and got into the car, saddened and, as the car drove away, acutely conscious of increasing distances.

Chapter Six

Benjamin seemed to be going out of his way to annoy our Spanish class in general and me in particular on Thursday. I tried, unsuccessfully, to block him out. Even Mrs. Ochoa told him to be quiet three times. Today his cap was purple with a Superman "S" on it. It reminded me of Dave's comment from the day before, and that bugged me too.

Geometry proved distracting enough to keep my thoughts occupied, but I was glad to escape to the cafeteria at lunch to meet Melanie, even though I wondered if Dave would be at the tables. I was sure the talk would be all about yesterday's games, and I really wanted to be there, but I resisted.

In study hall, Benjamin startled me by practically throwing himself into the chair across from mine. When the girl that usually sat there came in, she shrugged and found a chair elsewhere in the room. There was a ripple effect as everyone came in and found their seats occupied by others. It took a few minutes for the class to settle, but everyone seemed good-natured about it.

"Do you like my hat?" asked Benjamin, taking it off and putting it on my desk.

"What?" I said, though I'd heard him plainly.

"My hat. Do you like it? It's a DC edition Superman cap."

"I like Batman better," I said, and then hoped he wouldn't ask why.

He wrinkled his nose, put his hat back on, and said, "Batman's just a regular guy with a ton of money and a little muscle. Superman is an *alien* with *superpowers*. There's no comparison."

"I like regular guys," I said, annoyed with myself for responding to him at all.

"He's a playboy, scared of commitment. Superman has a heart of gold. I mean he's been with Lois Lane *forever*. Mostly, anyway. That's important, isn't it?"

It *was* important, at least to me, though it seemed like a very strange question to be asking. But my mind wasn't really on Superman *or* Batman. *What the heck is he bugging me for?* I sighed deeply and realized I was frowning.

He was still watching my face. "You don't like aliens?"

Another loaded question. As well as liking Westerns, my dad was something of a science fiction fan, and I usually watched those shows and movies with him. I tended to find the aliens much more interesting and infinitely more relatable than the "normal" humans in such shows. I'd even had character crushes on some of them, but I'd never admit that out loud. At least, not anymore.

I didn't like the question. "No." *Go away!*

Mrs. Ochoa came in, put some books on her desk, then looked around the classroom, momentary confusion evident on her face. Then she laughed and said, "Apparently we're all in need of a change of scenery."

I wondered if Benjamin had any idea what she alluded to. He didn't seem to.

On the way home, Mom asked, "Will you be staying after school tomorrow? I'm working, so you could stay with your friends and then come to the pool later."

In truth, I'd been stewing about this all week—whether to hang out after school with the others on Friday again. While I couldn't help wanting to be wherever Dave was, and he was likely to be hanging out, it seemed masochistic to go when I was convinced that none of that time would be spent actually with him in any meaningful way. Plus, I'd have to watch the other girls, especially Hannah and Roberta, getting the attention I so craved. And would Paola be there now too? The number of girls regularly receiving that attention was certainly growing.

"No, I'd rather just come home," I said quietly.

On Friday I tried to focus on the positive aspects of the upcoming week-end—riding and spending more time with Remmy, a lesson with Cheryl, hanging out at Bar 8—and to not think of anything else. I especially wanted to avoid Dave. Instead of going out to the tables with Robin after History, I told her I was going to go ask a question about my art project.

"Oh," she said, sounding surprised. "I guess I'll see you later then."

"Okay," I responded, feeling guilty. Not only would I probably *not* see her later, at least not later today, she probably thought I needed to talk to a teacher.

I would admit, if I had to, to avoiding issues, occasionally having selective hearing and memory—though most often I honestly hadn't heard because I was thinking my own thoughts and/or really had forgotten—and mostly keeping opinions, when I had them, to myself. But outright lying, purpose-fully fabricating misinformation or repeating something I knew to be untrue, really was almost impossible for me and I had very little practice doing it. Perhaps I just lacked that type of imagination. But even knowingly allow-ing someone to misunderstand me made me feel extremely uncomfortable, sometimes unbearably so. I usually felt compelled to explain, to correct the false impression, or to clarify what I felt was the truth. I knew it exasperated people and had caused me grief all through school; nobody likes someone who tries to correct everything, though it was never my intention to be that way. It was one more thing I didn't understand about myself, that seemed to be different from my peers, and another reason I tended to keep to myself.

Anyway, I always tried to be truthful, even when I didn't want people to *know* the truth. But I had definitely let Robin assume I was looking for my art teacher, and that bothered me.

I wasn't too sure where to find the person I actually wanted, but the gym seemed like a good place to start. A few guys in Panthers' colors, black and gold, were gathered on the court below one of the far baskets. Cris, dressed more conservatively than I'd ever seen him—buttoned shirt, at the moment unbuttoned and loose over a t-shirt, and nice pants but still wear-ing Converse—was holding a basketball and talking to the guys. He looked so different, so much older than how I usually thought of him. I stood just inside the door trying to decide whether to leave or wait.

A couple of the other guys noticed me, which caused a couple more guys to look my way, including Cris. He said something to one of the guys and shot the ball to him so fast it caught the boy off guard and almost knocked him over. Then Cris walked over to me. The guys milled around for a few moments, watching. Then the ball was put in motion and they seemed to forget us.

Cris was scowling as he approached, wary and not looking directly at me for more than a second.

"What do you want?" he asked, gruffly.

I felt immediately defensive. I just never knew how he was going to react to me. Most of the time he seemed neutral. It was true that he appeared to look out for me, but it always seemed grudging, like he didn't want to but didn't have a choice for some reason. Occasionally it seemed like he *almost* liked me and as if we could be friends. Then there were the other times. Like now. It occurred to me how little I'd seen him around, which reminded me of how he'd gone missing last June. That made me remember how worried and unhappy Dave had been, and no doubt the rest of his family too. And *that* made me remember how mad at him I was.

He was still scowling. "You needed something?"

I cast about in my head for the right subject to land on, but the only one that would come into focus was the last one.

"Why did you disappear last summer?"

"What?" he said, consternation plain on his face. He obviously wasn't expecting that.

Neither was I, but it was impossible to back down now. I was convinced that Cris must have some insight into why Dave was behaving differently toward me. It now occurred to me that Cris' disappearance might be linked to the changes in Dave; how, I had no clue. I tried to stay focused and pretended it was why I'd sought him out.

"You left without saying anything to anybody . . . without telling your family. How could you do that? *Why* did you do it? Didn't you consider for a moment how they would feel? How worried they'd be that maybe you were in trouble?"

He glared at me. "I needed to get away and was staying in Davis with . . . a friend. Would you be happier if something bad *had* happened to me?"

His comment bounced off me. I was trying to recapture the feelings I'd felt back then; trying to picture Dave, distraught over his missing brother. But it was difficult when that brother was standing right in front of me. Besides, it was months ago now and he was obviously, at least physically, fine.

In fact, he looked way healthier than the last time I'd seen him, before he went missing. At that time he looked too skinny and seemed so depressed. There had even been a suspicion that he was doing drugs.

I started to feel the awkwardness of my questioning him. I think Cris was feeling it too; his cheeks seemed to have reddened a little under his tan and the scowl deepened.

"What was your reason?"

"What is it to you?" His eyes searched mine for a moment, then hardened and broke contact. "Are you judging me?"

That threw me. I didn't know. I'd never thought of it that way.

"Everybody was really worried about you."

"Everybody?"

"Well . . . your family . . . especially Dave. He was really, really worried."

"Hmm."

"I . . ." I was starting to lose a handle on exactly why I was angry with him.

"Is it really any of your business?" he said flatly. "That's why you came to bug me?"

No. It was something else, but. . . .

"I don't understand what happened," I said, unable to let it go. A sudden weight seemed to press down on my chest. I was mad at Cris but so hoped he could explain about his brother. There was no one else I could ask. "Something's changed and I don't know what it is. Something about Dave."

I looked imploringly at him. He regarded me steadily. His expression changed, and he looked away and scowled deeply again, but I got the impression that it wasn't at or because of me or anything I'd said.

"What happened over the summer?" I asked, but it came out as a harsh whisper.

He looked uncomfortable, maybe impatient. "Are you asking about me or Dave?" He still sounded irritated.

I realized I must sound ridiculous to him, and I was taking up his time, too. No wonder he was losing patience with me. "Dave," I said, very softly.

His expression didn't change again, exactly, but I thought the scowl softened a little, and so did the look in his eyes.

"I told you before," he said, also in a slightly softer, more patient tone of voice, "there's nothing wrong. At least, nothing specific that I know about. He's just . . ." He thought for a moment. "I think he's just got a lot on his mind and his . . ." He paused so long this time that I didn't think he would finish the thought. Then, "Some of his interests are changing. I think he's just getting used to looking at some things differently."

I stared at him, trying to read him, but he still wouldn't connect with my eyes completely. So weird. But it worried me. Did he mean that I was one of those "things"? Was I an interest that had changed? I wanted to ask him to clarify but doubted that he would tell me anyway.

"I've got to get back," he said, indicating the guys behind him. He turned without another word and walked away.

I stood there a few moments longer, trying to assess what I'd actually learned from him. It wasn't much. Cris had simply been staying with "a friend," though the way he'd said it left me wondering. And his friend lived in Davis? I didn't even know where that was, though it sounded familiar. And I knew he and his dad hadn't been getting along. I guess he'd really just needed to get away.

More importantly to me, sometime over the summer there had been a shift in Dave's "interests." Going by his coolness toward me, I had to assume those *did* include me. It's not like I was completely surprised. After all, my whole life so far had taught me to be wary of people in general and extra cautious of those who took any kind of real interest in me.

I'd often thought that I'd made friends before, especially in elementary school, only to have them begin ignoring me coldly or turning on me nastily, sometimes becoming long-term bullies. And I never knew for sure what I'd done to deserve it. I had, in turn, learned to protect myself any way I could—mostly by avoidance and retreating within myself; learning, although usually just pretending, not to care. By the time I'd finished middle school, I had honed those skills and learned to be quite content as long as everyone left me alone. And when they didn't, I just retreated further into my own world and interests.

And then we moved to Douglas and I'd met Dave. Before him, Brenda had been the only person to really get to know me and still accept me the way I was and stand by me—even if that meant I sometimes bore the brunt of her frustrations and uneven temper. Even Robin had kept her distance from me at first, assuming—I'm not sure what. Dave's unconditional acceptance, his friendship, had completely disarmed my natural defenses. I sure had let my guard down where he was concerned; I had *known* it was too good to be true. Unfortunately, it didn't alter the way I felt about him one bit.

Still feeling the heavy weight on my heart, I turned away and left the gym. I stopped at my locker to make a necessary exchange and then realized I hadn't asked Cris what I'd actually sought him out for. I wasn't sure how much time remained before the bell rang, but I headed back to the gym, feeling incredibly stupid, and peeked inside. Most of the guys had gone, and Cris stood talking to two who were left. I entered and stood near the door again, trying to be inconspicuous.

One of the boys noticed me and seemed to think it funny that I was back again. He looked familiar, but I couldn't place where I'd seen him before. He said something that made Cris look my way. Cris said something back to the boys, apparently dismissing them, and then walked toward me. He didn't look happy to see me again, but I didn't care. I was hoping for some help, and there was no way I was asking Dave for it.

Cris said nothing as he reached me. He just glowered.

"I had wanted to ask you something," I said, then realized he might become even more defensive. "Something . . . different."

The scowl became an exasperated furrow.

"Do you think your dad would let me borrow the Spanish bridle?"

Cris' expression didn't change. Then his eyes narrowed slightly. "The Spanish bridle." It wasn't a question.

"Yes," I said. "I have an art project, and I'm drawing a still life with a horse theme, and I was going to draw my bridle and some other things, but I need my bridle to ride Remmy, but it's too hard to take it away and put it back again *exactly* the same way each time, and it's going to take a while to do the project, so I was thinking about the Spanish bridle you and . . ." *no, that's too dangerous*, "I used on Gold, and thought it would be perfect to draw." I took a deep breath. "Much more interesting than my plain bridle. If your dad doesn't mind and doesn't need it, of course."

Cris was no longer scowling; more like a slight, perturbed frown, his eyes still narrowed, his mouth a tight, thin line. I couldn't tell if he was amused, annoyed, or just thought I was really weird.

"I'll ask him," he said, very seriously. I still couldn't tell what he thought, but I didn't care. The bridle had been my original mission, and now that it was accomplished, I could leave.

"Thank you," I said, businesslike, then turned and left.

Something about this last exchange bothered me, but I was still feeling weighed down by other matters and couldn't allocate any real brainpower to figuring out what. I took my time getting to English, then buried my nose in Shakespeare and pretended not to notice when Dave came in.

After school, I made my way to the bus as quickly as I could, going the long way around and avoiding the quad. I had thought about walking to the pool to stay with Mom until she got off work, but I didn't want to make excuses if I saw the others. This was hard enough. I was miraculously able to get a place next to a window and put my backpack on the seat next to me to discourage anyone from sitting there. We weren't supposed to, and I'm pretty sure the driver saw me do it, but she also knew the other kids on the bus liked to bother me, for whatever reason. She didn't say anything, and nobody claimed the seat.

As preoccupied as I was, I still noticed several things when the bus finally progressed down the street and through town. First, a large, straggling group of kids walking down the road not too far from the school. I wondered if they—at least Dave and Robin—had waited for me, assuming I'd go as well. I was glad that nobody had asked. Now I felt terrible that they might have been hanging around waiting for me. I hoped not. As we approached, I saw Robin walking with Tanner and Matthew. Dave was more or less surrounded by girls. The group was too large to make out all the individuals, but I saw Roberta and Hannah. I looked down in my lap as we passed them, hoping nobody would notice me. Next time, I'd have to remember to sit on the other side of the bus.

Farther on, just after turning toward Old Town, I saw Ben, alone and riding—mostly coasting—on a skateboard. I didn't think he'd notice, but just as we were passing, he looked directly up at me, as if he somehow sensed me there. It was kind of creepy. He raised his hand; I looked down again quickly, feeling panicked.

Ugh, that's so stupid. Why do some people make me feel so uncomfortable?

It wasn't as if I disliked Ben, exactly, but he made me nervous, and I wished he would just ignore me. It occurred to me that I'd never seen him hanging out with anyone, though I assumed he was liked by others.

The final thing to distract me was seeing Cris' big, black Silverado parked just down the street from the hardware store. Was he working there again? I scanned what I could see of the lumberyard as we drove by, just out of curiosity, but I didn't see him. Nor could I see him through the glass storefront.

Not that I care one way or the other. . . .

I remembered a time that I'd talked to him there last year. Robin and I had asked him when Dave would be coming home from a family trip. I'd gone back to thank him, though at that moment I couldn't remember what for. I also remembered our last interaction today and that I'd felt uncomfortable about it. And now I realized why; I had said, "Thank you," to him, but I hadn't really meant it. They had just been words.

And now I remembered, *again*, that I still wanted to apologize to him for my barrel racing fiasco—the awkward situation I'd put him in, the misunderstanding and anger he'd endured from my father. I had felt such a hypocrite, and now I did all over again. And I *still* needed to thank him for what he'd done to help back then: he'd made sure that Remmy was taken care of, had gone to find my parents to tell them what had happened and where I was, and he'd found my broken glasses. I'd seen so little of him after that accident, and when I had, I hadn't thought about the accident or what he'd done. I was determined to make that right as soon as I could. My sense of justice wasn't going to let me completely forget the debt I felt I owed him, but I wanted to be out from under the burden of it.

Later that night Robin called.

"Where were you after school?"

"I came straight home today," I said, not having an excuse.

"Oh," she said, and there was an uncomfortable pause.

I was unhappy with what felt like a growing distance between us and didn't want her to doubt my friendship, so I said, "Can I come and hang out at your house sometime? I could use some help with geometry, too."

"Yeah, sure," she said. "Gran's been asking about you."

That made me feel much better. "Great! I'd love to see her too. And Gali, of course."

"Of course," she said, and we talked for a while longer. I couldn't help wondering, though, if she was the only one who had noticed that I wasn't there.

On Saturday I had a lesson on Fritz at Bar 8. I wished I could just ride Remmy there, but riding along my street would be dangerous, especially for me. There was very little shoulder, and cars tended to drive quickly along the narrow road. As far as lessons went, Remmy much preferred having things to negotiate and think about anyway, like poles or trail obstacles. Dave had warned me against doing the same thing day after day, so even when just riding around the house I tried to think of different things to do. Unfortunately, barrels were out of the question, at least for the time being. I hadn't exactly given up on the idea. I was just waiting for the right time, and it definitely wasn't yet.

We were getting really good at other things though. It had become one of our chores to pick up the mail in the evening. It would have been easier to get it right after getting out of the car or as I got home from the bus, but a lot less fun. Instead, as soon as I had Remmy saddled, I'd ride him around to the front of the house near the main driveway where the mailbox was and take out whatever mail was there. Once in a while, Mom had something for me to put back in. I hadn't figured out a way to teach Remmy to pick up and move the sprinkler, but on hot days it was fun to wear shorts and ride bareback, letting the sprinkler wave over us. Remmy seemed to like it too.

Cheryl said it was good for me to ride different horses for my lessons, and then apply whatever I learned when I rode Remmy. I'd already realized how different every horse was, so I more than agreed with her. Fritz was a fun ride, too; more of a challenge than Flash, the horse I learned on last year.

Today, a surprise awaited me at home.

"Someone stopped by today," said Mom, watching me and pretending not to.

I couldn't help my heart leaping, and I answered reflexively, "Who?"

Dad looked interested too, though perhaps more warily, as he continued on into the kitchen.

"Cris," she said, smiling. "He brought this for you."

She reached toward the kitchen doorknob and held Mr. Caldera's Spanish bridle up.

"It was a great idea to ask for it. Now you'll be able to finish your project, right?"

My heart had plummeted already, of course, but I was glad, too. I could now concentrate on the project. And the fact that Cris had remembered and brought it so soon was not lost on me. My emotions were confused, however.

I couldn't help wondering what would have happened if I *had* asked Dave instead of Cris. My eyes felt prickly considering this and I got mad at myself.

"He looks so different, doesn't he," said Mom.

"Hmm?" *Dave?*

"Cris," Mom clarified. "He looks very different with the mustache and beard."

No, not really. Well, maybe. Just a little . . . I guess.

I pretended it was a rhetorical question and didn't answer.

"It seems like such a long time since I spoke to him last."

I could tell Mom was leading up to something.

"It's been a long time since Dave called or stopped by, too."

There it is.

"Is everything all right?" she asked, gently.

This line of questioning was not helping the eye-prickling situation at all.

"Yes, Mom. Everything's fine," I said huskily, then escaped up to my room with the beautiful bridle. I had regained composure by the time I came down to dinner.

When we were all settled at the table, Mom tried to sound nonchalant as she said, "When Cris was here, he also brought an invitation to us from his father, but I wasn't sure how you'd feel about it."

Dad was watching her, but I focused on my plate.

"Next weekend is the Labor Day event at their ranch. Alex wanted to make sure we knew we were especially invited and that if any of us would like to help with the preparations, they'd like for us to be there on Saturday. I guess they have a work day, then a party in the evening, just for the people who helped during the day."

She paused, and I could feel her watching me. I was mechanically cutting and eating my food, but I didn't taste anything. I didn't look at Dad, and he didn't saying anything either.

"What do you think? We had a wonderful time last year, didn't we? I think I'm working on Saturday, but you two could go and help . . ."

Fork, knife, cut, mouth.

". . . and we could go together on Monday. Cris said they could bring Remmy over the day before if you wanted to ride in any classes . . ."

Chew.

". . . or just have him there to ride."

Swallow.

She sounded confused. It struck me that, this year, she probably wanted to go much more than I did.

"It sounds like it could be fun," she said, coaxingly or uncertainly, I wasn't sure.

And I wasn't at all sure about how I felt. Still—

I said, "I guess . . ."

"We'll see . . ." said Dad.

Mom looked unhappy and perplexed, but let it go.

The next day, I spent a long time with Remmy in the cool of the morning and then retreated to my room for the rest of the day. I put my desk chair in the corner and took a long time arranging the Spanish bridle over the top edge of it, just so, and then the other items accordingly. My boots were on the ground next to the chair. I opened the saddle blanket and draped it with deep folds on the chair. Remmy's soft body brush was set on it with the mane comb next to it. All this could be left in place until I'd finished the drawing. An apple and two carrots completed the still life.

I spent the rest of the day drawing and listening to music and reminding myself, very firmly, that Dave wasn't the one to formally invite us last year either. I still didn't have a concrete reason to be unhappy or worried. Even so, I skipped over certain songs that turned my thoughts in melancholy directions.

Monday dragged by, enlivened only by Ben's antics in Spanish. He had gone back to his old seat, thankfully, but didn't seem able to sit still or quietly. The tapping pencil, clicking pen, shuffling pages of his book and other repetitious behaviors he appeared incapable of controlling seemed designed to torment me, though he was probably completely unaware of doing them. No one else seemed bothered.

I went out to the tables, but Dave paid me no more attention than what seemed normal now. Paola appeared to be very close to him, both physically and socially, and Roberta was never far. Hannah didn't seem to be as close, but I saw her watching him. At least, I assumed she was watching him. He was sitting at the other table with Tanner and Matthew and some of the others that I wasn't as familiar with. Robin sat next to me. Stacie and Kyle were cozy together at the other end of our table, mostly oblivious to the rest of us. I tried to follow conversations, especially whatever Robin was saying, but it was difficult. My own thoughts were just so darn loud.

For some reason, during PE I wasn't as invisible as I'd begun to feel lately—invisibility being a *good* thing. I was unaware of having offended anyone or of doing anything specific to make life difficult for anyone else, but I seemed to be in everyone's way and, even in my distracted state, I was picking up on irritation all around me. My proximity elicited eye rolls and whispers. I tried to ignore it and stayed close to Melanie.

Mom was picking me up, so I went to the parking lot after school, but I couldn't see her car. Standing on the sidewalk, I became aware of a group of guys among the cars some distance away, and they kept turning to look at me. At least, I assumed they were looking at me as there was no one else nearby. It made me feel extremely uncomfortable and self-conscious.

Then I saw them: Varsity Jacket and the blond curly-haired guy from last year. The boy who had seemed amused when I'd talked to Cris in the gym was there too. The other guys who had been Varsity Jacket's accomplices last year might have been among the others, but I didn't recognize them and didn't want to look long enough to make it obvious that I'd noticed them at all.

Varsity Jacket—I didn't know his real name as he was at least a year ahead of me and I had no classes with him—had caused me quite a bit of grief and fear last year. For some reason he'd decided to pick on me, and it had been pretty clear that ill will toward the Calderas was the motive. Dave and Cris and some of the others had even gotten into a real fight over it, though I never heard any of the details about it. I didn't want to. I'd been furious with both of them—especially Cris. Since then, I'd tried to forget the incident just like any other bullying or meanness I'd ever endured. I guess I'd thought it was over. And maybe it was, but I could still see them out of the corner of my eye. I didn't like the way they kept looking in my direction, so I turned my back slightly. I doubted they would do anything out in the open like this. I hoped not.

"Are you waiting for someone?"

The voice would have startled me more than it did if it wasn't immediately recognizable. My heart had leaped at first—their voices were *so*

similar—but even before I turned to face him, I knew it was Cris. His voice was very slightly lower.

Relieved by his presence, I said, "My mom's picking me up here, but she's a little late—"

As I spoke, I heard my phone vibrating in my backpack. I set it down, dug my phone out, and read, "*Sorry! Be there in a minute!*"

Cris looked curious—at least, as curious as I had ever seen him look—so I showed him the message.

I wrote back, "*Okay.*"

"She'll be here in a minute," I said unnecessarily, now feeling not so much relieved as awkward. "You . . . you don't have to wait . . ."

Cris turned his head slowly toward the group of guys, expressionless, and looked steadily at them for at least a minute. I didn't want to look, but I was too curious. Their reactions varied from sneers to the appearance of self-consciousness, maybe something else as well. Most of them turned away as if they'd lost interest. Some decided to leave.

"I'll wait until your mom gets here."

He said no more, and there didn't seem to be much point in arguing. I couldn't lie to myself—at least a part of me was glad he was there. It bugged me too, but I was concentrating more on not feeling awkward than why I did. Mom arrived a couple of minutes later.

Cris said, "See ya," tonelessly, and walked away as soon as he saw her car, not seeming to expect a response from me.

I didn't give one.

"Sorry, sweetheart! I went over to Lowell to get an oil change, and they found a brake light out too, so it took a little longer than I thought it would. I had them both replaced. Better safe than sorry, though. Right?"

I nodded and tried to smile. It seemed an oddly appropriate thing to say for my recent situation.

"Wasn't that Cris?" Mom asked. When I didn't answer her, she continued, "Is he looking forward to graduating? I assume he's going to college somewhere?"

I stared blankly at my mother. I had no clue how Cris felt about those things. I had barely ever considered it, though a conversation was tugging at the edges of my memory. No, *two* conversations, but my mind wouldn't settle on anything but random words.

UCLA. Basketball. Army. Ric. Dreams. . . .

Ric was Dave and Cris' older brother, but he had been killed in a car accident shortly after he joined the army. It was the year Cris started high school. Dave had told me that Cris and Ric were very close and Cris was devastated by his death. After he died, Cris had admitted to his family that he'd planned to graduate early, like his brother, and join the army also. That had been one of Dave's fears when Cris went missing at the beginning of the past summer.

But I'd also had a cryptic conversation with Cris sometime before that. He had seemed very despondent and confused about his life in general. We had talked about dreams—hopes for the future—but he hadn't told me what his were. Not that I would expect him to. He *had* told me that his mother had died, but that was only because I'd asked him where she was.

Now I felt pretty much back to square one with him; not much closer than I was at the beginning of last year when I thought that he, if not hated me, at least greatly disapproved of me. Not that I wanted to be. Closer, that is. I figured he was probably relieved that Dave wasn't as interested in me— "interested" meaning friendship, of course, though *I* knew that *Cris* knew I felt much more than that for Dave. Yet Cris still seemed to grudgingly watch over me. There was only one reason I could think of for that, and I didn't like it. Not one bit.

"Allison?"

"What?"

Mom gave me a smile I was very familiar with. On most people, I was sure it meant, *"Space Cadet."* On my closer friends, it meant, *"Seriously?"* On Mom, it just meant, *"I love you."*

I tried to smile back, but I'd forgotten her questions.

We had just driven through Old Town toward home when I spotted Ben. He was walking along the side of the road, heading in our direction and carrying his skateboard. When he heard the car approaching he turned to look. I looked away.

"There's that boy again. Are you sure you don't know him?" Mom asked as we passed him. "I'm sure he was waving specifically at you, sweetheart, though I suppose he'd like a ride, too."

She slowed the car and pulled over as far as she could to the side of the road. In the side mirror, I could see Ben jogging toward us. Mom rolled down the window behind me as he caught up to us.

"Would you like a ride?" she asked him.

He said, "If it's not too much trouble. Thanks!"

He opened the back door and climbed in with his skateboard.

"How far are you going?" asked Mom.

"Straight up here," he said, then added, "Pretty much."

"Do you live out here?"

"Yeah."

"It's a long way to have to walk."

He laughed, but all he said was, "Yeah," again.

I was dreading him saying something directly to me. I didn't want Mom assuming we really knew each other, because we didn't. It was bad enough having him remain a mostly minor annoyance in my life. I didn't want him becoming a major one.

"Well, let me know when you'd like to be dropped off."

"Okay, thanks," he said.

Mom made a couple of observations about the countryside as we drove, to which Ben responded politely and appropriately.

Then she asked, "Have you lived around here long?"

"No, I just moved here this summer."

"Oh. We've only been here about a year," she said.

Then she tried to discuss an upcoming field trip with me, but I resisted. I didn't care to let Ben know what I was doing. Mom knows I'm not talkative at the best of times, and especially not around people I don't know, so she didn't push me.

Eventually, she said, "We're going to be turning up onto Brookside. Did you need a ride farther along the highway?"

"No, Brookside's good," he said.

I doubt that Mom knew what that meant any more than I did, but she turned and continued up our street.

"Well, this is our house. Do you want a ride farther up?"

I could tell my mother was now as concerned as I was, though certainly for entirely different reasons.

"No, this is good. I can walk from here."

Mom pulled into our driveway and stopped the car. Ben opened his door, and I heard him grab his skateboard and begin to get out. I didn't want to turn around, though I admit, at this point I was much more curious about him.

"I forgot to ask," said mom before he closed the door. "What's your name?"

"Ben," he said. "Thanks again for the ride." Then, sounding like it was directed specifically at me, "See ya."

"Goodbye, Ben. It was nice to meet you," said Mom.

He was already on the road and headed in the direction of Bar 8 when I opened my door and got out.

"Are you sure you've never seen him at school, sweetheart? He seems to be about your age."

"I didn't say I'd never seen him," I said, which was true. I didn't want to get into a conversation about that and went straight to my room.

Chapter Seven

The next two days were annoying, troublesome, and depressing by turn. I usually didn't like field trips, but I actually looked forward to going to the observatory on Thursday. Hopefully I'd spend most of the day with Melanie, and it would be nice to not have to deal with some aspects of my normal life for a day: the continued ill-will of certain individuals in some of my classes, especially PE where I guess they weren't observed as closely; continued lack of attention from Dave; and continued annoyance from Ben.

The latter could have been worse. I was afraid that Ben might assume we were really friends now and bug me even more. But apart from saying, "Your mom seems really nice," he didn't allude to the ride home or try to sit next to me in class again.

He did, however, continue the annoying noises and caused me a moment of concern when I realized he was following Robin and me after Geometry on Wednesday. He wasn't in our class and I wondered where he'd come from. Why was he following us? Robin didn't seem to notice. He said hi to several people at the tables, but I didn't observe his other interactions.

Dave seemed to watch him for a while. Paola took up most of the rest of Dave's attention, and they were often in conversation in a mix of English and Spanish. I found I could catch a few words of the latter here and there, but not much better than last year around Dave's family. I still had so much to learn.

Most of the talk surrounding me was about soccer and football, driving and cars—the latter being relatively new topics for the group—and the upcoming Labor Day rodeo and playday held at the Calderas' ranch. It was disheartening that Paola already seemed to know all about the event and she spoke very excitedly about it, mostly in Spanish, and mainly to Dave.

"You're going, right?" asked Robin.

I gave her the same answer as last time, "I'm not sure."

When the bell rang, Matthew, who'd been sitting at the other table, surprised me by saying quite loudly, "See you in the morning, Allie. Don't forget to come early."

I looked at him and nodded, but noticed Dave glance from Matthew to me.

"You guys going on that observatory trip?" asked Tanner.

"Yeah," said Matthew and smiled back at me. "Kind of lame, I guess, but who knows. It *could* be fun."

Matthew looked at Dave and, to my surprise, Dave gave him that steady gaze I'd seen him do several times last year. I didn't want to think anything more of it though; apparently it meant nothing. I walked to PE, found Melanie, and tried to stay out of everyone else's way.

To top the day off, Mom spotted Ben riding his skateboard down the street not far from the school and automatically stopped to give him a ride. He smiled and got in the car.

"Do you often have to get yourself home?" asked Mom. "It's an awfully long walk, even with your skateboard."

"Yeah, the skateboard's good in town, but doesn't work as well on the highway. Vivian doesn't always pick me up."

"Oh," said Mom, and I was sure she wanted to ask why and maybe who Vivian was, but said, "Couldn't you take the bus? Allison takes the bus sometimes."

No, Mom! The bus is bad enough as it is!

"Yeah . . . probably," he said.

This time, when we got home, Mom wasn't content to let me go straight to my room.

"Allison, I can tell that you don't like Ben. Is there a reason I should know about? Has he been mean to you?"

I winced and felt guilty.

"No, Mom. Nothing like that."

"Is he in any of your classes?"

I admitted that he was but didn't want to elaborate.

"Well, is there a problem with giving him rides home? He must live around here, and it's such a long way."

Yes! Yes, there is a problem. He bugs me, and now he'll probably bug me even more. . . .

"No, Mom."

She accepted that and seemed to think it made it okay to continue talking about him.

"He's an interesting-looking boy," she mused, "but cute. Don't you think so?"

I wasn't concerned with whether he was cute or not.

"If not for his auburn hair and light-colored eyes, I'd think he was Asian."

This had not occurred to me, and I was momentarily diverted. Not that it mattered, but it was interesting. It *had* occurred to me that he reminded me just a little of Hannah, and probably only because there wasn't a lot of racial diversity in Douglas. It was one of the things I had first liked about the table group, that there were *all* kinds of people there, in spite of the predominantly Caucasian population of the school.

I still thought Ben looked Elvish with his pale skin, delicate features, and straight brows and hair. But his hair color and impish grin were definitely more what I thought a leprechaun's might be. Or maybe a Hobbit's. I tried to picture Ben in suspenders with big hairy feet.

"He seems like a nice boy," Mom continued when I made no comment. "He's welcome to have a ride whenever he needs it. Okay?"

I didn't know whether this was a warning and establishment of what to expect in the future or a pronouncement for me to pass on to him should the need arise. Stifling what would have been a huffy sigh, I escaped outside to Remmy to share my woes with him. He commiserated affectionately and didn't judge me. It was so comforting to have such a sympathetic friend.

The observatory wasn't open to the general public and was still gathering donations and grants to update their displays and finish the planetarium. Donors and other members of the public were allowed to visit by appointment. The only reason Douglas High students were invited was that our Chemistry teacher, Ms. Wright, knew one of the resident astronomers.

On Thursday morning, Dad drove to me to school early before he went to work. I was thinking more about the weekend than the field trip. Nothing more had been said at home about whether we'd go to the Calderas' or not, though I knew it was on Mom's mind. I expected that we'd at least go on Monday—it would seem strange not to since most of Douglas would be there—but we hadn't discussed helping out on Saturday. Dad would be leaving soon for a trip abroad and wanted to be with Mom and me as much as possible. I assumed we *wouldn't* be going and, in light of my uncertain feelings, I figured it was probably for the best.

The busses were already at school when I arrived. I said goodbye to Dad and walked toward the first bus where Matthew and our other classmates were gathering, but then I saw Melanie. I lifted my hand in greeting to Matthew and continued toward the other bus. Matthew followed. I was surprised to see Melanie standing with Hannah. Paola was with them too. The girls smiled as we approached.

"So you guys get to go too? Great!" said Matthew. He was smiling, but it didn't look right. I'd seen him smile that way a lot lately. I almost got the feeling that he *wasn't* glad they were going.

Our teachers stood at the bus doorways and called us by class to board. Ms. Wright checked off names as we entered. I didn't know why Paola got on our bus. She was right behind me, and I think she might have tried to sit with me, but Matthew indicated a seat next to a window, and I was glad to take it. He sat down next to me. Paola looked at us, smiled, and continued past us.

I doubted that Matthew knew my feelings—I hoped it wasn't obvious—but I was thankful to be spared the bus ride trying to be sociable with Paola. Apart from other feelings about her that I didn't care to examine too closely, she was very talkative and would have exhausted me before we'd even arrived there. I didn't feel too bad though; she seemed to be getting along all right with everybody, especially the boys.

The busses remained another twenty minutes or so, long enough for people to start arriving early for school. I'm sure I saw Cris' truck turn in to the parking lot and I expected Dave was with him. I remembered last year how he came early to run and train for track since he was involved with soccer after school. I shook my head and determined *not* to think of him today. *Thinking of him does absolutely no good anyway.*

"What are we waiting for?" asked a boy from somewhere behind me.

There were several offered answers, mostly ridiculous. But about the same time, a red sedan drove up the street and parked on the other side of the bus lane. I watched with a sinking heart as Ben got out of the passenger side, stood for a moment as if listening to the driver, then nodded, waved, and closed the door. As he turned slowly in our direction, something looked different about him; he looked rumpled, his shoulders hunched up and his hands crammed in his hoodie pockets as if he were cold, though it was already relatively warm considering the sun hadn't been up more than an hour. He also looked paler than usual.

Someone said, "Hey. There's that Ben kid."

There were other comments, among them "weirdo" and "spaz," epithets I was personally well acquainted with. But I didn't think he was anything like me.

Then someone said, "He's a druggie. Said so himself."

Nobody denied this pronouncement, but someone else said, "That kid's all right. He's pretty cool."

The first kid said, "Seriously, though. He said he does drugs."

I watched Ben walk toward the rear of our bus and disappear.

I rested my forehead against the cool window. This was probably *not* going to be the relaxing, angst-free day I had hoped it would be. Trying to stay out of the way of Hannah, Paola, *and* Ben would be more stressful than just accepting my fate.

For most of the first hour's drive, Matthew kept me talking of this and that. He didn't bring up any awkward subjects, and I avoided asking any questions or making observations that might lead to them. The conversation was completely Caldera-free, and I was glad.

After a while, he got pulled into a discussion about planets and space in general, which evolved into a lively debate between hardcore Star Wars fans and those more supportive of Star Trek and its many incarnations, with occasional remarks on the relative merits of other sci-fi movies and television series. I had seen political debates on television before, but none as heated as this and definitely not as funny. I participated only as much as I was prompted to by Matthew and some of the other kids—I couldn't help having knowledge and opinions on the subject—but most of the time I preferred looking out the window and thinking my own thoughts. Arguing the subtler points of phasers versus lightsabers wasn't of monumental interest to me.

At long last we arrived at the small observatory, high on a remote mountaintop. Even though it was now late morning, the air felt crisp and fresh and smelled deliciously clean after the stuffiness of the bus. I stood with my eyes closed, just breathing in and out and feeling the sun on my face, until my hand was grabbed. I opened my eyes as Matthew pulled me along behind him.

"You're going to get left behind again," he said, smiling.

I smiled back and willingly followed but liberated my hand as soon as I could, trying not to be obvious about it. Matthew's hand on mine made me very uncomfortable.

The first part of our tour consisted of a lecture outside on the observation deck by one of the student astronomers. She told us about the observatory, its history, and what they did there. There was an incredible view from every side of the facility. Several binocular viewers were available to gaze at the surrounding landscape, and we were given some time to do so. It felt good to just walk around after sitting so long on the bus.

Then we entered the main building and were introduced to one of the resident astronomers who talked more in depth about how the telescopes worked and what the astronomers looked for and studied. I had a hard time following the lecture most of the time. I knew basically what stars and planets were, of course, but he used many terms and phrases that didn't mean much to me, in spite of my sci-fi knowledge. And without being able to picture what he said, I found it hard to follow. It wasn't a topic of vital interest to me anyway.

I looked slowly around the room. There were about forty of us, probably mostly sophomores and juniors. Some students seemed really interested, but some looked like I probably did—bored or confused. Even more were obviously involved in relatively quiet private conversations, or using the phones we'd been told to turn off. Melanie and Hannah were standing together and Ben wasn't far from them.

Melanie and Hannah appeared to be on cozy terms now, and I wasn't sure how I felt about that. They'd met inadvertently through me, I suppose, that day during PE, and had apparently gotten to know each other better through shared classes. A part of me was glad. I'd never seen Melanie hanging out with anybody besides me. The only other person I ever saw her talk to was Roger. I was glad she'd found someone else to be friends with and I had to admit that Hannah seemed genuinely nice. It wasn't that I was jealous of Melanie having more friends—at least I didn't *think* I was jealous, though I had little experience of it—but more that Hannah's relationship to Dave, whatever *that* was, made me feel weird about her relationship with *my* friend. I tried to shrug it off and not worry.

The astronomer explained what many of the exhibits in the building were and said that we'd get to examine them a little later. We then followed him around the facility and through the two domes to view the enormous telescopes themselves.

I found observing my classmates much more fascinating, except, of course, when they caught me. Then I just felt guilty and uncomfortable, wanting to avoid the question that such discoveries usually elicited: *"What are* you *looking at?"* I'd never found the appropriate response to that, so I tried to avoid the question.

When we came back to the main building, we were left to explore the exhibits. I went over to Melanie and wandered around with her, Hannah, and Paola, not really caring about the displays but glad to be with people I knew.

Matthew stayed with other boys. Ben followed behind Hannah most of the time and lingered at each exhibit but didn't say much. He seemed extraordinarily subdued and hadn't worn a hat today. I was just glad he wasn't bugging me. Our teachers circulated among us, trying to excite enthusiasm for the subject at hand. Some people really did seem interested, but apart from liking the pictures and models, I just wasn't.

I found one exhibit of photographs absorbing because of the colors and patterns in them—it almost looked like abstract art—and fell behind the others for a few moments.

"Hey, Allison," Ben said quietly. He had moved beside me. "I wanted to tell you . . . well . . . you and your mom . . . you don't have to give me rides home." He looked at me and smiled. He looked so tired and something else; a little out of it. "It's okay. Really."

I tried to think of what to say, but he'd already moved away.

After this we were able to get outside, gathering in the park-like setting not far from the buildings. Matthew found me again and steered me, his arm around my shoulders, to a table where no one else yet sat. It made me feel uneasy, and I wondered if he'd done it specifically to be alone with me. I was actually glad when Paola saw us and came to join us. Matthew's expression as she approached and sat across from us was hard to read.

"*Las montañas* . . . the *mountains*, they are *so* beautiful!" she gushed. "They . . . *remind* me of home. We lived in the *city*, but we would go to the mountains *en el verano* . . . mmm . . . in the *summer*."

Her smile was dazzling and I tried to smile back. By this time Hannah and Melanie had spotted us and came over too. I was glad, but Matthew didn't seem as happy. They all talked together and I was mostly content to just listen, but the conversation soon turned to subjects I would rather have avoided. I suppose it was inevitable.

"You will all go . . . *ya conoces el rodeo en el rancho del Sr. Caldera, no?*"

No one had trouble interpreting. I kept my eyes on my sandwich, which seemed to have become suddenly very dry and tasteless.

"I think we're going," said Hannah. "We didn't go last year." A melancholy look crossed her face briefly. "Are you going, Melanie?"

"No, I can't go. I'll be away this weekend."

Last year she hadn't gone either. She'd told me she was at a different equestrian event. I wondered if that's what she was doing this year, too, but I didn't want to ask in front of everyone.

"I don't have much choice," said Matthew, his mouth twisting a little, but I couldn't tell if he was unhappy or just joking. Then he looked at me—self-consciously, I thought—and laughed. "Of course, I'd go anyway . . ."

I was trying to figure that out when Paola turned her beautiful wide, dark eyes on me.

"A-lee-*sohn*," she pronounced my name the same way Angel did. "Will you go?" She watched me expectantly, and I quickly examined several potential excuses but discarded them all.

"I don't know."

Paola and Hannah looked vaguely concerned, which puzzled me, and Melanie looked thoughtful, which didn't. Matthew looked surprised and was now watching me closely.

We'd been given a long though late lunch break and I enjoyed the extra time sitting in the sun. It had been so hot down in the foothills where we lived, but up here the breeze was cool and the sun felt good on my face and shoulders. With my eyes closed, I could almost imagine myself at the beach.

Some distance away, Ben seemed to have found kindred spirits. They were alternately jumping on, over, and around some tables, low walls, and even tree trunks. A couple of them looked like they were pretending they had skateboards. It was the most energetic I'd seen Ben all day, though the effort seemed to cost him. Still, it was fun watching them.

"Do you know that guy Ben?" Matthew said quietly. "I saw you talking to him earlier."

My first impulse was to correct him—*Ben* had been talking to *me*. I hadn't actually said a word. I caught myself just in time, though, and then realized it meant Matthew had been watching me earlier. That was unnerving.

"Yes, he's in my Spanish class," I said, not thinking.

"Oh!" exclaimed Paola immediately, her eyes even wider. "*¿Estudias español?* It is *my* language!"

Yes, I know. Why couldn't I have just said we had study hall together?

"*Será divertido tener otra chica con quien hablar en español. ¿Entiendes?*"

I stared at her for a few moments. I recognized a couple of words, but she spoke so fast I couldn't be sure.

"I don't . . ." Feeling more inadequate than usual, I looked at the others and wondered if they had understood. "I don't understand that well yet."

She laughed then, but I didn't know why. "I am sure you will learn very fast."

I looked away.

Our teachers walked around, telling us to finish eating, gather our stuff together, and make sure we didn't leave any trash. We were to meet back at the main building and assemble in the exhibit hall again before entering the planetarium.

The ceiling of the latter was domed liked the telescope rooms but smaller. A few rows of old theater-style seats were installed in the center back of the floor, but there weren't enough for everybody. The few other people who were not with our school had been allowed to enter first and take the seats. Douglas students had filled in the rest, some sitting on the carpet at the front or standing at the back.

I had gone to the restroom first and was one of the last to enter. I looked around trying to find Melanie, Hannah, or even Paola, as I figured she would be close to the others. I caught a glimpse of Melanie sitting on the floor at the front on the far side of the room, but it would have taken careful maneuvering to get there. I didn't like navigating through people. Besides, the lights were slowly dimming. I wasn't afraid of the dark, but the room felt claustrophobic. I stood near the door and figured I could escape if I needed to.

As the room completely darkened, a cello began to play softly, soothingly, and our eyes were drawn to the ceiling by a projection of the night sky. Major constellations were outlined for us and the brightest stars named. This was interesting and held my attention. There were lots of "ooh"s and "ahh"s, and I felt drawn upwards and oddly weightless, though I could still feel my feet on the ground. It felt almost like floating in water. I liked the sensation but had to concentrate hard to keep my balance.

There was a slight jostling behind me and someone brushed against my back. I tried to move forward, but there were people in front of me.

"How would you like to be up there?" was whispered in my ear, making me shiver.

Matthew. I turned my head but could barely make out his features in the dark. I didn't try to answer. The presentation was wonderful and Matthew's presence, the sense of security I drew from it, allowed me to forget my surroundings and enjoy it even more.

It felt like we were being taken on a journey; first investigating the night sky, then looking back and circumnavigating the earth, watching cloud cover form and disperse with glimpses of ocean and continents beneath. Then we were pulling away farther and farther, the music changing, a full concerto getting louder and louder. The projection turned outward into space. The feeling of floating and motion was uncanny. Planets and moons, and then comets and asteroids, novas and quasars, drew closer and got bigger as if we actually approached them, then moved away behind us. The volume of the music, sound effects, and voice of our "guide" had grown extremely loud, which probably added to the whole sensory experience, but I was finding it stressful and had my fingers pressed against my ears.

Toward the end, our virtual speed made it seem as if we'd been catapulted forward even faster and deeper into space.

"Hyperdrive!" somebody shouted.

"Warp speed!" and "Kessel Run!" were added.

My balance was severely threatened. As the speed seemed to increase, I found myself unable to keep from leaning backward until I was pressing against Matthew. Immediately embarrassed, I tried to compensate and lean forward, but by that time he had lightly folded his arms across my stomach. I could feel him laughing. I tried to relax then, but it made me feel panicky, the sensation too similar to an incident involving Varsity Jacket last year and apparently still fresh in my memory. I was glad when the projection's speed abruptly stopped, hovering over earth once more. There were exclamations and laughing as the other kids coped with the abrupt change. I probably would have fallen over if Matthew hadn't been holding me.

"Wow, what a rush," he laughed, but made no move to release me.

But now I felt very awkward. This seemed entirely too intimate for the present situation. I gently removed his arms from around my middle and pulled away from him as the lights came back on.

We exited the planetarium and were given some time to talk and stretch our legs, revisit the exhibits in the main building, use the restrooms, or sit outside before getting back on the busses to head for home. I gravitated toward Melanie again. Hannah and Ben were with her too, but Paola was nowhere to be seen. The three of them were talking quietly together, but something seemed wrong. Melanie was her usual self, but Hannah looked very unhappy, and Ben was once more very subdued. In fact, Ben had seemed unusually quiet all day except for his brief exuberance during lunch. But I'd never seen Hannah look really unhappy before.

Around two o'clock we boarded the busses again for the long ride home. We'd been told we'd probably get back to school between four and five o'clock, but an accident on one of the mountain roads, and a brief snack and restroom break because of it, made it after six.

I was glad to see my dad parked along the street waiting for me. I was exhausted. We hadn't physically done much, but the noise and vibration in the bus on the way there and back and the volume and experience in the small planetarium had completely worn me out. Actively trying not to think of Dave throughout the day hadn't helped when so many things—and people—reminded me of him. I was looking forward to the quiet of my room and sleep.

As I got off the bus, I looked around for Melanie. She was just getting off the other bus, which was now in front of us. Roger had come to pick her up. That was interesting. She saw me and waved, and I waved back. By this time Matthew was standing next to me, and my dad was approaching us.

"Matthew," said Dad, smiling.

"Hello, Mr. Anderson," said Matthew, smiling back.

"So, you're in Allison's class?"

"Yeah, Chemistry and History," said Matthew.

"Good. So those grades will be good this year?" He said it jokingly, but I was embarrassed.

Matthew laughed. "Well, I'll help if I can, but she probably doesn't need it."

I looked at him and tried to smile. I was grateful though. He knew I had no natural aptitude or interest in Chemistry. If I did get decent grades in that class, it probably *would* be because of his help and presence there.

Matthew's dad honked his horn once and waved, obviously at all of us, and we waved back. We said goodbye to Matthew and walked to our car. Almost everyone else had disappeared already. Except for Ben. He wandered aimlessly around, his phone at his ear. We got in the car, and Dad pulled forward and turned around. Ben saw us and raised his hand slightly; a farewell.

"Who's that?" asked Dad.

"Ben," I said as we drove slowly past him. My conscience was nudged, and I added, "He lives near us."

"Do you think he wants a ride?" asked Dad, slowing the car even more and pulling over to the curb. "Why don't you go ask? It's a long way home, and it'll be getting dark soon."

I was thinking the same thing. I still didn't particularly *like* Ben, but I was ready to believe him relatively harmless. It would bother me to think that he was stranded. I got out of the car and began walking toward him. He had watched our progress and was already walking toward me.

"Do you want a ride?" I asked, still feeling cautious.

"That'd be great . . . if you don't mind . . ."

Now I felt guilty. Had it been that obvious that I *had* minded before? "No, we don't mind," I said, trying to let my guard down and walking back to the car with him.

"Dad, this is Ben. He's in my Spanish class."

"And Study Hall," Ben grinned.

"Did you miss your ride?" asked Dad.

"Not exactly. Vivian is out somewhere. Bill said he'd pick me up, but he's running really late."

"Oh," said Dad. "I know how that is. What work does he do?"

"He's in sales. Grocery. He travels around a lot."

Dad laughed a little. "I know how *that* is too."

Dad and Ben kept up an easy conversation all the way to our street. Dad is usually reserved with people, but he seemed to warm up quickly to Ben. And I guessed that was all right, but it also bothered me for some reason. Ben now seemed more his usual bright self, his color normal, his eyes clear.

"Where do you live?" asked Dad.

"Just up the street from you," said Ben. "I can walk from your house though."

Dad made a noncommittal sound and kept driving, but after turning right on Brookside, he drove past our house.

"Tell me when to stop," he said.

"Uh . . . okay," said Ben, but he sounded unsure. I got the feeling that he would rather have walked, for whatever reason.

There were no driveways or roads on the right for a long way. The first driveway on the left was probably at least a quarter mile from the south boundary of our property. The house could be seen standing in a park-like setting surrounded by trees. I knew the next driveway, quite a distance farther on and also on the left led to a house that couldn't be seen from the road. A sign proclaiming "The O'Dells" stood at the corner of the driveway.

"Here," said Ben, leaning forward and pointing between Dad and me toward that driveway.

I was surprised. In spite of his complexion, auburn hair, and Leprechaun grin, Ben didn't look like an O'Dell. Besides, I knew that wasn't his last name.

"Thanks a lot," he said, getting out of the car. "I appreciate it."

"You bet," said Dad, smiling, but I thought he was wary, too.

Dad backed out of the driveway and headed home.

"So . . . you two have classes together?"

Yes, Dad. We've established that already. "Mmhmm," was all I felt like answering.

"Seems like a nice kid."

"I don't really know him," I said.

It was true, and I think it was what Dad was hoping to hear.

"You don't hang out at school?"

I stared at him for a few moments before answering; long enough for him to quickly look at me a couple of times and verify that I was really paying attention.

"No, Dad," I said firmly. "Not at all."

He looked satisfied with that, but I couldn't help that my mind was in turmoil and my stomach was churning. And it wasn't because of Ben.

Ben seemed his usual bouncy self in Spanish the next day, Friday. He grinned and lifted his hand in acknowledgment to me on entering the class, but went back to his seat quietly enough. He wore no hat again today, but he was dressed with obvious care, and his hair was combed straight and smooth. I grudgingly acknowledged that he was cute.

After Geometry, Robin and I walked to our lockers to unload books for the afternoon. I kept my geometry book out for homework over the weekend, but Robin shoved everything in her locker and firmly shut the door.

"There's no way I'm doing homework *this* weekend," she said smiling, her eyes bright. It struck me that it was the happiest I'd seen her since school started. "You *are* going, right?"

Since there was only one thing she could possibly be referring to, I didn't pretend to misunderstand. But I was still conflicted. "I'm still not sure. Maybe," I said.

Robin frowned disapprovingly and said, "You don't want to go?"

"No. I mean, yes! I think." Not willing to tell her my real reasons, I added, "My dad's going away next week, so I'm not sure what we're doing this weekend." *Phew.*

"Oh," she said, as if that made sense. "Well, I hope you get to go. It'll be fun. You should definitely ride Remmy in some classes. It'll be good for you. *You* know . . ."

I knew she referred to my last disastrous attempt at a horse show. I wouldn't be trying anything like that again soon. *Probably.*

I smiled but let her have the last word on that. I so wished that I could confide in her—I considered her my best friend, after all—but her connection to Dave had always been too close for that. Last year I was sure that whatever I told her of importance was passed on immediately to him. So, for various reasons and at different times, I had kept my feelings for Dave to myself.

She and Dave didn't seem to be as close this year. He was obviously enjoying—and at least accepting, if not reciprocating—the attention of girls in general and a few in particular. None of them were me. Robin seemed much more introverted this year, sometimes even depressed, and seldom spoke of Dave as she used to. They obviously remained good friends, though, and I hadn't picked up on any real tension between them. But I still felt it safer to keep my emotions hidden and my thoughts to myself.

As we walked back across the quad, Ben appeared out of nowhere, greeted me briefly, and began talking to Robin enthusiastically about an assignment. Apparently they were in English together, which surprised me; I hadn't been aware that she had any classes with him. Robin responded to him somewhat tersely and at one point glanced at me and rolled her eyes. I knew that I'd caused her plenty of eye-rolling in the past and wondered what it meant regarding Ben. I also wondered if I sounded annoyed like her when I talked to him.

It was one of those days when half the school seemed gathered around our favorite lunch spot. Most of the time I didn't really care—I'd always been glad that the group was seemingly accepting of anybody. I felt that's why I was accepted there, too. But I had hoped that today there would be fewer people and therefore fewer distractions—for everybody.

One look at the crowd in Dave's general vicinity and those hopes dissolved. Robin and I found a place on the grass and sat down. Ben seemed unsure about following us. He hesitated, then walked over to another bunch of kids and seemed to fall into easy conversation with them. But after a few moments, he was back.

"Can I sit with you?" he asked.

Robin shrugged, and I thought that it was weird that he would ask—nobody ever asked that around here; you sat wherever there was room. I nodded. Dave was looking in our direction as Ben sat down next to me.

Okay, he knows I'm alive today. That's something.

I tried to seem occupied with my lunch and not gaze back as I wanted to. Ben had forgotten his lunch, so I gave him half my sandwich—I wasn't hungry anyway—and Robin gave him her pudding, which he ate by scooping it out with the lid. I'd never seen anyone do that before and watched with interest. Several other people had joined us, including Tanner, who seemed to be on friendly terms with Ben, and Matthew.

When the bell rang, the others said, "Bye," and went their own ways, but Ben remained beside me.

"Hey, I just wanted to say thanks," he said, looking more earnest than I'd ever seen him. "I know I annoy people sometimes . . . okay, a lot of the time . . . but I don't mean to." He grinned crookedly and added, "At least, I don't *always* mean to. Thanks for, you know, being nice about it."

I took a chance and searched his eyes—just for a moment and *very* uncomfortably—but I thought I read sincerity there. I was surprised and also felt quite guilty. I knew I hadn't really been nice about it at all. I was trying to think of how to reply—"You're welcome," seemed to imply that I *had* been nice and that it had been on purpose—when Dave walked up to us and all thoughts of Ben were put on hold.

"Hey," he said, his voice soft and low, the way I hadn't heard it in a long time. He looked at me long enough for our eyes to connect effectively, then he turned his attention to Ben. "Hey," he said again, this time a little louder, sharper.

"Hi," said Ben. He raised his hand slightly and looked like he felt awkward.

Dave showed no emotion and turned back to me. "Can I talk to you for a minute?"

My heart was doing its old Dave dance. I had *so* hoped to get a chance to talk to him today but all thoughts about why had fled. I was too nervous and happy to think at all. I followed him a few steps away from Ben.

"I was wondering if you're coming this weekend," he said. "I haven't had a chance. . . ." He frowned. "At least, it *seems* like I haven't had a chance to talk to you about it. The last time I asked Robin, she said she didn't know."

He asked about me? He asked about me!

I stared at his face. It seemed so long since I'd had an excuse to just gaze at him, study him, to closely admire his features—his straight nose, beautiful brows, dark lashes, the plane of his cheek, the angle of his jaw. His eyes. I didn't want to look away.

A sense of time and place returned when his eyes softened and crinkled very slightly in the corners. He was smiling. *That* smile!

I forced myself to look away and pull my wits together—another saying I'd never quite understood before that now made sense.

"I . . . don't know . . . for sure. Maybe." I realized that was not an adequate answer, and I was glad to have an excuse. "Dad's going away again . . . next week . . . so it depends on what he wants to do."

He nodded once slowly, his lips tight, his eyes harder again.

"So . . . who's your friend?" he asked with an almost imperceptible tilt of the head toward Ben. Ben had walked several more paces away but appeared to be waiting for me. "I don't think I've seen him before. Is he new?"

"His name is Ben. He's only been here since the beginning of the year." I hastily added, "He's in a couple of my classes, but I don't really know him . . . at all."

"Hnh. He looks like a Vulcan."

Dave's reaction to Ben shocked me. It wasn't like him to say mean things or label people, so I wondered what he meant by it. Perhaps he meant it as a compliment. After all, I'd been comparing him to fantasy beings, too. And I didn't think Ben looked at all like a Vulcan except maybe for his eyebrows, but I wasn't about to point that out to Dave. *Perhaps if his ears were pointed. No, he'd still look more like an elf. And what's with all the alien references lately?*

Dave turned and started walking toward the gym. I walked with him the few steps to where Ben stood. I could see a couple of girls lingering near the door of the gym, watching us. That didn't bode well for me, but I didn't care.

Stopping briefly, Dave said, "You should come. Angel wants to see you. You can bring Sp—" he paused and smirked, "your friend . . . if you want." He walked off ahead of us, then turned, walking backward just long enough to say, "See ya."

I lifted my hand slightly. "Bye."

Ben lifted his hand too, but his was higher, his fingers spread in a distinctive gesture as he said, "Live long and prosper."

Chapter Eight

Saturday, I awoke early and lay in bed feeling anxious. Dad hadn't said anything the night before about plans for today but had acted normal enough. Mom had seemed preoccupied and a little unhappy during dinner. As I still hadn't figured out how I felt about going to the Calderas', I was reluctant to mention it, but it left me hanging emotionally. I would have thought Dad had forgotten all about the work day, but I'd overheard my parents talking later.

On my way to the bathroom before bed, I thought I caught my name and wondered what my parents were talking about. Crouching at the top of the landing, I strained to hear but with the television on and their voices lowered it was difficult. I caught words and fragments of their conversation though—enough to be sure what they were talking about.

"... Allison ... tomorrow ..." Mom's voice.

"... Monday ... hasn't said ... riding?" Dad.

"... invited. You could ... later ..."

"There's a lot ... the yard ..."

"... friends ... Allison ... neighbors ..."

It's funny how names, especially your own, pop out of conversations even when the other words are muffled. I had plenty of experience with that from school. In those cases, I'd learned to pretend I hadn't heard. But these were my parents. I was such a wimp. I knew I should have gone downstairs and been a part of the conversation, but I didn't know what I would have said.

My desires were so mixed up; I honestly didn't know what I wanted to do. A part of me would be very disappointed if I didn't go to the work day. Robin and most of our other friends would be there. Dave would be there, of course, but our relationship felt so strained. Did he feel it too, or was it really just me? He had said I *should* go, that *Angel* wanted to see me, but he'd given me no indication of what *he* wanted. He'd even suggested, kind of weirdly, that I bring Ben, but I wasn't sure if he meant to the work day or the event itself on Monday. Either way, I wasn't about to invite Ben—that would be *really* weird—but it made me a little unhappy that he'd even suggested it.

I realized I was being nonsensical, too. I had to get over this longing to be more to him than a friend, especially now that our friendship didn't even seem as close as it had been. The best way to do that was probably to do the opposite of what my instincts told me and be around him as much as possible, to get used to the new status quo.

That, however, was one of the main problems. I had thought I'd more-or-less resigned myself to being just a friend. A buddy. Not anything like a girlfriend, but closer and more important than most of the kids that knew him, seemingly even closer than some of his older friends. But now it just wasn't the same. It didn't feel like he was avoiding me in any obvious way, and I didn't think that he *dis*liked me. He just seemed—at least most of the time—distant, almost as if he purposely had defenses up. And that wasn't like him. Not at all.

Was it because he knew how I secretly felt about him and he didn't want to encourage me? Although the subject had never been openly discussed between us, I knew Cris was aware of my feelings and *had* been aware, almost from the start. Had *he* told him? Incidents last year had made me ask this question before; I'd always felt that Cris was watchful of our friendship and somehow suspicious of me. But Dave had always, however unknowingly, allayed those fears by his actions and attention.

And now that was all changed.

Then there were the girls. He was, of course, a good-looking guy. Okay, *very* good-looking—though attraction being what it is, I was sure there must be girls that didn't find him handsome, sexy, whatever. They just didn't stand out at our school. And they weren't me.

But my attraction to him was so much more than just his face, or his athletic build and abilities. I'd asked myself many times whether I would have fallen in love with him had he been much less attractive and, honestly, I don't know. He'd certainly caught my attention—and captured my fourteen-year-old and very naïve imagination—the very first time I saw him: black t-shirt, blue jeans, cowboy boots, looking tall and slim, a little hot and dusty, vaguely dangerous, and riding a motorcycle. Of course, my perception of him had changed as I'd gotten to know him better—he was much younger than he at first seemed, and shorter too—but I could still picture how he looked that day. And I could remember how I'd felt. That hadn't changed much.

But it was his personality—his kindness, patience, confidence, humor, a million things—that had completely won me over. He'd initiated our relationship in the first place, too. And *he* had continued to seek *me* out—so many times I'd lost count—though his motivation remained a mystery to me.

Was I just last year's charity project? Going by how I felt about myself, *especially* last year, I could almost believe it. But that's *not* how he had treated me. Could somebody really make another person feel practically like family only to turn away from them after a couple of month's separation? I'd never understood social or even family dynamics, but to do that was completely beyond my comprehension.

Going to his home under these circumstances, and especially today when the public in general wasn't invited, would make me feel more than awkward. It was my chief source of anxiety at the moment. On the other hand, there were other people there I also loved and wanted to connect with again, Angel and Stevey in particular, though I was curious about Henry and Mr. Caldera too.

And Cris would no doubt be there, though I was never sure where I stood with him. I couldn't quite remember how things had been left between us after our last interaction—the memory was fuzzy—but he never made me feel anxious. I didn't always exactly *like* him, and I didn't always like what he said or how he made me feel or think about things, but anxiety about what he thought of me or how he would treat me was never an issue. At least, not since the beginning of last year. I guess that's one of the things I appreciated about him.

Robin would be there too. I hadn't had a chance to spend much time with her and today *could* be fun. I should want to go just because of her. And other friends would be there too, of course. I probably wouldn't even have to spend any time with Dave—or watch him interacting with other girls.

Which brought me back full circle to why I didn't want to go in the first place. I knew Hannah and Paola would be there at least on Monday, like probably half the population of Douglas, but what about today? Hannah was obviously much closer to Dave than I'd ever realized, but the way Paola had talked on Thursday reminded me that she was probably acquainted with Mr. Caldera, too. Dave had said that his dad and Paola's dad knew each other. It seemed there might be more between her and Dave than tutoring. *Ugh.*

I dragged myself out of bed and dressed to go feed Remmy. I stayed to talk to him while he ate but, though he appeared to be listening as he munched, even stepping closer to nuzzle my arm and face, he had no useful feedback to offer. When I saw my mother looking out the kitchen window, I stroked his neck and went back inside the house.

Mom was getting ready for work and making coffee. She gave me a couple of searching looks, then made some comments about Remmy and asked how my art project was going. But she said nothing about plans for the day.

Then Dad came downstairs. Mom poured him coffee and asked how he'd slept as she started making French toast.

"Pretty good," he answered, "except for a weird dream about an old lawnmower that wouldn't start and a guy dressed as Santa Claus."

Mom laughed. "What on earth would cause you to dream that?"

"Well, I've been concerned about getting things done around here, cleaning up the yards and making some flower beds. I'd like to get caught up before winter and wet weather comes, and I'll be leaving again soon. I don't know about Santa Claus, though." He shook his head and looked puzzled.

Mom laughed again.

When the bread was sizzling in the pan, Mom picked up her coffee cup and leaned back on the counter, facing us. Dad looked at her. She raised her eyebrows over the rim of her cup, took a sip, then tipped her head very slightly in my direction. I looked at Dad and he cleared his throat, putting his own mug back on the table carefully.

"So what do you say we head over to the Calderas' to help for a while?"

I couldn't tell what his feelings truly were but thought the lead-up indicated reluctance. "Only if you really want to."

He looked perplexed. "Don't you want to go . . . see your friends?"

"Sure," I said calmly, then reiterated, "but only if *you* want to. I could help you around here if you'd rather."

Dad stared at me. It crossed my mind that he might think I was trying to use reverse psychology on him or guilt him into being more enthusiastic about going than he obviously was. Then I got distracted wondering, if I was capable of imagining it, was I capable of doing it? I didn't want to think so. I realized I was hyper-analytical, but manipulation was right up there with outright lying; I had probably done it, but it wasn't something I wanted to do.

"No," Dad said slowly and looked back at Mom. "I think we should go. When you're ready though," he added, frowning. "There's no rush."

"Good," said Mom, brightly, and turned around to flip the toast. "Maybe I'll join you later . . . when I get off work." She set a plate of French toast in front of Dad and said, "How many pieces do you want, Allison?"

The toast smelled good, but my appetite had disappeared and anxiety kicked up a few notches.

"Um . . . I'm not really hungry. I think I'll just go ride for a while."

I went out the back door and started grooming Remmy while he finished his breakfast. I had an uncomfortable feeling my mom and dad were now talking about me, but I didn't want to know.

I saddled Remmy and rode him in the lower corral for a while, then around and through the creek. I tried to keep my attention on him and I talked to him almost constantly, but my thoughts kept racing ahead, picturing the Caldera Ranch, the house, Dave's family. Dave. It was just too hard not to. This led to Remmy being a silent stand-in for possible conversations with the latter, but I stopped every time I caught myself doing that. While it helped me process some things that were bothering me, it wasn't helping my anxiety. About mid-morning I rode back up the north side of the property, took care of Remmy, put his tack away, and went in to shower and change.

Dad and I didn't talk much on the way there. I really didn't have anything to say. He glanced at me a couple of times as if he might start talking, but he didn't. We weren't sure where to park when we got there, but there were a few vehicles pulled up between the big arena and the open space where the stage was being set up. I was surprised and a little disappointed that nobody was riding. The only horses I could see were in paddocks attached to the barns and a few on the hillsides behind them.

Dad stopped the car and we got out. I was immediately searching.

Dad said, "It's going to be a scorcher."

I nodded but couldn't speak. I'd spotted Dave walking down from the barns, just before he saw us. My stomach flipped, heartbeat quickened and, despite my determination to the contrary, hopes rekindled.

"Hey, Allie," he said as he reached us. He was smiling; a tight-lipped smile. No evidence of his easy charm. "Mr. Anderson," he nodded to my dad and gave him that direct look that always puzzled me, his mouth drawn even more firmly. "You came."

Just like that. An acknowledgment. I was already feeling more than awkward, like I'd misunderstood and come to a party I hadn't really been invited to. I knew what that felt like.

"Yes," said Dad. "Put us to work. Is your dad around?"

"Yeah, down at the arena, I think. I was heading there myself." Dave looked around, frowning, and said, apparently to me, "I'm not sure where Robin is. Around here somewhere." Then he looked steadily at me. "Angel's up at the house, though. She wanted you to go say hi if you came."

More awkward still. I knew I was probably overly sensitive—I couldn't help it—but I heard rebuke and dismissal in his words. My heart, fluttery and willing to soar a moment ago, took another nose-dive.

"Oh . . . okay." I turned to walk up the hill toward the house but did so hesitantly in case he would say more.

He didn't. Not to me anyway, though I wondered if he and Dad were talking and, if so, what was being said. I was halfway up the hill before I realized my eyes were watering and I took myself to task for it.

No! No brooding or worrying! As I had feared, today was shaping up to be an exercise in practicing fortitude and humility. I had to try to just go with the flow and expect nothing.

I walked past the angel statue, its basin dry as it usually was in summer, and stood uncertainly before the front door. Should I knock or just go in? I had never used the door knocker before. It was a bronze bull's head on the right side of the large double doors. Last year, I wouldn't have hesitated about just entering, but now—

I knocked. After a few moments, the door opened.

"*Ahleesohn!* You are here!"

Paola. She looked surprised but happy to see me, and I thought her smile looked sincere. I didn't exactly feel the same way.

"Come in! Are you looking for Anjélica?"

She pronounced her name *Ahn-he-leeka*. It had never occurred to me that "Angel" was short for anything.

"Yes," I said, stepping into the cool darkness of the entryway.

Merle, Cris' Australian Shepherd, stood at a little distance, watching. I crouched down and encouraged her to come to me, which she did, keeping one eye on Paola and wriggling slightly as she neared me. Eyes prickling, I scratched her lightly behind her ears and allowed her to lick my cheek once, thrilled that she acknowledged me. I was going to have to be very careful of my thoughts today.

The gentle trickling sound of the fountains in the back courtyard and a deliciously fresh breeze came through the tiled archway of the dining room. It cooled my suddenly flushed face. I blinked several times and followed Paola down the short hallway to the kitchen. Merle trotted behind me, her nails clicking lightly on the tiled floor.

And there was Angel, just as I remembered her, and tears threatened again. She was busy preparing food, I assumed for Monday.

"*Ahleesohn!*" she said, smiling warmly and wiping her hands on a towel.

She came toward me as I entered the kitchen, opening her arms wide and folding me in against her. She squeezed gently, and several tears escaped my eyes as if they'd been at the brim and were forced over. I'm not crazy about being touched by people in general and even less about being hugged—except sometimes by very close friends and family, and especially one in particular—but I was *so* happy to be received so warmly and familiarly by her. Perhaps all was not completely lost. I hugged her gently back.

"You have been well?" she asked, now holding me at arms' length to look at me closely. "*Ay!* You have cut your beautiful long hair! This is very nice though, no? It is more easy to . . . take care of. Yes?"

I quickly wiped my cheeks and nodded. "Yes."

"And where are your glasses, *amigata?* You no longer need them?"

Angel's observation and endearment made me feel self-conscious, but only because of Paola's curious stare. She, of course, had not known me before and was unaware of changes in my appearance. My face was feeling a little warm again, but I didn't want to appear embarrassed. Paola looked from me to Angel and smiled.

"If you don' need me, *Señora Anjélica*, I will go outside to see if I can help. *¿Está bien?*"

"*Si, si. Ve a buscar a los otros. Gracias, Paola.*"

"*De nada*," she said to Angel. Then to me, "You will come outside later?" Her smile was as open and charming as Dave's could be.

"Yes," I said. "I will."

"*¡Bueno!*" She smiled again and left.

"It is so long since I have seen you," said Angel. "You look very well. Not so skinny now."

So it is noticeable.

I laughed a little. "I guess so . . ."

"And *so* pretty! *Dah-veed*, he did not say. But of course, you were pretty before. You are just older. More grown up."

Pretty?

Not used to compliments, I wasn't sure what an appropriate response was and laughed a little again. Now I *was* embarrassed. I hadn't purposefully done anything to change my shape—just nature taking its course, I guess. And though I had longed for the day my "gangly" phase would be over, if that's what it was, now that there was hard evidence that it might be, I wasn't so sure I was happy about it. I changed the subject.

"Are you cooking for Monday?"

The warm smell of *masa* filled the kitchen; a tortilla press and stacks of fresh tortillas sat on the center island. Three large casseroles lay on the long counter. I couldn't tell what was in them, but they appeared to also be topped by *masa*.

"No," said Angel. "These are for today, for when the work is finished. We will sit *en la plaza* . . . to enjoy the evening."

I reflexively agreed and tried to smile.

"For Monday, the meat is all ready . . . for the barbecue you know. Alejandro and Miguel, they have all prepared. We have the cold storage, you see, near the barns. There is much . . . *supplies* for the workers. They are always hungry! We have the dinners *especialmente* sometimes also you know, for the men and their families."

I nodded. That made sense. I knew they had plenty of storage space in the house, but it probably wouldn't be enough to store everything they'd need for the Labor Day event as well as what they kept for the large family.

And if they had parties and sometimes provided meals for employees too, I could see how they would need more.

Angel wrapped the tortillas and covered the casseroles in foil, then put them away in one of the big refrigerators. She then poured glasses of lemonade for both of us and invited me to sit with her on the other side of the high counter.

"So!" Angel said covering one of my hands with one of hers. "Tell me . . . what did you do in the summer? *Dah-veed* said you would go to Los Angeles. To your family?"

I told her briefly of my time in the city, of the operation to partly correct my vision, of staying with my grandparents, my aunts, and Brenda. I didn't think there was much to tell, but she seemed very interested in my extended family. She had never met any of them and asked many questions, some of which I couldn't answer.

Her questions brought up questions of my own—questions about her relationship to the Calderas. When I'd first met her, I assumed she was the housekeeper and nothing more. But her position in the home seemed to be much more than that; much more intimate, permanent, and essential.

"Did you enjoy Hawaii?" I asked, partly trying to be conversational—a skill I felt massively incompetent at—but also to gain information. Dave had told me very little about the trip before he went and nothing since.

"*¡Si, como no!* I like it there very much, but I am always *very* happy to come home too. My *heart* is here." This last was said softly, almost shyly, which seemed strange.

"Do you stay with family . . . in Hawaii?"

"Yes! Maricela, the sister of Alejandro, she is married to a Hawaiian gentleman, Oscar. They have *un rancho*, though not so big as this one. It is very close to the ocean. The children, they work in the mornings and then they are gone!" She laughed. "They spend their time at the ocean. The boys, they love to surf, of course." Then, as if omitting something important, she added, "The girls also!"

Girls? I knew it! Though a part of me was warning against it, I couldn't help being curious.

"How many cousins does . . ." *not too specific!* "do Dave and Cris have there?"

"*¡Siete! Seven* cousins in Hawaii! Raúl, he is the oldest and is away at university. He is a very handsome and smart young man! He is studying the law. There are four girls. Jacinta is eighteen, almost nineteen; a most beautiful, beautiful girl. She was home from college for the summer. Noemi is sixteen. She is the quiet one. And Luisa and Olivia are fifteen and very lively. Twins! They had their birthday while we were there. They are all very nice and pretty and smart also, of course." She added this as if she did not want to be accused of favoritism toward the eldest.

"Then two more boys. Marcos is twelve years old and Gerardo, he is nine years old. *Tengo fotografías*," she said. She seemed excited. "I will show you, okay?"

No! I don't want to have pictures of them in my head! But curiosity won out over self-preservation. "Yes," I said meekly. Besides, I could hardly say no when she was so excited to show me.

She got up and went out into the family room, coming back with an envelope of pictures.

"*Es la manera antigua*," She waved her hand, looking apologetic, and said, "It's *old*-fashioned, *verdad?* The *paper* photographs." She chuckled a little as she sat back down and took the photos out. "I like to *hold* them."

I nodded.

She showed me the first photos, mostly pictures taken out of the plane window and some of the countryside, "On the way there," she said. They were pretty scenes of palms, lush green grasses, and brilliant blue sky; some of the ocean and some of open ranchland. Then she shuffled through them until she found what she wanted.

"It is *El Rancho de los Espíritus Azules.* So, *so* beautiful. Right beside the ocean!"

The picture was of a large sign, similar to the ones standing sentinel over the entryways to both the Caldera and Bar 8 ranches, but this was held up by slim, supported poles—possibly thick bamboo—painted white with no fences visible. Palm trees could be seen beyond the sign and green, green grass everywhere. Standing beneath the sign was a large, happy-looking group of kids, most of them with dark skin or deep tans; it was hard to tell the difference. Angel pointed to each in turn.

"Here is Jacinta and Noemi. And here is Luisa and Olivia. And there is *Dah-veed*, of course." I had spotted him first of all, surrounded by girls. "And Quique there, and Esteban there. There is Marcos and Gerardo."

Stevey's attention was to the side somewhere, off-camera, his expression neutral. All the others had smiles of varying intensity. There were lots of other girls as well as boys. Many were much younger, but some appeared to be teens. Henry had an arm around an older girl's waist and a smirk on his face. Two girls, not named by Angel, were hanging on Dave and laughing, one on each side. He was grinning in a familiar, mischievous way. It made my heart hurt. I hadn't seen that look in a long time. Had he left it behind in Hawaii? There were definitely far too many girls.

"Who are all the other kids?" I asked.

"They are neighbors and friends. Some are the children of people who work *en el rancho. Si*," she said, pointing to some of the smaller children in front. "*Estos.*"

"I don't see Cris."

Angel frowned in thought. "I do not remember where he was this day. He did not travel there with us. He came later. Perhaps . . ." She thought, then shook her head. "No, I am not sure. He was often with the workers. He was most interested in the animals."

She shuffled through a few more pictures, stopping at one of five girls—a heads and shoulders shot—smiling for the camera.

"Noemi, Luisa, Olivia, and their friends," sighed Angel. "They are lovely girls. And they had grown *so* much since we were last there . . ." She mentally counted. "Yes, *four* years ago. They will be so much older the next time we see them . . . unless they can come to visit us here."

It was of girls like these, at least the non-cousins, that I had tried to avoid thinking of, trying not to assume the worst was happening in Hawaii as I sat on my corresponding beach in Southern California.

The thing about assuming the worst—or something like it—is that things aren't supposed to actually be that bad. You tell yourself that you're preparing for the worst, but you're really counting on it *not* being that bad at all. So when you find out that the worst—or close to it—*didn't* happen, there will be profound relief, and an "all's well that ends well" feeling of closure on the whole thing.

Instead of the relief I had counted on and that had kept me from being worried and depressed all summer, I now worried about whether the worst—the *actual* worst—*had* happened. Something had obviously happened, and now all I felt was unhappy and kind of stupid.

Angel showed me more of the photographs: some of just the boys or only the girls, some of gatherings including the adults and friends, many of the ranch, and some of the other idyllic locations they had visited. It was interesting but alienating. The final photograph was the worst: all the teenagers—except Cris—on the beach smiling or laughing, and leaning or hanging on each other in some fashion. The twins were on each side of Dave again. A third girl, one of the friends, was on his back, her arms around his neck, her head laid against his, his arms under her bare legs.

I knew I'd hate myself for asking but couldn't help myself. "Who is that?"

Angel raised her eyebrows and said, "Ah," but I didn't know what that meant or how she felt about the person. "She is Aolani, a neighbor and friend of the girls. She was often there. She liked *Dah-veed very* much."

Now my heart felt like it was flopping on the floor like a goldfish out of water. I swallowed. I had to ask. I needed to know.

"And . . . did he like her?"

Angel raised her brows again and shrugged. "Is hard to tell. *Dah-veed,* he is a sweet boy and likes everybody. He likes to make people feel . . . *especial. ¿Tu sabes?"*

I forced myself to smile as she smiled kindly back at me.

"Yes," I answered. Was she thinking the same thing I was? Was this her way of putting me on my guard? "I should probably go outside and . . . find Robin. And help. Or something. Unless there is something I can help you with here?"

"No, *gracias!*" she said. "Is finished for now, until later. You go help your friends."

"Yes," I said, and left as quickly as I could.

Once outside, I walked slowly across the circular paved driveway and past the angel statue again, her arms folded over her breasts, her wings folded tightly against her back, face and eyes lifted heavenward as if longing to be taken away from the earth but resigned to stay. I thought I knew how she felt.

I noticed Cris' truck parked under the poplars on the north side of the house, close to where the garage entrance must be. A smaller, much older truck was parked close by, a patchy brown color. I knew Dave had a truck that he drove on the ranch and assumed this was his.

I continued slowly and thoughtfully down the sloping driveway back toward the plaza, getting a grip on my emotions and trying to reset my resolve.

"Allie!" Robin shouted and waved. "There you are! Come on. You can help me with these display panels. I need at least three hands, and everyone else is busy."

Apparently most of the people with any kind of real muscle were either helping put the stage up or were down near the arenas setting up more paddocks and making sure everything was in working order for Monday. There were a few women helping, but Paola, Hannah, and Jessie were the only other girls our age there. I could see them down at the smaller arena giving the rails a fresh coat of paint. It looked like Tanner and Henry were there too.

"Push harder *here!*" grunted Robin, pressing hard on one panel as I pushed back on another. "They're supposed to fit together but—"

Matthew, who'd been helping set up the stage nearby a moment before, was suddenly looming over me and with one shove locked the panels into place.

"Thanks," said Robin, wiping her hands on her jeans. "I guess there's something to be said for swimmer's muscles."

Matthew smiled. I hadn't thought about it before, but I guess he did have a good physique—from what I could tell. Tall and broad-shouldered, the visible muscles in his arms were certainly well-developed. He was looking quite mature.

"Do you need help?"

I turned from Matthew to Dave, who now stood next to Robin.

"Everything's under control," said Matthew.

"Yeah, we're fine. You're not needed," said Robin, but her smile was crooked. I could practically hear her add, *Poophead.*

Dave looked uncertain, and I wondered what he was thinking. But he just nodded once and walked off toward the barns.

Robin watched him go, frowning slightly, then turned back to me. "Let's get these other ones done then we can paint them."

"Do they paint everything every year?" I asked, thinking it was an enormous amount of work.

"No, they do everything spaced out over several years. They probably paint more often than they need to, but it brings everyone together, and it's fun to help."

"Besides, the food's great!" said Matthew.

"Yeah!" Robin nodded her head enthusiastically. "Some years there's not much to do. Last year we finished painting the grandstand. That had taken a few years. Before that, we painted most of the track fence."

Matthew stood back to survey the now connected art displays and frowned. "Wouldn't they have been easier to paint *before* putting them together?"

"They might not have fit together properly if they were," I said, thinking out loud.

"Yeah, that's what Cris said," said Robin.

Matthew looked around and said, "Well, I guess I'd better go find something else to do. If I can find a brush not being used, I'll come back and help you paint."

He smiled at us in turn and then walked off toward the arenas. Robin looked at me sideways, her head tilted slightly.

"So . . . what's up with you and Matt?"

I was surprised by the question. "Matthew?"

"Paola asked me yesterday if you guys were, you know, *together*. I said no, but she didn't believe me. And now I'm wondering too. He asked me earlier if you were here yet. I told him I wasn't even sure you were coming."

I stared at her for a moment. "Nothing."

"Nothing what?" she said, looking confused.

"There's nothing up with Matthew and me." I loaded my brush and went back to painting. She kept painting too, but I could tell she was watching me.

After a few moments, she said, "Why not?"

"Why not what?" I asked, though I was thinking of the main reason.

"Don't you like him? Do you think he's good-looking?"

"Yes, I guess so." *But that doesn't have anything to do with anything.*

She shrugged. "Most girls seem to think he's really good-looking."

"Hmm," I said as if considering. *Not really interested.*

She kept looking over at me as we painted, as if I was hiding something and she'd find out if she kept watching.

"Would you go out with him if he asked you?"

A third voice started, "Go out with . . ." but stopped abruptly on impact.

I had turned quickly to reload my brush but failed to notice that Cris had walked up almost next to me until it was too late. My brush continued to move forward enough to land solidly on his t-shirt, right about where his belly-button would be. It was a good thing the brush was relatively dry, but the white paint was very noticeable on his dark shirt.

My first reaction was slight horror; the feeling you get when you've done something wrong you didn't mean to do. My second was to laugh. I couldn't help it—he looked *so* surprised. He looked down at his shirt, then steadily at me.

"Oops," I said. Memories of cold snow shoved down my back made me shiver and laugh again, nervously this time.

Robin stepped forward and surprised us both by carefully drawing a line with her brush, from the top of his chest down to just above the splotch I had made.

"There," she said, very seriously. "That looks better. Nobody'll even notice."

Cris now had a white exclamation mark on his dark shirt. A large one. Robin and I looked at each other and burst out laughing. Cris looked steadily at Robin then back at me without visible emotion. Then he turned and walked away. As he walked, he took the shirt off.

"Uh-oh," I said, half smiling, half grimacing.

Robin laughed and made a face, then shrugged. "He's too serious. Gotta do something now and then to get him to lighten up."

I didn't disagree with her but hoped Cris would remember that, at least on my part, it had been accidental. I'd definitely be watching my back.

Robin and I continued painting throughout the afternoon. There were a lot of displays. Part of the event on Labor Day was an art show where artists throughout the area could exhibit and sell their work. The Calderas didn't charge for exhibit space, but a small percentage of anything sold went to one of the charities they supported, as did all of the proceeds from the food. Most of that, especially the beef, was donated by the Calderas.

Tables and chairs had been brought out from somewhere and were added to the picnic benches already occupying a part of the open space, and several awnings were set up. Three barbecue trailers had been moved to strategic locations around the plaza, ready for Monday's crowds. The smallest one was in use today cooking for everyone there. It was interesting to watch it all take shape. Last year had been something of a Dave-obsessed blur. Between that and the crowds, I hadn't noticed. Now I realized that I hadn't explicitly thought of Dave in at least an hour. I was glad I had come. I really loved it here and felt I was giving back to the Calderas somehow by helping. It was a satisfying feeling.

At one point I noticed some huge, dark birds flying in circles high up and to the south of us. I hadn't seen anything like them before. "Are those eagles?" I asked Robin.

She stopped and looked around, frowning. "Those are buzzards. You've never seen buzzards? They're using the thermals. Eagles are more solitary, and they're not as ugly. And they hunt for their food. Buzzards eat, you know, dead things."

I couldn't tell if they were ugly or not. They were too far away.

"Are they dangerous?" I asked. It seemed like a handy thing to know.

"Not as long as you keep moving."

She said this with a smirk, so I assumed she was joking. Still, from then on I kept an eye on them.

As I finished the panel I'd been working on I saw Miguel, the ranch manager, coming up from the arena. Stevey walked next to him, holding his hand, and Merle trotted beside him. Stevey looked the same as I remembered and I was surprised. I had expected him to have grown more noticeably over the months since I last saw him.

"How old are Stevey and Henry?" I asked Robin.

She thought for a moment. "Henry's nine, so Stevey's eight. Henry's just a little over a year older. Why?"

I shook my head slightly, still watching Stevey. "I was just wondering. Stevey seems a little small for his age." This was an understatement. Stevey looked barely five or six at the most, almost exactly the same as he had looked this time last year. I wasn't an expert but comparing him to my younger cousins, he seemed very small.

"Yeah. He has, you know, developmental disorders."

This wasn't a complete surprise. I knew he was different, yet knowing why affected me deeply.

"Are you okay?" she asked me. "You look a little pale all of a sudden."

"Yes," I said. "I'm fine."

I tried to smile and would have started painting a new panel, but Stevey had seen us and was pulling Miguel in our direction. I put my brush down and waited until they got close, wondering if Stevey would even remember me.

That question was answered when he let go of Miguel's hand and came to stand before me, then stood looking off into the distance.

"Hi, Stevey," I said, wondering what to do next.

"Hello, Allison," said Miguel. I started to feel normal again, pleased that not only Stevey but Miguel, who I'd met only once before, indeed remembered me.

"Hi," I replied, smiling at him. Some of the loose threads around my heart knit back together.

"I thought we were going to see *Anjélica, chico*," he said to Stevey. He then lowered his voice as if Stevey wouldn't hear and said to us, "He is acting a little s-l-e-e-p-y."

Stevey didn't look at him or speak but took my hand.

"I guess I can take him," I said. Then I saw Dave walking back down from the barns. Hannah was with him, her arm through his, and they were talking and laughing. "I need to use the bathroom anyway." I didn't need to go that badly, but it was suddenly where I wanted to be.

"Okay. If you're sure," said Miguel. "In that case, I'll take over from Alex. Barbecue will be ready in a little while."

He walked away toward the smoking grill where Mr. Caldera was adding chicken to the beef already cooking there. Merle followed him.

"I'll be back in a little bit, okay?" I said to Robin.

"Yeah," she said, watching Dave approach. "We're almost done anyway. I'll get Dave to help."

That seemed like an excellent idea. At this rate, I might be able to avoid him completely for the rest of the day. I turned and let Stevey lead the way up the hill. Once in the house, he let go of my hand and walked up to Angel, then took *her* hand and led her toward the rooms under the stairs.

"You can go by yourself, *niño*," she said.

He let go of her hand and entered the bathroom there. "*Aiee*," she sighed. "He estarted escuela this year. You know . . . *full* time, at Quique's school. Esteban, he is *en la clase especial diurna*. It has been very hard. He does not like to go. And now, some of his . . . *¿cómo se dice?* . . . abilities . . . they have gone backward." She made a motion with her hand. "It has been *very* hard," she repeated.

I didn't know what to say, so I just nodded.

"Did you need to use the bathroom?" she asked.

"Um," I hesitated, feeling awkward. That *was* the pretense.

"You can use the *guest* bathroom down the hall. You know where?"

"Yes," I said. I walked back toward the entryway and past the dining room entrance to the short hallway on the other side of the house.

To the immediate right was a bathroom. Dave had shown me this part of the house last year, but I'd never used this room. I'd always used the one across from the mudroom. I knew the next door on the right was a guest bedroom occupying the turret at the northeast corner of the house. Straight ahead was the entrance to the garage—I'd been told—and to the left, through dark wood double doors, was their beautiful formal sitting room. Those doors were closed.

When I came back to the family room, Angel was walking up the stairs with Stevey.

"He is probably a little sleepy," she said. "He did not have a good night."

"No," said Stevey, firmly, but it was impossible to tell what it was in response to. It occurred to me it was one of the only times I'd heard him speak.

She continued up the stairs, and I turned toward the family room. The lights were off and the doors to the courtyard closed, but the overhead fans in the high ceiling kept the cool air moving. I looked at the pictures on the fireplace mantle—the photos of the boys at different ages, including their older brother who had died, Ric. Younger Dave looked so much like Henry did now, but Dave's expression in the pictures was much more mischievous and less worldly-wise. Cris seemed so carefree and happy with his brothers, especially Ric. But there were no recent pictures there.

Angel still hadn't reappeared, so I thought it would be okay to go out to the back. Not wanting to open the family room doors—I assumed they were closed for a reason—I went back to the entryway and through the colorfully tiled archway, then through the dark dining room to the courtyard beyond. It looked just the same as the last time I'd seen it—that had been the previous year at Dave's birthday party—yet in some way, I felt as if I was seeing it for the first time.

*There's where he had sat so close to me, near the fire pit in the center.
There is the gray stone wall, water trickling down into a pool below.*

In the formal sitting room was a painted portrait of the family, of Mr.
Caldera and his five sons, with this stone wall as the background. In the
opposite corner of the courtyard was another fountain, this one concrete
and a more traditional design. The fountains trickled, and birds chirped
happily in the fruit and shade trees about the yard. A slight breeze rustled
the leaves. It would have been a very peaceful place except for the sound of
a bouncing ball.

The large door in the back wall stood open slightly. It had always been
closed before, and I hadn't thought much about what might lie beyond it; I'd
only been relatively sure it wasn't a swimming pool. Curious, I pulled the
door open enough to step through and was surprised to see Cris. I hadn't
realized that he'd come up to the house, though I guess it made sense. I was
also surprised that, just beyond a pathway next to the wall, there was a
full basketball court with poles and backboards, north and south. Cris was
apparently taking a break and shooting hoops—dodging and feinting with
invisible opponents, and jumping with the same natural grace he seemed
to do everything else; everything physical anyway.

I stood still within the doorway and watched silently for a minute or
two until he turned quickly to shoot toward the far basket and spotted me.
He froze for a moment then relaxed, bouncing the ball as he walked over to
where his graffitied shirt lay. He set the ball down, picked up the shirt and
wiped his face with it, then regarded me calmly as if expecting me to speak.

So I did. "Is it okay for me to be here?"

His eyes narrowed a little. He seemed to be deciding how to answer.

"I mean, out *here*," I clarified. "The door was open and . . . I've never
seen behind the house." It occurred to me that this sounded weird, but I
couldn't unsay it.

Cris regarded me a moment longer, then shrugged and turned to pick
the ball up again. "Don't wander off too far on your own."

With that, he walked away, but not toward me and the courtyard door.
He walked away to his left and the north side of the house, disappearing
around the corner toward the garage.

I looked around. The white fence and line of poplars that began down
at the main gate continued all the way back here on the north side, as did

the asphalt paving. The driveway ran up to a wide, closed vehicle gate and then continued to the west as a dirt road. I wondered where it went. The land beyond the white fence on the other side of the court, beyond the wide gate, appeared to be pasture.

To the southwest of the court were more trees—*many* more trees. The closest were old and tall, shading the south side of the house, but there were many more beyond. I could see something reflective, maybe metallic, even farther beyond. Taking Cris at his word—historically a good idea—I didn't walk toward it. That was the direction of the circling buzzards anyway, though I couldn't see them from here. Instead, I followed the pathway next to the courtyard wall to the southwestern corner of the house. The wall here had a curtained window in it.

I hadn't thought about it before—the only time I'd been in the courtyard previous to this I was *very* preoccupied—but the courtyard had six doors opening onto it. The family, dining, and formal sitting rooms all had wide, multiple hinged doors opening directly onto the large covered patio. The tall outer wall had the one arched, thick rustic door. I'd noticed a double doorway in the northern wall; I knew there was a doorway from the sitting room into that wing of the house but hadn't seen beyond it. But there was a corresponding wing on the south side with a sixth door. I hadn't considered it before; I had vaguely assumed the mudroom was here but now realized it couldn't be.

This was a whole separate area of the house. Coming around that corner, I saw that a door in the exterior wall of the house opened onto a small patio with its own wisteria-covered pergola shading the door and two windows, and was further shaded by the tall trees on the edge of the orchard. Another pathway led out to a vegetable garden. The path I was on continued to the back wall and door of the main house—*that* must be the mudroom—and then around the corner toward the front driveway.

It had taken only moments to observe all this, of course, but it seemed a more private area, and I felt like I was trespassing. I thought I should leave before someone came looking for me.

A strange rustling made me look up. At the back of the small garden was an old utility pole, the only one I'd noticed around here. Perched on the top was a huge dark brown bird with a bald, red head. It was quite ugly. Another flew from the orchard somewhere, trying to land in the same small space and jostling the other bird. There was some scuffling, but they made no other sound. They both watched me intently. Very creepy.

I would have considered continuing to the mudroom or following the pathway around to the front of the house, but the sinister birds deterred me. I moved slowly back around the corner again and quickly entered the courtyard, closing the outer door as I did.

My return to the house could only have been a minute or two after Cris left me, but he was already running lightly down the stairs, pulling a clean shirt on. I thought it strange that he'd gone all the way around the house, or perhaps through the garage, instead of just through the courtyard. Surely the latter would have been the quickest way. I was pretty sure his room was somewhere over the north side of the house. Of course, I'd been standing in the way. *Had he just been avoiding me?*

Cris hesitated on seeing me but then continued down the stairs more slowly, tugging his shirt down. His hair looked wetter than it had a few minutes before, too, as if he had washed his face and neck, if not taken a shower. It didn't matter, but I thought it strange; how had he had time?

As he reached the bottom of the stairs, he asked, "Are you planning to ride on Monday?"

Of course, I knew what he meant, but I didn't understand why he wanted to know. Last year I'd ridden Sam, the Calderas' calm schoolmaster. I guess I had vaguely assumed I might ride him again. Now I realized that was very foolish. Things were different. I couldn't, *shouldn't* assume anything.

"I . . . I'm not sure."

"We thought you might want to ride Remmy in some events," he said, then shrugged. "It's up to you."

Even though it had been suggested to me before, I hadn't really thought about it. This put a whole new slant on Monday, and I began picturing the possibilities. I was sure it would be fun to ride Remmy here, but I had no way to bring him. Cris was still watching me as if he knew how my brain worked and was giving me the time I needed to think it through.

"How . . . ?" I started.

"I can bring him here tomorrow night after we get home. It might be late."

"Oh," I said, still surprised and not sure what to say. "I guess." I realized this sounded indifferent and quickly added, "Yes, that would be nice."

He nodded slightly then continued past me to the entryway. I stood in the darkened family room for a couple of minutes longer, not wanting to follow him out too closely and wondering where Angel was.

By the time I rejoined Robin, Matthew had helped her to finish painting the panels. Meat sizzled on the nearby grill, smelling amazing, and almost everyone had congregated in the plaza, including my dad, Mr. Morrison, and Mr. Caldera. Paola, Jessie, and Tanner helped us move the dry display panels into positions around the plaza.

Paola kept looking around and asked a couple of times, "Where is *Dah-veed?*"

I was trying not to even think this question.

The afternoon felt like it was winding down when a portable PA next to the stage was hooked up and music began to play. Most of the adults had found places to sit or were getting paper plates and condiments ready. I thought this wouldn't be too bad—sitting out here and eating with everybody.

Cris and Henry walked up from the arena area, and then I saw Dave with Hannah. They were talking and walking close together, coming from the barns again. I looked away. As they reached the plaza, Paola went immediately to Dave's side, talking excitedly. It occurred to me that, like me, she might not have seen much of him today.

I also noticed for the first time that he looked exhausted. I wondered if he was having nightmares again, or perhaps he was the one who'd had a difficult night with Stevey. I knew Dave had nightmares—Cris had told me—and I also knew he often woke up when Stevey couldn't sleep. He chatted now with Paola and had smiles for everyone. Especially, it seemed, for Hannah. Still, I saw him yawn and squeeze his eyes shut when he thought no one was looking. I wished I could do something for him, but I mostly felt redundant.

Cris walked over to Dave and said something quietly. Dave nodded and said something back, then walked over to where Robin, Matthew, and I were standing. The others followed him.

"Let's get some food. We can go up to the house and chill," he said, looking around at us.

I thought his gaze lingered on me for a moment, but he frowned and looked away.

No, just wishful thinking.

Everyone agreed and moved toward the grill. I hesitated and looked over at my dad. He seemed to be enjoying a discussion with Matthew's father and an Asian man I hadn't seen before. Hannah walked over to the latter, obviously telling him where she was going. He smiled at her and nodded. She turned away back to Dave, who was waiting for her. Together they got plates and food and then started toward the house following Tanner, Cris, and Jessie.

Paola had a short but lively exchange in Spanish with the only adult woman there—I assumed her mother—and trotted as quickly as she could, carrying a very full plate, until she caught up with Dave and Hannah.

"Allie?"

"Oh ... um ..."

"You coming?" Robin had stepped back toward me, a plate in her hands already loaded with casserole, tri-tip, tortillas, and salsa.

"Hmmm?"

"Food?"

"Oh! Yes," I said. I had no appetite but knew I'd be harassed, at least by her, if I didn't get something.

I looked again at my dad. He looked back, smiled, and waved. He looked comfortable. It appeared we'd be here at least a while longer. I got a little of everything and walked up the hill with Robin.

As we neared the house, Angel came out, greeting us as she continued toward the plaza. The only evidence of the others, as we entered the house, was loud talking from upstairs. Everyone was up in the game room. Dave and Hannah were sitting on the floor and already playing a racing game on one of the big screens. Stevey sat in Dave's lap, giggling as Dave leaned ridiculously far into curves. Paola also sat near Dave on the floor while Jessie sat on the big couch. Cris was at the computer near the French doors, and Tanner and Matthew were setting up another game on the second screen.

"A Caldera work day tradition: video game marathon," said Robin, grinning.

When Matthew saw us, he said, "Hey ... come and play."

I thought he might be talking to both of us, but I had a hard time doing two things at once. I decided to eat first and just watch, sitting in the over-sized armchair. Robin took him up on the invitation and, though they argued over the decision a little, they were soon playing an old first-person shooter. When I finished eating, I got pulled into a four-way game with Jessie, but I wasn't very good at it. I kept dying, which got a little old for everybody, especially me, so I went and sat on the couch. Stevey came and settled beside me.

As time passed, games and players changed a few times and I wondered if I should say goodbye and leave. At one point Hannah sat on one side of me and Paola sat on the other, and they had a lively discussion across me, but I couldn't contribute much to it. I felt like the most boring person there, exacerbating my feeling of alienation.

I was trying not to conspicuously watch Dave, especially as I'd noticed Matthew occasionally looking at *me*, but I desperately wanted to talk to him—alone. It felt like I was missing something somewhere; some clue I was overlooking or hint that I just couldn't get—the piece of jigsaw puzzle you lost but keep stepping over because it blends in with the carpet. Missing or misreading social cues had always been a problem for me, but not so much with Dave; not until this year. I was sure it wasn't my imagination, and I needed to ask him about it. I needed him to just *tell* me.

I'd seen him stifle a couple more yawns and at one point he let Tanner take over his controller and then lay back, closing his eyes. Paola had immediately moved to sit next to him on the floor. Hannah got up and sat on his other side and began playing with his hair. I didn't think I could stand much more and had made up my mind to just leave when I saw my chance.

Dave got up and left the room. Paola got up too, as if to follow him, then changed her mind. I waited a few minutes then quietly got up and slipped out. I didn't think anyone had noticed except maybe Stevey; Matthew was busy fighting creatures with Tanner, Jessie, and Robin. Hannah and Paola were watching them and flipping through magazines, laughing and talking together. Cris must have left some time before.

The door to the bathroom at the end of the short hallway was open. The door to Stevey and Henry's room was open too. I could hear someone moving there and assumed it was Henry. The door on the opposite side, the door that might lead to Dave's room, was closed, but it didn't seem likely that he'd abandoned his guests to sleep, no matter how tired he was. I descended the stairs into the dark, cool family room. Dave wasn't in the kitchen, so I figured he might have gone down to the plaza. I planned to wait for him to return, but the outer doors were now open, and lowered voices reached me from the courtyard beyond. I moved closer. The voices sounded almost the same, one slightly lower at times than the other.

"I'm just saying, be careful."

"Careful? I'm not freakin' *doing* anything."

Freakin' is not the word he used. I knew I should leave, go back upstairs, but my feet wouldn't move.

It was quiet for a moment, then, "Maybe that's the problem."

"What's *that* supposed to mean?"

"Remember a certain conversation when you swore you'd never purposely hurt her? You said you were worried about it. Maybe you need to think about that some more." Quiet again, then the same voice, "Maybe it's better to just let go . . . completely."

I heard a huff that could have been a laugh. "Completely? God! It's not like I have much choice. There's nothing I can do about it. Right? Damned if I do and damned if I don't!" Sounds of muffled movement and he swore again. "Why can't I just hang out with . . . *be* with who I want? Sometimes it feels like I'm expected to babysit twenty-four-seven."

Oh god oh god oh god. I felt sick. It felt like all the blood had drained from my entire body leaving me weak, lifeless. I forced myself backward, slowly and silently—my feet and heart leaden—back past the fireplace mantel, past pictures of Caldera boys at every age smiling, grinning, laughing.

Laughing at me. *As if I could ever truly belong here. Belong with them. With him.*

I slipped through the hallway, put my shoes on in the entryway, and silently escaped out into the late afternoon heat. I knew it could be done; we had come in quietly once before almost exactly a year ago when my life had taken on new meaning and felt magical. *When my life had really begun.*

It occurred to me that someone might see me from the game room if they looked out the window, but it didn't matter. I just had to leave. Now. Dad looked surprised to see me approaching by myself and got up to meet me.

"Hey sweetheart, everything okay?"

"Yes, fine. I'm . . . fine . . . just tired. Can we go home?"

"Go home?" Now he looked suspicious.

I just nodded and tried to conceal the fact that I was shaking. It hurt my head to talk.

"Well, Mom was planning on joining us soon . . . I guess they usually stay here pretty late . . . but if you really want to go. . . ."

I nodded again.

Dad searched my face. I couldn't look at him.

"All right," he said. "Just a minute. . . ."

He walked back to where the other adults were seated, excusing us and saying goodbye. We walked back to the car together.

I briefly thought of Robin. I wondered how long it would take for her to notice I'd gone; how long before *anyone* noticed. But it didn't matter.

At the moment, nothing did.

Chapter Nine

Robin called before we arrived home, but I didn't want to talk, especially with Dad sitting next to me. Some measure of dissemblance would be necessary, and I wasn't sure I could do it. I didn't want to lie. I didn't want to talk. I didn't want to think. She didn't leave a message, but she called again right after we got home.

"Where are you?"

"In my room," I said.

"At home? You went *home*? I thought you were still here."

Ugh. Here we go. "I wasn't feeling well."

It was quiet on the other end for a moment. I felt awkward but didn't know what to say.

"You should have told me."

"Sorry. I didn't . . ." *what to say, what to say,* "I didn't want to interrupt you. You were playing."

"Did you see Dave before you left?"

"No. I didn't see him." Not a lie.

"So he didn't ask you about tomorrow?"

"Tomorrow." The word was apparently supposed to have meaning for me and earlier today would have sounded full of potential. But now it just fell from my mouth and disappeared into the carpet at my feet.

"Yeah, we're going to the beach." She paused. "He didn't ask you?"

No, why should he? My leaden heart felt even heavier. "I should probably stay home anyway. I've got homework to do."

"Oh. Okay," she said. "Well, I guess I'll see you Monday, right?"

"Mmm." I wasn't so sure about that.

Dad had already let Mom know we hadn't stayed. When she got home I could tell she was surprised and, I think, disappointed. I repeated that I was just tired and went to bed early.

I slept very little, waking up several times overwhelmed with a sick, anxious dread. I couldn't banish the conversation I'd overheard or the way it had made me feel. When I'd given up trying to *not* think of it, I turned it round and round in my mind and looked at it from every angle. Could they possibly have been referring to someone else? Paola? Hannah? Someone I didn't even know about?

It didn't seem likely. I appeared to be the only one he wasn't intentionally spending time with; not actively avoiding, but not seeking out in the same way as before and having little real contact with. I knew what *that* looked and felt like. Apparently now I was just a burden. It was a horrible feeling, but I had no intention of remaining that curse. I would not outstay my welcome.

If it weren't for Remmy, I probably wouldn't have gotten up on Sunday at all. I had no energy, no appetite, no interest in anything. But Remmy needed my attention. I finally got up, pulled on comfy clothes, and went out to feed him. I spent most of the day outside with him, bathing, grooming, and later, riding. For the first time, I felt completely dissatisfied with our usual orbit: down the dirt drive, across the covered cattle guard, around the hidden corral, through the trees and along the stream, then up along the north side of the property. There was also the area where we schooled, just beyond the stable. But I would have liked to explore farther. We had once gone a short way down the dirt road that continued past the lower corral into the hills but, seasoned and generally calm though he was, even Remmy acted nervous there, and I knew I wasn't a good enough rider to deal with any real trouble.

So I cleaned Remmy's stall and paddock and walked the wheelbarrow down to the corral to clean that too. Then I cleaned tack. I intentionally avoided homework. It was my back-up excuse for Monday.

The day dragged by, yet when evening came, it had gone by too fast. I had a difficult decision to make. I didn't want to go tomorrow. I wanted to completely avoid Dave, and that would probably be impossible if I went. I felt terrible about this. I felt no animosity toward him at all. And it wasn't because my feelings were hurt; I wouldn't be that petty toward him.

Rather, I didn't want to go because I was sure I wouldn't be able to respond to him normally or act normally around him—whatever constituted normal for me. I had some evasive and deflective skills, but I was no real actor. And he had always been fairly astute where I was concerned. I wished I could just stop thinking of him, just flip a switch and turn it off, but so far I hadn't been able to. He was still too important to me.

On the other hand, I was afraid that if I didn't go, he might become suspicious, especially after I'd left so suddenly on Saturday without saying goodbye to anyone. I would rather die than let him even suspect that I'd overheard his conversation, not for my own sake but for his. More than hating the way I felt right now, the thought of making *him* feel bad was even worse.

I just needed time to adjust. Time to adapt. Time to reinforce the crumbled walls of defenses that, over a short lifetime, I had erected to shield myself from such things. Dave had very effectively, if unknowingly, pulled those defenses to pieces.

Still, I wasn't so self-absorbed as to forget that other people might be affected by my decision. I hated letting people down. I knew my mother looked forward to going, especially as she hadn't been able to go after work on Saturday. She enjoyed the crowds and excitement. And if the truth were told, I was pretty sure my dad wanted to go, too. He might be resistant to the Calderas themselves, but he had made friends through them—Dr. James, Tom Reid, Mr. Morris—and, even though he wasn't generally a very sociable person, I knew he enjoyed talking and spending time with them.

And I wanted to see Angel and Stevey again. If Dave felt that way about me, who knew when I'd see them again? It might be a long time. Thinking of this just added to the growing depression and I tried to turn my thoughts from it.

The main reason I wanted to go now was for Robin. She was starting to seem more like her old self, but I wasn't convinced that all was well. Sometimes, like yesterday when we were painting but not talking, I still thought she looked unhappy, even haunted. I knew there were things that she had

never told me about herself, but that was okay. I was more concerned with simply being her friend; being there for her. Hopefully, I could just avoid Dave in the crowds.

I checked my phone a few times during the day, but there was no contact from anyone. I assumed they were all relaxing somewhere, maybe on the beach, and I tried not to let my imagination visit them. Finally, about eight o'clock, the house phone rang. Dad picked it up and then passed it to me. I hesitantly answered, sincerely hoping that it wasn't Dave.

It was Cris. Did I want him to bring Remmy to the ranch?

"Yes . . . please . . . if it's not too much trouble," I said.

I had thought about going without Remmy, but I wanted to be able to keep up with Robin. The best way to do that was to have Remmy there. I couldn't count on Sam being offered to me, and I didn't want to ask.

"No trouble," said Cris. "I'm picking Gali up too, and I'll go there first. Can you have him ready in about an hour?"

I said I could.

I wrapped Remmy's legs and tail and then brushed him again until Cris pulled in behind the house. He nodded to me, immediately taking Remmy's lead rope and leading him to the trailer. Remmy, old pro that he was, hopped right in. After stowing his tack in the trailer's locker, Cris turned back to me. He looked uncomfortable.

"We'll keep him in a stall tonight so he'll stay cleaner for you."

"Thank you," I said, humbled. I had never felt I deserved any attention from the Calderas, and this was more than thoughtful—especially under the circumstances.

Cris turned to leave, then stopped and said, "Oh . . ." He took folded papers from his back pocket and handed them to me. "If you ride in any events, you need to have your folks sign the release. You can enter classes right up until they close . . . usually about ten minutes before they start. It's pretty low key."

"Okay," I said. Then as he turned to go, I added, "And thanks . . . again."

Cris regarded me steadily for a moment then said, "I'm glad you de-cided to go."

All things considered, I wasn't sure what to make of that so just nodded.

This Labor Day play day was a very different experience for me than last year. I dressed carefully in clean jeans, my pale pink show shirt, black hat, and my now weathered and scuffed but much loved black boots. Looking in the mirror, I was surprised at my reflection, dressed in this outfit with my hair around my shoulders and no glasses. I still felt unsure about the way I looked. Once upon a time, Dave had thought me cute, though I'd never been sure what "cute" meant to him. Now I half felt that I looked good, attractive even. *Just not beautiful enough for him? Or maybe it's just the way I am.* I'd have to try to not let my thoughts run in those directions.

We parked in the allocated area just after nine o'clock. My parents told me to have fun and said they'd be in the grandstand. They wanted to watch me ride in at least one of the classes I planned to enter, so I said I'd come and find them. I wanted to get Remmy right away but wasn't sure exactly where he was, so I walked toward the barns on the far side of the arena. I was hoping to see Cris first, not Dave. But it was Henry who approached me.

"You're looking for Remmy, right?" he said, giving me an appraising look. "I can take you to him."

I smiled. This was even better. "Thank you," I said meekly.

He shrugged and said, "Yeah," and continued walking toward the barns. He led the way into the closest, biggest one.

As we entered I called, "Remmy!" and his sweet face appeared over a stall door. "There you are," I said, not feeling quite as nervous now.

"Do you need anything else?" Henry asked, not tersely but as if he'd been told to ask rather than through any inclination of his own. But that was okay.

"No," I said. "I'll be fine."

He turned to leave.

"Oh!" I said, "Do you know where Robin is?"

He turned back. "I'll tell her you're here if I see her. She's probably around the arena."

"Oh . . . right."

He gave me another longer, appraising look. "You look really different," he said. Then he smiled crookedly—a very familiar, mischievous smile—and left.

I wasn't sure, but I thought he approved. Perhaps it was pathetic to feel encouraged by an exchange with a nine-year-old, but I did.

Remmy's tack was on a rack right in front of the stall, his grooming tote underneath. I groomed and saddled him then led him out of the barn. After tightening the girth, I mounted and rode slowly toward the main arena. Cris was there on Laguna, his tall palomino, and Matthew, Jessie, and Tanner were close by. I approached them and was even more encouraged by their smiles.

"Hey, you're here," said Matthew.

He was riding the big brown horse I'd seen him on last year. Tanner was on a small roan mare. Jessie rode a stocky chestnut gelding.

"How's Remmy doin'?" asked Tanner. "You likin' him?"

I smiled easily. "He's wonderful!" I admitted, and it hit home again how incredible it was that I had him. And of course, *that* was because of Dave—him and his family. It was also because of Dave that I had these other friends. We might not be terribly close, but they accepted me. That felt wonderful too.

"Have you seen Robin?" I asked.

"She just finished a sorting class with Dave," said Tanner.

"Sorting?"

"There you are!" Robin's voice rang out over the surrounding noise, and I turned to see her riding toward us. "Did you see him? He did *so* good!"

I understood that her enthusiasm and praise was all for her pretty grulla horse, Galahad, and not for Dave, who was a little way behind her on Tee. Her eyes sparkled, and she looked happier than I'd seen her since before summer started.

"I . . . I just got here. I'm sorry, I would have come earlier if I'd known!"

"That's okay. I'm really glad you're here though."

This made me very happy. It was worth any discomfort I might feel today just to hear her say that. By this time Dave had ridden up, but I kept my attention elsewhere.

"Are you entered in anything?" asked Matthew.

"Maybe *not* the barrel racing," said Tanner.

"Subtle, Tanner. Good job," said Matthew.

"I think . . . maybe the trail class?" I said.

I actually had a few other classes in mind but felt awkward admitting it, especially in front of Dave. I didn't want him to feel he had to watch out for me for any reason like last year. I'd ridden in trail classes before, so I hoped he wouldn't feel the need to be involved at all.

"Everything okay?" he asked.

I looked at him to verify that he was, indeed, talking to me. He looked serious and his eyes searched mine—very disconcerting. I couldn't afford extended contact, or I'd be floundering all day.

"Yes!" I responded, looking down at Remmy and playing with his mane. "I feel fine. I'm sure we'll be . . . fine . . . no worries at all." This was true, yet the words sounded hollow, even to me.

"Okay, good," he said. "I have to stay over there and help, so I guess I'll see you later."

"See ya," said Robin.

The others uttered similar farewells, and Cris followed him. I was aware of him riding back slowly the way he had come but refused to actually watch him go. I wondered why he'd bothered to ride all the way over here just to turn around and ride back but didn't dwell on it.

"What's next?" asked Matthew.

"More sorting here," said Jessie, looking at a schedule. "Gymkhana ongoing in the small arena. I think I'll go get something to eat."

"That sounds good," agreed Tanner.

"I'm with you," said Robin. "I'm famished. Are you coming, Allie?"

"Oh . . . I think I'll stay down here," I said. They had probably been here for hours, but I wasn't ready for food yet. Besides, I had other plans.

"Okay," said Robin, not looking certain. "I'll be back."

I smiled and nodded. The others rode away and I turned Remmy toward the smaller arena. Matthew kept pace beside me.

"What are you up to?" he said, looking suspicious.

That actually made me laugh. "Nothing not already sanctioned by my parents."

He smiled.

When we reached the gymkhana arena, we sat and watched for a while. Riders were negotiating the quadrangle. I had studied the gymkhana classes carefully and as realistically as I could. I wanted to execute the runs, stops, and turns that Remmy and I had been working on, but I wasn't going to really race. I figured, the simpler the event, the less likely I was to come to grief. I had every intention of riding more assertively in future events, but today I was going to play it *very* safe. It would still be great practice. Half the battle for me—maybe more than half—was doing something like this in front of others. I just really didn't like having an audience.

"Is that where you sign up?" I asked Matthew, looking toward a table under a small canopy.

"Yeah," he said, nodding. "Got your release form?"

I pulled the folded paper out of my back pocket and held it up. Matthew held Remmy while I went and paid my entry fees for two of the events. I was going to avoid anything with barrels for now. I still had uneasy feelings about them and didn't want to communicate that in any way to Remmy. So, simple patterns without barrels it would be. After signing up, I walked back to Matthew and mounted again.

A couple of the events I might have been interested in had already finished that morning, but I had signed up for the single stake and keyhole. If those went well, I planned to enter the figure eight stake and birangle. I had also entered the advanced trail class for later in the day.

We watched a couple of events until the single stake started. Remmy and I were seventh to go and completed it at a leisurely lope, barely breaking our stride in the turn. Of course, we had gone nowhere near as fast as almost everyone else, but we had stayed on the correct lead, my seat was solid, and Remmy had remained calm. I was thrilled with that.

"Hey!" Robin had found us and joined Matthew by the fence. "You didn't tell me you were riding right now. I would have cheered you on!"

"Thanks, but I didn't want to stop you from going with the others."

This was true, but it was also true that I would have felt much more self-conscious if she'd been watching. For some reason, it didn't bother me that Matthew had.

After the single stake was the keyhole race and I was one of the last to ride. I was more nervous about this only because we hadn't actually practiced it within visible limits and I was concerned about staying within the chalk outline. Again, we entered at an easy lope and then stopped in the circle, Remmy's hindquarters well under him. We had been practising turns on the hindquarters so his turn was slow but pretty tight, and I urged him out faster but still in hand.

I came back to find that Matthew had left to get ready for the team penning and Robin had dismounted to stand with Hannah and Paola, who had joined her. They were all smiling, but Paola was clapping her hands excitedly.

"You did very well, yes?" she gushed. "*¡Felicidades!*"

A part of me knew that she was sincerely trying to encourage me, but it made me feel uncomfortable anyway. And the other part of me felt she was patronizing me as if she thought I needed *extra* encouragement for some reason.

Hannah was slightly more reserved, but still more enthusiastic than I thought the occasion warranted. "Well done, Allison!" she said, but I wasn't sure how to feel about it. I wished they hadn't been watching.

"Thanks, but it wasn't that good. I'm still learning." I hated feeling like I needed to make an excuse, but it was the truth, and their effusive praise had made me feel more defensive than anything else.

"Are you going to ride in any more of the races?" asked Paola.

I couldn't help it—her enthusiasm suddenly seemed superficial and *really* annoyed me. Perhaps it just made me feel what I was doing was unimportant. I quickly revised my plans.

"I think I'll just wait for the trail class later."

"Well, do you want to get something to eat?" asked Robin. "I didn't eat that much and I'm hungry again."

It had only been about an hour and a half since she'd eaten, but I agreed. It was already past noon, and I knew she had at least two more events coming up. We rode up to the barn, loosened girths, then haltered and tied the horses in their stalls where they could eat and relax for a while. Then we went down to the plaza.

Hannah and Paola were waiting for us; they made it clear they had saved us seats. I knew they were just friendly and considerate, but I wished I could have sat alone with Robin. There was nothing private I wanted to discuss, but I was having trouble. I had started the day feeling stressed and was already beginning to feel overwhelmed, though I didn't understand why. And I had prepared myself as best I could to see very little of Dave today—had actually hoped for it—but I felt so hollow inside. Making it worse was not being able to block out memories of last year when we had seemed so close. *Had it really just been babysitting?*

Now Hannah and Paola seemed to be the ones in his favor, and they seemed to have attached themselves to Robin and me, at least for now. I honestly believed Hannah to be a sweet and friendly girl, but I still found it difficult to be friendly toward her, and I didn't know why. I wasn't prone to disliking people—I usually didn't even feel badly toward people who were unkind to me—so it perplexed me greatly.

Paola, on the other hand, just plain bugged me. She was *too* much: too talkative, too loud, too nosy, too girly, too attractive and, most of the time, too darn close to Dave. Hannah, on her own, I probably could have tolerated, but Hannah and Paola together were almost unbearable. I was vexed by the situation, but I was even more annoyed with myself. I knew the girls were in no way to blame for the way I felt, but knowing that just made me feel worse.

The plaza was lively and noisy with a band playing on the stage while people got food, milled around the art exhibits, and socialized. The three other girls were also loud, talking and laughing as they ate, but I couldn't focus on most of what they said. I was beginning to think it was a bad idea to have come today after all.

"Allison, you do not eat very much," observed Paola.

"Um . . . I'm . . . I'm going to go get Remmy," I said, mostly to Robin. I needed to get away before I exploded or said something I'd regret.

Robin looked up, surprised. "You're done already? Okay," she said and shrugged. "Can I have your corn?"

"Yes. I'll . . . find you later."

She nodded and took the untouched corn from my plate.

I threw my plate away and went back to the barn. Talking to Remmy for a while in the relative quiet calmed my nerves. Then I led him out and adjusted his tack, mounted, and rode back toward the arenas. I thought I would just hang out by the big arena—I was pretty sure the barrel racing was starting soon and wanted to watch Robin ride—but I didn't see anyone I knew so kept riding around the track.

I *did* see Dave. He was on Tee and at one point looked straight at me. I know I should have returned his gaze. I should have tried to smile. I should have raised my hand in greeting. Something. But all I could do was immediately look away, then look at Remmy and smooth his mane, flustered and scared to betray the wrong emotion. By the time I realized my error and looked back, determined to be assertive and try to appear at least friendly, he'd already looked away and didn't look back again.

Okay, that's a good thing. The sooner he feels released from any responsibility for me, the sooner I can . . .

I didn't know. Since I'd fallen for him, whenever I'd thought of the future—rarely and even then, very vaguely—it had included him.

The rest of the afternoon progressed much more like the previous year, the main differences being that Matthew had replaced Dave as my main male companion and Paola was the one asking the questions—*many* questions—and receiving Dave's unflaggingly patient responses.

Cris was conspicuous much of the time and seemed watchful, but he also kept his distance which made me even sadder, if that was possible. I felt like I had some kind of disease that they'd found out about and wondered if this event today truly marked the end of an enchanted year, maybe the best one of my life, past *and* future. That thought didn't help the growing depression.

Robin rode brilliantly in the barrel racing, her face shining with triumph and pride in Gali's performance as she rode back to us. Dave nodded and said, loudly, "Nailed it!" as she passed him, which obviously pleased her enormously, and everyone acknowledged her great ride. She ended up coming in second after a much older girl's first, which still earned her a cash prize.

The team roping was next, and Dave and Cris would be competing together this year. Apparently Shane couldn't be there, and Matthew had declined, saying that he'd had no chance to practice.

"That never stops me," said Dave with just a trace of his mischievous smile.

"Unfortunately," said Cris, deadpan and riding away.

"Can you guys stay with Paola and Hannah?" This was said to the group at large.

"Sure," said Robin, without hesitation. A few others nodded their heads.

Dave rode away, following his brother toward the main gate and chutes.

I had other plans. "I'm entered in the trail class," I told Robin, quietly. "I'll find you after, okay?"

"Want us to come?" she asked, frowning.

Matthew, standing on the ground and holding his horse near the other girls, had overheard and looked like he might have followed too.

"No!" I said quickly, perhaps too vehemently. I tried to relax. "No . . . I'm fine. You stay and watch here. I'm going to find my parents first anyway. My dad wants to watch."

Dad hadn't seen me ride in a show since my birthday last year. I'd improved a lot, and I wanted him to see Remmy at his best. And I had something to prove to him. I didn't go to my parents immediately, however. I rode to the end of the big arena close to the grandstand and found a place to watch. I couldn't help wanting to see the brothers ride.

Dave rode header, but he had a hard time controlling Tee in the box. When the barrier released, he lost a couple of seconds getting Tee straight. The steer was halfway into the arena before he loosed his rope and he missed, the rope skimming over its back. Dropping the end of that rope, he grabbed his second and threw it more quickly than I would have thought possible, catching the steer solidly around its horns. He dallied and turned, allowing Cris to neatly rope its hind feet, but valuable time had been lost.

The steer was released and ran off, herded out by the previous team. Dave smiled ruefully and shook his head as he and Cris gathered in their ropes. They met in the middle and rode toward the exit gate together to wait for the next team to come in. I knew they wouldn't have been scored anyway, as they couldn't compete and win prizes at their own event, but I felt bad for Dave and knew it must grate on him. He was very competitive.

Kyle and Stacie were up next and, though they were obviously a couple at school now, I was surprised to see them doing this as a team. Kyle rode header and got the steer around the neck. When Stacie threw her rope, it looked like she would catch both heels, but the steer hopped one foot out a split-second before the rope grew taut. It was still a good round, and they looked pleased with each other. Tanner was up next with a boy I wasn't familiar with, and I wanted to watch him too but thought I'd better get going.

Moving closer to the grandstand, I located my parents and waved. They waved back, spoke to the Reids, who they were sitting with, and stood up to follow me. I'd already entered the class so went straight to the small arena to watch and await my turn.

The only obstacle I wasn't sure about was a raised wooden bridge that echoed hollowly as the horses crossed it. A few horses startled and shied before crossing and a couple absolutely refused to cross. I hoped, and thought it likely, that Remmy had negotiated this kind of obstacle before, but I didn't have the opportunity to ask Dave about it. I probably wouldn't have anyway.

I leaned forward and whispered to Remmy as another horse and rider crossed the bridge, "It's like the plywood over the cattle guard at home, just more off the ground."

The only other thing that we hadn't practiced was the lope over, but I wasn't worried about it. After many riders had entered the ring, my name was called to stand by. I rode Remmy closer to the gate. My mom and dad were now watching from the side, and I saw Robin and Matthew ride up near them. Paola and Hannah walked up, too, and stood close by. When the rider before me left the ring, Remmy and I entered.

One of the things I adore about Remmy is that no matter what job is set before him, he approaches it whole-heartedly, even though it may be something he's done a million times before. Like trail classes. When I first started riding him at Bar 8, before Dave gave him to me, he had been so patient—even over, around, and through the most mundane obstacles. He got excited around barrels, it's true, but I couldn't fault his enthusiasm. He had taught me so much already. If only I could learn to be as patient and generous as him!

We competently negotiated the gate, then a jog and stop before the next obstacle, a side step over a pole, backing through an "L" then sidestepping over another pole, which we nailed. From there we had to jog up to a pole box, step completely in and make a three-sixty turn in the center. On stepping out, we loped over four poles on the ground and halted squarely at a cone. We had practiced a little at Bar 8 last year, but I didn't have any poles at home so had only approximated it with small branches and mostly just jogged over them. Loping over them wasn't as easy as I had thought it would be and, though on the correct lead, Remmy clipped two of the poles. We'd have to work on that.

From the first cone, we jogged to a second cone then slowed again and walked to the bridge. Remmy approached it almost eagerly but hesitated a little before stepping onto it. Once he did, he startled slightly but continued over, if a little nervously, his hoofs echoing hollowly on the raised wood. The next was a mailbox. I had to put the flag down, open, take envelopes out, put them back in, then raise the flag again. No problem; our practice at home had really paid off here. The next was to jog a serpentine up to a pole with a plastic raincoat on it. I took it down and draped it over the front of my saddle. Remmy stood perfectly still as I did this and then replaced it. The final obstacle was my favorite part—jumping a log. We approached this from a quick trot and hopped over it easily. Then I walked him on a loose rein to the gate.

Our little cheering section broke out in whistles and applause, and I didn't mind too much. I stroked Remmy's neck as we exited the arena, feeling that we really had done very well. I didn't even care about the hiccup with the bridge. He had trusted me and gone over it. That felt almost as good as if we had won the whole thing. In the end, we came in third out of twenty, earning a second yellow ribbon to add to the one we'd won last year. And Dad actually looked proud, not just humoring me, and that was important. I decided that, regardless of anything else, this little victory and seeing Robin looking so happy were worth coming for today.

"I've got to go," said Robin. "The pole-bending is starting soon. But I'll see you later, okay?"

I nodded and waved as she set Gali back toward the big arena. Matthew, leading his horse, was already walking in that direction with Hannah and Paola.

"We're going to get something to eat before the big events," said Mom. "Do you want me to get you anything?"

By *big events* she meant the bronc and bull riding; not my favorites but the most popular here and the most important to Dave. Of course I had to watch.

"No thanks," I said. "I'm going to go watch Robin. I'll find you in the grandstand later."

I'd been thinking about this a lot. I had decided I would stay mounted to watch Robin in her last event, and then I'd settle Remmy for the rest of the evening. It wasn't that I didn't prefer riding, and he wasn't at all tired, but remembering last year—how the brothers had stayed so close to me—it just seemed best. No need for anyone to watch over me. No need for anyone to care what I thought. *No need for anyone.*

I also remembered how I'd apparently been observed last year by others from our school. It wasn't just fear of reprisals; I was determined to not be seen as needy. Did I still feel I needed Dave? His opinion? His presence? His affection? Yes, I couldn't imagine that changing. But I didn't want to *appear* dependent on him, and especially not to Dave himself.

I rode Remmy back to the big arena near the others. Hannah seemed content to talk to Matthew, but Paola insisted on talking to me. Between the general noise around us and the speed at which she talked, I couldn't process most of what she said.

Dave sat on the gate at the arena entrance. I didn't see Cris anywhere.

Robin had a great run, not knocking down any poles but not quite fast enough to place in the top four. She looked happy anyway. I met her on her way back to our place by the fence.

"That was great!" I said.

"Thanks," she said, looking pleased.

"I'm going to put Remmy in his stall," I said, patting his neck. "I think I'll sit with my folks for the final events."

Robin looked surprised. "Why?"

"No reason. I just figured I'd take care of him now rather than later." *And also try to avoid Dave.*

"Oh." I could see she didn't understand. She might even have been suspicious. "See you later?" she asked.

"Yes! Of course!"

She nodded and rode away. I didn't dare look toward the gate as I passed but rode on toward the barn, then unsaddled and rubbed Remmy down a little. He still had plenty of hay, so I left him to it and decided to walk up to the house. I didn't know when I'd see Angel again and wanted to see her once more before I left today.

I walked from the barn to the road, avoiding the plaza and any distractions that might be there, then continued up the drive to the house and through the unlocked door without knocking. Inside was dark and cool as usual, the only sound the light trickling of water on water coming through the dining room from the courtyard. Angel wasn't in the kitchen or family room, and the outer doors were still closed. I lingered near the mantle photographs, trying to commit them to memory, before walking back to and through the dining room,.

She wasn't in the courtyard. Disappointed but not wanting to remain in the house alone, I left.

I thought about checking for her at the plaza, but there were so many people there. Besides, I didn't want to miss seeing Dave ride even though it was sure to make me anxious, and he wouldn't know or care that I was watching.

I found my parents sitting in the grandstand in a group with Cheryl and the kids, Mr. and Mrs. Morris, and Mr. Caldera and Stevey. They all greeted me, smiling. Sitting near Mr. Caldera were the man I assumed was

Hannah's dad and the woman Paola had spoken to on Saturday with a man I assumed was her dad. I sat next to Cheryl.

"I heard you did great today!" she said. "Congratulations."

"Well, maybe not *great*, but I was happy with what we did, especially the trail class. But the speed classes were fun. I concentrated on control and balance." I knew she would appreciate that.

She smiled, patted my leg and said, "That's my girl."

This reserved compliment meant so much more to me than the earlier effusive praise from the others. Something about that made me feel guilty, but I pushed it away and refused to think about it. I didn't need to feel any worse today.

The poles had been cleared away and the arena was dragged again during a short break before the bucking events started. Mr. Caldera stood up to leave and held his hand out to his son, but Stevey shoved his hands between his legs and looked in the opposite direction.

"Stevey, come with me. Let's go and see *Dah-veed*. He will be riding soon."

He waited for his son to comply, but Stevey refused to look at him. Mr. Caldera remained very calm and said, patiently but firmly, "Esteban, *iva-monos! Ahora mi hijo, por favor.*"

Stevey still didn't look at him but stood up and, with his hands still tucked between his thighs, awkwardly tried to negotiate stepping down into the next row. He passed by my parents and Cheryl, but when he got parallel to me, he stopped.

"Esteban . . ."

"No," said Stevey, firmly.

The only response Mr. Caldera exhibited was slightly raised eyebrows. He looked toward the other adults and said with good humor, "Stevey has begun saying no. However, it does not always mean no. Interpretation is . . . challenging."

He said this with a smile and a soft look in his eyes. The same way Dave looked at his little brother. *The same way he sometimes used to look at me.*

"I must go. The next event starts in a short while, and I am judging. Cheryl, would you mind keeping an eye on him until one of the boys comes for him?"

"No, of course I don't mind," she said. "No problem."

"No," said Stevey again, but not as decidedly.

"*Mi hijo*, stay with Cheryl," he said. He continued down to the bottom of the stands and along the walkway toward the roofed observation deck.

"Come here, Stevey," said Cheryl. "Why don't you come and sit with me and Cody and we can watch together?"

Stevey looked around at all of us without focusing on anyone in particular and stood up straighter, his hands falling more naturally to his sides. He surprised me by climbing back up on the seat in front of us and came to stand next to me, then bumped gently against my leg.

"Hi, Stevey," I said.

He didn't respond. I didn't need him to.

The music from the stage came over the loudspeaker at the arena. Soon after, the announcer introduced the judges and the last events of the day. First would be the saddle bronc riding. This event apparently hadn't been offered for many years, and there were a lot of people entered. The first rider had an excellent ride and lasted the full eight seconds. As the rider walked out of the arena, Cris joined us in the stands, sitting near me on the other side of Stevey. Stevey was still standing and bumping against me gently, not watching the arena but looking off into middle space, thinking his own thoughts. I hoped they were happier than mine.

"Hey," Cris said in a low voice. "Has he been okay?"

"Yes, he's fine, but I guess he doesn't want to sit right now."

Cris nodded, watching his little brother.

"Aren't you riding today?" I asked, then wanted to clarify, "I mean, in the bucking events?"

Cris' gaze slid to me for a moment, long enough for me to feel the need to avoid it. "I've got a bull to ride in a little while."

My turn to nod. "Will someone be riding *your* bull?" Clarification seemed in order again. "Dave pointed him out to me last year."

Cris, like Dave, had a bull he had raised himself; a huge red speckled animal.

"Ol' Crackers? I think Colby drew him." I was surprised to see his lips tighten and curve in a smile, but he dropped his head immediately as if to hide it under the brim of his hat. When he looked up again, his expression was neutral. "I'm hoping that bull performs as well as he usually does. I have him up for sale."

I was going to ask about the bull's name, but his last words distracted me. I frowned. "You're selling him?"

He nodded. His hat shaded his eyes, which were fixed on the far end of the arena.

I couldn't help wondering why he was selling the bull and took a guess. "Is it to pay for college?"

His gaze slid sideways to me again for a moment, then back to the arena. "Something like that. Besides, I raised him for this. He needs a real job to do. A purpose in life. Not just standing around eating."

"I guess . . . he's probably worth a lot," I said, not knowing at all how much college cost except that it was very expensive, nor how much a bucking bull was worth.

"Enough for what I want," he said, still looking off into the distance.

We lapsed into mutual silence after that. Rider after rider took their turns. There had been twenty horses available to ride for the saddle bronc event, and there were riders signed up for all of them, including Tanner and Tom.

The bull riding was next. Dave came to replace Cris in watching Stevey, who was now sitting down next to me. When Dave reached us, he walked straight over to greet my parents first, saying hi to Dad and smiling warmly at my mom, but it wasn't his bowl-them-over charming smile. He gave a brief wave of acknowledgment to Cheryl and the others, saying "Hey," then turned and looked at me and then Stevey, smiling his softest smile. It was tempting to pretend that the smile was for me, too, but I scolded myself and didn't.

"I'll bring Remmy back to your house later tonight," said Cris. He stood and looked from me to my parents for confirmation.

I nodded and my dad thanked him. He and Dave looked steadily at each other for a few seconds, and then he walked away.

I was thinking about how much I hated feeling estranged from Dave. That he would probably ignore me now even though we were sitting so close, and how that would make me feel even more awkward and unbearably sad. But he surprised me by saying, "I heard you did really well in the advanced trail class with Remmy."

"Oh . . . yes. Yes, I think so. He wasn't sure about the bridge, but he went over anyway. He's so willing and always tries to do what I ask."

"That's because he cares about you and trusts you." He said this a little more softly and looked straight at me.

My foolish heart, refusing to listen to my much more cautious brain, leaped at the direct eye contact and the sound of his voice. Then his demeanor changed abruptly. He sat up straighter and looked like he was thinking of something else, looking away. *Far away.*

He continued in a gruffer voice, "And he probably hasn't had to cross a bridge of any kind in a long time. I don't remember the last time I rode him over one."

I was nervous about trying to keep the conversation going. I didn't trust my ability to act normally. I didn't know what my normal was, but I was afraid Dave would be able to tell the difference. I was also afraid I'd betray myself. Sometimes I said things that, in retrospect, didn't come out as I meant them to. I hadn't worried about it much around Dave before, but now it seemed to matter. And I was feeling so conflicted, not just about Dave and what I'd overheard on Saturday, but about the other girls. It seemed like a good idea to say as little as possible. Still, I didn't want him to think I didn't care at all. I braved another comment.

"I . . . I pretended it was just like going over the plywood covering the cattle guard at home," I said. "At least . . . I thought that's kind of what it sounded like. That's what I told Remmy anyway." I immediately realized how silly that sounded and added, "Though he probably didn't understand me." *Ugh. Even sillier to point that out.*

Dave looked at me again, and I thought there was just a glimmer of humor in his eyes. He smiled slightly and said, "That was a good idea. It helped you to be confident in that situation. But . . . yeah," he said, looking away with a slight frown and smirk, shaking his head, "I doubt Remmy actually understood the words." Then he looked back at me, and his voice softened again. "I'm really glad he's working out so well for you. I . . . we were pretty sure he would." He regarded me seriously for a moment longer, then nodded slightly as he said, "He's a good friend."

My stupid heart was misbehaving badly once more, and I didn't trust myself to say anything else. At that moment the first bull and rider left the chute and before the eight-second buzzer rang Hannah and Paola found us, coming to sit on the bench right behind Dave. I had no more direct interaction with him for the rest of the day.

In fact, it was all I would have for quite a while.

I felt very detached during the bull riding, watching but not letting my-self dwell on how dangerous it was. Still, I was glad Dave wasn't riding in the event. Kyle rode well and almost stayed on for the whole ride. I was a little more interested when I heard the announcer declare, "Colby Swift on Caldera Ranch's Firecracker Red," and Crackers, Cris' bull, burst out of the chute.

Roberta appeared at the same time, climbing the steps and coming to sit on the other side of Dave. I was distracted by the way she was dressed: purple jeans with a matching purple cowboy hat, fancy snakeskin boots, and a tight tank top imperfectly covering a lacy bra. I looked away immediately but wondered how long she'd been here at the ranch. Surely she hadn't just arrived?

None of my business, none of my business, none of my business!

Crackers was the biggest bull I'd seen today and, though he didn't become airborne to the extent some of the others did, he was talented and athletic, twisting and turning and throwing his head. His rider, a senior from our school, rode him well but failed to last until the buzzer. I had a feeling Cris had expected that. Colby managed to evade the bull's feet and butting head and ran to the side of the arena, hopping up on the fence until the bullfight-ers lured Crackers away.

I wondered if Cris was attached to the bull. Would he feel at all sad to part with him? Did he feel the same way about him as he did his horse, Laguna? Was it the same as I felt for Remmy? Or was it going to be easy for him to sell him? Were his plans for the money more important? I knew Cris had had him several years. I thought it was interesting though, that he called his horse Goonie and his bull Crackers; such funny, affectionate nicknames for such a serious guy.

There was a lot of conversation between the three girls, Roberta next to Dave, and Hannah and Paola right behind them, but I couldn't hear what they were talking about—not that I really wanted to. Paola, sitting closest to me, tried to engage me in conversation too, but it was so noisy that I couldn't make out what she was saying most of the time. I didn't want to keep saying "What?" over and over so pretended I didn't hear her at all. I *did* hear her interject lots of questions to which Dave very patiently gave apparently clari-fying answers, though I couldn't make out the words. It made my heart hurt.

When the last competing entrant had left the arena, the announcer said, "Cris Caldera riding Heatstroke for no score. Tear it up, Cris!"

Yells, whistles, and applause spread around the arena, and they cranked up the music. Then the chute door opened and a brown bull leaped out.

Have I mentioned that I'm not a big fan of bull riding? Don't get me wrong, I think the people that do it are talented, athletic, and brave—if a little crazy—and watching the sport itself is exciting. I can *appreciate* it, but I don't *like* it. My imagination is too vivid. I can't help feeling every twist, every lunge, and every point of contact. I imagine what it would feel like to fall off and have an eighteen hundred pound animal catch me with horn or hoof, fall on me completely, or chase me once I'm off. My accident last summer hadn't helped. I *knew* what it felt like to collide with something substantial. Watching the horses wasn't as bad for me. This probably had a lot to do with the difference in body mass, lack of horns, and less likelihood of the animal trying to murder you once you were off its back.

But Cris made bull riding look, if not easy, then natural. His body moved in almost perfect unison with the gyrations of the brown beast, as if the movements had been choreographed; each turn, twist, and jump practiced together until they got it down perfectly. And this was the final performance—a ballistic ballet. Except that was, of course, impossible. It was ridiculous to imagine such a thing could be rehearsed; he wouldn't even have known which bull he was riding until today, maybe just hours or even minutes ago.

I found myself watching his face, as I often tried to do when he was performing some feat of daredevilry. When the bull brought him toward the grandstand, I could see it from under his hat. His expression was the same as I'd observed while he snowboarded last winter: tranquil, relaxed. He wore a protective vest like most of the other riders, and I was glad to see it. He hadn't worn one last year. I wished he was wearing a helmet too. When the buzzer rang, he tumbled off the bull, not quite landing on his feet, but unhurt.

One of the bullfighters distracted the bull and coaxed it away to the other side of the arena. There he jumped into a barrel. The bull half-heartedly charged at the barrel giving it a good bump with his head, then stood looking around while the barrel rolled further away. When it came to rest, its occupant popped his head up and stuck his tongue out at the bull. The audience laughed and applauded.

Cris had immediately gotten to his feet and looked over his shoulder to make sure the bull was preoccupied. He then brushed himself off and walked out of the arena. Those gathered around the rails and the people in the stands had broken out into loud applause and calls for him, especially our section, and *especially* Paola. In fact, she screamed so loudly in my ear it hurt. I think I may have turned and glared at her, but it's hard to remember; I was already in surreal survival mode.

The bareback riding was well underway by the time Cris returned. Robin came with him.

"Wow. I was wondering where everyone was. Hi, Cheryl," she said as she stepped up and sat between us.

"Time for me to go," said Dave, standing to trade places with Cris once more. He turned, his eyes sweeping briefly over the whole group. "See you guys later, I guess." He grinned slightly, just a ghost of the mischievous smile I loved so much.

Roberta didn't speak, but patted his leg and looked very smug. Then she turned and looked straight at me. Her expression left me feeling deflated and inferior.

"Have a good ride!" said Hannah, smiling.

"Show 'em how it's done, cowboy!" said Cheryl.

"Knock 'em dead," yelled Robin.

"*¡Buena suerte! ¡No caiga!*" said Paola, very loudly.

He looked at each of them as they spoke, then his eyes rested briefly on me. I *wanted* to say, "*Please wear a helmet!*" but felt too awkward and said nothing. That probably would have been embarrassing for him anyway, though I knew he didn't get embarrassed easily. I looked down at my feet. When I looked back up, he was already halfway down the stands. I felt empty and was shaking a little.

Stevey was becoming restless, sometimes lying across my lap and yawning, occasionally getting up and trying to leave, sometimes repetitively bumping against Cris or hitting him, and even hitting himself. A couple of times Cris held his hands down to stop him, and he began to whimper. Cris finally stood and scooped Stevey up into his arms. Stevey chuckled as Cris swung him upside down and back up.

"I'm going to walk around with Stevey for a while, then take him up to the house," he said. "He's exhausted."

Everyone said goodbye and he walked away, occasionally dipping his brother head down then swinging him back up the way I'd seen fathers do to their much younger children. I thought it was a good thing that Stevey was still so small. Soon, no matter how strong Cris was, he wouldn't be able to do that anymore.

I was remembering my personal experience with how strong Cris was just as Cheryl said, "He's becoming more difficult."

"Hmmm?" I was still thinking about Cris and wasn't sure whether to agree or not.

"Stevey," she said. "He's going to school more this year and has a different teacher. Poor little guy just doesn't do well with change."

I still didn't know what to say, but I could understand Stevey a little; I didn't like change much either, but I coped better now than when I was very young.

"Maybe it'll be easier for him when he's older." I offered.

Cheryl smiled. "Well, I hope so for the family's sake. He's such a sweet, sweet boy, but . . . it can be difficult for them."

I considered what I knew of Stevey and how tired Dave had seemed on Saturday. I watched him now, far on the other side of the arena, helping to get horses settled into the chutes and riders prepared to mount. I wondered what part, if any, tiredness played in the changes I sensed in him. He seemed no less patient than ever, discounting the overheard conversation, but less—*what? Carefree?*

"Dave told me he doesn't always sleep well. Stevey, I mean."

Cheryl nodded. "Angel takes care of him most of the day when he's not in school or for special trips so they can get away sometimes, and Alex spends days and nights with him too, but it really often falls to the boys to get through the nights with him. I'm not sure how they cope." Then she said in a more optimistic tone, "I'm sure he'll settle into the new routine eventually."

Roberta, who had been talking to the other girls, stood and said, "I'll catch you later," and left. I soon saw her purple hat on the far side of the arena, not exactly close to where Dave was, but as close as she could get. I felt annoyed again but immediately recognized I had no right to. That just left me feeling guilty and sad.

Rider after rider entered the arena as the sun slowly disappeared and the lights at the arena and up at the plaza and barns came on. Hannah

announced that she and Paola were going to go hang out with Matthew and the others near the arena's main gate.

"Do you want to come with us?" she asked.

Robin looked at me, but I said, "No, I'll just stay here."

"Yeah, me too," said Robin.

Hannah and Paola waved goodbye and walked down the stands and away. I really just wanted to go home, but I couldn't miss Dave's ride.

Finally, the last contestant of the day picked himself up from where he'd fallen and left the arena. Wranglers drove his mount out the exit gate, and all attention turned to the chute where I'd been watching Dave's black hat rise and fall, its wearer dealing with a horse that didn't want to be mounted. The struggle continued for a couple of minutes. Dave climbed out of the chute, and I thought he was going to back out of riding. Then we saw that he was letting someone fit him with a helmet. I wasn't prepared for the intensity of feelings it provoked: relief, pride, pure happiness. I wondered what had caused him to put it on.

"Huh. He's never done that before," said Robin.

"The helmet?" I asked, but without much doubt.

She nodded.

He re-entered the chute and tried to settle on the horse.

"It seems to be giving him some difficulty," I said. "Maybe he's . . ." I wasn't sure what to say. I wouldn't dare say afraid or nervous, especially not in front of Robin. And I was sure that wasn't the case anyway. I'd never seen Dave show any fear, except maybe once, and not for anything like this. "I guess he's just being careful."

Robin looked at me then turned back, nodding. "Yeah, I guess."

The horse remained too agitated for them to open the chute for several more very long minutes. The announcer tried to fill the time with appreciative comments about the day's event, what a perfect day it had been, and how they felt sure it had broken a record for attendance and event entries.

Finally, the horse remained still long enough for Dave to get set. We saw his arm come up slowly then his hat tipped down sharply. The chute door swung open.

I'd only seen him ride a bucking horse once before, Medicine Hat Girl from Bar 8, who had been ridden today by someone else earlier in the competition. Back then, he had let Girl throw him and then pretended to be stunned, if not worse. I'd been terrified. He had thought it funny, which made me mad. I now knew that this, the bareback riding, was *his* event. I knew he could ride and work cattle more than proficiently, and he could rope but didn't feel accomplished at it and didn't take it as seriously. But this was the rodeo event he was known to love most and be best at.

The horse wasn't particularly large and didn't seem to be more talented than the others had been, but right out of the gate something seemed to be wrong. It's hard to say why, but Dave didn't seem happy; the confidence he usually exuded just wasn't there.

"One . . . two . . . three . . ." Robin whispered next to me.

The horse jumped straight up, all four feet off the ground.

"Four . . ."

Its feet landed almost squarely, but instead of bucking, the horse almost sat back on its hindquarters. Dave was already leaning back, preparing for a buck, and for a split-second it looked like he and the horse would tip over backward together. He managed to miraculously shift himself forward, allowing the horse to get its balance, but the next instant it had leaped up again with Dave slipping sideways. On Robin's count of six, as the horse came down, Dave fell right underneath it.

Robin, Cheryl, and I all gasped and leaped to our feet at the same time. Everything happened so fast it was hard to tell whether he'd been struck by the horse at all. We could see him curled up on the ground, but he got up quickly, looking to see where the horse was. A couple of men had already run out to him by the time the horse was at the far end of the arena. Dave removed the helmet immediately, but he was doubled over, holding his left side and limping badly.

I let out a long, shuddering breath. I'd held it as soon as I saw him falling.

"Well, that was an unfortunate and very unusual fall for David Caldera," said the announcer. "David, riding for sport and not for a score, of course, but we always enjoy watching the Calderas ride. Hopefully he's not hurt too badly. That was still a great ride, cowboy." The crowd erupted into whistling and applause for him.

In typical Dave fashion, he tried to straighten up and looked toward the announcer's deck. Then he held his right arm high, thumb pointed skyward. The audience whooped and applauded even more. The men helped him out of the arena where he was swallowed into a crowd of well-wishers.

Roberta's purple hat stood out in the glow of the arena lights. I assumed the other girls plus all his other friends would be there too. I felt unspeakably relieved. And completely unnecessary.

As the announcer thanked everyone for coming out for the day and invited them to stay into the evening for music and more barbecue, all I could think of was Dave and how he might be feeling. I longed to know that he was indeed all right, to make sure, but I could imagine all the other people crowded around him too.

"I'm going to go," said Robin. She looked slightly worried but mostly annoyed. "You know, make sure he's okay." She paused a moment as if she wanted to say something else. She looked at me with a tight-lipped smirk, shaking her head slightly, and I was sure I knew. My heart was broken, but I was ridiculously relieved as well, tears threatening to betray me. I was sure I was thinking the same thing.

Poophead.

Chapter Ten

The people around us began to stand and leave.

"Shall we stay for a while and listen to the band?" asked Mom. She was watching Dad.

"Sure," said Dad. They both looked over at me.

By this time I was shaking badly, my nerves shot and my emotions frayed. In truth, I felt panicked—all the anxiety I had felt leading up to today exacerbated all day by the crowd and noise and manifesting now, shoved even further over the edge of my coping ability by seeing Dave get hurt. I longed to know that he was all right, but I was done. If I tried to see him, it was sure to prove embarrassing for everyone. It was a long time since I'd felt this way, so close to complete meltdown. I couldn't pretend everything was okay. Not today.

"Can we go home?" I asked quietly, not wanting everyone to hear.

Mom sat down next to me. "You don't want to stay? Hang out with your friends for a while longer?" Her voice, already quiet, dropped even lower, softer, her head close to mine. "I thought you might want to go see how Dave is."

There was nothing in the world I wanted more, but my nose was already running, my eyes were stinging, and the shaking was getting worse. I just wasn't going to be able to hold it together.

"I'm *really* tired, Mom. I . . . I have a little homework to finish, too." This was mostly true. I had homework, but it wasn't due until Wednesday. I felt no

qualms about letting my mother think otherwise; under the circumstances, I was sure it was for the best.

Dad nodded. He didn't seem to mind leaving.

"All right," said Mom, but I could tell she was disappointed.

"Jen, if you want to stay for a while, we can take you home later," offered Cheryl, moving closer to me. "You can hang out instead of Allison. She looks exhausted, poor thing." She moved closer on the other side of me, put her arm around me, and rubbed my arm. Then she brought her head very close to mine and whispered, "I'm sure he's fine, hon."

I appreciated her perception and nodded slightly. I was really embarrassed, too. The last thing I wanted right now was attention. It just made it even harder. Her offer seemed to suit everyone, though, and I was glad Mom could stay. Dad and I left without anyone else seeming to notice. I was relieved to go but still felt a gnawing in the pit of my stomach—anxiety and guilt.

Once home, I retreated to my room and fell asleep in the dark. A couple of hours later, I heard a rattling sound coming around to the back of the house: Cris with the horse trailer. Feeling calmer, I got up and met him out back, watching as he unloaded Remmy. Then he held the lead rope out to me. He returned to the trailer and took out my tack.

"I'm sorry I didn't help load him and . . . my stuff . . ." I'd only now realized that I'd left it all to Cris. *Guilt on guilt.*

"Don't worry about it," he said, flatly. The only light reaching us came from the back porch and the front of the stable. He looked closely at me and his voice softened. "You look really pale. Are you okay?"

I was surprised by his concern, and the tone of his voice was almost more than I could bear. "Yes . . . yes, I think so." Then, because I *had* to, "Is Dave . . ?" I hated asking—we'd left so abruptly, perhaps Cris thought I didn't care—but I needed to know. "I saw him fall. He looked . . ." My eyes were filling, and I couldn't stop it. I was shaking again too.

Cris continued to regard me. I wondered what he was thinking then realized that, no, I really didn't want to know. I was pretty sure I already did. *Pathetic. Tiresome. Burden.*

"He'll live," he said in his usual tone. "Nothing broken."

"Oh," I said, nodding and feeling relieved. I wiped at my eyes and sniffled before I could stop myself. "I'm glad."

Cris opened Remmy's stall door for me, then took my tack into the far stall.

"Thank you!" I called after him.

He didn't turn around, just raised his hand in acknowledgment. Then he got in his truck and drove away.

I didn't sleep much that night.

Matthew watched me closely in Chemistry, so I tried extra hard to achieve "normal." My goal for the immediate future was to be no quieter than I usually was and avoid as many are-you-okays as possible.

Robin, so happy yesterday, seemed depressed again in History. I hated asking her—I was so tired of it myself—but I was concerned.

"Is everything all right?" I whispered.

She looked startled and a little flustered—extremely unlike her. "Yeah. Sure." She made it sound like I was being stupid, but I wasn't convinced. We went back to working on our World War I timeline, but after a couple of minutes, she whispered, "Gran's not feeling well. She's going to the doctor today. Angel's taking her. I'm worried."

I nodded. I knew Fiona found it difficult to walk and didn't drive, but I didn't know anything specific about her health.

After class, we walked to our lockers and then out to the tables. Although it was the first day of the week for school, it was actually Tuesday. I'd normally eat with Melanie, but my desire to see Dave—to verify with my own eyes that he really was okay—trumped routine.

Most of the kids were there already, talking over the previous day's events and giving Dave a hard time.

Kyle said, "Yeah, he should put sticky tape on his jeans. Maybe he'd find it easier to stay on."

Snickering.

"Gotta stop shaving your legs, dude," said Tanner. "You need the extra traction."

The laughter was a little louder.

"And lighten up on the skin oil. Then you won't slide off."

Everyone laughed, and Dave shook his head but bore it graciously with a slight smirk.

"It was just one of those days," he said. "I knew it as soon as I got on that sucker." Then he frowned and said, "No . . . even before that."

"Is that why you wore the helmet?"

A couple of people snickered but most just appeared curious.

Dave frowned then shrugged. "It just seemed like a good idea at the time."

"You have a premonition?" asked Tanner.

Dave looked over at him, but I was sitting right next to him, and Dave's gaze shifted to me. I held my breath and forced myself to return his gaze, not reflexively looking away.

He shrugged again. "Don't know. But if I hadn't worn it and he'd clipped my head instead of my hip . . ."

I let the breath out and shuddered.

"So, have you got a battle wound?" asked Tanner.

"Let me see, let me see!" cried Roberta, but her demeanor was hardly sympathetic.

She and several of the other girls jumped up from where they were sitting or moved closer to him, hoping for a better view. Hannah and Paola had gotten up and moved closer, but most of the guys seemed pretty interested too.

Dave stood up, unselfconsciously raising his shirt high enough to expose his flat, deeply tanned stomach. A large dark blue and purple bruise was developing high on his hip, spreading around toward his back and obviously continuing out of sight below the waistband of his jeans.

Several people said, "Ow," and made other appropriate sympathetic noises. I could see the fall all over again, imagining the pain of hooves against flesh.

Roberta moved right in front of him, reaching out to lightly touch the bruised skin, her fingers gliding slowly across his hip. He tensed as if shocked by her touch but stood very still. It probably tickled but he didn't betray it. I caught the look that passed between them though. Hers was openly provocative; his was intense. I couldn't read it, but I didn't like it and looked away, wanting Roberta to disappear; wanting Dave to pull away from her; wanting things to be different between us; wanting to be the person allowed to touch him so gently, so intimately.

Just wanting.

"I'll see you tomorrow, I guess," I said quietly to Robin. Dave was obviously fine and had all the attention he could possibly need. I wasn't going to torture myself any longer.

Robin looked surprised as I stood up and grabbed my backpack. "Hey, can you come over sometime soon? Maybe this week?" she asked.

I said, "Probably," and stepped over the bench, planning to get to English before Dave and the others. Unfortunately, my other toe caught on the bench, and I fell. I wasn't hurt but felt extremely embarrassed. I didn't look around to see if anyone had noticed but heard Robin start to say, "Are you—"

"I'm fine," I said, picking myself up and walking away as quickly as I could.

"Did you do the homework?"

Ben came into Spanish on Wednesday and sat at the desk next to mine. He looked expectantly at me and wore a ridiculous children's hat. It had stand-up ears and long braided ties hanging down. I wasn't sure if it was supposed to be a cat or a bear. In spite of the goofy hat, I was unaccountably glad to see him, but—

"Yes, but I don't know if it's right," I answered warily. I wasn't crazy about people copying my work.

He surprised me by sighing heavily and not asking for help at all. He moved back to his own desk just before the other seat's regular occupant came in.

What was that about?

"Mrs. Ochoa, do you like my hat?" asked Ben.

"Yes, Ben, but please take it off."

The class got started and progressed without more than usual distraction, but I was distracted anyway, reliving the scene at lunch yesterday and wondering about Ben.

I decided to spend lunch with Melanie. She watched me closely but pretended not to, and she didn't ask awkward questions. I always appreciated that about her, and I was getting *so* tired of people asking, "How are you doing?" If I couldn't answer honestly, which I couldn't, then I didn't want to answer at all.

Halfway through lunch, she said, "There's an event this weekend at Northfield. I was wondering if you'd like to come and spend the day with me. Maybe Sunday?"

My eyes flew wide and I stared at her. *Melanie is asking me to do something outside of school?* "That would be wonderful!" I said, very excited. "I can finally watch you ride!"

Melanie laughed. "I doubt it will be that exciting, but I've wanted to ask you over for a long time. My mother is very pr . . . protective." A shadow crossed her beautiful features, and the gentle smile disappeared. "She worries about things. *Too* many things."

I could relate. I thought my parents were overprotective and also worried far too much. I wondered what her mom worried about.

"I'll ask tonight," I said, and she smiled again.

Apparently my slight accident at lunch the day before hadn't gone unnoticed. Hannah looked like she wanted to ask me something as we dressed out for PE, but chose not to, only smiling instead. One of Roberta's friends, Lori, and some other girls were watching me, which just made me nervous in general. I tried to ignore them. As Melanie and I headed toward the door, they fell into step behind us.

"The *Fall* is such a nice time for traveling," said one of the girls, "*You* know . . . going on *trips?*"

"Oh yes," said another, enunciating in an overly clear manner and unable to stifle a giggle as she spoke, "*Fall* trips are the very best!"

"Hey, Allison," a third chimed in, "Have you taken any trips this Fall?"

They all laughed. Melanie was looking at me, obviously wondering what they were talking about. She didn't know about yesterday but might remember my klutziness from last year. We were outside now, and I was pretending I hadn't heard my name.

"Shhh . . ." Roberta had joined them. "Leave her alone." Any thought that she might actually be standing up for me was erased by the lowered voice that followed as she continued to say something to the girls around her. They all laughed again and walked away.

Melanie looked at me sharply. "What was that about?"

"What was what about?" I asked and continued to walk out to the field.

In Study Hall later that afternoon, Ben plopped into the seat across from mine again. "Hey," he said. I was slightly more prepared this time but distracted by today's hat. He grinned at me without saying anything more.

I looked at him warily. "What?"

"Do you sing?" he asked.

"Sing?"

"Yeah, you know, 'La la la la la.'"

This seemed like a very odd question. "Sometimes," I said. *When there's no one around.*

"You should join Choir," he said.

Where's this coming from? "I already have my electives," I said.

"It's after school . . . a new class. It's fun. You should join."

Mrs. Ochoa entered the room and Ben went back to his own seat, taking off his hat.

I shook my head. *Such a weird guy.*

He fell into step beside me after school and talked as if there had been no interruption in our brief conversation.

"Seriously, you'd like choir. You look like you could use some fun. Tuesdays and Thursdays. Why don't you come on Thursday? Mr. Tanaka is really great. I'm sure he'd let you join."

"Um . . ." We'd reached the front of the school. "I've got to . . ." I indicated where my dad was waiting in the car.

I wasn't interested in Choir. At least, I hadn't considered being interested in it. I was in Art because it was something I enjoyed and could do easily, was maybe even good at. I was in Spanish because—well, I didn't want to think about why I was in Spanish, but there was a reason. I'd sung in a choir in elementary school, and music, in general, was very important to me. But I had no reason to consider choir now. It wasn't something I was prepared to have an opinion on.

"Do you want a ride?" *What are you doing?*

"Really? Are you sure?" He looked hopeful.

I have no idea. I shook my head. "I don't think my dad would mind."

I was right. In fact, he seemed glad to see him.

"Hey there, Ben," said Dad, all chummy-like. Ben got into the back seat with his skateboard. As we drove down the street, Dad continued, "I

was hoping to see you this week. I was wondering if you'd be interested in earning a little cash."

I turned to look back at Ben. He looked even more hopeful. "Yeah, sure. I guess." Then he looked wary and said, "Doing what?"

"Just some yard work. I can show you when we get to our place."

"Okay," said Ben, grinning hugely. He looked at me and smiled even wider. I turned away and looked out the window. *Now what?*

When we got home, I went straight into the house, but I heard Dad begin, "I'll be going out of town next week for a while, and there are some things that need doing . . ."

I went up to my room and tried to focus on homework, but yesterday's scene at lunch kept intruding. I went out and told Remmy all about it, but he had nothing helpful to say on the matter. I wished he *could* talk. He probably knew Dave better than anyone. He might have been able to tell me what to think or, more importantly, what *not* to think. During dinner, after Mom got home from work, I told my parents about Melanie's request for the weekend.

"Does this mean we finally get to meet the elusive Melanie?" asked Mom. "You know, I'd almost started wondering if she was an imaginary friend."

I had told my parents about Melanie early last year and had assumed they would meet her at some point, but so far they hadn't. Mom referring to an imaginary friend bothered me, though. I knew she was just joking, but it made me feel uncomfortable, memories prickling at the back of my mind. I didn't want to look at them closely so pretended to ignore the comment.

Dad had no problem with the plan and even volunteered to drive me there on Sunday. He'd been to Northfield before and, when they had initially shopped for a house, he'd considered buying there. I was so glad he hadn't! He said he was still curious and would like to look around again. I didn't like the sound of that much but was happy he would get to meet Melanie. I knew Mom would love her, but right now it seemed more important for Dad to approve of her.

I now had something else to think about and look forward to, but my sleep was still fitful. As long as I was awake, all I could think about was Dave and his bruised side, how I wished I felt permitted to touch him as the other girls seemed to and, most distressing, the look that had passed between him and Roberta.

Matthew and Robin helped Thursday morning classes pass quickly, and I spent lunch with Melanie again. I told myself that I was just getting my lunch schedule back on track, but the truth was that I didn't want to eat with the others. I didn't want to be where I was sure Dave would be.

Melanie and I confirmed plans for the weekend, and I tried to keep my mind focused on that. Unfortunately, as I climbed the stairs to go to English, trying to get there early again, I heard voices on the half-landing.

"Come on," Roberta's voice was low but whining. "I *know* you want to. We'd be *great* together."

I paused as I reached them. Dave was leaning back against the wall near the corner, his hands under Roberta's forearms. I couldn't tell if he was pulling her toward himself or attempting to hold her away. Roberta stood in front of him, her hands on his chest. He looked over at me with no change of expression. I steeled myself, immediately looked down, and continued up the stairs. But I caught the quick movement of Roberta's head. My presence obviously wasn't a deterrent to her.

"Maybe," said Dave.

"Maybe?" said Roberta, sounding playfully scornful. "Well, if you want it, you'd better make your mind up fast, or the opportunity will be gone."

I climbed to the top of the stairs trying to get away quickly without appearing to do so and trying not to conjecture about the scene on the landing.

That, of course, was impossible. No matter what I did or tried to occupy my mind with, images of Roberta and Dave together as I had seen them—and worse, in ways I hadn't—tormented me for the rest of the day and beyond.

Friday passed slowly and dully. The only really memorable thing was being hit in the head twice with a soccer ball. Purposely or accidentally, I hardly cared. It left me unhurt but overwhelmed and on edge for the rest of the day. In Geometry, I agreed to go home with Robin on the following Monday, and I ate in the cafeteria, effectively avoiding Dave all day.

I'd never been to Northfield before. My friends, at least those that hung out with Dave and Robin, had previously indicated contempt for the whole area, but I didn't understand why. There had been some boys last year that had—well, they hadn't actually *done* anything, exactly. The boy I thought of as Varsity Jacket had grabbed me and said something nasty to me—at least, I was sure he meant it in an offensive way, but I could have misunderstood. I did that sometimes. Maybe he *hadn't* been speaking metaphorically.

But Dave had learned of the incident, even though I hadn't told anyone what the boy had said, and there had been a fight. I never found out too much about it except that the boys suspected of being involved, on both sides, got a warning from their respective school principals. The Northfield boys seemed to have avoided me after that, as I'd had no more trouble with them. I had a feeling that some of the girls that liked Dave and Cris and hung out at the tables might be from Northfield as well, but I wasn't sure about that.

The only other thing I knew was that the community of Northfield was considered wealthy, but I didn't see why that would make a difference. The Calderas might not be Beverly Hills rich—their relative wealth most likely tied up in land and livestock—but some of the other kids we hung out with, like Jessie and Kyle, seemed pretty well off, too.

Melanie had told me she would be there early—earlier than my dad wanted to get up on a Sunday—and had two rides in the early afternoon, so we had arranged to meet near the east entrance of the parking lot at about eleven.

As Dad and I neared the showgrounds, I was amazed at how green the surrounding landscape was; a stark contrast to the dry, summer-browned hillsides and meadows around Douglas, and even the Calderas' ranch. Some of it looked like parkland, but then I realized the area east of the road was really a sprawling, perfectly manicured golf course. To the west, on our left, was much less green; what looked like open fields bordered by forest and dotted with clumps of trees. Then I noticed what appeared to be obstacles—large rustic jumps.

Further up the road, on the golf course side, was a large building with a tall glass front set back from a beautifully maintained lawn and formal flower beds. I figured it must be the clubhouse. I'd been to golf courses with my dad when I was much younger, though he didn't play very often. I had enjoyed spending time outside with him and getting to ride in the cart.

The road leading off the main highway led straight to a guardhouse and gates, with the driveway to the clubhouse on the right just before it. Large, elegantly chiseled stone signs proclaimed:

Northfield Village

A little farther on we turned left. My heart sped up at the first sight of horses and riders. Across the corner of the road was a sign matching the others:

Northfield Equestrian Center

A huge building, open on one side, dominated the white-railed arenas and other features of the center visible from the road. International flags decorated its perimeter, giving it both an official and festive air. Just beyond was the entrance to the parking lot.

"I'll see if I can find a place to park," said my dad, "but it looks pretty packed."

"That's okay," I said quickly. "You can just drop me off here."

Although I wanted him to meet Melanie, I suddenly felt nervous about it. I didn't want Melanie to think that my dad had to approve of her or anything. Nor did I want to appear dependent on him, as if he had to hold my hand in an unfamiliar place. That was starting to bother me. A lot. I was no longer the little girl in the golf cart.

Dad hesitated then agreed. "Okay, but I get to meet her today, right?"

It also bothered me that I thought I detected a lack of trust on his part. *Who does he think I might really be meeting?* But the answer to that was as obvious as it was ludicrous, at least under present conditions and location.

"There she is," I said, having seen her standing in the shade of some trees. She hadn't seen me yet, but Dad nodded and seemed appeased.

I almost didn't recognize her. She looked even more mature and elegant than usual in buff-colored breeches, a navy show coat, shiny black riding boots, a cravat at her throat, and her hair pulled back in a thick bun. Melanie was older than most of my other friends and me. For reasons she hadn't felt inclined to tell me, she had missed most of her seventh-grade year and ended up being held back. Whatever the reason, I couldn't help being selfishly glad

of it. I was sure we wouldn't have become good friends otherwise. I didn't know when her birthday was, but she was probably close to seventeen, over a year older than me.

Right now she held a helmet by its strap and the free end of a lead rope in her left hand. With the right, she held a tall, dark horse covered with a sweat sheet. It was nibbling on the grass below the trees.

"I'm going to go check out the driving range. You can call me if you're ready to leave before I come back. Okay?"

"Thanks, Dad," I said.

I got out of the car and turned toward Melanie. She was already walking over, leading the horse.

"Hi!" she said, her smile wider and brighter than I'd ever seen it.

She was so beautiful. I had the ridiculous urge to draw her and wished I'd brought my sketchbook and pencils with me.

Her eyes were laughing. "I'm so happy you could come! This," she said, looking at the horse fondly and stroking his cheek, "is Digs."

"Digs? That's kind of a funny name, isn't it?"

"His real name is Professor Digory. But that's much too pompous for him, so we call him Digs."

"Professor Digory," I said, trying to remember. "The Chronicles of Narnia!" I had read the books when I was much younger and had almost forgotten the name.

"Yes, exactly. He does seem magical though. We did cross-country yesterday, and he did great. We worked a little just before you came, but he's cool now."

"Cross-country?" I asked, reaching forward to stroke Digs' nose.

Now that I was closer, I could see that he was indeed very tall—even taller than Gold had been—and a very dark brown all over, not black as I had at first thought.

"Did you see the advanced course as you drove up? It's just over there," she said, pointing south.

"Oh . . . yes! I wondered what the jumps were for. You jumped them? They look huge!"

"They're wide and sometimes tricky, but they're not as tall as the stadium jumps can be. But the training course I rode Digs on is over there." She pointed north. "I'm just starting to ride him consistently at preliminary level, the bigger course, and he's doing really well, but we're still competing at training level. This will be one of the last events of the year, and we'll be able to move into preliminary next season."

I nodded my head though I didn't comprehend what she was talking about. Last year I'd been introduced to the world of horses and riding through Dave, Robin, and Cheryl, but I had known Melanie's style of riding was different from theirs. I'd done research on dressage because of Melanie's interest and also because Gold had been highly trained in the art, but it was still mostly a mystery to me. And I knew even less about the other aspects of Melanie's sport of choice, eventing.

"Let me put him in his stall so we can go get some lunch. I have to get ready again in about an hour."

I agreed. We made our way through horses, riders, and spectators, around some large paddocks towards long rows of stalls, then past them to the back side of the facility. Four long stable blocks were here.

As we left the show area, Melanie pulled a small navy cloth mask out of her pocket and covered her mouth and nose. I couldn't help watching with interest as she secured it around her ears. She looked, not embarrassed exactly, but slightly self-conscious about it. I looked away.

"I have asthma," she said after a moment. "I've had it all my life. Sometimes it's really bad, so I wear a mask around the barns most of the time, especially when it's really dusty, or cold, and when I'm grooming. I . . . just don't like wearing it around the show grounds."

"It makes you look mysterious. Like an equestrian ninja." That made her laugh.

She opened one of the stalls and led Digs in, exchanging his bridle for a halter and tying him near the automatic waterer. A hay net hung from the same ring in the wall.

"He can relax there for a while. We have our stadium jumping later."

"Is he the new horse you were telling me about?" I asked.

"No, I've been riding him for a couple of years now, and I really love him. Hopefully, we can continue together for a while. Beau is over here." She led the way, farther along the line of stalls. "I'll be jumping him this afternoon, too. Beau has just started preliminary level, but he's still pretty young."

She led me to a stall where another horse, even taller than Digs, peered over the door. His head looked huge but his eyes were calm and soft. He was a bright reddish brown with a broad white blaze and a black mane.

"His name is Flambeau, but we just call him Beau. He's a little rough around the edges when it comes to dressage, but he loves to jump. Don't you boy?" She scruffed his forelock and Beau nodded. We both laughed.

"And this," she said, continuing to the very next stall, "is Kitty. She's a lot older, and we do mostly flatwork now. She jumps really well, but I don't event her anymore. I don't have as much time to just ride her either, which makes me feel bad."

Kitty, as I already knew, was Melanie's nickname for her own horse, Copper Copycat. She was a bright red chestnut, almost the same color as Robin's hair, and noticeably smaller and more lightly built than the other two horses. She rumbled a greeting to Melanie and snuffled at her hands.

"No, I don't have anything for you right now," she laughed, stroking the mare's pretty red face. "I'll see you later." Then she turned to me and said, "Come on. I've been up since five and I'm starving!"

As we neared the large covered arena, Melanie returned the mask to her pocket. We walked along its northern end to the other side, where a few concession booths stood with tables and chairs nearby. There were also smaller stands selling snow cones and churros. We got a large order of chili fries to share and found a place to eat in the shade.

From where we sat, I could see two small arenas separated by low white rails around their perimeter with platforms between them and at one end of each.

"Are those dressage arenas?" I asked. I'd been watching videos and recognized the letter markers placed around the perimeters.

"Yes. Dressage started Friday afternoon, the cross-country started yesterday morning, and today is all jumping."

I was very excited. I had a concept of all the things she said from the videos I'd watched, but I'd never actually witnessed them in person. But there was something else I was curious about. It wasn't the kind of question I liked to ask, but I'd been wondering for so long.

"Are your parents here . . . to watch you ride?"

I watched her face carefully, but she betrayed no change of emotion.

"No," she said, shaking her head slightly, but she didn't seem to mind the question. "My dad died when I was eleven, before we moved here. My mother is often busy on Sundays. She's not really into horses."

"Oh. I'm sorry about your dad," I said, not sure what else to say.

I thought about another incident when I was first getting to know Dave and Cris. Dad had been traveling for work ever since we moved to Douglas and they assumed I lived with only my mother. When they met my dad, they were surprised, which in turn had surprised me. I had said something like, "Everyone has a dad," and Cris had responded, "Not really." I'd never forget it because it had made me feel so stupid, so thoughtless. Later he'd told me that his mother had died and I'd felt even worse. And I *still* didn't know about Robin's parents. She never wanted to talk about her family, but I assumed her situation was similar.

"Do you live over there?" I asked, indicating the direction of the gated community.

She smiled softly, nodded and said, "For now."

I wanted to ask what that meant but figured she would tell me if and when she wanted to.

"Can you come to my house one of these days?" I asked. "I want my mom to meet you. And you've got to meet Remmy! Maybe you could spend the night?" I guess my enthusiasm was excessive as she laughed. I hoped I didn't seem childish. I just really wanted to know her better.

"Maybe," she said.

We were finishing up the chili fries and Melanie was explaining the rules for the stadium jumping when Roger walked up, dressed similarly to Melanie.

"Hey," he said, looking at her, then at me with guarded interest. He looked back at her. "All ready?"

"Of course," she said calmly. "Do you remember Allison? She's a friend from school."

Roger looked more closely at me and now seemed to recognize me. That didn't appear to be a good thing. "Yeah . . . sure. What's she doing here?"

This seemed like a reasonable question to me, but Melanie's cheeks looked pinker than they had a moment before.

"I invited her." Her voice was firm, and she held Roger's eyes steadily.

After a moment he said, "Whatever," seeming to back down unwillingly. Then he said, in a softer tone, "Have a good ride." I didn't understand his manner, either toward her or me, but it seemed like he really cared about her.

"Thanks," she said, her tone softening also. "You too."

He nodded then walked away.

Melanie looked at me, seeming self-conscious. "Ignore him. He's worse than my mother."

I was a little shocked. It was the most negative thing I'd ever heard her say, though I remembered an instance last year when her reaction to Roger was similar. Their relationship was so strange to me. At one time I had thought they might be brother and sister, but she had denied it. Then I thought it might be more of a romantic relationship, but she certainly didn't act that way with him. At least, not in the way I would expect. Something about it troubled me, but I wasn't going to think more about it now.

"Let's go get the horses," she said, looking at her watch. "We'll be starting soon."

She replaced her mask as we neared the stalls again and I watched her get Digs and Beau ready, helping wherever I could.

"Would you like to lead Digs for me?" she asked. "He's very mellow."

I very much wanted to lead him for her. When we arrived near the indoor arena again, a tall blonde woman wearing a frightening amount of make-up and even more jewelry walked over and made a big fuss of Beau.

"There's my handsome boy," she gushed. She spoke some nonsense to him and reached out but didn't seem very comfortable patting his neck. "How is he doing today?"

"He's doing very well, Mrs. Humph—"

"Because I saw his score so far and it didn't . . . well, it seems like it should have been much better."

Melanie opened her mouth to speak but a Black woman, slightly shorter than either of them and dressed simply in breeches, track shoes, and a polo shirt, had joined us and answered the first woman.

"Penny, we agreed that Mel's assignment this weekend was to get Beau around the course calmly and safely. Remember? He still gets too excited. We need to ease him into this level, and Mel did a great job of keeping him focused and calm. She's got the whole off-season to get him up to speed. We don't want to push him now."

The taller woman didn't look completely satisfied but apparently remembered the agreement.

The shorter woman subtly began to lead the other woman away. "Don't worry. He's got all the speed in the world, but if he's too worked up or becomes frightened, all Mel's hard work this summer will be wasted."

"Well," said the owner, "I look forward to seeing him jump this afternoon." She looked back toward us and smiled, but I wasn't sure the smile was sincere.

When she was gone, Mel blew softly through her lips and said, "That's Beau's owner . . . obviously. This is his first preliminary outing, and she thinks he should win it." She rolled her eyes slightly and shook her head. "He's a lovely horse, but he's a thoroughbred and originally trained for the track. She moved here recently and just brought him here in May. He came from another trainer that we feel moved him too quickly through the lower levels. The last thing he needs right now is to be pushed for speed."

"Does she ride him?" I asked.

Melanie's eyes danced. "No. I don't think she rides at all." She stroked Beau's cheek and said, "I think he's just a status symbol for her. And she wants him to win. Come on, I've got to get Digs warmed up."

The woman in the polo shirt came back to Melanie as we reached the warm-up arena. "Mel, do the same this afternoon as yesterday. Just get him calmly over the fences."

Melanie smiled and nodded, looking relieved by the woman's confidence in her. "Tatty, this is Allison, a friend from school. Allison, this is my friend and coach, Tatiana Reynolds. She's head trainer and manages the stables here."

"It's nice to meet you," Tatty smiled at me. Then she turned back to Melanie. "I'll hold Beau. You'd better get going. They're starting soon."

She took the reins from Melanie and led the big red horse away.

"We've got to start warming up," Melanie said, taking Digs' reins from me and indicating a nearby arena with several jumps set up. "Do you want to go find a seat inside and watch the others? I don't mind."

"I'll stay here and watch you for a bit," I said. I had wanted to watch her ride for such a long time but also wasn't quite ready to wander off by myself.

She led Digs toward the arena and used a mounting block to get on him. I'd seen them before, of course, but I'd never actually used one. *Except for those times when Dave gave me boosts, when I was first learning and when he helped me ride the Shire and Gold bareback. How many times . . . three . . . four?*

Then I pictured Dave swinging himself up onto Remmy's bare back without any kind of help. Thoughts of Dave warmed then saddened me. *I should try not to think of him again. At least not here.* Anyway, there was no comparison. Beau and Digs were extremely tall, both taller than Gold had been, and much taller than Remmy or his half brothers, Gali and Tee.

Melanie rode the dark horse calmly into the ring. Several other riders were there also, warming up their mounts. Melanie looked serenely confident and coolly elegant. She truly was the most beautiful person I'd ever known and, I thought, the kindest. I was so glad she had asked me to come. She seemed such a solitary, private person, too. I felt honored to be invited into this part of her life.

I watched her ride Digs, setting him at the jumps and gliding over them. She seemed to be taking her time, riding him at an easy canter between each, circling and changing leads across the arena, keeping him very relaxed. When her name was called to standby, she rode over to me.

"Here we go," she said. "Do you want to watch from inside? I'll be riding him and then changing horses. Okay?"

"Yes. Good luck!"

Melanie smiled at me and then rode Digs into the covered arena. I entered and made my way into the stands. I was amazed. The arena was not just covered, like the one at Bar 8, but almost completely enclosed on three sides. The jumps here were much larger and more elaborate than those in the warm-up ring. I'd seen pictures of show jumping, of course, and some video, but had never really *seen* it.

A horse and rider were just finishing the course as I took a seat. I was struck by how quiet it was considering the number of people and horses milling around outside. There weren't many spectators inside at all.

A man on a big grey gelding entered the arena. I watched with interest as he completed the course, the only sound being the horse's hoofs on the soft footing, its heavy breathing as it cantered, and the sharp, hollow sound of a hoof hitting a pole. On the second to last jump, the horse knocked a pole down, and it fell with a thudding bounce.

"Four faults for Adam Brannard and Sky Chief," a calm voice announced. Then, "Melanie Teodorescu riding Professor Digory, owned by Noel Lessard."

Melanie walked in on Digs, then set him at a canter. She looked very impressive, and I felt so proud of her. She rode Digs in a large circle then set him at the first jump. I held my breath in that moment of relative silence as they sailed over and continued to the next.

I tried to imagine what it felt like to jump a horse like that. I loved hopping Remmy over branches and small logs, but that couldn't compare with the height and breadth of these jumps. I'd been captivated last year by my first experience watching barrel racing, and I still wanted to be able to barrel race, too, but this captured my imagination even more. I wondered if it felt like flying to sail over the jumps. I was already wondering whether Remmy could jump like this.

Melanie's riding seemed flawless, and Digs' long strides devoured the ground, completing the course with calm efficiency. I had been impressed by what I'd seen in the warm-up ring, but she and Digs seemed to be one—confident and moving effortlessly together. It reminded me of the first time I'd seen Dave ride Remmy. He had ridden bareback and they'd moved as one creature. I'd been extremely impressed. *And you're thinking about him again. . . .*

Melanie circled once before leaving the arena, patting Digs' neck and smiling in my direction. I got up to meet her outside.

"What did you think?" she asked as I caught up with her. She had already dismounted and loosened Digs' girth.

"It was amazing!" I said. "I mean, I've seen videos of people jumping, but I've never watched it live. But," I felt foolish asking, "who will win?"

"The scores from the dressage and any penalties from the cross-country and jumping are totaled. The winner will be the person with the least penalties and best overall score in each division."

"Oh," I said, still wondering if she knew whether she'd win or not. But she didn't seem concerned.

Tatty was just leading Beau back to Melanie. They talked strategy for a few moments then Tatty led Digs off to walk him.

"Wow, you're really busy," I said.

"It's not bad when the show is here at Northfield. It's home, so we don't have to trailer the horses. And I'm only riding two horses this weekend. At some shows, I ride more horses in different divisions or ride multiple tests."

I remembered her telling me of other shows and, like the Calderas, many of her weekends were spent out of town at them, though with the Calderas it was cattle, quarter horses, or rodeo. They were often out of town for other reasons too.

I frowned as something occurred to me. "So, you compete on other people's horses because you want to? For fun? For practice?" I could understand it if that were true; I would ride any chance I got to improve my riding and ability to handle and understand horses. But she seemed to work so hard at it.

She laughed. "No, I used to though. Now I get compensated. It's my job. I've been training and riding horses for other people for quite a few years now. I ride Digs full time, and I've just taken Beau on recently, but I often ride for others as well. And then I give some riding lessons, too."

I smothered another, "Wow." I guess I shouldn't have been surprised she got paid for what she did, but I was still very impressed. I'd only recently started thinking of the *possibility* of getting a job.

"How old . . ." I thought the question might be rude—I knew you weren't supposed to ask really old people their age—so I asked something else that I had had been wanting to know. "When is your birthday?"

Her eyes laughed. "I'll be seventeen November twenty-fourth. Yes, I'm terribly old."

I wondered if she was offended, but she was still laughing slightly, her expression kind. And she didn't look old, of course, but very mature. I thought of Cris for some reason, who was also older than most of his classmates. I wanted to know more about why or how she had lost a whole year of school, but that was a topic she had always shied away from.

"Do you . . . do you know Cris Caldera?"

Melanie looked at me and then back to Beau. She tightened his girth a hole or two, and we began walking toward the warm-up arena.

"We went to different middle schools, and of course he's always been at least a year ahead of me. But yes, I know who he is. Up until a few years ago he hung out at the Center a lot. He and his brother used to go to the same youth group I did."

I wasn't sure what she meant by youth group or what "the Center" was, but the word *brother* stood out. "Dave?" I asked eagerly and then tried not to *look* eager.

Mel smiled again, a little sadly. "No, his older brother, Ric. Though Dave might have gone too, I don't know. He might have been in a younger group."

This was interesting. And perplexing. Dave hated Northfield but I didn't know why. I didn't know how Cris felt about it, but it seemed unlikely the brothers would feel too differently.

"I'd better start warming Beau up," said Melanie, and we parted ways once more.

I found a seat in the arena again and watched as horses and riders entered and completed the now higher course, some more successfully than others. I noticed that most of the riders were female. Then a boy entered on a striking appaloosa, black with a white spotted blanket pattern. I was surprised as, although I was used to seeing colorful horses at Western events, all the horses I'd seen here so far had been solid bays, grays, and chestnuts with a few blacks. And though my imagination was already transfixed by the sport itself, I literally couldn't take my eyes off this pair. The announcer said, "Bradley Scott riding Dark Side of the Moon."

There was nothing leisurely about the way the boy got the horse around the jumps. As he rode past where I sat, I could see his face more clearly beneath his helmet. His features were fine and even, reminding me of pictures I'd seen of the English princes when they were much younger. And he looked familiar. He wore a black coat and white breeches, his black helmet covering his hair except for some light blond curls at the back. He completed the course much faster than any other rider, only slowing once he was through the finish line. As he let the horse relax into a long-reined walk, he looked back over the course he'd ridden. He seemed to pause as he saw me, as if he thought he recognized me too. That was odd. Except for Melanie, and Roger I suppose, I was sure I didn't know anyone here.

Next into the arena was Roger riding a large bay horse. I didn't often cross paths with him at school, but he always looked impeccably dressed and groomed. The show clothes suited him. He was attractive too, I guess, in a quarter-would-bounce-on-his-bed, crusts-must-be-cut-off-his-bread kind of way. He'd made it plain that he didn't approve of me, but I didn't know if it was because I couldn't compare to Melanie or because I just didn't otherwise measure up somehow. Or maybe it was something completely different, like the company I kept. *Used* to keep.

No, don't go there.

And he was either very controlling or sincerely but overly concerned about Melanie for some reason. It had been apparent the first time I'd met him. I might even think him possessive if she hadn't made it clear there was nothing romantic between them. Kind of like Dave had been with Matthew when it came to his attention to me sometimes. *Once upon a time.*

Stop!

I was pondering these things, trying not to think of Dave and failing miserably as usual, when my dad called.

"Are you ready to go home?"

"Oh . . . can I stay just a little longer? Melanie's still riding."

"Where are you now?"

"In the main arena."

"All right, I'll meet you there."

And he did, just before the announcer said, "Melanie Teodorescu riding Flambeau, owned by Penelope Humphries."

As soon as they passed the starting line, it seemed Melanie had difficulty keeping Beau straight and calm. She fought to hold him in as he began rushing the jumps and at one point, about halfway through the course, he began tossing his head and looked like he would run off with her. She brought him around in a circle twice until he visibly relaxed and a buzzer sounded. Then she set him, now much calmer, at the next fence. She circled him one more time and brought him to a walk, riding him slowly out of the arena.

"What happened?" I asked, wondering why she didn't finish the course.

"The horse was too excited. He wasn't listening to her, so she chose to forfeit the class and school him instead of letting him have his way. She could have circled once and just got a penalty, but circling him more than that meant that she was off-course and eliminated. But she got him more relaxed and listening to her again and then took him over the jump to end on a positive note. It was a smart thing to do, though she's out of the competition on that horse."

I was surprised by my dad. It was the most detailed interaction we'd ever had about horses. We watched as the next horse and rider came in. "You know about jumping?"

My dad smiled, tight and mirthless. "This is what my dad did, your granddad. Isabel still competes but trains mostly hunters now. Dan competed, too, when he was younger, before he got hurt."

Daniel is my dad's younger brother. I knew he had hurt his leg from a riding accident. He was now an accountant in Denver and walked with a pronounced limp. He and his wife had come to California once, and he was the only member of my dad's family I could clearly remember. I knew my dad had grown up with horses and Mom had tried to explain why he was reluctant to let me be involved with them, but *he'd* never talked to me about any of it. Just like he never spoke of his home or growing up.

"Do *you* know how?" I asked. "To jump horses?"

Dad took a deep breath in and huffed it out. He gave a sharp tilt to his head and said, "I used to. It's exciting all right, but . . ."

I waited for him to finish but he looked like his mind was miles away. Maybe years away, too.

"Can I?" I said softly.

My dad didn't respond right away, as if he hadn't heard me. An older woman on a black horse was now in the arena, and we watched her progress around the course.

"Dad?"

He turned and looked at me—an intense look I wasn't used to from him. He seemed to be trying to look at me differently. It had happened a couple of times last year, too. I thought it might be a good thing, but it still made me feel weird.

He finally frowned and said, "What?" as if he really hadn't heard me.

"Jump," I said. "I'd like to learn."

He continued to frown and said nothing for a few more moments, then shook his head. "We'll have to see," he said. "I'm still getting over the last accident."

I felt indignant. Wasn't *anyone* going to let me live that down? And Dad made it sound like I was bound to have another accident—which might in fact be true, but I didn't want fear to keep me from trying. That was a decision I had made last year, and I was determined to hold myself to it.

"Let's get going, okay?" He seemed to have reached his limit of horse exposure for the day.

I nodded and followed him out into the bright sun. Melanie was close by, still on Beau and talking to Tatty. When Tatty had walked away, I led my dad over to her.

"Melanie, this is my dad. Dad, Melanie. And Beau."

"Hello, Mr. Anderson," she said calmly.

"Hello," said Dad. "It's nice to finally meet you."

I thought Melanie looked slightly self-conscious for just a moment, but she smiled back at him openly enough.

"You handled him well just now," said Dad, indicating Beau. "How long have you been riding?"

"Almost ten years," said Melanie.

Dad just nodded, then said to me, "Well, we'd best be getting home. Your mom will be off work soon. It was nice to meet you, Melanie."

"It was nice to meet you too," she replied, then looked at Beau, patting his neck. "I'm going to go and school him some more. I'll see you tomorrow, Allison."

I smiled and nodded. "Thanks, Melanie . . . for letting me come today."

She looked pleased. Dad and I went to the car and headed home. Once there, I spent the rest of the afternoon with Remmy, telling him about everything I had seen. Later, I helped Dad get dinner.

"So . . . what was it like?" asked Mom when we had sat down to eat, her eyes alight with curiosity. "You know, at Northfield?"

She looked at me. I looked at Dad.

"They've got a pretty nice club there. The course is nicely laid out, eighteen holes, immaculately kept. A guy there said they were having water rights issues, but you wouldn't know it to look at the course. He told me quite a lot, actually, about the area . . . and people."

"Aren't they building another course not far from there?" asked Mom. "I've heard things at the pool."

Dad shrugged. "That's the plan, apparently. A whole new community similar to Northfield, from what I've heard."

"What about you, sweetheart? Did you have a good day?"

I admitted that I had and gladly told her about Melanie, her horses, and the equestrian center.

"I would really love to learn to ride the way Melanie does. Do you think I could take lessons there? But I still want to ride with Cheryl, too."

Mom looked at Dad. "I'm sure that's something that we can talk about."

Dad was frowning again, but then he nodded. He seemed very distracted through the rest of dinner. I would have gone to bed relatively happy if I hadn't overheard the start of a conversation between my parents. I hadn't meant to eavesdrop—it was something I was trying to avoid—but I'd forgotten to tell them something important. I was just about to knock on their bedroom door when I heard Dad's voice.

"It puts a different perspective on things, for me at least."

"Oh dear. I admit I'd heard a few things at the pool, but they love to gossip. I'd put most of it down to that. Small town rumors."

"Well, from what I've heard, like father, like son. They've both got quite a reputation. I can't say that I'm unhappy that Allison's social circle is widening. And anything that keeps her away—"

At that point I knocked on the door. This was obviously something important, and I was tired of half-hearing about important or unpleasant things when they closely affected me.

Mom opened the door. "Hi, sweetheart. What's up?"

"What . . . *who* are you talking about?" I was pretty sure I knew, but I needed her to say it.

She looked nonplussed. "Oh . . . uh . . ."

"Are you talking about Dave?" I had no idea what was going on, but in spite of our strained or even *lack* of relationship, I was prepared to stand up for him.

"Oh," repeated Mom, looking at Dad then back at me. "No, sweetheart. Actually, we weren't talking about Dave."

Mom doesn't lie to me. Whenever I've asked her a straight-forward question, she's given me a straight-forward answer. But her hesitation made me doubt her this time.

"What were you talking about?"

She hesitated again and looked like she was deciding whether to tell me or not. Or how much. "It's nothing for you to worry about. Really! What was it you wanted?"

Mom was changing the subject and Dad had disappeared into their bathroom. I knew avoidance tactics when I saw them.

"I forgot to tell you that I'm going to Robin's after school tomorrow. Can you pick me up there?"

"Of course! I'd love to stop in and see Fiona. Maybe we can pick up pizza for dinner."

Mom smiled as if none of the previous conversation had happened. But it had.

Sleep seemed impossible. My mind kept dwelling on what I hadn't wanted to think about earlier in the day, about the way Melanie acted with Roger. He seemed to watch over her in much the same way Dave had watched over me last year. The only difference was that I had *loved* the attention, even if it wasn't romantic. Melanie seemed to *hate* Roger's attention, though she didn't seem to hate *him*. It was confusing and made me feel sad, but I didn't know why and wished I could stop thinking about all of it.

But I couldn't.

Chapter Eleven

Dad dropped me off at school before driving to the airport, but the rest of Monday morning slipped by me somehow. Between thinking about what I had observed at Northfield and the possibility of learning to ride English, the disturbing conversation I had interrupted between my parents the night before, and the ongoing confusion of where I stood with Dave, I was completely distracted.

Matthew and Robin kept bringing me back to earth in Chemistry and Geometry respectively—Matthew by lightly tapping on my notebook with his pencil and Robin by poking me in the ribs with the eraser end of hers—but I couldn't recall what we'd learned. That meant that homework would be harder and take me longer. Robin and I parted ways briefly after class to stop at our lockers.

"So, are you coming?" The voice made me jump.

Ben had been bugging me more again lately, just in general: being goofy and asking questions I'd already answered or shouldn't have to, and not remembering his lunch, and not doing his homework, and bothering me incessantly. Me *and* Robin. I was finding it easier to be patient with him—I guess I was getting used to him—but Robin always seemed short-tempered with him. This didn't seem to dissuade him at all.

"Coming where?" I asked. My mind was currently on the walk to Robin's house after school. I was a little annoyed by the added distraction.

"Choir. Tomorrow. Come on, it'll be fun."

I looked at Ben steadily for a moment then closed my locker, prepared to say no.

"Maybe," I said. *What? What are you doing now?*

"Awesome," he said and grinned from ear to ear.

"What's awesome?" asked Robin, and we began walking together.

"Choir," beamed Ben. "You should come too!"

Robin gave him a wary look. "Uh . . . no, I don't think so." To me, she said, "You're joining Choir?"

"Maybe," I said again.

"Huh," said Robin.

During lunch, I ate an orange and gave my sandwich to Ben, who said he'd forgotten his lunch again. I left the tables early to avoid Dave and Roberta, who were sitting too close together at the other table. I was one of the first out the door when English was over and finally breathed a sigh of relief in Art.

Miss Laski had told us to bring our projects in for a progress check, though we were currently studying and sketching old masters' still lifes in class.

"You still have four weeks left to hand in your completed project, but you should be just about finished by now," she said. "I'll be coming around to check your progress and make any recommendations for improvement. The best pieces will be displayed in the office during the next semester."

Melanie's piece was already finished and looked amazing. Miss Laski agreed it looked complete and accepted it. She picked up my tablet next.

"It looks like you still have quite a bit of work to do, Allison."

"Um . . . I wasn't sure," I flipped the page to show her the second of my pieces, "which one to finish." I flipped another page and then one more to the fourth incarnation of my still life.

Miss Laski laughed. "Well, you've certainly put enough time in on this. I think I'd like to see you finish *this* one," she said, flipping back to the second page. She pointed out a couple of areas for me to pay more attention to then handed it back to me. "Keep up the good work girls."

Robin met me at my locker after school, and we walked to her house. I noticed the front yard, though very dry, looked tidier than I'd seen it for a while and I commented on it.

"Yeah, Cris and Dave have been over a few times working on it since school started. It had gotten pretty bad. It's not the *only* thing they've been working on though."

She grinned and led the way back behind the old shake-sided bungalow. Gali whinnied softly when he saw us, walking away in his paddock and then circling back toward us again.

"Hi baby," she said in a high-pitched voice. "Look who's here to see you."

I started walking toward Gali, but Robin said, "Come and see," and went toward the side door of the garage. I followed her inside.

It was relatively empty as far as garages go. My dad was something of a neat freak, and everything stored in our garage was organized and out of the way. Compared to her room, Robin's garage was usually tidy and organized too: there were some boxes up on a broad shelf above the old washer and dryer, a pallet with a few bales of hay, two trash cans, the smaller of which held Gali's supplement, and a saddle rack and hooks on the wall holding her tack. The only other object, taking up most of the center of the garage, was the old Ford Mustang.

Before, it had looked like it hadn't been moved in years. Now the car had been turned around to face the closed garage door. The hood was up and the engine was missing. So were the tires, the axles resting on cinder blocks. Tools and rags lay on the front of the open hood and scattered on the floor. There were other mysterious mechanical bits and pieces lined up on newspaper nearby.

"They're fixing it up for me," she said, looking very happy. "It's going to take a while I guess, 'cause they can't always get over here, but they're getting a new . . . well, a rebuilt engine, and replacing pretty much everything. The interior's still pretty good though 'cause Gran's kept it closed up in the garage here. Dave said it's a good thing we keep the mice in check, or they could have done a lot of damage."

This was interesting and certainly something I hadn't been aware of. I was immensely curious about several aspects of this.

"Did the car used to be Fiona's?" I knew her grandmother didn't drive now but assumed she once did.

"No," said Robin, scooping up a measure of Gali's pellet supplement and pouring it into a small bucket. "It used to belong to my dad."

I looked at her closely, hoping she'd betray some obvious emotion or better yet, explain further, but she didn't. She had never once mentioned her parents to me, and for various reasons, I hadn't felt comfortable asking her. But we'd known each other a year now. I considered her my best friend, especially now that Dave seemed so indifferent. Before, I would have counted him as my best friend. He had seemed to understand and accept me, even care about me, on a deeper level than Robin did. But not now. Now Robin and perhaps Melanie were occupying that place. Surely it was okay to ask?

"Where is he?" I tried to say it lightly as if it were no big deal.

"Away," was all she said as I followed her back out to Gali.

She gave him the feed, petting and talking to him softly. Then we went into the house. Fiona was already in the kitchen making tea.

"Allison! How are you, dear? It's so good to see you!"

I flushed with pleasure, her heartfelt welcome touching me deeply. "I'm fine. How are you?" It was a reflexive response, but as I said it I remembered Robin saying Fiona hadn't been feeling well.

"Oh, fair to middlin'." She smiled. "I can't complain."

Robin made sandwiches as Fiona arranged the teapot, cups, and saucers on a tray. Then we carried everything into the sitting room.

Although somewhat small and claustrophobic, especially in warm weather, I loved this room. The furniture was old, covered in worn brocade and plaid throws. The standing lamp next to Fiona's comfortable chair and the one other lamp on the small dining table had fringed fabric-covered shades. Heavy curtains hung at the one window but, even though they were open, thick rhododendrons just outside allowed only patches of sky to peek through. This made the room very dark after the late summer brightness outside. It also probably kept it cooler inside than it otherwise would have been.

Like Robin's room, almost every square inch of wall was occupied by something: shelves for books, other shelves for knick-knacks, figurines, photographs that looked too old for even Fiona to be acquainted with their subjects, a couple of old paintings, and several framed pieces of embroidery.

My favorite of these was very simple: a bird's nest with blue-speckled eggs in it and a beautiful multi-colored butterfly on an adjacent leaf. The latter always reminded me of my grandpa's collection. The embroidered text said, "Life is Fragile. Handle with Prayer." I'd seen the sentiment expressed before in different places, but not as prettily or intricately worked as the embroidery on Fiona's wall. I wondered if she had done the needlework herself.

After our snack, Robin and I got our geometry done for the next day and worked through our history assignment, which was just as well since I hadn't been paying much attention in class. When we'd done as much as we could stand to, we went outside to play with Gali.

I felt thankful for Robin, not so much because of her help with homework, but because just being with her made me feel normal. More my true self—I think. By the time Mom got off work and came to pick me up, I'd made a decision, and it had nothing to do with Robin. Or Dave. At least, not directly.

"So, you're coming?" Ben asked during Spanish, much more enthusiastically than I thought was warranted.

"Yes," I said. "I'll see what it's like."

"Great!" he said. Then he frowned. "Did you do the homework?"

"Yes," I said, then frowned back at him. "It was just vocabulary. It wasn't hard."

"I know," he said, his mouth twisting. "I just forgot." He turned as if to go back to his seat, then turned back. "Actually . . . I kind of lost the list. . . ."

I didn't know what to say to him. I had a bad memory, too, for some things, especially things not immediately relevant to me. But not *that* bad. He went to his seat and had nothing to turn in. And I knew it wasn't the first time.

Lunch was angst-free; eating with Melanie was becoming more and more comfortable, and eating out at the tables less and less.

"I talked to my parents about taking lessons to ride English. I'd really love to learn dressage. And, maybe, learn to jump."

I knew things took time, and I was willing to take things slowly. I'd learned that lesson the hard way. But apart from the distraction it would give me—a definite plus—I really wanted to ride the way she did, the way Estephanie did, and the way Gold had been trained. As for jumping, it just looked like fun.

Melanie's face lit up. Her smile at times like these just about took my breath away.

"That's great!" she said. "What did they say?"

"Nothing yet, but I think they'll agree. My dad's out of town right now, but I'll ask again when he comes back."

I couldn't help thinking about that half-heard conversation, sure that my dad was amenable to my further association with Melanie and Northfield, and probably equally if not more glad of anything putting distance between me and the Calderas. I wasn't happy about the latter but, at present, saw no way of changing things.

She smiled widely again. "Do you think you could come again this weekend? I don't have a show, I'll just be working with the horses, but you could . . ." She blushed slightly.

"Watch?" I asked. "I'd *love* to watch you ride. Can I help you groom too?"

She looked pleased again. "Yes, of course!"

We walked together to PE talking of horses, and she seemed even more excited at the prospect of my going to Northfield again than I was.

Ben approached me at the beginning of Study Hall looking sheepish.

"I was wondering . . ." he said, scratching the top of my desk slightly with his thumbnail. "I was wondering if we could work together on our Spanish?"

I was trying to work on an essay for English, but now I was frowning at his thumb and wishing he would stop scratching. I'd been having a hard time concentrating on the essay as it was, and it was due tomorrow. I still had chemistry to finish, too.

"I . . . can't right now," I said, then felt bad when he looked disappointed. "We could work on it tomorrow at lunch . . . if you want."

His face brightened immediately. "Yeah! That would be great! You wouldn't mind?"

"No, I wouldn't mind."

After school he walked with me to my locker and then to the choir room. I felt very awkward walking through the door, sure all the other students milling around the room or sitting and talking on the risers had been in this class since it began. I didn't even know when that was. A group of kids were gathered around a grand piano with a man, obviously the teacher, Mr. Tanaka.

I had a sudden stab of panic, the general anxiety affecting my every thought and action lately spiking sharply. *What on earth were you thinking? That you were going to sing? In front of everybody? What if he makes you audition . . . right now?*

I stopped just inside the door and took a step back, ready to flee.

"All right," said Mr. Tanaka. "Let's get started." Then he looked toward us and beckoned. "Benjamin! Have your friend come on in."

"Come on," Ben urged gently. "You'll be fine."

I followed him slowly into the room as everyone gathered around the piano. There seemed to be no order for positions, and I was glad I could remain next to Ben. Mr. Tanaka began a vocal exercise that was easy enough to follow, and I relaxed a little, singing very softly. I looked more closely at the other students. I was surprised there were so many of them. I recognized some people from different classes, but I was perturbed to see both Hannah and Paola at the end of the piano, smiling at me as they sang.

Again I considered leaving—this was supposed to be a distraction, not a torment—but I couldn't, of course. The last thing I wanted to do was draw more attention to myself. And what about Ben? Would that embarrass him? Disappoint him? I really didn't want to do that. No, I'd make it through this and then explain how I felt later—or something.

After several vocal exercises, and with no discernible cue from Mr. Tanaka, everyone moved to the risers, seeming to take preassigned positions. I didn't know what to do and again considered bolting, but now it would be even more noticeable.

"What's your name?" Mr. Tanaka asked me.

Ben remained close by and looked ready to answer for me.

"Allison," I said.

"Do you know what part you sing, Allison?" he asked.

I knew what he meant, but I had no answer. I hadn't sung in an organized way since elementary school, and then we mostly sang in unison or simple equal parts. I shook my head.

"That's okay," he said and smiled. "Why don't you join the sopranos for now? Can you stay a few minutes after class to do a voice placement?"

I nodded, wondering if I'd be able to slip out before. Or maybe I could just tell him then that I'd changed my mind.

But a funny thing happened. Somewhere between being directed to stand between two girls I didn't know—one of whom got a folder with music for me—and the final notes of the last song, I relaxed and got lost in the music. While I wasn't used to reading in multiple parts, I had played the clarinet for a couple of years and was able to follow the soprano line quite easily. The physical exercise of singing was extremely satisfying, and my

spirits were lifted considerably. So I was sad when the class came to an end. I had really enjoyed it.

"Allison!" Paola came over when we were dismissed. "You are singing too!" Her eyes and smile were wide.

I answered warily, "Maybe. I'm not really sure . . ."

"Hi, Allison," said Hannah, joining us and also smiling. "I didn't know you sang."

I wasn't sure what to say to that, but Ben came up, and I was glad of the interruption.

"Mr. Tanaka wants you to sing for him."

"What?" I said, panicked.

"No, no," Mr. Tanaka had walked over to us, too. "Don't worry, I just need to hear what your range is and see if you can repeat simple lines."

I looked nervously around the room. Quite a few students remained, talking or picking out parts on the piano.

"We can go into the office if you'd like. No one can hear."

"I'll wait for you," said Ben, smiling encouragingly.

I nodded and followed Mr. Tanaka.

The office itself was large, and although he closed the office door, the upper half of the wall was glass, so I could still see into the music room and also be seen. We went to an upright piano next to a desk. He assured me the office was soundproof and had soon put me at ease. I faced away from the classroom and followed his directions.

"I think we'll keep you in the soprano section for now. Okay?"

I agreed, realizing that I really *did* agree. I *wanted* to do this. He gave me some papers to take home, to read and get a parent's okay to take the extra class. Ben smiled as I came out of the office.

"What do you think?" he said excitedly. He waved goodbye to Mr. Tanaka and grabbed his skateboard as we walked out the door.

"I . . . I liked it." I acknowledged. "Why is it after school though? I mean, why isn't it just a regular class?" I hadn't been interested enough to question it before.

Ben shrugged. "I heard Mr. T. wanted to make it a regular class this year, but whoever decides those things didn't think enough people would join. So he teaches two music appreciation classes as well as band and other choir classes. Right now there's just the men's choir—that's my other elective

—and the women's choir. But no mixed choir. So this is great. I mean, it's fun to just sing with the guys, but it's a lot more fun to sing with everybody."

We had reached the front of the school. "I'm walking to the pool," I told him. "Mom's working. Do you have a ride?"

Ben grinned and held up his skateboard.

"I mean a ride all the way home? You can come with us if you want." I was surprised when I realized I not only meant it but *wanted* him to.

Ben agreed, and we walked into town to the pool. We worked on homework due the next day until Mom got off work and drove us home.

"See you tomorrow!" Ben said as he got out of the car at his house. "Spanish at lunch!"

"Yes," I confirmed.

He shut the car door, and we waved at each other.

"He's a nice boy, isn't he," said Mom.

"Yes," I agreed. *Annoying as heck sometimes, but nice.*

As we drove back toward our house, I realized I hadn't thought of Dave again since entering the music room. The distraction had worked.

So why do I feel so sad?

Matthew seemed extra attentive and upbeat Wednesday morning, but just before Chemistry was over, he seemed to become self-conscious, as if he wanted to say something but was nervous about my response. It seemed unlike him.

Finally, the bell rang and he said, "You know, my birthday's coming up."

"Oh . . . yes." I frowned, realizing that his birthday was indeed just weeks away.

"Yeah, we're probably doing the barbecue/pool thing again. It's become something of a tradition, I guess." He half-laughed, but I wasn't convinced he was happy about it. "So . . . you'll come . . . won't you?"

I was flattered to be so explicitly invited. Last year I had found out about it at the last minute. Matthew thought he'd asked me, but I'm sure I would have remembered. Up until then, getting invited by others to do anything had been extremely rare.

"Um . . . I probably can," I said. "Robin's going too, right?" I'd feel very awkward there without her.

"Yeah, sure," he said, a half smile not reflected in his eyes. "And no getting grounded this time. Okay?"

I nodded as we reached the door. There seemed little possibility of that and, nonsensically, I felt sad again.

I walked to lunch with Matthew and Robin after History. The tables were already pretty full, just like they'd become about this time last year. Back then, the group had a definite "Caldera Fan Club" vibe to it, at least where the girls were concerned. It was subtly different this year. There were still obvious fans of Dave—they got as close to him as they could, participating in conversation and even, if they could find the slightest excuse for it, touching him in some way.

Hannah and Paola were the ones who obviously felt more comfortable around him. Their interactions had a natural appearance, though still troublesome for me. Roberta's appeared more possessive as if she had some sort of right to have her hands on him. That was bad enough, but he didn't seem to mind, which made it far worse.

Other girls, those varying from day to day and less familiar to me, looked on with differing degrees of curiosity and longing. I understood how the latter felt but was very conscious of not letting it show. I couldn't afford to.

Cris was seldom there, as were the other seniors. When Cris *was* there, he would catch and return my gaze just long enough for me to know he was aware of me. I didn't know exactly how I felt about that; I guess, somehow, it was comforting. I wondered if that's why he did it but doubted it.

To give the impression that Dave was the only boy getting attention would be false, however. Kyle was obviously with Stacie and everyone knew it, so he seemed exempt from undue female attention. But many other boys attracted admirers, even from girls who might have preferred Dave but found the others more accessible.

Chief among these was Matthew. He'd been nice-looking last year, but there was no denying that he'd gained a more mature appearance, which in itself was attractive. I guess I'd become more aware of it myself since Robin pointed it out at the workday. Like Dave, he seemed to accept the attention without letting it go to his head, mostly, unlike some of the others who either became almost obnoxiously arrogant or even goofier than they were to start with.

Of course, the same could be said for the girls, although Paola was the only one noticeably singled out by multiple guys. And she, while obviously appreciating the other boys' interest, gave most of her attention to Dave.

Robin and I found a place on the grass, and I got my lunch and my Spanish textbook out. Ben, who'd been sitting at the far table, jumped up and came over as soon as he noticed us.

"You actually brought a notebook?" I asked.

He held it up and grinned. "I know, it's amazing."

He copied the assignment, and we began working on translating the simple English sentences into Spanish. We got stuck several times and spent some time flipping forward and back in the textbook looking for answers. Ben often looked enquiringly to Robin, but she just shrugged.

Finally she said, "Quit looking at me. I barely know how to say 'Hi, how are ya?' "

At one point Paola materialized over my left shoulder between Ben and me and it startled me.

"Ah! You are studying *español, ¿verdad?*"

"*Sí!*" grinned Ben.

"Can I help you?" she said excitedly.

Ben opened his mouth but I beat him to it. "No. No . . . really. We're fine."

"But I don't mind. I would love to help."

"No . . . thank you. I learn better if I have to figure it out for myself."

Liar. It might be true, but that's not why you don't want her help.

"Okay," she said and looked a little sad. She got up and wandered back to Dave's table and was soon chatting and laughing again.

Refusing her help made me feel bad, but it didn't outweigh the annoyance of her asking in the first place. Or the confusion I felt. I'd so hoped I could count on Dave for help in Spanish, even indulging in imagining private tutoring sessions. But now I wasn't sure how I'd react even if he *did* offer. Again I wished he was just an average guy: not so smart, not so cute, not so ready to help and watch out for people, and not tutor material for *any* subject. Or anyone.

"Are you gonna eat your apple?" Ben asked.

"No," I said, distracted. "You can have it. I'm . . . I'm going to get to class. I'll see you later, okay?"

"See ya," said Robin. Ben nodded, his mouth already full.

I gathered my things, got up, and began walking toward the quad. I walked past a group of girls also sitting on the grass but didn't pay much attention to who they were. Suddenly a leg was thrust sideways as if the girl were stretching. But her timing was impeccable. I tripped, my backpack slipping off my shoulder and hitting the ground just before I did. My knees hit first, and I barely got my hands out in front of me fast enough to prevent my face hitting too.

"Oops," said the girl. She was in my PE class; one of Lori's friends.

I tried to pick myself up quickly, glad I hadn't worn a skirt today.

"Oh, did I do that?" asked the leg's owner.

I stood up and checked my hands.

"Did you hurt yourself?" Lori asked, but her voice was cold. She sat facing the group I'd been sitting with.

Was that an accident?

Robin and Ben had jumped up and were at my side, making sure I wasn't hurt. The grass had been enough to cushion my fall and avoid serious injury, but I doubted that was the intention anyway. I looked around quickly. Dave had jumped up from where he'd been sitting, too, and was looking our way as if deciding whether to approach or not.

Klutz factor off the charts. Humiliation achieved.

"I'm fine. Really," I said for Robin and Ben's benefit, ignoring the girls on the ground as if they weren't there.

I dawdled at my locker, now hoping that Dave would get to English before me. I dreaded him asking the question everyone kept asking, though I longed for him to care, too.

The bell rang just after I entered English and I slipped into my seat as quickly and quietly as possible, not looking around at all. Miss Saunders was writing an assignment on the board. Hannah was suddenly at the edge of my desk, crouched down.

"Are you alright?" she asked, her voice lowered.

Ugh. "Yes."

"We saw what happened. Was it really an accident?"

Well, I didn't purposely trip over her leg. That's what I wanted to say, but I knew what she really meant.

"Yes," I said. "An accident. I'm fine."

"Okay," she whispered and moved back to her seat.

I half turned to look behind me but caught myself. I wouldn't know what to do if Dave was watching and I'd feel hurt if he wasn't. And I was very aware of who else was likely to be observing.

I could *do* this. I could come to school and go to class and deal with these little failures as long as I didn't sabotage myself with useless longing or regret. I got my notebook out and wrote the assignment down. I participated in class and worked hard to not think about anything else.

As soon as the bell rang, I was out the door.

That evening I checked my email to find that Estephanie had sent me one. She had sent it the week before.

> *"Dear Allison,*
>
> *"How are you? I hope you are fine and doing well with your riding. How is Remmy? I would love to see a picture of him.*
>
> *"I have sent some pictures to you. There are a couple of Gold. He is doing very well. Look how long his mane and tail are now! And also, very exciting, he is going to be a papa! I have also sent pictures of the mares he is bred to. They are very lovely horses with good minds. We are very excited to see what the foals will be like. We hope at least one will be golden like its papa.*
>
> *"That's all for now. Please send some pictures to me, too!*
>
> *"Estephanie"*

The first two pictures were obviously of Gold, but I barely recognized him. One was taken from the near side, his beautiful mane cascading down his shoulder to the top of his foreleg. He was in motion, and his tail fanned out behind him. The other was similar but from the off side. His neck, shoulders, and hindquarters looked even more heavily muscled than they had been before. He was very impressive. I waited for a sharp pang of regret or longing but found I was happy with his situation. He was being taken care of, developed, and appreciated by someone who loved him. I knew I wouldn't really have been the right owner for him.

I slept fitfully that night. I dreamed of singing in Spanish. I dreamed of palomino foals gamboling around. I dreamed of Ben and Matthew having a discussion about chemistry that I couldn't understand. That was the weirdest one. But each dream ended abruptly with me tripping and falling hard. And each time I startled awake with my heart pounding in my chest.

At lunch the next day, Melanie said, "My mother said I could use the car on Saturday. That means I can come and pick you up . . . if you can come."

I nodded. "My mom's working so I'll ask her. I'm sure it'll be okay."

I felt delighted, and Melanie smiled, obviously pleased. *Now if I can just make it through the end of the week without any mishaps.*

As usual, Melanie was changed and ready for PE before I was, but somebody told her Coach wanted to talk to her, so she didn't wait for me as she usually did. I continued putting my track shoes on. When she'd left, I became acutely aware of how quiet the changing room had become. Although I always preferred quiet places, here it felt ominous. A locker door slammed on the next aisle, making me jump. Lowered voices murmured then laughed.

"Has he agreed yet?"

"No, but he will. He *has* to, right?"

I recognized Roberta's voice. I had little doubt of who "he" was.

"How could he refuse a sure thing?" another girl said.

"I bet he's *really* good at it," said a third voice.

Muffled laughter.

"What about the dance? Do you think he'll ask you?" The first voice again—it might have been Lori's.

"I'm working on that too. I'm sure I can get him to."

Another locker slammed shut, and a moment later four girls walked past my aisle toward the outside door. Roberta led them and looked very slightly in my direction then looked away, smiling. The others walked by without seeming to notice me at all, but I was sure they knew I was there.

I struggled intensely not to jump to conclusions, but it was almost impossible. Specific memories of Dave with Roberta—her touching him so intimately, them together on the stair landing—tortured my imagination; it wasn't such a leap to imagine even closer interaction between them. That made me feel sick to my stomach and short of breath. It also brought up all the other doubts and fears I'd had about Dave so far this year.

One thing tempered these reflections: Roberta's assertions of getting Dave to do—whatever it was. Dave wasn't the kind of person to be easily manipulated, if at all, and Roberta was hardly subtle if even I could read her. I couldn't imagine her getting him to do anything if it wasn't something he already wanted to do.

This was both heartening and depressing.

Friday started with, "Hey."

I think I jumped about a foot off the ground, then turned to face Dave.

His eyebrow quirked slightly. "Still jumpy," he observed.

"Yes." *Great response. Come on, you can do better.*

"So . . ."

Please don't ask how I'm doing!

"You haven't been around much."

This wasn't much better. It was such a ridiculous statement, it was all I could do to not disagree with him. *Of course I've been around. I just haven't been* close.

I stared at him, noting how smooth and beautiful his skin still was, though a line of fine, light colored hair now grew along his jaw and chin. He stared back. Amazingly, he seemed to reach uncomfortable status before I did. My turn to say something.

If you were smart, you would just agree with him. Or disagree—that would at least start an argument.

But I didn't like arguing, especially not with Dave. "I guess," I said. *Ugh.*

"I have to work later," he said, "but we're going for coffee right after school. Want to come?"

Yes! No! Who is "we"? I really didn't want that clarified. "Maybe," I said. *Another cleverly nonspecific answer. Good grief.*

He narrowed his eyes at me. I knew that look.

"Maybe?" he said after a moment.

I felt uncomfortably caught between inclination and survival. "I . . . I have homework I'm doing with a friend . . . after school . . . today." This was true. Since Tuesday, Ben and I had walked to the pool after school and worked on homework together. Then Mom drove us home. I was starting to not mind his company, and he was getting at least some of his homework done on time.

"Homework? It's Friday."

Dejá vu. Again.

"I have a lot of homework."

His expression changed again; not happy but not disappointed either. Resigned?

Yes. This is the way it is.

"Okay," he said, finally. "Well, see ya."

"See ya," I echoed as he walked away.

After school, Ben and I walked to the pool and I didn't mention coffee.

Chapter Twelve

As we had arranged, Melanie came to pick me up on Saturday morning at about eight o'clock. She was dressed similarly to the way her coach, Tatiana, was on the day of the show: polo shirt, breeches, and track shoes. Her hair, like mine, was pulled back in a ponytail. I was glad that she was able to meet my mother and now knew where I lived.

"It's wonderful to meet you at last!" Mom said, beaming. "I've heard so much about you. Perhaps you could come to dinner sometime?"

I felt a little embarrassed by Mom's effusive greeting, but Melanie responded graciously, "I'd like that very much."

"Come on," I said, leading the way out the back door. "I want you to meet Remmy!"

He was still eating his breakfast, but when he heard the back door open, his head appeared over his stall door. He continued munching as he watched us walk toward him, ears pricked forward, eyes bright. Just adorable.

"He's so cute!" laughed Melanie.

I smiled, glad she thought so too. Instead of opening the stall door, I entered the gate in his paddock and called to him. He came out immediately to greet us. Melanie's eyes grew bright with an appreciative gleam.

"He's lovely!"

I could tell she was looking at him critically—the same way Dave looked at horses—and felt doubly gratified. She reached out to stroke his neck, then walked around looking at his back, his legs, his feet.

"He looks very athletic," she said.

"He's *way* more athletic than me!" I laughed.

Melanie smiled but looked thoughtful. "He could probably do just about anything you want him to. Though he's a little small for Grand Prix." Her eyes danced and I assumed she was making a joke, but I didn't know what she was talking about. "Do you still hang out much with Dave?"

The question took me by surprise. I had told Melanie about Remmy, of course, and how I had gotten him but without any specific or embarrassing details. And I was sure she at least suspected how I felt about Dave, but she'd never questioned me about him before.

"No," I said, trying to keep my voice light. "Not much. He's been busy . . . I think." Visions of Hannah, Paola, Roberta—girls in general—and his responses and open attitude toward them filled my mind. "He doesn't . . ." *Doesn't what?* The words just hung in the air for a moment.

"But you still like him?" she asked softly, and I knew what she meant.

"Yes." *Forever.* "I like him a lot." *But I think he has a girlfriend. Or two. Or more.* "It just . . . it's been different."

I felt uncomfortable talking on this subject with her, but who else could I confide in? Brenda? She was hardly sympathetic at the best of times. Robin? No, she didn't seem to be as close to Dave as she was before either, but she still seemed much closer than me. No, that definitely wasn't an option. Mom? *Hardly.*

She was thoughtful for a moment, stroking Remmy's neck. "Do you talk at all?" she persisted, and I wondered why. It wasn't like her to press me about him or my feelings in general.

"Yes, sometimes. He asks how I'm doing." I thought of Friday. "He asked me to hang out after school . . . you know, with everybody. But. . . ." *But I don't feel like he really sees me anymore.*

". . . he doesn't seem the same," said Melanie, very gently, as if she truly understood.

I nodded. Remmy stood quietly before me, seeming content to be near me and to listen to us talking. My throat felt tight. Then I remembered a cryptic conversation with Melanie. She had once cared for someone, too.

"Did . . . did something like this happen to you?" I asked, hoping she would let her guard down as I had.

She frowned slightly, absently scratching around Remmy's jaw. "Yes. And no. The circumstances were probably very different." The frown disappeared then and she smiled, her eyes laughing. "And my friend never gave me a horse."

That made me smile, too.

Back in the house, Melanie asked Mom, "Would you mind signing a liability release? It's just for today, for the equestrian center." She seemed embarrassed to ask, but Mom said it was fine and signed the form.

"Have a great day," said Mom as we walked toward the front door. "I'll be off at six as usual. Allison, you can just come to the pool if you want, if you're back before then."

We hadn't talked about how long I'd stay with Melanie today, so I agreed. Melanie was, so far, the only one of my close friends who was driving, at least legally. I'd been excited to hang out around the horses with her today but was very interested in driving with her, too, as if I could have that level of independence vicariously through her. I was surprised when I saw her car, though. I suppose I had been expecting something similar to the Mercedes that Roger now drove, possibly a BMW or Lexus.

But the car that she led me out to was a Honda sedan, dinged up, the paint peeling a little. Definitely not a recent model. It was apparently her mother's car. Still, the drive to Northfield with Melanie felt much more of an adventure than driving there with my dad, and I was definitely open to adventure. Adventure, occupation, distraction, anything to keep my mind busy.

The equestrian center looked very different today as we drove by. International flags still flew gaily around the large covered arena, but there weren't many cars in the parking lot and few horses and riders in that area. Melanie stayed on the road, driving past the main parking lot and past arenas and paddocks I hadn't seen before. She turned up a narrow side road that led past the back of the barns, then entered a smaller lot and parked.

Melanie leading the way, we walked through the side entrance of the closest barn and straight through to the next, where the horses Melanie rode were stabled. The only one watching over the door was Kitty. She whinnied softly when she saw her owner.

Melanie smiled and said, "I'll ride her a little later. I need to get the boys exercised first."

She grabbed a halter from the hook in front of Digs' stall and held it out to me.

"Do you want to bring him out?"

I nodded and took the halter from her. We soon had both geldings cross-tied in the breezeway and began grooming. Digs was so much taller than Remmy that I had trouble brushing his back with any muscle. Melanie suggested I use a nearby mounting block, which I did. Digs stood quietly, lifting his big feet easily for me to pick out and obligingly lowering his head for me to brush his face and forelock, his eyes partially closed.

When Melanie was satisfied with the grooming, she led Digs back to his stall and tied him, then saddled Beau, showing me what she did. It didn't seem much different from Western except for how the girth was fitted. She led him out to a paddock near the barns, mounted, and began walking him.

It was a gorgeous day, a slight breeze cutting the heat that had been re-lentless since I'd come home from Los Angeles. There were lots of tall trees around the barns which probably helped. A few other horses and riders came and went but, compared to how busy it had been on the day of the show, it felt like we almost had the place to ourselves.

After a while, Melanie began trotting Beau in schooling patterns. She told me what they were doing as she rode—shoulder-ins, quarters-in, lateral work across the arena—and lots of circles. Beau was, for the most part, complacent enough, but when she worked him at a canter, he sometimes appeared to have his own ideas about where he wanted to go and how he wanted to get there. Melanie was very patient with him, ultimately getting him to do what she wanted.

As she finally walked him out around the ring, Tatty came up beside me. "Hi there," she said. "I met you last weekend, didn't I?"

"Yes," I said, happy for the acknowledgment. "Allison. My name's Allison."

"Of course. Do you ride, Allison?"

"Yes!" I said happily again. "But not like Melanie. Not English. And nowhere near as well."

"Hmm," she said.

When Melanie reached us, she stopped on the other side of the fence. "I brought Allison to hang out today," she said.

"I see that. I hope you got a release form signed." Tatty's manner seemed business-like but not unfriendly.

"It's in the car," said Melanie, jumping down from Beau. "I'll get it now."
Tatty nodded. "I'll be in the office."

We walked back to the barn, Melanie leading Beau. She unsaddled him, giving the tack a quick wipe, then threw a cooler over him and led him through to the other side of the barn. About twenty yards away was a hot-walker that she clipped him to and set it going slowly.

"Like a carousel," I said, then realized how silly it sounded.

But Melanie laughed and said, "Not quite as much fun I'm afraid, but Beau doesn't mind it."

She showed me where the emergency shutoff switch was, "Just in case." We walked back to the car so Melanie could grab the release form and then walked to the office close by. I waited outside, watching Beau. She was in there a few minutes and when she came out, she went back to Beau and set him going in the opposite direction. Then we went back into the barn to get Digs ready. Melanie let me try to saddle him and only adjusted the tack slightly when I was done.

"You're getting the hang of it already," she said, smiling.

I smiled back, so happy I was finally getting to spend some real time with her and getting to see her ride. I found it fascinating. As much as I loved Bar 8, I thought I would like it here too. That there were no physical reminders of Dave here was a plus. I'd barely thought of him since Melanie picked me up.

Melanie stabled Beau and then rode Digs for about an hour. She rode similar patterns to those she had done with Beau, but Digs was noticeably more focused and balanced.

"He's such a good boy," she said, stroking his neck as she rode him back out of the arena. "Let me take care of him, and we'll go get some lunch, okay?"

"Sure," I said, wondering if I was going to get to see where she lived.

When Digs was unsaddled, cool, and back in his stall, we got in the car again. Instead of going back to the main highway, Melanie pulled out of the stable lot and turned right along the side road. After a while, a slight right, and straight ahead across another road brought us to a large complex. The side closest to us looked like some kind of large auditorium.

"What's that?" I asked, pointing to the huge structure ahead. I thought perhaps it was a mall.

"That's the community center," she said. "They have just about every-thing in there. I'll show you around."

She parked the car near the farthest end of the parking lot, where there were the fewest cars, and we walked toward the closest doors leading into the complex. A white wall hung with artwork faced us as we entered, much of it similar to what we were doing in Art class. A handwritten sign said "Mrs. Bell's Class – Lowell High School." A long corridor stretched to our right. There was no one in sight, but a distant clash of sounds came from that direction. To our immediate left was a glass wall and doors. A sign showing through the glass said, "Closed."

"That's the youth center," she said.

Visible in the room beyond were tables and chairs, cabinets, foosball and pool tables, and open doorways leading to other rooms. Melanie had pulled her silver locket up from under her shirt and ran it back and forth lightly along its delicate chain. I hadn't noticed her play with it for a long time.

"Do you come here much?"

Looking like I'd pulled her back from another time, she frowned slightly and said, "No, not anymore. I used to though, in sixth and seventh grade. Or, at least, a part of seventh."

She looked a little sad and as if her thoughts were far away again for a moment, then she seemed to snap out of it. She smiled, dropped the locket, and said, "The church runs it on Sunday mornings and Thursday nights for their youth groups. The rest of the time it's run by the community after school until about seven o'clock and also during the summer. There are basketball and volleyball courts out back. Come on, I'll show you the rest."

I followed her along the hallway. A wider corridor opened to our left and we turned there. On the left side of this was a long wall broken only by two pairs of double doors.

"Those are the banquet rooms. It's where they hold community meetings and events. They've had art shows, wine tasting, dances; things like that. We had our middle school graduation dance here." She rolled her eyes slightly and smiled, but I thought there was still a trace of sadness.

I couldn't help asking; I so wanted to know more about her. "Did you go with someone? You know . . . a date?"

"No, I went all by myself!" She said this with a decided nod of her head. Then, as if to clarify, "I got asked by a couple of different boys, but there was nobody I really wanted to go with. I thought it would be better to go on my own."

I was trying to picture her, slightly younger—though she would have been older than her classmates—and dressed for graduation, arriving alone at the dance. I hadn't even had a graduation dance.

"Did you have fun?"

She smiled and said, "Yes, I really did. I didn't think I would, but I did."

She smiled again and led me through a wide opening in the wall halfway down the corridor.

"That's the gym. Obviously."

There was a small seating area to the right and a long counter with a girl working behind it. Behind, on the other side of another glass wall was an enormous room filled with various machines and free weights. A boy stood on our side of the counter talking to the girl. He wore shorts and a tank and had a towel and a slim gym bag over one shoulder. I assumed he was going in. His general height and build, and the slightly long, curly blond hair looked familiar. I guess I stared too long as he turned his head and looked our way.

It was the boy I had seen at the horse show, the one riding the Appaloosa. He had looked familiar then too, and now I knew why. In English riding clothes and with a helmet covering most of his hair, I hadn't recognized him. Memories from last year—at school near the drink machines with Varsity Jacket and at the mall in Sacramento—made my heart feel like it flipped and not in a good way. I suddenly felt a little sick. The boy looked at me—I couldn't tell if he recognized me—then looked at Melanie, giving her the slightest of nods. I didn't see if she acknowledged him.

"This is the swim center," she said, indicating another counter across from the gym's, but there wasn't much to see. Openings on either side of the counter led into short angled hallways, one side labeled for men, the other for women. I was happy to leave and get back into the corridor. We continued to the right and out through the back doors. A low wall with a high chain link fence bordered a large area with two enormous pools.

"The local swim teams train and compete here," said Melanie. "This pool is for the community."

Both pools were in use but the closest, the public pool, was much more crowded and noisy. On the other side of the walkway were several basketball and volleyball courts, and fenced tennis courts beyond them.

"There's more," said Melanie. She led me back into the corridor and back to the front of the complex and turned left, continuing along the original corridor.

This was where all the noise came from. Past the back wall of the gym, an immense area opened up with an arcade and a small food court. Beyond these, at the back of the building, was a bowling alley with at least ten lanes. I was amazed. Although huge, the complex hadn't looked big enough from the outside for all this.

"It's a lot busier during the week," said Melanie. "And especially Friday and Saturday nights because . . ." She hesitated, a droll expression on her face.

"Because there's nothing to do anywhere else," I finished for her.

She laughed. "Too true. Of course, there's the multiplex in Lowell and some shopping. But a lot of the kids from Lowell and Douglas end up here."

Except for at least one significant person.

I shook off the thought and continued to follow Melanie. Past the food court was a ticket window, movie posters, and more glass doors.

"The theater, obviously. One screen is usually a children's movie, and the other doesn't play anything over PG-13, so mostly kids and families come here. So that's the community center. Do you want to get something to eat here? Or we can go around the corner by the market."

I wouldn't have minded eating in the food court, but between the deafening noise—always a problem for me—and the possibility of the blond boy coming this way, I chose the latter. We left the complex and got sandwiches, eating them inside before heading back to the stables.

"That boy at the gym. . . ."

She seemed to think for a moment then said, "You mean Bradley?"

"Yes. Do you know him?"

Melanie shook her head. "Not really. His horse is stabled here, and he competes at most of the shows I do, but we've never really talked. I think he just moved here the summer before last."

"Like me," I said.

Melanie smiled, "Yes. And I'm so glad you did, too." She was quiet for a moment then said, "Do *you* know him?"

"Oh, no," I denied. "Not at all. I've just . . . you know . . . seen him around."

"He's good-looking," she said, watching me.

He obviously was so I nodded.

When we got back to the stables, she said, "I'm going to ride Kitty for a while, then I'll take you back, okay? You're going to saddle her though."

I agreed and spent the next half hour happily occupied with grooming and saddling Kitty, and then watching as Melanie rode her. When she walked the beautiful mare back to me, she surprised me by saying, "Would you like to ride her?"

I didn't need to be asked twice. Again Melanie surprised me after dismounting by taking off her helmet and putting it on my head.

"It's policy, for safety's sake," she said. "Riders have to wear helmets."

I was okay with that and stood still as Melanie adjusted the strap below my chin. Kitty was smaller than the geldings, and I was able to mount without help. Once in the saddle, Melanie adjusted the stirrups and showed me how to hold the reins between my fingers with both hands, similar to the way Dave had taught me how to ride Gold.

Heels down, toes forward, elbows in, hands soft and low and just above Kitty's withers, eyes up and looking where we were going—similar basic technique to Western, and very comfortable, but it felt different from the way I had become used to. Melanie seemed very pleased. She told me to use my lower legs to ask Kitty to walk forward, maintaining very light contact with her mouth. As I was more used to neck-reining Remmy, this was a little harder because I wanted to let the reins become too long.

Melanie walked along beside us for a few moments then stepped away toward the center of the paddock to observe us. From there she instructed me in halting, backing, and turning Kitty, all of which made perfect sense to me but was accomplished in a slightly different manner than I was used to. After a turn into the long side of the arena, I saw that Tatty had joined Melanie and was watching us. We continued to walk around until we reached them.

"I was thinking," Melanie said, loud enough for me to hear too, "that maybe I could get Allison riding Kitty for me. And she might be looking for a riding coach if you have time."

I was stunned and looked at her in awe. "What?" I whispered.

Tatty looked at me and said, "I'll have to see a little more of how she rides. But you can take her on if you want to. Just get the paperwork to me." Then Tatty walked away to one of the barns.

"What?" I asked again. "Paperwork?"

It felt as if something good was happening, but I couldn't quite grasp it, like some of the conversations at school where I understand all the words but seem to miss the meaning.

"Don't worry about it. I'm just planting seeds." I know I gazed at her blankly and she looked apologetic. "Tatty doesn't like to have things sprung on her. She kind of likes to think things are her idea."

I was still looking at her in amazement. She was setting up riding lessons for me? With Tatty? Or possibly with herself?

My mind was full of new experiences and hopes as Melanie drove me back to Douglas and dropped me at the swimming pool. The day had been enlightening in many ways, both in getting to know Melanie better and in trying to understand my place in the world again. Perhaps a world without Dave.

Mom asked Melanie if she wanted to get some dinner with us in town, but she said she had to get home—her mother might need the car and she had homework and babysitting to do. We agreed we would see each other in PE on Monday and she drove away. On the way home I told Mom all about the stables, the horses, the way Melanie rode, and of course riding Kitty and what Tatty had said.

"Well, that sounds very exciting, but what about Remmy?" she asked.

I had already thought of this. "I won't be able to go there all the time. I'll still ride Remmy a lot. Melanie has *three* horses to ride."

Mom seemed to be thinking. "You really want to do this, don't you?" she said.

Learn something new. Ride a lot more and get better faster. Keep busy. Be distracted. All with horses . . . .

"Yes, I really do."

Mom nodded and said we'd talk to Dad when he got home. But I thought she looked troubled.

"Are you staying for the game?" asked Robin.

It was Tuesday; third period, World History.

"Game? Staying?"

There had been talk about it last week, though I hadn't heard any details.

"The first home games. You know . . . Dave. Soccer. You're coming, right?"

"I . . . didn't know it was a home game," I said.

I *should* have known, but I was trying so hard to *not* be aware of what Dave was doing. It's not that I didn't want to know, but that I couldn't afford to.

"Junior Varsity's playing first. You should come over after choir for the Varsity game. Your mom won't mind, will she?"

"I don't know," I said, trying to think of an excuse. "I have a lot of homework . . ."

"Whatever," she said, obviously dissatisfied with my answer.

When the bell rang, we walked together toward the quad. Dave was just ahead of us.

"I guess I'll see you later . . . maybe," Robin said and walked toward Dave.

I continued by myself but looked toward them once. Robin shrugged as she spoke to Dave and he looked over at me. I set my face toward the cafeteria and kept going.

In English, I kept my eyes down as everyone entered the room but was very aware as Dave came in. With Roberta. Hannah was right behind them. I left the room as quickly as I could when class was over, but Hannah caught up to me.

"Hi, Allie. I was wondering how you like Choir?"

"It's okay," I said, feeling a moderate response was appropriate under the circumstances.

I hadn't entirely made up my mind yet. The fact that both Hannah and Paola were there was at least slightly against it. The fact that Roberta was *not* there was in its favor. I'd take both Hannah and Paola over Roberta any day.

"Are you going to the game?" she asked, and I started to feel a little annoyed.

I shook my head. "I don't . . ."

I was going to say "I don't think so," meaning no, but I'd never watched Dave play soccer. The game wasn't about me and whether I liked his other friends. It was about him. It was one of the things he was really good at, and he'd had to work so hard to get on the Varsity team. He'd had to prove himself. It was important to him. As his friend, I wanted to show my support.

"Maybe," I said.

"Great!" she said. "I'll see you later!"

Later, Choir was just as enjoyable as it was the first time and I felt more comfortable, a little more confident. Ben joined me as I left.

"So, I'm going to stay and watch the game. Are you walking to the pool?"

"Um . . . actually . . . I was thinking maybe I'd watch for a while."

He smiled widely, "Cool! I'll walk with you!"

A lot of other kids from Choir were going, too, so we walked over together to the upper field. There were a lot of people in the stands on both sides. Robin saw us coming and stood up, waving to get our attention. I sat next to her. Ben sat in front of us, next to Paola and Hannah.

"You came!" Robin seemed thrilled, and I was happy that *she* was happy. "JV's still playing," she informed me. "There's Matt." She pointed to him running on the field. "And there's Tanner." Tanner had the ball and was trying to get a clear shot to a teammate. "Dave and Cris will be playing soon."

I got my phone out to text Mom and let her know what I was doing. She replied that she'd pick me up when she got off at six if I wasn't at the pool before then. Ben too, if he wanted.

It was fun watching our guys play. The visiting team was Lowell, which explained why the visitor's stands were so full with more people arriving all the time. In fact, soon there were noticeably more spectators on their side than ours. Our team, the Panthers, dressed in black and gold. The Bearcats' colors were red and white.

"What's a bearcat?" I asked Robin, amazed I'd never heard of one before.

She burst into loud laughter. "Nobody knows!" she said loudly, still laughing. "That's why they're *losers!*" This last word was yelled at the top of her lungs toward the field, but it was so noisy, I doubted anyone beyond the people around us heard.

The JV game continued for another ten minutes or so and ended with a close score: Douglas 6, Lowell 5. Our side of the stands erupted into loud applause and whistling.

"I can't *wait* to see *Dah-veed* play!" Paola said loudly. She turned toward us, her eyes bright, her smile dazzling. "*Futbol*, it is my *favorite* sport. We watch all the time in Cuba. My brother . . ." She abruptly stopped, and her expression was more solemn for a moment. She smiled again but not quite as openly. "I loved to watch my brother play . . . when he was younger."

I heard someone behind my right shoulder say in a low voice, "As if we care."

I was shocked to hear someone say something so mean out loud. I was even more shocked to realize that I'd been thinking something similar.

"Seriously. I wish she'd just give it a rest. It's not like he's ever going to be serious about someone like *her*." This was almost whispered by a different person further to the right behind me, but I still heard it plainly.

I couldn't help making assumptions—I had little doubt who "he" was—and I wondered why they thought he wouldn't want to go out with Paola. She was gorgeous and friendly. She seemed to be happy *all* the time. She was smart, too. It would be too obvious if I turned around to see who was talking, but I had my suspicions.

"Ugh. As if slant-eyes wasn't bad enough. Dah-veed this and Dah-veed that. Black girl's all over him in study hall. And then when she needs extra *help*, they go off to the library together so they can *talk*." The emphasized words were whispered disdainfully as if the speaker made quotation marks with her fingers.

"Bitch is so smug about it too. But I think she's faking. She speaks English good. I just want to slap her."

Now I felt sick. I couldn't imagine what Paola could have done to be called that. I would admit to not feeling very friendly toward her, but I had a growing awareness that it was due to my own shortcomings. It certainly had nothing to do with her appearance. And their offhanded slur obviously aimed at Hannah really surprised me. I'd thought they were friends.

I wanted to move away so I wouldn't hear any more, but there wasn't room to sit on Robin's other side or in front. Instead, I turned around enough to verify who it was—Lori and two others. One of them glared at me as if I were being nosy. Then Lori looked at me haughtily and said, "You want something?"

I felt the blood drain out of my face and I almost turned back without saying anything. I actively avoid confrontation, and I rarely tackle important topics unless I've had time to think them through very carefully. But I couldn't stand what I'd heard and didn't want to listen to any more. Instead, I threw caution to the wind. It wasn't so much for Paola's or Hannah's sake as due to my own frustration at their meanness.

My heart pounded, and there was a tingling in my cheeks I'd never felt before as I responded, "No . . . but you should probably talk a lot softer. Unless, of course, your *intention* is for everyone to hear the ugly things you think."

As hard as it is for me to look most people in the eyes, I forced myself to look steadily at each one of them in turn, my heart thudding uncomfortably.

I'd kept my voice just loud enough for them to hear me, but both Robin and Ben had turned to look. Lori now glared at me too, and her jaw seemed to jut out slightly as if stopping herself from responding. All three girls looked shocked—and very angry—that I dared to speak up at all. That was both frightening and oddly exhilarating. I turned my back to them again.

"What was that about?" asked Robin, frowning.

"Nothing," I said, now shaking and feeling a little sick.

Robin turned to glare at the girls.

"It's nothing," I repeated, not wanting to drag her into anything.

I could still hear the girls behind me and caught random words. I was pretty sure I was now the primary object of their resentment, but I tried to ignore them. I was also sure they weren't going to forget my interference, but I'd deal with that when I had to.

The Varsity teams had taken the field and were warming up. Dave was number nineteen and it was hard to keep my eyes off him. His hair was now so long that he'd tied most of it back and kept having to sweep the shorter front lengths out of his eyes. I'd never seen him wear his hair like that. I wondered if he was ever going to cut it.

Robin surprised me by echoing my thought. "Dave needs to cut his stupid hair."

"Why hasn't he?" I said and then wondered if it was a weird thing to ask.

Robin shrugged. "Maybe he's going through a hippy stage. Or maybe he's just lazy, I don't know."

"Maybe he's saving his money," said Ben, who had overheard.

She laughed at that, but he appeared to be serious.

Then the Varsity game started. Within the first few seconds, Dave had the ball and appeared to be in place to shoot toward the goal. The goalie was obviously ready for him. Instead, Dave passed the ball right between two Lowell players so fast that they couldn't react in time. The ball found its real goal—Cris. Cris ran two steps with it and shot straight through a gap in the other team's defense. It had happened so fast, the goalie couldn't throw himself to the other side of the net in time to stop it. Our side erupted in cheers. Even I clapped my hands like crazy.

The stands on our side had now filled out, probably due to parents getting off work, and I saw the whole Caldera clan arrive. Mr. Caldera saw us and waved, then Angel did too. Henry's eyes were on the field, and Stevey looked in our direction but didn't respond in any way.

An impromptu cheering squad had gathered on the home sideline. They were led by Roberta, who had appeared from somewhere but included several other girls including Hannah, obviously all cheerleaders.

"Wait till the football team hears about this," said Robin, smirking.

"Doesn't soccer have cheerleaders?"

Her expression let me know how hopeless she thought me. "No. Not that I've ever heard of anyway. They've never done anything at a soccer game here. Just football and basketball. The coaches don't acknowledge it, but there's already rivalry between the football and soccer teams. This isn't going to help."

As if that first goal had been a good omen, it seemed the Panthers could do no wrong. By half time, our team led four to nothing. The guys all came off the field, Dave looking our way for several moments. The cheerleaders had immediately run over to the coolers to pass out water to the team. Roberta approached Dave, effectively distracting him from us. Lori and the other two girls got up and made their way down toward the field too.

Robin surprised me by jumping up and saying, "I'll be right back." She looked like she was following them.

I had a bad feeling about that and got up to follow as well. When she got to the field, Lori grabbed a bottle from the biggest cooler and approached Cris with it. Perhaps he just hadn't seen her, but he turned his back on her and walked in the opposite direction. That made Lori hesitate just long enough for Robin to catch up to her.

"Hey!" Robin shouted. "Were you talking trash about my friend?"

Lori seemed confused, then looked beyond her and saw me. Her lips spread in a sneer. "Getting your friends to fight your battles? That's pathetic."

Robin launched toward Lori and shoved her hard with both hands. "*You're* pathetic! Just leave her alone, skank!"

I felt sick again. "Robin!" I said and tried to grab her arm.

Lori shoved back before I could grab Robin, her face a mask of fury.

Suddenly Cris stood between them. "Stop now," he said, calmly but sternly, "before you get into real trouble. Go back to the stands." I assumed he was talking to Lori and Robin, but he seemed to be glaring at me.

I took Robin's arm and tried to pull her away. Lowering my voice, I urged her, "Robin, don't! *Please*. You misunderstood. Come *on*." I continued to draw her away. "They weren't talking about me."

"What . . . who were they talking about then?"

I considered telling her the truth, but there didn't seem to be much point. They already hated me, and they probably *had* been talking about me too. I couldn't see any good coming from telling anyone. I shook my head.

I managed to lead Robin away, her face stormy. Dave was some distance away, but he'd been watching the altercation. He looked concerned but didn't seem to feel his intervention was necessary. I was very glad of that. Roberta looked—amused? Certainly not worried or surprised.

We headed back toward the stands, and I looked back toward Dave once. He seemed to nod to Roberta, raising the water bottle as if thanking her for it, then walked away from her to where Hannah, Paola, and a few others were standing. I was glad. And then I wasn't.

Cris had immediately walked away from Lori and the other girls.

Ben met us at the bottom of the stairs. "Wow. What was that about? I thought you were really going to fight!" He seemed impressed.

"So you stayed a safe distance away?" said Robin.

"Yeah," he said as if it were the obvious and smart thing to do. He was probably right.

When Lori and the others came back up, they sat further away and I didn't look at them again.

The second half of the game seemed to slow down, the ball going out of bounds more often and all potential goals, on both sides, being blocked by defense or the goalies. The Bearcats finally got a goal, but our team didn't allow them to get any more, even though they didn't score any more themselves. A Panther had almost scored when I got a text that Mom was waiting in the parking lot.

"My mom's here," I said to Robin. "It looks like they'll probably win though."

Robin smiled. "Slam dunk."

Her choice of metaphor made me pause, and I almost said something but just smiled back instead.

She frowned and laughed. "You know what I mean."

"Do you want a ride?" I asked Ben. I was a little surprised that he hesitated as if not sure.

"I guess so. The game's almost over. Right?"

Robin nodded.

"Do you need a ride?" I asked her.

"No, I'll wait for Dave and Cris. They always take me home."

I pictured her sitting between the two boys in Cris' truck and felt good about that. At least some things hadn't changed.

Later that night, trying to fall asleep, I kept thinking about Lori and her friends, Roberta too, and wondered if I'd just provided them with more reason to target me. I wasn't sure why I'd felt compelled to say anything; it wasn't like I really considered Hannah or Paola my friends. That thought led to thinking about *why* I couldn't see them as friends, which in turn led to thinking about Dave, of course. It also made me feel as pathetic as Lori had accused me of being. And guilty, too. *That* made me confused and sad, and I barely slept.

Chapter Thirteen

I took too long getting ready the next morning and was almost late for school. Very unlike me. I spent most of that time trying to decide what to wear and the rest putting makeup on only to take most of it off again—and then putting some back on. Also unlike me. I wasn't even thinking about how other people would see me; I was just dissatisfied with myself but unable to pinpoint the problem.

I had been feeling more than usually on edge at school: guilty, afraid, and irritable. It seemed to get worse as the days passed which was also unusual. In the past, if something, some event, triggered the nameless fear, it dissipated at least somewhat over time: a few days, maybe a week. It had been a part of my life as long as I could remember, but I was only recently recognizing it for what it was and putting a name to it, *anxiety*, though I still didn't understand it. And I hadn't suffered from it this much since middle school. Today it was worse than ever.

I tried to be very aware of my friends—Robin, Melanie, and Ben too—trying not to isolate myself from them, but I didn't trust myself, afraid of unintentionally offending them. I was easily startled—Dave called it *jumpy*; very preoccupied and often staring at nothing—*super* space cadet; irritable—even less sleep than usual probably didn't help; and somewhat paranoid—the anxiety and its attendant but incomprehensible guilt dogging me like some vaguely imagined yet very real monster.

I tried to avoid interacting with Hannah and Paola, as much to protect them from my irritability as to defend myself from their good-natured but ultimately aggravating attention. Having to watch and listen to them, especially around Dave, was like letting someone pour lemon juice on a still very open, ugly wound. And starting today, I would actively go out of my way to avoid Roberta, Lori, and the others in their group, though Roberta was most often somewhere in Dave's vicinity.

I also decided, on the days I went to lunch with Robin, I would try to make sure we sat on the grass a little distance from the tables—close enough to be a part of the bigger group but far enough away from the tables to be unable to hear or participate in their conversations.

Today Cris was at the tables and I realized that I missed him when he wasn't. For some strange reason, even if he wasn't close by and didn't obviously acknowledge me, his presence gave me a greater sense of well-being; a respite from the relentless dread that haunted me. But those days were few and far between now.

"Cris is hardly ever around."

"He's taking classes at the college in Lowell," said Robin, looking over at him.

He seemed to sense us looking at him and regarded us solemnly for a few moments before turning away again. He was sitting near Dave and being much more sociable than I was used to seeing him. He wasn't talking much but was paying attention to those who were.

"I guess he's working, too, but I'm not sure where. He's only here for a couple of classes and to play his last year on the Varsity teams. Then . . . I guess he'll be gone."

"Gone?" I immediately thought about his disappearance last June.

"University . . . somewhere . . ."

Dave had told me his brother was supposed to go to UCLA like their dad had, but from what I knew of Cris, he wasn't necessarily going to do what was expected of him.

A disturbance at Dave's table attracted our attention. There was a lot of loud laughing and talking there, especially from Roberta. She was sitting across from Dave as they ate and there seemed to be food swapping going on. As we watched, Roberta got up and grabbed something from in front of Dave, then walked backward away from the table. He jumped up immediately,

stepping onto and over the table to follow her. She shrieked and ran a few steps, but he caught her around the waist. It was very apparent that's what she wanted; she hadn't run very fast.

"Give it back," Dave said, trying to grab the item out of her hand.

She changed hands and tried to keep it out of his reach. It looked like a juice box. He finally grabbed it back, let go of Roberta, and walked back to the table.

"Ugh," said Robin. "I wish he'd just tell her yes or no, and then maybe she'd leave him alone."

It was the first time she'd ever shown real aggravation because of Roberta or any of the other girls for that matter. I had a stab of fear that there truly was something more serious going on between Dave and Roberta.

"Yes or no?" My stomach felt like it did on amusement park rides—the ones I *didn't* like. I needed to know, to put the subject to rest one way or the other, but I was dreading enlightenment.

"Class president," was her unexpected answer.

I stared at her, wondering how to form the next question without sounding like a complete moron. I vaguely remembered some sort of student body election process at the end of the previous school year, but I hadn't taken any interest in it.

"Brian is moving. I heard his parents split up. Anyway, I guess he's moving away with his mom, so someone's gotta take his place."

"Isn't that what a vice-president is for?"

She shrugged. "Some kids wanted Dave to run for it last year, but he wasn't interested. Now that Brian is leaving, Roberta's trying to convince him to run. They're going to have an election in a few weeks. I guess Brian told her about it before anyone else."

"Why does she want him to do it?"

"Why do you think? More opportunity, I guess. She's class secretary."

I wasn't exactly sure what *more opportunity* meant, but I got the general idea. "Do you think he will?"

She shrugged again. "He said he's thinking about it. It looks really good on transcripts, of course. I guess he'd be as good as anyone else."

Not knowing what the position entailed, I just nodded, but I was sure he was more than capable of filling it.

I was even more circumspect than usual in PE, bearing in mind the incident at the soccer game the day before. But the girls completely ignored me which was a relief. Ben and I walked to the pool after school since my dad was still away. I was looking forward to him coming home, but I actually enjoyed the walks after school—and was enjoying Ben's company.

As much as he aggravated and distracted me in class sometimes, outside of it, I found I could relax with him. Sometimes he was extra hyper-active and silly—that's when he was the most annoying—and other times he seemed exhausted and almost depressed, like the day we went to the observatory. But no matter how despondent my own mood, he could usually make me laugh. I was starting to really appreciate that.

He usually did most of the talking as we walked, telling me of movies he liked or TV shows he watched, his favorite foods, and the places he'd been. The latter sounded fascinating and made me wish I could travel too. It occurred to me that he'd never said anything, ever, about his family. As we lived so close to each other, I couldn't help wondering about them. Today he opened the subject by asking about mine.

"Your dad's been gone awhile, huh," he said.

"Yes, but he'll be home this weekend . . . I think."

I felt a twinge of guilt for not being sure. When I was younger, I used to mark the days off on a calendar and always knew exactly when my dad would be gone and when he'd be back. But I rarely kept track anymore. It's not that I didn't care—I loved my dad and *usually* preferred it when he was home—but my life was filled with other people and things now, and my own concerns most often occupied my mind. I didn't miss him the same way.

"I want him to see what I've done in your front yard," said Ben.

"You want him to *pay* you," I said.

"Well, yeah, that too."

After a moment I asked, "Do you have any brothers or sisters?"

"Nope. Only child, like you." He grinned and then frowned. "At least, as far as I know."

"Oh," I said. That told me nothing. Try again. "I've never seen your parents. But I guess you haven't lived here that long, right? Are you going to take the O'Dell's sign down from in front of your house?"

Ben frowned again. "Why would I do that?"

I frowned back. "Because it's not your name."

"Yeah, but it's Bill's last name. He's lived there for years."

I thought of the red-haired man I'd seen dropping Ben off the day of the field trip.

He was quiet for a few moments but kept stealing glances at my face. Finally, he said, "Bill and Vivian are my foster parents."

"Oh," I said, trying to process the new information; trying to match it to anything I was familiar with but failing. "What's that like?" I asked, wanting to find out more but not knowing what to ask.

"What's it like to *not* be a foster kid?" he countered good-naturedly.

He had me there. I laughed a little. "I guess I don't know. I wouldn't know how to compare it."

Ben nodded and was quiet again. After a moment he said, "Hey, I'd appreciate it if you don't say anything though. Okay?"

I was confused for a moment then understood what he was asking. "I won't," I assured him. It wouldn't be a problem. I was very good at keeping things to myself.

He changed the subject then, describing a trip to New York.

The heavy cloud of guilt and anxiety that was becoming my constant companion followed me around all day Thursday. The only respites were moments during lunch with Melanie and during Art, and also in choir after school when I was distracted enough to forget it for a few seconds or even minutes. But it was there, lurking.

Mr. Tanaka asked for volunteers to come up with choreography for a couple of the songs and I was surprised when Ben raised his hand excitedly. Hannah and Paola also formed a part of the group, and they all made arrangements after class to start working on it during lunch periods. Our first performance was in about a month.

On Friday, Hannah and Paola and three other people that I didn't really know, two girls and one boy, joined Ben on the grass with us, making our group much bigger and noisier than usual. It was fine as long as everyone was eating and brainstorming how the lyrics of songs could be physically interpreted, but when they stood up and started executing moves, Robin and I felt safer retreating to one of the tables where there was room for us. Matthew, who had been sitting at the other table with most of our regular group, including Dave, came over and sat next to me.

"So, you remember it's my birthday next week, right?" he said, with a hopeful smile.

"Oh yeah," said Robin with a mouth full of sandwich.

"It's just at my house again. Kind of lame for a sixteenth birthday, I guess, but . . . you know. . . ."

He seemed apologetic and I searched his face for clues as to why. I found none. "I don't think it's lame," I said. "It was fun . . . last year."

"I'm glad you thought so," he said, smiling.

But I was already distracted by thinking about what it had been like last year and *why* it had ended up being really fun—at least for me. I looked toward Dave just as Matthew reached out to move a strand of hair that had blown across my eyes. I tried to smile at him but could still see Dave. He was looking our way now; in fact, he had stopped chewing for a second and was watching us too intently, making me squirm inside. Matthew turned his head to follow my gaze and the two guys regarded each other for a moment. Matthew frowned and shook his head slightly, then turned his shoulder toward Dave, leaning his arm on the table, head in hand, effectively cutting off the line of sight between us.

So *that* weirdness still seemed to be there.

Just before the bell rang after lunch, Paola ran over to Dave.

"*Disculpe, Dah-veed,*" she said, quite loudly. She said more in Spanish that I couldn't follow, then, "*. . . en la biblioteca?*"

Dave said, "Yeah, of course. I'll meet you there later."

I couldn't see his face, but I could see Roberta's. I wondered if her sour expression was what my face looked like most of the time these days. I hoped not—it wasn't at all attractive.

"So . . ." Matthew's voice brought me back to the subject at hand.

Um . . . right. Party. Pool. Next Saturday.

"Oh, I think . . . probably. I probably can." I couldn't think of any reason that would prevent me. My parents both liked Matthew, especially Dad.

We went our separate ways to our next classes—PE for me—and I later tried to concentrate on homework in Study Hall but kept picturing Paola and Dave in the library.

Copper

Maybe they're sitting where I used to meet with him. Maybe he's sitting next to her. Then I'd chastise myself—*It's none of your business!* And then I'd picture Dave's expression as he watched Matthew, an expression I could never read. And *then* I'd imagine Paola talking to him so easily, so animatedly, and his relaxed rapport with her.

My heart hurt, but I felt something else, too. Something as nebulous as it was sinister. Something I couldn't put a name to but was feeling more and more and with growing intensity. Something I really didn't want to look at too closely but was finding hard to ignore.

Dad came home very early Saturday morning. He slept in, and when he was up, he brought his coffee outside to hang out with Remmy and me. Well, probably mostly just me. I'd already warmed Remmy up in my makeshift, fenceless arena and was working on my aids for lateral work. I could get him to do a nice shoulder in at the walk. And our side pass was very good, though that was something he'd probably already learned from Dave.

"He's looking good," said Dad, "and so are you. Have you been to Bar 8 lately?"

"I had a lesson last Saturday, and I'm going this afternoon too," I said, glad he'd brought the subject up. "But . . . remember Melanie? She can give me lessons too. English. Dressage. I really want to learn. I brought some forms home from the equestrian center. She's an instructor trainee and will be certified next year, but she's been riding and teaching for a long time already."

Dad looked gratifyingly impressed and nodded his head. "I think that would be great for you. I'm sure we can work something out."

I smiled, glad he seemed so open to the idea of me spending even more time—and, I supposed, more money—on horses and riding, especially given his previous hesitation to let me ride at all. But I was also very aware of the whole Northfield/Caldera connection. Or rather, *dis*connection. A part of me was okay with that and agreed it would be good for me, for many reasons. But the part of me that still couldn't let go of Dave, to let go of the relationship that seemed to be gone, resented that Dad was so transparent about it.

Later in the day, we looked over the personal information and liability release forms to not only take lessons at the equestrian center but to ride and enter shows there. That was immensely exciting to me.

I still had trouble sleeping that night, and when I did, I had my old dream—Gold being led away and me trying to run after him. But this time it was different. One moment it was Gold being led away, the next it was Dave walking away, his arm around the waist of a girl, though it wasn't obvious who it was. I tried to call out to him, but I choked, my voice getting caught in my throat. My heart was breaking. I was sure if I could just get to him, somehow things would be okay. I tried to move forward, to go after him, but I was held fast by someone behind me. When I turned, it was my father and the dream immediately changed. I was at Northfield riding Digs. If I hadn't woken up right then, I probably wouldn't have remembered the previous part at all. It seemed like a long time since I'd had that dream, but it made me feel haunted, as if I'd had it many times in exactly that way but just hadn't remembered it on waking.

On Sunday afternoon Ben walked over to see Dad. I sat on the porch as they talked. He'd mowed the front and back yards twice since Dad had been gone and had weeded and dug up the ground around the front and south side of the house. He'd worked on it mostly on the weekends, but he had come and gone without any fuss. I was usually in my room at the back of the house or out with Remmy, and I wasn't always aware of him being there. Dad was pleased with what he'd done and gave him a hundred dollars. Ben seemed thrilled.

"Would you like to stay for dinner, Ben?" Mom stood in the open doorway.

"Oh . . . uh, thanks," he said, looking from her to my dad then to me and back and forth between dad and me a couple of times more.

Dad's expression was benign; he seemed to really like Ben. I tried to mirror his expression but wasn't sure if I did. I was surprised that I didn't mind if he stayed.

"I guess that would be okay," he said.

"Do you need to call your parents?" asked Mom.

"Oh, no," he said. "Bill's on the road. Vivian won't mind."

Mom and Dad exchanged looks, and I realized they probably thought it strange he used their first names; they didn't know he lived in a foster home. But I couldn't see why it would matter, and I'd promised not to say anything, so I didn't. My parents went back inside. Ben sat next to me on the porch.

"Your parents are really nice," he said.

I smiled. I thought so too, most of the time.

"So, what do you do . . . you know . . . for fun? You have a horse, right?"

Apparently he hadn't been formally introduced to Remmy, so I led him around the house to the stable.

"Do you ride?" I asked.

"I rode a horse once, a long time ago," he said.

He seemed very nervous when we were close to Remmy. I remembered my first time around horses and how I'd felt, too, though my nervousness had been from excitement for various reasons. He seemed fearful.

"He won't hurt you," I said, stroking Remmy's head and neck.

Ben reached out, gingerly touching Remmy's nose. When Remmy didn't move, he stroked his face a little more boldly. Then he pulled his hand back and stepped away, laughing a little.

"He looks hungry," he said.

I laughed. "He can't be *that* hungry. He would never want to eat *you*."

But Ben seemed to have had his fill of Remmy. We wandered back toward the front of the house, the late September afternoon sun painting everything in dull golds and pale yellows. We sat on the porch again and talked about school, which led to talking about Choir, which led to talking about music in general.

"What do you like to listen to?" he asked.

"All kinds of music," I said, trying to think of specific bands he might know. "I like music you can move to, so I guess I like some pop music. But I don't like all of it. I like music that I can sing along with, and that makes me feel happy. Or sad. I guess I just like music that makes me *feel*. I like some electronic music too. It's great for drawing. It depends on my mood."

Ben nodded. "I guess I like those kinds of music too. I like hip-hop and rap too. I listen mostly when I'm doing my homework."

I looked at him and raised my brows the way Robin did to me when she didn't believe me.

"What? I do homework . . . sometimes."

I laughed and shook my head. "I can't listen when I'm doing homework. Except for art."

"Why?"

"It distracts me. I listen too closely and can't focus on what I'm supposed to be doing."

Ben laughed. "Really? I'm the opposite. I can't focus if I *don't* have music on." That seemed very strange to me. "I listen almost all the time. Especially when Vivian's not home."

He asked me what bands I liked and said he liked them too. I hadn't heard of most of the ones he mentioned.

"Can I hear some?" he asked.

I agreed and led him into the house and up to my room.

"Whoa!" he said, halting at the threshold.

"What?"

"Does your room always look like this?"

I looked around to see what was amiss. "Yes. What's wrong?"

"Very neat," he said, but it seemed to trouble him.

He walked in, toward the corner where I had my still life arranged. He reached toward my hat, hung over an edge of the chair back.

"Don't!"

He jumped and turned wide eyes to me.

"Sorry," I said, more softly. "Don't move those. I'm still working on an art project."

"Really? Let me see!" he said.

So I did.

"You're pretty good, aren't you?" he said.

I sat on the end of my bed, unsure of what to say.

"Why did you do so many drawings of the same thing?"

I shook my head. I didn't have an answer for that either. It was just something I wanted to do.

He moved toward my desk and the rack of CDs, pulled one out and held it up, eyebrows raised. I nodded and he put it in the player. Then he sat on the floor and I joined him. We listened to music and read the lyrics together, talking a little, until Mom called us to dinner.

Ben got Dad to tell him about some of his travels, but I noticed that every time my parents asked him about himself, he turned it back into a question about them. I figured he had his reasons. About seven o'clock, just as Ben and I were helping to clear the table, there was a sharp rap on the front door, and the doorbell rang too. Ben and I both stopped what we were doing and watched as Dad opened the door.

"Good evening," said a male voice. "I'm from down the street there. I was just wondering . . ."

Ben and I both moved to see who was there. It was the red-haired man that I'd seen before. Ben raised his hand and grinned.

"Benjamin," said the man, seriously but not unkindly. "I just got home and didn't know where you were. I thought you might be here." Then he spoke to my dad. "Forgive me, I don't mean to be rude. I'm Bill O'Dell."

He held his hand out, and Dad shook it willingly.

"Greg. Greg Anderson. Ben's been doing some yard work for us. I hope that's all right."

"Yes, that's fine. He'd said something about it which is why I thought I'd check here first. He does have some unfinished business at home, though. Right, Ben?"

He looked meaningfully at Ben as if to jog his memory, but Ben looked unenlightened. I noticed a vague resemblance between them: the fine, straight nose; the wide mouth, impish when smiling; freckling across nose and cheeks, though it was very light on Ben. And Ben's hair was very dark, much darker than Mr. O'Dell's. Ben's eyes were shaped differently and his brows were very dark and straight. Mr. O'Dell's eyes were blue while Ben's were somewhere between green and brown. The shape of Ben's face was different too, more square with almost delicate features and a pointed chin. Mr. O'Dell's face was rounder with an indefinite chin that looked like it might one day succumb to jowls. Still, the resemblance was interesting.

"I guess I've got to go," said Ben. "Thank you for dinner," he said to my mom, who had come out of the kitchen to see who was at the door.

"You're welcome, Ben," she said. "It was nice to finally meet you Mr. . . . O'Dell?"

"Bill. You can call me Bill. I'm afraid I'm on the road a lot. I should have introduced myself long before now. But we'd best be going." He looked at Ben again.

I followed Ben to the door and watched as they walked to Mr. O'Dell's car in the driveway. He was saying something to Ben, but his voice was very soft. Ben turned once and waved, grin impish and eyes laughing.

"Well, it's nice to finally meet one of our other neighbors," said Mom. "Do you know anything about his mother, Allison?"

I hadn't given it any thought after he'd told me he was fostered and obviously hadn't wanted to answer any other questions. I still didn't see much point in telling my parents that though. Ben was Ben, and I was starting to feel pretty comfortable with him. It occurred to me for the first time that we must really be friends, though it had happened so gradually I hadn't realized it.

"No, I don't know anything about her," I said, and finished helping with the dishes.

Dad picked Ben and me up after school the next day. When we turned down our street, Ben said, "I can walk home from your house." When we got there, he seemed to linger a few moments as if he wanted to say something. Dad went into the house. I waited. Then Ben said, "See you tomorrow." He looked a little sheepish, then waved before walking off.

I raised my hand too, wondering at his hesitation. I didn't have much experience with boys—last year was the first time I'd had any consistent dealings with them—but his behavior seemed weird enough for me to compare it against what I thought I knew.

Dave had acted like that with me a few times last year. It had caused me to hope that maybe he *more* than liked me, as hesitation didn't seem to be a normal part of his behavior. But nothing had come of it. I thought of Matthew, but he'd never acted that way with me at all, and even my friends seemed to think he was interested in me. I guessed that kind of hesitation, slight awkwardness, meant something else. Relieved, I went into the house to start on homework.

Dad and I had dinner ready for Mom when she got home.

"You'll never guess who came to the pool today," said Mom brightly.

Once upon a time not so long ago, before I had so many other things on my mind, I would have taken her up on the game and offered suitably ridiculous guesses, or maybe turned it into a game like twenty questions. But right now everything was filtered through varying degrees of angst, and I had no inclination to guess. Dad's eyebrows had gone up slightly, but he didn't seem to want to guess either. Mom's looked slightly disappointed.

"Paola's mother, Rosa Bernal."

I kept my eyes on my plate.

"I'm off on Thursday, so I invited her family to come to dinner."

I glanced at her, shocked, then looked down again quickly. I didn't want her to see the aversion I felt. The hope that the sinister cloud hanging over my life would dissipate any time soon was obliterated.

"I wasn't aware of their situation, how and why they moved here. Were you, Allison?"

I shook my head and played with my food, what little appetite I'd had completely gone.

"Her father . . . Edmundo?" Dad asked. Mom nodded. "He talked about his son. I believe he's a teacher in Cuba, but there was some trouble of a political nature? I think he said he'd met Alex when they were younger, in Spain."

"Yes, they met in boarding school. They've stayed in touch all these years. With Alex's help, the Bernals were able to come here. But it took several years, and they are still concerned about family in Cuba."

I heard the words but wasn't processing them. All I knew was that I was going to somehow sit through a dinner with Paola and whatever else their visit entailed. I wasn't good at that sort of thing at the best of times. Under these conditions, I feared disaster. I excused myself to the kitchen to clear my plate and escaped outside to Remmy.

Tuesday morning Mrs. Ochoa gave me a reminder about getting my school picture taken the next day in the library during Study Hall. I felt more than usually reluctant about having my photo taken. I was having such a hard time coping with dismal thoughts and negative emotions, trying to keep them buried, not daring to examine them too carefully. And I *hated* having to sit and look at a camera. I always wanted to close my eyes or look away. And I doubted I could fake a smile. Difficult under most circumstances; probably impossible now.

And what would be revealed by that picture? Would the ominous cloud hanging over me be at all visible? Would my expression look like the one I'd seen on Roberta's face when Paola was talking to Dave? I had no way of comparing, of course, but I was pretty sure that whatever emotion had caused it was the same one I was feeling now.

Wednesday morning I was almost late again. I changed my clothes several times and fussed over make-up—putting it on a little at a time, hoping it would help the way I looked if not the way I felt, and trying to take some of it off again when it did neither. I wasn't sure which was worse for posterity: my iniquitous heart evident on my face or looking like a sociopathic doll.

Once the make-up was completely off again, I looked unseasonably pale with dark circles under my eyes from lack of sleep. My face looked a little thinner than it had when school first started, too.

I wasn't eating. I'd always had trouble with this anyway, but I *purposefully* wasn't eating, and I knew it was wrong. The problem was, it seemed like the only thing I had any kind of control over—whether I ate or not and how much. I had gained a little weight last year and even more during the summer, which had seemed to be a good thing. But then I'd gradually lost it again as the semester wore on and my daily worries and aggravations exponentially increased. It didn't help that Ben's bad memory now provided me with an excuse. Knowing these things only added to the vague sense of guilt I carried around and reanimated the feelings of inadequacy I thought I'd mostly left behind in freshman year.

I thought about not getting my picture taken. *Just skip it. No big deal.* They'd have one of those generic female-shaped icons where my photo should be in the yearbook. And no one would care. Decades from now people would see it with my name at the side, frown, and try to remember who I was.

'Allison. *You know, that weird girl.*'

'Oh yeah. *Space Cadet. Huh. I don't remember what she looked like . . .*'

"Allison?" Mrs. Ochoa was frowning at me.

It had been one of those black hole days—it had just disappeared, and here we were in Study Hall already.

"Aren't you supposed to be getting your picture taken?"

I sighed. *No getting out of it, I guess.* I looked behind me briefly, toward Ben. He was watching, of course. He smiled widely and pointed to the corners of his mouth with his index fingers. He looked goofy and almost made me smile back. Almost. By the time I arrived at the library, only a few other kids were waiting to have their pictures taken.

"You are getting your picture today also?"

Paola had appeared next to me, smiling.

"Yes." Then I realized that, of course, she hadn't been here the first time the photographer came.

"I have already had my picture taken," she said, still smiling. "I very much look forward to coming to your house tomorrow."

She continued to smile at me, expecting me to say something back, but I couldn't. Not only did I not find appropriate words currently available to me for the situation, I just didn't want to say anything. I couldn't say I looked forward to it too. I was pretty sure that's what was expected of me. But I just couldn't make myself lie about it, and there was nothing else I could think of to say.

"Allison Anderson?"

I looked around at the photographer, who was motioning for me to take my place on the stool, then I turned back to Paola. She lifted a hand and backed away, smile not quite as wide as it had been.

And there was Dave, sitting at a table in plain sight on the other side of the room, watching and obviously waiting for Paola to return. The photographer repeated my name. I sat and did what he told me to, then left the library feeling—nothing; for a few moments just numb. Then feeling *every-thing*. Stupid, lonely, sorry, ugly, longing, clumsy, angry, guilty, hurt. Feelings bombarding me in waves, one after the other and repeating. Horrible.

Just horrible.

The next day was horrible too. I'd slept a little but didn't feel rested. I had, on top of all the other specific anxieties, a feeling of impending doom, as if I was running out of time for something vitally important, but I didn't know what. I kept thinking about summer vacation and how hopeful, how naively optimistic I'd been about the possibility of being more to Dave than just a friend. Those days and nights watching the horizon or the waves or the stars, digging my toes in the sand; imagining him doing the same and feeling cosmically connected to him somehow.

So stupid.

Now I pictured that sand in an hourglass; it was running out, and the glass might never be turned again.

I ate lunch, very distractedly, with Melanie. She was trying to talk to me about lessons and Kitty, but my mind wouldn't stay on topic, and some of the words didn't sink in at all.

"I'm sorry, what?" I asked for probably the third time.

Melanie smiled kindly. "Are you all right? Something's really bothering you, isn't it."

"I'm sorry," I said again, but I really meant it this time.

"You look worried. Actually, you haven't seemed yourself for quite a while. What's going on?"

If I could talk to anyone, it would be Melanie. She was the least connected to Dave and also seemed the least judgmental of anyone I knew. But I didn't know what to say. The only words that came to mind sounded either pathetic or self-condemning. I didn't want to dump either on her.

I tried to smile and shook my head. She played with the silver chain at her neck.

Except for choir after school, Paola and I had no regular classes together so avoiding her was easy. Hannah wasn't quite as easy to avoid. Most of the time she hung out with Paola and some of the other girls. She was usually near Dave too, of course, if he was around. Today she stayed close to Melanie and me during PE.

As the shower bell rang and we headed back to the locker room, she said, "You're going aren't you, Allie? To Matthew's?"

I realized with a stab of guilt that I had forgotten all about it. It was his party on Saturday, and I hadn't gotten him anything.

"Um . . . yes. I think so." It was hard to look beyond today's fears and abstractions.

She smiled brightly. "Oh, good. I was hoping you were."

As with Paola's friendly words yesterday, I had nothing to say in return. This made me feel even worse. Instead, I just nodded and followed Melanie to our PE lockers. Melanie looked at me once or twice, curious. It occurred to me she might not know who Matthew was, but she asked no questions, and I didn't want to explain anything. I avoided looking at either Hannah or Paola in Choir. Their smiles left me feeling unbearably uncomfortable.

Paola called out, "I will see you tonight, Allison," as I was leaving.

I turned back to her and nodded. It was the least I could do.

Dad was there to pick Ben and me up. I had nothing to say on the way home except, "Bye," as Ben and I parted ways. Mom was already cooking. I rode Remmy for about thirty minutes, then fed him, took a shower and changed my clothes, then buried myself in *The Three Musketeers* for comfort.

About six o'clock the doorbell rang. I slowly closed my book, avoided looking in my mirrors, took a deep breath, and headed downstairs determined to at least be polite. Paola beamed when she saw me descending the stairs. Why couldn't she act more neutral? Her excess made my deficiency feel so pronounced. There was just no way I could match her affability. I couldn't fake it. I probably wouldn't even if I could.

I said hello to Paola's parents, who said they remembered seeing me at the work day and play day, and how Paola had been so impressed by my riding and had told them all about my joining choir, too. I felt myself blush, but it wasn't from pleasure. *Why did she want to talk about me?* I couldn't remember even mentioning her to my parents—or anyone else.

The dark cloud that I'd been trying to fend off found all the chinks in my flimsy armor and descended, enveloping me. It took every ounce of control I had to force a small smile. Mom excused herself to the kitchen, and I was going to follow her—to help of course—but Rosa had followed her too, and Paola wasn't far behind. The kitchen felt suddenly very crowded. When my dad and Mr. Bernal also came in and crossed through to the back door, I indicated to Paola that we should follow them.

My dad was explaining how we'd moved from Los Angeles and this was the first home they'd ever bought. I led Paola down to Remmy.

"Ah!" she said.

His face had appeared over his stall door to see who was coming. He was still munching on his dinner, but he waited for us to reach him and allowed Paola to stroke his nose before returning to his hay.

"¡Es muy hermoso! También es amigable, ¿verdad?"

I basically understood what she'd said, that Remmy was both beautiful and friendly, but was surprised she had spoken only Spanish to me. Her English was becoming better and better and, except for a slight difference in accent and syntax sometimes, she was starting to sound very American. I knew why, too.

"I'm sorry," she said, looking at me closely. "I thought you would understand. I can help you—"

"I understood," I said. I didn't want to sound terse, but I think I did. "Remmy is very . . . good." I added, "And kind." He was so much more than that, but I didn't feel like elaborating.

"You have had him a long time?" she asked, and I realized that she didn't know how I'd gotten him.

A part of me wanted to tell her, not so that she would understand there was a connection between Dave and me, but because I wanted to hear the words myself. But the last thing I wanted to do right now was talk about Dave. *No, the last thing I want is to hear Paola talk about him.*

"No," I said after a moment, "not very long."

Mom spared me any more prevarication by calling us all in to dinner. I was relieved. The adults would keep up adequate conversation from now on, I was sure. I wasn't expecting to have to pay much attention, but the first topic was hard to ignore.

"How are you adjusting to school, Paola?" asked Mom. "Is it very different?"

Paola admitted that it was quite different. She had gone to a public school but had to wear a uniform, like I had in private school. She also took extra classes in English and gymnastics. "It is different, but I like it here very much."

"Alejandro's son, David, has been most kind and helped her so much," said Edmundo.

"And Hannah!" added Paola.

"*Sí!*" said Rosa. "Hannah Liu. *Una chica tan dulce.*"

I sank a little lower in my chair.

"I believe we met her father at the Calderas'," said Mom, looking at Dad for corroboration. He nodded. "But her mother wasn't there."

A sad look came over Rosa's face. She spoke in Spanish and her husband translated for her. "No, her mother has died . . . only last year, I think." More Spanish. "Yes, late last summer, I am sure."

My mother made a suitable reply, and they talked about Hannah for a few minutes. I wasn't processing the information well. It was as if they were talking about someone I didn't know at all. Dad changed the subject first, and I was glad.

"So what are your plans now? You're here to stay, right?"

"Yes," said Mr. Bernal, "but we have unfinished business in Cuba concerning Rosa's brother. In fact, we will go next week to speak to the Ambassador in Washington, DC."

"And Claudio, our son," interrupted Rosa with a concerned expression.

"He is still there," said Mr. Bernal.

"Yes, you were telling me a little about that before," said Mom. "He's a teacher?"

"Yes. He *was* teaching," said Mr. Bernal, and Rosa made an affirmative sound. "It is . . . complicated. My wife's brother, Raymón, who worked on a government farm, became involved with members of a dissident group many years ago. He gave them some food and supplies, but swore he did not know who they were.

"Unfortunately, one of his own people, one of the men who worked with him, betrayed him," he continued. "Soon Raymón was under investigation by the government. He got word to us because he was afraid. And then he was arrested and imprisoned for aiding them.

"I knew what would come next," said Mr. Bernal, "so I wrote to Alejandro Caldera. We had attended secondary school together in Seville and became good friends there. We had tried to keep in touch over the years and had often spoken of meeting again but had never managed to do so. He could not easily enter Cuba, and it was even harder for me to leave. But finally I was able to leave for a short business trip and was able to visit him. While I was here in the United States, I was able to make some contacts with Alejandro's help that would help me get a job. Between Alejandro's sponsorship and with the guarantee of employment, I was able to get the visa process started.

"But it took a long time. That was years ago. As soon as I returned to Cuba, I found my trip was under investigation and my son, Claudio, also. I'm sure our connection to Raymón has much to do with it. Claudio was at a small university teaching history. The police seemed determined to find something against him, and we were worried. We know that he has democratic leanings and often talked of these things at home. We were afraid even though we knew he had never done anything against the government. We wanted him to come with us, to come to the United States and be able to teach freely, without fear, but it was no good. They went so far as to interrogate some of his students. And they took his computer."

That didn't sound good, but from the way Mr. Bernal said it and the look he exchanged with his wife, it was obviously far worse.

"He had some correspondence . . . *innocent* correspondence . . . with a friend, someone he had gone to school with. He was a librarian. This friend," Mr. Bernal looked at his wife again, "he had been watched for some time. He was suspected of having ties to democratic groups. It made the conversations Claudio had with him appear to have anti-regime sympathies. Claudio was detained and then suspended from the university. We were afraid he would lose his position . . . or worse."

"He is now waiting," Rosa said, haltingly, and lapsed into Spanish again. Mr. Bernal translated, "to see if he can return to his position, but they watch him very closely. We want him to leave, to join us here, but now it is even more difficult, and he says he will not go."

"We are going to the embassy next week, mainly to see what we can do for Rosa's brother. We are hoping to be able to get him released to join the rest of their family, who are now in Barcelona. Unfortunately, we must go to Washington, DC. Paola will have to miss some school."

"She can stay here," said Mom, jolting me out of the Bernals' story.

I had heard everything that they'd said and had tried to picture it, like a movie, but it hadn't sunk in as real. What my mother had just said seemed *too* real.

"We have a spare room," she continued. "Paola is welcome to stay with us until you return."

Paola . . . stay here?

My dark cloud was now aided by a miasma, chipping away at my incompetent armor from the inside. Soon there would be gaping holes. More than anything, I feared its unleashing. Once let loose, I was sure I'd have no control over it. My toes, fingertips, lips, and temples felt burning cold, icy hot, throbbing, numb. My ears were ringing more than I could ever remember. My eyes were stinging from the light, from unsheddable tears, from the very air around me.

I had felt this way before many times—completely overwhelmed, overly stressed, ultra-sensitive to my surroundings—but never so close to what I suspected could be a violent explosion. I needed to leave but how could I? No one would understand. *I* didn't understand.

The adults were still discussing matters, but my own personal noise drowned them out. Out of the corner of my eye, I was aware of Paola eating her dessert very slowly, silently cutting the apple pie into small pieces with her fork. I realized I was just staring at mine.

She seemed to be trying not to draw attention to herself.

I wished I could completely disappear.

I was aware of my father frowning at me, and it wasn't a frown that meant he was concerned about how I was *feeling*. Mom was enjoying the conversation, but she finally noticed me *not* eating the apple pie, my favorite. I had barely touched dinner. Now she was watching me, too, but trying to appear not to. She gave me a couple of meaningful glances. I avoided looking at either of them. It felt like I was hanging on to the edge of a waterfall, the noise in my head like surging water drowning out their words. I was hoping they'd see me hanging there and, if not help me to safer ground, at least not push me over into the abyss.

Mom threw me a lifeline. "Let's go sit in the living room and I'll bring some coffee. Allison, come and help me in the kitchen." Rosa and Paola both started picking up dishes as if to help too, but Mom said, "Please, go and relax. We'll be right there."

They smiled and agreed. We gathered up the dishes and retreated to the kitchen. As soon as we had set the dishes in the sink, Mom started a fresh pot of coffee, then turned to me and said, her voice lowered, "Okay, what's the matter?"

The roaring in my ears had already dissipated slightly, and I heard her just fine, but I didn't know what to say.

"Why don't you take Paola to your room? You can listen to music or something."

Alone with Paola—not a circumstance I was comfortable with, especially not right now, and mostly for her sake. I shook my head. "Can I just stay here and do the dishes?" I asked quietly.

"Allison, what's going on? Have you had a fight of some kind?" When I said nothing, she frowned. "I thought you and Paola were friends."

"We haven't had a fight," I said.

"You know, Paola had told her mother about you . . . how you're also friends with the Calderas, especially Dave, and now in choir together, too. Rosa was certainly under the impression that you were friends. That's why

I invited them to dinner. That's why I suggested Paola stay with us while her parents go and see how they can help her uncle and maybe her brother, too. I thought it would be a good opportunity to get to know her better."

Mom stood looking at me; it was obviously my turn to speak, but I had nothing to say. Not out loud anyway. The internal noise was increasing again and pressure and pain were growing behind my eyes.

"I don't feel very well. May I go to my room?" I asked quietly.

Mom looked at me seriously for a few moments more. "No, I think you need to stick this out. It would be very rude of you to go to your room while we have guests. This isn't like you at all. We'll have a talk later."

I hated it when my dad was mad at me, which was almost never. Last year had set some kind of record for that. But I couldn't remember my mother ever looking this unhappy with me, even when I hadn't told them about Gold, and about the Caldera brothers, and even though she had been really upset with me over the barrel racing incident. Those had been because she was worried about me. This seemed like something else.

Mom gave me a small jug of cream and the sugar bowl to take out and followed me with cups of fresh coffee. I turned to Paola and quietly but as politely as I could, said, "Would you like something to drink? We have grape juice or apple juice or . . ." I wasn't sure what else we had. I drank mostly water.

Paola smiled at me and said, even more politely, "Oh, no! But thank you very much for asking."

Now I felt like a complete jerk but didn't know what to do about it. The roaring in my head had diminished again, but I really did have a headache and felt exhausted. The skin on my face felt pulled tight as if my skull was trying to escape it. It still felt like I could explode at any moment. I tried to respond appropriately whenever I was spoken to but otherwise continued to hold on to my cliff edge as calmly and securely as I could. Paola tried to make conversation with me a couple of times, but I have no memory of what she said or what I answered.

At last Rosa said, "I think we should be going."

Dad and Edmundo shook hands, and my mom and Paola's mom hugged.

"I will see you tomorrow, Allison," said Paola, but she didn't sound convinced.

I just nodded, assuming she was literally correct but not at all sure about actual interaction.

My parents followed them out to their car, and I escaped to my room. I didn't even turn on my light but closed the door and sat on my bed in the dark, feeling immediate relief as the stress began to dissipate slightly, enough to relieve my headache. With my eyes closed, I tried to empty my mind, but I'd never been good at that. So I thought about Remmy standing out in his paddock. Or perhaps he was in his stall, his head over the door, looking toward the house. Or maybe he was lying down in the shavings. I imagined what it would be like out there sitting with him, *leaning against his shoulder, stroking his coat, burying my face in his neck, his mane—*

A soft knock on the door then Mom's voice, "Allison, I'd like to talk to you."

The *last* thing I wanted to do right now was talk about anything, but I reached forward far enough to open the door then sat back on my bed again. Mom stood in the doorway, a black form cut-out with the light from the landing behind filtering into my room around her. It reminded me of the negative space exercises we'd done last year in Art.

"I know you don't care for company, that people make you nervous sometimes, and I don't expect you to be entertaining. But I do expect you to be polite. Paola seems like a very nice girl, and I think she'd like to be your friend. Just because you made good friends last year isn't a reason to reject others. You should be thankful and remember what it feels like to be in a new school and not know anyone. I know it's never been easy for you . . . to make real friends . . . but you have to be open to them. You have to try. Is there something I don't know? Some reason you feel you can't be friends with her?"

I tried to pull together all the things I felt about Paola, but my mind wasn't synthesizing at the moment. It was still relatively shut down and comfortable out in the stable with Remmy.

"I know Paola is different from you in many ways and perhaps you don't have much in common, but I never would have expected any kind of differences to matter to you. I'm disappointed in you," she said, and I could see from her shadowed expression and hear it in her voice that she really was.

I felt guilty and sick but wasn't entirely sure why. And I had nothing to say in my defense. How could I explain about Dave? What was there to tell? Nothing. There was nothing.

But her words confused me, too. Paola different? Maybe because Spanish was her first language? But that made her no different from Angel, who I loved.

I was the one who was different. I'd never really understood completely how or why but knew it to be true. It was what made it so difficult to read and understand people, to recognize motives or see social interactions from their perspectives. The little things that seemed so important to everyone else, the things that other people seemed to be able to easily read and comprehend, I often misinterpreted or just missed completely.

It wasn't a lack of empathy. I often felt things too strongly; physical things and life events I usually understood and, historically, was far more affected by for the sake of others than for myself. Someone once said it was something about the way my brain worked. It was probably why watching or even envisioning others in dangerous situations, especially people I cared about, affected me so much on a physical as well as emotional level. I was prone to emotional and sensory overload and, except for some vague, imperfect coping strategies, there wasn't much I could do about it.

So I puzzled over Mom's words as I got ready for bed—quietly and slowly—still feeling very wrong and now totally exhausted. I still hadn't turned my bedroom light on, but on returning to my room, I took matches out of my bedside table and lit the candle Robin had given me last year. I hadn't lit it in a very long time.

I thought of the other girls in Dave's life, the ones I felt had replaced me. Paola: effervescent and sweet, undeniably pretty, petite. Hannah: slim and graceful, gentle and also pretty, even stunning when she wore make-up. Both girls had never been anything but kind and considerate to me. Why was it so hard to like them? There were a lot of other girls, too, I didn't even know the names of most of them, and Dave was always unfailingly pleasant and attentive to them, though he didn't seem to pay any more attention to one than another. And then there was Roberta. I didn't even like thinking about Roberta. She was as tall as I was, blonde, attractive, athletic, and obviously strong-willed. She knew how to influence people and get what she wanted. I especially couldn't stand thinking about her and Dave together.

And then it hit me. I was jealous. Not just a little jealous. Not like last year, when I realized I was a bit jealous of Cris with Gold. No, this was storm-cloud, ugly-thought, green-eyed, mind-melting, heart-breakingly jealous. I'd never felt this way before—not about *anything*—and I didn't know what to do about it. Last year I'd had to deal with the other girls at school, a few of

whom had gone out of their way to make me feel bad, but many more who'd watched me in a way I couldn't understand. Until now.

Now I was one of them, and that realization cut me to the core, not just because I was admitting to my inferior place in Galaxy Dave, but because now I really hated myself. And now, maybe, I knew what they had felt.

It's one thing to recognize and accept if not embrace your limitations, but completely another to admit to such a destructive flaw. I could hear Robin's voice. *"Some girls are just drawn to what they can't have, I guess."* She had been talking about Cris' fans, but didn't that describe me with Dave, too? Pathetic. I'd always known it, but now I hated it. It wasn't how I wanted to be.

Tears ran down my face, and I wasn't going to stop them. I'd bottled this up all semester, refusing to give in or look at it closely. Instead, I had let it fester. I wanted it out. *Now.*

I forced myself to continue thinking about the girls.

Paola, whose parents had fled the country of their birth, leaving a brother in prison and a son in danger. And for what? For giving food to hungry people? For having and sharing independent thoughts? Paola must be so worried about them, especially about her brother, yet she never let it show. She never took it out on anyone.

Now I was really crying.

Hannah, whose mother had died so recently. I had envied her last year when she got to dance with Dave in PE and had shared "Best Smile" in the yearbook, but I hadn't felt this overwhelming jealousy. That had begun to grow on the first day of school *this* year. Now I knew that she and Dave had been classmates for a long time. They'd grown up together like he and Robin had. They were comfortable with each other. Their fathers were friends. I'd been sure she wasn't at the Caldera's rodeo last year. It must have been shortly after her mother had died. It occurred to me that she and Dave shared that heartbreak, too—the loss of their mothers. I thought of my own mother and how I would feel if she died.

I cried harder.

I knew nothing about Roberta except that she was smart enough to be in more than one AP class and therefore shared a lot of Dave's classes. She was a cheerleader and very athletic. Now I could see how much she and Dave really did have in common. And she hated me. She herself hadn't overtly done anything to me this year, but she was one of the jealous ones last year. *Ugly* jealous.

And that's why I didn't want to think about her. I didn't want to *be* her. It was easier to dislike Hannah and Paola and be passive aggressive with them than to have to compare myself to Roberta. And I thought Roberta was more attractive than me and obviously more likely to have a real relationship with Dave. She was *exactly* the kind of girl Dad had said he thought Dave should be concentrating on. Maybe my dad had been right all along.

And if that is true, then it must also be true that he really is no good for me. And I'd be no good for him.

I don't want to feel this way anymore. . . .

I allowed myself to dissolve completely. Every horrible thought, every angry, jealous feeling—I wanted them gone. If loving Dave—no, *desiring* Dave—caused me to be this way, then I had to learn how to *un*-desire him. I was sure I could never not love him. I still felt it would take mountains falling into the sea or stars falling from the sky for that to happen. It would take much more than Roberta to make me believe him less perfect than I'd ever thought him, or less worthy of love. No, I would love him forever and die unmarried and unfulfilled. An old maid. I was sure of it.

That made me feel lonely—being so sure it was impossible I could ever feel the same way about someone else—but not half as hopelessly lonely as the thought of not even being Dave's friend. Last year I'd been mostly unsatisfied with mere friendship. Now I would give anything to have it again.

I found myself pleading, trying to make deals with an unknown supreme being.

Please forgive me. Please make me better . . . a better person. Please, please, please let Dave be my friend again. Just friends. I'll do anything. . . .

I sobbed my heart out for what felt like hours.

The thing is, if anyone had ever asked me if I believed in God—a specific entity who actually cared about the human race in general—I would have said yes. That opinion was not based on any research I'd done, in-depth discussions or revelatory experiences I'd had, or family traditions. It was just there.

But I also imagined God a little like my Grandma and Grandpa—people who cared about me in the big picture but weren't in the immediacy of my life. And they had been there much more—more *tangibly*—when I was very young.

I vaguely remembered Grandma cooking and cleaning, but it was Grandpa who had fostered my love of language, reading, and words in general. They had most often been the ones to babysit me while both my parents worked, but as I grew older they became more distant, Grandpa preferring the more boisterous company of his grandsons, and Grandma thinking me a "strange child" and finding it difficult to relate to me at all.

God seemed like that. I had accepted his existence as a small child—that he was there somewhere watching over me—and took it for granted. But as I grew, he seemed more and more removed from the reality of my life and, if he really existed, less interested in me. He probably thought me a strange child too.

Now I found myself torn and bleeding inside and it was by my own hand. No one had done this to me. But I didn't know how to stop the hurting; how to stop ripping myself to shreds emotionally. How to stop everything. The jealousy that I'd allowed to dominate my thoughts and feelings since August, had completely taken over not only my emotions but whatever I had left of logic.

The girls I'd come to dislike so intensely had done nothing to deserve my hatred, and it was doubly devastating to realize that it was indeed something like hatred that my jealousy had turned into. *Hatred!* Even Roberta, who I knew looked down her nose at me and I was sure was involved in actions against me, didn't deserve my hatred. I didn't have to *like* her, but I could see that the way I felt about these girls was destructive—not to them but to me.

I really hated myself.

And why? Because of a boy. A boy who, wonderful though I still believed him to be, didn't return my depth of feeling. I had allowed myself, deep down, to become just like all the other girls that vied with each other for his attention, even though outwardly I had not. I was just as bad as any of those girls who had hated and been jealous of me last year. And my heart was breaking, not so much over lost love and the longing to be physically desirable and close to him, but over the loss of the friendship I knew we'd shared. I had to face the fact that it was gone.

I prayed and cried as I hadn't cried since Gold had been taken away and the memory of *that* loss exacerbated the deeper longing I felt now. I didn't allow myself to think about the other important aspect of the day that Gold left, the memory that had been so dear to me and that I had drawn on for almost a year now.

No, I couldn't let myself think of that—or anything like it—ever again.

As exhaustion and my guttering candle won out over misery, and I began to slip into sleep, my mind landed back on my mother's parting words: *'I'm disappointed in you.'*

I pictured Paola, her beautiful smile, bright eyes, and bubbly personality, and only one thing occurred to me.

Chapter Fourteen

I awoke remembering a new dream, no doubt influenced by my directed thoughts of Remmy the night before. In the dream, I was in a stall with him, but it wasn't *his* stall. I didn't recognize it but thought it might be in Heaven. Outside was storming but inside was warm and dry. Remmy was lying down, curled up in very deep wood shavings, more like they had at Northfield, and I was curled up against him, my hand on his warm coat, feeling safe. That's all. Now that I was awake, I felt tired but calm and clearheaded. I felt comforted too, even though I clearly remembered everything I'd thought and felt from the day before.

I got up and went downstairs to feed Remmy and eat something myself, then went through the motions of getting ready for school. Yesterday I had agonized so much over what to wear for my pictures that I didn't even want to think about it today—*any* of it. I grabbed the closest pair of pants in my closet, which happened to be an old pair of brown pants I now only ever wore to play with Remmy. They were still dusty from the last two afternoons, smelled vaguely of horse, and had suspicious green stains along the hems. I didn't care. I opened a drawer and pulled out the first clean t-shirt. It didn't coordinate at all with my pants, but I didn't care about that either.

Then the sense of calm started to dissipate and I began to feel nervous. I put my contacts in, brushed my teeth, and began brushing my hair smooth as had become my habit since cutting it. It had already grown out quite a bit and was well below my shoulders.

My stomach churned and I found it suddenly hard to breathe. The calm had gone, and all I felt now was loss. Numbing loss, like after Gold had left—no, even *before* he had left—but this was even worse, threatening to overwhelm me again.

I'd always known that Gold wasn't mine and I'd never seriously entertained the idea that I could possibly keep him. And he had been taken away by others. If he could, he might have chosen to stay with me. That bond was intact, though he was thousands of miles away in a new loving home.

This was different. I was making myself give up on Dave, and no matter how unlikely it had seemed, I *had* allowed myself to fantasize about him. Being with him. Loving him. Being loved by him. This was an even more challenging dream to let go of; the most difficult thing I'd ever done. And unlike with Gold, I had to do this all by myself. There were no friends to comfort me because no one else knew.

Looking at myself in the mirror, I felt ugly. The more I brushed and smoothed my hair, the uglier I felt until tears were streaming down my face. That just made me mad at myself. I thought I'd finished with this—this self-pity. I also wanted to be finished with caring about impressing anyone. I began brushing my hair back roughly, smoothing it back over the top of my head and gathering it into my left hand. I thought briefly about braiding it but decided against it. It would feel like I was trying to recapture something that was gone. *I can't let myself do that. Not anymore. This is me moving forward.*

I found the pink and gold scrunchy Robin had given me last year and left my hair in a high ponytail, the way I wore it when I worked around Remmy at home. The scrunchy didn't match my clothes either and I was glad. Then I went back into my bedroom, took my contacts out, and put my glasses on. The black framed ones.

The girl looking back at me now was not the same girl that had her picture taken yesterday, but neither was she the same girl she'd been last year. This was the girl who cared about her friends and loved her horse. This was the girl that Remmy loved. And that was good enough.

And I'm going to let it be good enough. . . .

I wasn't looking forward to school, exactly, but I wanted to go. I was glad that Dad took me instead of Mom, though. I remembered what she probably

thought and didn't feel up to discussing it. I knew it wasn't true, and while it made me very sad that she might think that of me, it could wait.

I'd grown up listening to my dad's stories about all kinds of people, and he had never ridiculed or put anyone down—certainly not for things like the color of their skin, their religion, or their nationality. And businessmen from all over the world had come to dinner at our home when we lived in Los Angeles. I sometimes have trouble telling people apart and recognizing people I don't know well, like Jessie and Stacie last year. So I've learned to notice external details. But I don't usually differentiate between exteriors to be critical. I was sure Mom would understand when I had a chance to explain. I just had to figure out how much I wanted to tell her.

Matthew sat down next to me in chemistry, looking expectant. "Are you coming?"

My heart sank. *I'm such a horrible friend!* I'd completely forgotten about his birthday. Again. It was today and the party was tomorrow. *This day's not off to a good start.*

"Happy birthday!" I said as sincerely and enthusiastically as I could. I think I even managed a real smile for him, but I was also stalling.

He smiled back "Thanks. But are you coming?"

"Um . . . yes. I think so. I'm pretty sure."

I felt so bad. I'd been so wrapped up in my own problems and distractions I hadn't even asked if I could go. Under normal circumstances, I wouldn't have doubted it. But after last night I wasn't so sure. Also, Dave and Matthew didn't seem as close as they'd been last year, but they were obviously still friends. I was sure Dave would be there, but I couldn't let that stop me from going. Matthew was my friend too. Besides, I couldn't let Dave's presence or opinions influence any of my decisions. *Not anymore.*

Matthew seemed pleased at the prospect of my going on Saturday.

"And you can stay longer, right? And really swim? You know, with appropriate swim attire this time?"

That might have made me blush if it wasn't Matthew saying it. Instead, it made me laugh. I didn't let myself think about the incident he was referring to though.

"Yes, and yes," I said, glad to make him happy but also wondering who else would be there.

"I'm sure we could give you a ride if your parents can't bring you. I'd pick you up myself," he said, looking slightly self-conscious, "but my license will only be provisional, and I won't get it until next week."

"That's right," I said, sidestepping the party issue. "You'll be able to drive. That's great."

"Yep. It opens up all kinds of possibilities."

He looked at me again, very directly, and I looked away quickly, not wanting to read into it at all. If there was a deeper meaning behind the words, I didn't want to know. Not now.

Class started and Ms. Wright began talking. Matthew leaned over and whispered, "Noon to . . . you know . . ."

I nodded.

As we walked to history together, he told me about his car, which he sounded very proud of. I guessed driving was something I really needed to ask my parents about, in spite of my ophthalmologist's warning. I wouldn't know until I tried.

After class, we walked out to the tables together. The atmosphere there was light-hearted today—it was Friday, it was Matthew's birthday, and a lot of people were talking about the party tomorrow. It was also the second day of October. The days were noticeably shorter and the nights were getting chillier, though the weather remained dry and hot during the day. Still, the season was changing, and that seemed to affect everyone.

Matthew insisted that Robin and me sit with him at one of the tables. It was uncomfortable sitting so close to specific *other* people. And as Matthew was the center of much of the attention today, I was in the middle of most of the conversation.

Robin, Tanner, Jessie, Kyle, and Stacie were going to the party. Last year there had also been a lot of people I didn't know, mostly Matthew's friends from the soccer and swim teams. Dave was a given, but I couldn't tell from anything said or from their expressions whether Paola, Hannah, or Roberta were invited. I tried and mostly succeeded not to care.

The conversation eventually turned to cars. Matthew's new Honda CR-Z was discussed, of course, in deference to the occasion. Tanner would get his license soon and could drive his mom's car when she didn't need it, but he'd still get around mostly by skateboard. Jessie was getting a new car, her parents being very well off. Kyle was teased, again, for being the youngest.

He wouldn't be sixteen until January, after my birthday, but Stacie made up for it by holding up and dangling her set of keys. Kyle grinned and wagged his brows.

"Are your parents okay with you driving this guy around?" asked Matthew.

"My parents are fine. It's *his* parents that have the problem."

Several people laughed, but I thought she looked serious and Kyle's expression supported the observation. I wondered if it was just typical parental concern; Stacie was just a little older than Kyle but seemed *much* more mature. Kyle's family was apparently much more affluent than Stacie's. And, given my own mother's apparent assumption last night, it could be something else entirely. They seemed to belong together but, considering recent experiences, perhaps not everyone would think so.

"Well, this time next month, I'll be driving my Mustang," said Robin with a wide smile. Then it faded. "If I can afford gas. Ugh. I need to get a job." She sighed and slumped forward, her chin on her arm. There was a general murmur of empathy.

I had been listening to them but mostly watched Ben, Hannah, Paola, and the other choir kids working on their choreography over on the grass, keeping my eyes averted from Dave at the other end of the table. They were at the putting-it-together stage now, and Ben was emerging as something of a creative leader, though a rather goofy one. I envied his apparent lack of self-consciousness. They looked like they were having so much fun, but sometimes Hannah glanced wistfully in our direction. I wondered if she was wishing she was closer to Dave. I hadn't looked in his direction once and had heard his voice a little but not much. I also knew that Roberta was right next to him. Her voice was more constant.

"What about you, Caldera?" said Matthew. "Are you going to just keep driving that old ugly beast you call a truck? Or are you getting something new and shiny for your birthday too?"

I could picture Dave's truck parked under the trees by his house, an older model Chevy patched with gray primer. Everyone turned to look at Dave. I finally did, too.

"Ugly beast, huh? Nothing wrong with my truck," was all he seemed to feel needed saying. But there was a smirk on his face, a very slight one, like the ones I'd seen on Cris once or twice. I didn't know about the others, but I had a good idea what it meant and wondered what he was thinking.

"So, what about *your* birthday," Matthew persisted. "Big plans?"

Dave looked steadily at him, which included me just beyond. His gaze moved from Matthew to me and back to steadily regard Matthew again. Then he looked down and shrugged. "Haven't decided."

"I can't wait!" said Roberta, very clearly.

The conversation shifted to soccer and football.

"What about you?" asked Matthew.

"Oh . . . I don't . . . I haven't," I shook my head slightly. "Sports. . . ."

Matthew laughed. "Yeah, I know. We've had that discussion. I still think you should try out for the swim team. But I was really referring back to driving and cars."

"Oh!" I said, then thought it was funny because my response would be basically the same, *'I don't . . . I haven't,' head shake. 'Cars. . . .'* but I tried to form a coherent sentence instead. "My birthday's not until January. I haven't started diving yet." I wondered if it appeared too odd to not be concerned about it. And no need to mention my still imperfect eyesight and spatial awareness.

When the bell rang, I took my time moving away from the table, giving Dave, Roberta, and the others a chance to get well ahead of me. Matthew stayed behind too.

"So . . . you're going to *try* to come tomorrow, right?"

In spite of everything else on my mind, his insistence made me smile. "Yes, I'll do my best," I said.

Dave, walking up ahead with Roberta, looked over his shoulder and turned to walk backward. It had been a long time since I'd seen him do that and it caused me a momentary pang. I willfully quelled it. *No reminiscing. . . .*

"Hey! Are we getting coffee later?" he called loudly. "You know, the last walk into town before you're driving everywhere?" He was obviously talking to Matthew, but he was definitely, unnervingly, looking at me.

"Yeah, sure," returned Matthew, just as loudly. "Are you buying?"

"Yeah. It can be your birthday present."

"You're too generous."

Dave regarded us a moment longer, his expression unreadable to me. I looked away, and when I looked back, he'd turned back around and appeared to be listening to Roberta as they crossed the quad.

"Are you up for coffee after school?" asked Matthew.

Somewhere deep inside, a small part of me—the part that would probably always long for Dave's affection—wanted to say yes. But the part of me that knew I couldn't afford any weakness, said, "No, not today. Another time, okay?"

Matthew nodded. It wasn't until I was sitting in English that I felt bad for saying no. It was Matthew's birthday; the least I could do was go for coffee. I felt very conflicted about it. I hoped he wasn't disappointed or offended, but I wouldn't want him to read too much into it anyway, whether I went or not. I sometimes felt he expected more from me—more of a response, more of a relationship, especially lately. It made me uncomfortable and, if I overthought it, very sad. But not for him. Did he feel about me the way I felt about Dave? I found it hard to believe. More to the point, did Dave feel about me the way I felt about Matthew? *That's what doesn't bear thinking about.*

After English, I hurried toward my last class hoping to catch Paola before hers. The music room was right behind the portable that my Art class was in, and I'd seen her heading in that direction on Art days. I checked the music room first, but she wasn't there yet. When I did see her, she was coming from the gym with Jessie. They both smiled but looked surprised to see me.

"Hi," said Jessie. I still didn't know her very well, but she seemed to accept me, which I appreciated.

"Hi," I said, smiling at her as best as I could. Then I looked at Paola. "May I talk to you for a minute?"

"Of course," she said, but I thought I detected hesitation and tension. It made me feel awful.

Jessie continued walking. I looked steadily at Paola. "I want to apologize," I said.

Paola looked surprised again but relaxed visibly. "You don't have to—"

"I do," I said. "I was rude to you yesterday, but I didn't mean to be. And I haven't . . ." I wasn't sure how to continue. "You tried to be friends with me and I . . ." I got stuck again.

"You have a hard time trusting people?" she offered.

"Yes . . . but no . . . that's not it. I wanted to let you know it's got nothing to do with *you*, really. I've just been dealing with—" No, I didn't want to admit to jealousy but only because I didn't want to discuss the cause. Nor did it seem appropriate to explain the anguish it had caused me. That was my problem, not hers.

Paola watched me patiently and didn't look judgmental. A sudden fondness for her almost overwhelmed me as I recalled her unflagging good humor and friendliness. Every barrier I had erected between us fell in a pile of rubble, and tears rolled down my cheeks. "My mother thinks I don't like you because you're Black," I said, bluntly but honestly. "But I need you to know, that isn't it. That would never . . ." I struggled to find the right way to say what I wanted but failed. I gave up and looked her straight in the eyes. "I'm not like that."

I was shocked to see tears well up in her eyes, too. "I didn't think so at first, but then. . . ."

I felt like sinking through the ground at the realization that she *had* thought the color of her skin was the reason I wasn't friendlier. Racism is far worse than jealousy, and even if she had suspected that was the reason, she had never treated me coldly.

"I want you to stay," I said.

She looked confused.

"At my house, while your parents are gone. I would like it very much."

Paola's expression transformed immediately. She practically glowed.

"Just one thing . . ."

"Yes?"

"Well, I usually don't talk very much."

She laughed then. "Allison, I had noticed that. I will try not to wear you out."

I searched her face, trying to tell if I had offended her, but she still seemed happy and maybe relieved, like me.

"Are you coming after school?" she asked as we turned toward our classes.

"Oh . . . no . . . not today," I said, almost wishing I hadn't decided not to go. But those reasons hadn't changed. "I will another time though."

Paola nodded and smiled her most dazzling smile as we parted ways.

I dawdled again after Art, taking my time clearing up materials and sorting through my backpack for no real reason except to waste time. Melanie lingered with me.

"I was thinking," she said, "if your parents agree, perhaps you could come with me one day during the week. I always go straight to the stables to work. You could get a ride with us. That way I could give you a lesson during the week. Weekends tend to be very busy."

I knew she was often away at shows. I smiled and nodded. That was *exactly* what I needed—more distraction, especially after school.

"What about Roger?" I asked, thinking of his disapproving looks whenever I was around.

She smiled again and said, "Roger's okay. A little stuffy maybe, but he'll warm up to you, I'm sure." Her voice softened slightly as she added, "He's actually a really great guy."

I searched her face but could read nothing into what she'd said. "I'll talk to my parents about it. Oh! But . . ." I'd remembered choir. "Would Mondays or Wednesdays be okay?"

She smiled again. "I think that would be fine. I'll fit you in somewhere."

She gathered up her things, saying she had to leave. I waved goodbye and dawdled some more, finally leaving the classroom to walk slowly to my locker. I didn't really need it, but I pretended to swap books. I just didn't want to run into the others and have to say no to joining them again. It would be too hard.

When I got to the front of the school, I was surprised to see Ben loitering there, skateboard in hand. He smiled widely when he saw me and walked over.

"I thought maybe you'd left already."

"Sorry," I said, not sure whether I was happy or annoyed that he'd waited for me. It wasn't as if we had any kind of arrangement for walking together or anything, and sometimes I really liked being left to my own thoughts. But I decided I was glad to see him anyway.

"I've never seen you wear glasses before," he said, trying to peer into my face and walk at the same time. "Do you usually wear contacts?"

"Yes," I said, and reflexively pushed my glasses up.

"Hmm."

"What?"

"You look really different. I mean, with glasses, and your hair's pulled back."

"Well, this is how I look now," I said, not really caring how he felt about it.

He grinned widely. "Looks cute."

"Don't be silly."

"It does."

"Tell me a story."

He told me of a trip to Thailand, describing the landscape beautifully, and about how he got to ride an elephant. I thought it was a little strange considering how nervous he'd been about Remmy. Surely elephants were scarier than horses. As we reached the pool, I heard noise behind us and turned to see who it was.

Everybody. At least, everybody that I had tried to avoid. They were still some way behind us, but Robin and Matthew waved at me. I waved back. Dave and Tanner were carrying their skateboards as were a few others. It seemed like *all* the girls were there. We stood and waited until they reached us and I talked for a minute with Robin. She wanted me to go home with her on Monday; I didn't think it would be a problem. A few of the kids who knew my mom followed Ben and me toward the pool and called, "Hi!" to her through the fence. Mom was happy to return their greetings. Dave had continued walking with everyone else. I don't know if he had even looked at me or not. I was purposely *not* watching him.

We parted ways with the others, Matthew saying, "Don't forget. . . ."

Ben looked at me in question, but I didn't want to say anything until I could talk to my mom alone.

"I invited Paola to stay with us," I told her after we dropped Ben at his house.

Mom looked at me quickly then back to the road. "Well, I hope you'll be able to put any differences you have aside and be kind to her."

That stung. "It wasn't about differences," I said. I looked out the window but could feel Mom turning to look at me again.

After Dad got home, during dinner, I brought up Matthew's birthday. Mom's mood had already lightened considerably—I'm sure she was already thinking about Paola's visit—but she brightened even more.

"Is it that time already? Hasn't time flown!"

I agreed that it certainly had but tried not to dwell on the passage of time. By this time last year, so much had happened and, even though I had been grounded, I'd been happy. Now I felt like I'd gone through a long, dark tunnel and was finally coming out the other side but was in some kind of holding pattern, not sure what to do or how to feel. And it seemed like nothing exciting or of any real importance had happened since school started.

My parents agreed that I could attend Matthew's party for as long as I wanted. Dad would be home and could pick me up later.

"Robin asked if I could go over to her house on Monday."

They both nodded their heads as they ate. I then broached the subject of lessons at Northfield. It was important to get these details ironed out before Dad left next week. Again, they agreed with a slight reservation: they didn't know Roger and weren't sure about letting me go if he was driving.

"Maybe I'll drive you the first time. This Wednesday?" asked Mom.

"I'll double-check," I said, starting to feel like I needed a planner to keep all my engagements straight. I wished it made me feel happier but, even though they were things I really wanted to do, it felt too much like I was trying to fill the minutes and hours, to keep busy and not let myself have brooding time. And maybe that was a good thing, but I couldn't think about it too much. I needed to keep specific thoughts at bay and hopefully with them, anxiety and depression. Paola coming to stay was probably an excellent thing.

"Do you want to get Matthew a gift?" asked Mom.

This had occurred to me, but I hadn't come up with any ideas. In spite of knowing him for over a year now, I didn't know him very well. I had got him a bookstore gift card last year but didn't know if he was really that interested in books.

"Allison? What does he like?" she asked, accurately reading my thought process.

"He's on the swim team," I said, but that didn't help. "And plays soccer." Either did that. I knew he rode but had no idea how much. I'd seen him ride the same horse at both of the Caldera rodeos, but didn't know if it was his. It certainly wasn't kept at his house. "Oh! He got a new car. A Honda."

"Ah! Car stuff," said Dad, taking a mild interest now. But I still didn't know how that would help.

"We could go into Lowell earlier if you want," said Mom. "I'm sure we can find something."

I nodded. I was pretty sure he wouldn't mind if I didn't bring a gift, but I preferred to not go empty-handed.

Saturday morning I groomed Remmy and cleaned his paddock while he ate breakfast. I'd made a decision to work on homework as much as possible during school from now on—even lunchtimes—and ride as much as I could the rest of the time. I was even more motivated than before. While I'd been taking care of all Remmy's needs, it felt like I hadn't been spending as much quality time with him. That was going to change.

Later, I wore one of my newer bathing suits under shorts and a tank top. No excuses for not wearing one this year. I'd try not to be too self-conscious. Most if not all the girls there would have better figures than me, especially Jessie and Stacie, and even more if Paola and Roberta were there, but I didn't really care anymore. I doubted that anyone would notice me much anyway. I was going to keep the tank on though, not because of exposure but because of the very noticeable scar my accident had left.

Mom and I drove over to Lowell and stopped in the auto store first. Dad had suggested a few things that Matthew might already have but would probably appreciate anyway and could keep for spares. The first, a steering wheel cover, made me laugh as I imagined giving it to him.

"Here. It's for your steering wheel." How exciting.

But I couldn't think of anything better and the other things Dad suggested seemed even sillier. Not knowing what color his car was and hoping it wasn't white, I chose a black cover that was supposed to be "for superior grip and sporty appearance." I hoped it would be okay. As we neared the cashier, I noticed racks of key chains. I was sure he probably already had one of those too, but as I found one that not only had the Honda insignia on it but also incorporated an "M," I bought it also.

We bought a gift bag and tissue paper at another store to make the gift look presentable, then drove to Matthew's house.

Nobody was out front, but a sporty, dark metallic gray car sat in the driveway. The front door of the house was open slightly, so I went through the spacious living room to the glass wall leading out to the patio and pool area.

A lot of people were there already, including Hannah, but no Dave and no Robin. Matthew came over, smiling widely as soon as he saw me. He was barefoot and wore board shorts but didn't look like he'd been in the water yet.

"You came!" he said as if he'd doubted I would.

"Yes," I said, handing him the gift bag and trying to smile.

"Thanks, but you didn't have to. Did you see my car?"

"Yes! It looks . . ." *What do you say about cars? He might not appreciate "cute."* "It looks nice."

Setting the gift bag down on one of the patio tables, he pulled the steering wheel cover, wrapped in tissue paper, out of the bag and began to open it.

"You . . . probably already have one of those," I said, feeling very awkward.

As he lifted the plastic box free of the paper his eyes crinkled a little. "I *do* already have one," he said, "but it'll wear out. This is great. Thanks!"

I thought he was just being considerate. "There's something else."

He looked in the bag and pulled out the smaller package—the keychain, also wrapped in tissue paper. "Oh, cool," he said. "I *don't* have one of these." He reached across the table to a set of keys that had been left there and worked the keys onto the new ring. "Perfect," he said, holding them up and smiling.

I still thought he was being generous, but he seemed genuinely pleased, so I felt happy.

"Come on, I want to show you," he said, and indicated that I should follow him back through the house.

I looked toward the others, but only Hannah seemed to notice. Matthew led me back through the front door and over to the new car.

"Get in!" he said, opening the passenger door.

I hesitated and looked around. "Is . . . Robin coming?"

"Yeah, they're supposed to be here. They were working over at her house this morning."

This answered the unspoken part of my question, *'Is Dave coming?'* which I *wasn't* going to ask, but apparently Matthew read into it anyway. I wasn't sure what to think about that.

"Come on," he said again. "You've got to see the inside."

A little reluctantly—I never knew what might be misinterpreted—I lowered myself into the seat. Matthew closed the door and moved quickly around the car, getting in the driver's side. I could tell how proud of it he was as he pointed to the dashboard features and talked about the engine. I didn't know anything about engines.

"Let's go for a quick ride!" he said and started the car.

"No!" I said reflexively.

"Why not? Just for a minute. Come on, put your seat belt on."

The car started backing out of the driveway.

"I don't—"

The car had come to an abrupt stop. Matthew looked in the rearview mirror and didn't look happy.

I turned also and was surprised to see Cris' truck across the driveway right behind us. The passenger door opened and Dave jumped out followed by Robin. Matthew turned the engine off and huffed slightly, putting the car in park again. But when I looked at him, he smiled his usual smile, shrugged his shoulders, and got out. I opened my door and got out too, feeling relieved and a little guilty for some reason.

By this time Cris had joined the others in admiring Matthew's car. Dave and Cris were dressed in old jeans and slightly grease-stained shirts, but Dave had a gym bag over his shoulder. Robin was dressed like me. I felt Dave looking at me, but I concentrated on saying hi to Robin.

"Trying it out?" she asked loudly, her eyebrows lifting a couple of times.

Embarrassed, I reminded myself that it didn't matter what Dave thought. By then it was too late to think of anything to reply. It didn't seem to matter anyway; the brothers were asking questions about the car and Matthew was happily showing it off.

"Come on. They'll be a while," said Robin, and walked toward the house.

I looked back once to see Matthew standing at the driver's door and Dave sitting behind the wheel. They were both talking animatedly as if I hadn't been there at all, which was a good thing. But Cris stood near them and was definitely watching me with a strange expression—at least, strange for him. *Puzzled? Speculative?* It made me feel uncomfortable. I told myself that I didn't care what he thought either and followed Robin into the house.

By the time Dave walked into the backyard, changed into board shorts, Robin was already in the pool and Matthew had joined me on the side. I had shed my shorts but kept the tank on.

The afternoon progressed pleasantly, though Matthew spent more time with me than seemed usual or even appropriate considering he had so many

other guests there. I spent much of the time talking with him or Robin—who spent most of *her* time in the pool—or watching everyone else. I went in the water too, but tried to stay at the opposite end from Dave.

The only other thing I really noticed, apart from the fact that Paola and Roberta were *not* there, was Hannah's behavior. Most of the time she seemed her usual happy self, and she was usually near Dave, which didn't surprise me. But a few times I caught her looking in my direction looking sad. This was disturbing and perplexing. I couldn't remember ever being purposely rude or unfriendly toward her and wondered what I'd done wrong now. I already felt utterly weighed down by guilt; I didn't need any more. I determined to try to find out what was wrong and set things right with her as soon as I could—as soon as Dave wasn't around.

And I tried *not* to watch Dave—I hoped the more I practiced, the easier it would get—and so was unaware of his actions most of the time and whether or not he noticed me much, which was also good. By mid-afternoon, almost everyone was in the pool playing with an inflated ball, including Matthew. It was noisy and boisterous and looked like fun, but I was happier sitting in the shade, watching. A few kids, including Tanner, Stacie, and Kyle were still on the patio eating and talking to Mr. Morrison. The latter had barbecued for us again and the food had been delicious. I just wished I'd felt hungry enough to enjoy it and eat more.

A few hours later and after a couple of other people had left, I called my dad. Robin noticed me on my phone and came over, dripping.

"What's up?" she asked.

"My dad's coming to pick me up."

"Can I get a ride home?"

"Sure," I said, surprised she wanted to leave already. "I thought you'd be leaving with Dave."

"He'll be here until Cris comes for him, and who knows when that will be. I think he's working somewhere today. Anyway, I don't want to wait that long." She looked worried for just a moment, then smiled. "I've got stuff to do at home."

"Me too," I said. And it was true but more accurate that I was reaching my threshold for sun and noise and proximity to Dave. I'd simply had enough. But I was a little proud of myself too. I didn't feel jealous of anyone, not even Hannah. I actually felt more curious about and concerned for her.

Robin found her towel and wrapped herself in it, then sat next to me under one of the cabanas. We talked about school and horses. Then she told me of a show that was coming up; the same one she had ridden in near her birthday.

"You should enter this year. I'll give you a copy of the entry form."

I agreed that it sounded great. When my dad arrived, he called to say he was out front. Robin walked toward Dave, yelling to get his attention. He went to the side of the pool to listen to her then looked at me, nodding. Then he surprised me by getting out of the water and walking over with her.

"Leaving already, huh?"

"Yes." Brevity seemed safest.

Suddenly Matthew was with us too. "Leaving?"

"Yes," I said again but felt he deserved an explanation. "My dad's here."

"Oh, okay," he said, but obviously planned on walking out with us.

Robin put her shorts and tank on over her wet suit and gathered her things. When we walked toward the house, Matthew came with us. So did Dave.

Dad was out front with Mr. Morrison, admiring Matthew's car.

"Hello, Matthew," said Dad. "And happy birthday! Sixteen, I assume?"

"Yes, sir. And thanks," said Matthew.

"I was just admiring your car. It's a beauty."

"Yeah, I think so too."

I noticed Dave was wearing a slight smirk again. Dad noticed too, and his smile faded a little. They regarded each other for a moment, just long enough for me to feel uncomfortable. I hated it when they did that. I hated it all the more now that there could be no reason for it.

"Well, we'd better get going," said Dad, turning back to Mr. Morrison. "It was good to see you again, Zach." Then he turned back to Matthew. "Congratulations on your car. Take good care of her," he said, "and drive safe."

Every once in a while, I feel like I'm picking up on hidden communication, which is weird because I so often miss meaning in regular conversation completely. I felt Dad was saying something to Matthew and felt embarrassed and indignant. His approval of Matthew was as useless as his disapproval of Dave; neither was going to influence me. But I didn't need Dad sending Matthew signals when I was trying to *avoid* them.

"Thanks, Matt," said Robin. "It was fun. And thanks, Mr. Morrison. The food was great."

"Yes, thank you," I said, glad that Robin had pretty much said everything I would have. Then to Matthew, "Happy birthday . . . again."

He looked really pleased and said, "Thanks for coming . . . and for the gifts. It means a lot."

Now I really *was* embarrassed, especially with Dave standing right there. I tried to resist glancing at him, but I couldn't help it. He was looking away, frowning into the late afternoon sun.

We dropped Robin at her house then went to the grocery store. Dad wanted to cook dinner for Mom.

"That's some car Matthew's got, isn't it?" he said.

"Yes," I agreed. "I guess. It looks nice."

I didn't know what else to say about that and lapsed into silence, but it did remind me of something important; important to me, at least. After a few moments, I said, "Can I start learning to drive?"

I don't think that's the conversation he'd meant to start, but it was the only one I was interested in.

"You really want to drive already?" he asked.

"Yes. I'd like to be able to get around on my own, so I don't have to bother you or Mom. Like for going to Northfield." I was sure he could understand what a drag it would be to take me there every week. "And babysitting for Cheryl. And maybe I could get a real job. In town."

Dad was quiet for a moment then said, "Okay. Let's start tomorrow."

I nodded, not excited but determined. Starting tomorrow, things needed to be different for a lot of reasons.

Chapter Fifteen

My father's easy capitulation to teaching me to drive left me feeling slightly nervous and vaguely suspicious. I'd thought it would take some time to convince him, which would have bought me more time to steel myself for actually doing it. But true to his word, early the next morning we headed out to the car—Mom's car. Dad wanted to take me to the high school parking lot, but I quickly vetoed that idea.

We agreed on the parking lot at the strip mall instead. Even on the busiest days, the parking lot was mostly deserted. In fact, it was close to the old gas station, mercifully abandoned by even middle school skaters this morning, that Dad parked and we switched places.

I wish I could say that my first driving lesson was successful, but I don't think it was. I tend to lack coordination and my spacial judgment has always been questionable. It was mostly because of the latter that I'd been warned I might have trouble driving.

I have a tendency to misjudge distances in general even while walking—corners of walls, edges of tables, doorways, etc. I also trip easily and have general balance issues. My enemies have always picked up on this quickly and used it against me. They still did. It wasn't because of my eyesight but the way my brain works, apparently. My ophthalmologist wasn't able to do anything about it. He had said I might be able to compensate adequately as I got older.

After getting too close to light poles a couple of times, freezing every time another car came anywhere near me, and generally failing to stay within the parameters I'd been asked to, we decided to call it a day and head home. It hadn't been the confidence-building experience I was hoping for, and vehicular autonomy seemed as far away as ever. I took comfort in working Remmy around and through the makeshift obstacles I'd set up in my imaginary arena. Perhaps Remmy compensated for me, but I didn't seem to have any noticeable spatial or balance issues while riding.

After unsaddling, I got him to stand close to his paddock fence and used it to boost myself up onto his back. It wasn't the first time I'd ridden him bareback—I'd practiced a little around the field at just a walk and slow jog—but today I rode him down to the stream. There we relaxed, playing in the cold stream and sitting—well, I sat and Remmy stood—in the shade. I was disappointed about the driving experience but not crushed, and I was far from giving up. But I definitely felt more and more at home on horseback. It was more than adequate consolation for both driving and companionship, but I didn't let myself dwell on the latter.

"What on earth?"

Robin and I were walking to our lockers after Geometry, but she had stopped suddenly, staring open-mouthed at a wall. Several flyers were posted there at eye-level. Dave's face stared back at us. It was last year's yearbook picture, though I almost didn't recognize it without the facial hair and glasses he'd drawn on my copy.

"*Your new class president!*" it boldly proclaimed. We looked around and saw it wasn't just this wall that had been so decorated, but every vertical surface within sight.

Robin frowned. "He decided to run?"

It didn't surprise me that I hadn't heard the news, but it was disconcerting that Dave hadn't told her.

We continued walking to the tables. Dave wasn't there. When he appeared, he walked straight up to Roberta, who was already eating lunch at one of the tables. He held several of the flyers in his hand.

"Was this you?"

She looked surprised and pretended her mouth was too full to answer him.

"You got out of History for *this?*" He wasn't furious—I knew what Dave really angry looked like—but he was obviously annoyed. "Well, you wasted your time."

He crumpled the flyers up and tossed them into a trash can close by. Then he turned to look around at the rest of us. Everyone was watching with great interest. Well, almost everyone. Ben was sitting with some of the other choir kids on the grass nearby, looking in Hannah's lunch bag.

Dave focused in our general direction and said, "Will you help me take these down? They're all over the freakin' school."

"Freakin'" wasn't the word he used, but I felt included in the request and gladly got up to join them. I walked over to Ben and gave him the rest of my lunch. He looked up and smiled.

"Thanks!" Then it seemed to dawn on him what was going on. "Hey, do you want more help?"

Dave regarded both of us for a moment. "Could you check around the gym?"

I nodded. He, Robin, and Tanner walked back toward the quad and the main school buildings. Hannah and Paola got up and ran after them. I glanced toward Roberta, still eating her lunch as if nothing had happened. She was talking to the other girls as if she didn't care, but there were bright spots of color in her cheeks. She looked up, saw me looking at her, and glared back. I walked away and couldn't help smiling. This proved that the school council was at least one thing she couldn't manipulate Dave into. I thought she was foolish to try manipulating him at all, but I tried not to think too deeply about it.

Ben and I found plenty of flyers posted around the outside of the gym. We took them all down and threw them in the closest trash cans, but I felt funny about it. It seemed almost symbolic—crumpling up Dave's picture and throwing it away—but I tried not to overthink that either.

Ben checked in the boys' locker room, and I checked the girls'. There were plenty of posters in there. Luckily the room was empty or I would have felt even odder taking them down; I dreaded having to defend or explain my actions to anyone. I wondered if Ben had found any. I wouldn't put it past

Roberta to go in the boys' locker room, though she must have had help to get them all over the school so quickly.

I took a flyer off the top of the stack I'd collected and looked around quickly, then dropped the rest of the pile in the trash can near the door. Dave's face stared back at me from the flyer in my hand. He definitely looked different now. The picture seemed to represent a simpler, perhaps more innocent time. It made my heart ache.

It wouldn't hurt to keep just one, right? I began to fold it carefully as I moved toward the door.

Ugh! You're so hopeless. I crumpled it in my hands and walked back to the trash can, throwing it in.

Pointless, idiotic, masochistic.

I began to open the door—*but you don't have a real picture of him. . . .*

I went back to the trash and picked up an uncrumpled copy just as Ben opened the door. "What's taking you so long? Were there a lot?"

"Yes. Lots," I said, dropping the picture in the can and moving toward him. The door shut behind him and I ran back to grab the copy, folded it neatly and put it in my pocket, then left the room.

We had gathered and thrown away a lot more copies by the time the bell rang.

"That was a lot of paper," said Ben.

"Mmm," I concurred.

"She must really like him."

I didn't feel like sharing an opinion on that.

"Or she really thinks he'd make a good president."

I had no doubt that Dave would be terrific at whatever he put his mind to, but I was also convinced that the well-being of the sophomore student body was not Roberta's motivation. I highly doubted that she had Dave's best interests at heart either, but I kept these things to myself too. Ben was watching me closely, so I scrambled to find something to say.

"I guess he didn't like the idea," I said and was slightly ashamed of how pleased I felt about that.

He *would* make a great president. He was smart, cared about people, and was popular enough to probably win. It was the kind of thing I was sure any of the Calderas would want on their transcripts for university. But, for whatever reason, he didn't want the job. I wondered if it was because it wasn't his idea, or because he wouldn't allow himself to be manipulated by anyone, or specifically Roberta, or because he just didn't want to do it.

It doesn't matter anyway. What Dave chooses to do or not do is none of your business.

Still, I would have supported and voted for him. As a friend.

After Study Hall, Ben followed me to the front of the school.

"Oh . . . I'm walking over to Robin's house today. Sorry, I forgot to tell you." And I *was* sorry, but I also felt a little guilty and resented it. I hadn't given a thought to how Ben was getting home, but I didn't want to feel responsible for him.

"That's okay. Can I walk down the street with you?"

I didn't know how to feel about that. "I guess."

Then I saw Robin walking toward us. With Dave. The boys acknowledged each other with sharp nods. Robin and I began walking down the street, and the boys fell into step with us, carrying their skateboards, Dave beside Robin, Ben beside me. Robin and Dave continued an argument they already had in progress. When Dave finally let her have the last word we were almost to Main Street. He looked over at Ben with a calculating look I was very familiar with.

"So . . ." He still seemed unsure of Ben's name. "Can you really ride that?"

Ben grinned his best Leprechaun grin and said, "This old thing? Yeah. Sort of."

Dave looked at Ben's skateboard in much the same way I'd seen him look at horses and cattle. He'd even looked at me that way once or twice. It just looked like every other skateboard to me.

"Well, I gotta go this way," said Ben as we reached the corner. He glanced at Dave and Robin, and I could have sworn there was more color in his cheeks. I'd never seen that on him before. He looked at me and said, "See you tomorrow."

"Okay. Bye."

In one fluid movement, Ben dropped the board, seemed to step onto it before it fully hit the ground, and glided away.

Dave's eyes narrowed slightly before we turned and headed the other way. "So what's the story with Spock?" He seemed to be asking me, though he'd said it brusquely and wasn't looking at me.

Indignant, I said, "What do you mean, 'What's the story?' And his name is *Ben*."

Now his gaze was intense. "You seem to hang out a lot."

"We have a couple of classes together. I help him with—" I almost said *Spanish*. "Homework."

"And feed him," said Dave.

Now I was even more annoyed. *He can't be bothered to talk to me, but he's keeping track of what I do?*

"He forgets things," I said.

"He lives near you, right?" offered Robin.

Not helping, Robin.

"He does?" said Dave.

"Yes. We sometimes give him rides home."

"Really," said Dave.

"Didn't he do some work for your dad?"

Still not helping, Robin.

I was a little surprised Dave wasn't already in possession of all this information, but as I'd already observed, he and Robin weren't as close as they had been.

"Yes. Some yard work. He mows the lawn and things like that and is helping with a little landscaping."

"Hnh," said Dave.

Robin had lost interest. We fell into an uneasy silence—extremely uncommon for the three of us—and I continued to feel awkward around Dave. Weirdly, he seemed to feel uncomfortable around me, too. I knew why I felt that way but couldn't imagine why he did.

Cris was already at Robin's house. I followed the others through the now open garage door. The hood of the Mustang was up, and a new-looking engine was being installed.

"How's my metal pony?" said Robin.

Cris looked up at us but continued to ratchet a bolt in the depths of the Mustang's innards. "Coming together," he said.

Dave set his skateboard down in a corner and picked up a rag. He leaned against the car facing his brother, his back toward me. It seemed purposeful.

"We should be able to start it up by the weekend," said Cris. "Then we'll get new wheels and tires and get it cleaned up and painted. It should be ready for your birthday."

Robin was obviously very excited, and I was truly happy for her, but it felt like Dave was turning a cold shoulder to me and my feelings were extremely conflicted.

I was sad, but I wasn't going to let myself dwell on it. I couldn't afford to. I felt confused, too—why he cared who I hung out with was beyond me. Mostly, I felt annoyed, as annoyed as I'd ever been with Ben. And why did Dave feel he could keep making fun of Ben around me, which is what it seemed like he was doing? And why was he doing it at all? It wasn't like him and made me more than annoyed.

"I'm going to go see Fiona," I said, moving toward the garage's side door. "I'll help her with tea or something."

Robin looked up and seemed surprised. "Huh? Oh . . . okay."

Fiona was happy to see me, and I helped to get tea started. She'd gone back to the sitting room when Robin came in to the kitchen.

"So, what's going on between you and Dave? Another *misunderstanding?*"

Curse her good memory. She was referring to the status of my relationship with him early last year. It hadn't been a misunderstanding so much as me not being able to interpret Dave's intentions, my overwhelming crush on him, and my fear of being badly hurt because of it. Looking back, everything now seemed obvious and simple. I wondered if it would seem that way next year about our present status. I hoped so.

Robin cleared her throat loudly, eyebrows raised.

"Oh . . . um . . . what do you mean?"

Robin looked severe. She knew me too well and wasn't fooled.

"It feels weird when you talk to each other, like you've had a fight or something. At first I thought it was just my imagination, but," she shook her head, eyes narrowed, "it's not."

"Everything's fine. It's just . . . different."

"Yeah, that's pretty much what he said but . . ."

I couldn't resist. "But what?"

She shook her head again. "It's not like him. Then again, I guess he *has* been acting differently." She frowned and looked thoughtful.

I wondered if she was thinking of the same things I was. *Roberta . . . Hannah . . . Paola . . . Hawaii. . . .*

I shook it off. These were the things I couldn't afford to think about. Trying to analyze interactions between Dave and myself only led to hope or despair—neither of those emotions any good for me. Things were going to be weird between us now, and that's all there was to it. The only hope I would let myself hold onto was that we could somehow indeed be friends again; no weirdness, no angst, and no nonsensical romantic ideas. I was glad that I wasn't the only one who thought he was acting differently though.

Robin made sandwiches for the guys and took them out to them. We finished our own sandwiches and tea in her room and worked on geometry for a couple of hours, letting Gali eat his snack and leaving the guys to work without further distraction from us. By the time we went back outside, they had gone. I felt genuinely relieved. And I was *relieved* that I felt relieved.

Even so, my mind was restless trying to fall asleep that night. I wondered how long it would take to feel completely content about the whole situation. I tried to think about other things: Paola would be coming home with me after choir tomorrow, and I'd be having my first lesson at Northfield with Melanie on Wednesday. We had the math part of State tests to take tomorrow too. *Math . . . not my strong point.* And my art project was due Thursday; I had finished and was going to turn in *all* of my drawings.

This should have been more than enough to occupy my mind but, traitor that it was, other thoughts nudged through too. It was the Fall Dance in less than two weeks. Posters had been up for a while, and I'd made myself look away every time I'd seen one, but my brain had made notes. Obviously there was no chance of going to it with Dave, as I had so dearly hoped back in the summer. Then the following week was his birthday. What was that going to be like? And thinking about *that* stirred up a multitude of memories.

I had almost decided that I may as well get up and study or draw, when a strange, almost scratching noise startled me. My window was closed—though the days were warm the nights were becoming cold—and I wasn't sure if the sound had come from inside or outside. I looked at my clock: twelve thirty-seven. I was sure my parents had gone to bed.

I lay listening for the sound to repeat. Now it sounded slightly different: a light *tick, tick, tick, tick, tick* in rapid succession, then quiet again. It had come from the back window. I crept out of bed and pulled the curtain aside slightly.

The moon was full and the sky cloudless, everything washed in deep blues and grays and black, with moonlight shimmering white and silver along some of the edges. I could see Remmy standing in his paddock, head over the rails, facing the house—a large dark shadow.

And, standing under my window, a boy.

Opening the window enough to speak through, I whispered, "What are you doing?"

"I couldn't sleep," Ben whispered harshly back. "Come out and play!"

"What? No!"

"Come on!" His voice had solidified from a whisper to his normal volume. "It's amazing out here."

"Shh! You'll wake my parents up!"

He whispered back, "Then come outside. Just for a little while."

Ugh. So annoying.

I pulled a sweatshirt over the tank top I slept in and crept downstairs carefully in the dark. I unlocked the back door and stepped into my flip-flops just outside. Remmy was watching Ben with interest. Ben stood several feet away murmuring to him, as if trying to make friends but afraid of getting too close.

"What are you doing here?" I whispered as I got closer to him.

"I couldn't sleep," he said.

"Yes, you said that already. But why are you *here*?"

He shrugged. "I wanted company."

"Oh . . . thanks for thinking of me," I said, hoping I sounded sarcastic.

He just grinned. "Besides, I've always wanted to do that . . . throw pebbles at my beloved's window. You know . . . romantic."

"What?" I said, genuinely shocked. "I am *not* your beloved."

"I know," he said, still grinning, "but I figured I could practice on you since you're so handy."

"Gee, thanks," I said, quite sure I sounded adequately sarcastic this time.

"We could pretend to be star-crossed lovers. If it'll make you feel better, I'll ask you out and you can tell me why you can't accept."

"No. Definitely not."

His face fell. "Does that mean you don't think I'm worthy?"

"What? No . . ."

He nodded his head sadly. "I'm not good-looking enough."

"Don't be silly."

"Is it because I don't have a car? It's because I don't have a car, isn't it?"

Now he was just confusing me. "I just . . . I don't feel that way. I don't see you like that." And now I felt bad, for him but for me too, my confession too close to other, similar issues. He and I weren't the star-crossed ones. "You don't really—" I started, suddenly worried and not wanting to hurt him.

"No, not at all." His grin was back full force. "I like someone else. And so do you. I mean, like someone else. Not the same person." He frowned comically. "At least, I don't think so."

That startled me too. There was no way he could know. "What are you talking about?"

He shrugged. "It's obvious. He's always making googly eyes at you, and you don't seem to mind."

"Would you stop it?" Now I was really irritated. "There is no one making *googly* eyes at me. You've imagined it. Besides, that sounds gross."

"He is too making googly eyes," he said, and now I *knew* he was just trying to annoy me.

"I'm going back in," I said, walking away.

"Don't go." He sounded sincere, so I turned back. "I was just giving you a hard time. I'm a little jealous 'cause the person I like barely knows I exist."

"Who do you like?"

He smiled slyly and shook his head. "Hey, remember the trip to the observatory?" He looked up at the sky. "We can't see much tonight because the moon is full but," he pointed up at the stars, "it'll be *really* great in a couple of weeks when the moon isn't visible."

"You know a lot about astronomy?"

"Oh yeah, tons. My dad taught me all about it. That's Ursa Major," he said, pointing north. "And that's Ursa Minor. I'm going to be an astronaut. It's a prerequisite that you know all the stars. That way if you get lost in space, you can find your way home again."

"Really," I said, not believing a word of it.

He laughed loudly, and I put my finger to my lips. I didn't know if my parents had their window open or not.

"No . . . I don't know. I want to travel though."

"More travel? It seems like you've already traveled a lot."

A strange look crossed his face. If I didn't already doubt his sincerity on every topic, I would have thought he looked sad, maybe just guarded.

"I think I'm always going to want to be somewhere I'm not," he said.

I had no idea what to say to that, but his words gave me an empty feeling. "Do you get along with your foster parents?"

He smiled, but more seriously. "Yes. No. Sometimes. Most of the time. Bill is my uncle. Did you know that?"

That did surprise me, in spite of the vague resemblance I'd noticed. "No, I didn't."

"Yeah, my dad's brother. I guess that's where the red comes from," he said, pointing to his head. "Mom's hair was dark brown."

He was quiet for a few moments as if thinking of the past. I didn't want to interrupt his thoughts, but now I did have questions. Unlike with some of my other friends, I didn't mind asking.

"Was?"

"Yeah," he said, giving me a sidelong look, "she died . . . when I was younger."

"Oh," I said. "I'm sorry." I hated saying "I'm sorry" for something that I couldn't really be sorry for. It always felt wrong. I mean, it's not like I'd done anything. But what else can you say? I tried to imagine a younger version of Ben suddenly losing his mother. "That must have been really hard for you. What about your dad?"

"Yeah, he died too." He paused for a moment, and I waited for him to continue. "A car accident. That's why I'm an orphan."

"And that's when you came to live with your uncle?"

That sidelong, slightly calculating look again. "Yeah."

His words echoed a memory: a child losing a mother, a brother killed in a car accident. Then a memory of Dave distraught over a missing brother and the reason for it; a memory of Cris answering a simple question with even greater, though heartbreaking simplicity:

'Where is your mother?'

'She's dead.'

"But you like your uncle, right?"

"Yeah! He's great. His wife, Vivian, she's not as . . . happy . . . about me living with them. I bug her. I try not to, but it seems like everything I do annoys her."

"Oh," I said.

"Yeah," he said softly.

He certainly could be annoying, but I felt bad for him. Sometimes I was sure he was annoying on purpose, but not *all* the time.

"I've had people treat me like that," I offered, thinking back to elementary school and early middle school, before I learned how to shut down and keep to myself, especially my thoughts. Then I thought of Roberta, Lori, and the others. "Sometimes they still do."

"Like those girls?" he said, knowingly.

I didn't want to talk about it.

"We should make a pact," he said.

"A pact?"

"Yeah, you know, make an agreement to stand together against the forces of evil and unreasonable expectations. But we should seal it with blood."

"*Blood?*" Now I was alarmed.

The alarm increased when he drew a pocket knife from his pants pocket and opened it.

"Yeah . . . I saw it in a movie once. We cut our palms and shake on it. You get a little of me, and I get a little of you. Then we can stand together against anything! What blood type are you? I'm not sure if we have to be the same blood type. What do you think?"

"I think you watch too many movies. Put that away, please."

A grin split his face, his eyes laughing. He pocketed the knife.

A light went on at the back of the house—my parents' bathroom.

"You need to go!" I whispered harshly, but I wasn't sure why. We weren't doing anything wrong. I couldn't immediately think of a reason my parents would be mad but didn't feel like taking chances. "I'm going back inside. See you tomorrow."

"Sleep well, my love," he said, gallantly.

"Cut it out!" I turned and glared at him in the moonlight.

"Just practicing," he said.

I sneaked back into the house, trying to fabricate an excuse for being up and failing. But no one came downstairs, and there was no discernible light under my parents' door. I was sure the encounter with Ben would keep me awake, but the silliness of the whole thing made me smile in spite of the sad story of his parents. I fell asleep quickly.

Chapter Sixteen

I made it through the math exam the next day—more or less—and then had lunch with Melanie. I didn't see Ben or Dave that morning, and I was okay with that. Melanie and I talked mainly about my upcoming lesson, and she told me stories about Kitty, who I'd be riding.

"Oh," I said, remembering an important fact, "Paola . . . my friend . . . is staying with us for a few days. Is it okay if she comes with me?"

Melanie's easy smile assured me that it was.

Choir after school was fun. The kids doing the small group choreography were getting really good at it, and Ben and Hannah had worked on a duet for another song that they showed Mr. Tanaka. Mr. T. approved enthusiastically. I was impressed too; Ben was a terrific dancer. He was also still very annoying. Today he wore black thick-rimmed, lensless glasses and smiled like a Cheshire Cat every time I looked at him.

Mom and Paola's mother were waiting for us after choir. They transferred a suitcase and a smaller bag from Rosa's trunk to ours. Then Paola and her mother embraced tightly. Rosa spoke to Paola intensely in Spanish before releasing her.

"Thank you so much," she said, haltingly, looking from Mom to me. "*Qué bendición*. Please, you will pray for us? They will hear us?"

We all willingly agreed. I briefly wondered if Mom really prayed. Though I wasn't at all sure where I stood with the recipient of my prayers, they seemed to be doing me some good. I was certainly more at peace with my situation. I didn't mind beseeching deity for Paola's family's sake. It was the least I could do after my hateful jealousy.

Ben and Paola kept up a lively conversation about the upcoming choir concert all the way home. When we got there, Mom invited Ben to have dinner with us. I tried to maintain a benign expression. He grinned and asked if he could use the phone to call Vivian. She wasn't home, but he left a message.

We got a snack and worked on homework together in the kitchen, Paola helping us with Spanish—especially Ben—and me helping her with some English definitions for her history. Ben provided comic relief. It seemed very strange, having these kids sitting at my kitchen table. I'd only recently considered them even *possible* friends. I couldn't help thinking of a different time with very different kids, and my heart hurt—but only for a few moments. Then Ben said something ridiculous and Paola laughed her rich, bubbly laugh and I felt happy.

Happy enough.

Wednesday sped by. It seemed like I'd spent most of the day with Ben—Spanish in the morning, Study Hall later—and Robin and I had sat with him and the choir kids on the grass during lunch. I sat with my back to the tables so I *couldn't* see Dave and only saw him in passing during PE.

The Sophomore students definitely had been split into two PE groups, at least during our period: those who were or expected to be involved in after-school sports—considered the real athletes—and those that weren't. The athletes were most likely to continue with specific PE electives next year.

Students in the more intensive part of the class were concentrating on running, track and field sports, and general fitness training, including using the weight room. I'd rarely see Dave at all anymore unless both groups were involved in the same unit. It also meant that, except for changing in the locker room, I didn't have to worry too much about interactions with Roberta and Lori. Win-win.

Dad picked Paola and me up after school and drove us to Northfield. I changed into my boots before getting out of the car. There was no sign of Melanie, but Tatty saw us and walked over.

"Hi there," she said, smiling and extending her hand toward Dad. "You must be Allison's father."

"Greg Anderson," said Dad. He smiled and looked pleased to be meeting someone obviously in charge.

"It's nice to meet you," said Tatty. To me, she said, "You're starting lessons with Mel today, right? And you've brought a friend?"

"Yes," I said happily. "This is Paola. She's staying with us for a little while."

"Nice to meet you, Paola."

Paola smiled widely and said excitedly, in her precise but now only slightly accented English, "It is so nice to meet you also."

"Do you ride? Do *you* ride, Mr. Anderson?"

"Not anymore," said Dad. "I rode when I was younger."

Tatty looked at Paola.

"Just a *very* little," she said.

Tatty smiled—almost smirked—and said, "Well, we can always fix that. Mel's in the barn. I'll see you later. It was nice to meet you both."

We all said, "Bye," as she turned and walked toward the office.

"I'm meeting James at the driving range," said Dad. "Just give me a call when you're done."

I nodded.

We found Melanie in the first barn, wearing a dust mask and overseeing three young girls grooming two ponies.

"Hi Allison. Hi Paola. We have a couple of classes together, don't we?"

Paola smiled widely. "Yes, I have seen you!"

"I have a group lesson right now and then a private lesson. Your lesson will be about five-thirty. Okay, Allison?"

"Yes," I said.

"I need Kitty right now, though. Jacqueline is going to ride her, but I want you to get her ready. Do you remember where she is?"

I looked around. "Through there, right?"

"All the way through. Her tack is out already."

I was very nervous. Melanie seemed different, a little distant and very business-like, which made sense. After all, she was at work. But I was also worried about handling Kitty. There was something *knowing* about her as if she could gauge a person's experience and respond accordingly—positively or negatively. And, fanciful though it might have been, I was sure she had me pegged as an *almost* intermediate rider who still lacked confidence; someone safe enough to give a hard time to.

Paola followed me to Kitty's stall and stood back as I led her out and cross-tied her nearby. Kitty remained aloof but allowed me to check her feet, groom, and saddle her. I led her back to Melanie, who double-checked and adjusted her tack then led her out to a small arena where the girls and ponies waited.

"It is very nice here, isn't it?" said Paola.

I looked around. Compared to Bar 8, and even the Calderas' ranch, everything appeared much newer and better maintained. Buildings and railings looked recently painted. The footing in the arenas was regularly groomed, the open spaces were kept raked, and the surrounding areas were mowed lawns, green in spite of the season and complete lack of rain. I liked it a lot, but I was sure my heart would remain elsewhere.

"Yes, it's beautiful. I guess they can afford to take care of it well."

"It must cost much to keep a horse here."

I hadn't thought about the cost before, beyond the fact that it cost money to keep horses anywhere, but I supposed it did. I was glad I had Remmy at home; it must have cost my parents quite a bit just to keep him at Bar 8. It probably cost even more here.

"I don't know," I said.

"How long have you had Remmy?"

She had asked that question before, but I had avoided it. I thought about how to answer, how much to tell, but there didn't seem to be any reason to avoid the subject now. For anyone else who knew I had Remmy, *how* I got him was common knowledge.

"Not very long. Just since January. For my birthday."

"Ah," said Paola, her smile wide and her eyes alight. "My birthday is in December! Your parents, they give him to you?"

"No," I said, determined to be as open and honest with her as I could. I'd state the facts and only the facts. "The Caldera family gave him to me." Though I'd continue to think of Remmy as a personal gift from Dave, my revised answer was technically correct and seemed a more judicial response.

"Ah!" she said again, her eyes even brighter. "David must like you *very* much."

This was said wistfully, and I briefly wondered exactly how *she* felt about him. But I didn't really want to know. I didn't want to think about it at all.

When the girls were done with their lesson, Melanie loosened Kitty's girth and asked me to walk her for a bit then hold her while an older woman on a huge black horse had her lesson. They moved to another arena where a couple of jumps were set up in the center, the poles set low. I was very interested in the lesson, though I shivered slightly most of the time, and paid close attention to everything Melanie said and that the woman did. When the lady's lesson was almost over, Melanie came and tightened Kitty's girth again, handed a helmet to me, and told me to mount and walk her in a nearby paddock. Feeling very nervous, I led Kitty to a mounting block and did as she said.

In spite of a few minor miscommunications with Kitty, I enjoyed the lesson and felt that I'd learned a lot. It seemed to go very quickly and consisted mostly of getting used to holding the reins differently, keeping my heels down and toes in even more than I already did, and learning about diagonals at the trot and how to rise in the saddle. It was wonderful, but I think I was right about Kitty. She seemed to take any weakness on my part as an excuse to "misunderstand" my aids. Melanie just told me to be clear and firm with her.

"She may test you, but I think you'll learn quickly with her, especially as you've already been riding a lot. She'll never let you be lazy! If you'd rather try a different horse, we can."

"No! I like Kitty," I said. I thought she was right about improving faster with her. "How soon do you think I can learn to jump?" I asked.

Melanie laughed. "I think we'll make sure you're riding confidently at the basic gaits first. Okay?"

Which didn't exactly answer my question. I guessed it would depend on me. I was already thinking about how I could practice on Remmy without English tack.

On the way home, Dad asked about the lesson, which I described in as much detail as I could—probably *too* much detail. I was excited that he seemed so open to this new phase of my equestrian life and was happy to include him.

"So this is something you'd like to continue?"

"Yes!" I said. "I'd have a lesson every day if I could!"

Dad laughed. "I don't think that's going to be possible. Of course, if we lived closer, you could ride there more." He became thoughtful and I felt vaguely uneasy.

When we got home, I helped Paola get settled in our guest room and showed her where everything was. She helped me feed and groom Remmy and even helped clean his paddock as I cleaned his stall. I felt much happier than I had for quite a while and was very content with her being there.

"Have you heard from your parents, Paola?" asked Mom at dinner.

"Oh! Yes!" said Paola, smiling. "They arrived in Washington DC at twelve-thirty. They sent me a text message."

I felt horrible that I hadn't thought at all today about *why* Paola was staying with us.

"They have a meeting with someone at the embassy tomorrow morning. I hope . . . I am praying *so* much . . . that they will be able to help."

I tried to picture Mr. and Mrs. Bernal in a strange city, waiting for the opportunity to intercede for Rosa's brother, maybe their son as well. It must be nerve-wracking.

"Are you getting along all right at school?" Mom asked.

"Yes!" said Paola. "People are so kind and helpful."

I thought about Lori and the other girls and felt uncomfortable.

"You speak English extremely well," said Dad. "Did you learn mostly at school in Cuba?"

"Just a little. We have English but," she looked slightly embarrassed, "I learned most at home from my father and also from Claudio when he is with us." This caused her to look sad for a moment. She continued, "He lives . . . he lived . . . near the university, so we did not see him often. But he would stay with us when there was," she searched for the words, "*fiestas y vacaciones.*"

"Holidays?" asked Dad.

"Yes, holidays."

"Are you getting help at school?" asked Mom.

"Yes!" Paola beamed, a rosy glow burnishing her cheeks. "The teachers are so kind. And David." She, like the older Calderas, pronounced his name "Dah-*veed*," which made my heart ache, but just a little. "David Caldera is *very* helpful, always."

And that word, *always*, was painful too. I swallowed. Mom smiled at her, a curious light in her eyes. Then she looked at me. I looked down at my plate.

"But *you* know how generous he is also. He has given Allison such a beautiful horse."

Dad cleared his throat, and Mom looked even more searchingly at me.

"He . . . they . . . gave Robin a horse too," I said. "They just do things like that."

"Yes," said Paola, "but I do not think he gives *everybody* a horse."

Paola helped Mom and me clear the table. She chatted almost constantly, obviously happy to have my mom to converse with. But now that Dave's name had come up, he seemed to be *all* she wanted to talk about. Mom was more than happy to help her by asking pertinent questions. I stayed out of it unless I was asked something directly, and then I tried to sound neutral. Which I was, of course. I *had* to be. I just wished that Paola would talk about something else, some other absorbing interest, and that my mother wasn't always watching me.

"*El habla buenen español*," Paola said. "*Very* well . . . so he is able to explain things quickly to me."

"That must take a lot of extra time," said Mom.

"Not so much. *Tenemos permiso* . . . we have *permission* to be in the library during the study hall so that we can talk a little more. I like that *very* much."

Her cheeks were glowing again. It was becoming impossible not to picture them, heads close, talking softly together. I loved it so much when Dave spoke softly to me.

I washed the dishes while Paola dried and handed them to Mom to put away. Mom seemed to be watching *both* of us much more closely. But she looked more thoughtful than curious now. I hoped she was figuring things out for herself so that I wouldn't have to talk about it. Ever.

"What do you like most about Dave?" asked Mom.

Please stop, Mom! Let's change the subject already!

"*Es muy guapo* . . . *very* attractive. Do you not think so?" This was asked of me.

"Yes. Of course," I answered without looking up. It would just be ornery not to agree.

"But it is his kindness I like the best. He is very . . ." She searched for the word but seemed to be having trouble.

"Thoughtful?" offered Mom.

Paola frowned slightly.

Not the right word at all. "Patient," I said.

"Yes!" Paola was beaming again. "He is *very* patient and does not make me feel stupid *ever.*"

Yes, that's Dave. Soft words, encouraging gestures, patience. At least, once upon a time. . . .

I washed the last fork, dried my hands, and said, "I'm going upstairs to finish some homework and get my art ready for tomorrow." I didn't want to listen to anymore.

I had carefully rolled up my still lifes and secured them with several hair bands when Paola came up the stairs. Something had occurred to me while she and Mom were talking and I called to her. She came in and sat on my bed, smiling.

"I need to ask you to do something, and it's very important to me."

Her eyes widened slightly. "Of course! Anything!"

This was awkward and perhaps even selfish, but I felt sure it was the right thing to do—at least for my own peace of mind.

"Don't say anything to anyone about Northfield. Especially Dave." Something passed across her face, and I felt sure she'd already planned to tell him all about it. "Please?"

"But why?" she asked, obviously very surprised and, I think, disappointed.

I could understand that. I would have loved to tell him all about it myself if things were different. But what to say to Paola? There were all kinds of reasons why telling Dave or anyone else would be a bad idea. I thought I'd lived down the original assumption that I was a snob, but some people still might get the wrong idea. And I didn't want to be thought a traitor but resented the thought of having to defend myself.

The truth was that I just didn't want to be influenced in any way about it. I didn't care if Dave knew about choir. And the way he'd acted about Ben was annoying and perplexing but wasn't going to alter that friendship. But having lessons with Melanie was already taking on a vital aspect for me. It was going to be more than just a distraction, and I didn't want to know Dave's opinion concerning it.

"Dave really hates Northfield," I said. "I just don't want him to know. Actually, it would probably be best not to say anything to anybody. Even Robin." *Especially Robin.*

Paola looked unsure but shrugged slightly and said, "Okay."

"Thank you," I said, feeling relieved. In spite of her very social nature, I thought I could trust her.

Thursday passed quickly, too. I showed the different finished versions of my still life to Miss Laski and Melanie, and they helped me choose the best one. I added it to the others now attached to the whiteboards with magnets. When all the projects were up, we began the presentations.

I usually feel very anxious about speaking in front of classes, but I actually enjoyed explaining my theme, what the items in the still life were, and how I'd used light and shadow. It was fun seeing everyone else's projects too. Melanie's was probably the best in the class. Hers was a collection of antique china figurines and glass bottles that belonged to her mother.

"She loves old things," she said.

Choir was fun, though the constant reminders about our upcoming performance were making me feel nervous. At home, Ben did homework with us and gladly stayed to dinner again. Then he and Paola did an impromptu performance of a choir song Ben was dancing to, but he was so goofy about it that he had us all laughing.

I went to bed that night feeling like I had accomplished a lot. And I'd done it all without thinking about Dave. Well, mostly, and not in a moony, dejected way. I finally felt like I was getting somewhere—socially, emotionally, and riding, too—and Dave had *nothing* to do with it.

Paola's parents were still in Washington over the weekend. They had spoken to both my mom and dad, as well as Paola, of course. They were finding the process of diplomacy and appeals frustrating and worrying but were hopeful for some kind of resolution early the next week.

Paola and I were getting along just fine. She still wore me out a little with her constant chatter, but she also seemed to sense when I needed to have time alone and either spent time in her own room, outside, or with my mother. I appreciated it immensely. We were enjoying working on languages together too, though I needed far more help than she did. I also let her ride Remmy, and she helped me arrange a new obstacle course.

Saturday evening she came with me to babysit Cody and Zoe and taught us new games. Ben came over on Sunday to do yard work and stayed to hang out with us and Remmy, though he still kept his distance from the latter. It was an enjoyable weekend, and every time my mind wandered to similar times spent with different friends, I firmly redirected it. I was *not* going to let myself be sentimental for what used to be. Or might have been.

The whole next week continued in the same way—mostly positive, productive, and enjoyable. Even Ben was getting his homework done; at least his Spanish. Robin and I routinely sat with the choir kids now, especially Paola, Ben, and Hannah, and it was a fun group I felt relatively comfortable in. I was aware of Dave, of course, but chose to sit facing the field whenever I could. Matthew tried to wave us over to sit with him a couple of times, but I avoided that too.

Cris and some of the other seniors were at the tables more often now. A couple of the older girls were in our choir class, and I suppose some of the guys were on the soccer team, but except for Cris and Shane, I didn't know them.

I *did* notice Cris watching me more often, but he found no reason to approach me. I had mixed feelings about that. I was oddly comforted when he was there, his presence adding a veneer of normalcy to the new social structure and a link to the old. But it was unnerving too. A part of me wanted to talk to him, but I didn't know why or what I would have said. He always made me feel like I was bugging him. Still, there was something I liked about talking to him and, at least a couple of times, I'd *almost* thought he felt the same way.

Almost.

By that Wednesday, all conversations led inexorably to the Fall Dance on Saturday, the first dance of the year. I had wanted to go last year, dancing being something I really enjoyed though I knew I wasn't very good at it. Of course, back then I'd hoped that Dave might ask me to go, but he'd been out of town. I had hoped to dance with him during the dance unit in PE, too, and maybe Winter Formal, but that hadn't happened either. I *had* danced with him at Bar 8, and it was one of those memories I'd held on to and romanticized. But I wouldn't do that anymore. No, I had no expectations or desire to go to the dance.

Paola's parents had come back and they picked her up after school. I was both sad and relieved. Sad because it had been fun having her at my house and I liked her a lot; relieved because she really did wear me out, especially when she insisted on talking about the boys at school, and Dave in particular. Mom always encouraged her, too, as if she wanted to know what he was doing and what everyone thought of him, which I found very disconcerting. I had escaped whenever they started the boy talk.

Dad was there to give Paola her stuff and then take me to Northfield. He stayed long enough to visit the horses and chat briefly to both Melanie and Tatty. I was glad but still uneasy about his easy approval of everything having to do with Northfield. As for my lesson, I felt more at ease with Kitty, though she tested me a lot. Melanie laughed afterward and said it was good for me; I couldn't be lazy and really had to *ride* her.

I spent the evening finishing homework and then looking online for riding clothes, appalled at how expensive everything was and hoping my parents would help me purchase what I needed. I had some money saved from babysitting for Aunt Kate during the summer and from Cheryl since we'd been back, but only enough for a pair of the cheapest breeches and paddock boots.

Still, just the idea of new riding clothes kept me perfectly distracted all the next day—so much so that both my geometry teacher and Robin had to get my attention in class. That I was picturing myself looking even half as elegant as Melanie did in riding clothes was something I would never admit to. And of course, I avoided imagining what Dave would think. Mostly.

All in all, I was quite pleased with how well I'd made it through the last couple of weeks. I had just about all the distraction I could handle and was keeping busy enough to easily redirect my thoughts whenever necessary. And it *was* necessary, but I was doing better. I'd planned on not adding anything more, but something came up that changed my mind.

"Are you going to the dance?" Ben asked as we walked to the pool after choir.

"No," I said automatically.

"Why not?"

Because no one has asked me. Because I wouldn't go by myself. Because the only person I'd want to go with is Dave. And it was very possible he was going with someone else. "I don't want to."

"Really? Or is it because Mr. Right hasn't asked you?"

Shut up! I didn't answer.

On the drive home, it came up again.

"Do you have any plans this weekend, Ben?" asked Mom.

"Uh . . . sleep . . . eat . . . sleep some more. Vivian's threatening to call the CDC if I don't clean my room, so I guess I'll have to do that. I kind of wanted to go to the dance on Saturday, but. . . ." He didn't finish the thought, just grinned and shrugged his shoulders.

"Oh, I didn't know there was a dance." Mom looked over at me, but I was looking out the window and pretending not to listen. She didn't say anything more until we were sitting down to dinner with Dad.

"You never mentioned that there was a dance this weekend, sweetheart. Did you want to go?"

I was truly surprised by the question and again automatically said no.

"It sounded like Ben would like to go. You haven't," she started but seemed to re-think her words before continuing, "you haven't done much with your other friends lately. It might be fun."

It might be. . . .

Dad hadn't said anything, so Mom appealed to him. "You wouldn't mind her going to a school dance with Ben, would you?" Then she looked at me again, not waiting for an answer. "Are any of your other friends going?"

Dave. Maybe. But probably with Roberta.

I sighed and, after mentally setting those two people aside, said, "I don't know. Robin doesn't dance. At least she didn't. Melanie went last year, though." Mom continued looking at me searchingly. "I don't know about anyone else."

But now I *was* thinking about it. I said good night to Remmy thinking about it. I went to bed thinking about it. It occupied most of my thoughts on Friday—that and Dave's birthday, but I knew nothing about his plans for the latter and wasn't going to worry about it.

The matter of the dance was different though. I remembered how much fun it had been dancing with Gerald in PE last year, and he had asked me to Winter Formal. I should have gone but had been unwilling to consider going with anyone except Dave. Matthew had asked me too. I never found out what my answer to him would have been because Dave had practically told him I didn't like to dance. I still didn't understand that.

I liked the line dancing we'd done in PE too, and you didn't have to have a partner for that. Maybe Melanie would be going. Or Paola. She'd probably be a lot of fun at a dance. Or even Hannah, or Jessie, or Stacie. I was starting to realize I actually had a lot of people, at least friendly toward me, who I was sure I could hang out with.

I might never have a boyfriend, but I can at least enjoy dancing, can't I?

So I brought it up to Ben on the walk after school.

"Do you still want to go to the dance?"

"Yeah . . . kind of." Ben looked at me speculatively.

"I was thinking . . . maybe we could go together? You know, just for fun."

Ben raised his face to the sky, pumped his fists, and shouted, "Yes!"

His reaction startled me. "It's not a *date*," I said sternly, just wanting to confirm the nature of the proposition.

"Of course not," he said, then grinned widely and added, "my love."

"Please stop that."

"Okay," he said, still grinning and looking wholly unrepentant.

"I mean it. Or I won't go."

"Yeah." He was still grinning from ear to ear. "Got it."

Dad agreed to take Ben and me to the dance and pick us up after, though he seemed to want confirmation that it wasn't an actual date. In fact, my parents decided that *they* would have a date, a late dinner, then pick us up later. We could be there at least a couple of hours. I was pretty sure Robin wouldn't be going but thought Melanie might, so I called her. She verified that she was in fact going and we agreed to find each other there.

"I don't know what to wear," I admitted. I'd never been to an organized dance before.

"Almost anything," said Melanie. "As long as it's dress code. I think Lori got sent home last year for wearing something too sheer. Some people get very dressed up, but you don't have to. It's not like Winter Formal."

I didn't have any clothes I hadn't already worn to school at least several times, so I didn't stress too much over it. I wasn't concerned about impressing anyone. I just wanted to feel comfortable and look nice. Opting for one of the cute tops and skirts Aunt Audrey had bought me, I wore my hair down and put on just a little mascara. I looked much more like I had at the beginning of the school year, but I didn't feel at all the same. I was nervous, but it was an excited, not worried nervous.

We picked Ben up about seven-thirty and drove together to town. Ben always wore nice clothes, but he sometimes looked rumpled, as if he'd slept in them. Tonight his shirt looked ironed, and his pants looked new. His dark auburn hair was clean and wispy around his face—unadorned by silly hats or lensless glasses. I told him he looked really nice.

"You think so? I wasn't sure if Vivian would let me go, but she seemed glad and even pressed my shirt."

This sounded strange to me, but he looked happy—his eyes bright and his grin as impish as ever.

There were other people also getting dropped off at the back of the school near the gym, but most of the older students had probably driven themselves. Ben tried to buy my ticket, but I insisted on purchasing my own. He was starting to be such a brat about things, I didn't want to give him any reason to tease me about being his date.

While not specifically a homecoming dance, the gym was decorated with balloon arches, crepe garlands, and streamers in gold, white, and black—Panther colors. The bleachers on the west side were locked away, making it feel even bigger than usual. There was a long, wide platform on that side large enough for a full band to play on, but a DJ was set up there instead. Tables near the open bleachers on the other side held refreshments. The whole event had a simple, comfortable vibe to it, and I was glad. I could handle this.

No one was dancing, but people had begun congregating in small groups. I was surprised when Robin approached us. She had come with Tanner.

"What are you—" she started.

"You didn't tell—" I said at the same time.

We both laughed. I looked at Tanner—I'd never seen him look so neat—and marveled that he'd gotten her to go with him. Then I noticed Robin was looking speculatively at Ben.

"We just thought it would be fun," I tried to explain.

"Yeah . . . us too," she said, but *she* was blushing.

We laughed again. I think we both felt a little embarrassed.

The gym filled up pretty steadily. Stacie and Kyle arrived, obviously *very* much together, and Hannah and Paola seemed to have come together.

Jessie was there with a boy I didn't recognize. The gym wasn't crowded by any means, but it seemed like a good turnout.

There were still very few people actually dancing when the DJ decided to get things moving. A disco beat played on a loop while he had us all stand in lines and taught us steps. He did a couple of these—I guess to loosen everyone up—then began playing more familiar pop songs again. The lights had all been on while line dancing, but now several banks were turned off leaving the stage and refreshments well-lit and the center of the gym a little darker, just enough to lower inhibitions. The bright lights bothered me, so I liked it better anyway.

I could see what the kids had meant last year about dances being too well-chaperoned. There were at least five adults there I recognized as teachers and another five or six who must have been parents, but it didn't bother me.

"Come *on!*" said Ben, grabbing my hand and dragging me out toward the center of the floor.

It was fun to dance with him. He acted goofy again, but I think it was just to keep me at ease. I'd seen how well he could really dance. When that dance was over, Gerald appeared in front of me. They were playing something with a Latin flavor, and we had enormous fun trying to remember the salsa steps from last year. From the general laughter I heard around me, a lot of other people were too. After that, I danced with a boy I didn't know, which I felt very awkward about, and then with Ben again.

Melanie came a little late with Roger and found me to say hi, but I was glad Robin was there. She looked like she was having fun, too. I won't lie and say Dave never crossed my mind. I was thinking of how it would be even *more* fun to dance with him, when I saw Roberta arrive. And she wasn't alone.

I had noticed Lori and a large group of their friends earlier, and Roberta made her way to them immediately. Her escort saw me right away and walked over.

"I didn't know you were coming," he said, looking happy to see me.

I wasn't surprised to see Matthew, just surprised by his date. He was dressed neatly, his hair carefully gelled as I'd seen it on several occasions before. But I already knew he cleaned up nicely.

"Did you come alone?" he asked, looking around the darkened gym.

"Ben came with me," I said, unapologetically. By this time I was happy we'd come.

Matthew's eyebrows shot up, and he looked at me oddly. "Oh," he said, and I think he would have said more if Gerald hadn't come up to me again.

I was glad that Dave had *not* come. I imagined seeing him instead of Matthew arrive with Roberta; it would have pretty much ruined my evening. I probably would have felt more self-conscious about dancing with the other boys, too, especially Ben for some reason. And I knew I would have wasted too much energy hoping he would ask me to dance with him, all the time knowing that I shouldn't.

As it was, I got to dance to a lot of the songs and had people to stand and sit with in between. At one point I saw Ben dancing with Robin, and it struck me how adorable they looked together. From the way I saw him looking at her sometimes, I even wondered if *she* was the one he secretly liked. But when the song was over, he noticed me sitting and came over right away.

"Are you having fun?" he said, smiling.

"Yes!" I said and smiled back. "Yes, I am."

"Awesome," he said, then wandered off again.

Robin came and sat next to me, but Tanner immediately led her out to dance. *They* made a cute couple too, but I didn't think there was anything there—not on Robin's part anyway.

"May I have this dance?" Matthew stood in front of me, his hand held out.

I hesitated but couldn't think why, so I took his hand.

"So, I hear Ben lives near you," he said after a few moments. "Do you guys . . . hang out?"

"What?" I wasn't sure I liked the question. It was starting to grate on my nerves how interested everyone seemed to be in my friendship with Ben. "Not much," I answered, trying to make light of it. "We have some classes together, and he gets rides home with us sometimes."

He acknowledged this with a nod and one of those weird not-quite-smiles. I decided to turn the tables on him. Besides, I was curious.

"I was surprised to see you come with Roberta."

He gave a short laugh. "I wasn't her first choice. I hadn't made up my mind whether to come or not when she called asking if I'd meet her here." He shrugged his shoulders. "She didn't want to show up alone."

"Oh," I said, not sure whether to feel relieved or sorry for him. He didn't look exactly heart-broken.

"Now, if I'd known *you* were going to be here, I definitely would have come sooner." He was laughing again. "But then Roberta wouldn't have had a date."

I looked around and saw her dancing with an older boy nearby. She obviously noticed that I was dancing with Matthew and didn't look happy about it, but I couldn't see why she'd care. Everyone knew he wasn't the one she wanted, as Matthew had pointed out.

Ben was close to the refreshments and also watching us. He pointed at his eye, at Matthew, mouthed *googly*, and then wagged his eyebrows. It was a good thing I wasn't eating or drinking or I would have sprayed.

The evening seemed to go by so fast. I danced again with Ben as well as Tanner, Kyle, and another boy I didn't know. When the DJ finally announced he would be playing the last song, I got my phone out to text my mother, then looked up to see Matthew again.

"May I have the last dance?"

The music was slower than anything else the DJ had played all evening, and I'd already made up my mind to say no, just in case someone asked.

"I . . . don't really want to dance anymore." Then I felt bad, not wanting him to take it personally. "We could talk . . . if you want."

I thought he looked disappointed but he smiled and sat next to me. Some of our friends were soon gathered in our general vicinity making private conversation impossible, which I was thankful for. When my mother messaged that they were waiting in the parking lot, I made a point of finding Robin and saying goodbye, and then got Ben and left.

It had been a fun, almost angst-free and, concerning my friends' inter-relationships, somewhat enlightening evening.

Chapter Seventeen

On Monday Ben's foster dad, Bill, who was apparently also his uncle—I was still confused about that—was away on business and Ben hadn't gotten up early enough to catch the school bus, so he rode with Dad and me. It wasn't the first time it had happened. I was seriously starting to wonder about his home life. But he hadn't volunteered any more information, and when I might have had an opportunity to ask, he kept me so distracted by stories and nonsense that I'd forget.

It quickly became apparent that we were definitely the objects of speculation at school, which was funny and, of course, very annoying. Extremely puzzling too. Why anyone cared is beyond me. It wasn't as if Ben was highly sought after, though he was friendly enough and I didn't think there was anything wrong with his appearance, barring the goofy accessories he sometimes wore. Today he wore the fake glasses and a Peruvian hat with long, dangly ties. I wore my glasses too, with my hair pulled back in my now usual ponytail.

I felt myself the object of observation before Spanish started, and there was some whispering and laughing, which may or may not have been about us. Ben sat in his regular seat to the side and behind me and may have heard what they were saying, but he never told me, and I didn't want to ask.

I was blissfully unaware of anything except Robin's presence in Geometry. Matthew met us after class and walked with us to our lockers and then to the tables.

"Did you both enjoy the dance?" he asked.

"It was all right," said Robin, as if she had no strong feelings about it. But I was pretty sure she'd enjoyed it very much.

"It was fun," I said and meant it but didn't elaborate.

Robin and I joined Paola and Hannah on the grass and were soon joined by Ben. Matthew went to the tables, but I didn't even look in that direction. Tanner walked over from the tables and joined us too. There were often more people on the grass now than around the tables.

When the bell rang, I said, "See ya," to Robin and Ben and began walking toward the gym with Hannah.

"Hey."

I was brought up very short by the voice and turned around. Hannah stopped too. Dave glanced once at her then looked steadily at me. Hannah said she'd see me in a minute and, it seemed somewhat reluctantly, turned and walked away. Roberta, Lori, and about three other girls also walked past. Roberta looked intently at Dave as if she'd love an excuse to interrupt us, but Dave looked in the other direction for a moment, long enough for the girls to walk out of hearing distance.

"I heard you went to the dance," he said without preamble.

"Yes."

"With that Ben guy."

"I went to the dance with Ben. Yes."

"Why?"

"Because I wanted to. It sounded like fun. And it was."

He looked confused; a rare expression that I loved.

"Dude, you're not her dad." Matthew had walked close by and heard us. "You're not even her *brother*." He said the word as if it had special meaning between them. As he continued to walk away, he said, "You can't tell her who she can or can't go out with."

Dave glanced at him then turned quickly back to me as if ignoring him, but Matthew's words obviously bothered him.

"So . . . you're going out with him?"

He sounded nonchalant as if he were only curious, but he didn't look it. I thought about the question, imagining myself with Ben. If circumstances were different, I might have laughed.

"Um . . . no. Not exactly."

Dave seemed to relax slightly but still looked bugged. I was bugged too. *You've barely talked to me at all so far this year and you're mad because you think I'm going out with Ben?*

"Um . . . I've got to go," I said, feeling uncomfortable, confused, and wanting to end the conversation.

"Yeah . . . okay." He didn't sound okay, he sounded aggravated. But that didn't make sense. And it really wasn't my problem.

I walked to the left side of the gym, he toward the right. Roberta glared at me as I walked past her in the locker room. I took extra care during class, watching out for extended legs.

The conversation bothered me for the rest of the day and well into the night. I tried not to think about it, and tried not to read anything into it, but it was impossible. And the conversation itself wasn't even what disturbed me the most. What really bothered me was how differently he acted; so different from last year, and not just toward me but in general toward everybody. It definitely wasn't my imagination.

I still wondered what had happened over the summer. What had changed him? And why did he act so weirdly around me? I didn't feel like I had changed . . . not *that* much. I was still obsessing over him, wasn't I? Yet I'd also been able to function quite well—exceptionally well, for me—without his attention or help. Without *him*. That was certainly different and had to be a good thing. Right?

Did I feel differently toward him? Before eventually falling asleep, I examined this in great detail, from the way I felt every time I saw him, to the way I saw him interact with others, especially girls—in particular, Roberta and, even more particularly, me. I came to the conclusion that, though my hopes and expectations had altered immensely, my feelings were the same as ever. I'd been sure they would never change, and nothing had happened to alter my opinion.

I loved him. I would always love him. It was pathetic and nonsensical, but it seemed even more ridiculous to imagine I could ever feel like this for anyone

else, that I could possibly ever want someone else. Ever. Poetic metaphors like mountains having to crumble into the sea made perfect sense to me.

So that was the way it would be. I had hoped—no, not just hoped, I had *prayed*—for a return to a close friendship, but that seemed as unlikely now as a romantic relationship. And I was just going to have to live with it.

I awoke with a start, remembering Dave's birthday. It was tomorrow. *Should I get him something? What could I get him?* I had no clue. I knew what a lot of his interests were, but not enough to know what he would like or what accessories he could use. And when would I be able to give a gift to him? There had been no mention of a party or anything. At least, not around me.

What if he just didn't invite you? The thought made my heart crumble around the edges a little. *Would he do that? Exclude me?* It didn't seem likely. He obviously still cared about me in some way. *Enough, apparently, to take notice of who I was spending time with.* I thought of Matthew last year, and now Ben. *Enough to still interfere.*

In Chemistry, I thought about asking Matthew if he knew anything about Dave's birthday plans, but decided that, considering his remark to Dave yesterday, it would make me feel even more uncomfortable. I hoped Robin would say something in History. She didn't, though she did seem grouchy. I didn't hear anything at lunch and hoped something would come to light during English, but apart from Roberta literally hanging on Dave as they walked in, nothing did. At the end of class, he was out the door before I'd closed my notebook.

October twenty-first: Dave's actual birthday. I was determined to find a way—any way—to wish him a happy one. I didn't have anything to give him, not even a card, but this seemed less important than letting him know I was thinking about him and wishing him well.

The mystery of whether there would be some kind of big party like last year was solved at lunch; there wouldn't be. There would be no movie or other event where everyone was invited. For his sixteenth birthday, Mr. Caldera and Cris were taking him and his closest friends—*guy* friends— surfing and camping in Big Sur. This went a long way toward explaining

Robin's grumpiness and should have served to allay any worries of mine, but I still felt uneasy.

I thought I might be able to wish him a happy birthday on the way to PE, but Roberta and Lori and some of the others were staying so close to him, it would have been weird and intimidating. He looked in my direction once before walking off with them, but the memories of our last interaction and the current crowd prevented me from doing anything.

After school, before going our separate ways, Robin asked if I wanted to come to her house since my dad was gone and mom was working. I said, "Maybe Thursday?" and she agreed. I did tell her that I was hanging out with Melanie after school on Wednesdays, but I didn't say where or why and she didn't ask. She had always seemed vaguely disapproving of Melanie, though she didn't know her.

On the other hand, my dad approved so wholeheartedly of Melanie—and Northfield in general—that I would be allowed to go there with her and Roger on Wednesdays, even though he had never met the latter. I felt guilty about not telling my other friends what I was doing, but I didn't want to have to deal with anyone's judgments or opinions.

Melanie sat in the front passenger seat while Roger drove the dark blue Mercedes. I sat in the back. They talked easily back and forth about their day and horses and people I'd never heard of. Just as I'd always envied the comfortable relationship between Dave and Robin, I envied how comfortable Melanie and Roger seemed with each other. I'd never felt that way with *anyone* but had begun to think, before summer, that I almost had that kind of friendship with Dave. But now. . . .

I got my phone out. *'I didn't get a chance to tell you earlier—Happy Birthday!'*

My phone sat in my lap all the way to the stables, but I received no reply.

I had a good lesson on Kitty, though. Melanie and I got changed in a room in the office, then I went to get Kitty ready for Melanie's first lesson. While she was busy with that, I wandered around visiting the other horses and even got some homework done. I considered walking to the community center—it wasn't that far and I was a little hungry—but decided against it.

Melanie worked me hard during my lesson. I was getting the hang of diagonals, and she seemed pleased with my rising trot—said I wasn't throwing myself out of the saddle so much. But she mostly had me doing leg work and circles at a sitting trot. Kitty behaved, for the most part, and I felt satisfied and encouraged. Afterward, I got Kitty walked out, cooled down, and put back in her stall while Melanie gave her last lesson. My mom arrived to pick me up about the time she was done.

"How is it going?" asked Mom.

"Great . . . I think," I said, realizing that Melanie and Kitty might have a different opinion.

"She's doing very well," said Melanie. "She has a good foundation and basic aids. She should be able to pursue any discipline she chooses."

I wasn't exactly sure what she meant by that, and it didn't look like Mom did either, but I felt incredibly encouraged.

We gave Mom a quick tour of the stables as she'd never been there before, and of course I introduced her to Kitty, Digs, and Beau. She seemed appropriately delighted. On the way home, I told her about my lessons and about Tatiana and anything else I could think of related to Melanie and Northfield. Then I remembered my phone and dug it out of my backpack.

Dave had replied, '*Thanks.*'

I don't know what I'd expected, but I guess more than that. Maybe enough to reply back again, some semblance of conversation.

But that seemed to be that.

I was tempted to go the tables Thursday, a familiar need gnawing away at my heart, but I resisted. It would be stupid and serve no purpose. I was not going to rearrange my life on the off-chance that Dave might glance in my direction or might talk to me. *Definitely not!*

So it more than surprised me to find him waiting for me after English. He'd left the room immediately and I had taken my time. Though Art was at the other end of campus, I didn't need to make any stops along the way, and Miss Laski was lenient. Anxiety about bumping into Dave had trumped concern over being late, and taking my time after class usually helped in avoiding him. Now, I couldn't.

"Hey," he said.

"Hi," I responded, probably looking as surprised and wary as I felt.

"We're hanging out tomorrow . . . at the Marlow station. I just wanted to make sure you knew this time."

"Oh," I said, my brain scrambling to decide if this was an actual invitation. These sudden meetings always threw me completely.

"Yeah," he said, "it might be the last time we all walk there. Drinks are on me."

He was watching my face closely. I tried to concentrate on the words he was saying but was too distracted by the movement of his lips.

"Okay," I said. I think.

"Okay," he repeated, his expression unchanged, unreadable. He started to turn away but turned back and added, "You can ask that guy . . . Ben . . . to come. If you want." He took a few steps backward as he said, "Tell him to bring his board."

Then he walked away.

The Marlow Station is the abandoned gas station on the west side of town near the strip mall. A large group of us gathered after school on Friday and walked, more or less together, to the coffee shop where, true to his word, Dave treated everyone to the beverage of their choice. It must have cost him at least a couple of hundred dollars. I'd never held that much money all at one time. A lot of the kids took the opportunity to order expensive drinks. I didn't want to feel like I was taking advantage of his generosity, so I ordered a small iced tea. Robin and Ben did the same.

From there the group straggled over to the old station, some taking their time and a few remaining at the coffee shop. Those of us who were there purely for Dave and not just the free drinks walked over to the station immediately.

I thought about Dave going out of his way to invite me. He could have just asked Robin to tell me as he'd done on other occasions. So apparently it was important enough to ask me personally. I hoped this was a good sign, an indication that my friendship was still meaningful to him. But I wasn't going to read too much into it. And telling me that I could invite Ben? That had surprised me, given his general attitude toward him, but I supposed it was just his generous nature winning out.

What had struck me even more was, "It might be the last time . . ." That had left me feeling sad and a little empty. Not walk together anymore? It wasn't as if we did it a lot, but I treasured my memories of walking around town with Dave—and other friends. But almost everyone was driving now.

Not Ben and me, but most of our other friends drove or would be driving soon, though they were all walking today. To think there would be no more days like this was depressing.

Robin, Ben, and I sat on the end of a pump island and watched the skaters warming up. There were only about twelve on skateboards, including three girls. One of them was Jessie. I was a little surprised Ben didn't join them right away, but he seemed content to sit next to me, watching the others and sipping his tea through a straw.

There were apparently several skate-worthy areas of the station: the spaces between the pump islands and the low curbs at the front of the station; the front of the building, which had no railing but had an access ramp and higher curbs; and the back corner where the hillside had been paved to prevent erosion and included railings and a low wall. Dave and Tanner and a few of the others favored this last area and were already taking turns working the corner.

I realized someone was missing. "Where's Cris?"

It wasn't that he always hung out with us. In fact, except occasionally during lunch at school, we rarely saw him anymore. But it seemed like he should be here today.

Robin frowned and shook her head. "Don't know. He might be at school . . . you know, college. I don't know when his classes are."

I'd forgotten about that. Somehow the fact that he wasn't here on this historic occasion just aggravated my proactive nostalgia and feelings of regret. Would we ever gather like this again?

Ben finally stood up, set his drink next to me, dropped his board, and began skating. At first he just skated near us, working the board at angles and doing small flips. It was fun to watch him though. It struck me that he had a similar grace to Cris, making his moves look not just easy but effortless. Except when he miscalculated. Then he was all arms and legs and goofy grins.

Robin watched him, too. "Do you know how to really use that thing?" she called to him.

His face lit up at that, smile wide, eyes laughing. He seemed thrilled by her attention. "A little," he called back.

I looked toward the corner and watched Dave, though he was just standing and holding his board. He and Matthew were talking to some girls, but he kept looking toward Ben. Ben dropped his board again, skated around to the front of the building, up the ramp, flipped his board as he turned at the top, and then sped down the ramp again and hopping his board on and off the curb.

"Not bad," said Robin when he returned to us.

"Not bad?" he said, still smiling. He popped his board up and held it out to her. "Here."

She looked embarrassed. "I didn't say *I* could skate."

He grinned.

"Hey! Ben!" Dave called to him.

"Uh oh," said Ben as if he were in trouble, but his eyes were laughing.

He skated over to the others, and they talked for a couple of minutes, inspecting boards and seeming to get to know each other a bit better. A few of the skaters had been half-heartedly using the back corner as a one-way ramp, running up carrying their boards and skating down. Dave and Tanner had done flips at the bottom, but nothing more. Now the immediate area cleared of all but the most serious skaters. Last year I had watched from a distance, from the coffee shop, as Dave, Cris, and others skated—and crashed. Now I could see how high the back of the lot really was, how steep the corner.

Tanner was the first to go to the top, set his board down, ride to the bottom, across the corner, and up the other side. His board crept up to the upper edge, then he came back down. There was general murmur and most of the other kids came over to watch. Robin and I were already pretty close and could see just fine so stayed where we were.

Ben went next, receiving his own murmur of approval. Dave nodded to him and did the same, followed by a few others, some of whom didn't quite make it up to the edge. A couple of them lost control of their boards at the bottom, but nobody fell. When everyone that was interested had had a turn, there was a little more talking.

Dave was the first to attempt more than a simple run. He got enough momentum coming down the first side that he shot up the other, leaving the pavement completely, then skated down, flipping his board again on reaching the bottom. Tanner went next and did more or less the same. After a couple of other boys and one of the girls, Ben took his fake glasses off and walked over to Dave, holding them out as if expecting him to look after them. Dave frowned and narrowed his eyes but took the frames. A couple of people smothered laughs. Robin rolled her eyes.

Ben went to the top of the hillside, set his board down and put one foot on it, then crouched low, taking a moment as if gauging something. Then he dropped with surprising speed, his body lowering even more into the curve, and shot up the other side. He cleared the top by at least two feet, tucking his knees up tight and grabbing his board, flipping it on the way down and shooting up the first side again. When he got to the top, he jumped off, catching his board and grinning from ear to ear.

The approval was much more than a murmur now, and Dave was smiling widely too—his dangerous, mischievous smile. In spite of what I was sure it meant, I was so happy to see it. It had been a long time.

Dave tossed Ben's glasses back to him, and Ben came over and gave them to me, along with the hat. Things escalated pretty quickly from there, the impromptu competition narrowing to Dave, Ben, Tanner, and three other boys. Matthew had dropped out when Dave began incorporating the railing. That's when the falls started. And that's when I started feeling anxious. I couldn't help it; I felt every impact as if I'd fallen myself. Dave fell twice and I practically fell off the curb both times. But I admired them all. They looked like they were having so much fun—I wouldn't have changed that for the world. And it was fun to watch them, especially Dave and Ben.

We'd been there about an hour when a tan-colored squad car pulled into the parking lot and drove slowly in our direction. A few kids looked worried, but Dave walked over to speak to the officer inside. Hannah and Roberta followed. The car stopped near where Robin and I sat.

"We got a concerned citizen call," the deputy said. "I'm going to have to ask you to break it up and go on home. This isn't a skate park."

I thought maybe if it were just up to him, he would have left us alone.

Dave smiled back. "Okay. No problem."

"Appreciate it," said the deputy. He backed up and just as slowly drove away.

"I guess we're done," said Dave, looking disappointed but not angry.

Everyone else sounded disappointed too, but most of the kids took it in stride. Some of them wandered back to the coffee shop or down to the taco place, probably to wait for rides. A large group of us walked back toward town, our numbers diminishing as kids went their separate ways. Tanner, Robin, and Dave were some of the first to leave. We stopped on the corner of Robin's street while the others kept walking.

"You're good," Dave said to Ben. "Really good."

"Thanks!" beamed Ben, bumping Dave's offered fist.

Dave glanced at me and his expression changed slightly. He looked at Ben, said, "See you around," and then looked back at me.

"I'm going to be bored tomorrow," Robin said. "So call me. Okay?"

"Okay," I said, nodding.

We began to go our separate ways, Ben and me toward the pool and the others turning down the street, Dave obviously hanging out with one of them. But I had to say something.

"Dave!"

He and the others stopped and stared at me, curious.

"Happy birthday," I said. "I hope you have a lot of fun this weekend."

He regarded me for a moment too long, and I realized that my wish for his happiness was *so* much more. I wondered if he realized it as well.

"Thanks," he said earnestly, then turned and walked away with the others.

Ben couldn't stop talking about the skating the rest of the way to the pool. He seemed thrilled to have been included and was especially admiring of Dave.

"Did you see it when Dave . . . ? What about when he . . . ?"

If he were a girl, I would have suspected he had a crush on him. But he didn't wait for responses from me, and I was happy to let him rave.

Later that night, I lay awake puzzling over Dave's attitude toward both me and Ben. I could come to no conclusions except that he perhaps still felt some responsibility for me. But responsibility wasn't the same as affection. On the one hand, it was nice to know that he cared at all. On the other, I didn't want his charity. Or his interference. Or his leftover attention. I just didn't understand him at all.

A light rattling noise at my back window alerted me that Ben was lurking. I went to the window to let him know I'd heard him, but the waning moon was just coming up behind the hills and I could barely see him. I pulled on a sweatshirt and put my flip-flops on outside.

"I couldn't sleep," he said.

"So I see."

"Do you mind?"

"No. I wasn't sleeping either."

I could just barely see his grin and nod. He was wearing a sweatshirt too, hood on and hands in pockets. He looked up at the sky and said, "See! I told you it would be easier to see the stars now."

He was right. It wasn't the first time I'd seen a clear, moonless night sky here, of course, but it was the first time since the observatory trip and the first time really seeing it and sharing it with someone. I joined him in leaning back against Remmy's paddock rails, looking up. Remmy came to stand beside me, and I played with him and kept him from bothering Ben. Ben pointed out constellations and told me about Florida, the Everglades, and alligators. He said he'd lived there briefly with his mother.

After a while I went back into the house and back to bed, falling asleep quickly. I dreamed of Dave skateboarding with Ben and dancing with me.

I called Robin the next day as I'd promised. Remmy and I were hanging out in the shade by the stream. Robin was apparently also outside and playing with Gali, but she sounded very disgruntled.

"All summer surfing, and what does he choose to do for his birthday?"

I pretended to commiserate. "Yes, it's very unreasonable of him."

"Ugh! It wouldn't be so bad if it wasn't so hot here. All I can think about is going to the beach. I keep picturing Dave surfing, and it makes me mad."

Now I was picturing Dave surfing, too: exuberant and soaking wet. Dave wore water so attractively.

"Still," she said, "I think I know why he did."

I wouldn't have thought that Dave needed a reason for choosing to celebrate his birthday this way, but I said, "Why?" anyway.

"Cris'll be leaving for university next year. Dave said he was missing him already and that they'd hardly ever get to do stuff together anymore. I think it's really bothering him. At least, something is, but he won't tell me what."

"Hmm," was the only response I felt safe in making. I hadn't thought much about Cris going away—indefinitely. As close as the brothers were, it made sense that it would weigh on Dave's mind.

"So, next Wednesday's the last home game. Are you going?"

Somewhere in the back of my mind I'd known this, but with everything else going on and not really being in that conversation loop anymore, I'd forgotten. Plus, Wednesday—Northfield.

"Oh . . . no, I don't think I can."

"That's too bad. You could have spent the night or something."

I agreed it would be fun but said I wasn't sure. We decided to talk about it at school. As soon as I was off the phone, I remembered something else affected by Northfield—the choir concert later that evening.

Dad came home on Monday and solved one problem by saying he'd pick me up from Northfield and drive me back to Douglas for the concert. I'd have to get myself changed and tidied up in between. At Tuesday's rehearsal, Mr. T. said we could bring our concert clothes in the morning and keep them in his office if we weren't going home first. This worked well for Ben, and we gave him and his clothes a ride to school Wednesday morning.

I took my dress and shoes with me to Northfield and changed in the office after my lesson. Mom and Dad had picked up a hamburger and drink for me, but I was so nervous I couldn't eat. I was thinking through all the words to the five songs we were singing—three by ourselves and two with the combined men's and women's choirs. I was even more worried about the choreography and hoped I could fake it through anything I didn't remember. It wasn't the actual performance I was nervous about but the audience. If we could just perform without one, I'd be fine!

The concert was at the Presbyterian church, not far from school. A lot of the kids had attended the Junior Varsity soccer game but were now dressed and ready at the church. Some of the other kids had stayed for as much of the Varsity game as they could, including Ben, Hannah, and Paola. That made me nervous too, worrying about whether they would get there on time. It was clear that I was the only person from our extended group who hadn't gone to the game. I tried not to think about that, though. A few weeks ago I would have wondered if I'd been missed. Now, I was really hoping my absence wasn't noticed. I couldn't afford to feel bad about it either way.

The two regular choirs—men's and women's—would perform separately first, so those of us not in either group sat in the front row on one side of the church. There weren't many of us.

It wasn't the first time I'd been in a church, but it wasn't an environment I was used to. Most people seemed to be keeping their voices lowered, which was calming, and the stained glass windows were a welcome distraction.

As time drew closer and closer to the start, I tried not to keep looking back to see who had arrived. It only made me more nervous. I wasn't surprised

to see Paola's parents. They sat near mine. Hannah's dad was there too. I wondered if Ben's folks would come.

When Stacie arrived with Kyle, I felt a bit better. I assumed it meant the others were on their way, whether the game was over or not. Jessie arrived next, loudly, with another boy I didn't recognize, both dressed for the performance.

Last year I'd had trouble telling Jessie and Stacie apart; they had been similar in many ways: both about the same height, similar length blond hair, and usually dressed in jeans and t-shirts or sweatshirts. But they had changed this year too, and now it was easy. Jessie was the glamorous one— her hair usually curled, her make-up perfect, and her clothes more stylish and often a little dazzling. Stacie had gained some weight, wore very little make-up, and still dressed plainly but was just as pretty. She came across as very down-to-earth and seemed the most mature of all of us, which made sense since she was the oldest. It seemed like she and Kyle were never far from each other.

At a quarter to seven, Hannah, Paola, Ben, and quite a few others finally came in just before Mr. Tanaka called us to warm up in a little back room.

"You should have come to the game!" Ben whispered between vocalises.

"Did they win?" I whispered back.

"Sure did! Eight, zero! I think I want to take up soccer next year."

I smiled and shook my head, glad to have him near. Who'd have thought Ben could be a stabilizing influence on me!

The women's choir sang first while the rest of us sat in the front pews. I loved their songs—so different from ours. They sang in Latin, German, and Finnish, and the harmonies were beautiful. I'd never heard music like it and loved hearing the different languages.

The guys sang next, and I was entranced by their songs too. The first was a boisterous sea chanty and the second a stirring spiritual. The third was in Spanish with a little choreography, a rousing *canción* that Ben performed with gusto. He was the only boy I really knew, so I watched him most of the time. He noticed, smiling at me often, and I smiled back.

The men's and women's choirs combined for two more songs, then Mr. Tanaka introduced his newest choir—us!

Most of the guys sat down while the rest of us, plus quite a few of the girls from the women's choir, arranged ourselves on the risers. I was wishing

I'd been placed with the altos so I'd be closer to Hannah and Paola—what a turnaround!—when I noticed that a group of boys stood along the back on one side of the sanctuary; some of the soccer team, including Dave and Tanner. I tried to keep my eyes glued to Mr. Tanaka or to the other side of the building, over the audience's heads so I wouldn't look at anyone in particular, sitting or otherwise. I could see Cris, too, leaning against the wall in the shadow of the entryway.

Our first song was a Disney medley that most of the group had seemed embarrassed about when we first started learning it, but now everyone adored. There were solos—Ben and Paola each had one—and lots of different parts. The second was an African folk song. There was some tricky choreography involved, but I thought I did okay. Our last was a heartbreaking folk ballad that I loved and always got a little choked up over while singing. Seeing the guys at the back made it even harder; I was emotionally affected by the lyrics and music and distracted by their presence. Especially Cris. I remembered what Robin had said about Dave missing him already.

When our group was done, the audience applauded appreciatively, but shrill whistles came from the back. A lot of people turned to see who was making the noise, which made me feel embarrassed but even more proud of our performance. I thought we sounded pretty good, too. I was really glad I had joined choir.

We remained on the risers as the rest of the women's and men's choirs joined us for two last songs. I'd been looking forward to this as we had never rehearsed with the other choirs. I was curious about how we'd sound. By this time I was almost wholly distracted, but I thought we sounded good. Our first was the pop song that Ben and Hannah had sang and danced to at my house. Our last song, a medley from *Les Mis*, made me choke up a little again and was met with more whistling and loud calls for an encore from the back, I think mostly from Tanner and Dave.

As we didn't have an encore prepared, I went immediately to my parents. They were smiling widely and seemed very happy. I saw Dave talking in a group with Robin, Stacie, Jessie, Hannah, and some others, but I didn't let my glance linger. I looked for Cris, but he didn't seem to be in the building any longer.

Robin joined us as Ben bounced over. Dad congratulated him on his solo, choreography, and dancing duet with Hannah. It truly was terrific.

"Thanks!" he said. Then, "I think I'm going to be a choreographer."

"I thought you were going to be an astronaut?" I said.

He seemed to consider. "I can do choreography in my spare time. Or maybe I can be a part-time astronaut."

My parents laughed.

Robin looked skeptical, but said, "It was really cool. The whole concert. I've never been to a choir performance before."

I was pleased that she liked it. "Do you have a ride home?" I asked.

She thanked us but said that Cris was giving her and Tanner a ride home when Dave left.

I looked once more in Dave's direction to see that he was watching us steadily, but he made no move to approach and didn't smile. Then he turned back to the others. Robin said bye to us, and I left with my parents and Ben. The latter kept a conversation going with Mom all the way home, which I was thankful for. My mind wouldn't settle on one thought long enough to participate. Feelings of elation from a good riding lesson and the choir performance along with the positive physical aspect of both were at odds with the emotions stirred up by at least two of the songs and Dave's presence.

And Cris. Now I was missing him already, too.

Chapter Eighteen

November arrived feeling much the same as October, which is to say, much the same as summer. The nights were cooler, but the days varied between bearably warm to uncomfortably hot and no sign at all of rain. Personally, it meant I was still setting sprinklers on the back lawn, there was nothing for Remmy to nibble in the corral down by the stream, and the surrounding countryside remained a crispy tan and brown.

At Bar 8, I became aware of much greater concerns and realized that the Calderas must be facing the same problems: less grazing, higher hay prices, and greater risk of wildfires. It was the latter that seemed the worst to me, but I overheard conversation at the tables that enlightened me on several aspects of the former.

Apparently water, or the lack thereof, was the most significant issue to the farm and ranch community here in the Douglas area. Water was routinely rationed through the dry months of May to September, so after the last crops of the summer, the fields were most often left fallow. But rain in October could usually be counted on to at least prepare the earth for planting, if not to saturate the soil. Good rain in October would saturate enough to sink into watersheds and provide runoff to reservoirs. But it was November, and there hadn't been one single rainy day. Last year had been considered a drought, in spite of the rain we'd had. This year wasn't off to a good start.

Tom and Cheryl didn't grow their own hay; they usually bought from local ranchers. The Calderas, I knew, grew enough hay to meet their own needs for most of the year and especially through the summer and fall under normal circumstances. But apparently even they were already buying from other ranches. Lack of rain throughout the West had driven the price of hay and other feed up, and many people were buying from Oregon and as far away as Idaho and Washington, and that was expensive. I didn't comprehend the complexities of the situation, but I was now aware they existed.

On the first day of the month, Sunday, I called Brenda. I had avoided talking to her while I was miserable; I doubted I could fake it well to her and dreaded any mean remarks, unintentional or otherwise. But I was doing better, and it had been quite a while since we'd talked.

"Hi," she said. Her voice sounded unnaturally soft.

"Hi," I said, already wondering what was going on. There was a silence—very unusual—and I wasn't sure what to say. I'm horrible at small talk, and Brenda had always led the way. "How is school?" Not something I really wanted to know, but the only question I could think of.

"It sucks. How about you?"

I was beginning to think I'd caught her in one of her peevish moods. That was never fun.

"Mmmm . . . it's okay. I like some of my classes." Silence on the other end again. *Okay, not peevish.* "How's Trevor?" Then I realized that he might be the problem. "Are you still going out with him?" *Then* I realized I probably shouldn't have asked. I certainly didn't want to talk about *my* current situation.

"Yeah," she said, still very softly. "I think so." Then it sounded like she was crying.

"What's wrong?" Now I was concerned. This wasn't like her at all.

She sniffled. "I think he's mad at me."

"Why?"

No response, just more sniffles. I was trying to picture Brenda crying—I don't think I'd *ever* seen her cry before.

"I'm just being stupid . . . sorry. Tell me what you've been up to."

I didn't know how to comfort her, so I thought distracting her might be just as good. I told her about Melanie and riding at Northfield, about choir and our performance, and about Paola and Ben. She asked a few questions on these topics, and I even made her laugh when I described some of Ben's antics. By the time we hung up, she sounded happier, but I was still worried. Then I realized that's what *she* was. Worried.

Monday was a full moon. I knew the moon would be full because Ben had told me so during Spanish. And he'd said it with such a gleam in his eye that I wasn't surprised when gravel rattled lightly on my bedroom window that night. I even welcomed it.

"Did I wake you up?"

"No," I said. I didn't tell him that I'd been waiting. It was cold enough now after dark to need coats on, so I'd gotten fully dressed after I heard my parents go to bed.

Ben looked around. "It's so light, you can see almost everything."

I could see Remmy standing in his paddock, watching us. Light gleamed off the lighter colored surfaces, the tops of trees, and the water in Remmy's trough. But the shadows were too dark to see into.

"I was wondering," I said, "do you know what's out behind us? Behind the hills?"

Dad hadn't gotten around to going for any extended walks with me, and the one time I had tried to ride there, Remmy had become increasingly nervous. I hadn't felt confident enough to push him, but I was very curious.

Ben shook his head. "I haven't thought much about it."

"How do you get here? Do you walk on the road?"

He shook his head again. "There's only the Fredericks between us, and they're old. They must go to bed about nine o'clock. At first I was afraid they might have dogs. But they don't. So I just cut across the back of their yard and climb through the fences. I tore my shirt going back last time though. Vivian threw a fit." He frowned. "She gets upset about a lot of things."

I wasn't sure how to respond to that, so I tried to change the subject slightly. "So, she's your aunt?"

"Yeah. Only, she's Bill's second wife. They haven't been married that long . . . maybe three or four years. She wigs out a lot. Especially about me."

"Like how? Why?"

He shrugged. "I get on her nerves. I forget stuff. And I guess I'm messy and noisy. I don't mean to be. Other stuff too, I guess. And she sometimes talks in Korean, so I don't know what she's saying. I think it has something to do with my mother. Vivien doesn't trust me. She's always saying that I don't know how lucky I have it and that if Bill hadn't gone looking for me, I'd still be at that group home. Or in Juvenile Hall. Or out on the street."

"Group home?"

Ben looked uncomfortable as if he'd said way more than he'd meant to. He shrugged again. "Hey . . . let's go explore!"

I looked back toward the house. "I don't know . . . if my parents find me gone, I don't know what they'd do. I'd better stay close. Besides, it's school tomorrow."

He was frowning, grinning, and shaking his head. The truth was that I very much wanted to explore but was already starting to shiver a little, and not because it was too cold.

"Chicken," he taunted.

"Yes," I acknowledged.

"Your parents aren't going to wake up, and even if they do, would they go into your room?"

I admitted that it was highly unlikely.

"Come on," he said, walking away toward the dirt road. "It's practically daylight. We won't go far."

I hesitated a moment more, then said, "Okay, but let's cut across the stream *this* way. It'll be quicker."

He agreed, and we walked almost straight back behind the stable, down the hillside, and through the remaining brush closer to the stream. The stream itself was barely two feet wide right now, and we jumped across easily. Then we headed through the trees until we reached the dirt road.

"How far have you gone?" asked Ben.

"There's a wide gate across the road that's locked and a smaller gate next to it that isn't." That gate had been wide open when I'd first seen it, and I assumed it was how Gold had gotten onto our property last year. "There's a 'no motor vehicles' sign on the gate, but it doesn't say anything about horses. I took Remmy through the side gate, but he started acting really nervous when I mounted him on the other side. I'm not sure why. It might just have been because I was nervous."

"I don't know anything about horses," he said as we reached the fence. "Just camels."

"Camels?" Completely diverted, I followed him through the smaller gate, and we continued down the road.

"Yeah. I never owned one, of course, but I rode them when I was in Egypt."

"You've been to Egypt." Not a question; a request for confirmation.

"Cairo and Giza. It's awesome. And really pretty in the spring."

As we walked farther out along the fire road, he talked about Egypt and how to ride camels, walking bow-legged, and swaying from side to side to demonstrate what that was like and making me laugh. We kept our voices lowered, though it was doubtful anyone could be near enough to hear us.

The road itself and the steep hillside to our right were illuminated brightly, but the trees and underbrush to our left were deep in shadow and kept me watching nervously. Still, the worst thing I could think of lurking there was a mountain lion, and hopefully one wouldn't randomly attack two people.

As we came around a curve the road split, the second road climbing slightly up the hillside on our right, toward the south.

"I wonder where that goes?" said Ben. "Maybe it goes near my house."

"Maybe it heads away from *both* our houses," I said. "I need to go home."

Ben was obviously ready to continue exploring, but I'd reached my limit. Listening to him tell stories had helped, but my stomach was tied in a knot, not only from what could be lurking in the shadows but from what would likely happen if my parents found me gone. Being grounded probably wouldn't phase me—spending time with the one person I really wanted to be with *not* being an issue—but I didn't want anything to jeopardize my riding or going to Northfield.

Ben and I parted ways back at the stream. Moonlight still made it too light in my room, and I had a hard time getting to sleep. When I woke, I vaguely remembered a dream of barrel racing camels with Ben. But the *last* thing I remembered was watching Dave walk away, limping and holding his side.

Dave, Tanner, and some of the others were missing at lunch on Wednesday. Track training had started. If this year was anything like last year, we wouldn't be seeing much of them for a while unless it rained. There was no sign of that happening anytime soon.

"What are you doing for your birthday?" I asked Robin.

She sighed. "I don't know. It's so hot! I want to go to the beach, but I doubt that will happen. I'm getting my license on Friday, but," her mouth twisted, "I don't think I'd be allowed to drive that far."

"Mmm," I murmured. *Even if she were, I wouldn't be allowed to go with her.*

She sighed again.

"Is there a show?"

We'd been to a show the Saturday after her birthday last year, but I felt a little out of that loop, too, and hadn't heard anything about one this year.

"Moved to the following weekend," she said. "But I'm not sure if I'm going."

I assumed she simply hadn't decided whether to go or not. Later, I realized that it wasn't just her decision. She couldn't do it on her own. As inextricably interwoven with my emotions Dave had become to me, Robin's *life* was dependent on him and his family in many ways. It had been the Calderas who had made it possible for her to do almost everything in the past. I didn't think those bonds had been broken, but there was a definite change in their relationship, not just in ours.

Dave and Robin had seemed practically inseparable last year, each knowing the other's concerns and actions. Although she still knew where Dave was and what he was doing most of the time, she seemed to know far less about what he was thinking or feeling. Apparently he wasn't communicating that to her. Maybe there wasn't much to communicate. But that didn't seem likely; he couldn't match his brother for brooding, but as Robin had said, something seemed to be bothering him. It seemed more likely that someone had taken her place as his confidante. That made me feel horribly sad for both of us.

"You can come and spend the night though, can't you?"

"Probably," I said. "When?"

"Whenever," she said, and it occurred to me for the first time that she might be lonely. "You could come on Friday after school. Maybe stay Saturday night, too?"

"Sure. Oh . . ." I remembered a commitment. "I have a lesson with Cheryl and babysit for her some Saturdays. I can maybe get out of it. . . ."

Robin's eyes lit up. "I can hang out too! Cheryl won't mind."

I agreed it sounded like a plan, said that I would check with Cheryl, and was happy that *she* seemed happy.

I met Melanie after school. Even though Roger still seemed suspicious of me, I was enjoying the rides out to Northfield. It felt like I was leaving everything else behind, everything that bothered or confused me. The experiences at Northfield were still new and exciting and kept me perfectly distracted.

Kitty kept me completely busy too. I *had* to focus on her or she would take shameless advantage of me. She never did anything mean and didn't give me cause to fear her, but she kept me on my toes. Literally. If I didn't keep my heels well down, I would find my seat wrong and my balance off, and she was quick to feel it and use it against me, especially on circles and corners.

"Keep your heels down and your leg on her! Inside on the girth! Don't let her cut the corners!"

It had become Melanie's mantra for me, and I actually recited it to myself.

Tatiana walked over at the end of my lesson. "How's she doing?"

"Very well," said Melanie, smiling proudly at me. "We have a lot of work to do on circles and leg aids, but her hands are great, her seat is pretty good, and she's doing very well with Kitty."

"Excellent," said Tatty. "Is she ready for a show?"

"Probably," said Melanie. "Perhaps a novice pleasure class. What do you think, Allison? There's a show here next weekend. You could ride Kitty in a couple of flat classes."

My heart had leaped with excitement for just a moment, then I remembered—that was Robin's birthday weekend. One way or another we'd be doing something. I loved being with Melanie at Northfield but was beginning to feel that I'd neglected Robin. Being with her right now was more important.

"I don't think I can," I said. "Not right now. Besides, I still don't have the right riding clothes. I'd rather wait . . . just a little while."

They smiled and said that was fine, and I was glad they didn't try to pressure me.

On Thursday I had lunch with Melanie as usual then went to English. I was surprised to see Dave standing alone near the entrance to the Language Arts building—waiting, apparently, for me.

"Hey," he said softly.

"Hi," I said, trying to sound normal but steeling myself for whatever might come next.

"It's Robin's birthday next week."

Okay, this is a good, neutral topic. "Yes."

"We want to do something for her . . . beyond fixing up her car. She probably wouldn't tell me if I asked . . . you know how she is."

I certainly did. She couldn't stand people feeling sorry for her, and it was difficult to give her much without her taking offense.

"Has she said anything to you . . . about anything she wants? Or something she wants to do?"

I shook my head slowly, trying to think of anything she'd expressed a desire for, but he'd probably spent more time with her so far this year, in *and* out of school, than I had.

"Oh!" I said, suddenly remembering. "She wants to go to the beach."

"The beach?" He didn't sound surprised; more as if he was considering the idea.

"Yes. Because it's so hot and . . ." I wasn't sure whether to say it. It was one of those situations when I didn't know if my reasons for saying it might be misunderstood, or perhaps I was just obtuse in not knowing how it would be perceived.

"And . . . ?"

"She was . . . frustrated," *yes, that's a good word*, "that she didn't get to go with you. You know . . . on *your* birthday."

"Oh," he said, looking at me a little too earnestly. "Yeah . . ." He appeared to be thinking, but it felt almost like he was stalling. Unlike him. "I couldn't exactly ask her to go . . ." I got the feeling he wanted to explain, but instead he said, "We should get to class. Thanks, though."

"Of course," I said, the supportive friend, glad to help him in any way and even more happy to be a part of helping Robin.

He nodded slightly and entered the building. I instinctively hesitated, letting him go ahead, and he didn't wait.

That was good. Neutral. I can do this.

When I thought he had enough of a head start to avoid awkward conversation with him, I followed.

In class, Miss Sanders was allocating assignments. We'd already done an overview of Shakespeare's historical plays and had been doing partner readings in class, getting used to the language, examining the characters, exploring his choice of words, and discussing his use of literary devices. I loved it, and Miss Sanders had expressed her approval of my work in and out of class so far. That meant a lot to me, though I doubted it helped me in the social aspect of the class.

I also loved hearing Dave read Shakespeare out loud; not because he was good at it—he had as much trouble as anyone wrapping his tongue around *thees* and *thous* and *forsooths*—but he obviously *understood* it, able to read with inflection and emphasis on the right words. That was more than a lot of the other kids could do. Besides, I would have enjoyed hearing him read a dictionary. I just loved hearing his voice.

I was glad that we were never paired to read aloud together in class; I was sure I'd have trouble concentrating on the text and would probably stutter. As it was, he'd read with both Hannah and Roberta and, though the passages had been far from romantic in nature, it was still a little painful for me. And that was stupid. I knew I had to learn to direct my thoughts better, and I was determined to do it. *He's just another boy . . . just like Matthew or Tanner. Or Ben.*

Yes, if I could just think of him the same way I thought of Ben, that would be perfect.

We were beginning a survey of Shakespeare's comedies and tragedies. Miss Sanders had written ten plays on the whiteboard, five of each. In her hand, she held a seemingly empty tissue box. Another sat on her desk.

"In this box, I've placed twelve girls' names. They will draw one name from the other box to be their partner. I will assign one of these plays to you. Your project assignment is to read the entire play and choose an appropriate scene between two characters—any characters, any gender. Once you've agreed on a scene, you will analyze it for character motivation. Finally, you will interpret and modernize the language then read either version dramatically in class with your partner. You must be ready two weeks before winter break. We'll discuss the scenes after each one. Any questions?"

Many hands went up asking everything from how long the scenes had to be to whether there were any kissing scenes. I prayed that I *wasn't* paired with Dave.

I wasn't.

I pulled Kyle's name and looked at him a little shyly. He smiled widely back and gave me an enthusiastic thumbs up. I felt profound relief. He was probably the best person I could have been paired with. I knew him well enough to be comfortable around him and had no negative or conflicted feelings about him. I liked Kyle and thought we would probably do well together.

Hannah pulled Dave's name and gave a tiny squeal of delight, her eyes bright and happy. Roberta's got drawn by one of the other girls and she looked murderous.

Miss Saunders assigned the plays, and we spent the class time discussing what to look for in an appropriate scene, and so on. Miss Sanders gave us the last five minutes of class to confer with our partners and discuss strategy. Roberta attempted to persuade Hannah to switch partners, causing most of us to look to the back of the room where they were all sitting. Dave looked intensely at Hannah. She began to say something but was saved the trouble by Miss Sanders.

"Let's stick with who we drew from the box, shall we?"

Dave and Hannah both looked relieved, and the whole room seemed to relax.

"So . . . how should we do this?" asked Kyle. "Read the play first, obviously." We'd been assigned *Twelfth Night*.

I nodded agreement. "Maybe we should read it over the next couple of weeks and come up with ideas. Then meet after Thanksgiving?"

"Oh, yeah. Thanksgiving. I almost forgot. I doubt if I'll get much done that week. *Big* family and they all come over to *my* house."

I smiled. "We'll probably go to Los Angeles. But I'll be able to read it." I'd be glad of an excuse to get away by myself.

"Okay. Make a note of any parts you think might be good."

I agreed and we exchanged phone numbers.

"It would have been kind of cool to get *Othello*. Though I wouldn't want to be typecast . . . you know," he said with a wry smile. He looked at me to see if I understood. I thought I did but wasn't sure if he was joking. "But I'm glad we didn't get *Romeo and Juliet*."

"Yes," I agreed, but I was surprised he'd voiced it. "It would be . . . awkward."

"Oh . . . no!" he said, looking worried. "I don't mean because of the romance. I meant the whole Capulet-Montague thing. You know, families at war and thinking their kids aren't good enough for each other. It's too close to real life for me."

This puzzled me and I would have asked about it, but the bell rang. It would have to wait.

On Friday morning, Robin asked if I could hang out after school. I was more than happy to and called my dad to say I'd get a ride home with Mom. Later we met at our lockers and began our walk toward Main Street. Robin was describing the epic fail of something she had cooked in Home Ec. when two short bursts from a car horn interrupted her. We both turned to look behind us. Moving slowly in our direction was a truck—a black Chevy truck—but it wasn't Cris'. It was a much older model but looked brand new, the black paint shining. And unlike Cris' completely black vehicle, chrome gleamed everywhere.

Dave was driving.

"Here comes the sexy beast," said Robin with a smirk.

I was shocked. "What?"

She laughed. "Dave's truck. It's always been called 'The Beast' because it's old and looked so beat up, you know? Then Matthew started calling it 'The Ugly Beast' after he got his new car, so that's what everyone else started calling it, just to tease Dave. I guess he unveiled the makeover over the weekend, you know, for his birthday . . . and shut everyone up. So now it's 'The Sexy Beast.'"

The truck pulled over beside us. Dave leaned slightly toward the open window and Roberta, sitting on the passenger side. "Need a ride?"

"No," Robin's brow wrinkled as if it was a stupid question. "We're good."

Dave looked from Robin to me. I thought Roberta looked at me haughtily as if daring me to say yes. I had no desire to.

I shook my head.

Dave nodded once and pulled back into the lane. My heart felt like it descended into my stomach as he drove away. I half expected some kind of disgruntled comment from Robin, something about Roberta's constant presence. I rarely saw him without her somewhere in his general vicinity. Or right next to him, like they were joined at the hip or something. *And now, next to him in his truck?*

"Right?" said Robin.

"What?"

"I was *saying*, I need to get a job so I can buy gas for my car and then I won't have to walk everywhere. Where have you been?"

Pulling Roberta out of that truck.

I sighed, tried to throw off the sinking feeling—*I should be over this by now*—and gave my attention entirely to Robin. "Where do you think you could get a job?"

We brainstormed all the options we could think of, but there weren't many. Our town just wasn't very big.

"What about you? You're driving, aren't you?"

"Oh . . . um . . . sort of. My dad's teaching me."

I didn't want to admit that it wasn't going too well. And my options for a real job weren't any better than Robin's. Anywhere I worked would have to be within walking distance of school for the foreseeable future or fit into whenever my parents could drive me. Right now I babysat about every other Saturday for Cheryl. I didn't make much money, but a part of my compensation was lessons, which were even more valuable to me. Even without lessons, I enjoyed being at Bar 8, and I loved Cody and Zoe. I didn't want to give it up. And working in town on weekends would be difficult anyway unless I could drive.

"Wait till you see the pony." Robin's eyes were bright.

"Gali?" I asked, wondering if she'd given him a weird haircut or something.

"No, silly, the Mustang," she laughed. "It's all finished, and it's *gorgeous!*"

Indeed it was. She had told me what color it was being painted, but knowing wasn't the same as seeing. A bright metallic green, the car shone like new in the light of the garage. Like Dave's truck, chrome gleamed everywhere from the bumpers and window edges to the classic wheel covers the Calderas had gotten for it.

"I love the color!" I said.

"Yeah. When they asked what color I wanted, I almost said red or black. I knew Dave's truck was going to be black. And black is cool, right?"

I smiled, thinking of Dave's truck. "Yes. Very sexy."

"Exactly. Red would have been cool too, but they said I'd have to drive like an old lady or the cops would target me. And you know *that's* not going to happen."

No, I couldn't imagine my pole-bending, barrel racing friend driving anything like an old lady.

"Then I thought of that sweater you got me, the green one. I *love* that color. So I made them take the sweater to match paint. They gave me a hard time about it, but I didn't care. It suits me too well, don't you think? It turned out *perfect!* And it's a real classic too, like Dave's truck. Only mine's way older—nineteen-sixty-six. The trucks's an eighty-five. They said if I ever have to, I could probably get a lot of money for the Mustang. But I don't ever want to sell it."

"It matches your eyes, too."

"Right?" She looked ecstatically happy as she lovingly ran her hand over the hood.

I was happy to see *her* so happy. She still seemed subdued and even troubled so much of the time. I wasn't sure where I stood with God, if I stood anywhere at all, but I couldn't do anything for her. Maybe he would.

Please let Robin find a good job so she can keep her car and help her Gran. . . .

It didn't hurt to ask.

On Sunday afternoon Robin called, very excited. "Okay, so next weekend . . . you know, for my birthday . . . can you come over and spend Friday and Saturday night?"

"Probably," I said.

"Great! You'll need to bring shorts and a bathing suit."

"So, we're going to the beach?" I started picturing what that might be like under present circumstances.

She laughed. "I don't know . . . Dave won't tell me. He says it's a surprise. Maybe he'll tell you, and you can tell me."

"Then it won't be a surprise," I said.

"I hate surprises."

I could understand that—I didn't like surprises either *most* of the time. The big exception so far had been anything Dave was involved with. And he seemed to love surprising people.

The week went by quickly and, as I'd expected, there was never an opportunity to ask Dave about Saturday. I was glad, too. He seemed to be actively avoiding me this week, and that was fine with me. But by Wednesday, Robin was extremely grouchy.

"What if I don't want to do what he has planned?"

I considered this. "Have you ever *not* wanted to do something with him?"

"Good point," she conceded, but still wasn't happy. "I hate that everyone else knows except me. *So* annoying."

"*I* don't know," I said.

She rolled her eyes. "*You* don't count."

I didn't take that too seriously.

By the end of the week, we both felt philosophical about Saturday. Robin had adopted an *I'll-just-go-along-with-whatever-it-is* attitude, which just seemed best whenever the Calderas were involved anyway. I was feeling more *I'm-just-going-for-Robin's-sake*, which was true. Since it was some kind of outing to celebrate Robin's birthday, I wondered exactly how many people were invited and who they were. I usually didn't like large groups of people, but in this case I was hoping for it. If there was any background to blend into, that's where I wanted to be.

Cris and Dave took Robin after school on Thursday, her actual birthday, to take her driving test, and she drove her car to school for the first time on Friday. After school, a large group gathered near it and the Sexy Beast, which she had parked nose-to-nose with. Everyone admired her car and wished her a happy birthday. I was in full sidekick mode, not wanting any attention but enjoying her animated happiness.

"You're going tomorrow?" Matthew stood next to me.

"Yes. I'm staying over at Robin's."

"Oh," he said, looking a little disappointed, which surprised me. Then he looked self-conscious and said, "I mean, I'm glad you're going. I just thought maybe I could give you a ride there."

"Oh . . . no, I think Cris is picking us up." It occurred to me that he should know better because he couldn't legally drive us, but there wasn't any point in saying anything. Then I thought it was worth trying for information. "Where exactly are we going?"

Matthew smiled and shook his head. I assumed this meant he knew but wasn't telling. I was glad that going for coffee wasn't suggested, though. Tomorrow was going to be awkward enough, whatever we were doing.

As the group began breaking up to go home, Robin called out to Dave, "You coming over later?"

He shook his head. "Gotta work. We'll meet at your house around ten tomorrow, okay?" He smiled at her though, a touch of mischief in his eyes.

Robin huffed, though I wasn't sure whether it was because he wasn't coming over or because she still didn't know what we were doing.

I wasn't completely sure about driving with her to her house, but she assured me she *would* drive like an old lady, just for me, and that it would only take a couple of minutes to get home. Which was true.

Angel was there sitting with Fiona and we had tea together, which was nice. Angel exclaimed that she hadn't seen us in such a long time. She had picked up a decorated cake Fiona had ordered from the local bakery and had brought a small present for Robin.

"You shouldn't have," said Robin, holding the gift and looking uncertain. "The car is enough for ten birthdays. A *hundred* birthdays."

"No, no," said Angel. "*Es un cumpleaños especial.* Fixing the car, it is from Alejandro and the boys. *This* is from *me.*"

Robin smiled and began to open the wrapping very carefully, revealing a small velvet-covered box. When she lifted the lid, she breathed out a soft, "Oh." Then she turned the box so we could see. A bright gold cross lay against red velvet. It was about the size of a nickel and delicately wrought.

"It's beautiful," she breathed. "Is it . . . is it really gold?"

"*Si,*" said Angel. "You must never forget that you are highly valued. You are *very* precious. And you are *never* alone."

There was a tightening in my throat and a fierce agreement in my heart I didn't quite understand, beyond agreeing that Robin was a special person. There were tears in Fiona's eyes, and I was surprised to see a similar brightness in Robin's.

"Thank you," she said softly.

We finished our tea and Angel left, but not before giving both of us long, tight hugs and expressing the wish to see us soon at the ranch. This was hard to hear, especially as I was still feeling a little emotional from before. It was even harder when she whispered to me, "We *miss* you."

I tried not to think too much about her last comment; it would have distracted and subdued me, and I wanted to be good company for Robin. Besides, I was sure Angel's "we" meant her and maybe Stevey. Maybe even Mr. Caldera in a benevolent way. I doubted anyone else actually missed me.

Later, I gave Robin my gift. I felt a little embarrassed by it but knew she'd at least find it useful. I'd bought her a CD I thought she'd like—still trying to broaden her musical horizons—but wanted to get her something else, seeing as it was a special birthday. Mom and Dad had agreed and contributed generously to it.

She opened the card and a gift card fell out. She looked at it with interest. Then her eyes grew wide.

"Are you *kidding* me?"

For a second I was afraid she was offended at the mundane gift. Or that she just thought it was really weird, which is how I felt about it, especially after Angel's beautiful and thoughtful present. But then her smile grew wide, too.

"It's *perfect!* This is *so* great! Thank you! This will last me a long time, I'm sure." She took the gas card and put it in her wallet, looking so happy and confident. "Now I just need a job." She smiled crookedly, but her voice had a determined edge.

"I'm sure you'll find a good one," I said, feeling determined for her.

She opened the CD and played it while we talked about beach trips, pool parties, and what Dave could possibly have planned for the following day.

Dave called Robin about eight in the morning saying that a job he was doing with Tom was going to take longer than they thought.

"He said he'd spread the word about meeting later, but that we'd still have plenty of time. So probably *not* a beach trip."

She sounded slightly disappointed but brightened quickly. We spent the morning talking to Fiona over breakfast and then playing with Gali. By noon we'd changed into bathing suits and shorts and were waiting in the driveway, sitting in the green pony.

When Tanner arrived, he jokingly said, "Take me for a ride," so she told him to get in the back and she started the engine. We didn't actually move but imagined all the places we *could* go once everyone had been driving long enough.

About twelve-thirty Dave pulled up in The Beast. Cris was right behind in the family SUV with Hannah and Paola in the back seat. And no Roberta. I told myself it wouldn't have mattered, but it did. Dave didn't get out of the truck but yelled out the window, "Sorry! I had to go home first to get the food. Come on, let's go!"

Robin and I climbed into the SUV while Tanner ran back to his mom's car. We all followed Dave through Old Town, out onto the highway, and eventually past Brookside—my street.

"Where is he going?" I asked.

Cris said nothing. Robin was frowning. "Maybe Tahoe? But that's kind of far. We wouldn't have much time. Maybe one of the lakes?"

I knew there were several lakes in our county, though I'd never been to them. Most of the road was vaguely familiar and I realized we had come this way last year when we'd gone to the snow. But there was no sign of snow, not even on the very tops of mountains in the distance. It was at least eighty degrees today, and the countryside was still brown and thirsty-looking.

After a while, Dave turned onto another road heading southeast. It wound mostly between tall pines and firs, and the air smelled deliciously fresh.

"Oh . . . my . . . God . . ." Robin uttered, and her face lit up. "I *know* where we're going. We haven't been here since we were kids!"

We drove quite a way farther and eventually a small river became visible intermittently between the trees on our right. Dave eventually turned onto a smaller road and parked next to a couple of other cars. The sound of moving water splashed gently beyond the trees. Dave and Tanner unloaded a large cooler and a huge drink thermos that had been bungeed in The Beast's bed.

"I asked Kyle and Stacie to get here early to make sure we have a table," Dave said. "I didn't think they'd mind getting some alone time. Remember this place, Robin?"

Robin, since the first time I'd known her, seemed utterly at a loss for words. Her eyes were very bright though, and slightly red. She nodded.

Dave watched her intently for a moment, but then he smiled and said to me, "Could you grab those blankets?"

Glad to be given a job to do, I took the old quilts out of the bed and followed the others along a dirt path through the trees. Cris locked the SUV and ran to catch up, taking the quilts from me without a word as he passed. He had books under his other arm.

"Welcome to Cuprum Creek," said Dave.

"How come I've lived in Douglas all my life and never been here?" said Tanner.

"We used to come a lot when I was a kid," said Dave, "but it's tricky. Earlier in the year, there's too much run-off, and the water moves too fast. Not safe. Too cold, too. In the summer, there's too many people. Not fun. Usually around this time of year, the water's already too cold. But right now, it's perfect."

I could see what he meant. The area was a glade in the pines surrounding a natural pond. At the head of the pond was a waterfall, the width of a small river. The flow of water was gentle but steady, amply feeding fresh water into the basin below it. The pond itself was a little smaller than the pool in town. I couldn't see the bottom. The most interesting features were the flat rock surfaces just below it. Huge granite boulders, worn smooth from millennia of erosion, continued gently downhill for about twenty feet, ending in a much smaller pool. After the lower basin, the creek continued as a narrow but more lively stream.

Tanner grinned hugely. "Slip and slide!"

"It's *so* much fun," said Robin, excitement replacing whatever emotions had choked her up before.

We greeted Stacie and Kyle, who had been sitting close together on top of a picnic table under the trees. Jessie had apparently arrived just before us.

"We've got the place to ourselves," said Kyle. "At least for now."

"Another good thing about coming this time of year," said Dave. "No tourists. I think that's why we stopped coming. There were always too many other people here."

"It's perfect," whispered Robin. She looked *so* happy.

"Just be careful not to swallow any water," said Dave. "And keep your shoes on."

Matthew had arrived by the time Robin and I had spread out the old quilts between the tables and the pond. The boys put the coolers between the tables. Cris took some sandwiches and sat at the farthest table, apparently studying.

Dave and Hannah paired up almost immediately. I told myself I was glad. Hannah was truly lovely, and I much preferred to see him with her than with Roberta. In a lot of ways, they seemed made for each other, and I was determined to be okay with it.

Since it was now well after one o'clock, we all ate first. Dave was the first one to enter the pool. He walked in as far as he could without a tremor as if the water were comfortably warm, then swam to the middle and disappeared. He came up right below the waterfall.

"It's perfect," he shouted. "No diving, but jumping between here and the middle is fine."

That's all Tanner needed to hear. He vanished through the trees and reappeared a moment later at the top of the falls. Letting out a whoop, he leaped out, grabbed his knees, and landed close enough to Dave to drench him.

"Hey!" shouted Dave and swam after Tanner.

Tanner came up whooping again, this time from the cold water, then swam away backward, splashing Dave as he did. Once Tanner reached the shore, he ran back toward the path leading to the top, Dave hard on his heels. Robin peeled off her shirt and ran after them. Dave caught up to Tanner just before he jumped and both tumbled over the edge together. I thought it looked dangerous, but they both came up laughing, and then waited while Robin prepared to jump. She giggled nervously and had a couple of false starts, which had the rest of us laughing too. When she finally jumped, we all cheered and applauded. That seemed to be the cue for everyone else to enter the pool one way or another.

Matthew came and sat next to me on one of the quilts. I'd just taken my t-shirt off, leaving my shorts and shoes on like everyone else. I felt a little self-conscious about my scar though, especially with Matthew sitting so close. Dave took notice of us too, which didn't help.

Matthew looked toward Dave and then back at me. "I sometimes envy him," he said.

This surprised me—not that it might be true, but that he'd admit it out loud. I didn't know what to say in response.

"It's so easy for him, you know? He always falls on his feet, whether it's sports or girls or whatever."

Now I felt *very* uncomfortable. He'd spoken lightly—didn't sound bitter or anything—but it felt wrong. Was it just a little envy talking? I knew what that felt like. Or was he actually saying something else? A warning? I hated the fact that I was curious, but I *didn't* want to know.

"He has a generous nature," I said, as matter-of-factly as possible. "I think you do, too. I don't think you should be envious."

He smiled and looked at me more intensely. I wondered if I'd said the wrong thing.

"Yeah, he's *generous*. He definitely likes to spread himself around. He's always had all kinds of . . . *friends*. I guess that's easy for him, too."

I wasn't sure what that implied and felt even more uncomfortable. I didn't like talking about other people like this. Especially Dave.

"Like you, for instance." He looked squarely at me again. "I mean, don't get me wrong . . . you're cute and everything, but not his usual. . . ." He looked back toward Dave and let the phrase hang unfinished. My stomach churned. What was he implying? "You've probably noticed that the girls he's *really* close to are . . . well . . ." he glanced at me, "*not* as quiet and shy as you."

We were both watching Dave. He *did* always seem to be in the middle of everything. Right now both Jessie and Paola were laughing, trying to get a ball away from him and not at all shy about physical contact.

"Actually, he once said that's what he liked about you. You're quiet and don't harass him. I guess he likes that for a change sometimes." He laughed as if he'd said something funny, but my stomach was twisting even more. "I think he's wrong, though. I think you're smart and have a lot more going on inside than he gives you credit for."

Matthew's last comments were troubling, to be sure. I couldn't process them right now. And his opinion of my appearance and intelligence level didn't make me feel any better at all. As for Dave's nature, he was right. There was no way that Dave wasn't happy being the center of attention, especially with girls. He was many things, and maybe not all of those things were entirely positive, but I'd never seen him pretend to be something he wasn't. He was what he was.

"Aren't you going to jump in?" Matthew asked as if we'd just been discussing the weather.

"I'll . . . just go in the pond," I said, standing.

"I'll go with you," he said, smiling.

The water was freezing and took some getting used to, but with all the splashing going on, I was soon soaked. Both Paola and Hannah were all over Dave, and he seemed to reciprocate. I tried to keep my back turned. When Tanner, Robin, and Jessie moved toward the smooth rocks where Stacie and Kyle were, I went with them. So did Matthew.

One at a time we took turns sliding down the slippery stones on our backsides, ending in the shallow pool below. Then we trudged back up the incline to do it all over again. Stacie and Kyle retreated back up toward the tables, and I was thinking of doing the same after one more slide.

Right before I sat down, Matthew slipped an arm around my waist from behind me. "Let's do it together," he said, a little too softly and much too close to my ear.

I had a stab of pure panic, but I wasn't sure why so I didn't object. Then we were sitting and sliding over the rocks together. When we reached the pool at the end, I got up and out right away and tried to make myself laugh, but there was nothing inside to laugh with. I put distance between us as quickly as possible. Jessie and Robin were heading back up toward the tables, and I caught up with them. Matthew followed. He was making me nervous, but my senses and emotions were too jumbled to analyze exactly how I felt about him and what was happening.

I was surprised to see Dave following not far behind Matthew—he must have seen us slide down together—and soon everyone was back at the picnic tables or in the upper pool. Matthew hesitated near the table as if deciding what to do next, but then followed Tanner back up the path to the top of the falls. I breathed a sigh of relief and went to sit alone at one of the other tables. Dave came and sat near me while he ate a sandwich, but he didn't say anything.

After a while, I looked at him and said, "This was a wonderful idea. Thank you for organizing it. Robin looks so happy."

She was in the pool having a splash fight with Tanner, laughing and shouting loudly. Dave grinned and watched her for a moment, his eyes crinkling at the corners. Then his expression became clouded, troubled.

"I wish I could do more. We've been friends for so long." He turned and looked intently at me. "I'd do anything for her."

Flustered, I tried to keep my thoughts on Robin and not let any personal longings resurface.

"I'm sure she knows that. She knows you and your whole family care about her. That's . . . that's . . ." I couldn't think of the right word. "Important," I said, but it felt inadequate. There were so many other adjectives I could have used that would have been more heartfelt and accurate, though I didn't think I could say them without my voice catching. "Knowing people really care about you is sometimes all you need."

That wasn't exactly what I was thinking either, but it was the closest I could say under present circumstances.

He nodded, still looking steadily at me, but his expression seemed strained as if he also wanted to say something else but was holding back. Then Matthew called to him, a water polo ball raised in his hand. Hannah called, too, then several others.

Dave looked back at me, still intense. "Allie . . . don't forget what I said to you last year." He continued to look at me as if sure that words had magically popped into my head. He got up and took a few steps backward, then turned and walked into the water.

We stayed for several hours. Then there was talk of what to do afterward; the sun had already disappeared behind the surrounding hills, and it was cooling quickly. Matthew offered to have the party move to his house where the water theme could continue with warmer water and hot food. He said he was sure his parents wouldn't mind. Dave countered with video games or movies at his house. Both sounded wonderful. And terrible.

Kyle said he had to get home—his parents weren't aware that he had come with Stacie today, but they knew she could drive and they weren't happy about it. He needed to be home before dark. Tanner said something about Cinderella and pumpkins, and everybody laughed. But I remembered what he'd said about Romeo and Juliet and wondered.

"I should probably get home to Gran," said Robin. "But thank you . . . everybody. It really was *perfect!*"

Matthew came over as I picked up a blanket to fold. "Hey, I can give you a ride home if you'd like."

"No, it's fine. I'm spending the night with Robin."

I didn't say that we'd be at Bar 8 later. I'd had all the attention from him that I could handle, flattering though it was, and I felt bad about that. Still, it seemed safer to remove myself from all aggravation right now. I was glad that we weren't going over to *either* boy's house.

"Okay. Well, see you at school, I guess."

"Yes," I said.

Stacie came over and picked up the other quilt. "So, has Matthew asked you out yet?"

"What? No! No, not at all." I wasn't completely surprised by the question but didn't want to discuss it.

"It's just a matter of time," said Kyle, helping Stacie fold the quilt.

Cris and I were both taciturn on the way home. It occurred to me that I'd barely noticed him the whole time we were there. He'd swum briefly when everyone else was sliding but otherwise appeared to be studying. I guessed he must have a lot of homework from his college classes. He dropped Robin and me off first, then drove off with Hannah and Paola.

Tom picked us up a little later to babysit while he and Cheryl went to a movie. Cheryl had baked a small cake for Robin and ordered pizza for us, and we had fun watching a movie with the kids. About eleven, Tom drove us home again.

That night I dreamed jumbled but extremely vivid images and feelings. Hannah kissing Dave which morphed into Roberta kissing Dave. Matthew pushing me into the arms of Varsity Jacket, which then became Dave roughly shoving me backward into the arms of Matthew. Matthew held me by my upper arms from behind, whispering something into my ear that made me feel very uncomfortable while I watched Dave walk away with his arm tight around Roberta's waist. And then Dave was walking away alone, and I was trying to run after him—a more familiar dream. But it was no longer Matthew who held me. I couldn't turn far enough around to see who it was but I was sure it was either Cris or my dad. Maybe both. I woke up on the floor in Robin's room, panting, my heart beating fast, and Dave's last words in my ears.

"*. . . don't forget what I said to you last year . . .*"

Chapter Nineteen

Those last words were now a new source of torment. My mind latched on to them as some sort of lifeline, some hope, and of course, a puzzle to solve. The problem was that Dave had told me a great many things last year, but I had poor conversational recall. The only thing I kept thinking of was, *Don't worry so much.* "Don't worry," had been a sentiment he'd repeated several times, but it didn't seem to make much sense at the moment. Why would he want me to remember that?

My first impulse was to ask him to clarify as soon as I had a chance. I couldn't afford to think about it all the time, which I was sure to do until I found out one way or another. Then I decided that, no, all these little confrontations and conversations with him weren't doing me one bit of good. If I'd thought less highly of him or had more reason to doubt him, I would have suspected he said it on purpose to tease me, to keep me guessing, to keep me off-balance—not hard to do at the best of times. And the things that Matthew had intimated made that seem almost plausible.

But that's not the way Dave acted when I was with him. When it was just *us*. Was it? Was I just blind to it?

By Monday, I was completely annoyed with both boys—Matthew for paying too much attention to me, and Dave for paying any. If I could just turn my brain off, I thought I'd do pretty well. But since it was neither possible nor advisable, I'd have to live with feeling more or less on edge again. And *that* had a tendency to make me cranky and become overwhelmed easily. I was actually glad there was only one more week until Thanksgiving vacation, and then we'd be gone.

It was going to be a busy week, too. Choir on Tuesday as usual and a combined band and choir rehearsal after school on Thursday, a lesson with Melanie on Wednesday and, on Saturday, my first show since before summer vacation: a gymkhana I was going to with Cheryl. I was looking forward to all these things and hoped to just get through the rest of the week without any added concerns or angst.

No such luck.

At lunch, Robin sat with Dave and Matthew. I purposefully sat next to Paola on the grass. "How is your brother?" I asked. "Is there any news?" I had been wondering about this, but probably not as much as I should have.

"Oh . . . thank you for asking! I believe he is well. He has been allowed to return to teach again, but he is probably being watched very carefully. It is very dangerous, and he cannot write to us anything of importance. He says only, 'I am fine. The wind blows. The sky is blue.' "

I nodded, not wholly comprehending but feeling the severity of the situation.

She sighed heavily. Then her eyes brightened and she said, "*You* are being watched also . . ."

"*What?*" Considering she had just been referring to the Cuban government, I was very startled.

Paola giggled. "It is not a *bad* thing, I think. David . . . he watches you."

Flustered, I glanced his way before I could stop myself. He was engaged in lively conversation with the people around him, especially Roberta sitting next to him.

"He is cute, no?"

"Um . . . yes," I said. We had already established this; there was no point in lying.

"I think so also. But he does not really see me."

I wasn't sure what she meant.

She continued, "I think he sees *you.*"

"What are you talking about?" In spite of any communication difficulties, I had a feeling I knew. I felt just as sure that she was very mistaken.

"David, he watches you very much. All the time. He never looks at me that way." She sighed.

"He *talks* to you all the time," I countered, then hated myself for it. *You don't care. Remember?* I also didn't want to seem jealous in any way, because I wasn't. *Really.*

"Yes, he talks to me. He *talks* to everyone, no? It does not mean so much. He is very . . . friendly. But he does not *look* at me, I think, the same way he looks at you."

The words were out before I could stop them, "What way is that?"

Paola's brow furrowed. "I am not sure," she said slowly, thoughtfully, "but he watches you. And sometimes, he looks worried . . . a little."

I was *not* going to play into this. For some reason, Dave had opinions about who I could hang out with and what I could do. I did have a dad for that and it wasn't him, as Matthew had so kindly pointed out to him. "It's because he thinks I can't take care of myself. He's just acting like a brother. You know, watching out for a sister."

"My brother, he loves me, I think, very much, but he did not watch me like that. Not when he lived at home. And we were very close."

I almost blurted my old excuse, "He's just a friend," but had to stop and think about it. I didn't know a lot about friendship, but whatever there was between us now didn't feel like it at all, in spite of whatever either of us said. We had definitely been friends last year, I had no doubts about that. And I *did* have other friends now. Our relationship was not the same as last year, for whatever reason and whoever's fault it was. It wasn't anything like my other friendships either. Still, I didn't know what else to say. "We're just friends," I muttered.

Paola looked unconvinced. "Hmmm. You might not think it could be so, but I was very popular at my home. I knew many boys, and many of them were friends." She shook her head. "I do not think they look at me like that either."

I resisted turning to look at Dave again. She was wrong. I was very sure she was. He was probably looking at her. Maybe he just wondered what we were talking about. Perhaps he could tell we were talking about him somehow. Or maybe he assumed we were. But that would be very paranoid. Or narcissistic. I was sure Dave was neither.

But apparently I was—paranoid at least. I began to gather my stuff. "I . . . I've got . . ." I couldn't think of an excuse, but I didn't want to remain where I was. It wasn't her fault, though.

"I'm sorry!" she said, looking worried. "I should not have said—"

"Oh . . . no . . . it's fine. But I really need to go." I tried to smile at her. "I'll see you later, okay?"

She smiled back. "Yes!"

Ben was sitting next to Hannah and they were talking and laughing, which made me feel happy. It seemed like choir had helped Ben connect with a lot of people, and since the choir concert, he was practically popular. He still wasn't much better at remembering things though. I crouched beside him long enough to give him the rest of my lunch: half of my sandwich and a pear. I wasn't hungry.

He looked up and smiled. "Thanks!"

Hannah smiled too, a soft, gentle smile that eased my heart a little. She probably thought that Ben and I were a *thing*, but it didn't bother me.

Since I had PE next, I began walking toward the gym. I thought I'd just go sit on the bleachers inside and read if there was no one else there. But as I reached the open doors, I heard the sharp, resonant bouncing of a ball and thumping and screeching of shoes on the courts. There were a couple of small groups talking in the upper bleachers and one or two other people sitting alone, reading as I had thought to do. A whistle shrilled loudly and someone on the court shouted, "Wake up, Caldera!"

Cris was looking my way from the middle of the court, a ball bouncing away behind him. There was no expression on his face except perhaps mild curiosity—or slight annoyance, it was hard to tell the difference—but he rarely showed more than that anyway. It occurred to me he might have thought I'd come looking for him again.

Far from it! Embarrassed and sorry to have inadvertently interrupted the practice, I left and headed toward the upper field. It was deserted. I walked past the long jump, across the track, and stood on the grass playing field in the center.

A few memories teased me here, but that was okay. It would do me good to examine them realistically. As meaningful and tender as I had wanted to believe them, it was so easy to see all those interactions with Dave for what I now considered them to be: the good intentions of a kind-hearted boy; a boy who knew pain and sorrow and saw me as someone to protect. Someone like his brother, Stevey.

But he wasn't the same boy this year. He was very obviously not only older but more mature in every way. Less mischievous, seemingly, but no less dangerous to unguarded hearts. *And I'm okay with that. Not fantastic, but okay. It's time to really move on.*

I was different, too. I felt I had really, *finally* reached equanimity with my status. I had friends: Robin and Melanie were more important to me than ever; Ben was turning out to be a person I cared about and enjoyed being with, without the angst of attraction; and Paola and Hannah already had secure places in my heart. They were all people I was growing to trust more and more.

And I had plenty to keep me busy, too, to occupy my traitorous thoughts. Taking care of Remmy, riding him and Kitty, lessons with both Cheryl and Melanie, and choir. I sometimes even wished I had more free time; more time for drawing or reading or just listening to music. But overall, I felt very content.

I closed my eyes and sighed deeply. The sun felt good on my skin, though a slight breeze cooled my face. I had come to what I felt was a final decision concerning Dave. There would be no sparkly-princess happily-ever-after ending for me with him. I knew it as surely as I knew I'd never be a track star or a beauty queen. He and I were too different, and he just wasn't attracted to me. It didn't change the way I felt about him, but it changed the way I felt about myself feeling *for* him. I imagined being on the outside, looking at and really *seeing* myself the way I truly was.

And I'm okay with it—with me. I actually like myself. For the first time in my life, I can honestly, informatively say it. I'm okay with who I am, with my idiosyncrasies, weaknesses, challenges. It's who I am. And I have strengths, too. I don't need Dave or anyone else to approve of me or like me or—

"You're avoiding me."

My eyes popped open.

"I . . ."

Dave's brows curved down in that dangerous way that never failed to make my knees go a little weak. I was already being drawn down into soft brown eyes. I tore my gaze away and looked back across the field.

"*Are* you avoiding me?"

"A little."

"Why?"

"Just . . . feelings . . . I can't help."

Dave's frown deepened. "Is it something I've done?"

"No! It's . . . me. It's just easier for me this way."

He looked away, still frowning, then looked back. "Is it that Ben guy? You're . . . together?"

In spite of feeling the awkwardness of this conversation and how impossible it was to confide the truth any more than I just had, this struck me as very funny, tempered by the fact that it also made me a little angry. *Just as well. At this point, I'd hate to laugh in his face.*

"No, we're just friends."

The phrase was so used and worthless to me that it sounded hollow and meaningless, even to my own ears.

"Like *we're* just friends?"

Something about the way he said it—almost bitterly, as if at some time he'd offered more to me and I'd rejected it—struck icy cold to my heart. "No. You're special to me," I said, still avoiding looking directly at him. "*Really* special." He had opened this door; now was the time to try to express what was in my heart—what I could never say before. "You've been much more than a friend to me. And I want you to know that I always *will* be your friend. I'll always be *for* you, on your side, no matter what." My voice faltered a little, sounding unnaturally husky. "I only wish good things for you."

"Why are you saying that?" He looked and sounded worried, maybe even angry. "Why does that sound like some sort of goodbye?"

"I just want you to know. It's hard for me to tell you . . . to say it. I don't want you to ever . . ." Tears began to prickle behind my eyes as my own painful doubts sprang to mind, but I refused to let them form. "I don't want you to ever doubt my friendship. It's yours, whether it's important to you or not."

"What the hell? Of course it's important! How could you even think it's not?"

His response didn't surprise me much. For all his apparent concern, he never seemed to understand how he affected the people around him, except when he purposely turned on the charm. And I hadn't seen him do that in a long time.

I tried to choose my words carefully. "You've been very . . . preoccupied . . . this year." He started to interrupt me but I stopped him. I needed to say this. "It's okay! I understand. Really! I think I understand a lot of things I didn't before. I guess I've been very selfish, that's all. So if I'm not around all the time, that's why. I'm just finding other things to do and think about. Okay?"

He was still frowning slightly, thoughtfully, but then his eyes narrowed, something I'd noticed he only did when he didn't trust somebody or thought they were hiding something important from him.

The bell conveniently rang. I tried to smile and waved goodbye. He had an adorably perplexed look on his face—one of my favorite expressions on him—but I valiantly ignored it and tried to immediately forget it.

No moping over cute Dave expressions for you!

I suppose he followed me back to the gym, but I was determined to hang on to my new sense of independence, flimsy though it was. I walked around to the girls' locker room without looking back.

Today the girls were on the tennis courts behind the lower field. Roberta, Lori, and two girls I wasn't familiar with were choosing teams to play on the two courts. It didn't surprise me that I was one of the last picked. I didn't care at all except for feeling confused by the poisonous glances thrown my way. The degree of animosity seemed strange until I realized that either they had known Dave was coming to find me at lunch, or someone had seen us together on the field. In spite of tennis being a non-contact sport, if I understood it correctly, I got hit several times by balls, and even a couple of times by rackets. By accident, of course.

I was on my guard by the time we went back to the changing rooms and completely avoided everyone except Melanie. Hannah came over and changed near us too.

"Is everything okay?" she asked.

I felt I had things under my tenuous control—namely, how I reacted to things. "Yes. No problem."

Hannah smiled and looked like she would pursue the topic, but instead asked Melanie and me about our plans for Thanksgiving. I was grateful that she made a point of walking out of the changing room with us. I didn't look around, so wasn't aware of anyone possibly laying in wait, but I didn't want to know.

I met up with Robin after school to accompany her in her quest for employment. "If I can get a job that I don't need to drive to, it'll be great."

"Can I come too?" asked Ben.

Robin looked at me instead of Ben, expressionless. Then she looked at him sternly. "Only if you take those stupid things off," she said.

"Which stupid things?" he said, obviously more than willing to do whatever she wanted.

Robin stared hard at him for a moment. He sheepishly removed the lensless frames and the red Ernie hat and stuffed them in his backpack. Then he smoothed his mussed hair and cleared his throat self-consciously.

The Beast passed us as we walked, Roberta very conspicuously inside, but Dave didn't appear to notice us.

We headed east first, toward downtown, and then on toward Old Town. Robin went into every prospective place while Ben and I either waited outside or tried to remain inconspicuous nearby. Most places either told her they were not hiring at all or said they didn't hire under-eighteens. Ben and I tried to stay positive and keep her spirits up.

A few places said they probably had all the extra holiday help they needed already, but gave her application forms anyway. We examined these together with great interest. By the time we had walked all the way back through town, my mom was almost ready to get off work, so we waited at the pool for her. Mom tried to answer all the questions Robin had about the forms. We gave her a ride home, and Mom went in to say hello to Fiona for a minute. Ben and I stayed in the car.

"I need to get a job too," he said.

I nodded. "Me too. But I don't drive, so it's got to be in town. I should probably go around and get applications too."

"Yeah. But it looks like there aren't many jobs."

I nodded agreement. We sat quietly for a few moments. "I would hate to get a job before Robin does," I said. "She really needs one. Much more than me."

"Yeah, more than me too, I guess." He perked up and said, "Hey, let's agree to not even look for jobs until she gets one. Okay?"

I readily agreed. "I can ask Mom to keep her ears open at the pool."

Ben seemed to get even more excited about the idea. "Let's have a code word. You know, like *koala*."

"What do we need a code word for?"

"So people don't know what we're talking about. Like, 'Hey, have you heard of any koala's around town?' That way nobody can overhear and apply before she does."

"That's really silly," I said.

When Mom came back to the car, I asked if she'd let me know if she heard about any potential jobs for Robin. Ben looked like he was about to explain the code word, but I tried to glare at him. He just grinned.

Tuesday was perplexing. I had hoped that my conversation with Dave would make things easier, smooth out the rougher spots, and help us leave each other alone—literally. So it was perturbing to find him not only buying food in the cafeteria while I ate with Melanie but also seeming to be more demonstrative with Roberta, at least whenever I looked their way. Which I tried not to do.

By Wednesday it was apparent that it wasn't only Roberta that was receiving the extra attention. It didn't seem like he was instigating it, but he certainly returned all such attention in a way I'd never seen him do before—wholeheartedly. But he still wasn't the carefree guy he'd seemed for most of last year. It occurred to me he was acting more as he had at the beginning of *this* year, appearing to enjoy the physical advances of several girls bold enough to put themselves forward, yet not really happy.

I wondered if Hannah or Paola noticed the difference, but Hannah behaved the way she always did with him—playful and very familiar—and Paola seemed to admire him even more. It made me feel sick, but not because of my own feelings for him. I was beginning to wonder if this was who he really was. And I couldn't help still being haunted by some of the things Matthew had said. Had I really only seen him the way I wanted to? Whatever had subdued him since August seemed to be gone. I didn't think it had anything to do with me, but the timing seemed strange. I was more than normally glad to get into the car with Melanie and Roger and leave school—and everything connected with it—behind.

My cares had dissipated, at least temporarily, by the time we reached Northfield. I was surprised to see Dr. James' truck there and even more surprised to see Cris. He was walking toward the truck as Roger dropped us off. Melanie looked from him to me and back, smiling, acknowledged him with a brief, "Hi," and then walked past him, saying she'd meet me in the barn. Cris returned her greeting with a nod as if they had at least a slight acquaintance. He stopped what he was doing and regarded me. Neither of us seemed to know what to say, and I wondered if he was thinking the same thing I was: *What are you doing here?*

I broke the silence. "You're here with Dr. James?"

He nodded slowly. "Yeah. You are . . . ?"

"Taking lessons," I said. "English." There didn't seem to be much point in avoiding the truth. I'd never felt the need to do that with Cris anyway, for some reason.

"You looked . . . unhappy . . . Monday," he said, and I remembered interrupting his practice.

"Oh, no. I was just looking for a place . . ." *to be alone. No, Mr. Perspicacity would read into that.* "To read," I said. "I was looking for a quiet place to read." I hoped that was an adequate explanation as to why I didn't remain in the gym. It was true enough.

He nodded but, from his expression, I felt like I'd wasted the effort.

"So, you're helping Dr. James?" I asked. His expression still didn't change, but he looked away.

"Yeah. But," he frowned, not the scowl but as if he were concerned, "I'd appreciate it if you didn't say anything. To anyone."

That surprised me. Then I realized I felt the same way. "Oh . . . me too," I said. He nodded. "So . . . is this where you've been working?" I asked.

He looked sideways at me before his gaze slid away again. "Not just here. I'm working with James when I'm not at school."

I frowned. "You're family doesn't know?"

He gave a stifled laugh—a strange sound coming from him—and shook his head once. This was perplexing, but he didn't give me more time to consider it. "You haven't told," he paused then said, "your *other* friends . . . about this?" His gaze encompassed our surroundings.

He had me there. I couldn't think of an excuse, so I just shook my head too.

"So . . . we're a couple of traitors." He seemed to like this idea a lot because it surprised a real smile and another laugh out of him. It transformed his whole demeanor, which coaxed a genuine smile out of me as well. "Okay. I won't say anything. I'd better get this to James." He indicated the items in his hand and began to walk away but turned back and said, "You're really doing okay with . . . everything?"

I wasn't sure how specific *everything* was meant to be, but Cris wasn't one for platitudes. And at this particular moment, I felt strong, hopeful, and happy. I smiled easily again. "Yes."

His expression remained neutral, but for a moment his gaze felt intense. He nodded and walked away.

I changed my clothes and found Melanie, who told me to get Kitty ready. I thought it strange that Melanie wanted me to get the mare ready instead of the girl who would be riding her first, but I was more and more glad each time she did.

Kitty had little idiosyncrasies and issues that Remmy and the other horses I'd known didn't. She was fussy about her feet, not lifting them as automatically as I was used to, sometimes pulling away slightly if I took too long picking them out. She sometimes pawed the ground while cross-tied too, even while I groomed, and she wasn't always easy to bridle. At first I thought she just didn't like me; not mean, but grouchy. Melanie had insisted I continue to be firm with her and not nervous, to make her move when she was impatient, and to not let her bully me. Sure enough, we were already getting along much better, and my confidence around horses in general had risen to new heights.

Apparently Saturday, the day of our river trip, had broken records for how hot it was at this time of year. But every day since then had become a little cooler. Today there was a fresh breeze and Kitty, although she'd already been ridden, was a handful during my lesson. Melanie had me working her at a trot and in circles until she began to relax and behave, then opened the gate and led us to a different paddock, adjacent to one of the bigger jumping arenas. This one had a scattering of wooden 'x's connected by poles to form very low obstacles.

My heart leaped. "We're going to start jumping?" I asked, very excited.

"*Start*," affirmed Melanie. "These are *cavaletti*. We'll be doing this for a while."

That was fine with me. I was so excited that everything—*everything*—else disappeared. Melanie had me working in two-point position at a trot around the arena for much of the time until my thighs were burning, but she seemed happy with my efforts. Then she had me do the same over the lowest *cavaletti*. Kitty was still a handful and even kicked her heels up over one of the poles, but I didn't let it disturb me. I kept her straight and forward. Melanie seemed very satisfied.

As I walked Kitty toward the gate, I saw that both Cris and Dr. James had been watching. Tatty was walking toward them. "Looking good," she said to me as she passed us. Brief but high praise coming from her. "Dr. Emory, thank you so much for coming out on such short notice. I know Dr. Simon's practice doesn't normally service this area, but we didn't want to wait."

"Any time," said James. "I personally have no problem coming out at all. Feel free to call me directly."

These comments were said as if there were underlying meaning, and I looked at Cris, wondering why it was a big deal. He wasn't looking at me though and, as usual, there was nothing but a slight scowl on his face. Dr. James gave Tatty a business card and they shook hands. Then Tatty walked off toward one of the barns. I dismounted, ran the stirrups up, and loosened the girth. My legs felt like rubber.

"Well, Allison," said Dr. James, "it looks like you're doing a little moon-lighting yourself."

I didn't exactly know what that meant, but his eyes looked merry and, considering what had been said so far, I got the idea. "Who's your friend?" he asked.

"This is Kitty, but her real name is Copper Copycat," I said, stroking her cheek.

Then I realized he was looking even more amused. I could tell Cris was trying to keep a straight face too. Melanie was smiling.

"Oh, sorry," I said, not as embarrassed as I might have been in different company. "This is my friend, Melanie. She's a trainer here." I couldn't help boasting a little—I was proud of my friend and I liked telling people. I felt it necessary to add, "But I'm still working with Cheryl, too." I didn't want to be thought disloyal.

"Well, good for you! And how is Remmy doing? Not getting neglected for your other new friend here, is he?"

I lit up. I couldn't help that either. "No! He's *great!* I practice everything I learn here on him . . . except for the saddle and stuff. And I've been riding him bareback a lot. You know, just around."

Dr. James smiled kindly, but I was surprised by the expression on Cris' face. Approval? Or just amused? He looked instantly uncomfortable when I looked at him, then frowned and looked away.

"You know, I think I saw that Remmy's due for shots and is probably ready again for deworming, too. Why don't you have your mom or dad give me a call and we can set something up?"

I agreed. We all said goodbye and they left, but I felt strangely elated the rest of the evening, excitedly telling Mom about my lesson and not thinking about Dave. Well, not much.

Mom made dinner while I fed and spent some time with Remmy. Dad had gone out of town on Monday but planned to be back by Friday. We had just begun eating when the phone rang, and we assumed it was him.

"Hello?" Mom said. "Dan! How are you? It's been a while!"

Mom was smiling, obviously happy to hear from Dad's younger brother. "Yes, we're all fine. Greg's out of town right now but . . . mmhmm . . . Oh no! Is she all right?" Mom looked over at me, her brow furrowed. "Where is she now?" she asked, and I wondered who "she" was. Dan's wife, Diana? Dan's daughter, my cousin Estelle? Dad's older sister, Isabel? Or his younger sister, Emily? "I see. So they don't know yet?" Mom was quiet for some time, her concern obviously growing. "Yes, of course. I'll call him right away. Perhaps he can change his travel plans." Another pause. "You too, Dan. Give everyone our love . . . Yes, we'll talk soon. Bye."

Mom hung up the phone and stood looking at it for a moment, seeming slightly shocked and pale.

"What is it?" I asked, more curious than alarmed. I hadn't seen Uncle Dan in years. I hadn't seen the rest of Dad's family since I was six and I barely remembered them. I didn't really feel connected to them at all.

"It's your Aunt Isabel," said Mom. "She's had a heart attack. Luckily her manager was nearby and saw her collapse. He knows CPR and probably saved her life. He got her to the local clinic, then they airlifted her out to the closest hospital." Mom was looking even paler now, and her eyes filled with tears. "Poor Isabel! I'm so glad she wasn't all alone!"

I couldn't remember Isabel at all. The only images of her I had in my mind were from photographs. *Old* photographs. In them, she was anywhere from adolescent to maybe in her early thirties. She always appeared pale and expressionless, especially if her two youngest siblings were in the picture as well. Dad shared a close physical resemblance to her—tall, slim, ash brown hair. In the photographs, Daniel and Emily were shorter, darker hair, more vibrant—their expressiveness directing the eye to them.

Mom took a deep breath and went to find her cell phone, then called Dad and relayed Dan's message. I could feel, through her, his shock and concern.

We were more subdued for the rest of the evening, Mom browsing through a magazine in the living room while I did geometry at the dining table. Dad eventually called Mom back. She listened eagerly, but at the end of the conversation, she seemed resigned.

"Daddy talked to Uncle Dan and has been able to change his flight home so that he can go see Isabel and everyone. She's apparently in stable condition, so that's good. But he doesn't know when he'll be home. This might change our Thanksgiving plans."

Every year we had always spent both Thanksgiving and Christmas with my mom's family: Grandma, Grandpa, and Mom's two sisters and their families. This had been easy when we lived in Los Angeles. Last year I'd been unhappy about being away for the holidays. But this year, except for the long drive there and back, I'd really been looking forward to it. I was especially looking forward to seeing Aunt Audrey, but I also thought it would be a relief just to get away. Of course, Aunt Isabel's well-being was much more important.

I wouldn't usually have seen much of either Dave or Cris the next day, but I saw them both several times. Cris made no secret of noticing me, our first acknowledgment of the day having a delightfully conspiratorial feel to it. Dave acted as if I wasn't there, not once catching my eye, not even in English, but seeming to bask in the attention paid to him by others. Very unlike him. I was starting to feel like I really *didn't* care—a significant victory for me—and I was glad when Miss Sanders gave us most of the period to confer with our partners about our Shakespeare assignments.

Kyle and I had both finished reading *Twelfth Night* already and had some definite ideas, both about character motivations in general and which scenes we should choose from. We agreed to meet in the library during lunch

on the day we returned from vacation. I think he was as happy as I was with our progress and our partnership. Dave had already left the room by the time Kyle and I were done talking.

We had an extra long choir rehearsal since our concert would be the week after Thanksgiving. Mom was almost ready to leave when Ben and I got to the pool. And she had news.

"Isabel is doing well. Dad says she seems to be in good spirits and delighted that he's there."

Her droll expression made me question the veracity of the last part of that. I knew that Isabel and Dad didn't exactly get along. We drove home and, after dropping Ben off, she told me more.

"The doctors are considering an operation, so Daddy's waiting to find out. He also felt he should stay there so Uncle Dan could get back to work and his family. So he'll probably be gone at least over the weekend. They'll know more then."

I tried to not feel disappointed that our plans were changing and really thought about Aunt Isabel. It was difficult. I knew she was older than my dad, but I couldn't picture her as anything but a girl or young woman. And I had only the vaguest memories of the farm in Colorado. But she wasn't there now anyway, she was in a hospital. I *hated* hospitals.

I made a point of praying for her. I hadn't thought about God much lately, but if he could make her better, it seemed appropriate. It didn't hurt to ask.

Excitement seemed to hang in the air on Friday, everyone looking forward to our first long break and a week without school. Whether we went to Los Angeles or not, I was looking forward to it, too.

"So, are you going to the gymkhana tomorrow?" asked Robin.

"Yes," I said. "I wish you were going with us though."

When I first asked her about it, she had immediately said the Calderas weren't going. They would be away at a different show for the whole weekend. I was surprised that I felt relieved about that. Truly relieved. I had urged her to talk to Cheryl about coming with us, but she said she wanted to save her money and not spend anything on entry fees.

I felt bad—I sometimes forgot that she and her Gran didn't have much to spare. I would have offered to pay for a couple of classes for her, but I knew the reception that would get. She said that she planned to spend the day filling out application forms and taking them back to the stores. I wished her luck and added it to a growing mental list of things to bring to God's attention. At least it felt like I was doing something for her.

I considered avoiding the tables at lunch but wanted to spend the time with Robin. We were the first ones there and claimed one of the tables. I sat across from her and Matthew came and sat next to me. He hadn't said or done anything to single me out or make me feel uncomfortable since Robin's birthday, and I was trying not to have defenses up around him. I really didn't want anything to affect our friendship.

We had already started discussing Thanksgiving plans by the time most of the others got there. I didn't mention the situation with Aunt Isabel but said we usually spent the whole week in Los Angeles. I knew the Calderas usually had a large gathering of family, friends, and workers at Thanksgiving. Tanner, his mom, Robin, and Fiona always spent the day with them, and it sounded like Paola and Hannah and their families had been invited too. I was sure they would have a wonderful time, but I wasn't jealous. I was still hoping to be miles and miles away.

"I wish we were going," said Roberta, pouting. "We've got to spend it with family."

Dave sat on the other side of Robin, and when he wasn't jokingly giving her a hard time about her *not* driving the Mustang they had slaved over, he seemed to be flirting with all the other girls around. Except me, that is. He actually seemed to purposely ignore me. *So* unlike him. I wasn't upset but was tired of trying to guess what he was thinking or doing, what I had done wrong, or what, if anything, I was expected to do. I was so exhausted from trying to meet *anyone* else's expectations.

I leaned close to Robin and said, quietly, "I'll meet you by the lockers after school."

She had been actively listening to the surrounding conversation and had a mouthful of fruit roll, but nodded acknowledgment. I wanted to go off by myself but didn't dare. I couldn't imagine Dave following me again—not after the last time and not after the way he'd been acting—but I didn't want *anyone* assuming that I was leaving in hopes he *would* follow me. Instead, I found a spot on the grass near Ben and Paola. They were in a very lively and jovial discussion about the trials of traveling.

I was enjoying just listening to them, clearing my mind of other thoughts, when I became aware of someone coming to stand next to me. My first thought on feeling someone close was, of course, that it was Dave. But only for a second. One glance at the person's shoes and I knew it was Matthew. Then he sat down by me.

"So you don't know where you'll be for Thanksgiving?" he asked.

"Oh . . . no, but we'll probably go to Los Angeles, to my grandparents' house. It's kind of a tradition."

"Yeah, we have to go to my grandparents' too." He didn't sound too thrilled at the prospect. "They live in Bakersfield."

"I don't think I've ever been there, but I've seen the signs . . . you know . . . on the way to LA."

He nodded and was quiet a few moments. I was quiet too; I had no more to say on the subject and was too tired to work at a conversation.

"I wanted to ask you . . ." He paused and seemed to be seriously considering how to proceed. "I'd like to ask you to go to Winter Formal with me."

I suppose I shouldn't have been as surprised as I was—there had been plenty of hints for a long time now that even *I* had picked up on—but I really wasn't expecting that. I wished that he hadn't asked me yet; another week or two of emotionally distancing myself from Dave and I might have said yes. I'd had a lot of fun at the last dance and would love to go again. And Matthew was a person I *mostly* felt comfortable with. But at that moment I was still vacillating, at least slightly, between longing for, being annoyed at, and defending my heart against Dave. I needed to feel more detached from him. I couldn't think about Matthew at all right now and felt sorry, but the last thing I wanted to do was encourage him to think of me as more than a friend when I knew I couldn't, for the foreseeable future, return the interest.

"Oh . . . I don't know." I panicked a little, trying to find the appropriate thing to say; to stall without hurting him or slamming the door, at least until my feelings changed or I knew my own mind better.

The bell rang and, as we both got to our feet, he said, "That's okay. Just think about it. I'd really like to take you."

He was smiling, but it was that smile that I didn't understand. I appreciated his attitude though. He began walking with me—odd because I was heading toward the gym. Then he put his arm across my shoulders as he had several times in the past. I didn't think too much of it, though I was surprised and uncomfortable.

"I hope you have—"

The thought was never finished. His arm was forcefully pulled from my shoulder, and he spun immediately to face Dave. They glared at each other for a moment. I felt shocked and didn't know what to do.

In a low and menacing voice, Dave said, "Keep your hands *off* her."

I had seen Dave in various degrees of annoyance, even anger, but I'd never seen Matthew anywhere close to it. For a few seconds only, he looked furious, like he might lash back, maybe even physically. He glanced at me and appeared to make himself relax.

"What's the matter with you?" he said. "*You* have no interest here. And *you* don't get to decide who Allie likes or who she can go out with."

This little speech made me feel like sinking into the ground for several reasons, and Dave looked like he'd explode.

"*Stop!*" I cried, shaking violently. "*Please* . . . just *stop* it. I don't want to go out with *anyone*. Okay?"

Dave looked from me to Matthew, his eyes glittering and hard, holding Matthew's glare a moment longer. He backed away slowly, seeming reluctant and really angry. A group of girls and guys were waiting for him and had no doubt heard and witnessed the whole thing. I didn't look directly at them.

"Hey, sorry about that," said Matthew. "I seriously don't know what his problem is."

I had nothing to say, completely shaken. I hoped he couldn't tell. "I . . . I need to get to PE."

"Yeah, sure," he said, smiling again slightly and trying to sound upbeat. "Have a nice Thanksgiving, okay?"

"Yes. Thank you. You too."

He turned and walked away.

I continued to the gym, still shaking but trying very hard not to. I just didn't know how to make it stop.

Chapter Twenty

I avoided everybody I could in PE and was relieved to get to study hall. Ben and I met Robin after school and she walked to the pool with us, me keeping my eyes on the sidewalk in front of me. It was noticeably much colder than it had been earlier in the day and a very slight breeze felt even colder, plucking at my cheeks and nose and ears like icy little fingers.

"So, what happened at lunch?" asked Ben.

I'd heard him but hoped he was talking to Robin or asking a vague, generic question like, "How's it going?"

"Yeah, what the hell *was* that?" added Robin.

I glanced at them to make sure, but they were definitely talking to me.

"I . . . I don't know." This was very true. "You should ask *them*."

"I did. At least, I asked Dave. He said," she lowered her voice and muttered, "'Nuthin,'" grumpily to mimic him. When I didn't respond, she said, "If I didn't know better, I'd say he was jealous. But that doesn't make sense. Right?"

"Right," I agreed.

She didn't look satisfied. "He's never asked you out. I mean, he's never acted like he *liked* you." I could feel her eyes on me though mine were back on the pavement. "*Has* he?"

"No. Never," I said, but I was more confused about that. I'd been trying so hard to convince myself of that fact, *again*, and then he does something like this. I didn't know what to make of it. *Unless. . . .*

There was only one other thing I could think of. Last year, my dad had gone to their house to talk to them—about me. I never did find out exactly what was said, but I had suspicions.

"*You* obviously aren't interested in *him*," she said, decidedly.

I couldn't respond to that because I didn't want to lie, especially not to her, but my cheeks were growing warm. This was not a comfortable topic for me. "I just don't know," I said again. *Time to change the subject.* "But I didn't tell you about my aunt." I proceeded to tell them the little I knew about Aunt Isabel's present status, leaving out my dad's history with his family.

"So your dad's still in Colorado?" asked Robin. "Is he going to come home for Thanksgiving? Are you still going to your grandmother's?"

"I don't know yet, but yes, he's still in Colorado. I guess we find out on Monday."

She nodded. Ben had been unusually quiet throughout the conversation. I wondered what he was thinking, but he kept his thoughts on the matter to himself.

When we reached the pool, Robin said, "Call me tomorrow . . . after the show. Let me know how you did!"

"I will. Good luck tomorrow!"

"Yeah, good luck with the job hunting!" said Ben.

She grimaced and waved as we parted ways.

On the drive home, Mom said she'd heard from Dad. Aunt Isabel was doing much better and already insisting on leaving the hospital. Dad had checked into a hotel nearby, and Dan had gone home to Denver. Their sister, Emily, had been to visit but couldn't stay, so went home again too. Dad was trying to keep Aunt Isabel occupied by playing cards and watching TV with her, but she was used to being up and active, was very worried about her farm and horses, and hated the hospital. Apparently she was being difficult.

We dropped Ben off and I fed Remmy as soon as we got home. I spent a long time grooming him and would have liked to bathe him for the show the next day, but it was too late and too cold. Instead, I washed his legs, feet, and tail, and sponged his face and ears. I also would have liked to borrow the Caldera's clippers for his fetlocks, but there was no way I was going to

do that. I brushed him until he was sleek and shiny then put the light rug on him, more to keep him clean than warm, though the temperature did seem to be dropping quickly. I braided and wrapped his tail then added extra bedding to his stall and made sure he was settled for the night.

After dinner, Mom and I built our first fire of the season, and I brought all my tack in to clean while we watched a movie.

"You still seem unhappy. Has something happened?"

"No, Mom. Nothing has happened."

"Is everything okay with you and Paola?"

"Yes, fine. We're . . . fine. We get along great."

She was quiet for a moment, and I hoped she was done questioning me. Then, "You never mention Dave anymore. Has something happened between you and *him?* It seems strange that we never see him at all." After a few moments more, she said, "I miss him."

My immediate response surprised me—lump in throat, blurry eyes, leaden heart. I felt like shouting, *"You have no idea!"* but just nodded and busied myself by taking Remmy's bridle apart.

"What shall we watch?" she said brightly, maybe sensing my discomfort.

"I don't mind," I said.

"Princess Bride?"

I was torn. *The Princess Bride* was one of my favorites; a go-to choice for escaping into a different but very familiar and comfortable world. I could quote long passages of dialogue by heart but usually didn't anymore—not out loud. Choosing it would indicate that my mother was right. I weighed the relative values of comfort over secrecy and nodded my head again.

Sleep was elusive and I was wide awake way before my alarm went off. A mixture of very vivid dreams, memories of the previous day's altercation between Dave and Matthew, and excitement for today's show chased sleep away. I got up, fed Remmy and made sure he was ready for the day, gathered my clean tack and grooming kit on the back porch, then went to get ready myself.

I was happy to get dressed up, my show clothes fitting a little differently now but still looking good. At least, *I* thought so. I never did get the chaps

I had hoped to, but I didn't mind. Now I was more interested in getting breeches anyway.

When Cheryl arrived, we loaded Remmy and his tack and I climbed into the back seat of the truck. Originally, my dad was supposed to be home and we would have followed in our car. Mom was scheduled to work today and so couldn't go, but I didn't mind.

Two other students were going. I didn't know them at all, which made me feel a little uncomfortable in the truck. It also didn't help the knot of anxiety growing in my stomach, but once I had Remmy unloaded at our destination, I felt better.

Remmy was relatively calm, as he usually was, eyes bright and ears active but not at all nervous. His calmness always helped me relax too. The show was at a small horse farm I'd never been to—at least, small compared to Northfield, the Calderas', and Bar 8. I took Remmy's blanket off and walked him around, getting a feel for the place and seeing where our classes would be held.

There was a small covered arena, open on all sides with a small stand of bleachers on one side. Some distance away was another arena, larger but uncovered. The gymkhana games would take place there later in the day. First were the reining classes, and people and horses were already warming up in it. I had an equitation class and a pleasure class this morning, both in the smaller arena. Another small arena was also being used for warm-ups.

I took Remmy back to the trailer and then went to sign in with the other girls. They were much younger than me and mostly acted as if I wasn't there, which was fine with me. Neither of them were in my first classes. I felt calm and focused and, thankfully, confident.

Remmy and I took fourth and third respectively in classes of about ten riders, and I was thrilled. He was so responsive and our movements were accurate, which really helped us in the equitation. We definitely weren't as showy as most of the competition, so getting third in pleasure was a big deal to me. I took Remmy back to the trailer, loosened his girth and made a big fuss of him, then left him to his water and hay net.

There was a real nip in the air today, but the sky was clear. By noon there was a breeze, too, that seemed to cause quite a few riders grief. There were no flags here, as there were at Northfield, but there were tall poplars and eucalyptus trees that swayed and rustled, awnings that flapped, and the occasional piece of paper or plastic bag that flew off before someone could grab it. Our horses, Remmy and two of the Bar 8 horses, were unphased by it all, but not everyone was as lucky.

I went to watch the reining while Remmy relaxed for a while. I watched all the riders closely and admired their skill, storing up details to relay to Robin, though this was not an event I was interested in doing myself. After a while, I wandered back to the small covered arena where an English equitation class was taking place. This was more what I could imagine myself doing, and I tried picturing Remmy and me in English tack and riding clothes. This was quite easy to do and it became a solid goal.

About twelve-thirty I got Remmy ready again, then led him over to the bigger arena for the gymkhana games. Remmy's quick, calm response was great in the pleasure, equitation, and trail classes, but there was still something of a disconnect between us at faster speeds. My skills and reactions were a little too slow sometimes, so I had promised Cheryl to keep him in hand and only go as fast as I could and still maintain control. Of course, this meant that I didn't have a chance of placing in the games, let alone winning anything, but it also took the pressure off. Remmy behaved impeccably at home but still got a little excited in the speed events at shows. Today, I might not have ridden really fast, but I was able to keep Remmy happy and relatively calm—a skill in itself.

I rode the games at a fast trot or controlled canter. I also did poles at a trot, but mainly because I had no way of practicing at home and I hadn't learned to cue leads competently enough for fast changes, though I knew Remmy could do them. That was another goal.

The only event we performed at a real canter, though not a gallop, were the barrels. Even though I'd been practicing around obstacles at home, this was the first time competing at them since my accident last year. I tried to focus and relax, but I admit I was anxious. Remmy saw the barrels and wanted to race, but I sat deep and didn't completely give him his head, and by the second barrel he settled into a more relaxed speed. We negotiated the barrels with precision and, I thought, aplomb, and I was pleased with that.

It also made me happy that Cheryl seemed very proud of me. My confidence soared, and I felt the whole day had benefitted me, even if Remmy was capable of so much more. We watched the other contestants, including the girls I'd come with, both of whom rode much faster and bolder than me. I leaned over to whisper to Remmy and promised, "One day I'll let you really *run!*"

Sunday was a quiet day. It was cold and breezy again, and my hair was driving me crazy—sticking to my face and seeming to reach out to anything else I came near. I even got shocked several times from walking around the house with just my socks on. It was too cold without them, but I hated wearing slippers. Static electricity had rarely been a problem when my hair was longer and braided all the time.

Glad of Remmy's company, I spent most of the day with him, cleaning his paddock and stall to perfection, or close enough, then letting him out to nibble on grass while I raked and tidied outside. I almost wished Ben would come over to distract me, but I was just as glad that he didn't. I had things to work out and I didn't want to have to act social for anyone.

On Monday, I worked specifically on lead changes, something I was sure Dave could do with no problem, but I was still honing my communication skills. I wanted to be able to do pole-bending seriously and not just trot slalom between them. Of course, I needed actual poles, too. I hadn't gotten up the nerve to ask my dad and had no idea how or where they were to be obtained. For the time being, I moved large rocks into a straight line, pacing off strides between them.

After lunch, Mom wanted me to pack. We still hadn't heard what was decided about Aunt Isabel, but Dad wanted us to go to Los Angeles, one way or the other. He was waiting to hear from the doctors and then he'd make appropriate plans with Dan and Emily.

Around five o'clock, the house phone rang. It didn't ring often, and before now it would have caused my heart to leap and beat faster; it *could* be Dave. Now, that was extremely unlikely. I let Mom answer it.

It was Dad. Mom talked to him for quite a while, and I picked up "flights," "operation," and "Mom's," meaning Grandma's house.

Once off the phone, she explained. "Isabel is doing well physically, but she's fretting so much about being away from home that her blood pressure is too high for them to consider operating right now. They do want to

operate, though. Her doctor is releasing her tomorrow, and she'll stay with Emily, as she lives closest to the farm. They'll keep an eye on her and make sure she doesn't overdo things. I don't know her very well, but I remember she didn't like to be in the house or sit still much.

"Dad wants us to go ahead down to Grandma's. He'll take Isabel home so she can pack some things. And he knows she won't rest until she's seen her animals and is convinced the farm isn't falling apart. Then he'll drive her to Emily's and fly out to Los Angeles, hopefully no later than Wednesday."

Mom sighed, looking tired, but then smiled and rubbed my arm, I think more to comfort herself than me. I realized she must be sad, thinking of Dad so far away and having to do so much for his sister. I was sure she wished she could be there with him. I gave her a hug and she squeezed me back.

She snuffled a little then said, laughing slightly, "This has probably been difficult for both of them, but good too." She nodded her head. "They need to reconnect and forgive each other. I'm not glad that Isabel is unwell, but I *am* glad something happened to force them together again."

I nodded and felt a funny twinge; my mind always leaped to Dave and my uncertain relationship with him at the least provocation. He'd been something like a brother to me last year, and perhaps still was—a grouchy, meddling, perplexing one now, at best—but I also realized that at least we *did* have a connection, though I couldn't begin to define or understand it at all.

I wondered if he could.

Early Tuesday morning Tom came to take Remmy to Bar 8 for a little holiday of his own. I actually felt glad about this; he'd be happy where there were lots of other horses and things going on to watch and people to interact with. Everyone loved Remmy. Tom promised to take him out on the trails at least a couple of times while I was gone.

Mom and I loaded our bags and headed out about nine o'clock. Unlike this time last year, when I was very sad to be leaving, I relaxed more and more as the miles swept past and put distance between me and my world.

My world.

I loved my home so much: my friends, my house and neighborhood, Remmy and the other horses in my life, and even school—mostly. But many things still existed within the confines of how I felt about Dave and, more affectively and changeably, how he seemed to feel about me. Nothing had changed on my side. I still couldn't imagine ever caring for anyone else as deeply as I did for him. I couldn't even think of the possibility. But heartache combined with almost constant confusion was wearing me out emotionally and mentally. I was relieved to be getting away.

Mom and I talked some of the time about school, riding, and Aunt Isabel. She asked about Dave a couple of times. Was he home for Thanksgiving? Was he driving now? I answered affirmatively for those questions so don't know what she assumed, but I said no more. I didn't want to talk about him at all. It seemed strange that she didn't ask about any of my other friends' plans.

I called Brenda that evening from my grandmother's house to let her know we were in Los Angeles. She seemed very subdued but denied that anything was wrong. Then she said she'd been sick and still wasn't feeling very well. She went on to assure me that she was still dating Trevor and that her other friends were fine, though I hadn't asked about them. It was the weirdest phone call I'd ever had with her and it left me wondering what was really going on.

Mom and I picked Dad up from LAX on Wednesday as planned. It felt like he'd been gone a very long time. We went out to lunch to get caught up with each other before going back to Grandma's where there was sure to be little privacy. We talked of his trip, my gymkhana, and life in general until we'd ordered our food, then Dad explained what was happening with Isabel.

"I took her home to pack what she needed for the coming weeks and to prove that the horses weren't starving and the place wasn't falling into ruin without her. Which of course it wasn't. Her current clients and students have all been contacted, and everyone is very supportive, sending cards and flowers and assuring her they look forward to her recovery. I think that set her mind at ease. Her neighbor, Jose, is there. He's been helping her manage the place for the past few years. He's the one who was there when she collapsed. His cousin and one of his sons are taking turns with him actually staying at the place while she's away."

"Wow," said Mom. "What wonderful neighbors!"

"Yeah, well," said Dad, then hesitated. "There's a lot of history between our families. . . ."

A meaningful look passed between them. I got the feeling a lot more would have been said if I weren't there.

"So anyway," continued Dad, "she'll stay with Emily until Sunday, then Dan's picking her up to stay the night in Denver. Her surgery is scheduled for Tuesday. They'll keep her in the hospital for a while, depending on how quickly she recovers, then she'll stay with Dan and Diana."

Dad paused and looked at both Mom and me. "The thing is, they had planned to come out here for Christmas, to spend time with Diana's family up in Redding. They were wondering if Isabel could stay with us while she gets her strength back. We all agreed the only way we'll keep her from going back to work is to keep her away from the farm. It may be well into January before she's fit to go home by herself."

I wasn't sure how to feel about that. The idea of someone I'd never really met staying with us for a long time weighed against a growing curiosity.

"It would mean staying home for Christmas," he said, watching Mom closely. "And I've got a trip scheduled for the beginning of January."

But Mom looked intensely back at him and said, very decidedly, "Of course! It would be wonderful to have her come. And we can really get to know her."

Mom's warmth and sincerity made Dad noticeably melt and pretty much won me over too. Dad looked at me and I nodded, not exactly sure what I was agreeing to but willing to go along with their plan.

Grandma was not as complacent about it when Mom explained the situation and was a little huffy about it that evening. She seemed more than usually impatient with me for some reason too. That made me feel as if it were somehow my fault we wouldn't be spending Christmas with her.

By the next day, all seemed forgiven if not forgotten, and my grandmother put me to work peeling and slicing apples for apple sauce and pie filling. Aunt Audrey and Aunt Katharine and their families were with us by noon, and the house became noisy and jolly and smelled warmly of apple and cinnamon and turkey and stuffing.

I was especially happy to see Audrey and wore one of the outfits she'd bought me.

"Allison!" She came and hugged me tightly. I hugged her back. "You look so pretty! Your hair's getting long again, isn't it? Are you going to let it grow?"

I hadn't thought about it.

Grandma stopped what she was doing and looked at me critically. "She's certainly filled out a little. That's nice. Yes, she's looking quite pretty but could still stand to put a little weight on. Boys don't like skinny girls. She should keep her hair shorter, though. It suits her."

I don't know why my grandmother sometimes talks about me as if I'm not right there, but I didn't hold it against her. I was surprised her off-handed compliments didn't make me feel uncomfortable, but her next words did.

"Still no boyfriend?"

I managed to distract myself enough to not blush.

Mom looked at me apologetically and said, carefully, "She has lots of *friends*, Mom. Girls *and* boys."

"That's not the same thing, Jennifer."

Aunt Audrey, my hero, changed the subject. "Are you doing anything special for your sixteenth birthday, Allison?"

I gave her a grateful look but didn't have an answer. "I don't know."

"But it's your *sixteenth* birthday," said Grandma. "Sweet sixteen. She *has* to have a party, of course. What do the kids do these days? Renting halls and limousines?"

I saw no necessity for *having* to have a party but didn't dare contradict her. She would just think I was sullen. Or worse.

"We really haven't talked about it yet," said my mom. "I'm sure we'll do something special."

The conversation turned toward the doings of my cousins, and I escaped outside to the cool and quiet of the backyard.

Later that day I ate enough to not be scolded by anyone, spent time in the same room as my boisterous cousins, and didn't brood about whether I'd hear from my friends, which was just as well. I didn't. We came home on Saturday, and Tom brought Remmy home to me on Sunday.

I'd made it through the whole week without feeling too depressed, but now the thought of returning to school the next day had me feeling low. Trying not to think about Dave and keeping busy didn't change the way I felt. The sense of loss was just as real.

I vaguely remember Matthew and Robin asking me questions in class on Monday and I must have answered, but I'm sure it was mechanically. I met Kyle in the library at lunch to talk about our Shakespeare assignment, and I was glad to have an excuse to not go near the tables. We agreed to meet every day there to talk about and practice our scene. Then we walked to English together and, though I was very aware of him, I was able to avoid looking at Dave.

Dad picked Ben and me up after school and told me he was going to take Mom out for dinner and a movie. Except for their summer vacation and the night I went to the dance, it had been a long time since they'd gone on a real date together, and with Isabel coming, he wanted to take the time while he could. I didn't mind having an evening to myself.

It was about eight o'clock and I was thinking about checking on Brenda when the doorbell rang. I was hesitant to answer—home alone and all—but curiosity got the better of me. I peeked out the dining room window and recognized the truck in the driveway. Extremely surprised but actually happy to see him, I opened the door.

"Hi," I said.

"Hey," said Cris with his brother's voice.

He was wearing a hoodie, which wasn't unusual, but something about the *way* he wore it seemed strange—completely zipped up with his hands in the pockets. He was holding it out slightly in front of him, too. He seemed to be trying to look me in the eyes but kept looking away.

He'd shaved; the light mustache and chin hair were gone. And his hair was shorter. He'd finally broken down and gotten a haircut. I wondered if that meant Dave had too. Cris looked younger again. Something about it flooded my mind with vague memories. I didn't understand why, but I had a lump in my throat. I supposed he looked more like he did last year and it made me feel nostalgic for that time, but I wasn't sure. I was never sure about much where Cris was concerned.

"I was at the clinic today and someone brought a lost kitten in. Dr. Simons was going to send it to the shelter but," his right hand came out of his pocket to reach under the edge of the hoodie, pulling out a puff of gray fur, "I said I might be able to find it a home."

"Oh!" I gasped, both at his words and at the sight of the ball of fluff.

He held the kitten out to me as I instinctively reached for it. The simple action pushed me over the edge; there were tears in my eyes.

"It's so little!" I breathed, cradling the small, warm body in my hands. I laid my cheek gently against its back. "So soft!"

Cris stood quietly, just watching and looking serious.

"Oh, but I can't!" I said, and a couple of tears rolled down my cheeks. If it had been anyone but Cris there, I would have tried to wipe them away, pretend it hadn't happened. But I never bothered much about pretending with Cris. "My mom's allergic."

He frowned and his mouth twisted sideways slightly as if aggravated. "Oh, sorry. I didn't know. I thought maybe . . ." He shifted to the other leg. "I can't take her home with me. Merle . . . I wouldn't trust her around a kitten. She doesn't like cats, and she kills vermin. I don't know if she'd be able to tell the difference. I'll take her for just tonight, then I guess I'll take her back."

"No!" I cried, holding the kitten close. It mewed sleepily, barely a fraction of a sound, then began whirring as if it had a tiny motor inside. A surprisingly loud motor. "She can stay with me tonight at least. Maybe I can keep her until we find a good home?"

Cris' expression, though unsmiling, lightened noticeably. "Are your parents home?"

"No, they're out for a while. But she can stay in my room tonight. She won't bother my mom there."

He nodded and looked relieved, maybe almost happy—at least, as happy as I'd ever seen him. "I have some stuff for her," he said and went back to the truck.

The "stuff" turned out to be a small litter box, a box of litter, and a paper bag with food and a couple of toys in it.

"Did you buy all this?" I asked.

He didn't answer, but I thought his cheeks darkened—it was hard to be sure in the half-light. The mental image of Cris shopping for the little toys made me smile. He followed me into the kitchen and got the litter box set up.

"Do you have something to put food and water in?" he asked.

I didn't know. We rummaged through cupboards looking for something suitable. We decided on two small, shallow containers, which I carried, and Cris followed me up to my room with the bag and litter tray. He put a little

soft food into one bowl while I got water for the other from the bathroom. I set the kitten down in front of the water, and she obligingly drank with tiny, delicate laps.

"Does she have a name?"

Cris shook his head. "Name-free."

"What should we name her?"

A gentle smile momentarily transfigured his face into something light and beautiful before he remembered himself. But I'd seen it. I knew that smile; I'd just never seen it on him.

"You're asking the guy that named his merle dog Merle?" Then he shrugged. "You can name her whatever you want."

"Oh. I'm not very good with names."

He almost smiled again but looked sad too. "I'm sure you'll think of something."

We sat there on my bedroom floor for a while, watching the kitten explore. She ate a little and exhibited interest in the litter box.

"She looks like she'll be fine," said Cris after a while. "You should probably keep your door closed all the time, so she doesn't get out. Have you ever had a cat before?"

I shook my head.

"Have you heard the expression 'curiosity killed the cat'? There's a reason for that. They like to get into everything and'll try to fit into ridiculously small spaces . . . not the greatest judgment. She could get into trouble." He frowned then, and a strange look came over his face, but he didn't immediately say more.

We sat a while longer in silence, just watching and playing gently with the little creature. It was strange how content Cris seemed, to stay and watch the kitten with me—certainly he must have better things to do. But I assumed he just wanted to make sure the kitten would be okay in my care.

Finally, he said, "I better get going."

I nodded. We left my room, closing the door carefully, and I followed him downstairs. He opened the front door and stood in the doorway a moment, frowning again.

"You won't get into trouble for this, will you?"

"No, of course not," I said, wondering why he'd even ask. "But I don't know if I'll be able to keep her."

Cris nodded. "Just let me know tomorrow."

I agreed and he left. I hurried back up the stairs to the kitten. She was stalking the laces of my shoes by my closet. I sat back on the carpet and waited for her to come to me. She soon did, mewing adorably, and curled up in my lap. She played with my fingers and her own tail for a while, then fell soundly asleep. I sat like that, marveling at her and gently stroking her fur, until my parents got home.

Mom instantly fell in love with the kitten and wanted to hold her but didn't. Dad grumbled something about puppies but otherwise didn't object to her. He seemed more concerned about the fact that Cris had been here when they weren't home. But he didn't actually complain about it, only looked meaningfully at Mom.

I made a soft bed for the kitten in a corner with some old sweaters. She was on my pillow next to my head when I woke up.

Tuesday passed quickly, and Wednesday, and the rest of the week, each day my thoughts more on the ball of fur at home than anything else. Cris seemed to be around more, or at least made his presence known to me more than usual by enquiring after the kitten. He said they had put flyers up around town about her. He also seemed unusually satisfied that my parents were okay with me taking care of her—unusual in that I'd never actually seen him look satisfied about anything. He said he'd done some investigating and thought the kitten was a Russian Blue, and that mom might not be allergic to her.

I told my friends about the kitten, of course, and enlisted their help in thinking of a name, but nothing stuck. I could tell by about the third day that they were tired of hearing about her, so I kept her latest antics to myself. I looked up "Russian Blue" on the internet and agreed with Cris it was likely that's what she was.

Still working on our *Twelfth Night* presentation, I realized how much I identified with Viola, which was just one association away from calling the bluish-gray kitten Violet. And that was her name.

Thursday night I awoke to gravel on my window. I was wide awake immediately and not averse to adventure. I left Violet asleep on my bed and went out to talk to Ben for a while.

"It's really bright out," he said. "I was thinking we could explore more."

"Okay," I agreed. "But not for too long."

The moon was full and the sky was clear, but it was very cold.

"I tried to find that road we were on before from my house, but ended up in someone's back yard. They have a Cujo."

"You'd better be careful or someone's going to call the police on you. You don't always carry that knife, do you?"

"Only at night. You know, for protection."

"That's what I was afraid of."

He laughed. "I'm not *doing* anything."

I didn't reply but followed him. We walked through the gate at the back of our property and found the fire road cutting south across the hillside. We followed this for quite a way, moonlight flooding the open road before and behind us and the slope to our right, but casting deep shadows around the trees and undergrowth to our left. It was beautiful and exhilarating and creepy.

As we walked, he told me about Louisiana and New Orleans and Mardi Gras. It sounded noisy and crowded and humid and smelly and not a place I would like to be, but I was fascinated anyway.

"The air smells of old moss, spices, jasmine, and fried chicken. Only sometimes it smells kind of rancid, too, like old cigarette butts and barf, depending on the season, where you are, and which way the wind's blowing. It's colorful too, people dressed up in gold and green and purple and red for Carnival. There's music everywhere. You could be walking down the street and hear one band playing, and before you leave that sound behind, there's another, then another."

I loved hearing his stories but was starting to feel uneasy. "How old were you?"

"What?"

"When you were there. How old were you?"

"Oh . . . I don't remember. Pretty little, I guess."

"And you remember all that? I can barely remember anything from when I was little. *Why* were you there? Who were you with? Your mother?"

"Yeah," he said, giving me that sideways look I was starting to mistrust. "Mom was . . . an actress. She was there filming a movie." I would have asked much more about this, but he abruptly changed the subject. "So . . . Cris Caldera."

I frowned. That was out of the blue. "What about him?"

"*He's* who you like," he said, looking at me knowingly.

"What are you talking about now?"

"It's all right. I'm not jealous or anything."

"You talk so much nonsense," I said.

"No, really. I like him much better than Googly Eyes. But I think he's too old for you."

I stopped dead in my tracks, covered in moonlight, facing him in the middle of the road.

"Will you please stop? There is no *Googly Eyes*. Have I told you how gross that sounds? And Cris has just been asking about the kitten. We're . . . friends. I guess."

I suddenly wondered if that were true. He'd thought of me for the kitten, in spite of our differences and in spite of Dave's current *in*difference. And I'd noticed him watching me more lately and even seeming to care how I felt. I was sure it was just because he knew that I liked Dave and that Dave didn't return my feelings. He might understand that I felt hurt, but he didn't seem unhappy about the actual situation. The reason for that was obvious to me—he was relieved for his brother's sake. I wondered if they ever talked about me, then I remembered the conversation I'd overheard. I didn't want to think about that.

"You have an overactive imagination. I could just as easily talk about you and Hannah."

He grinned widely at that and wagged his eyebrows. "How'd you guess? And I thought we'd been so discreet."

"*Is* that who you like?" I asked, glad to get the focus back on him.

He looked sideways at me again. "Why? Because we look the 'same'?"

Perturbed, I struggled to understand why he would say that. "You don't look anything alike. Except maybe . . . oh." Hannah was one of the few obviously Asian students at Douglas High. Ben was less obvious. I hadn't thought much about it until now. "Is . . . was your mom Asian?"

His expression made me feel stupid for asking, and I wondered if it was an insensitive question, but I was really curious.

"I'd never heard of your last name before," I said. At the beginning of school, I'd thought it was Newin or some similar spelling. Since then I'd seen it written down and now knew it was Nguyen.

"Yeah. She was . . . I'm half Vietnamese."

"Oh." I thought that was interesting. I'd never met anyone that was Vietnamese before. "I only said Hannah because you always sit next to her and bug her during lunch."

He laughed. "Well then, no, Hannah's not the one. Though I think we'd have beautiful children." He pretended to sigh and look off in the distance as if picturing their hypothetical offspring.

I shook my head. "You're impossible."

We continued walking, finally coming to a fence just before a crossroad. There was another wide, locked gate and a smaller, unlocked gate next to it.

"Where do you think we are?" he asked.

"I don't know. Maybe the road across from Bar 8?"

We could only see a short way in either direction along the crossroad. Our road continued across it and disappeared into shadows.

"That would mean my house is that way." He pointed northwest. "Somewhere on the other side of this hill. Want to climb it?"

I regarded him, considering he might genuinely be crazy. "No. Let's go back."

We turned around and headed back the way we'd come.

"Chicken," said Ben.

"Yes," I agreed.

Chapter Twenty-One

"We're going to Sacramento tomorrow," said Robin in History, her eyes bright.

"You are?" I asked.

"*We* are. You and me. You can go, right?"

"I . . . I don't know. Maybe."

"It'll be the first time I've driven there myself."

I could tell she was extremely excited at the prospect.

"Gee . . . in *that* case, I don't know. . . ." I pretended to doubt her ability.

She gaped at me, then laughed. It was a good sound I hadn't heard in a while.

"How dare you question my skills. Come on, it'll be fun. Gran is going, so it'll be legal and everything. Sort of. We probably won't stay too long, but I think she's really looking forward to it. She hardly ever goes anywhere outside Douglas. And I promise to take excellent care of you."

Later, I asked my parents, and with only slight reservation, they agreed. I was looking forward to it and even dressed up a little. I had some babysitting money to take but not as much as I would have liked.

Saturday morning Mom drove me over to Robin's and stayed to visit with Fiona. After Mom left, we did too. Fiona tried to insist on sitting in the back seat of the Mustang, but she would have had too much trouble getting in and out. We convinced her to sit in the front. Robin filled the car up with gas in town using the gift card I'd given her, and we hit the road talking and laughing and singing along to the radio.

"The others are meeting us there," she said at the end of a song.

My heart sank. "Others?"

"Yeah, you know . . . Dave and them. I'm not exactly sure who all's going."

The carefree shopping trip with just my best friend and her Gran suddenly had an aspect of ordeal. Not only would I have to deal with—or try *not* to deal with—Dave, who knew who else would be there. Matthew? If so, I dreaded his attention and the tension that might cause. Hannah? Paola? I guessed I could handle that. It would be better without boys involved though. Roberta? I didn't really care anymore—I was sure I didn't. I just didn't want to hang out with her.

"What's the matter?" asked Robin.

I guess I was too quiet on the subject. "Nothing," I said. "It's just . . . I thought it was only us."

"Oh," said Robin. She didn't take her eyes off the road, but she looked concerned. "Well . . ." Her face brightened again and she smiled widely, "we can always ditch the others. I've got my own keys!"

I laughed at that and she did too.

It ended up not being too bad. It definitely could have been worse. Roberta could have been there, but she wasn't. Jessie had driven herself. Hannah had come with Paola and her mother. Paola was very excited to see us, but I saw Hannah pause and look—disappointed? Then she smiled and said hi and gave no other indication she wasn't as happy to see us as the other girls. I had such a hard time reading people anyway, it was probably nothing.

Tanner had come with Dave. Matthew had come alone.

Rosa and Fiona insisted they were happy for us to go on without them; they'd walk together at their own speed and rest whenever Fiona needed to.

We spent several hours there, and I began to relax when neither Matthew nor Dave paid any particular attention to me. Actually, Dave avoided contact with me completely, though I caught him looking my way a few times. He looked away immediately each time, so I didn't become uncomfortable about it. Matthew didn't ignore me, but he didn't bug me either, and he seemed conscious of keeping some space between us. That seemed very considerate and I was grateful.

Paola appeared to have the most fun and Jessie definitely bought the most stuff. Hannah was subdued and stayed near Dave, sometimes even walking arm-in-arm with him, and I couldn't help wondering about them; about her. But I wasn't jealous. I just felt a little sad—the way Hannah looked.

As usual, we passed a lot of stores without even looking in the windows, but I was surprised when Dave stopped in front of a men's store. The storefront mannequins were all dressed in stylish suits, some elegantly conservative and others more flamboyant in color and design.

"Dude . . . you gonna go all GQ on us?" laughed Tanner.

Dave looked over his shoulder at him and enigmatically said, "Maybe," a little too seriously for my peace of mind.

He and Hannah remained there talking as the rest of us continued on, but then they followed behind us. After a while we all split up, agreeing to meet for lunch. Hannah and Dave walked back the way we'd come. Matthew and Tanner went in search of a video game store. Paola and Jessie went off together, giggling.

I breathed a deep sigh of relief when Robin and I were left alone. We took our time looking in various stores. Robin found a soft knitted angora throw in a pretty heather pink I agreed Fiona would love. Though I would have liked to have had more money to spend on really nice gifts for my parents, I was kind of glad I didn't. Robin probably wouldn't care, but I would have felt awkward spending it. Instead, I bought my mom some earrings I thought would look pretty on her. Later I was able to sneak in some cute pajamas with ponies on them for Robin while she was elsewhere in the store. I hoped she'd love them. Dad was much harder to buy for, but I finally found a big coffee mug with a cute robot on it. It said, "Robots need love too." I felt pleased about the day so far.

When we got to the food court, everyone was there, including Fiona and Rosa. Jessie and Paola both had twice as many bags as they'd had before and everyone else carried at least one. Hannah still looked subdued and appeared even more clingy to Dave. He had a bag from the men's store they'd been looking in earlier, but he didn't seem happy either. In actual fact, he looked—tired? I'd avoided looking at him closely for so long, I was shocked. His hair had gotten so long that he kept having to push it behind his ears to keep it out of his eyes. And there was something wrong about his eyes, but I couldn't, *wouldn't* meet his gaze long enough to figure out what.

After lunch we began to go our separate ways. Tanner asked Robin if he could hitch a ride since he lived close to her. I had a stab of something like fear that I might be expected to switch places with him and ride with Dave, since he technically lived closer to me than anyone else. Hannah was looking in my direction, and I wondered if she hoped Dave would offer her a ride instead. My heart was flip-flopping and I hated myself for it; the fear that Dave would offer me a ride at odds with the stupidly desperate hope that he would.

"I could give you a ride," said Matthew from behind me, softly, so only I could hear him.

"Oh, I . . ."

Dave turned to Hannah. "Want to ride with me?"

She looked distracted for a moment, then smiled and said, "I'd better go back with Rosa."

He shrugged. My heart sank, but I turned to Matthew, "I'll just go back with Robin. But thanks."

Dave might not care, but I didn't feel comfortable going with Matthew. I felt terrible about it though, as if I were being unfair to him. I was having a hard time justifying my hesitation to myself. He was such a nice guy. I had a feeling it was just a matter of time before I'd say yes to him—yes to *something*. I also had a feeling he knew it. These thoughts prompted others, though. Matthew had asked me to Winter Formal. How would I feel about Dave by then? Perhaps enough time would have gone by for me to consider going with Matthew if we could go as just friends. Right now, I still couldn't.

Fiona was visibly exhausted, and we insisted that she sit in the front seat of the Mustang again. Tanner sat squished into the back with me all the way to my house. He kept up a steady conversation with Robin about the relative merits of individual people and their horses as it applied to competition. I didn't know many of the people and watched out the window instead. When we got to my house, I thought about inviting everyone in—Robin hadn't seen the kitten yet—but she seemed anxious to get her Gran home, I wasn't sure how Tanner would feel about meeting my parents, and I was socially and emotionally exhausted myself.

"See you Monday," said Robin.

I agreed, briefly said hi to my parents in the house, made sure Remmy was happy, and spent the rest of the afternoon in my room, in the dark, eventually falling asleep on my bed with Violet.

The next week went by quickly, thankfully. I spent as little time in Dave's proximity as I could. It was just easier for me. I was trying so hard to function normally—at least trying to find something that felt like normal, which had always been elusive anyway. The highlight was on Tuesday.

"I got a job!" said Robin, meeting me before Geometry.

I was excited for her. "Really? Where?"

"At the bakery in town. I'll be working early Saturday mornings and Mondays after school, and maybe more if they need me to cover someone else's shift. And the great thing is, I won't need to drive, so I can really save money."

She seemed so excited at the prospect. I was glad for her and would have liked to know if she was saving for something specific, but by that time we were at our desks and the class was starting. I'd try to remember to ask later. It occurred to me that between my activities and her working, we wouldn't have much time together outside of school. I'd already spent much less time with her this year, and it made me feel bereft somehow. My universe was shifting again, and it seemed like Ben and I were the only ones without cars and jobs.

On Thursday Dad picked Ben and me up from school after choir, then later we all came back into town for the holiday concert. This was very different from the first one and took place in the school gym. The bands were also playing, so we needed a larger space to accommodate all the singers and instrumentalists and the larger audience. While it lacked the ambiance and better acoustics of the church, it was interesting to be in a combined concert.

I was less nervous about performing this time but more stressed about the noise and crowd. Still, it was mostly fun. Our after-school mixed choir sang only two songs by ourselves and one combined with the other choirs. In between, we listened to the bands play.

I was surprised to see not only Stacie playing the trumpet but Tanner playing percussion with the concert band. He was a lot of fun to watch as some of the songs required the percussionists to play two or more different instruments.

Looking around, I saw Kyle sitting in the stands and couldn't help scanning them for Dave, too, but I didn't see him. I thought he might have come to see everyone, especially as Tanner and Stacie were also performing. It was doubtful that he didn't know about it, and soccer was over. I thought I saw Cris a couple of times but they were passing glimpses, and when I looked back, he wasn't there. My distance vision being what it is, it might have been someone else, and perhaps I'd grown too used to the shaggy head and facial hair to recognize him clearly without them.

On Saturday, I had a lesson with Cheryl and would later babysit for her. I was thrilled when she asked if I'd like to go for a trail ride with her after my lesson.

I was riding a dun-colored mare named Sunset I'd only ridden a couple of times before and didn't feel entirely confident on yet. Cheryl had me riding her for lessons now; she said her stride most closely resembled Remmy's and we were starting to work more on pole-bending. She was a little more spirited and unpredictable than the other horses I'd become used to, but Cheryl assured me she generally didn't become spooky on the trail.

I let Sunset snooze while we waited for Cheryl to saddle up, and then we headed out on the trail next to the road leading to Brookside, my street. We talked a little as we rode. She told me that reservations were completely filled through July for the guest house already, which meant they were financially stable, but there'd be precious little quiet time for the family in the busy seasons.

"I might want you to babysit more so Tom and I can get away now and then. Would you be up for that?"

I assured her enthusiastically that I would if I could. I, in turn, told her what I was learning with Melanie. She was very encouraging. I also told her about Robin getting a job, and a little about Aunt Isabel, indicating that I might be more available over Christmas break since we weren't going away. She became thoughtful.

"Robin's working, huh? That's good, but I miss seeing her. You should tell her to come out to just visit sometime."

I assured her I would.

"And Dave, too," she said, and I thought she seemed expectant, perhaps watching for a reaction. "He's working with Tom a lot, but I rarely see him anymore. Now that he's driving, especially. I really miss that guy."

I wanted to say, "Me too!" but said nothing.

"I guess you're all just growing up and going your separate ways, but I miss having everyone around." She was quiet for a moment and I felt her watching me. "I suppose you see him at school?"

A direct question—no dodging a response. "Yes. Most days." We lived on the same planet. I *saw* him. It felt like that was about it.

"Hmm," she murmured.

We rode on in silence, completing the ride around the perimeter of most of the ranch and having some lovely canters along the way. When we got back and had the horses turned out, Cheryl told me to go up to the big kitchen for some dinner. Then I could come over to the bungalow.

"And Allison," she said as I began to walk away. She paused a moment as if second-guessing whether to say anything, then continued, "Stay close to your friends, hon. Don't let them slip away."

I thought about what she said and searched her face for any hidden meanings. I might not have been able to read them anyway.

"That's what I want, too," I said, then went up to the guest house and Phyllis' excellent cooking.

Monday was Kyle's and my presentation day for English, and I was very nervous about it. We went over everything at lunch, sitting on the grass with Robin, Stacie, and Ben listening in. Cris was there, too, and appeared interested in what we were doing, very uncharacteristically coming to sit between Kyle and Ben. I didn't mind. Dave and Hannah sat together at one of the tables and were probably also working on their scene, but I didn't watch them.

We had chosen to perform our contemporary interpretation as we both lacked confidence in speaking the old English out loud, but Kyle had found a three-cornered hat with a huge feather and had a long fringed sash to wear on his hip where a sword would have hung. He had wanted to rent a real one but doubted school administration would be cool about it. He'd already changed into a loose shirt and some dark suit trousers to complete his Orsinio look.

I had no real costume pieces to play the gender-swapping Viola, but had worn my black show jeans and my cowboy boots, and wore my hair pulled back in a low tail with a black ribbon. I noticed that Dave had worn black jeans and boots too. I also wore a white shirt of my mom's that was too big for me, and I had an old fashioned vest to put on that she'd found in the back of Dad's closet. We had pinned it up the back to make it smaller for me. Right before the bell rang, Robin drew a small mustache on me with an old eyebrow pencil I'd borrowed from Mom. She assured me I looked great, but I felt a little sick and extremely self-conscious walking to English.

I had hoped we'd be the first to go, and if not first, then at least before Dave and Hannah's Romeo and Juliet scene. I wasn't sure how it might affect me. But they actually went before us and it turned out to be a good thing.

They had also chosen to do their own interpretation. Hannah's hair was braided and she'd hidden the length of it down the back of her shirt. She held a long blond wig and two long shawls, one pink and one white. Dave held a large piece of shiny black fabric, but I couldn't tell what it was. Hannah placed two chairs sideways at the front of the class as Dave, very serious, explained the famous balcony scene and what had led up to it.

Right before starting, they exchanged items, Hannah sweeping what we could now clearly see was a Batman cape over her shoulders with a flourish, and Dave wrapping the pink shawl around his hips like a skirt, and the white one around his shoulders. Then he put the wig on, smoothing it down and pretending to be as self-conscious as I probably felt. Hannah stepped back and knelt as Dave stepped onto the chairs amid the class's giggles.

Hannah started with a short paraphrased "What light through yonder window" speech, referring to Dave as "Jules."

Dave's first words were, "Oy vey," in an only slightly higher than normal voice followed by a huge sigh. After Hannah's paraphrased aside, he began his next dialogue with, "Hey, Romey, where you at?"

It was very funny, mainly because I would never have imagined Dave doing anything that silly. They both exuded confidence in their performance and received a loud round of applause when they were done.

Miss Sanders asked them why they had chosen to switch parts and perform it comedically.

Hannah said, "We thought about doing a different scene because this one is so cliché, and the language is so over the top romantic and flowery, but the actual story is so sad. And then Dave said how funny it would be to swap roles and completely rewrite the dialogue."

Dave added, "We both felt uncomfortable with the intensity of the characters. I mean, they really don't even know each other."

I thought about what Dave had said while Miss Sanders asked a couple more questions, and then Kyle and I were next.

Kyle set the scene, describing Viola's transformation into Cesario and Orsinio's amorous pursuit of Olivia. We played the scene straight, and I know I was a bit wooden physically, but I think I read the lines well. We received polite applause and took our seats.

"Kyle," said Miss Sanders, "what is Orsinio's motivation?"

Kyle frowned. "To be honest, I'm not sure. I think he's just rich and bored and more in love with the idea of love than he is with Olivia. He's built up all these fantasies about her without knowing anything about her. He's barely even seen her before but is crazy about her because she's beautiful. That's just really shallow. She's rich, too. He denies interest in her money and land, but you can't help wondering if he'd be as crazy about her if she were poor."

Miss Sanders nodded. "Good points, Kyle. Allison, tell us about Viola."

I had been mentally preparing to answer the motivation question while Kyle spoke, but for me, Viola had been the one character not easily pigeonholed into one. She was also the only character I identified with. Miss Sanders' broader directive was a little easier to accomplish, but I wasn't sure where to start.

"Why do you think she agreed to enter Orisinio's service?" she said.

"I think it was just a place to start," I said. "Viola had lost everything, including her brother. At least, that's what she'd thought. In Shakespeare's time, a woman with nothing wouldn't have any good options for the future. As a man, she might make enough money to start over somewhere."

Miss Sanders' brows rose and she inclined her head. "What do you like about her?"

I tried to think of why I identified so strongly with her. One of the reasons was because she seemed more comfortable around men than women, but I didn't want to say that. "She's honest and doesn't really lie, even though she's pretending to be something she's not. That's actually very difficult for her. And she's very loyal. She's intelligent and kind, too, or at least, more than most of the other characters." Then I felt compelled to add, "Even if she does fall in love with someone as shallow as Orsinio."

The class laughed, but Dave was frowning at the floor and I felt like falling through it.

Roger drove Melanie and me to Northfield on Wednesday. Roger usually dropped us off at the equitation center and then continued to the market where he worked.

"Aren't his parents rich?" I had asked Melanie, surprised that he had a job. Then I felt terrible. Melanie worked too, and for all I knew she was as wealthy as him. I hadn't meant to imply anything negative.

She smiled and said, "He doesn't *need* to work, but his parents want him to learn what it's like to earn his own money and work for someone else. I'm sure he'll own his own business one day like his dad. I think it mostly just pays for his gas money and insurance."

That seemed reasonable, but I couldn't help comparing it to Robin, who had so little and wanted to work to help her Gran and save for something in the future. She had to *avoid* buying gas for her car.

Then there was Dave—and Cris, too—who also had a relatively wealthy family and also worked very hard. I wasn't sure how they used their money. *Renovating old trucks and buying fancy suits, I guess.*

Today, I hadn't been hungry at school and had given most of my lunch to Ben, but I realized I should probably eat something before my lesson. Hesitantly, I asked if I could ride to the community center with Roger, then I'd walk back. Melanie seemed okay with it and Roger, though not looking thrilled at the prospect, agreed.

When we reached the market's parking lot, I thanked him and walked around to the community center where the food court was. It felt strange being there on my own, but I thought it was good for me too; I wanted to be independent and able to function without anyone helping me or *with* me all the time.

I had just bought a hamburger and was debating whether to eat it there— noisy and garish from the adjacent bowling alley and arcade—or take it back to the relatively quiet stables, when I saw Matthew with a bunch of other boys.

One of the other boys looked familiar, but I couldn't immediately place him. They all carried gym bags. There was nowhere to disappear to so I turned away and stood very still, hoping Matthew wouldn't see me. But he did.

"Hey," he said, walking over. "What are you doing here?"

"Just getting something to eat," I said, holding up the burger bag.

He frowned, laughing, and said, "No . . . I mean, what are *you* doing *here?* At Northfield?"

Now he looked suspicious. I felt uncomfortable, as if I were somewhere I shouldn't be.

"I'm with a friend," I said, but when he looked around, I added, "She's . . . waiting for me. Outside." All perfectly true.

"Oh," he said. "*She*, huh?" He seemed satisfied with that and looked about to ask something more.

I didn't want to be asked anything else, so said, "You're here for?"

"Regional swim team every other Wednesday. Plus meets. So have you given any thought to joining the school team this spring?"

"Oh . . . um . . . no. Not yet. I'm . . ." I was going to say that I was very busy with choir and riding, but I didn't feel like explaining or avoiding the truth anymore. "I don't know. But I'd better get going or my friend will wonder where I am."

"Do you need a ride somewhere?" was his immediate response. I felt a stab of annoyance, then felt guilty for it.

"No. No, really, I'm fine. I'd rather walk."

His lips tightened and he nodded. He didn't look mad. Disappointed? Speculative?

"Bye," I said and walked toward the nearest exit, still feeling uncomfortable.

"Yeah . . . see you," he said.

I wondered if he would tell Dave that he'd seen me there, then assumed he wouldn't. After all, why would he? *And so what if he does? It's none of Dave's business. Right?*

On the walk back to the stables, I considered the issue of *trust.* I wasn't sure why I hated the thought of being talked about, but I did. I guess I just wasn't sure how I felt about Matthew. He was nice. He'd never done anything to make me think otherwise. He even seemed to look out for me, but I always felt I owed him something for it somehow. Dave, and even Cris, never made

me feel that way. I didn't think Matthew did it on purpose. *Was* it a trust issue? Did I trust Matthew?

I thought about my other friends.

I trusted Robin beyond the fact that anything concerning me might still be relayed to Dave. I doubted she shared personal information about me to anyone else. And I still trusted Dave as far as personal things *not* related to him went, though he apparently told Cris at least *some* things. I trusted Melanie. I highly doubted she would ever repeat something said to her in confidence. And I trusted Paola but doubted I would ever share anything too personal with her. That was more for her sake than for mine. Hannah had proven herself discreet and sincere as well, though her recent sadness troubled me.

And Cris?

I thought over everything I knew or *thought* I knew about Cris, thinking over the few real conversations we'd had, and realized that I probably trusted Cris most of all. He might not like me much, and it was obvious he didn't want his brother in a real relationship with me, but I trusted his character. Completely. This seemed strange, even to me, but it was true.

In contrast, trusting Matthew was a nebulous thing. In spite of time spent with him, I didn't feel like I *knew* him. And that was probably wholly my fault. I'd spent way too much time focusing on Dave to pay adequate attention to Matthew. He, on the other hand, seemed determined to pay attention to me whether I reciprocated or not. And I didn't know what to do or how to feel about that.

What if he *did* ask me out—something more than just Winter Formal? And would I go to the dance with him?

I thought about how he had acted and how I had felt at the river, especially when he had gone down the rock slide with me. I disliked being touched by anyone, especially suddenly—with one exception. And being *held* wasn't something I took lightly at all.

When Matthew had held me in that situation, I'd had a severe stab of panic. Why? Because it was too similar to that time at the planetarium? Because both incidents reminded me of the experience with Varsity Jacket last year? Because I was worried about what everyone else would think? Because of what *Dave* would think?

All of these issues were probably true to some extent. I didn't want to push Matthew away but was afraid my lack of negative reaction was encouraging him. Did I *want* to encourage him?

I was still preoccupied while riding. Kitty took enormous advantage of the situation, and Melanie scolded me roundly for it. I apologized to her, chastised myself all evening, and promised myself I wouldn't let stupid boys interfere with my riding ever again.

We received our school pictures during first period on Thursday morning. I didn't think mine were as nice as the year before, but I did look older, which I figured was a good thing. I thought my hair looked decent too. So, all in all, I was okay with them. Ben wanted one of mine, so I asked for one of his. I exchanged photos with Robin during Geometry. I cut up the rest of my wallet sized pictures when I got home and put them in an envelope in my backpack, in case anyone else wanted one. I assumed I'd exchange pictures with Melanie, but there was one other I wanted. I just wasn't going to ask for it.

The last day of school before Winter Break came and went. I felt relieved but even more hollowed out inside. Saturday morning I awoke feeling inexplicably depressed. I didn't even feel like riding but took care of Remmy and then moped around the house, unable to settle in any one place or on any one occupation for long. I wasn't hungry all day, and by the afternoon I had closed myself in my room with Violet and *Jane Eyre*.

And then it hit me. On this Saturday last year, Gold was taken away. I put the book down and sat for a while listening to music with the curtains closed and the lights off, the picture Cris had taken of me riding Gold laying in my lap. Violet came and sat on it. I shed some tears, but it's questionable whether they were for the memory of my loss or for something else. Eventually, I curled up with the kitten and slept until dinner time.

The next day, Sunday, I got up early and went straight out to Remmy. I cleaned and groomed and rode, spending the whole day with him and not letting myself think of anything else. Right after dinner we put the Christmas tree up, turned out all the lights except for those on the tree, and watched *Elf*. I took comfort in the lights twinkling in the darkness, the sense of tradition and memories of similar times spent with my family, and my parents' presence. And I was thankful for all those things. I slept deeply without remembering any dreams.

On Monday, Uncle Dan and his family arrived with Aunt Isabel. Her surgery had gone well and she was strong enough to travel. And she was expected to completely recover her strength and health, but she needed to be observed and kept from trying to do too much until then. Dad said he'd sit on her if necessary, but I think he was joking.

I'd been looking forward to their visit with equal parts curiosity and anxiety. Curiosity because it had been several years since I'd seen my uncle, his wife, and my cousins, and I couldn't remember Isabel at all. Anxiety for the same reasons, especially because of Isabel.

It's not that I was afraid of meeting her, but knowing that she would be staying with us in the bedroom right next to mine for an indefinite period, and not knowing what kind of person she was, made me uneasy. I hoped she wasn't like Aunt Katharine or Grandma, who didn't understand a person's need for quiet and privacy sometimes; who even walked in on you without knocking. My home, especially my room, was my refuge. I usually didn't mind guests, but the thought of someone I didn't know staying with us made me feel uncomfortable, even defensive, but I didn't know why. That in itself was troubling.

Plus, I knew Isabel and Dad had a history of not getting along. *Would they fight?* My stomach churned at the thought.

They arrived in time for a late lunch which, with everyone around the dining table, would make becoming acquainted much easier. Dan was quite a bit shorter than my dad, with darker hair and a more square face, but he had the same shaped eyes and nose. He smiled easily but was a little intense and business-like with a loud voice. His wife, Diana, seemed really nice but spent most of the time interacting with, almost policing, my cousins. The latter were both much younger than me and, though well-behaved for the most part, were very talkative and active and apparently required my aunt's constant supervision.

It was Isabel I was more interested in anyway. I had studied her when she'd first walked in—under her own steam but her brothers hovering closely as she walked from the car to the couch in the living room.

"Do you want to rest upstairs?" asked Dad.

"Your room is all ready," said Mom.

"We can wait to eat for a while," added Dan.

"Stop fussing," said Isabel in a very no-nonsense way. "I'm not completely decrepit."

She certainly didn't look decrepit. She was almost as tall as Dad and just as slim, though she had a wiry, slightly weathered look that Dad lacked. Her hair was shoulder length, pulled back in a low tail, and a light ashy brown color with some white already mixed in. She wore a navy pantsuit that didn't fit her quite right and looked like it was from several decades previous. In spite of the rest of her appearance, she had a youthful face and very bright, intense eyes the same color as my dad's. The same color as mine.

I retreated to the kitchen to help Mom and didn't sit down at the table until she did. Dad had put the extra leaf in the table to make it bigger, and I sat next to Mom instead of across from her. Dan sat on Dad's right, and Isabel sat next to him, across from me. Diana and my cousins sat at the other end.

Isabel didn't say much unless required to by a direct question, and after a while, it occurred to me that I was the same—always content to let conversation happen around me but not contributing much unless I had to. Uncle Dan was very lively, and he and Mom talked the most.

At one point, I look around the table. Mom, Dan, and even Dad too, were discussing something animatedly together—it could have been sports or politics or something else I wasn't interested in. Diana kept a running commentary going of what Steven shouldn't be doing with his fingers and how many more bites Estelle needed to eat, while the children were both commenting on completely different things or arguing with each other.

Both ends of the table were lively and noisy, and the center, Isabel and me, quiet and almost still. I looked at her to find her regarding me, but she looked away almost immediately. Not, however, before I registered the sparkle in her eyes. She didn't smile, but she was clearly amused. I looked down at my plate and smiled.

Maybe Isabel and I would get along just fine.

She went upstairs to lie down in the spare bedroom soon after lunch. Uncle Dan and his family stayed for a little while longer. I took Steven and Estelle up to my room to see Violet, but I didn't want to disturb Aunt Isabel next door and it was hard to keep them quiet. So I took them outside to see Remmy. They were actually very sweet, though lively and rather noisy children. I liked them. I led them both by turn around the field on Remmy and showed them how to brush him.

Remmy was so cute with them, interested in watching them and very careful around them. My heart felt like it would burst, I loved him so much and was so proud of him, but the emotions were bitter-sweet. He still reminded me of Dave for a lot of reasons, and that would probably never change.

Dan, Diana, and my cousins left around five o'clock, though Aunt Isabel hadn't gotten up again yet. They still had a couple of hours to drive before reaching Diana's parents' home, their destination for Christmas. Dad checked on Aunt Isabel around seven o'clock, but she wanted to stay in her room and sleep, and he conjectured on how tiring the trip must have been for her.

I didn't see Aunt Isabel again until the following morning.

I had just fed Remmy and was filling up his water trough when Isabel joined me outside. She wore a very baggy sweater, old but clean breeches with thick socks pulled over the leg cuffs, and old hiking boots. She looked comfortable and kind of cute in an odd way.

I suppose it was evident I noted her attire. She stared straight at me and said in her brusque, forthright manner, "I hope nobody minds me wearin' my regular clothes. I dressed up fer Dan and Diana, but I can't stand wearin' those clothes fer long. I don't mind gettin' dressed up fer church and parties and such, but not fer every day."

I couldn't help but agree with her and indicated my own slouchy sweater, comfy non-denim pants and, though I'd only had them about a year, well-worn cowboy boots.

She smiled and nodded. "So tell me about yer pony."

That I was more than happy to do. "His name is Remmy. At least, that's what he's called, but his full name is Remington Bronze. He's half quarter horse and half mustang, and he's fourteen years old."

"And you ride him Western?"

"Yes. But I'm learning to ride English, too. My friend Melanie . . . she's the one giving me English lessons . . . says he could probably do almost anything."

"Maybe so. Except maybe *Puissance*."

"What's Pweesonts?"

"The highest jumps that horses can clear."

I smiled. "Melanie said he probably couldn't do Grand Prix."

Her response was a loud, "Ha!" Her mouth didn't smile, but her eyes were bright and looked merry. "Yer dad told me 'bout him when I was stuck in the hospital. He said the family of a friend gave him to ya fer yer birthday. They got a cattle ranch."

"Yes," I said. I could feel my cheeks growing a little warm. I wasn't sure this was a safe topic. I didn't want to end up talking about Dave. "They raise and train some horses, too." I hoped she wouldn't ask any more questions and was glad she appeared to be done.

She turned abruptly and said as she walked away, "I'm gonna get some breakfast. I'm starvin'. Didn't get no dinner last night."

I noticed her walk was odd: her upper body seemed a little stiff, her arms hung almost still at her sides, and her knees seemed to bend a bit more than they really needed to. I'd never seen anyone walk that way. It made me wonder what I looked like when I walked, and I became self-conscious about it for weeks after and then periodically long after that.

I took my time with Remmy and finally went back into the house, drawn by the irresistible smell of bacon. I came through the back door just as my dad entered the kitchen from the living room.

"Iz, you're supposed to be taking it easy!"

Isabel had been busy. There was a full pot of coffee ready, a whole mess of bacon on a platter, and a stack of buttered toast on a plate. She was now scrambling eggs.

"Don't fuss at me, Gregory," she said, calmly but firmly. "I'll be more difficult if I go crazy from boredom. Bring a plate over fer some eggs."

And that's pretty much how things went for the next few weeks. Dad worried that Isabel wasn't taking it easy enough and scolded her, and she talked sternly back to him and refused to be "molly-coddled."

After breakfast, Isabel came back outside with me and watched me put Remmy through his paces. She wasn't at all hesitant in giving feedback, saying, "You need to do this," or "Don't do that." I bristled a little at first, feeling

she was only finding fault. I was used to Cheryl's firm but diplomatic comments and Melanie's more gentle approach to coaching. But I soon realized that it was just her way and that she really did know what she was talking about. I even began to appreciate her clear, concise instructions.

"I'd git on him m'self and show ya, but I'm not supposed to ride at all fer at least another four weeks. I've never gone so long outta the saddle."

"I had to go without riding while I was in Los Angeles," I said. "It was actually longer than that. I had a riding accident."

"Okay," said Isabel. "Tell me what happened."

So as I continued to walk Remmy around my makeshift arena, I did. I explained my impatience to be able to ride as well as my friends, how I'd entered a barrel racing competition before I was anywhere near ready, and what followed after. Well, *some* of what followed after, leaving a few names and details out.

"Well, that was stupid," she said, and again I was taken aback by her frankness. But then she said, "But good fer you fer gettin' out there and tryin' somethin'. We all have to make mistakes and take some bumps along the road. I guess we wouldn't learn much if we didn't. I'm sure ya learned a thing or two."

Telling her of the incident and hearing her response on the subject had brought it back vividly: the helpless feeling of not being in control of the situation, the pain, the embarrassment, the trouble it caused, the misunderstandings. Dave's unflagging goodwill. *Although he'd said it was stupid too, even called me an idiot. And Cris! I still haven't thanked him for all he did!*

This was still in the back of my mind—along with other broody topics—while Mom, Isabel, and I watched television that afternoon. And then the doorbell rang. Mom was closest and got up to answer it. I thought it might be Ben and was surprised to see Angel.

"I hope I am not interrupting your afternoon," she said.

"No, no. Not at all," said Mom, obviously happy to see her.

Angel stepped into the house and saw Isabel. "Oh! I'm sorry! You have a visitor."

"Please, come in!" said Mom, and offered her the chair she'd been sitting in.

"*Gracias*," she said.

"This is Greg's sister, Isabel, visiting from Colorado."

"Oh, it is so nice to meet you!" said Angel warmly. The sound of her voice, accented and musical, gave me a pang of regret. I'd missed her!

"Isabel, this is Angel, one of our friends," said Mom.

"*Es un placer conocerte también. ¿Vives cerca?*" said Isabel. I hoped my astonishment wasn't apparent.

"Ah! *Gracias. ¡Hablas muy bien el español! No, no vivimos muy cerca. Vivimos al otro lado de todas estas colinas. Tal vez cinco millas.*"

Angel's attention turned back to Mom and me. "Please forgive me, I have only learned today that you do not go to Los Angeles. You did not tell David? I think he learned this from Cheryl Reid and only told me this morning."

I felt another pang at the pronunciation of Dave's name. "Oh . . . no . . . I suppose not," I said, trying to act like it was no big thing but feeling everyone's eyes on me.

"Well," she said, looking slightly troubled, "we would like to invite you, you know, to our *Fiesta de Nochebuena*. You are all *very* welcome. We have very much food and *musica* and dancing and is very good fun. Family and friends and neighbors. We *hope* you will come, even for a short time." Here she paused and looked at me, fondly I thought. "It has been *too* long since you have come to the house. You are missed."

This completely disarmed me, my cheeks growing warm and tears surprisingly ready. "I miss you all, too," I said, but the words barely came out. It felt like a great weight was crushing my chest.

"I'm sure we'd love to come," said Mom.

"*¡Bien!*" exclaimed Angel, looking extremely pleased. "You are welcome any time, but most people will come around five or six. Robin and Fiona will be there earlier."

She stayed to chat with Mom and Isabel, she and Isabel sometimes speaking easily in Spanish, which I found interesting. I was wrestling with my feelings.

Of course I want to go! And Dave apparently prompted this visit. What does that mean? Is it just a thoughtful inclusion? And should I go? I want to go! But I don't want to go. It'll be awkward. There will be too many people there. But Robin will be there. Probably Hannah and Paola, too.

I had mixed feelings about that possibility, though no harsh feelings toward them personally.

I want to see Stevie. And Henry, too. And Merle. I wonder who else will be there? But it will feel so uncomfortable.

I was praying, too, though nothing actually put into words. And I realized I still wanted too much. Surely it would just be masochistic to go.

Chapter Twenty-Two

The next day Dad went to work and Mom, Isabel, and I went to Lowell. I was glad of the distraction—if I'd stayed home I probably would have moped—and there was still a little shopping I wanted to do. Although Isabel had no obvious trouble getting around, we walked slower than we might have done normally and I had difficulty dealing with the crowds of people. So Mom went off by herself sometimes, and I was happy to sit with Isabel, glad she wasn't the kind of person who needed to talk or be entertained all the time. I had a feeling she felt the same way about me.

Although I'd already gotten her the cute pajamas, I also found Robin a green T-shirt with a Mustang logo I knew she'd love. I couldn't resist buying something for Dave, too, but I wasn't sure when, where, or even if I'd ever give it to him.

We passed a Disney store and Isabel wanted to go in, so we did. I was delighted to find Lady and Tramp stuffed toys and thought it perfect for Stevey. I knew the movie was one of his favorites. I picked up a Tramp toy at first, thinking he'd obviously like the boy dog, but then put it back. Something told me the Lady would be better, so I chose it instead.

I even got Ben a Goofy hat for no real reason except that I knew he loved hats and Goofy was the goofiest character they had. I wanted to get Melanie something too, but in spite of all the time I now spent with her, I felt like I knew the least about her.

On the day of the Caldera's party, Christmas Eve, I was still undecided about going and my stomach was tied in knots. It didn't help that Isabel said she didn't feel up to a party of people that she didn't know. She'd rather stay home, though she thought Angel very nice and hoped to see her again. I knew how she felt; I didn't even feel up for a party with people I *did* know. Dad announced that he was happy to stay home with Isabel, and I didn't even question his reason—I was too confused about my own.

In the end it was Cris, indirectly, who made up my mind. It had been bothering me so much; I still wanted to properly acknowledge everything he'd done for me last year. I just hoped I wouldn't feel too awkward around the rest of the family and that we wouldn't stay long. I wrapped Dave's present and put it in a bag with the ones for Robin and Stevey, just in case an appropriate moment presented itself.

We arrived around five-thirty. It was already dark and the front courtyard had many vehicles parked around its perimeter. Cris' truck and Dave's Beast were parked where they usually were, under the trees to the side of the driveway. I pointed to them and suggested Mom park there too, as there was more room.

Mr. Caldera answered the door. He seemed delighted to see us and took our coats. Beyond the tiled archway, the dining room was brightly lit. I could see the long tables beautifully set with white cloths, candles, and decorations.

But we were not led through there, nor left toward the kitchen and family room, but right and along the hallway that led to the formal sitting room Dave had shown me last year. The double doors were open into the beautiful room, all burgundy and cream, cherry wood and brass. An elegantly lit and decorated tree stood in a corner, there were tasteful but not excessive decorations around the room, and flames burned brightly in the fireplace. But I knew none of these things were the cause of my mom's sighed, "Oh!"

Her eyes were fixed on the painting hanging above the mantle—the arresting portrait of Mr. Caldera and his five sons.

"That is a magnificent painting, Alex," breathed Mom. "You have such a handsome family! And this is such a *lovely* room."

"Thank you, Jen. It is gracious of you to say so." Mr. Caldera smiled and even bowed slightly, seeming very gratified. Then he laid our coats over the back of the couch with some others. I set the bag with the gifts down there too, then took Robin's and Stevey's out.

Unlike the day that Dave had shown the room to me, the arched doors leading into the dining room were wide open. So was the wide doorway into the back courtyard, lit so brightly it seemed like day. We stepped through into a wonderland.

The pergola over the patio was lit with tiny white lights, but that was nothing new. What made me catch my breath were the hundreds, maybe thousands of white fairy lights all around the courtyard, threaded through the trees and bushes and running around the fountains. The trees—orange, olive, and lemon—had other decorations among the leaves, too, the fairy lights twinkling off their shiny surfaces.

A fire burned in the center pit and *Mariachi* music played from somewhere beyond the back wall. People were everywhere, standing or sitting and talking, and coming and going through the huge open door at the back of the courtyard.

Mr. Caldera smiled warmly at us and said, "Let me help you find someone you know," then continued to lead us through the outer door to the basketball court beyond.

A warmer glow presided here, the soft light of hanging lanterns zigzagging across the court with pagoda lights around the back and sides. Fires in clay *chimeneas* at three corners added to both the warmth and glow. A group of musicians playing acoustic instruments performed at one corner of the court, and many people were dancing. Small groupings of chairs, many of them occupied, were placed around the perimeter of the court.

"Fiona, look who I have found," said Mr. Caldera, having led us to where Robin's grandmother sat.

"Jen! Hello, Allison. It's lovely to see you here. Sit down, sit down, and keep me company for a moment. Robin's off somewhere with Dave, I expect. When she told me you weren't going to Los Angeles, I hoped we might see you here. You know, it's really the only big event I still go to."

She and Mom settled into a conversation about Robin's new job and car and Aunt Isabel's visit, while I scanned the dancers and small groups of people. I recognized Matthew's, Jessie's, and Paola's parents, as well as Tom and Cheryl, all dancing. Paola sat on the other side of the court with Hannah, Hannah's dad, and Kyle and a couple I assumed were his parents. There were many other people I didn't think I'd ever seen before.

I left my mother and Fiona and headed back into the courtyard. Phyllis, the cook from Bar 8, greeted me as we passed each other. Manuel, talking to the Caldera's veterinarian, Dr. Simons, smiled and nodded to me. I tried to smile back.

I peeked into the dining room, lit entirely by candles, and saw that some food had been laid out on the side tables but was still covered. So I moved back toward the family room doors. Only one partition of the multi-paneled door stood open, obviously not inviting casual guests in. But I thought—I *hoped*—I might still be considered more than that.

The family room was only partially lit from the large, open kitchen. I slipped inside and gasped at the other source of dim illumination, an enormous lighted tree standing in the corner near the door. This one had gifts sitting beneath the boughs.

Robin was helping Angel in the kitchen. I approached them after placing Stevey's gift under the huge tree.

"Here she is," said Angel, as if she'd been waiting for me. That was comforting. They both smiled as I approached, but Angel said, "Just in time for dinner! Robin, go and ask Manuel to come and help, *por favor.*"

Robin shot me another smile as she bounded past me toward the courtyard. I heard the front door close, and a moment later, Dave walked in.

"You came," he said, but I couldn't tell what emotion, if any, lay behind the words.

"Yes," I said, and almost added, "Mom wanted to come," but didn't.

He looked like he wanted to say more too, but Angel asked, "Did your aunt come?" as she continued working.

"Oh . . . no. I don't think she cares much for parties. At least," I tried to remember what she'd said, "not with a lot of strangers."

She said she understood and then Manuel walked in. They all began moving trays and dishes and casseroles full of food into the dining room. I asked if I could help, but Angel said, "No, no, you must go and enjoy the party!"

I felt awkward and a little in the way, not sure if I should wait where I was or move. I was wrestling with this—*Wait for what? Move where?*—when a tinkling bell rang out in the courtyard. Mr. Caldera announced that a buffet dinner was ready in the dining room. I moved back toward the outer door, but raised voices and the sound of many people moving right outside caused me to remain where I was.

Angel and Manuel went back and forth to the kitchen a couple of times, and some kids, including Matthew's younger brother and Henry, came down from the room upstairs, followed by Stevey. Cris came down last. It was rather dark where I stood—the only direct light coming from the Christmas tree—and he didn't appear to notice me as he walked past the kitchen. But Stevey had looked my way with his dreamy little smile.

I thought about stepping farther into the light and speaking to Cris right then but waited too long. I didn't want to keep him from dinner anyway; I'd seek him out after he'd eaten. At that moment, Dave walked through the door right next to me.

"You still standing here? I was looking for you."

I didn't know what to say and just stared at him.

He frowned. "I wanted to talk to you."

I still stared at him.

"I heard you were at Northfield."

"Yes."

"Why?"

"I was there with my friend, Melanie." True.

"That's not a good place for you to go." He looked, not exactly angry, but upset.

"Why not?" It was a reflexive question. I really didn't want to know "why not" right now.

His frown deepened. "I can't protect you there, and there are people who could hurt you." His eyes were hard, glittering.

"There are people who like me there, too." I was getting upset as well.

He looked annoyed, but I couldn't help it. He was being unreasonable. I *knew* he was. I just didn't know what to make of it or how to feel about it. And it was none of his business, after all. I considered saying as much, but the doorbell rang and immediately there was a loud disturbance from the entryway. It sounded like an exuberant group of people had arrived.

Dave turned as if to move in that direction, but the disturbance had already poured through the hallway and into the family room, all seeming to talk at once.

"It's so dark in here!" said one of the girls.

"We should have gone through the dining room," said another.

"People are getting their dinner. It's too crowded. We have to put these somewhere first anyway," said a woman. She seemed to be the only adult.

The woman and five teenage girls brought in light luggage. An older girl and a boy about Henry's age carried bags of wrapped packages followed by Cris, also carrying luggage. I assumed he had answered the door. Then the girls saw Dave. Four of them dropped what they carried and flew at him, one squealing loudly and jumping toward him, almost knocking him down. He staggered back slightly but wrapped his arms around her. It was hard to tell if it was an affectionate or defensive action. She in turn jumped up and wrapped her legs around his hips, her head next to his, hugging him tightly.

I recognized the girl from Angel's photographs.

The woman must be Mr. Caldera's sister; most of the kids must be Dave's cousins from Hawaii. The other three girls gathered around him. The girl currently hugging him tightly was *not* a cousin. After a moment, hands on her waist, he set her on her feet.

"You haven't cut your hair!" said the not-cousin, her fingers exploring its length. "Does that mean you've been waiting for *me?*" She laughed loudly and said, "I cut mine *ages* ago!"

These comments were as incomprehensible to me as the visitors' sudden appearance. Feeling extremely uncomfortable and having seen and heard much more than I wanted to, I slipped out the door to the courtyard.

People were still mingling there, but most people were either in or near the dining room or had returned to beyond the wall where music was playing again.

I was ready to leave. I hated feeling like a party-pooper, but I wasn't sociable at the best of times and I'd had about all the devastation I could handle for a Christmas Eve.

I went through to the basketball court looking for Robin and my mother. Everyone from school seemed to be gathered in a big group, eating around a *chimenea* at the far corner of the court-turned-dance-floor. I joined them since Mom was currently dancing with Tom

"Merry Christmas, Robin," I said, offering her my gift.

She put her plate down on a nearby table. "Oh! Thanks! I got something for you too. Wait here."

She went to where Fiona sat with Gloria and Phyllis and exchanged packages from a bag nearby, then returned to me. "It's not much."

"Thank you!" I said, sure it was a lot.

"Oh," she added, "and, don't kill me, but I need another picture of you. I seriously can't believe I lost another one!"

That made me laugh, but I couldn't think of a witty comeback, so just said, "There's still plenty where that came from."

"Where's Dave?" she asked, as if she assumed I knew.

It was annoying that she was right. "In the house. Some people came. I think his cousins are here." I tried to say this without emotion.

Her eyes flew wide. "Really? They weren't supposed to get here until tomorrow!" She sounded very excited. "I haven't seen them in forever!"

"You've met them before?"

"Yeah, years ago. They came during one of the Calderas' stay-at-home summers."

That shouldn't have surprised me, but it did and made me feel even more like an outsider again.

"Come on," said Robin. "I want to go say hi."

"I . . . I need to talk to my mom. I think we might be leaving soon. We weren't going to stay very long. You know . . . Dad and Isabel are at home." I was glad I had this excuse.

"Oh." Robin looked surprised, but she nodded. "Well, Merry Christmas, Allie." She stepped forward and I was happy, comforted even, to return her hug. "Call me tomorrow, okay? And thanks for the present."

I watched her run off toward the house close to where Cris stood on the opposite corner of the court, nearest the door. He was talking to some men I didn't recognize. When he saw me walking toward him, he appeared to excuse himself and turned toward me, waiting. I was a little surprised.

"Hi," I said, suddenly feeling uncomfortable. I had gone over this in my mind so many times—sometimes effusive, sometimes nonchalant, and sometimes out loud—but all those imagined conversations now deserted me.

"Hi," he replied, expressionless but giving me his complete attention and direct eye contact. This just served to disconcert me more.

"I don't think I ever thanked you for what you did last year."

Now *he* looked disconcerted. He stared hard at me for a moment, that searching look that made me feel strange. Then he looked down, frowning. "For what?"

"You know, for last summer when I . . . when I fell. Everything you did at the horse show. Wasn't it you who took care of Remmy? And told my parents? And went and found my glasses?"

He didn't acknowledge doing these things, but he didn't deny them either.

"I never thanked you."

His brow cleared and he searched my eyes again briefly before looking away.

"I can't . . . I don't know how to thank you enough, but I wanted you to know that I knew. That I was aware and that it matters. If there's ever anything. . . ."

"You still don't owe me anything." His soft tone was at odds with his very intense expression. "And you're welcome. Again."

The song that had been playing finished and Mom returned to Fiona. She looked happy and I felt terrible that I wanted to leave, but I did. Now. I looked back at Cris, shaking slightly and trying not to feel sad but tears just a thought or two away. Just then Dave, Robin, and most if not all the visitors from Hawaii came through the courtyard door.

"I . . . have to go. But I hope you have a Merry Christmas!"

I didn't hear whether Cris replied or not; I turned and walked quickly to my mother and quietly asked if we could leave. She raised her brows then looked concerned. *Then* she obviously noticed the group that had just arrived.

"Okay, if you want." Looking at the other women, she said, "We should probably get home to Allison's dad and aunt. We hope you all have a lovely holiday."

We all said goodbye. I saw Cris walking toward his brother, who was introducing our school friends to the girls. Mom and I retreated through the courtyard and through the sitting room to pick up our coats. I picked up the bag I'd brought and followed her out to the entryway.

"Allison!"

Dave must have run through the family room to catch me before we left.

Mom put her coat on and looked from Dave to me, clearly curious. But she said, "I'll go warm up the car and pull up in front here. All right?"

I nodded and put my own coat on, already tensing for whatever this encounter held.

"Merry Christmas, Dave," said Mom softly.

"Merry Christmas, Mrs. Anderson," said Dave in his normal voice. His voice softened as soon as the door closed behind her. "Hey . . . I'm sorry . . . about earlier," he said.

My mind raced, picturing the girls, their ecstatic expressions, the extreme familiarity. I looked into his eyes but didn't linger there, afraid of what I'd see.

"I didn't mean to sound . . ." he huffed as if impatient. "I just don't want anything bad to happen to you."

My stomach was in knots, and not in a good, happy, my-idol-is-noticing-me way. He was referring to his attitude about Northfield, not the girls. He was concerned about his pet, the misfit he'd adopted, even though he'd so obviously outgrown me. I didn't know what to say but looked at him again, though not directly making eye contact. He frowned and seemed dissatisfied with my lack of response. I told myself I didn't care and still had nothing to say.

"I want . . . wanted to ask you . . ." He now sounded much less sure of himself. "I want to take you to Winter Formal."

The words were important. They were supposed to mean something. Something good. Something happy. Highly desirable.

I shuddered violently.

"Will you go with me?" he asked, a slight crease between his brows.

I could tell his eyes were seeking mine, but I couldn't focus there—could barely stand his attention at all. I dug deep for strength. For willpower.

"No."

I awoke with a start, bolting to a sitting position, my heart pounding. Panic attack. I reached for Violet and cradled her in my lap. What had I done?

Did I really say no to Dave? Or was that just a dream? Did he even ask me or was that a dream too? We were in his house . . . there was a party . . . the look on his face!

I hadn't been able to meet his eyes for more than a split second or two, but I'd never seen that expression before. He had paled. He certainly hadn't expected my answer. It took a while for me to calm down enough to sort through the memories of the night before.

Dave was mad about Northfield. I got mad right back.

Cris was there. I finally said what I needed to. We're even . . . I think.

Something about this made me feel sad and slightly guilty. And nervous, like I'd still forgotten something. But I'd think about that later, if I remembered. Right now other things crowded out thoughts of Cris.

Dave's cousins . . . and their friends. . . .

I could clearly recall the exuberant—what did you even call that? *Embrace* didn't seem to cover that interaction between Dave and the not-cousin. Dave hadn't cut his hair all that time because of some agreement between them? This made me feel sick, and not because of his hair. I didn't care how he wore it.

And then, out of the blue and as if nothing else has happened, he asks me to Winter Formal? Too, too bizarre. And heartbreaking. And infuriating, too!

I assumed it was Matthew that told him about Northfield. And why shouldn't he? I had hoped he wouldn't, but I hadn't asked him not to, though what conversation or motive could have brought the subject up was beyond me.

And Cris probably alerted Dave that I was leaving last night—motive also unknown—but he wasn't the type to blab about everything. And he had agreed not to tell about Northfield. No, I trusted Cris.

And if Matthew had told him about Northfield, he might also have told him he'd asked me to Winter Formal. I couldn't imagine Dave asking me otherwise. That should have hurt, but it made me mad instead. It was almost like last year when he'd told Matthew I didn't like to dance. At the time I'd thought he was just trying to save me embarrassment for being grounded. A part of me—a *big* part of me at the time—had hoped he was interfering for his own sake, to leave the way open to ask me to the next dance. But he hadn't and I'd given up on those fantasies. Now everything he did just seemed—I wasn't sure. Controlling? *Meddling . . . interfering. . . .*

And the most infuriating thing of all was that it *still* didn't alter how I felt about him.

I hadn't given him the present either. Not because I was mad at him. I'd just forgotten what I was holding. I sincerely wanted to give it to him, but I also didn't want him to feel compelled to give me something in return. I wouldn't be able to stand that.

A soft knock on my bedroom door startled me.

"Allison, are you awake?" Mom's voice. "Merry Christmas!"

I'd completely forgotten. It was Christmas today. Now I felt guilty again.

Here I am trying to be on God's good side—though I guess he doesn't have any other side—and I can't even focus on Christmas? No wonder I don't make friends easily. Always so distracted!

I prayed a quick but sincere apology and got out of bed. I made sure Violet had food and water, then scooped her up and headed downstairs in my pajamas.

"Good morning, sweetheart!" said Mom.

We rarely had big breakfasts, but on Christmas day it was a tradition. The house was filled with the smell of pancakes, bacon, and maple syrup. Dad was making the pancakes, and Isabel was eating already.

Mom started, "What would you . . . ," but didn't finish, her eyes drawn to the kitten cradled along my arm.

"Can Violet be downstairs today?" I asked. "For at least a little while?"

Isabel's face lit up like our Christmas tree the moment she spotted the kitten. "Oh! Let me hold her!"

I gladly passed Violet to her and went out to feed Remmy, wishing he could also join us in the kitchen. It was very chilly but not freezing, so I took his blanket off and opened the door to his paddock. I gave him a couple of treats—from Santa, I told him, just because it was Christmas—and hugged him, laying my cheek against his neck while he munched. I allowed myself a few self-indulgent tears, hopefully getting them out of my system, then wiped my face dry, gave him his hay, and went back to the house, determined to at least *appear* happy for everyone else's sake.

"Oh, Allison!" said Mom, frowning at me as I sat down at the table. "What have you been doing? Go wash up!"

I went into the downstairs bathroom and peered at myself in the mirror. Of course, my face was smeared with dirt from crying and hugging Remmy, then wiping my face with stable hands. I smiled at myself and sighed. *Such a loser.*

But I suddenly also felt more at peace about everything. About Dave. About myself. Would I have said yes to him if it weren't for Northfield? If it weren't for the demonstrative girl and the implied agreement? I thought about it carefully and came to the conclusion that, no, I still wouldn't have said yes. I had to move on. I definitely couldn't let him dictate what I could or couldn't do, and I would *try* not to let him invade my dreams. My life would go on and become something on its own. Something without Dave.

Daveless.

I felt I had done the right thing, saying no to him. Then I marveled at that realization. I once thought I could never say no to him about anything, but I was actually getting quite good at it.

Chapter Twenty-Three

Christmas day passed by peacefully, enlivened mostly by Violet, who thoroughly enjoyed having the run of the house and took the opportunity to explore *everything*. Unfortunately, she liked getting underfoot, and Dad almost stepped on her a few times. In his efforts to avoid this, he'd contort his body, step too wide, or hop on one foot, almost falling over. It was especially funny if his hands were full. It reminded me of a cartoon, but I kept that to myself.

Static electricity kept me on my toes too. Every time I touched a light switch or anything metal, I got shocked, sometimes just enough to make my skin tingle slightly and occasionally strong enough to make a popping sound and make me jump. I finally pulled my hair back in a tight braid and took my socks off in the house.

I talked to Robin on the phone for a while about inconsequential things. I think we were both comforted by the conversation, though I didn't know why she would be. She said she was working over the weekend, but maybe we could do something during the week? I agreed that would be great.

If I thought of Dave at all, and I confess I did, I pictured him miles away on a snow-covered slope somewhere, even though they might not have left yet. It was his family's custom to have a large Christmas Eve party and then head to the mountains for skiing and snowboarding. I wasn't sure if their visitors would alter that tradition, but there was no reason to think the fam-

ily wouldn't still go. Maybe the visitors were going too. Except, of course, I *wasn't* letting myself think about that.

So I was extremely surprised the next day to hear a familiar engine sound: Dave's motorcycle. Isabel and I were in the living room reading. Senses straining, I waited for the doorbell to ring. When it didn't, curiosity got the better of me. I got up and peeked through the sheers.

Dave was talking to my dad just a few feet from the porch. I hadn't known Dad was outside. Dave appeared to be doing most of the talking, standing squarely and looking respectfully confident. Dad had his arms crossed over his chest. I couldn't see his face, but he stood listening rigidly. His defenses were up.

"Good-looking boy."

Isabel's voice made me jump. Violet in hand, she peered through the sheers over my shoulder. I hoped Dave couldn't see us, but he hadn't looked our way at all, his eyes firmly fixed on Dad.

"Friend of yours?" Isabel asked.

"Yes. He's . . . yes. A friend." I wasn't sure if that was still accurate. I wasn't exactly sure *what* he was.

"Do you have feelings for him?"

The question seemed almost impertinent, but I couldn't deny it and found I didn't want to.

"Yes."

"Well, if I were you, I'd git my butt out there and not leave them to decide things, if those things have anythin' to do with you."

It seemed like an odd thing to say, especially coming from someone who didn't know much about me and even less about Dave. But it made sense, too. I looked at her and she lifted her brows as her mouth slid sideways.

I hesitated then moved slowly to the front door, wondering what I would say. I got a shock from the door handle, then grabbed and opened it.

". . . kept my word about everything," Dave was saying. His eyes shifted to me as I stepped quietly through the door, then back to Dad.

"Yes, I think you have. It doesn't change my reasons for concern."

Dave looked the way I felt—suddenly very uncomfortable.

"Hey," he said in my direction, but I got the feeling he was alerting Dad to my presence. Dad turned and acknowledged me.

"So we can start work on that soon?" said Dave, very businesslike.

"Oh . . . yes," said Dad and seemed off balance for a moment. "Whenever Tom can get over here to level it out."

I was confused, wondering what on earth they were talking about. I was sure there had been a shift in the conversation, but I'd been unable to follow it and couldn't at that moment remember exactly what was said before.

Dave nodded his head and looked at me as if he'd like to say something. I would have liked to say something back. But Dad wasn't moving, and the awkwardness between all of us was so jagged and repelling, there was nothing for it but to back away. Dave moved first—a few steps backward, a hand lifted slightly, expression heartbreakingly neutral. I returned the gesture and moved backward toward the door. He mounted and started his dirtbike, put his helmet on with another look back at me, then rode away.

Not wanting to talk to Dad—curious but doubting I'd like whatever he had to say—I turned to go back in the house just as Mom came out.

"Was that Dave?" she asked.

I nodded and waited to see if Dad would say anything. He watched Dave disappear then turned to face us.

"We were talking about making an arena for Allison to ride in. It would be a bigger area to turn Remmy out in, too. And safer than the old corral."

Mom smiled complacently and said, "Oh. That'll be nice."

I nodded but wasn't convinced that was what they were really talking about. At least, not the only thing. I went back into the house. Isabel was sitting on the couch, reading again and stroking the kitten, but I got the feeling she was pretending. Dad sometimes did that when he was listening to a conversation he didn't want to actively participate in. She and Dad were alike in a lot of ways.

I went out to Remmy, spending the rest of the afternoon with him and avoiding everyone else.

On Monday morning, Robin called. "Whatcha doin'?"

I was in my room sketching Violet, which was very challenging. The only time she was completely still was when she was asleep.

"Nothing much," I said.

"Dave and them left this morning. They won't be back till Sunday."

This didn't surprise me. "I thought they usually left Christmas day?" That's what she had told me last year.

"They usually do, but his cousins were here, so they stayed here a couple of days. I think they all went together though."

I wasn't sure what to do with this information, so stored it away with the other unknown factors currently regarding Dave; an ever-expanding catalog. *That I'm not going to think about.*

"So do you want to do something?"

"Like what?"

"I don't know. . . ."

I got the feeling that she *did* know but didn't want to ask. "Do you want to come over? You can meet my aunt. And Violet."

"Okay," she said, sounding like she didn't mind one way or the other. But I think she did.

"Do you want us to pick you up? Or do you want to drive?"

She was quiet a moment, then said, "Do you think your mom would mind picking me up? I'm . . . I'm trying not to use gas."

Arrangements were made and Mom and I drove into town to pick her up. We both went into the house to say hello to Fiona. I invited Robin to spend the night, but she said she was working early in the morning and declined.

"I wish we had a horse trailer," I said on the way home. "Then we could bring Gali over too. We could ride around and Gali could hang out with Remmy."

Robin laughed. "They could have a play date."

I laughed too. "Yes!"

Mom said, "I suppose we ought to think about getting a horse trailer. . . ."

Robin and I exchanged hopeful smiles.

We had a fun day in spite of being unequally horsed and the fact that I static-shocked her at least three times.

"What on earth?" she said after the last one.

"I don't know. Ever since it turned cold, it seems like I build up static electricity like crazy. It hardly ever happened much before I cut my hair."

I went upstairs and braided my hair. Then, just because she had given it to me, I put the pink scrunchy in too. I didn't wear it often as I didn't want to wear it out. It was too special to me. She noticed it and smiled.

Isabel sat on the back porch while we played with Remmy. She seemed content and quietly interested in my friend. Mom and I took Robin home after dinner.

"What's the story with your friend, Robin?" Isabel asked the next day.

She had taken to hanging out with me while I fed and groomed Remmy in the mornings. At first I wasn't too happy about it—that time had always been *our* time—but I didn't mind too much now. She didn't invade my space otherwise, physically or mentally, and I found we got along quietly and very well.

"What do you mean?" I asked back.

"Jen says she lives with her grandmother. Why?"

I felt uncomfortable. Her question implied that I should know this, but it was the kind of question I used to get in trouble for asking when I was younger. By middle school, I had learned not to ask them. I'd almost ceased being curious about her family myself—her living arrangement now seemed normal and Fiona was the only family I could imagine her having. But Isabel's question stirred curiosity up again.

Dad worked the week after Christmas, so Mom drove me out to Northfield on Wednesday and Isabel wanted to come. Since there was no school, I was able to have my lesson much earlier. Melanie had said that she'd have her mom's car, too, and could drive me home if I wanted to hang out longer than my lesson.

We got there a little early and took Isabel on a tour. Melanie was in the middle of giving a lesson to a girl I hadn't seen before. I introduced Isabel to Digs and Beau, both of whom she immediately made fast friends with, and Tatty who had seen us and walked over.

"This is my Aunt Isabel," I said. "She's from Colorado."

Tatty introduced herself and Isabel complimented her on what she had seen of the center so far, stating that she had a much smaller training stable herself. The two women fell into conversation as we walked toward Kitty's stall. I haltered her and led her out to crosstie in the breezeway.

Isabel and Tatty were deep in discussion, comparing opinions on everything from eventing saddles to grass hay. It was the most lively and talkative I'd seen Isabel since she'd arrived, and I'd never heard Tatty talk so long to anyone. I guessed they'd "hit it off" as Grandpa would say.

As soon as there was a lull in the conversation, I caught Isabel's eye and said, "This is Kitty, the horse I'm taking lessons on. She belongs to Melanie. Her real name is Copper Copycat." I frowned and amended, "I mean Kitty's name, not Melanie's."

Tatty laughed but Isabel just looked intensely at Kitty. "She's a pretty little thing," she said. Kitty being around sixteen hands, "little" was obviously relative. "Thoroughbred . . . and Arab?"

Tatty smiled widely and agreed. "The best of both, I think. Melanie's going to have a hard time letting her go. They've been together a long time. Ever since I've known her."

"Letting her go?" I repeated, not understanding.

"She doesn't have a lot of time to ride her and seldom competes with her anymore. She uses her mostly for lessons these days, which is financially counterproductive for her and, frankly, a waste of Kitty's real talents. She's an older horse, but still has plenty of potential. She'll make someone a nice intermediate horse . . . dressage, eventing, even hunter/jumper."

My heart fell. I was becoming very fond of Kitty and was just starting to feel like we were really getting to know—and trust—each other. I wasn't as attached to her as I was to Remmy or as I had been to Gold, but the thought of losing her as a partner made me sad.

I finished grooming and saddling Kitty in silence and led her out toward the warm-up paddock, then mounted and began walking her. When Melanie approached my mom and Isabel, I rode over to introduce them.

"Melanie, this is my Aunt Isabel that I told you about . . . from Colorado. The one with the horses." That came out more awkwardly than I would have liked, but Melanie's face lit up.

"Oh, yes!" she smiled brightly. "Allison told me you're a trainer."

"Goin' on thirty years," said Isabel matter-of-factly. "But it looks like you started early, too."

Melanie looked slightly self-conscious and smiled again. "Well, this is only my second year training professionally." She turned her attention to me and said, "We'd better get started. Let's continue in the *cavaletti* ring today."

I happily agreed and walked Kitty alongside her. Mom and Isabel watched long after my lesson had begun. That made me self-conscious at first, especially wondering what Isabel thought, but soon I was focused entirely on what Kitty and I were doing. Mom and Isabel had left by the time we were done.

"I don't have another lesson today," said Melanie. "My last person re-scheduled and had theirs earlier. Would you like to go for a short ride? I rode Beau this morning, but I should take Digs out for at least a good walk."

"I'd love to!" I said.

I dismounted and waited for Melanie to saddle up, then we headed down a trail beside the road leading to the community center. Along the way was a gate, which we passed through. That path led into and through a wooded area very unlike the landscape around my house and Bar 8. The trees were tall and met overhead. Late afternoon light filtered through, casting a green glow all around. The air now held a chill, but it had been warm earlier and the wonderful smell of fir and pine still hung in the air.

"It's so pretty here!" I said. "You could almost believe in fairy tales!"

"You don't?" was Melanie's surprising response. I hadn't figured her to be a very fanciful person.

"Sometimes I want to," I admitted. "But that sounds foolish. It hasn't been my experience of life so far."

She gave me a knowing look and nodded. "Me either, but I still like to believe. At least in the happily-ever-afters."

I smiled back, thinking this was an odd conversation and wondering if we were talking at all about the same thing. The "happily-ever-afters" reminded me about her mare.

"Tatty said you're going to sell Kitty."

Melanie looked sad and a bit apologetic. "I really don't want to, but I can't justify keeping her. Almost all of my students have their own horses, and I'm considering taking on two more horses for training. I just won't have time for her. She needs someone who's going to ride her more or she'll get fat and lazy. Plus the food and board. It . . . it doesn't actually cost me much to keep her. I don't have to pay for her board myself." She went quiet for a moment as if considering what to tell me. "But entry fees cost a lot. At least, for the big shows. I just don't have time to ride and show her, but I'll miss her terribly. I've had her since I was nine."

We rode on through the trees without speaking until we reached a huge field. I could see cars passing by on the highway in the distance, just beyond a hedged fence. Large logs, brush oxers of various sizes, and other rustic but solid-looking obstacles dotted the large field. Little colored flags flapped in

the breeze at each end of the jumps. Unlike most of the equestrian center, the ground was hard, the grass brown.

"This is the beginning through training level course. Stay here for a minute, okay?"

She rode Digs around the field at a relaxed trot and canter and occasionally set him over smaller hurdles. After about fifteen minutes she returned, walking Digs on a long rein and patting his neck.

"I'm afraid I might not have Digs too much longer either. His owner's daughter is coming home from college and will probably take him on." She sighed deeply. "He's a really great horse. I'll miss him a lot, too."

"That's sad," I said, wondering if that was the right thing to say. I didn't want to make her feel worse, but I did feel sorry for her. I knew what losing a horse friend was like.

Melanie smiled. "Well, at least he'll probably still be here for a while. And his owners are wonderful people. Not like . . ." She seemed to regret saying that much and didn't finish, so I did for her.

"Penny?"

She grimaced slightly. "Well, I'll be happy if we can find the perfect home for Kitty. We even talked about maybe just leasing her out but haven't decided. Anyway, I'm going to have you begin really jumping her soon. We'll start in the cavaletti ring, but eventually we can work back here too. Okay?"

I'm sure my face must have been glowing; I could feel it tingling. "Yes! Oh, yes, please!"

We continued our ride, through a fence closer to the highway, around the front of the showgrounds, past the huge arena and show paddocks, and back to the barns. After we cared for the horses, we got into her mom's car. She started the engine and said, "I'd really like my mother to meet you. Are you in a hurry?"

Meet her mother? Finally? And, I suppose, see where she lives. . . .

"No, I'd love to meet her!"

She smiled and began driving. I wasn't surprised when we drove back around the equestrian center and across the highway, past the golf club driveway and up to the Northfield security gate. The guard smiled and waved her through. I'd never been to a private community before and was intensely curious about it. It also felt like an illicit adventure—entering the heart of enemy territory, a forbidden zone. I couldn't help thinking of Dave, then pushed thoughts of him away again.

There wasn't much to see as we drove through the gates, except for what looked like open parkland—trees everywhere and lush green grass—and a large building with gardens around it.

"They call it 'Northfield Hall'," said Melanie. "It's just a pretentious clubhouse really. You know . . . like at a trailer park."

While I didn't have first-hand experience of that, I knew what she meant. I thought the analogy very strange, though, especially coming from her.

She looked apologetic. "It's not that bad. They do a lot of social events there . . . brunches and parties and fundraisers. It's primarily the domain of the women here. I think most of the men prefer the golf club. They have similar functions over there. There's always *something* going on."

She said this matter-of-factly, but I thought I detected a note of disdain too, which also puzzled me. It didn't seem like her.

She'd driven slowly around the parkland and the Hall's grounds but now drove faster. Houses came into view between tall hedges; *large* homes on beautifully landscaped lots. It reminded me strongly of the neighborhoods around where Brenda lived, though these houses were much newer and often much grander. Luxury cars could sometimes be seen on long, sweeping driveways, and trees and beautiful green lawns were everywhere.

Many of the houses still wore holiday decorations and were just starting to light up as daylight waned. It gave the whole neighborhood a festive if ostentatious appearance, though there were few people visible and the only noise seemed to be from our own vehicle.

We'd soon left the more easily accessible houses near "The Hall" and drove along a quiet road, the properties to either side mostly protected from view by high hedges or close stands of trees. Every once in a while I'd catch a glimpse of the residences and caught my breath each time.

I remembered seeing the Calderas' home for the first time. It had looked like some kind of Mediterranean castle to me then. I still loved the beautiful warm-colored, asymmetric exterior, but I was also aware of how homey and practical it was on the inside. The homes here were grander still, some even built to look like real castles or old Tudor mansions. I couldn't help being curious about the interiors. The properties seemed to become more magnificent

and the grounds more extensive the farther we drove. I'd already assumed Melanie was somewhat wealthy, but she lived in one of *these?*

She finally pulled up before a massive black wrought iron gate. She held a device up toward the gate and it opened inward slowly. We drove through. The driveway wasn't as long as many others had been but passed along a vast expanse of immaculate lawn toward a massive three-story house. "Chateau" came to mind and made me think of fairy tales again.

"You live *here?*" Obvious, perhaps, but I couldn't help voicing it.

She smiled slightly and nodded once. She drove through an archway between the house and a single story building on the right. The latter turned out to be an enormous garage, though I would have thought it another house except for the multitude of wide doors. Melanie turned into the paved area behind the garage and parked a little farther beyond it in a carport hidden from view by a tall vine-covered fence.

I got out of the car and looked around in the quickening dusk. A perfect lawn spread generally downhill from an enormous brick patio behind the house. Beyond it, toward what I assumed was the back of the property, I could see a large pool and a tennis court.

"This way," she said, and led me toward the house.

We walked back toward the archway and through a side door that I hadn't noticed before. This led into what appeared to be a large storage room of some sort. Cupboards lined one wall and two upright refrigerators or freezers stood against another. There were a lot of boxes, too. We continued through into an enormous kitchen, much larger than the Calderas' but not as prettily decorated. Everything here was white marble and stainless steel. A short, rather stout woman alternately sliced vegetables on the far side of a wide island and stirred something in a large pan behind her.

"Hi, Marcy," said Melanie, taking a seat on the near side of the island. I pulled out a stool and sat down too.

"Ah, here you are," said Marcy, giving me a curious glance then going back to her chopping. "Your mother was wondering where you were."

As if on cue, a slim, modestly elegant woman walked in, her face expressionless. "I thought you were going to be home earlier today," she said, her gaze sweeping over me, around the kitchen, and back to Melanie. She had an accent I couldn't place.

"I *am* earlier than normal. I needed to ride Digs, so we went for a short ride. Mom, this is my friend, Allison, from school. Remember? I've told you about her. I wanted you to meet her."

"Oh," said Melanie's mother, taking a closer interest in me, though she seemed extremely reserved, perhaps even guarded. "It is nice to meet you. Melanie has spoken highly of you."

There was nothing offensive in what she'd said or the way she'd said it, but it made me feel uncomfortable, as if I were being considered for some lofty position I couldn't possibly be qualified for. I was suddenly very conscious of my dirty stable hands and dusty boots. She gave a strong impression of "high standards" and I doubted I'd measure up.

She spoke to her daughter again. "You remember you said you would watch Eva tonight?"

"Yes, Mom," she said.

Melanie's mother looked at her watch. "Family dinner is at six o'clock. They'll need you by seven." Her glance flickered to me for a second, then back to Melanie with no hint of emotion. "Will you be ready?"

"Of course," said Melanie, mildly. "I'll take Allison home and be right back. I'll change before I go."

Mrs. Teodorescu nodded and said, "It was very nice to meet you, Allison." She turned to go back the way she had come in, but stopped and faced me again. More graciously, she said, "I am happy that Melanie has made a good friend." Then she walked out of the kitchen.

I looked at Melanie. Her cheeks were pink, but she got up from the stool and said, "We'd better get going. We can wash our hands over here."

We both washed up at a large sink at the back of the kitchen, then she led me down a short corridor to what I assumed was the back corner of the house. She opened a door and we walked into a small living room. A window looked toward the garages.

"Home, sweet home," she smiled and seemed to relax. "This is my room through here."

She opened another door into a neat bedroom with a single bed. The room was pretty but quite small. A light yellow, gauzy bedspread, frilly pillow covers in a matching fabric, and pastel pictures in gold-colored frames made the room bright and cheerful. The images were watercolor paintings bearing the mark of Melanie herself.

"I love your paintings!" I said and looked more closely at each one. They appeared to be of the equestrian center and the grounds of the house or somewhere similar. "They're beautiful! I hope I can paint like this someday."

Melanie had drawn the shade down at her window and began to get changed. "They're not really that good," she said modestly. "I did them a long time ago but don't have much extra time for it anymore. The perspective's not very good. I know we'll be doing more painting next year. You're taking Art 3, aren't you?"

"Definitely!" I answered, still focused on the pictures while she changed into jeans and a sweater.

"Well, we'd better get going. I need to get back to babysit. I'll show you something first, though."

She turned off the light in her room, and I followed her back through the small living room into the corridor and back into the enormous kitchen. Behind the wall where Marcy still stirred was a small alcove with a table and chairs. A long corridor lay across from it on the far side of the kitchen. I supposed it also led to the back, parallel to the hallway we'd come out of a moment before. Melanie's mother had appeared through here. A door lay on the left near us, leading almost directly into the kitchen. It was toward this door Melanie led me. Opening it slowly, she looked around then waved me through.

This proved to be a dining room, though it seemed small and simply decorated for such a grand house. Melanie led me out another door into an immense hall.

The first thing I noticed was the enormous Christmas tree beautifully decorated in reds and golds and standing within the arcing sweep of a grand double staircase. It wasn't too big a leap from our earlier topic of fairy tales to imagine Cinderella running down the stairs and leaving a glass slipper behind. At least, that's what I was thinking. This was Melanie's home and I supposed she was used to it, though it seemed strange that her bedroom and the living room were tiny in comparison. Perhaps it was her own apartment—her private part of the house. That would be pretty cool.

The Christmas tree itself almost rivaled the one at the mall in Sacramento, reaching almost to the top of the second story. Which was the second thing I noticed: not only was the entryway vast, it was completely open to the ceiling of the second story. The ceiling itself had a plaster relief and was painted a soft sky blue, making it seem to soar even higher. I was speechless.

"I wanted you to see the tree before they take it down. It's decorated differently every year. What do you think?"

I struggled to find something appropriate to say. "I think you could hold a dance here," I said, overwhelmed by the size and scope of the room and staircase and still imagining fairy tale scenarios.

Melanie laughed. "That's what the ballroom is for."

"Ballroom!"

She laughed again. "I'll show you around another day. We'd better go."

Bemused, I agreed and followed her back out to the car. We were quiet as we drove along. I got the feeling Melanie was waiting for me to say something, but I was still struggling, trying to process what she had just shared with me.

"Your mother seems . . . nice," I said.

Melanie smiled, but there was a grimness in the line of her mouth. "I apologize if she made you feel uncomfortable. She just always has a million things on her mind. She's had a hard life and worries too much about me."

I wasn't sure what to say to that so figured I'd play it safe by stating the obvious. "You have an amazing home."

The grim smile again. "It's all right . . . until we can afford something else."

This seemed like such a ridiculous thing to say, I had no idea how to respond. I knew I was completely missing something but wasn't sure how to articulate the confusion. "You don't like your house?"

Melanie looked sideways at me—not judgmental but slightly speculative. I was getting used to these looks from my other friends, but Melanie had rarely done it. "It's not our house," she said. "We just live there." She looked sideways at me again and continued, "The house belongs to the Farringtons."

Since I had never heard of the Farringtons, that meant nothing to me. I opened my mouth to ask a question—something like "Do you rent it from them?"—but realized how stupid that sounded and closed it again.

Correctly interpreting my silence, she explained, "My mother is the Farringtons' steward."

Chapter Twenty-Four

Melanie was silent for a minute, giving me time to process this. At least some things were less of a mystery now. Although I wasn't entirely sure what a steward did, I understood the owners of the house employed her mother. Melanie not having her own car and the less than new condition of her mother's car now made more sense. Other things weren't as apparent. Kitty wasn't a backyard kind of horse; I'd done some research and had a good idea what a horse like her must be worth. And it must cost a fortune to keep her at the equestrian center, even if she worked there. And *who* was Roger?

I looked over at her as she drove in the dark, wanting to know more but not knowing where to start. And I didn't want to ask a *wrong* question.

She smiled and continued explaining on her own. "After my father emigrated here from Romania, he worked for a wealthy actor in Hollywood. But he was just one of many gardeners working under another man. That's how he met Noel Lessard, Roger's dad, who was the actor's friend. Noel comes from money—*old* money and a very wealthy family—but he took a liking to my dad. He eventually offered my dad a job being in charge of the grounds of an estate he'd bought in Bel Air.

"Noel eventually helped my dad bring his parents over from Romania. In fact, if my father hadn't gone back to Romania to help my grandparents come here, he wouldn't have met my mother. But that's a long story. Noel got married, too, and he and Dad became good friends. Roger and I grew up together. That's how I got into riding, but that's a long story, too."

"You grew up near where I did!" For some reason I was pleased with the realization.

"Really?"

"Well, not Bel Air, but the Santa Monica area. Wow."

"At that time, my dad was Noel's head groundskeeper, but he dreamed of owning his own company. That's why he had come to America in the first place. Noel wanted to help him do that. He had bought this huge property, what is now Northfield, as an investment with some partners many years before. By the time Roger and I were ten, Noel decided to move his family here."

"But you still lived at the estate in Bel Air?"

Melanie nodded. "My dad was putting things in order there and training someone to take his place overseeing the estate. The Lessards would still spend time there, but they were moving to Northfield to help get it established. Then we were going to move to Northfield too, and Noel was going to help Dad start a landscaping business. There were plenty of new properties being developed and already an established outlying community in need of landscaping and ongoing groundskeeping.

"When I was eight, I had complications with my asthma and got very sick . . . I almost died. I recovered, but my lungs have never been the same. The smog from the city along with other things made continuing to live in Los Angeles a bad idea for me. So that's one of the reasons my parents wanted to move up here. The air quality is so much better. I still have trouble with high pollen and dust. Because I'm so involved at the equestrian center, I have to be careful and wear the mask there all the time, especially around the stables where there's a lot of bedding and horse dust, and sprays, and other things floating around. But I refuse to wear it at school, so I agree to limit my outside time exposed to allergens and dust. That's why I spend lunch in the cafeteria. My mother trusts that it's kept clean."

"So . . . what happened?" I almost whispered. Obviously something had gone wrong with their original plan.

"We're not sure why, either my dad was trying to get a job done quickly, or he was showing someone else how to do it, but he felt it necessary to do some tractor work himself instead of one of the workers. He was riding a lawn tractor, a big one, on a hillside. There was an accident." She shrugged, an uncomfortable one as if to shrug off the painful memory. Her mouth looked very grim. "It was different after that."

"I'm so sorry. I . . . I had wondered. . . ."

"It's okay," she said. "It feels good to finally tell you. I've wanted to for a long time, but it's not the kind of story you just dump on someone. Roger knows, of course, but I've only ever told one other person besides you. My mother . . . well, she's . . ."

"Protective," I said, remembering a previous conversation.

"Yes, but she's also very proud. We have arguments about it. The Lessards wanted to help us, like family. We had been so close from the beginning, in spite of the difference in wealth and position. Noel was devastated . . . probably almost as much as we were. He felt completely responsible for Dad's death, though we knew he wasn't.

"They offered to let us stay in our house on the estate. I think they even wanted to support us so Mom wouldn't have to work, but my mother wouldn't hear of it. She insisted she would take care of us and work. But the only work she'd ever done was housework for a large family in Romania before she met and married Dad.

"The Lessards then wanted us to come and live with them in Northfield. They offered her a home and employment with them, though I doubt they'd have made her work much."

"But she wouldn't accept it?"

Melanie shook her head. "No. But she wanted us to move away from Los Angeles, away from the city and the smog. And, I think, she wanted to stay close to the Lessards. They really are about the closest we have to family. My grandparents died before my dad did, and my mom's parents are still in Romania. I've never met them, but she doesn't want to go back there. My mother asked the Lessards to help her find suitable employment. So they did. The Farringtons are very busy socially and entertain a great deal. They have a daughter, Eva, who also has chronic asthma, so Mom was perfect. She's had a lot of experience with keeping allergens out of the house. They're really nice people, but . . ."

I thought about what it would be like, to live and work in someone else's home. "It must be difficult sometimes."

Melanie nodded. "Mom's been saving all this time. Noel's the one who developed the equestrian center, and he still owns it. He insists on taking care of most of Kitty's expenses. They also make it possible for me to work and train there, and to compete as much as I do. My mom might not have allowed that, except that most of the money I earn or win goes into my college fund. *That* has her approval."

"And Roger?" I couldn't help asking; I had wondered for so long and was too curious now.

Melanie smiled, but it was slightly tight-lipped. "*He* has her approval, too. She would never admit it, but I know she hopes that one day I'll fall madly in love with him and live happily ever after."

"The fairy tale?"

She laughed. "Cinderella, I suppose. And I think that's the main reason she wouldn't let us live with them. You know, so it wouldn't appear. . . ." She made an odd face and shrugged. "That's a little more complicated."

"But . . . you don't feel that way about him?"

She looked over at me, then back to the headlight lit road. "No. Roger was my very best . . . my *only* friend when we were little. He's still a really good friend. I don't know what I'd do without him really. But no, I don't feel that way."

I was sure there was something, maybe a *lot*, she wasn't telling me. We had reached Douglas and were driving through Old Town.

"My mother would like to open a little store . . . antiques and china and things. Then we could live closer to Douglas and have our own home. She says maybe next year."

Her voice sounded neutral, but her expression looked wistful, almost sad.

"Would you still ride?" I asked, wondering if that's what she was thinking of.

"Oh, yes! We're not sure what we're going to do about Kitty, but eventually I'd need to find a home for her anyway, before I go away to college. It makes sense to do it sooner than later, especially as I can't give her the attention she should have. But I'll keep training and showing." She looked over at me again and smiled. "It's what I do."

When we reached my house we said goodbye; she needed to get back immediately to babysit Eva, and it would probably take another forty minutes to drive all the way back. I felt in possession of so much more information now about my friend and would have liked to retreat to my room to process it all, but dinner had been held for me, and Mom had news. I ran out and took care of Remmy, then came back in to eat.

"Angel called," she said as she brought plates out to the dining table. "Apparently the rest of the family is away, but Stevey wasn't well enough to travel, so she stayed home with him. He's feeling better now, and she has invited you, Isabel, and me over for lunch on Friday. Fiona and Robin will be there too. It's New Year's Day."

She looked immensely pleased about this, but I had reservations. "The others will still be away?"

A strange look came over Mom's face. "Yes, that's what she told me. Did you not want to go if they're not there?"

I could feel Dad, Mom, and Isabel all watching me closely, and I would have loved to escape. "No. That's . . . fine," I said, not wanting to give my feelings away but relieved Dave wouldn't be there.

"Good," said Mom. "And Isabel suggested we go out tomorrow and get you some proper riding clothes."

My eyes grew wide at that. "Really?"

"If yer gonna take ridin' seriously . . . dressage and jumpin' . . . ya need the right gear," said Isabel.

"Tatiana told us where to go. There's a store in Lowell."

I wasn't going to argue with that!

Thursday sped by, most of it taken up with our trip to Lowell. We had lunch out first then spent over an hour at the tack and clothing store. I couldn't help looking longingly at the English saddles and wondering again what Remmy—my adorable half-mustang barrel racer—would look like wearing one. I had almost despaired of ever owning one because they were so expensive, but Isabel found a section of the store with used saddles. She said some of them were very good and reasonably priced.

Mom got us both back on track. Our purpose today was clothes for me, not Remmy. Isabel and I tore ourselves away from the intoxicating smell and feel of leather to concentrate on the opposite end of the store. I usually hate trying on clothes, but I enjoyed trying on several pairs of riding pants and breeches and boots. Isabel said I should try a show jacket, too, just to see what it would look like. I happily complied.

In the end, I got a pair of navy riding tights for schooling, a pair of buff-colored breeches and a white shirt in case I had the opportunity to participate in a show, a helmet, a pair of paddock boots, and some half chaps. Isabel assured Mom these things would suffice until I started seriously showing. I couldn't wait to get home to try riding in them.

And I did. I was going to keep the breeches for my lessons for now, but I rode Remmy all over the property bareback in the stretchy pants, chaps, and boots.

I was having trouble falling asleep that night—my brain overflowing with riding, riding clothes, Kitty, Melanie, lunch with Angel and, lurking behind all these, Dave—when I heard a familiar rattle. It was cold and I didn't really want to get up, but I obviously wasn't falling asleep anytime soon and didn't have to get up early, so I did. I put a coat on, put my cowboy boots on downstairs, and went out to meet Ben.

The moon was full but scudding clouds covered it periodically, making everything look shrouded and spooky. The wind appeared to be faster higher up, but down at our level there was just an icy breeze.

"It's getting cold," I whispered.

"Yeah, I didn't think it was this bad. Maybe it'll rain." He was just wearing a t-shirt and hoodie and looked frozen.

I looked in Remmy's stall to see that he was lying down. The swivel of his ears betrayed his awareness, but he was obviously too warm and comfortable to move. I closed the top half of his stall door to keep it even warmer.

I looked up in the sky. "I think you might be right. It's hard to see the stars tonight at all."

He was looking up too. "Yeah," he said quietly.

"You should go home and get warm," I said, just as a few drops of rain hit us. "And dry!" I added.

"I guess so. Can I come over tomorrow?"

I almost said, "Sure," but then remembered lunch. "Oh . . . we're going to be out tomorrow. But maybe later?"

"Yeah. Okay," he said, and started moving away in the direction of his house. "See ya."

"Bye," I said, and walked toward the kitchen. By the time I reached my room I felt bad. I wondered if Ben had needed to talk.

The next day was very cold with a light steady rain—finally! The parched countryside needed it so badly, and I looked forward to seeing the hills green again. I opened Remmy's half-door in the front and the whole door to the paddock, but left his blanket on. I'd groom and probably ride him later in the day. I hoped he wouldn't go out and roll.

Robin drove Fiona to the Calderas' and they were already there when we arrived. The rain came down more heavily, so we parked next to the green Mustang and another car, just beyond the angel statue. We made a dash for the door and I entered without knocking, hoping it was all right and glad to get into the dry and warm. We hung our coats on the hooks in the entryway and took off our shoes, then went through to the family room.

Everyone was gathered there: Fiona, Robin, and Stevey sitting on one of the small couches facing the huge fireplace. It was the first time I'd seen a fire lit in it. Paola was there too, sitting on the other small couch, and I was surprised by how happy I was to see her. Rosa was in the kitchen with Angel. Manuel was helping too. Merle, who had been sitting on the threshold of the kitchen, trotted over to greet me.

"¡Hola!" called Angel, beaming at us. "You are here! I hoped we could enjoy lunch on the patio, but is too cold and wet."

We agreed that it definitely was. It also made me happy to see Stevey holding the Lady toy I'd given him for Christmas. I sat down near him and Merle came and leaned against my leg.

"Stevey . . . do you like Lady?" I asked him.

He didn't look at me but hugged the stuffed dog more tightly, his vague, sweet smile all the thanks I needed.

"Ah," exclaimed Angel. "David told him that it was from Allie. He told him, 'Now you have a dog, too, just like Cris.' He has not put it down since Christmas!"

That made me even happier.

We ate in the dining room with only the very center panels of the outer door open to the patio and courtyard beyond, and one of the *chimineas* near the door to stave off the chill. It was lovely, watching and listening to the rain but eating inside in the beautiful dining room, warm and cozy.

A lot of the conversation revolved around Isabel, as she was the least known member of the gathering, and that was fine with me. Angel asked about her house and family, Mom asked about the closest community, Rosa asked about the countryside and neighbors, and Robin and I wanted to know all about the stables and horses. As reticent as she usually was, Isabel enthusiastically told us about all these things.

Her home, she said, was a large ranch house once also occupied by her parents and three siblings, but now she was the only one living in it full time with occasional working students and clients there for training. She said it was nothing fancy, but it was her home and she was happy there. I was glad she didn't mention Northfield as a point of comparison, though I wondered. The closest real town of any size was over thirty miles away, but she was very close friends with her nearest neighbors, the Salcedos to the northwest and the Chapmans to the south.

"Joe Salcedo's my manager. If it weren't fer him, I'd be dead." She said this bluntly, seemingly without emotion. "And he weren't supposed to be there. He was *supposed* to've gone home fer the day. He said God told him to stay longer." She shrugged. "I'm just glad he did."

Robin and I exchanged glances and I wondered what she was thinking. Mom didn't say anything, but Fiona and Angel made understanding sounds, nodding, and didn't seem surprised at all.

"He's got family 'round here somewhere . . . his sister, Victoria . . . but she's married. I don't remember her husband's name." She looked at us expectantly, and we all looked at each other, but apparently no one knew anyone named Victoria.

"Some of the boys, Joe's sons and nephews, and some of the girls, too, work around the place and keep the horses exercised. We've got five hundred and twenty acres, mostly pasture and uncultivated land, but we got acres under grass and timothy too. The Salcedos work it and we share the harvest. It's enough to get me through the winter. They raise some beef and can always use more feed. I help the kids get started with their trainin' and showin' and some stay on to help me out if I don't have workin' students. Works out pretty well fer all of us."

I was intrigued and tried to picture it all, based mostly on my knowledge of Bar 8, Northfield, and the Caldera's ranch.

"I usually have four or five horses in trainin' at any given time, but I rarely show 'em myself anymore. I take on clients or their horses on a limited basis. No quick fixes at *my* place," she said proudly. "I got a large indoor barn surroundin' an indoor school large enough for small jump courses. And a

smaller barn with a covered round pen attached. So in the winter, when the snow is too heavy, we don't have to go out in it at all. We can exercise the horses inside or just turn them out."

Robin and I exchanged glances again, wide-eyed with interest.

" 'Course, most of the time we work outside if we can. It's awful purdy country 'round there."

"It sounds wonderful," said Angel. "You must be missing your home. The manager, he is taking care of everything?"

"Yep, Joe and some of the kids. Somebody's there all the time, watchin' the place and takin' care of the horses."

There was a little talk about Robin's job and car, then the conversation turned to the Calderas.

"So they all went skiing together?" said Fiona as if verifying something they already knew.

"*Si!* Maricela and *all* the girls, and Marcos and Gerardo, too. They all came here this year except Oscar. He stayed, you know, to tend the ranch. They do not often get to come from Hawaii. And they brought the friends of the twins also. It is a shame Robin was not able to go."

I looked at Robin, not realizing she had been invited. She looked regretful but just shrugged.

Angel sighed and shook her head. I half wanted, half dreaded to hear what more she'd say. But she continued, "We have . . . what do you call . . . the timeshare . . . a cabin every year, close to the resort and the lifts. Esteban and I, we do not ski, but we enjoy going. The cabin is very big and has many rooms, so there is room for everyone. The main lodge is also very nice. But Esteban and I, we do not enjoy the snow like the others."

I remembered hearing that before. I couldn't picture the cabin, but it sounded like everyone was in pretty close quarters. That was kind of depressing. It made me feel lonelier than I had for a while, and I tried not to think about it. But I missed Dave. I couldn't help it.

"I would have liked to go this time," continued Angel, "to spend more time with Maricela and the children. They will come back and stay with us a couple more days before they have to leave. But Stevey and I have had a nice quiet week here, too."

She actually did look very rested and happy. Not that she ever looked *un*happy, but there was a glow to her skin and high color in her cheeks.

Robin and Fiona had to leave around two o'clock as Robin was working at three-thirty, and I was glad that Mom, Isabel, and I left at the same time. It was lighter now but still raining, and I noticed the base of the statue already had an inch or so of water. I couldn't remember ever seeing water in it before. It also struck me for the first time, with her eyes lifted up and the rain falling on her face, how sad and lonely the angel looked.

But that's just fanciful. I'd never thought she looked anything but pretty and content before. *It's just a statue.*

By Sunday afternoon all signs of rain were gone except some muddy spots on our dirt road and in the old corral down by the stream. The stream itself was already deeper, wider, and faster. By Monday morning a few high, wispy clouds were the only hint of moisture in the air, but at least the static in my hair was gone. I'm sure Violet was relieved.

Back to school routine on Monday: Spanish and Geometry; Ben then Robin. Then lunch. I couldn't help searching for Dave as we approached the tables and, sure enough, he was there surrounded by *everybody.* Even Cris and some of the other seniors were there. The grass was slightly damp, so many of us were gathered near the tables, standing or sitting on the pavement. I could only hear a little of what was being said, but all conversations seemed to be about winter break. I was sure Dave was talking about his snow trip. Under normal circumstances, even estranged as we were, I would have wanted to listen, too. But I didn't want to hear about the other girls. I just didn't.

For some reason, I'd expected that his hair would be cut. The exact nature of the agreement he had with the twins' friend was one of the things I didn't want to know, but I was surprised his hair was still long—thick, wavy, and almost brushing his shoulders. He looked my way once and stared hard at me for a moment. *That* was different. And unnerving. And I noticed that he appeared really tired, which also surprised me. Dave was the kind of person to thrive on being around other people, especially girls, and he loved the snow and snow sports and anything active and fun. If I had expected anything, it was for him to look rested and energized. But there were definitely shadows around his eyes, and his smile was not as ready as usual.

I was trying not to watch him, but he finished what he was saying to the people closest to him and looked toward us again. He started to get up as if to walk over, but Ben bounded up just then, and I gladly followed him toward the grass. Robin stood indecisively for a moment, then walked over to join Dave.

Ben found a relatively dry spot on the grass and a few people wandered over to join us. I wasn't able to sit facing away from the tables. If I looked up, I could see Dave clearly. In fact, Dave had moved and I had a clear view of him, so I kept my gaze on my lunch, the ground, or the people sitting to my left. Thankfully they included people from choir who were friendly, though I barely knew them. Hannah and Paola were at the tables near Dave. And Roberta, of course. The only two times I allowed my gaze to wander to him, he was looking my way, so I looked away immediately. It felt almost like a game, but one I didn't want to play.

When the bell rang I tried to get away quickly, but he was beside me before I'd taken four steps.

"I want to talk to you."

Okay, this isn't fair at all. I was trying so hard to be complacent and disinterested and calm, but I could *feel* him, even though he hadn't touched me.

"I . . . really don't want to talk," I said, not daring to look at his face.

He stopped and I walked on alone again, wondering what he thought, wondering what his expression was, and making myself think, *It doesn't matter anyway.*

We were outside for PE, and then it was Study Hall. Ben and I did our Spanish vocabulary. After school we walked with Robin. The Sexy Beast passed us and I looked away, but not before noting that Roberta was *not* in it. I almost let myself go down the "wonder why" rabbit trail, but stopped. *Too many girls . . . I don't want to keep track. . . .*

Tuesday was more normal except for English. I left Melanie early enough to get there before anyone else; I didn't want to be waylaid before class. I was aware of Dave walking in, but he didn't hesitate or look my way. There was some murmuring and sounds of movement behind me though, and when Mrs. Sanders looked up to begin speaking, she paused for a moment as if something had surprised her. I looked back quickly and saw that Dave and

Hannah had switched seats, putting Hannah between him and Roberta. That seemed odd, but I didn't want to speculate about it.

On Wednesday, I brought my riding clothes in a bag and dropped it off at my locker before my first class, though I had a hard time opening it. I almost avoided the tables at lunch but was glad I didn't. Dave wasn't there anyway, along with the others training for track. We weren't likely to see much of them now until Spring unless it was raining. Which was a *good* thing.

I can just relax and enjoy my other friends now. . . .

And I enjoyed my lesson at Northfield more than ever, feeling very proper and comfortable in my breeches and paddock boots and wearing my own helmet. Melanie and Tatty both commented on the appropriateness of my attire, which made me feel good. *And* I was feeling proud of myself for not letting Dave dominate my thoughts. My *life.* I thought I was really moving on.

It was a good day.

Thursday was almost exactly like Tuesday except for the dark looks—I felt more than saw—from Roberta's group. In English, Miss Sanders began speaking, then stopped, looking toward the back of the room.

"Is there something wrong with your own seat, David?"

Everyone looked back. Curious, I glanced back for just a moment. Instead of sitting in the middle of the back row, his regular seat, he was now in the far corner seat, Kyle's. Hannah was back in her own, and Kyle was in Dave's. Roberta looked peeved.

"Nothing wrong. I'm doing research. For science. And math. It's a probability experiment."

Miss Sanders hardly looked convinced but chose to continue with the class. I didn't look back again and hurried out as soon as the bell rang.

During dinner, my parents wanted to talk about my birthday.

"Have you thought about what you'd like to do?" asked Mom.

Not exactly.

It's not that I hadn't thought *of* my birthday, but the *fact* of it posed some problems for me. If it weren't for my parents and certain friends, I would have ignored it altogether, or perhaps just done something quiet at home. But I doubted they'd allow that.

When I had thought—a bit abstractedly—about my sixteenth birthday, back in the summer, I had assumed it would be similar to my fifteenth. Without getting another horse, of course. But I'd already found out that the Bar 8 schooling show was set for a different weekend, so that was out. They had changed the date especially for me last year but were reverting back to its regular day. But with Dave being all weird, I thought it might feel uncomfortable for both of us, and especially for me, if I invited him to anything *not* held at Bar 8.

Then he'd had his "boys only" trip for his own birthday, which had also seemed weird but I'd been kind of relieved by. Girl-less was a good thing. So then I started thinking that maybe having girls only, whatever we did, would also be a good thing. At least potentially angst-free. I actually had a great group of girl friends now, too: Robin and Melanie, of course, and Jessie and Stacie from the old group, and now Hannah and Paola. It could be really fun.

But then I wouldn't be able to invite Ben, which for some reason made me feel sad. And Matthew had made a real point of asking me to *his* party; I felt I should reciprocate. I'd hate to hurt his feelings. And if I invited Ben and Matthew, I should ask the others—Kyle and Tanner, at least. At that point it would be impossible and appear *very* odd and particular *not* to invite Dave.

And then I thought of Cris. I wasn't sure why, except that he had been there for my birthday last year and was most certainly a part of my life. I was sure he wouldn't come, but should I ask him, just to be polite? It was all very perplexing.

Mom and Dad were still watching me, waiting for me to process the simple question.

"I don't know," I said truthfully.

I looked at Isabel to see if she had any words of wisdom on the subject—which she often did—but she was very focused on her mashed potatoes.

"What about bowling?" asked Dad. "They've got the lanes over at Northfield . . ."

I had bowled before and knew I was quite hopeless at it. Still, it *could* be fun. If it weren't at Northfield. *Or if Dave wasn't invited.*

"Mmm," I said, just to prove I was listening.

"Why don't you talk to your friends? See if they have any suggestions," said Mom.

I nodded. I would have liked to put it off, but it was less than two weeks away. Plans had to be made. Invitations needed to be given.

On Friday, Matthew asked if I wanted to hang out after school—some of the kids were going for coffee. He even made a point of inviting Ben. Ben had grinned widely and wagged his brows at me meaningfully. I might have considered it except for two things. Well, three.

Robin couldn't go because she worked at three-thirty. So, stalwart companion not available for moral support. Hanging out without her, with this group, would feel wrong at the moment. Awkward, even if Ben came. I was trying to avoid any extra awkward.

The second reason was that Dave was staring at us at that moment. It almost made me want to say yes just to annoy him, but I couldn't. I hated thinking that I was in any way responsible for the tension between him and Matthew. Even though I was convinced it wasn't Matthew's fault, and even more sure it wasn't really mine, with Dave's gaze currently boring a hole into the back of Matthew's head, I didn't want to give him any excuses to interfere.

And that led to the third reason, the same thing that tempered almost everything concerning Matthew: I didn't want to encourage him. In fact, that was one of the things I was most mad about when Dave asked me to Winter Formal. I was convinced it was to keep me from going with Matthew. I didn't understand it but was sure it was so. And I *did* want to go, but now I realized I couldn't say yes to Matthew about that either, for the same reasons. Matthew might take it more seriously than I wanted him to. I was beginning to feel like a pawn in a game I didn't understand. And I still didn't want to play.

Looks like I won't be going to Winter Formal again this year. I sighed deeply.

"That was a deep sigh over coffee."

Sense of place jolted me back to the present. Dave was, if possible, watching even *more* closely, almost scowling and looking oddly like his brother. I was starting to feel cranky.

"No . . . I was . . . sorry, I started to think about my birthday," I said, floundering for something to say, then realizing too late that it probably wasn't the best choice of topic. "I mean . . . no, I can't go. For coffee. I'm . . ." a valid excuse occurred to me, "I'm babysitting for Cheryl." Not until *later*, but the babysitting was true enough.

"Your birthday. Right," said Matthew, unfortunately grabbing hold of my lapse in judgment. "That's really soon, huh. What are you doing?"

"I don't know. That's the problem."

"We could have a party at my house," he said, a little too earnestly and *much* too softly. "The weather's warm enough and the pool's heated all year."

That, of course, would not do at all. Dave was still scowling, and if his eyes really had been lasers, a hole would have been appearing through to Matthew's forehead.

"Oh . . . I don't think—" I started.

"We should go to Disneyland!" offered Ben, not very helpfully, but saving me from having to fabricate another excuse.

"That's too far for a party," said Hannah.

"It is?" said Ben, as if he genuinely had no concept of the distance involved. "How about miniature golf? That's fun." More people were now watching us.

It went rather quiet, and I didn't know if that meant everybody was considering it or they were too embarrassed to comment.

"I've never done it," I confessed.

"Me either," said Ben, still grinning.

"It's kind of fun," said Hannah, "though I haven't been since I was a kid."

"What's kind of fun?" Dave had apparently given in to curiosity; he'd walked over to see what we were talking about.

"The mi-na-ture golf," said Paola precisely, her eyes alight. But by Dave's presence or by the thought of mini-golfing, I don't know.

Further conversation was halted by the bell.

It seemed very hot over the weekend; at least, hot considering it was January. I had a lesson with Cheryl on Saturday and called Robin that night.

"How's work?" I asked, practicing conversation.

"It's okay," she said. "It's pretty easy." She talked a little about the work and her co-workers, then, "Cris and Dr. James came in for donuts and coffee today. Cris seems to hang out with him a lot."

"Mmm," I said, not wanting to say too much, but I added, "I think they're pretty good friends." I knew this to be true from last year and doubted it was news to Robin.

"Yeah," said Robin. "He said he starts college classes again on Monday, so he won't be around much."

"Mmm," I murmured again, not having much of an opinion on that at the moment. "Have you ever been miniature golfing?"

She laughed, but I didn't know if it was because of the question itself or my abrupt change of subject. Preamble isn't one of my strengths.

"Yeah. When I was little. Why?"

"My parents want to know what I want to do for my birthday. I don't really want a party. I'd rather do something with just you . . . like go to the beach or something. But I guess I need to do something else. Ben suggested miniature golf."

It was quiet on the other end of the phone.

"Is it lame?"

"Yeah . . . kind of. But I guess it *could* be fun. Especially if there was a big group of us. Who would you invite?"

I went down the list—five boys and six girls, not counting me. I *did* count Melanie; I knew she was friendly with Hannah and Paola, so didn't think she'd feel out of place. I would have to make sure she didn't. "So that's twelve of us."

"Hmm. More girls than boys."

I didn't have a problem with that. I thought about who else I knew. There was Gerald, and we were *friendly*, but we didn't hang out or anything. And Cris, of course, but the thought of inviting him to miniature golf made me smile. It might be worth inviting him just to see his expression.

"Oh well," said Robin. "It'll probably be fun. Especially if they've got bumper cars and a good arcade. The guys would like that."

I said I'd talk to my parents about it and see her on Monday.

I mentioned the mini-golf idea to Mom. She liked it and talked to Dad about it on the phone. Plans would be made. Those who weren't driving or didn't want to drive themselves could come with us. My parents could drive separate cars if necessary.

I felt increasingly uncomfortable about it though. First, because it just seemed sillier and sillier the more I thought about it. I wondered what my friends would *really* think. Was it too childish? What did people—ordinary people, not rich or celebrity people—*do* for sixteenth birthdays? Brenda had told me about her massive party at a hotel ballroom with about a hundred people and a DJ and everything. The thought made me shudder. I'd enjoyed the Fall Dance and was disappointed I wouldn't be going to Winter Formal, but to be the center of attention at an event of similar proportions would have me seeking escape from the start. At least miniature golf would keep people busy, right?

On Sunday, Isabel stayed home and Mom and I went into town to do some shopping and buy some small, blank cards to make invitations with. We went into the bakery—not a usual stop for us—just to say hi to Robin. We got some cookies for the ride home, and I got extras for Isabel. At home, I spent the afternoon drawing and painting doodles and designs on the cards while Mom neatly printed the where, when, and why on the inside. I set the best one aside to give to Dave, and Isabel put the others in their envelopes while eating the cookies.

By Monday morning I was stressing pretty badly. I wasn't too worried about anyone else, but exactly *how* was I going to give Dave his invitation? And when? And what would he say? I realized it was idiotic to worry about it, but I just couldn't picture myself doing it without extreme awkwardness. Not the way I could imagine the other girls asking him.

'Yo, Caldera,' Robin would say. 'It's my birthday. You better be there . . .'

Hannah would be a little more demure, but the exchange would be friendly and relaxed.

I could picture Paola bounding up to him excitedly, smile huge and eyes sparkling. 'You will come to my birthday. Yes?'

And Roberta—I didn't even want to imagine how Roberta would approach him.

I supposed I could give it to Robin to give to him, but that was too cowardly. I tried very hard to think from Dave's perspective: how would I feel if he did the same to me? Last year I wouldn't have minded; I would have been and, on other occasions, *had* been thrilled just to be included. But as things stood right now, if Dave had Robin give me an invitation to something as important as his birthday, I'd feel alienated. I'd think he was avoiding me or, at best, the request was an afterthought. And, of course, I was avoiding him, and he probably wouldn't care. But I couldn't do it anyway, on principle.

I gave Ben's to him on the ride to school and he seemed really thrilled. I gave Matthew his at the beginning of Chemistry. He opened it and raised his brows as he read.

"Miniature golf it is," he said, but I couldn't tell what he really thought about it.

I gave Robin, Tanner, Jessie, and Hannah theirs before History started.

"I already asked for the day off," said Robin, "but do you think I could get a ride with you?"

"Of course!"

At lunch, I sat as far away from the tables as I could and didn't face them. I wanted to find a way to give Dave the invitation without so many people around, but if I became aware of him looking at me, I was going to lose my nerve. I *did* take the opportunity to give one to Paola. She seemed delighted and I was glad.

I took my time getting up when the bell rang, hoping Dave would get well ahead of me. He stopped and looked in my direction, and I immediately looked down. I didn't mean to; it was just becoming a reflex. I realized with a sinking feeling that I was reverting to ingrained evasion and defensive tactics. With *him*. Something I never would have imagined I'd do. Were my feelings about him changing? Had they already changed and I'd been too preoccupied and busy to notice? I'd promised myself to stay open to whatever kind of relationship he wanted—buddy, sister, *some* kind of friend—but I didn't feel like any of those things anymore. *And it's probably all my fault.*

When I looked up again, he'd turned away and walked toward the quad with a group of kids. I said bye to Ben and caught up with Kyle and Stacie. They were lingering together, as they often did, before going their separate ways.

"My birthday's on Sunday. We're going miniature golfing. I hope you can come," I said, holding the small envelopes out to them.

Kyle smiled widely and looked genuinely pleased. "Thanks, Allison."

Stacie smiled too, a *kind* smile, I think.

I turned to walk up the hill, leaving them to finish "talking." After a few moments, Kyle ran to catch up with me and we walked to English together.

This time Dave sat against the opposite wall, still toward the back. I made a mental note not to look in that direction. Kyle went back to his original

seat laughing. Miss Sanders looked around the room before starting class, obviously making a note of his position too.

"And how do you like that location?" she asked him. I couldn't tell if she was amused or annoyed.

"Definitely a different perspective here," he said. "It's interesting. I'll have more data by the end of class."

Everyone laughed.

When the bell rang I looked over at him; he was looking back. Roberta then planted herself at the edge of his desk, blocking him from view. Or blocking me from his. "What are you doing?" she said.

He didn't pretend to misunderstand her. "Like I said before, it's a project."

"We're not doing any projects in Ag. Science. *Or* math."

"It's for extra credit."

"You're such a liar!" she said, sounding angry.

I was surprised Dave still sat at his desk. Almost everyone else had left. Miss Sanders was erasing the board but was obviously aware of what was going on. I took my time, pretending to organize my binder.

"You're not changing your seat in any other classes," said Roberta, confirming my suspicion that they had most if not all their other classes together.

"No, just this room. It's an older building and . . . and we're upstairs . . . and the light comes through the windows differently."

"You're an a—"

"I think you'd better get to your next classes," said Miss Sanders, looking around sternly at them.

Roberta had moved and I saw Dave smirk slightly, almost imperceptibly. Roberta huffed and moved reluctantly toward the door. Dave got up slowly, looking at me again. It was now or never—at least for today.

"Um . . ." Always a great opening. *Argh!* "Dave?" I stood up with the card in my hand and took a step, but my foot caught on my chair leg and I had to steady myself against the next desk. The envelope went flying just as Dave started forward as if to catch me. Luckily he was too far away, and I was already stable again. He took another step and picked up the envelope.

"For my birthday . . . on Sunday," I said, feeling embarrassed and breathless and *very* aware of both Miss Sanders and Roberta.

I forced myself to focus on his face and look him in the eyes. And got a shock. Not only was his return gaze *intense*, but there were deep shadows around his eyes. I'd never seen him look so exhausted.

"Yeah . . . I heard about it," he said softly. He held the envelope up slightly. "Thanks."

I glanced at Roberta, looking on disdainfully from the doorway and obviously waiting for Dave. I turned back to my desk to gather my things. When I looked up again they were already gone. I was acutely aware of Miss Sanders' attention and students filing in for the next class. I hurried to Art and gave Melanie the final invitation. She looked pleased and said she'd try to make it.

I didn't see Dave at all on Tuesday, and he wasn't at lunch on Wednesday. Since Tanner, Jessie, and some of the other kids were missing too, I assumed they were training. When I got to English, he was not only already there but occupying the desk directly behind mine. My heart immediately beat faster and my face started tingling, but it could have been as much from anxiety as embarrassment. *What the heck is he doing?*

He was reading or wanted it to appear as if he were, leaning back in his chair with his legs stretched straight out, ankles crossed almost under my seat. He didn't move, but as I reached my desk his eyes met mine and then returned to his book. His expression gave away nothing. All my internal energy was taken up in trying to quell the blush that was just one dangerous thought away. *You can't go there!*

I sat down without acknowledging him, trying not to betray the slightest discomfort, and got ready to take notes. Of course, I hadn't believed his ridiculous "project" excuse any more than anyone else obviously did, but as the class progressed, I fervently hoped and tried to make myself believe that it *was* true. I wasn't prepared to deal with anything else.

I also wasn't prepared for the rumbling and shuddering.

One moment I was gazing sightlessly at the book on my desk and the next, the world was moving beneath me. Desks, loose objects, and windows rattled. My pencil rolled off my desk. An alarm began ringing somewhere close—much too loudly—and a couple of girls behind me shrieked, in terror

or just surprise, I don't know. A cracking sound came from the glass in the old multi-paned window above my head.

Miss Sanders' face had gone completely white and she yelled something loudly to us. I felt calmly detached and hadn't quite got to the mental place of deciding what to do.

And then Dave was beside me, grabbing my arm and pulling me gently off my seat. "Get under your desk," he said, still holding my arm and crouching next to me.

I suddenly realized what he'd done—what he was still doing—and tried to back away, pulling my arm free. I only succeeded in banging my head on the bottom of my desk. "Get under yours!" I said back to him.

The rumbling and shaking had already ceased when Miss Sanders' voice came from the doorway where she had chosen to stand. "Please get under your own desk, David."

A snickering and giggling pervaded the room now as Dave moved back to the other side of his desk, but the tension in the room had relaxed too.

"Please stay as you are until the all-clear signal," said Miss Sanders. "There may be aftershocks."

Everyone seemed content to remain where they were.

"Allie," Dave whispered. The back of his desk was in the way, and I couldn't see his face. "Go to Winter Formal with me."

Another, shorter wave of movement kept me from speaking.

I waited for a few moments and he repeated, "Go to Winter Formal with me."

"No."

"Why not?"

I didn't have an easy reply so remained silent while we waited. The principal's voice finally came over the PA and I was glad for the interruption. I still couldn't organize my thoughts enough to think of what to say. There *was* a reason—I was *sure* of it.

We all got up slowly, adjusting clothing as we did. I was really glad I hadn't worn a skirt. Miss Sanders bustled back into the room, scanning it to make sure everyone was all right and behaving themselves, and took her handbag from a drawer of her desk. The principal's voice said to make our way carefully to the upper or lower field, whichever was closest, while they inspected the buildings for damage. Miss Sanders reminded us to take our belongings, and we began filing out of the room, down the stairs, and out toward the track with all the other students in the building.

Dave was right behind me. When we were out of the building, he fell into step beside me.

"Well, that was fun."

"Fun?"

He grinned and shrugged. "Did it scare you?"

"No," I said, honestly. "I've felt worse."

I think he nodded, but I was watching where I was walking. I was much more likely to get hurt by tripping over my own feet than in an earthquake.

"Why won't you go to the dance with me?"

I just shook my head. I didn't want to discuss this now. My thoughts were much too scattered, and I felt very vulnerable—vulnerable to his ever-present charm—and I didn't want to say the wrong thing.

"You're inviting me to your party, but you won't go to the dance with me? Hardly fair."

Flustered, I said, "And hardly the same."

"Allie . . ." he said, obviously not going to let it go.

I stopped in my tracks and turned to face him. I tried to look at his eyes without connecting too deeply, and said, "I don't want to go with you. I just don't. Please don't keep asking me."

Something diminished in him; he looked disappointed and a little stunned. It occurred to me that he probably wasn't used to being told "no" about anything. At least, not from friends. *And especially not from girls.*

I continued on toward the field and didn't look back.

Chapter Twenty-Five

I successfully avoided Dave the rest of the week; he trained for track during lunch, and I only saw him on Friday during English. He still sat behind me, which surprised me, but he didn't talk to me or otherwise try to get my attention. He still looked very tired, and I was concerned but didn't want to initiate conversation. I still suspected his motives and wanted it to be clear that I wasn't interested in playing games.

I also had real trouble opening my locker. I entered the combination several times, jiggling and pulling the catch really hard to get it open. It looked like I would have to go to the office about it again.

Later, I babysat for Cheryl. She had asked if I could spend the night as she and Tom were leaving early for a special event in Sacramento and wouldn't be home until very late. She put blankets and a pillow on the couch for me and made sure the baby monitor was working. I noticed a small stack of casserole dishes near the door, but I assumed they were from the guest house and didn't think any more about it.

Cody, Zoe, and I spent the late afternoon exploring around the barns, visiting the horses and barn cats and, at least on Cody's part, looking for bugs. We had a nice early dinner with Phyllis in the guest house kitchen and then played in the yard. It was a beautiful, warm evening and I had a lot of fun with them, laughing and feeling more content than I had for a very long time. As the sun went down, we went into the house and got cleaned up. A little later I got the children ready for bed. Cody brought a comforter from his room and we spread it out on the floor. Then we all sat on it and watched a movie he had chosen. The children were soon fast asleep.

About eight o'clock I was thinking about moving them to their beds when I heard a vehicle drive up close to the bungalow. I thought Tom and Cheryl must be home early for some reason. A few moments later, a light knock fell on the door. Not sure whether I should answer or not, I went to the door and listened.

Another knock, slightly louder. "Cheryl?"

I'd have known that voice anywhere. It was one of two people, and it wasn't Cris. I would have recognized the sound of his truck. I opened the door.

"Allie." Dave looked genuinely surprised. "Cheryl called earlier and said she had some things of Angel's . . . asked if I could pick them up. . . ." His eyes narrowed as he talked.

"Oh," I said, keeping my voice lowered. "They went to Sacramento. I'm watching Cody and Zoe." I looked back toward the children, still fast asleep on the comforter.

He nodded slowly. He didn't say anything for a moment, but his expression looked strained.

I picked up the dishes and turned back to him. "I guess that's what these are," I whispered, lifting them toward him.

"Allie . . ." He frowned at the dishes but didn't reach for them. "Can we just talk for a minute? Please?"

I froze, dishes in my hands, trying to process the situation. I still wasn't prepared to talk to him at all right now. I didn't want to upset the sense of contentment I was clinging to. I thought I'd gotten to a place of relative neutrality concerning him, but that state was probably pretty fragile. I needed to be very careful for my own sake.

I turned and put the dishes down again as noiselessly as I could. If the children woke up completely, it could cause problems. And if they knew Dave was here, they would definitely wake up. I could have used this as an excuse not to talk to him—it *did* cross my mind—but I didn't want to. If he really, seriously wanted to talk, then so did I.

"Hold on," I whispered.

I closed the door to keep the cold out and went back to the sleeping children. I was able to gently lift Zoe and move her to her crib without waking her, but Cody was too big. He whined a little bit but held my hand down the hallway and climbed into his bed. I grabbed the monitor receiver and my coat, then went back to the door.

Dave waited just beyond the front porch. We strolled to the backyard of the guest house nearby, then toward the pergola, lit slightly from the lights around the swimming pool beyond. It was a moonless night and, except for the pool area and the porch lights of both houses, it was very dark. I wondered what he wanted to talk about and tried to remain calm and aloof—as aloof as he'd been with me all this time. I waited for him to speak.

I could just see that he was frowning. "It's been kill . . . bothering me, why things are so . . . weird between us."

I continued to wait, not sure if he'd say more. When he didn't, I said, "I don't know. Everything is just . . . different."

"How? *I'm* not different."

"Yes, you are," I said softly. "You're *very* different."

I wasn't sure if he looked angry or exasperated. I tensed, my defenses going up. I couldn't help it.

"I think you're the one who's changed," he said. "At least toward me. And I don't know why."

I thought about this and answered, carefully, "If I've changed at all, it's in response to the changes I sense in you."

He shook his head. "I don't understand. Explain it to me."

Girls, avoidance, expressions, your indifference, lack of contact. Lack of anything.

My mind was disorderly and cluttered—Brenda's bedroom floor, Robin's bedroom walls. The information was all there, but it was tangled up with conflicting memories and very confusing emotions. I couldn't grasp hold of any one thing or put it into a form I could verbalize.

He waited. I could tell he was making a great effort to be patient, but I still felt pressured to come up with a response that would satisfy him. I knew there was one—at *least* one—but it was impossible for me to articulate it right then.

I sat down on the bench swing. I thought back to the beginning of the school year. It seemed like the right place to start. After a few moments I said, "I thought of you over the summer." *Huge understatement.* "I thought that . . . was hoping . . . things would be the same . . . the same as *before* summer," I said, not wanting to admit to too much. "I had really looked forward to seeing you again."

It seemed like a time for openness, but my heart was beating uncomfortably fast and not just because of his nearness. I feared his reaction. I was still afraid he was somehow finished with me, and I wasn't sure I could handle finding out right now.

"I had looked forward to continuing . . ." *What? What was it?* ". . . to get to know you better. But you acted so differently, especially toward me. Or it seemed like it."

He opened his mouth as if to deny it, then closed it again, frowning. The light wasn't good enough to see nuances in his expression, but it still looked strained.

"It made me feel, at first, as if I'd done something wrong. You didn't seem to . . ." I struggled with admitting this, but it really went to the heart of the matter for me, "You didn't seem to care at all anymore. It felt like . . . like we weren't even friends."

The irony of me, the one obviously lacking in social skills, telling *him* he lacked in *anything* was not lost on me. I still couldn't quite make out his expression, but his shoulders seemed to fall slightly. He sighed heavily.

"I didn't know," he said, very softly. "I . . . didn't know I was coming across that way. I was trying to . . . I didn't mean . . . Allie, I wouldn't purposely hurt you for the world."

It was quiet for a moment and I looked down at my hands in my lap. I felt he was waiting for a response from me again, but I didn't have one. I felt so clueless and confused so much of the time—the price of being me—but I knew I hadn't imagined everything.

Very softly, he said, "What . . . how can I fix things?"

Normally, I'd at least have had some internal promptings, but my mind was blank.

"I don't know," I said, honestly. I wasn't sure that "things" could be fixed. I wasn't even sure what "things" were. I wanted to be in Dave's life, but I didn't want to be just a pet or an afterthought. I looked up and met his gaze—as much as I could in the near dark. "I want to be friends, *real* friends again, but I'm not sure I can handle it."

There didn't seem to be any point in explaining that. I don't think I could have brought myself to do it anyway. It would sound like I was blaming him for just being himself.

He stood staring at me, and I wished the light were better so I could see his face more clearly. This time he was quiet so long I was sure I had finally, *really* said the wrong thing. He took a deep breath and let it out again.

"I want that too," he said, his voice so low and soft that I wouldn't have heard it if it weren't so quiet out here.

I nodded, still not feeling much. Except for cold. The night was beautifully clear and still. I could see the stars between the lattice and vines overhead. But it was definitely much colder. I shuddered.

"I should get back in and check on the kids," I said, standing up.

"Allie," he said, stepping closer. His lips tightened and he shook his head slightly, jamming his hands deeper into his jacket pockets. "I've been kind of figuring some things out lately, about myself, and . . . I'm sorry. Really. I want to ask you one more time, and if you say no, I promise not to bug you about it anymore, but . . . please . . . go to the dance with me."

I didn't answer right away, my brain arguing with my faltering heart. I wanted to say yes but was so tired of being unhappy. I couldn't see how going to the dance with him would change anything.

We walked back to the house and stood in the porch light. I watched his eyes for a few moments; his searched mine back.

My heart started skipping.

He looked worried.

"It'll be fun. I promise," he assured me. "We'll go as friends. I mean . . . you can do whatever you want, dance with whoever you like. Okay? Just . . . *go* with *me*." He waited a moment more. Then his lips quirked very slightly. "You *know* I can dance," he said.

I smiled, but reluctantly. *Yes, you certainly can.*

"Okay," I said, and some devil prompted me to add, "but only because I *really* want to go to the dance."

He smiled slightly, frowning and nodding. "Understood," he said, but his expression seemed to say something else. Still, he looked genuinely happy, and I couldn't deny that made *me* happy. "You better get inside. It's cold out here. But I'll see you Monday for sure, okay?" His eyes now danced and his smile slid sideways. "Miniature golf."

In that instant, he looked like *my* Dave. Really tired with very long hair, but definitely the Dave I missed so much. Heart still skipping, I watched him back away into the dark.

Tom and Cheryl came home at about two in the morning. I was still awake—reliving every moment and word and barely seen expression from Dave's visit—but I pretended to be asleep. I'd forgotten to give the dishes to him and didn't want to be asked about them. In the morning, Cheryl made me eat some breakfast but never questioned me about anything besides how the children had behaved. Then Tom drove me home. I spent a good part of the rest of the day getting homework done and trying not to waste time reliving the night before.

When I came downstairs Sunday morning, Isabel was already in the kitchen and seemed excited.

"Happy birthday!" she said heartily and began cracking eggs into a bowl. "Your mom says you like French toast. You like French toast?"

I actually wasn't crazy about French toast, but I didn't have the heart to tell her. "Sure," I said.

I went out to feed Remmy. We didn't have any plans for today and, as my homework was done, I planned on spending the whole day with him. When I returned to the kitchen, Mom and Dad were both up and made a big deal about me being sixteen and everything. I didn't feel any different. Not about that anyway. I was still mulling over developments with Dave but trying not to read too much into it. I thought I was being very calm and mature, considering. Maybe *that* was a result of being sixteen.

When we were done with breakfast, Mom and Dad cleared the table but Isabel told me to stay where I was. She still looked excited about something, her eyes wider than usual and her mouth a firm line, as if she were trying not to smile. Dad sat down while Mom went out of the kitchen, coming back with several large, wrapped boxes. She put these on the table with a few envelopes and sat down.

"Okay," said Dad, looking a lot like Isabel did right now except he was smiling very broadly. "We talked a lot about this . . . what we were going to get you for your sixteenth birthday . . . and, well, if you're not happy about it, we can still change the situation . . ."

Confused, I looked at Mom. "If you'd like it, we're going to lease Melanie's horse for you. At least for a while. Just a half lease."

"But it will give you a chance to ride at Northfield more and work on English riding," said Dad.

"Work on your dressage," said Isabel. "And really learn to jump."

My eyes grew wide. "*Kitty?*"

"Yes," said Dad. "Just on a trial basis for now. You seem to be doing very well with her, and we knew that Melanie was thinking about leasing instead of selling her. Tatiana and Isabel agree that she's a good partner for you. If you really like her and Melanie decides to sell her—"

"Lease?" I was picturing myself riding Kitty around Northfield, practicing in the dressage courts, really jumping her in the big arena. But I wasn't sure how leases worked.

"She'll stay at Northfield," said Mom. "Melanie would still like to use her for a couple of her other students; she'll work out some kind of schedule. You'll still have your lesson but you can ride her more often."

"Of course, you can't neglect Remmy," said Dad.

I felt a twinge of uncertainty. I would make very sure I in no way neglected Remmy. It didn't even bear thinking about. It would be like preferring another horse over him. *It would be like—*

I stopped myself from making any other comparisons. There was no way I would ever give Remmy up.

"Thank you!" I breathed, feeling overwhelmed and sure the reality of it would hit me later.

"Come on now, open yer presents!" said Isabel, unable to contain herself any longer.

I smiled and reached for the envelopes: cards and money from Dan's, Emily's, and Kate's families. Then I reached for the first box.

"The top two are from Grandma and Grandpa," said Mom.

The top box contained a long sleeved dress shirt and a beautiful navy show jacket. It looked like the same one I had tried on at the store in Lowell.

"Yer gonna wanna show Kitty sooner or later," said Isabel. "And ya never know . . . that little mustang out there'll probably do just as good as her if ya train him right. Learnin' on Kitty'll teach ya."

I had no doubts about that. I opened the next box: a pair of glossy black tall boots. Also probably the ones I had tried on.

"Oh . . . wow," I breathed, otherwise speechless. The boots were gorgeous.

"You'll eventually wanna get a different helmet too . . ." Isabel was saying, and I nodded but didn't really hear the rest of what she said.

My mind was swirling with possibilities: visions of riding at shows at Northfield, riding Kitty, riding Remmy. I suddenly thought of Dave, our recent interaction still so fresh in my mind. I imagined him seeing me looking as elegant as Melanie. What would he think? And I'd be seeing him tomorrow. There were no doubts he would be there for my party and I felt a sudden thrill of happiness.

Other possibilities began slipping through my previous resolve; fantasies that I'd banished but were now clamoring to be considered once more. I brutally pushed them away. I was not going to let myself do that again. That's what I'd been concerned about—I'd doubted I was strong enough to keep those thoughts at bay and was struggling already. I needed Dave to be like Matthew to me. Like Ben. We would be friends, and I would have to figure out—all over again—how to accomplish my side of that relationship. And I was going to have to be very careful. I would have to guard my heart.

"Allie?"

I focused back on the shiny black boot in my hands. I'd been running my fingertips lightly over the highly glossed leather.

"This is *so* wonderful," I said, knowing the words were inadequate.

"You're going to have to work hard," said Dad. "Apart from continuing to take good care of Remmy, we expect you to keep your grades up. I think that's going to keep you very busy. You'll have to stay *very* focused."

He said this with what seemed like great satisfaction. I got the sense that, in his mind, a problem had been solved or at least averted. My grades so far this year had been excellent, for me. I'd even received a 'B' in PE in spite of not doing that great in the fitness testing.

"I will," I said.

The bottom box was from Audrey. It had some cute long-sleeved tops, a gift certificate to one of my favorite stores, and a new leather journal.

"This is from me," said Isabel, handing me an envelope.

I opened it slowly. Inside was a card with a gift certificate from the saddle store in Lowell.

"I wanted to get you a bridle and saddle . . . nothin' fancy, ya know, just a used all-purpose for you to start usin' here with Remmy. They'll let you try a few before buyin'."

"Oh!" I gasped, amazed at her thoughtfulness and generosity. I was sure she'd had a hand in the show coat and boots gift too, even if my grandparents had paid for them. "Thank you *so* much!"

I jumped up and gave her a hug. She patted my arm but seemed uncomfortable. That was okay; I understood. I hugged Dad and Mom by turn, and they all urged me to go put on my new show clothes. Dad insisted on taking pictures which I usually don't like, but he took a great one of Isabel, Remmy, and me, which I planned on framing for my room. It would go next to the others of Gold.

I called Grandma and Aunt Audrey before changing again and going outside. Writing thank you notes to the others would take a while, so I'd do it later.

There was still something I needed to tell my parents—no, ask them—no, *tell* them. I didn't feel any kind of permission was necessary; it was *my* decision, after all. Even so, it seemed judicious to choose the right timing. I'd wait until *after* miniature golf.

Monday morning I was as nervous as I'd ever been about anything, still worrying about whether miniature golf was too silly for a sixteenth birthday party and hoping at least a few of the people I'd invited would come. Robin and Ben were coming for sure—we were picking them up. Dave had pretty much promised to be there. I hoped Melanie could come. Even if it were just us, we would probably have fun.

In the end, *everyone* came. A part of me hoped and almost expected Dave to get there first, but he didn't. Robin, Ben, and I played in the arcade until most of the others came. Stacie and Jessie drove themselves and arrived soon after we did. Matthew was there next. I was thrilled when Melanie arrived. She hadn't scheduled any early lessons for the school holiday specifically so she could come. Paola and Hannah came with Rosa, who asked if she could stay too. Mom was happy about that and so was I.

Finally, Dave arrived. Cris had driven the family's smaller SUV and they'd picked up Tanner and Kyle. Dave smiled at me in a way he hadn't done for a very long time, almost mischievously, but he kept his distance. Which was a good thing. It suddenly occurred to me that Winter Formal would be a real *date*. A date with *him*. But I couldn't afford to dwell on that today.

Dad rallied us to follow him so he could pay for everyone, but I noticed Cris holding back. He looked slightly uncomfortable, so I walked over and said, "You can play too. I would have invited you but I wasn't sure . . . I thought you'd probably be busy or something. You know, work or . . . something."

He frowned, his lips tight, but he didn't look mad or upset. For him it was almost a smile. "I'm fine. I'll hang out here."

"Okay," I said, and began to walk away, then turned back. "Thanks, though, for bringing the others."

He nodded and looked uncomfortable again.

Ben bounded—literally—over to me and led me the rest of the way back to where the others waited. Apparently I had to go first.

It soon became very apparent that, like just about anything else incorporating skills with balls, I had no natural aptitude for golf. Only a couple of people missed the first and easiest hole like me. The others moved on in twos and threes. Dave, Matthew, and Robin all got it on their first try and stood back at the second hole, letting others play through while they waited for me. And Ben. It was hard to tell if Ben was really that bad at playing or if he was missing on purpose. I felt embarrassed when we finally got to the second hole. The others let me go first again, but when I missed, I insisted they play ahead.

"I don't want you to wait for me. Really. I'm sure I'll get the hang of it."

Robin went first and moved ahead. The boys insisted I try again so I did, but I missed and felt even more embarrassed. They were careful to hide any impatience, but I was sure they felt it.

"Really," I said. "I want you to have fun. You should catch up with the others. I'll catch up with someone, I'm sure."

Dave and Matthew looked at each other.

"We're not going to leave you playing by yourself," said Dave. "Try again. We can wait."

And so it went for several holes. Tanner, Stacie, and Kyle were nowhere to be seen. Robin, Melanie, and Ben had played together and caught up to Jessie. We eventually caught up to Hannah and Paola, who were also struggling.

The boys finally let competition win out and soon disappeared from view. It was fun playing with the girls, but even they were much better than me. Ben seemed to be stuck at the eighth hole, a pagoda with a tricky up-hill approach, and was waiting for us. I saw Robin and Melanie talking and playing together and was glad. I hoped they would get to know each other a little. Soon Hannah and Paola had moved ahead too, and it was just Ben and me again.

At one point we could see almost everybody from where we were. Dave and Matthew seemed to have forgotten all about me and were battling it out in good-natured if somewhat boisterous and vocal competition. It made me happy to see them together.

"Looks like he's having fun," said Ben when I hadn't acknowledged his latest ineffectual swing.

"Oh . . . what?"

"You know . . . Mr. G—" he stopped himself and wagged his straight eyebrows. "Your boyfriend," he said.

"He's not my boyfriend."

I realized he was talking about Matthew but felt no need to enlighten him. After all, Matthew and Dave were both just friends. That's all.

Ben didn't look convinced, but I wasn't going to feel annoyed with him today. I was enjoying myself too much. Every friend I had in Douglas had *wanted* to come today. And Dave—I didn't want to think anything beyond the fact that he was here, and my friendship *was* important to him. It was the best present I could have gotten.

At that point I felt the pressure was off and I really started to have fun. It was ridiculous how poorly we played. I ended up laughing so much that my sides hurt and my cheeks ached from smiling. I felt exhausted by the time we'd completed the last hole.

Most of the others were back in the arcade. Hannah and Melanie were talking with the adults but came with us to find everyone else. Dave was waiting near the door looking sheepish.

After the others went in, he said, "Hey, I'm sorry."

"For what?"

"For not waiting for you. Matt and I have this . . . thing. *Competitive* thing."

"I didn't want you to wait for me," I said gently. "Did you have fun?"

He grinned. "Yeah. Whipped his ass."

"Then that's good. I mean, good you had fun. That's all I wanted today. I'm really glad you came."

He had a strange look on his face and said, "Of course I came. Are *you* having fun?"

I nodded, smiling easily. "I haven't laughed so much in a *really* long time."

He looked at me more intensely, frowning slightly, and might have said more but the others saw us and came over. Melanie and Stacie both said they'd had a lot of fun but had to leave, and I thanked them for coming. Kyle disappeared with Stacie for a few minutes, saying goodbye out of view of the adults. I realized I'd provided them with something of a clandestine date and was glad.

The rest of us rejoined my parents and Rosa outside for pizza. Cris sat at an adjacent table and appeared to be studying. I put two slices of pizza on a plate and set it down by him, then sat down across from him.

"Have you had anything to eat?" I asked, thinking he must be bored out of his mind.

"Yeah. But thanks."

"You don't have to sit by yourself over here."

"I'm okay."

"You'll come on the bumper cars with us, won't you?"

He squinted at me briefly, then looked away. "Seriously, I'm fine."

"Come on, it's my birthday," I insisted. I wanted to insert "Grumpy" in there somewhere but didn't think I'd get away with it, even if it was my birthday.

A look that could have been resignation—or almost a smile—passed over his face. He closed his book, left it on the table near the adults, and went to stand behind his brother. He ate the pizza *and* he went on the bumper cars. I had been a little nervous about the latter but ended up loving them. I got bumped a lot—I think maybe more than my fair share—but so did Cris. I took the bumps from my friends as signs of affection.

It had been a fun but exhausting day. I felt happy and content but was glad to get home to the quiet. I spent time with Remmy and went to bed snuggling Violet, wondering what would happen the next day. I had a feeling I should have been asking myself some questions—*serious* questions—about Dave, but if I'd started doing that, I wouldn't have slept

and might not have remained happy. Instead, I firmly focused on the fun I'd had and the friends who had made me feel accepted and important to them. Silly or not, it had been another excellent birthday.

I slept very well.

"That was fun yesterday," said Matthew, walking with me after Geometry.

"Yes," I agreed. "It was. I really had fun."

"So, Winter Formal on Saturday. . . ."

My happiness dissipated immediately. I'd forgotten something. *Two things!*

"Have you thought any more about going?" he said, then added, "With me?"

I hadn't. Not once, even before Dave had asked me again on Friday night. I also hadn't told my parents yet. I'd been so distracted all day yesterday it had just slipped my mind. *Oops.*

"I . . ." My brain felt like it was spinning like a clockwork toy. "Um . . . I *am* going . . ."

"But you're going with someone else."

I nodded. Apparently Dave hadn't told him. Should I? Things had been so volatile between them, and I hated thinking I was the cause somehow. I also didn't want to hurt his feelings, but I didn't want to be made to feel guilty either. I did that enough to myself.

Had Dave told *anybody?* I hadn't—yet. I wasn't sure if I would. I was trying so hard to play it cool, but it also occurred to me that not telling was probably a good thing. Me going out with Dave was likely to cause a stir among friends and foes alike no matter how platonic the date was. My heart sank a little—but just a little. This had always been the reality of being his friend, at least for me. But I would rather not deal with any fall out until *after* the dance.

"You're going with Ben again?"

"What? Oh . . . um . . ."

Robin joined us at that moment, talking about something that had annoyed her in her last class, and I said that I was eating with Melanie and would see them later. I never answered his question. It got me thinking though. I knew that Dave couldn't legally drive me to the dance yet, so I had no doubt my parents would make sure he didn't. Transportation must be found.

PE was fun. Just like last year, this week, the week leading up to Winter Formal, was devoted to dance. It was a strategy to motivate both those who danced well and those who were still learning to buy tickets and go.

I'd learned that the junior and senior proms in May were held off-campus at rented venues, the money collected from ticket sales going right back into the student association fund for the next year's proms. The fall dance and Winter Formal were held in the gym. The PTO of Douglas High raised money and paid for the expenses of the fall dance, but the ticket sales of the fall dance went directly into costs for decorations, DJ, and refreshments for Winter Formal. All proceeds from Winter Formal went to sports scholarships. Almost everyone went to Winter Formal.

Before I'd even exited the locker room, my heart was beating faster in anticipation of what Dave might do. Would I get to dance with him?

No. Like last year, members of the track and wrestling teams were conspicuously absent. But Gerald and I partnered up and enjoyed the class immensely. He asked if I was going on Saturday and I assured him that I was, trying to repress the feelings provoked by even thinking about it.

I took my time leaving Study Hall. Ben didn't wait for me but left the room talking to a couple of the guys from class. Dave walked up just as I left the Language Arts building.

"Are you leaving now?" he asked.

"I have Choir."

He wasn't standing that close to me, but the fact he was close at all, actually talking to me like he used to and not with unusual circumstances or unspoken angst, had me on edge. In a good way.

"Hmm. Choir." His nose wrinkled slightly and I wondered what that meant. "Tuesdays, huh?"

"Tuesdays and Thursdays," I said, flattered by him taking an interest but trying not to be.

He leaned against the wall, away from the doorway and the students passing through, and frowned. "I've got track at lunch tomorrow. I might not see you."

"That's okay," I said, wondering why he was bothering to tell me that and struggling even harder to keep my feelings reserved, a blush just a slip of the mind away.

He was watching me—a little too closely. "Okay," he said.

"Oh!" I'd almost forgotten a critical matter. "I haven't told my parents yet, and I don't know . . ." I paused, wondering if I should say anything. Maybe he already had it all worked out.

"If they'll let you go with me?" he asked, making a reasonable assumption and suddenly very serious.

"No . . . at least . . . I don't know that either but . . ." Now I was flustered and losing my train of thought. What if they *didn't* let me go with him?

"I'll come over and ask," he said, his brow clearing. "No problem."

"No," I said firmly. I remembered unanswered questions, partially overheard conversations. "No. *I'll* tell them."

His expression softened, a small smile—*that* smile—lurking on his lips.

"It's just that I don't know how I'm going to get there." But then the answer was obvious: one of my parents.

"Right," said Dave, frowning as if he hadn't thought it through either. "My dad would probably drive us. Or I can ask Cris."

I nodded but didn't like the thought of inconveniencing *his* family.

"Let me know tomorrow?" He began moving slowly toward the quad and, presumably, the parking lot beyond. Turning suddenly, he said, "I haven't told anybody except my family. I don't want to deal with . . . everyone."

I nodded again. I felt the same way, though I wasn't sure it was for the same reasons. I was actually surprised he would even think about it. I'd never known him to care what anyone else thought.

"I wasn't going to say anything either," I said.

He nodded as if satisfied. "I'll see you later." He began walking backward, still watching me. With a mischievous smile, he said, "Enjoy yourself at Choir." Then he turned and walked away.

I went to Choir, happy and nervous, and still purposely avoided overthinking everything.

Later, the conversation with my parents didn't go as smoothly as I thought it would, but it wasn't *too* bad. Dad picked me up from school, but I waited until dinner to have Mom and even Isabel as possible reinforcement.

"Dave asked me to Winter Formal," I said soon after we'd sat down to eat. "I said yes."

Dad had trouble swallowing. Mom looked surprised. Isabel looked curious.

"I thought you weren't hanging out with him much," said Mom, watching my reaction.

"We're still friends." I tried to say it lightly and was proud of myself for remaining calm. "I want to go to the dance, and Dave asked." No need to say that it was the third time he'd asked me, nor that Matthew had asked me first.

"Who's this Dave feller?" asked Isabel.

"Dave is one of the Caldera boys," said Mom.

"Dave gave Remmy to me," I clarified.

"Oh, right, right," said Isabel. "You should go. You can give him at least a dance or two, right?"

I knew what she meant, but it came out sounding funny and I had no chance to stop the blush this time.

"She doesn't *owe* him anything," said Dad, not looking pleased.

Isabel regarded him steadily as if trying to understand why he was unhappy with what she'd said.

"That's not why he asked," I said, trying to remain calm. "He would never . . ." *Never what? Use his gift against me somehow? Ridiculous!* "I don't think he even considers it anymore."

Dad didn't look convinced. He ate for a few moments, then said, "He can't drive you."

I wasn't sure what the terms of driving licenses were and knew that Dave did, in fact, drive other people from time to time, at least for short distances, but said, "No." I figured this was in his favor right now but couldn't resist adding, "Not yet."

"How fun," said Mom. But she looked like she was trying to take a cue from me on how to feel about it.

I tried to appear calmly content. *No big deal. Just Dave and me. On a date.* I still wasn't allowing myself to feel anything beyond glad to be going, and going with someone I liked. A lot.

But just friends.

"It sounds nice," continued Mom. "Of course, we can take you both. Or I guess he can meet you there. Right?"

"Yes," I said, thankful that at least she was prepared to move ahead without too much discussion or asking too many questions I couldn't answer, even if I wanted to.

"I suppose we'll need to go shopping," she said.

I stared at her.

Dress.

I certainly had nothing formal in my closet. I wasn't even sure what *formal* meant as far as clothes went. I suddenly had visions of movie stars on red carpets in glamorous satin gowns with billowing trains, and ladies from historical movies in poofy, frilly ball gowns. I couldn't picture myself in either.

"If we had a little more time, we could have gone to Sacramento. But we can probably find something very nice in Lowell. Let's go after your lesson tomorrow, shall we? We'll be halfway there already."

Now I was excited. I couldn't help it—it was becoming too real. It was going to be much more challenging to remain stoic about it now.

I'm going to Winter Formal. With Dave!

I felt uncomfortable working with Matthew in Chemistry the next morning, knowing I'd left him under a misconception. But he didn't bring the subject up again.

I sat with the kids on the grass at lunch, as I usually did, but I sat so I could see Dave without turning my head too much. I certainly wasn't avoiding him anymore, and I didn't want it to appear to him that I was. I was surprised to see him at all since he'd said he'd probably be running, but he sat with the others at a table.

He looked my way several times, not exactly smiling but looking—happy? It was the same expression he'd had several times last year, like on the beach just before he'd fallen asleep. His expression seemed lighter than it had been since school started somehow. Clear. The way my heart was beginning to feel.

Content?

That thought and his expression affected me profoundly, and I was sure everyone could see my feelings. Like in a video game where people have hearts over their heads if they're in love with you.

On the other hand, my mind was still a cluttered mess that I was refusing to organize, but I was finding it easier to ignore it.

The subject of Winter Formal came up, of course. It was the biggest dance and social event of the school year in terms of how many people usually went. It suddenly occurred to me that I had no idea if any of my other close friends were going.

"Are you going?" I whispered to Robin.

She shook her head but looked pensive. "Tanner asked me, but I don't want to spend money on a dress I'm going to wear maybe once. And," she shrugged, "I don't know. It's not a big deal. You?"

It occurred to me that perhaps I should have told her right away when Dave asked me—that's probably what most girls would have done, right?—but I just didn't think that way. Except for Matthew, it never crossed my mind to tell anyone specific. Why should it? Besides, things were—complicated.

I nodded but kept my voice lowered. "Dave asked me."

She almost choked on her sandwich and her eyes grew wide. "Seriously? Wow. He goes to all the rodeo dances and dances at parties and stuff, but he's never been to a school dance before."

"Who?" asked Ben, having only heard Robin's response.

"I'll tell you later," I said quickly, caution asserting itself.

Several other people now seemed to be watching and listening to us. I was sure there would be gossip soon enough—there always was—but I didn't want to be robbed of this; this wonderful feeling of having Dave back in my life. I wanted to hold on to it at least until after the dance. I'd deal with reality after that.

Unusually perceptive, Robin changed the subject. Luckily Ben was easily distracted.

I left the group early hoping to have a word with Dave before English, even hoping that he might follow me, but he didn't. I stopped at my locker and struggled with it for almost fifteen minutes without success, reaching class right before the bell rang without the book I needed.

Dave had moved again. Now he sat sideways in the seat right in front of mine. He looked up as I walked in, his eyes meeting mine briefly. Mischief clearly lurked there.

He continued sitting sideways for the whole class, and I couldn't help being distracted by his profile. I wondered if that's why he did it. Although

he seldom looked directly at me the rest of the period, I could see the hint of a smile playing at the corner of his mouth. He was amused; maybe pleased. Or perhaps just up to something.

We were given an assignment; a poem to read. We were to look for figures of speech, making notes, then we would compare notes as a class. I had paper and pencil but no book. Dave had his book but nothing to write with.

I hated raising my hand for any reason. Through most of elementary school, I'd raised my hand a lot because I either had an answer or a question. Sometimes I just had extraneous information that seemed important enough to share.

By the end of elementary school, I had figured out that raising my hand all the time was not socially acceptable and by the end of middle school I rarely offered answers or opinions or information of any kind. It had become a negative reflex, and I'd learned really well to keep everything to myself. Now people sometimes assumed I was stupid, but I didn't care much. At least, I didn't use to.

"Can I share my book with Allison?"

Dave's voice roused me from decision making. Miss Sanders looked toward me, surprised.

"You forgot your book?" she asked.

"Um . . . no . . ." I almost said something about my locker but didn't for the same reasons I hadn't raised my hand.

"Very well," she said, but she seemed suspicious. "No talking."

Dave laid his book sideways on my desk so we could both read it. We pointed out words and passages to each other wordlessly, and I wrote them down. We were now leaning close to each other—we had to. Not that I minded, of course, but I knew it wouldn't go unnoticed by others. Precisely the kind of attention I was trying to avoid. And I was using everything I had to stay focused on our task and not let his nearness affect me and *not* focus on his hair, his hands, his mouth, his eyes. *Definitely not his eyes.*

After class, Dave asked, "So where's your book?"

Roberta walked by, interrupting. "Did you enjoy your miniature golf?"

Even I could hear insult in her voice. She obviously wasn't talking to me, but for my benefit. I looked down, closing my notebook slowly and taking my time putting my pencil away.

"Yeah," said Dave. He made no move to get up. "It was a blast."

There was no edge to his voice; it was a neutral answer as far as his tone went, but it made me happy. I didn't think he was just saying it because I was there.

Roberta still stood as if waiting for him.

"Did you need something?" he asked.

"Yeah, I need to talk to you," she said.

I still hadn't looked at her, but she didn't *sound* happy. I pretended to look for something in my backpack.

"In a minute," he said. He waited for Roberta to walk away before turning back toward me. "Your book?"

I thought his persistence strange, but said, "It's in my locker. I couldn't get it open. It's been getting stuck lately but won't open at all now."

He seemed to be trying to suppress a smile, his eyes bright and the corners of his mouth suspiciously twitchy. "Want some help?"

Of course I do. "Yes. Thanks."

"Need to get into it right now?" He frowned slightly and looked toward the door. Roberta hovered there.

"No. I just need to get into it before I leave school."

"Okay," he said, getting up for an incoming student. "Meet you there after school."

I nodded, not sure what to think. He joined Roberta without a backward glance at me, but she shot me one that made me uncomfortable. Hurt? Definitely hostile. They disappeared together. I sighed and got to Art as quickly as I could.

I had a chance to talk to Melanie in class, and it occurred to me that she was probably knowledgeable about such things.

"Are you going to Winter Formal?" I asked.

She smiled slightly, not in a *wow-I-can't-wait-to-go* way. "Yes, I always go to the dances. It makes my mother happy. Are you?" Now her eyes were bright with curiosity.

"Yes, but I'm not sure . . . I don't know what to wear."

Melanie looked thoughtful. "Can you come home with me after riding? I might have something. I can take you home later. I don't have to babysit and I don't have much homework."

I looked at her dubiously. "I don't think we're the same size." She had curves I doubted I'd ever have.

Now she smiled widely, her eyes laughing. "I *always* go to the dances. Remember? And I have *all* my dresses. I've tried to give them away, but my mother wants me to keep them."

I smiled back, feeling excited again. "I'll call Mom after class."

And I did. Mom thought it was a great idea, and if I had no luck at Melanie's, we could still go to Lowell on Thursday or Friday. Then I rushed to my locker.

Dave was waiting there as he'd said. "What's the number? I forgot."

This didn't seem strange. It had been over a year since I'd needed his help with it. I might not have remembered either. I told him as he dialed.

"Huh," he said after several tries with no success. "It's really stuck this time."

He tried again, hitting it with his fist just below the catch several times. It finally popped open.

"So, what did your parents say?" he asked, leaning on the locker next to mine.

"Um . . . it's fine. They'll take me. And pick me up."

"Good," he said, smiling slightly. "Are you going home now?"

"Oh . . . no." I wasn't sure how much to tell him. "I'm meeting a friend."

He watched me for a moment then smiled. "Okay. Well, I'll see you tomorrow."

"Yes," I said, thankful he wasn't going to ask questions. He was usually a lot more inquisitive.

I watched him walk away, then dropped off my books and went to meet Melanie.

In spite of my growing excitement about the dance, I rode well during my lesson and was able to remain focused. We worked on seat and aids, mostly without stirrups. Melanie finally let me uncross my stirrups but then had me practicing in two-point position for the rest of the lesson. By the time we were done, my legs felt like wet noodles.

"I won't talk to you for a week if I can't dance on Saturday," I joked.

She laughed. "You'll be fine. It's good for you. We'll start in the jump arena next week."

That was *very* exciting.

After Melanie's last lesson of the day, her mother picked us up. She looked surprised to see me, but said, "That's a good idea," when Melanie explained our plan. "You are welcome to join us for dinner," she added. This seemed like a gracious offer from her very reserved mother.

"Yes. Thank you very much," I said as politely as I could.

When Melanie and I were alone in her room, she reached under her bed and pulled out several vacuum sealed bags of mostly pastel-hued dresses.

"I think this one has something that might work," she said, opening one of the bags.

"Wow. You have a *lot* of dresses," I said, stating the obvious but wondering how a high school sophomore, even one who had repeated a year, had so many.

"I've attended a lot of social events both here at the Farrington's and at the Lessard's. Community events too. Believe it or not, I've worn some of these many times. My mother wanted me to keep them." She shrugged. "I'd rather have the extra space under my bed, but I'm glad if it helps you."

She pulled out four dresses: two full-length and two much shorter.

"I wore this one in eighth grade, but not to a school dance. The first time I wore it was to a wedding."

She gazed at the dress and looked wistful, almost sad. The satin dress was a soft dusky rose—my favorite color—sleeveless but otherwise demure enough to satisfy my parents and any dress code for the dance.

"I wore it at a social event at the community center, too, but nobody at school would recognize it."

I tried the dress on and it fit very well.

"What do you think?" she asked, smiling.

I was looking at my reflection in her mirror. "Do I have to wear my hair up?"

"I usually do for formal dances, but you don't have to," she said.

She stood behind me and gathered my hair in a ponytail, then twisted it around, coiling it at the back. I shook my head and she let it loose again.

I looked at the other short dress, a soft apricot color. I thought of Robin and felt sad.

"Did you want to try this one on? You can—"

"Oh! No, I think this one will be perfect! I really like the color." I smiled and smoothed the rose satin. "I was just thinking of Robin."

"Is she going?"

"She. . . ." I wasn't sure what to say—Robin was so prickly about some things.

"You can take it if you like. I'd love for Robin to be able to go. Do you think she'd wear it?" she asked softly.

At that moment I was sure Melanie was the best person on the planet. Yes, even better than Dave.

"Are you sure?"

"It doesn't fit me anymore, but my mother. . . ." Her expression indicated she didn't understand her mom.

I tried on the dress and it fit perfectly, though it was a little short on me. It would be perfect for Robin. Melanie seemed very pleased. I got changed back into my own clothes, and we joined her mother in the small dining room off the kitchen for dinner.

Melanie drove me home soon after and I thanked her with all my heart for the dresses and also for the ride home. She came in to say hello to my parents and Isabel, and then left, saying she'd see me tomorrow. I showed everyone the dress she had lent me, then went up to my room and called Robin.

"Hi," she said. "What's up?"

"What if you had a dress for the dance . . . would you go?"

"I don't have one."

"But what if you *did?*"

"I don't know. Maybe."

"I have a dress I think would fit you. It's really pretty."

She wanted to know the particulars of the dress and I described it the best I could.

"Where'd you get it?" she asked, suspiciously.

"Does it matter?"

She was quiet for a few moments. I imagined she was weighing her desire to go to the dance against her dread of any kind of charity.

"Yes," she said.

"I'm borrowing a dress from Melanie. You know, you played miniature golf with her."

Silence on the other end of the phone.

"I didn't have a dress. Mom and I were going to go shopping, but Melanie said she might have something that would fit me. And she did. I was going to spend some money I got for my birthday, but now I don't have to. She had another dress that made me think of you. I've got it here with me."

Still silence.

"I didn't even ask. She just offered. Please? It'll be way more fun if you come."

"I'll think about it," she said.

That was all I could do. The rest was up to her.

I wasn't expecting to see Dave at all on Thursday, which would have been fine. It was so much easier to stay calm and focused on other things if he wasn't around. But we were dancing again in PE, and this time all the track and wrestling kids were there too. Dave looked my way and my heart skipped a few beats, but Gerald was right in front of me before I could find out what Dave's intentions were.

Probably just as well.

Dave was soon claimed by Roberta, and I was surprised I didn't mind. In fact, until Monday at least, I thought it was better for me. If Roberta was happy maybe she'd leave me alone.

On the way to study hall, I got a text from Dave. *'Locker after school.'*

I wasn't sure if this was an assumption that I needed help or something more like a command, but I texted back, *'Okay,'* and continued to class.

When the bell rang, Ben left with me, but Robin was waiting right outside the Language Arts building. She eyed Ben steadily for a moment and, when he didn't move, said, "I need to talk to Allie. Privately?"

Ben retreated quickly, saying, "O . . . kay," to her and, "See you in Choir," to me.

When he'd gone, Robin said, "Yes."

Locker. Ben. Choir. None of these subjects seemed appropriate for her affirmative statement.

"The dress. I'd . . . like to borrow it. For the dance."

I lit up. "That's great!" I said. "We can probably bring it over tomorrow."

We agreed it was a plan and continued toward our lockers together.

Dave was already there and opened my locker without too much trouble when he saw me coming. Robin punched him hard in the arm as she passed on the way to her own locker. He frown-smiled at her and rubbed his arm.

"I was thinking," he said in a soft voice, "what if Cris came and picked you up with me? He offered and everything. It seems weird to go separately if we're, you know, going *together*."

I had thought the same thing, but since Dave couldn't legally drive me, we had no choice. I assumed most of the sophomore class was in the same situation. I *was* a little surprised that Cris would put himself out for us though.

"I'll ask," I said.

He nodded, smiling gently—*my* smile.

"You're not worried about anything, are you?"

"No," I said, very calmly and truthfully. "No worries at all."

"Good," he said, walking backward away from me and still smiling. "Have fun at Choir."

"I will," I said.

And I did.

By Friday morning, plans were finalized. Dad had vetoed Dave's suggestion, which didn't surprise me too much, insisting that either he or Mom would take me and pick me up. Dad didn't give a reason, but Dave didn't seem to have a problem with it.

"What color are you wearing?" was the only other thing he asked. I thought it strange that he'd care.

"Rose," I said.

He squinted at me. "Rose. Like . . . pink?"

I smiled at his expression. "Yes. A soft, dark pink. I like pink."

He nodded very slightly, frowned, then walked away. But I heard him say, "Pink," again to himself.

It was becoming harder and harder not to feel excited about the dance. I kept telling myself it would be just like the fall dance only fancier, and that helped. I had really enjoyed that dance and hadn't been nervous at all. And every time I thought about *who* I was going with, I reminded myself, very firmly, that we were definitely just friends.

He had kept his distance at school, except in English and helping me with my locker, and I tried not to allow any thoughts even approaching romance about him. As well as preventing Matthew from taking me, for whatever reason, I thought he might be trying to make up for ignoring me so much before. I wasn't sure how I felt about that, but I didn't want to think about it too much. Besides, we weren't actually *going* together at all.

Isabel came with Mom to pick Robin and me up from school, and they had brought the dress for Robin. She looked very pleased with the fabric and color, and I couldn't wait to see her wear it. We all drove to Lowell to shop for shoes. Robin had decided that she didn't mind spending a little of her hard earned money on new ones.

Isabel tried to help but her taste in shoes was definitely different. She seemed happiest looking at hiking boots and track shoes.

When we'd both found shoes we liked—Robin buying some gold strappy sandals with heels and me buying simple white flats with a pearly sheen—we drove back to pick Fiona up and then all went out to dinner at the steak house.

I went to bed feeling happy—it had been a great day—but I had troubling dreams.

On Saturday, I spent the day outside with Remmy, trying to stay busy and not think too much about the evening to come. Isabel came out with me and set up some makeshift *cavaletti* with my branch poles and some bricks left over from flowerbed borders Ben and Dad had made. I had told her about starting to ride two-point and about using the *cavaletti* at Northfield, and she seemed as excited as I was that I'd be jumping. I didn't have an English saddle yet, but I was able to ride Remmy over the raised poles bareback at a trot.

Earlier had been clear and chilly, as it had been for the past few weeks, but in the afternoon an icy breeze drove me inside. I put Remmy's light blanket on him before going into the house.

I had skipped breakfast but Mom insisted I eat something for lunch. I couldn't force myself to eat dinner, even though Mom had made it early. Around five-thirty I went upstairs to get ready and checked my phone—you never know, Dave could have called. There were three messages.

Robin: *'The dress fits perfectly! Looks really cute with my shoes, too. :)'*
Ben: *'I got a ride to WF. Can I get a ride home with you?'*
Dave: *'What time are you leaving for the dance?'*
The last message got immediate attention, of course: *'7:30.'*

Then I thought that maybe I should have said more, but I didn't know what more to say.

To Ben, I texted, *'Sure'*, not worrying if the answer was too short.

'I can't wait to see you! :D' was sent to Robin.

After showering, I borrowed my mom's blow dryer—I almost never blow dried my hair—and she came and helped me with the curling iron. I didn't expect the waves to stay in, but it was fun to see my hair really wavy for a change. I wasn't stressing too much over how I looked. My appearance never seemed to matter to Dave. Melanie's dress was pretty and very flattering on me. I just wanted to feel comfortable and look nice, and I was pretty sure I did.

At about seven-fifteen, the doorbell rang. I was still upstairs, worrying a little about my hair; I'd just brushed it again and strands were sticking to my neck and face, a few floating in the air with minds of their own. Violet was staying clear of me.

"Allison," Mom called up the staircase.

I thought it might be Ben at the door.

It was Dave, but I was shocked when I saw him and froze for a moment halfway down the stairs.

It's hard to say what hit me first about his appearance. He stood just inside the closed front door in a dark grey suit that fit him perfectly and made him look taller than usual, with a black shirt, and a tie. A *pink* tie. It was a darker shade than my dress, but it was still pink. And his hair was short. Gone was the shaggy mane, the long washed out waves he'd worn all school year so far. It was actually shorter than I'd ever seen it and looked darker styled with gel. I'd *never* seen him wear gel before. He looked immaculate, standing tall and straight, holding something in both hands.

I felt all kinds of things I'd never have been able to express, surprise being the least affecting. Recent thoughts of fairy tales occurred to me, but I couldn't imagine any fairy tale prince looking more handsome. "Charming" wasn't the impression he made on me, though. *No, too dangerous for Charming.* And his face! I'd almost gotten used to him looking kind of scruffy and more often than not tired, though the past week he'd seemed a little more his old self. There were still hints of shadow around his eyes now, but he looked rested. Vibrant. Ready for anything. I was starting to feel that way myself.

He smiled widely when he saw me and looked about to say something but stopped, his eyes darting toward the living room where my parents and

Isabel were. He was probably trying to be on his best behavior and make a good impression on them. I hoped he was successful. Then he said, "I wanted to bring you something," indicating the small plastic box in his hands.

I felt suddenly shy—he looked so *him*, only amplified to eleven—and I knew my face was turning pink. I couldn't help it. Now I *was* concerned about my appearance, afraid the borrowed dress wasn't fancy enough to complement his appearance. *Maybe I should have put my hair up. And put*—things *in it*. I suddenly realized I still had slipper socks on. Afraid I'd trip just because he was watching, I walked slowly and carefully down the rest of the stairs.

"I hope it's okay," he said, opening the box. But he didn't really seem concerned.

Inside was a beautiful pink rose corsage. He took it out of the box and held it out to put it on my wrist, but the moment my hand touched his, there was a static shock that made us both jump and then laugh.

"Sorry," we said at the same time, then laughed again.

I was very aware of my parents, standing in the living room with different expressions on their faces. Isabel too. Dad's face was relaxed but his gaze was intense. Mom looked happy and about ready to cry. Isabel looked exuberant and like she was holding it in with great effort.

"Well . . . I guess I'll go. But I'll wait for you there, okay?"

"Yes," I practically whispered, still overwhelmed by his thoughtfulness *and* his transformation.

"Oh, wait! Let me get the camera!" said Mom, then disappeared into Dad's office.

Much as I hate having my picture taken, this time I wanted it too. *Me and Dave? Dressed up like this? Yes, please!* Just having a photograph like that would help to get me through the future angst that I wasn't allowing myself to think about yet. After all, I *knew* this was just for tonight. No other wishes or expectations involved. I couldn't allow it.

Mom took several pictures of me with Dave, which he played along with admirably. Then he left, promising again to be waiting. I ran back upstairs and exchanged slipper socks for shoes, thinking vaguely of Cinderella. Mom loaned me a pretty, white crocheted jacket to wear into the dance, but I put my best winter coat on to wear outside. She and Dad almost argued over who would drive me to the dance, but Mom won, which was probably a good thing.

Chapter Twenty-Six

"I remember the first party I went to with your dad," said Mom on the way into town. "He hadn't danced much before and only went because I really wanted to go. We had a lot of fun though."

I smiled but didn't have anything to say, my mind fully occupied with my own immediate future.

"Do you know if Dave likes dancing? I mean, I suppose he doesn't mind too much or he wouldn't be going."

I had already thought of everything I knew about Dave and dancing. He had pretended he couldn't dance much when we'd had dance units for PE last year, but I was now sure that had been for the benefit of the girls around him—he obviously *so* enjoyed them trying to help him. I suspected he found the class more entertaining that way too. The one time I'd danced with him at Bar 8 had been the most exhilarating experience of my life, not counting my botched attempt at barrel racing, which had just terrified me. But Mom didn't know about that impromptu work day dance. In my opinion, he danced *very* well. I tried to picture him dancing at "all the rodeo dances and parties," as Robin had said, but had no idea what that was like. For some reason he liked those situations better than school dances.

"I think he likes dancing," I said, then lapsed into silence, trying to quiet my mind and remain calm.

We got there just before eight. The parking lot was very busy as we drove through it following a line of other cars, both parking and dropping people off. I could see people lingering outside the open gym doors, probably waiting for their dates to arrive, and wondered if I'd have to wait too. I hoped not; waiting around made me nervous, and I was trying so hard not to be.

As we reached the front of the line of cars and stopped close to the gym, I began to open the door, but Dave was right there, opening it for me. He reached down to take my hand and got shocked again for his gallantry. He frowningly smiled but held on and helped me out of the car.

"Sorry!" I said.

He frowned again and shook his head. I took the warm coat off and left it in the car.

"Have fun, you two," said Mom, looking happy but wistful. "Dad will be here at eleven to pick you up, Allison."

Dave said, "I'll make sure she's out on time," which I thought was a little weird, but I wasn't focused on anything but him and trying to act like I thought other girls would.

Dave took my right arm and wrapped his left around it, then we walked toward the gym. We were given glow sticks in exchange for our tickets and told to save them for later. Dave put them in his pocket. I left the lighter jacket with a parent hanging outerwear on a garment rack. She gave me a numbered receipt which Dave took and also put in his pocket.

There was already a crowd of kids inside, and I was aware of heads turning before we'd left the coat rack. And it wasn't *me* drawing the attention. I caught a few people's stares shifting from Dave to me briefly, then back again. I don't think most people even registered who I was, and that was fine with me.

The gym had been transformed into a fantasy place with the lower half of the walls and closed bleachers covered with silver paper or foil of some kind and huge white glittery snowflakes decorating that. Blue and silver reflective decorations hung from the high ceiling and raised court hoops; I felt vertigo just imagining having to put them up there. The gym lights were on at the moment, but banks of automated light projectors were attached to a massive metal structure standing on thick pads in the middle of the floor. A large ball hung from the center of this.

"Oh!" I breathed as we continued into the room.

"What?" asked Dave, looking concerned.

"A mirror ball!" I said, and smiled widely at him. "I've always wanted to dance with a mirror ball on!"

His lips curved—that soft smile that was still mine. He laughed gently, but I wasn't sure why. It didn't matter though; he *looked* happy, and I *felt* happy, and that was all that mattered tonight.

"They decorated so well!" I said. "Much better than the Fall Dance. But that was nice too," I added, not wanting to sound critical.

"Yeah, leadership did a good job. I think Roberta headed the decorating committee." There was a wry twist to his lips as he said this, but I didn't know what it meant. I certainly didn't want to talk about Roberta, so I didn't ask.

The DJ occupying the stage beneath the structure was obviously much more professional than the one for the last dance, and from the sophistication of his equipment, I assumed that he wasn't a local. Twice as many tables were laid out for refreshments along the opposite bleacher wall, too, with white tablecloths and silver colored serving trays and bowls. Blue and silver reflective centerpieces dotted the tables.

It was barely past eight and there was already a crowd of people talking, eating, and milling around. Techno played in the background but there was no one dancing yet.

"So, what do you think?" said Dave, his left arm still beneath my right. It seemed an oddly protective gesture for such a benign situation, and I thought he was really asking, *"Are you okay with this?"*

I looked fully into his eyes then. I ignored the suit, the tie, the hair cut, the decorated gym around us, and looked at *him*. This was the boy who had patiently taught me how to ride last year, who had seemed to know what I was feeling without me saying a word, and who had been my greatest comfort during very difficult times. He was noticeably more mature now and, at least at the moment, much more elegant. But he was the boy I had fallen in love with. Still.

At that moment a wave of emotion washed over me, and I allowed it. It was okay. *This* was okay. I suddenly realized my prayer for restored friendship seemed to have been heard and much more than answered. I was so grateful that my eyes starting watering. I felt a little guilty that I hadn't even thought of God for a while now, but I made a mental promise to talk to him soon.

Dave looked worried and his eyes searched mine, stirring up even deeper feelings. Feelings better not felt for a friend. He was waiting for an answer. I rewound recent memory to his last words.

"Perfect," I almost whispered, still gazing into his eyes.

"What?" he said, frowning slightly and making me aware once more of our surroundings.

The music had gotten louder and even more people had arrived. It seemed like everyone was talking and laughing loudly, and I vaguely heard the DJ say something, but I wasn't paying attention.

I smiled and looked around, then said, louder, "It's perfect!"

He smiled back. "Well, have fun tonight. Okay? Do whatever you want. Just find me if you need anything." He looked around at the crowd of kids, some of them starting to dance closer to the structure. "If we get separated and you need me, wait over by the hallway. I'll see you."

I looked in that direction. The hallway at the back of the gym led to the bathrooms, boys to the right, girls to the left. The interior doors of each, the doors leading to the changing rooms and showers, would be locked. Next to them were the weight room and mat room respectively. The rear exit had been taped off; we'd already been told it was an emergency exit only tonight and off-limits, but two teachers were stationed nearby anyway. If you left through the front doorway, you wouldn't be allowed back in. The gym lights had now been turned off, but the DJ's lamps illuminated the whole room softly. The light in the hallway was on and would easily be seen once the room darkened.

I smiled at Dave again and nodded, wondering how much time I'd actually get to spend with him, and did he have other plans? Then I chastised myself. It didn't matter. We were here *together*. We were friends. We didn't have to be glued to each other, and I hadn't expected to be. I looked around again. I'd probably get to dance with other boys I liked, and I would have a lot of friends here. I was *happy*.

I assured him that I'd be fine.

"If you have any trouble with *anybody*, you let me know," he said, becoming more serious.

I wondered what kind of trouble he meant and who potentially would cause it, but I wasn't going to worry about it. I wasn't going to let *anything* stop me from enjoying this night.

"I'll be fine. Really."

He seemed satisfied and smiled again as the lights changed and a new song started.

"All right," he said, putting his arm down and allowing mine to drop from his. "Just one more thing, though." There was mischief in his eyes. "I get the last dance. Okay?"

I nodded, wondering what *that* meant.

"Come on," he said, leading me further into the growing press of people. "I get at least the first dance, too."

I laughed and danced happily if a little self-consciously with him to the end of the song. Dancing with him, like this, was very different than our dance at Bar 8. I kind of missed the contact and movement of swing dancing. But this was fun too. He moved so easily and with such great rhythm, at ease and confident. It helped me feel the same.

As the song ended, Ben danced over. His black pants and white long-sleeved shirt were normal enough, but the colorful bow tie, red suspenders, and fancy black top hat were pure Ben. And it was difficult to tell exactly what, in this light, but he'd done something to his hair. It looked lighter. He spun in front of me, swept off the top hat and bowed, then held his hand out to me. "My dance, I believe," he said in a mock stuffy accent.

I laughed and took his hand, then looked back at Dave. His eyebrows were drawn up and together, as if he didn't know what to make of Ben.

As we danced, I asked, "What did you do to your hair?"

"Do you like it?"

"I don't know. I liked it before. Now it looks . . . orange."

"It's red," he said, pouting. "It's just the yellow lights in here right now." The lights were, indeed, predominantly yellow for this dance.

"It was red before," I said.

"It's redder now."

I didn't know what to say to that, but I didn't think it was an improvement. Ben tried to talk to me more while we danced, but the music seemed to be getting louder and louder, and most of the time I couldn't separate his words from the music and other sounds. I danced with him through two songs. When the music changed again, I heard him say, "Where's you-know-who?"

"No, I don't know who," I said, not even wanting to guess.

"*You* know. Mr. G." I stared at him, uncomprehending. "Didn't you come with him?" He wagged his brows at me.

I now realized who he meant but was too happy to be annoyed with him. "His name is Matthew," I said. "You know that. And no, I didn't come with him."

I almost told him I was here with Dave, since he didn't seem to have made the connection, but decided against it. Only Robin knew. Apart from just not wanting other people commenting on it, I was afraid it would sound like bragging if I said it out loud. I didn't want *anyone* to think that.

"My mom dropped me off. And my dad's picking us up at eleven so don't hang around after, okay?" I wanted to keep Dad in a good mood. Making him wait for us late at night was not likely to do that.

Ben grinned his best leprechaun smile, grabbed my hand, and twirled me under his arm. When I'd come around full circle, he held my hand up and lightly touched his lips to the back of it.

"Your wish is my command," he said, still grinning.

I pulled my hand away. "Cut that out," I said seriously, hoping no one was watching.

He continued to grin and I walked off in search of other friends.

Melanie was currently dancing with a boy I didn't know, but she saw me and waved, smiling. I smiled and waved back. I found Robin with a group of people toward the front of the gym where the lighting was a little better. She looked so pretty, the apricot dress complimenting her lightly freckled skin and enhancing the coppery red of her short hair. She wore a bit more eye makeup than usual and had a pretty golden clip in her hair. She looked pretty *and* happy.

"Allie!" she said. "You *are* here."

"Hi," I said "The dress looks great on you! Melanie was right. It really suits you!"

She looked self-conscious for a moment but smiled. "Thanks. Yours too! Wow. Look at us all dressed up, right? I," she paused and scanned the dance floor. "I wanted to thank her. Is she here?"

"Yes, I just saw her over there dancing. Do you want to go find her?"

Robin nodded, so arm in arm we headed back the way I had come. By this time there was an incredible press of people everywhere. It seemed like the whole school had turned out for the dance.

As the music had gotten louder, the lights had gradually dimmed, and it was already very dark except for the light display. A much slower song now played and fewer people were actually dancing. Most were gathered in groups talking or heading toward the refreshments or just wandering around like us.

At one point our way was blocked by a large crowd of people and I got separated from Robin. I was jostled to the side, lost my balance slightly, and fell against a large guy, touching the back of his suit jacket.

"Oh! I'm sorry!" I said immediately.

He turned around, a creepy smile spreading his lips thin as he looked me up and down slowly. He looked at Robin, just returning to my side, then looked back at me.

"Well, if it isn't my favorite little. . . ." The guy I knew only as Varsity Jacket didn't finish the sentence but licked his lips and leered more widely.

The guys with him, along with a few older girls, were watching and had a variety of expressions from mild curiosity to disdain and worse. Only Bradley looked neutral, gazing straight at me with no expression at all.

Robin took my arm and said, "Leave her alone."

"Hey, I wasn't the one copping a feel," he said loudly and laughed, holding his hands up slightly. He dropped his voice lower so that only those closest to him could hear and said, "But look me up later if you want to explore more privately."

"Ugh. You're disgusting," said Robin, and dragged me away.

He shouted something after us, but it was lost in the crowd and the music. We walked a little farther, making our way to the side of the gym where there were fewer people. I stopped and pulled her to a stop, too.

"Don't tell Dave," I said.

She frowned at me but nodded solemn agreement. We both knew it could be disastrous if he found out. I didn't even want to think about it.

"But if that douchebag *ever* bothers you, you've got to tell someone."

"I will," I promised. "You too."

She smirked, her emerald eyes suddenly hard and cold. "He'll regret it if he messes with me, and I think he knows it."

There was no humor behind her expression or words; no false bravado. She really meant it, and her attitude intrigued me. She'd always come across as a tough girl—though in a pretty apricot dress it was harder to think of her that way—but this was different, as if it were *personal*. Yet I was pretty sure she hadn't had any other dealings with him besides that one time last year. I hoped she'd confide in me one day.

"I don't know why he picks on you, except he probably thinks he can get away with it. And I guess he's right. You're too . . ."

I wondered what she would say. *Too what?*

"You've got to stick up for yourself," she said, and left it at that.

Brenda used to say that to me, too, but I was never sure how to accomplish it. Words failed me in stressful situations; I was usually too surprised and confused. I'd always thought that if I could understand *why* someone would treat another person like that, I might know how to talk to them. But I *couldn't* understand. I didn't even want to think about it. Especially not tonight.

We continued around the room and found Melanie with a group including Paola. They all smiled as we approached.

"You look fantastic . . . both of you!" Melanie said loudly above the music.

"Thank you!" I said, happy that she approved.

Robin seemed suddenly shy, and said more softly, "Thank you . . . Melanie." It was the first time I'd heard her say her name.

"You're welcome," said Melanie. "I'm so happy to have helped. And really, they look *perfect* on both of you."

I became aware of Roger standing nearby, staring at us, but I couldn't read his expression. It seemed slightly disapproving, but he always seemed to look like that, at least when I was around. I wondered if he recognized the dresses.

Roger's left eyebrow went up slightly and I thought it was because of me, but then realized Dave stood at my elbow. The two boys regarded each other, nodding slightly without betraying emotion. Melanie's eyes were a little wider than usual. She looked toward Dave, then back at me, her expression definitely one of curiosity and, I thought, approval.

Robin said to Dave, "You sure clean up all right. Haircut and everything. You were waiting for Winter Formal?"

"Nope," was all he said.

The lights had come up quite a bit, and the DJ was calling everyone to form lines. Suddenly Ben was on my other side, between Robin and me. He said something almost loud enough for me to hear that sounded like "Retro."

"What?" I wasn't sure I'd heard right.

"Come on," he said, and grabbed my hand, leading me to one of the lines forming in the middle of the floor.

I looked back to see everyone else pairing up and following us. Robin was with Dave and looked happy, which made *me* happy. I assumed we'd be dancing a line dance similar to those we'd learned in PE, but the DJ explained it would be more like Follow the Leader. He was going to play a mix of dance hits down through the decades set over a techno beat and would call out the dances—*old* dances. Four girls from the dance classes, including Roberta and Hannah, stood up on small platforms at each corner of the stage and gave short demonstrations of the dance moves. Then the DJ told us to activate the glow sticks and put them on our wrists if we hadn't already.

Ben seemed ecstatic. "This is *so* great!" he said excitedly.

I have no idea why, but I was ridiculously elated about it too. It seemed we weren't the only ones. The room buzzed with excitement and probably some nervousness, the music adding to the charged atmosphere. The first song was Chubby Checker's *The Twist*, and everyone laughed so hard because we all looked so goofy doing it. After that, it didn't seem to matter anymore, and everyone had a blast.

Ben was in his element, dancing to everything almost as if he'd choreographed it in advance. But it was Dave, on my other side, that made it all the more fun. He split his attention between Robin and me and, with Tanner and Ben on our other sides, it would have been impossible to not have fun. The lights gradually dimmed as the music became more and more contemporary. For a mix of songs from the sixties, large circles of primary colors swirled around the room. We were able to see Roberta and the other girls dancing and followed them through several dances with simple moves. Around the seventies' *The Hustle*, the disco ball lit up and threw spots of light over everyone. A strobe accompanied a mix from the eighties, which I found a little disorienting and had to close my eyes through a part of, minimizing my movement so I wouldn't lose my balance.

"Okay?" I heard Dave's voice say close to me.

I opened my eyes to see he was very close and watching me intently.

"Yes. The light . . . I'm okay."

He looked concerned a moment more, then nodded as if he understood. He took my hands and said, "Close your eyes." We danced like that until the music became contemporary to us and the light show switched to lasers.

Now we were just dancing any way we wanted, many just jumping up and down. The atmosphere was supercharged, and I felt flushed with the exertion and excitement, and the pleasure at Dave's consideration. It seemed like he genuinely was back—the Dave I knew and loved.

When the extended mix was over, Dave asked, close to my ear so he wouldn't have to yell, "Want something to drink?"

I nodded but also took myself to task for the shiver down my spine his nearness and voice had caused.

No, you're not feeling that way.

I thought I'd convinced myself and felt a certain satisfaction about it. In fact, I felt elated in general, so much happier than I had felt in a long, long time. In spite of the loudness of the music and the crush of people—both things that usually triggered my anxiety and made me feel overwhelmed—I was having a *great* time.

A small group of us gathered at one of the refreshment tables. The music was now just a little softer and slower, and the lights had come up slightly, making it much easier to see people's faces. Some couples were even slow dancing, though the music wasn't really right for it. Several teachers were lingering near the tables too, including Miss Sanders and Mr. Tanaka.

"That was fun," said Dave, and I agreed. "Will you be okay for a while?"

"Yes!" I assured him. I didn't want to monopolize his time. That thought prompted a happy memory and I was able to smile wholeheartedly.

"Good," he said, smiling back. "I'll find you a little later. Have fun, okay?" He backed away slightly then disappeared into the crowd.

I started to wonder where he'd gone and if he was looking for someone specific to dance with, but stopped myself. It was none of my business, and it was fine anyway. I was determined to dance with anyone who asked me.

"Where's your date?"

Matthew had joined us. I didn't know if he'd figured out *who* my date was, so it took me a moment to decide what to say. I looked in the direction Dave had disappeared and was about to say, "He went that way," when Ben grabbed my hand.

A faster song had just started and he said, "Come on! I *love* this—"

"Actually," Matthew interrupted, "I was just going to ask you to dance." He was talking to me but looking a little sternly at Ben.

Ben grinned at him. "Oh, yeah. Sure, it's cool," he said and looked meaningfully at me. He spun around and begged Robin to dance with him.

She stared hard at him and said, "*What* have you done to your *hair?*"

"Will you dance with me?" asked Matthew politely.

I laughed a little and said, "Yes," following him to the edge of the nearest group of dancers. I didn't hear what Ben's reply to Robin was but saw them dancing a few moments later, Ben matching his steps to Robin's reserved movement.

"I hope that was okay," said Matthew. "I didn't mean to come between you and your date."

I frowned, trying to figure out what he was talking about. "My date . . ." Then I realized that both he and Ben thought each other were my dates for tonight. I wanted to set him straight right away but immediately became distracted.

I saw Dave across the room. He was dancing with Paola and they looked so cute and happy together. I examined my feelings and found no trace of concern or jealousy, which made me happy too. I *could* do this. Dave and I really were friends again, or headed in that direction. He was free to do whatever he wanted. So was I! He owed me nothing and I would get over my obsession with him. The *remnants* of the obsession I *used* to have for him.

Yes. Remnants.

Still, the tension between Dave and Matthew hadn't dissipated much from what I could discern. I'd been about to tell Matthew that I was here with Dave but changed my mind. I didn't know for sure if he'd care or not, but I was avoiding anything negative tonight. This evening was going to be one of those memories I'd cherish. I wanted nothing to spoil it.

"You didn't," I said finally and very honestly.

He seemed satisfied with that but said, "So, am I ever going to get you to come to a dance with *me?*"

The question was a reasonable one, all things considered, but it made me feel uncomfortable. It seemed likely; I'd often considered going with him. The situation had just never been right. After tonight, Dave and I would do our own things as we always had. There were no expectations for the future. I almost said, "Probably," but didn't.

"I don't know. Maybe," I said, but tried to smile naturally at him—always a challenge. It was difficult to fully meet his gaze.

Time seemed to fly by. The DJ's choice of music was excellent, and I danced to at least half the songs which, throughout the evening, was a lot. I danced at least once with Tanner, Kyle, Matthew, and Gerald, along with a few of the boys from choir who often sat with us at lunch. I lost count of how many times I'd danced with Ben, but I'd turned him down at least twice because I needed a breather.

Dave had only danced the first dance and the one group dance with me, but I was completely okay with that. And I was surprised that I was okay, and a little proud of myself, too. I guess I really had made progress. I tried not to look for him throughout the evening but couldn't help seeing him dance with Robin, Hannah, Paola, and a couple of other girls I wasn't at all familiar with. But whenever I saw him with Roberta, which was several times, they were talking in a group of people. Sometimes he was watching me. I tried *not* to feel satisfaction about that but wasn't very successful.

About ten thirty, the DJ began playing one of my favorite songs. You know that feeling when you hear it, no matter where you are, it just transports you to a different plane and everything else melts away? That's the way I felt. It was too perfect for them to be playing it here, now. The lights went down leaving sultry reds and calming blues by turn, then mixing together in lavenders and purples. Suddenly my hand was taken and Dave led me away.

Dancing with Dave to one of my favorite songs. It can't get better than this.

The relatively slow tempo and heavy bass line of the song, reverberating right through my body to the deepest part of me, made it easier to dance and made me less self-conscious. Or maybe it was because I'd been dancing almost all night. Or maybe, probably, it was due to Dave, dancing so close to me, accepting again, sometimes reaching for my hand and turning me or holding me against him briefly—not long enough to alert the chaperones, but sufficiently long enough to set off sensations I had outlawed.

I closed my eyes and imagined we were alone, letting the music, his touch, the scent of his nearness, and all the other sensations inside just flow through me. I knew I should be resisting but I couldn't. I wouldn't. He was just being himself, as always, and couldn't possibly realize how he was affecting me. I was sure he'd be surprised, perhaps chagrined, if he knew.

No, I was going to enjoy every touch and every sensation. I'd deal with reality tomorrow.

"I need to talk to you," he said close to my ear as the song neared the end. His voice sounded a little rough, but it was probably just to make himself heard above the music. I opened my eyes, feeling disoriented by the lights and other dancers, but gazing at him in a way I hadn't allowed myself to for a very long time.

He looked at me strangely, almost as if he'd forgotten what he was going to say. I remembered something Robin had once said. *Maybe I'm starting to rub off on him again.* The thought made me smile.

His gaze became more intense, but he seemed to recall what he was going to say and looked around as if disoriented himself. I waited expectantly.

"Not here," he said.

The music had changed and the lights were brighter again. We were still dancing, but he maneuvered us closer to the far end of the gym. He seemed to be watching that whole area very closely. Then we stood still, halfway between the corridor and the closest refreshment table. I watched his face, trying to figure out what he was up to. He looked back at me, his eyes glittering as the shifting lights caught them.

Miss Laski stood nearby talking to Mr. Tanaka. Dave led me closer to the corner of the corridor. I vaguely hoped we wouldn't get into trouble for whatever he had planned, but I had no thoughts of *not* following his lead.

"We're just going to step outside for a minute . . . or two. It's too noisy in here, and I don't know when I'll have another chance." He was looking at me oddly again—half severe, half mischievous. "We have some stuff to discuss."

I was still watching his face and wondered what "stuff" he was referring to. Then the logistical difficulty sank in.

"If we go outside, we won't be able to get back in," I said. Not that I cared at that moment, but I thought it was worth mentioning.

"Don't worry," he said, mischief even more apparent on his face. He now watched the stage area closely. "I'm going down the hallway. You'll know when to follow me."

I wasn't so sure of that. There were too many things I just didn't pick up on. It gave me the first twinge of real anxiety that evening. On the one hand, I didn't think Dave could have anything horrible to say to me. He looked too happy. And I was very curious to know what was so important it couldn't wait for another time. But disregarding school rules—really *any* rules—made me extremely uncomfortable. Given sufficient time, I might have been able to logic it away and reconcile myself to it, but there was no time and not enough information to make that kind of informed decision. Still—

This is Dave . . . the boy that I love and my friend that I thought I'd lost. Decision made.

Since I was still closely watching his face, I caught the slight nod to the side of the gym behind me, near the refreshments. Almost immediately, raised voices could be heard, a girl and a boy.

"You think that's okay?" the girl's voice yelled.

"I didn't mean anything by it," the boy returned loudly, placating.

A lot of people close by were focused on them, including Miss Laski and Mr. Tanaka.

"Oh, right, like it's the first time it's happened!"

"You're causing a scene—" the boy started, but was cut off.

"Don't *touch* me, you jerk," the girl screamed, and I finally saw who the couple was.

I was shocked. Then I almost laughed as I realized it must all be an act. Stacie and Kyle, causing a diversion. The two teachers nearby moved toward them. At the same time, Dave moved backward toward the restrooms. In the next instant, the light went off in the hallway.

Was that the signal? Was I supposed to go too? I was still thinking it would be too obvious if he opened that back door, when *all* the lights went out. The music kept playing and people kept moving, the general response being a loud, "Wooo!" and other exclamations. *Was* that *my signal?*

I moved into the corridor, feeling my way and hoping the boy's restroom door wouldn't open suddenly.

"Allie!" a harsh whisper farther along the hallway beckoned.

I slid along the wall and was surprised to be grabbed by the hand. A door opened and I was pulled inside. Dave closed the door carefully. Feeble light from high windows illuminated the weight room.

"How . . ." I started, then realized it didn't matter.

Dave led me to the back door, smiled, and said, "I got the key. Stay there."

He moved quickly to a desk in the far corner, hanging the key on the edge of a shelf bracket by its lanyard, then ran back to me as if he were in a race of some kind, almost colliding with the wall. He opened the back door slightly and looked around before grabbing my wrist and pulling me through.

"Dave!" I whispered, not comprehending what he was up to but now much more concerned about getting locked outside and getting in trouble. I also started wondering again, now fearfully, what could be so important that he couldn't wait to tell me and that he would go to all this trouble to get me alone.

He stooped and grabbed a large rock laying right outside the door, a little *too* conveniently, and slipped it between the door and the jamb to keep it from closing all the way. Then he led me around the corner of the gym, away from the rear light. It was darker here, but there was enough light to plainly see his face. He stood very close and still held my wrist, as if afraid to let go.

"I'm not sure . . ." he said softly, staring back at me.

That caused a stab of fear for what he'd say next. "Dave, I—"

Before I could say anything more or even begin to formulate theories on his behavior, he looked at my lips then planted his own firmly on them.

A few moments later, he pulled slowly away.

I was stunned, not even sure what I felt. My heart had leaped into my throat the moment we had reached this dubious destination. Now I couldn't grasp the fact that Dave—*Dave!*—had not only taken me to this dance but had literally dragged me outside to a forbidden and isolated location to—what? Kiss me? He just *kissed* me?

Dave just kissed me!

My heart became the most erratic it had ever been, thumping and skipping crazily as the reality of that sank in to my poor befuddled brain. I was speechless. My assumptions about this evening were spinning in ever-widening circles as the ramifications of this whole scenario beat in on me.

Could it really be true? Is this really happening? To me?

"I . . ." He looked embarrassed. "I don't really know how to do this."

I was still staring at him in shock, my mouth open in surprise, and he looked . . . nervous? I'd never, *ever*, seen him look that way. But I didn't know what else it could be. Was he scared about how I would react?

Really? Are you kidding me? This is his first kiss? I'm his first kiss? And he's . . . scared?

Heart beating even harder now, I understood that he was waiting to see my reaction; to see whether I *liked* it. *Seriously?* I could hardly breathe. I reached up slowly and touched his cheek in wonder, hoping he'd read anything he needed to in my eyes. Apparently he did, as he bent slightly toward me again. He kissed me more softly but longer this time. Eyes closed, I was scared to move in case I inadvertently discouraged him or woke myself up.

After a few more moments he drew back and looked into my eyes again. "Was that okay?" he asked, looking more his usual, confident self, though still sounding like he wanted reassurance.

After a moment I said, "Yes." I wracked my brains for something else to say, but all I could think of was, "It was nice." Because it was.

He narrowed his eyes, smiling crookedly, as if trying to decide whether I was teasing him. I wasn't, but I didn't mind him thinking I was.

"Haven't you ever kissed anyone before?" I asked.

This had the desired effect of throwing him even more off-balance. His eyebrows shot up, but his eyes were laughing. "Have *you?*"

"I asked you first."

Still smiling, he said, "Yeah . . . but I'm not sure if it counts."

Now he was laughing at me. I could tell.

"Why wouldn't it count?" I asked, really curious.

"Because it was like this." He leaned forward quickly and barely touched his lips to mine before leaning away again.

I pretended to frown in thought as if truly deliberating on the matter. I was actually hoping he couldn't tell I was wondering who had received that first kiss.

"Hmmm," I said. "It was *barely* a kiss."

He laughed. "It also happened in the third grade, and she took her shoe off and hit me in the head with it." He smiled very crookedly. "She was *really* pissed."

And I *really* laughed. It felt good. "Well, then I don't think it counts. Unless *you* want it to."

Still smiling, he said, "No. Not anymore. It doesn't count. You officially have my first kiss." He became serious. "We have to go back inside, but I need to make sure you know . . . don't *ever* think I don't care about you. Okay? But . . . I'm not sure what's going to happen after this."

I wasn't sure if *after this* meant for the rest of the evening or the rest of our lives, but it didn't seem to matter at that moment. Dave had asked me to the dance. He wanted my friendship. I was still, apparently, important to him. He'd *kissed* me for heaven's sake! It wasn't clear to me exactly what

that meant to him, but all these things assured me that we had some sort of relationship. That was so much more than I'd hoped for.

I nodded and followed him back to the rear entrance of the weight room. He removed the rock and closed the door behind us. Now we were in complete darkness. I was hoping for another kiss, but he took my hand and led me back to the hallway door.

"Wait a sec," he said, opening the door slightly.

It was still dark except for the DJ's laser lights, lime green and pink.

"Let's get out of here before someone turns the corridor light back on. When I say, 'Go,' slip out. I'll leave after that."

This seemed like a reasonable plan. When he gave me the cue, I slipped out of the weight room and across to the girls' bathroom. There were quite a few girls in there, all in front of the mirror. They looked at me as I came in, but I ignored them and went into one of the stalls. I didn't need to go but figured a few moments of reflection might be a good thing before facing everyone.

Dave kissed me!

It was going to take a while to get over that. Maybe I never would.

When the girls finally left, I came out and confronted myself in the mirror. My eyes were bright. Two spots of pink highlighted my cheeks and my lips looked darker than usual. I thought *maybe* I looked pretty. I still didn't know what Dave saw in me, but I was happy. Maybe happier than I'd ever been in my life. I smiled at myself and rejoined the crowd in the gym.

It was ten forty-five. Dave was nowhere to be seen, but I wasn't worried about that. I wandered around until I found Robin. She dragged me over to the refreshments and we both got a last cup of punch.

"So?" she said. I waited for her to finish, not sure if she'd known what Dave was going to do. "Pretty cool, huh?"

I breathed a sigh of relief, assuming she just referred to the dance. "Very cool," I replied. *Off the charts cool!* "Are you glad you came?"

"Yeah. It's been fun. You glad you came?"

"Yes. Very." I smiled at her. *Understatement of my life!*

"Grab that special guy or girl," the DJ announced, "or whoever's handy, for the last dance."

He said some other things, but I didn't hear. I was watching Dave walk across the gym toward me. Roberta followed.

"May I have the last dance?" Matthew was suddenly beside me, bowing gallantly.

I couldn't help laughing a little at his manner again, and I *was* flattered, but this dance was reserved. I didn't think even Roberta would keep Dave from it. That sent a thrill of excitement *and* relief through me.

Matthew smiled. That thrill must have been apparent, but he'd misread it.

"Oh . . . I . . . ," I looked toward Dave.

He had stopped to talk calmly to Roberta for a moment but was coming my way again.

It was then that I noticed Hannah, unmistakable longing in her expression. And she wasn't looking at Dave.

Epiphany. *All this time?* She and Dave were friends. They'd been friends forever. But it was *Matthew* she really liked!

"My dance, I think?" Dave barely acknowledged his friend. He put his hand lightly under my elbow and I more than willingly went with him.

That last dance was everything I could have hoped for at that point, and so much more than I had imagined any time before it. Dave held both my hands, low to our sides as we danced, keeping us close. He also came up with a lot of conversation, excuses to bring us even closer and keep his head near mine.

"Everything all right?"

"Yes!"

"Are you okay . . . you know, with before?" He leaned away, searched my eyes.

Still unsure? Amazing.

I couldn't help staring at him, watching him watch me. I could have done that all night. I wanted to reply with a kiss. *Probably not a good idea. Not on the dance floor with who knows who watching.*

"Perfectly okay," I said finally, a little huskily.

He looked content with that, an extra curve to his lips.

"You'll be relieved to know that Kyle and Stacie have made up already."

"Really?" I replied, feigning surprise.

"Yeah, it's remarkable. Apparently, it was all a *big* misunderstanding."

"Well, these things happen sometimes."

"Yeah, they do. They even happen to me."

I frowned. "No! How can that be?"

"I *know* . . . stranger than fiction."

It went on like this, him asking silly questions easily answered or making simple remarks I could readily respond to. And keeping me close. I was storing it all up, sure this was just Dave's effort to re-establish rapport with me—for whatever reason. Except it didn't explain the kisses. Still, I'd spent far too much time looking for meaning in his behavior before now only to be disappointed, confused, and ultimately hurt. I wasn't allowing myself to read *anything* into his actions. Even those kisses. No, I was just going to enjoy right now. I knew I'd be sorting through everything *ad nauseam* later.

When the song came to an end and the lights came up, we took a step apart, dropping each other's hands.

Dave smiled—*my* smile. "Did you have fun?"

Fun wasn't the word I would have chosen to describe the experience I'd had this evening, nor the sensations I was still feeling, but it was close enough. I nodded. I think I smiled back. I mostly felt like quietly imploding somewhere. I wouldn't have imagined it possible earlier, but I actually wanted to go home. I was looking forward to the dark quiet of my room. I *didn't* want to leave Dave, though. If I could, I would have taken him with me.

His mouth quirked slightly, but he regarded me steadily, speculatively. "Let's go get your jacket."

I nodded again, reluctant to speak any more than necessary.

He gave me the coat receipt then kept a respectable distance between us, leading the way toward the front doors. I reclaimed my mother's light jacket and put it on, looking around for Ben. Dave stood nearby watching me, hands in his pockets, looking like some kind of male model. *That* prompted memories, too, but I pushed them away—for now. I would allow myself to enjoy them later. I wished we could have just a minute more alone together, but the whole area was busy with people walking to their parked vehicles, getting in cars waiting for them at the curb, or waiting for rides to arrive.

Ben ran—partly *skipped*—up to us, smiling. "Sorry . . . I was getting phone numbers."

He turned his hand in various angles, looking at his palm as if reading something. Most guys would have made it sound like conquests had been made. He just seemed happy to have more people to talk to.

I was glad to see that it was Mom who had come for us, and not Dad. We all walked over to the car, and Dave opened the front passenger door for me.

What do you say in these situations? Feeling shy in front of Mom and Ben, I said, "I guess I'll see you . . . Monday?"

Dave smiled. "Yeah. You'll see me Monday." It wasn't so much the confirmation as the way he said it—his voice dropping in pitch and volume—that set my pulse racing again. "Hey, Mrs. Anderson," he said, voice normal, as Ben got in the back seat.

"Hello, Dave," said Mom. I felt she was looking too closely at both of us. I was trying not to have "Dave kissed me" all over my face.

I looked him straight in the eyes—as well as I could in the lights of the gym and parking lot. "Thank you for . . ." I wasn't sure what to say. ". . . *for taking me to the dance,"* wasn't technically accurate. *"Thank you for kissing me."* I obviously couldn't say that—at least not with Mom and Ben listening in! I decided anything else I could say would sound pathetic, and I was tired of that. "Thank you for *everything,"* I said as sincerely as I could. *That covers it.*

"You're welcome," he said and seemed equally sincere. "Thank you, too."

My heart flipped like mad. It would have been bad enough if he'd just smiled, or if his eyes just laughed. I could put that down to Dave's charm; a response to girls—people in general, I think—that was intuitive to him. Instinctive. But this response was so genuine and *intentional*—as if he wanted me to *really* take him seriously.

Then, "See ya," he said in more his usual manner.

"Yes," I said confidently.

He closed the door and Mom drove away.

"Well," said Mom, just like I knew she would. "Did you enjoy yourselves?"

She was full of questions that Ben conveniently answered. He kept her entertained by descriptions of everything and everybody. I wondered if he'd finally figured out where my allegiance truly lay, but he didn't mention anything specifically about me and I was grateful.

We dropped him off at his house and I waved, then prepared to be targeted for further questioning. But Mom was either out of questions or understood I was pleasantly otherwise occupied.

I was processing—as I'd known I would be once Dave wasn't near. Every sensory experience, every emotion, every word, and every expression was being replayed; some analyzed, mostly unsuccessfully, and some just enjoyed. I'd sort through them more thoroughly later. Isabel had already gone to bed, but I was still processing as I said goodnight to my parents, and as I undressed, and as I finally lay in bed, my room blissfully dark and quiet.

I wasn't expecting to sleep much, if at all. And I wasn't too surprised when, about an hour later, I heard a sharp *tink, tink, tink* at my back window. But I definitely wasn't in the mood. Tomorrow I'd think of all the reasons why Dave couldn't possibly be serious, but for tonight, I was going to fantasize as much as I wanted and stay in the fairy tale. And I didn't need goofy neighbors interrupting.

My window was closed but the curtains were open, the moon half full and glowing through gathering clouds. I opened my window just enough to whisper harshly to the figure shrouded in shadow on the ground.

"Ben, not tonight!"

The figure below stood silent. Then, "Ben?"

Chapter Twenty-Seven

Dave!

"Oh!" I whispered harshly, grasping for rational thought.

This had never occurred to me. I was still on the *"Did that really happen?"* phase of ruminations and hadn't gotten to *"What might happen next?"*

"Wait!" I whispered out the window, then closed it, pulled sweatshirt and socks on, and quietly hurried down the stairs and out the back door.

Miscalculation. The only shoes on the back porch were flip-flops or my big rubber boots that I used for messy horse tasks. Not wanting to risk Dave disappearing while I searched for more appropriate footwear, I chose the boots—comfort over appearance. It was too cold for flip-flops.

Dave was waiting with Remmy, who had his head over his stall door. I approached him slowly, focused on not tripping in my less than elegant boots. He looked like he was trying to keep a straight face but was finding it difficult. As I reached him, he frowned sternly.

"So . . . Ben?"

"Um . . . yes," I said, determined to not feel guilty, but not sure how I was supposed to feel. *Sheesh. It's not as if we've done anything wrong.*

"He's come over like this before? At night? Thrown pebbles at your window?"

"Gravel," I said.

He frowned again.

"I think he throws gravel. It sounds different."

"*Throws?*" he said. "He's done it more than once?"

He looked very stern *and* perplexed. Cute, but a little too close to expressions my dad had worn in the past year or two. It hadn't occurred to me how Dave might perceive my nocturnal meetings with Ben, but I couldn't begin to make up an excuse. His frown deepened.

"Ben lives just over there." I waved vaguely in a southerly direction. "He comes over sometimes when he can't sleep."

I could see Dave's face clearly in the half moonlight, though I couldn't interpret his expression. Doubt? Hurt? Worry? I didn't want him feeling *any* of those things.

"How many times?" he asked.

I thought it was a weird question. "I don't know. I haven't kept track. Four . . . no . . . five?" That didn't seem to make him feel better.

"So . . . he *likes* you?"

I really wish that word didn't have so many degrees of meaning.

"We're just friends," I said, and the phrase was so used and worn that it sounded hypocritical, but it was true.

"Like *we're* just friends?" His voice had dropped to its softest, but it wasn't comforting. We'd had this conversation before.

His expression was intense and I didn't know what to say. "Yes," was the most appropriate answer, as I wasn't expecting anything more from Dave, but I hesitated to agree with him. His kisses implied something more, but I still didn't want to assume anything.

"You never answered me . . . earlier," he said, still frowning.

"Answered?"

I wasn't trying to appear obtuse or stall for time; my brain was still dealing with too many other things—recent experiences, the present situation, Dave's presence here now—and trying to think of the right answer to his previous question. I thought the question itself might imply we *were* something more. His tone of voice suggested something else. And he still didn't look happy. I obviously wasn't keeping up with this conversation, and there was no trace of amusement left on his face at all.

"Your first kiss."

His eyes scanned mine intensely and he looked *so* severe. But those words, coming from *him*, made me feel so relieved and struck me as so funny that I laughed. I was starting to shiver, too. My sweatshirt and boots were warm enough for now, but my pajama pants weren't. And here was Dave, questioning me about first kisses. I was having a tough time with this. *Still—*

"Is that why you're here?"

His eyes narrowed. "Are you avoiding the question?"

"No. And no, I've never kissed anyone before you. And no, I've never wanted to. And no, Ben does *not* like me. And no, I do *not* like Ben. At least, not that way." I wanted to add, "silly," but I couldn't call him that. It felt like taking a liberty he might not appreciate. He *wasn't* Ben, who I wouldn't have hesitated to call silly.

He watched me wordlessly for a moment with a more neutral expression. I wondered if he thought I was lying. Then his frown relaxed and he half-smiled. He finally said, "Yeah," his voice pitched low and dangerously quiet. "That's why I'm here. That . . . and practice."

"Practice," I said, still watching his face for clues to what he was feeling and how I should respond.

"Yeah. I believe in practicing. Natural aptitude only gets you so far." He was smiling his dangerous smile.

"So that's why you're good at running . . . at soccer and track. And skateboarding."

My heart beat harder as he leaned close and his intentions became clear. His smile grew even broader—a touch of arrogance.

"And *not* so good at roping," I added.

His brows rose and he drew back slightly, now looking like he would laugh. "So you remember that."

I remember a lot of things.

At this point I wasn't sure which I wanted more, to be kissed immediately or to continue just talking to him, especially when it felt like this. I had envied Robin and the way she bantered with him. Maybe it felt like this. And I liked it. A *lot.* I especially liked surprising him.

"So do you want me to kiss you the way I play soccer or the way I rope?"

I gave it due consideration, then said, "Your roping seems a bit hit or miss. So definitely not roping."

"Well," he said, leaning close again, "I'll try to never miss." He leaned closer still and demonstrated his accuracy.

The kiss was soft and sweet and lingered longer than before. But I was still thinking of comparisons.

"I think dancing is a better metaphor for kissing than soccer or roping," I said.

He looked ready to laugh again, but I wasn't sure why. "So, do you think I'm a good *dancer*?"

I gazed at him steadily, trying to decide whether we were still speaking metaphorically. He continued to look amused, but I thought I should give him a serious answer.

"Dancing with you is one of the most enjoyable things I've *ever* done. I *love* dancing with you."

His eyes narrowed again, and I thought he might also be wondering about metaphors. "Ben seems to be a good dancer."

I thought this a weird observation for him to make, but it was true enough. "Yes, Ben's a wonderful dancer."

"Better than me?"

"Are we really talking about *dancing*?" I said, wanting to make sure.

He was quiet for a moment, then smirked. "Yeah. Dancing."

"I love dancing with you way more than with Ben or *anyone* else," I said, trying to avoid the issue a little. Not being an expert myself, I wasn't sure what the *right* answer was.

"Hnh," he said, but still looked suspicious, or pretended to. "Okay. As long as he's not *better* than me."

I was pretty sure he was now joking and laughing at me, so I ventured to add, purely out of fairness to Ben, "There *is* something that Ben does a lot better than you, though."

His brows shot up again and he almost smiled. "And what's that?"

I frowned, trying to appear serious. "He's a much better singer."

"Hnh. Do I need to practice that too?"

"I don't think so," I said, and tried to maintain a straight face, but failed. "I'd rather you didn't spread yourself too thin when it comes to practicing things." Feeling a sudden stab of fear, afraid I might have gone too far, I added softly, "I'm just joking. You don't need to do anything. I like you just as you are."

That, apparently, was a very acceptable answer and earned me another kiss. I was enjoying this immensely, but I was feeling cold in spite of Dave's nearness.

"Um . . . I'm very underdressed for this situation," I said, also starting to feel self-conscious again. Dave still wore his beautiful suit. "You didn't go home after the dance?"

"Nah, I was just hanging out."

"Oh." Trying to picture this raised some of the questions I wouldn't think about before, and now they began occurring to me again. I smoothed the fine fabric of his lapel. "Did you buy this the day we went to the mall? Just for the dance?"

"Yeah," he said.

I got the feeling he could sense the underlying question, so I voiced it. "Were you planning to go with someone else?"

"Nope."

"But I'd already said no."

He shrugged and smirked. "I don't give up easily." Then, more seriously, "You had me worried for a while, though."

More questions—there were *so* many of them—were popping into my head. But asking too many questions—or perhaps the *wrong* questions—had so often gotten me into trouble, especially when I was younger. I'd learned to internalize most of them. But there were things I wanted to understand about him. I would have to be very careful. I asked the one uppermost in my mind at that moment.

"What happened between you and Roberta?"

He frowned slightly and I thought he looked guarded. "What do you mean?"

I had another stab of fear that perhaps this wasn't the best time to be asking such questions, but I'd already opened the can of worms, as Grandpa would say. There was nothing for it but to come out and ask. I needed to know.

"You seem so . . . close. At school. You're with her a lot. I thought you were going out with her. I had thought you'd go to the dance with her."

He appeared thoughtful, then he shrugged and said, "She's in almost all my classes."

I considered this, but I could remember too many instances, too many *close* encounters.

"Hey," he said, ducking slightly to catch and hold my gaze again. "There was . . . and *is* . . . nothing between me and Roberta." His brow lifted slightly. "Or anybody else."

I was still wrestling between the desire to take him at his word and the sting of memories from the past few months. "It didn't seem like it," I said softly.

He looked suddenly uncomfortable—a very rare occurrence for him. "Look," he said and shrugged again, "I'll admit that I thought about it . . . asking her out. At least at first. My dad and her dad were doing more business last year. We were thrown together a lot. And there were other . . . things . . . going on. I thought about asking her out before . . ." He didn't finish the thought but was looking squarely at me.

I waited, not sure I wanted to hear more but wondering, *"Before what?"* He regarded me intensely as if expecting or *willing* me to understand without him having to explain. I was trying my hardest.

"I was jealous," I said, hoping that admitting to that flaw wasn't a mistake and that sharing it might help him open up more about himself. "I was *so* unhappy. I don't ever want to feel that way again."

Dave nodded. "I got jealous too. I just . . . I didn't figure out that I *was* jealous for a long time. I've been kind of messed up." He looked down at our hands, entwined between us. "Messed up in the way I was thinking about . . . things. It took Matt comparing me to—"

His lips became a hard line. He didn't finish the thought, but it sure looked like he wanted to.

"I promise I'll try to never let you doubt me again," he said, looking at me intensely again. "So . . . will you be my girl? No matter what happens after this?"

My heart melted and I felt like a balloon quickly losing its air. I leaned against him, questions and concerns scattered. He let go of my hands and encircled me lightly with his arms. I put my arms around him too. All I wanted right now was to hold him. To stay like this. Forever.

"Yes," I said against his shoulder, eyes tightly shut, soaking the moment in—this moment I had believed impossible.

A very light drizzle began to settle on and around us. Considering the drought, I took it as a good omen, a blessing, though I suppose it could have been the opposite. I leaned away to look at his face again. The clouds, moving slowly across the night sky, now covered the moon more often than not, making his expressions even harder to read.

"What do you mean, 'No matter what happens after this'?" It had finally sunk in that it sounded ominous.

He was quiet, frowning. The fact that he had to spend time thinking about it worried me. "I know . . ." He paused and seemed uncomfortable again, maybe even embarrassed. "I'm *aware* that people have given you a hard time. I'm not exactly sure who or why. I don't want to be the cause of more problems for you, but I won't . . . *can't* ignore you. I don't *want* to leave you alone."

This confused me greatly. He made it sound like someone had *told* him to.

"It's been killing me, not being able to just talk to you like, you know, normal. Feeling like there's something wrong between us. But it may not be best for you if we seem *too* close, at least at school. God, that makes me sound so arrogant! I'm sorry. It's just . . . I'd change things if I could. If I knew how to. Right now, the only people that know . . . that know how I *really* feel about you, are Tanner and Kyle. And Cris, of course. Not even Stacie knew why she and Kyle played their little scene for me, though she probably does now."

He was smiling again and looking up into the darkness, the light drizzle becoming a sheen across his face. I tipped my head back too, closing my eyes, feeling my own face getting wetter and trying to process what he'd said.

"I'm going to come over and talk to your dad. Maybe Monday."

"Why?" I looked back at him and frowned.

"Because I'm going to be gone tomorrow. Tom has a job in Chico. We'll be gone all day."

"No, I mean why are you going to talk to my dad?"

He shrugged. "I'd rather come right out and tell him and deal with . . . anything . . . right away. I don't care about what people at school say, except for how it might affect you. But I don't want to mess with family. Your dad, well, I don't think he trusts me at all."

"I don't want you to talk to him. There's no *reason* for you to talk to him." I was uncomfortable with the idea of Dave talking to Dad right now for any reason, but I felt a little angry that he thought it necessary. I mean, I guess this meant we were officially now *more* than friends—a realization that distracted me for a moment—but he didn't need Dad's *permission* for heaven's sake. Dad had said I couldn't date until I was sixteen. And now I was. I felt that was all the permission I needed. "I'll talk to him."

Dave frowned back at me for several moments and I thought he would argue, but he smiled and shrugged slightly. "Okay."

Taking into account past situations, I wasn't sure I trusted his easy capitulation, but echoed, "Okay."

The fine drizzle was becoming heavier, and my hair, face, and pajama bottoms were decidedly damp. "Your suit's going to be ruined. You should get dry. Where's your truck?"

"Down the street. But you should get inside too. And I should probably go anyway. We're getting up in a few hours to get an early start. The job's too far for me to help Tom much after school, so we're getting as much done tomorrow as we can."

"Okay," I said again, softly, looking at him and hoping for one last kiss before parting.

He smirked. "Any more questions?"

I shook my head slightly, watching his lips. "Not at the moment."

He leaned close and kissed me once more. Releasing me, he said, "Go get dry."

He stood, hands in pants pockets and shoulders hunched against the chill, watching me walk back to the house. I turned and raised my hand, slipping slightly on the wet grass in the process. He raised his hand as well, smiling, and I went into the house. I slipped my boots off quickly and set them back outside, then ran as quietly as I could up the stairs, into my room, and across to my window. He was already gone.

Suddenly freezing cold, I took off all my wet clothes and got into bed, curling into a ball under the covers and folding my bare arms and legs as close to my body as I could—not just for warmth but to try to contain myself. I felt ready to explode.

It's real! Dave's my boyfriend!

Isabel sat at the kitchen table doing a crossword puzzle while I ate breakfast. She had fed Remmy for me but didn't say anything about it or the night before. I hadn't slept much and felt groggy. In fact, I was in a daze all day, happy but completely preoccupied, reliving—over and over and over— everything that had happened at and after the dance. Everything Dave had done and said. Every expression. The feeling of his hands and arms. The feel of his lips on mine. There was room in my mind for little else.

I thought of telling my parents about us. I wanted them to know, to establish the fact that Dave was firmly in my life. But Dad was going out of town tomorrow for at least a few days, maybe more. Thinking of similar times, I thought it might be better to wait until he was home again. Perhaps I'd just tell Mom. I thought she might actually be pleased. But that was the other problem—what, exactly, to say.

"Dave is my boyfriend." It was true but sounded so odd when I said it out loud to Remmy.

"I'm going out with Dave." I wasn't sure of the accuracy of this. I *had* gone out with him, to the dance, and now I was happy to acknowledge it as our first date. But would I really be "going out" with him? He couldn't drive me anywhere; not legally anyway. I didn't know what to call it when you have a boyfriend but real dates aren't likely. At least, not for a while.

I realized I was probably far too meticulous in this train of thought, but I was still hesitant to assume too much about Dave, and accuracy was always important to me. In the end, it was Isabel who helped me decide. I was too restless to relax in the house, preferring to ride and deal with the cold and drizzle. She joined us as I groomed Remmy in his stall.

"So I hear yer gonna get a real arena out there."

"Yes, I think so."

"I guess yer young man's gonna come over and work on that."

I wanted to correct her—*He's not my young man*—but then I realized, *Yes, he is!* This distracted me all over again. It made me want to laugh, too. Thinking of Dave as "my young man" was too funny.

"Why doesn't yer dad like him?" asked Isabel.

"I'm not sure. I don't think he *dis*likes him . . ." I wasn't sure what more to say and wondered how Isabel had come to that conclusion.

"But *you* like him," she said.

I'd always had a hard time admitting to this, but maybe I should practice owning up to it.

"Yes. I like him very much."

"Yer gonna be seein' more of him?"

"Yes. Yes, I am." What a thrill to feel so *sure!*

"Well, he seems like a real nice young guy. And his family's good and cares about ya too. Don't let yer dad er anyone else decide yer feelin's fer ya."

This was easy. "I won't."

"And never let anyone convince ya that ya can't do whatever ya put yer mind to. Ya understand?"

"Yes, I think so."

"Now, I don't wanna go gettin' in trouble with yer dad. And I wouldn't want ya gettin' in trouble with him either, but ya stand yer ground. If ya want somethin', ya have to go fer it. Jes' make sure it's the right thing. And make sure he's the right guy before doin' anythin' ya can't undo."

"Yes. I will," I said, wondering what she was thinking of or perhaps remembering. I'd never seen or heard her so intense before. She'd been watching the rhythmic motion of the brush on Remmy's flank, but now she looked beyond us and seemed far away.

As for making sure Dave was the right guy before doing anything I couldn't undo, I thought I knew what she meant but wasn't sure. *Dave would always be the right guy. How could that change?* But I'd already decided not to say anything to my parents. I wasn't going to discuss it at all until it came up.

"Where're ya gonna ride?" Isabel asked as I tightened Remmy's girth.

"Just around here."

"What's back over there?" She indicated toward the creek.

I explained about the fire road and the government land.

"But I haven't gone very far. When I tried, Remmy was nervous and I didn't feel confident. Ben and I have walked around back there a little." I didn't add that it was in the middle of the night and I wasn't sure exactly where we'd gone.

"Well, I feel like goin' fer a walk. Wanna come? Ride yer pony? You could call yer friend . . . Ben. The more the merrier. I could use a good walk."

Her wanting to invite Ben surprised me a little, but I was happy to include him and smiled when I thought about telling Dave. I was sure he'd eventually get used to Ben. I couldn't imagine his generous nature not winning out over his misplaced jealousy. I didn't want to give up Ben's friendship. And that surprised me too, considering how little I'd wanted it at first and how annoying I still sometimes found him.

I texted Ben. *'Want to come for a walk with me and my aunt?'*

He texted back immediately. *'Yeah!'*

That made me happy. So much had happened in the past twenty-four hours that it seemed an age since I'd seen Ben instead of less than a day.

Isabel coached Remmy and me through bending exercises at a walk until Ben arrived. His hair was even lighter in color in daylight, definitely a soft orangey color. It made him look so different. I introduced him to Isabel and we set out down the dirt driveway, over the cattle guard, past the old corral, and out through the back gate.

We talked as we walked, and I could tell Remmy was extremely happy; relaxed but interested in everything and glad to be on an adventure. I wished I could get him over to Bar 8 more often to ride him there. He knew those trails well and I felt safe there too. Then I thought about riding him at the Calderas' ranch. That distracted me completely until Ben brought my attention back by relating one of his stories. He recounted a white water rafting trip in Idaho.

Isabel listened without interrupting, except to say, "I've been to Idaho. There's some good horse country up there."

I listened to his detailed account with mounting suspicion but said nothing.

We walked straight out along the fire road, not turning to the south as Ben and I had before. The dirt track continued weaving through the hills, mostly uphill. There was no sign of anyone else, though we took precautions where visibility was limited, Isabel insisting on leading the way about five yards ahead of us. We'd been walking about an hour when the trail climbed to the crest of a hill.

Smaller hills continued to the north and we could see for miles, but higher elevations sided in snow to the east seemed much closer than I had imagined they could be from our house. To the south, the steeper neighboring hills made it impossible to see further. Looking back the way we'd come was unnerving. There was no sign of my house, no sign of habitation at all, just more rolling hills and trees, but I thought I recognized a hill at Bar 8. We'd come a long way.

The sun had come out and, though the countryside was still obviously parched, moisture glistened on the coyote brush and scrub oaks covering the hillsides and made manzanitas stand out with their dark red and orange branches. And the recent precipitation had caused the earth to darken.

Instead of a washed out, predominantly tan landscape, colors stood out vibrantly. The previously dusty ground was a rich variety of browns, from dark chocolate to almost chestnut like Kitty or Beau, to the lightest buff where the soil was probably sandy. The greens of evergreen foliage seemed more varied too. And the smell! The air was sharp and tingly with aromas I couldn't name, but they all smelled green and exciting. The sky was still mostly gray clouds, but some of the edges were lined with gold, and the gaps between them were heart-breakingly blue.

I took my phone out of my coat pocket to take pictures and saw that Dave had texted me. I wrestled with whether to read and answer right away but didn't want to have to explain to anyone. I took a few pictures and put the phone back in my pocket.

On the walk back, I asked Isabel more about her home and her horses.

"It's flat in the valley where I live. Not like this. But it feels a lot further away from people, even though it's only three miles to town. Town's a lot smaller than yours though, nothin' more'n a small grocery store, a gas station, a few other buildin's. It's over thirty miles to get to a town the size of Douglas. Even longer from any real city." She was quiet for a moment, then said, decidedly, "I like it."

She told us of her horses. She had five of her own. Two were retired and she didn't ride them much. "I've had 'em since I was a girl, probably about yer age." She called them Salty and Jasper. " 'Course those er just their barn names."

She'd competed for years on Riley, a thoroughbred bay, but now used him mostly for students. Mandy, a chestnut warmblood mare, had begun eventing the previous spring. Fox was a "youngster" that she had just started over poles.

"Full of personality. And real purdy. He's still dark right now, just startin' to dapple. Should gray out real nice."

"Could you send me some pictures? I'd love to see them," I said. "I'd love to see your home, too."

"I'll try to remember to send 'em. You might have to write 'n remind me. Internet and mobile's real sketchy where we are, so emails and phone texts don't always go through. Write a real letter and I'll get it though."

The thought of staying in touch seemed to make her as happy as it did me. We didn't talk much the rest of the way back, but it was a comfortable quiet. Ben said he should probably go straight home. I took care of Remmy before getting away to my room.

'Hey,' said Dave's text. *'That was fun last night. ALL of it.'*

An enormous smile on my face, I responded, *'Yes!'*

I waited for a while but realized he probably couldn't text back right away. Then I realized I hadn't said anything for him to respond to. This was so weird. And wonderful. I wrote what I never would have dared to before, *'I can't wait to see you again.'*

A few minutes went by, then, *'I want to see you too but won't be home till late.'*

I almost texted back, *'Come over?'* but decided not to. I thought it would be too selfish. Much as I wanted to see him, he'd be tired. He still looked like he needed to catch up on sleep. Instead I wrote, *'That's okay.'*

He sent me a picture of a line of fencing with some cattle in the background. *'What I've been doing all day. What have you been up to?'*

I sent him the prettiest picture I'd taken from the top of the ridge. *'Went for a ride. Isabel and Ben walked with me.'* There. That was as upfront as I could be.

He texted back immediately, no trace of angst, *'Cool!'* I was glad. After another moment he said, *'Sorry g2g.'*

'I'll see you tomorrow.' A fact.

'Definitely!'

That had my heart skipping, and I couldn't help smiling the rest of the day. I didn't know what tomorrow would bring, and I admit to some nervousness. I wasn't nervous in a negative way about *him*, but very unsure what would happen with everyone else. But I was as ready as I could be.

Bring it on!

My world was so different Monday morning. Dark, of course, as it was still midwinter. Rain fell steadily. It wouldn't get very light today and was growing even colder, too.

But that wasn't the real difference. I felt accepted and excited and deliciously content. I felt loved, though Dave hadn't used that word and I didn't expect him to. I had no doubts about him, at least not at the moment—ab-

solutely none about how he would treat me. That knowledge, along with attendant feelings, was exquisite.

At first I wanted to look my best and couldn't decide what to wear. Then I decided not to worry about it. The last time Dave had seen me I was in soggy pajama pants and rubber boots. I doubted my apparel would make much difference now. Jeans, comfy shirt, a sweater, and my warm jacket. A little mascara and lip gloss. Since the weather had turned colder, I'd begun to wear my hair down again. I left my contacts at home, though. I'd just continue to use glasses at school for reading.

I couldn't help wondering how long it would take before everyone at school knew about us. But just thinking about the whole school knowing, or even only our class, made me anxious, so I tried not to think of it. Not that I really cared what anyone actually thought, exactly, but other people's opinions were things I didn't want to deal with, especially about this.

On the drive to school, Dave texted, 'Locker.'

That elicited a smile that Ben noticed. He certainly was the most observant of my friends—even when he got things *wrong*—and I thought I should probably take him into my confidence. But not right now. Not yet.

Since we had Spanish together first, Ben walked with me when we got to school.

I asked him something that had been bothering me. "Why did you change the color of your hair?"

He looked at me as if he was worried. "You don't like it? It's not really the right color. It's supposed to be darker."

"It's okay," I said, not meaning to make him feel bad. "I just liked the color it was before."

My locker stood open, and Dave was leaning against the neighboring one. "Hey," he said to Ben, but the soft smile was mine.

Ben's face lit up. "Hey!" he said. His face looked pink as he launched into a one-sided skateboard discussion about modifications he'd made to his trucks and deck.

I took my Spanish and Geometry books out and closed the door. Dave was listening to Ben but glanced at me, raising an eyebrow and tilting his head very subtly. He wondered if I had told him. I gave one very slow shake of my head.

"Maybe . . . maybe we could hang out and skate some time . . ."

"Yeah," said Dave, glancing at me again, then back to Ben. "Sure. You drive?"

"Uh, no," said Ben, looking crestfallen.

Dave looked at me again, then said, "Well, we can probably figure something out."

Ben beamed. "Great!"

"I'll see you later," Dave said.

"Yeah! Later!" said Ben.

I just smiled as Dave walked away.

"Wow. He's really great, isn't he?" said Ben.

I laughed. "I think you have a crush on him."

Ben went pink to the tips of his ears.

Oh.

"What are you talking about? I mean, I just think he's a good guy. You know?"

"Yes," I said thoughtfully. "I think he is too."

Was *Dave* the person he really liked? If so, I was even less sure how to tell Ben about us.

I wish I could say that was the only cloud over my day, but it was more of an omen. Real clouds covered the sky, gray and even more ominous, and sporadic rain drove us inside for lunch. I considered heading to the library—I was sure Dave would seek me out, and I longed to be alone with him—but I followed Robin, Jessie, and Tanner to the Ag. Science room after Geometry instead.

After winter break, the track team members usually trained during lunch, but not when it rained. Mr. Cooper's room was crowded and stuffy and very loud; all the chairs and most of the desktops and open floor were occupied. Mr. Cooper wasn't in the room, but a door connecting it to the next room stood open.

Dave and Tanner had been sitting in desk chairs, but they got up and offered them to Robin and me as we walked in. Then they nudged the boys off the desktops and took their places. I was surprised by it and happy, but I wondered if the gesture wasn't too focused under the circumstances.

Dave didn't talk specifically to me at all, giving his attention entirely to everyone else, but he was laughing and a little boisterous and seemed happier than I'd seen him at school for, well, *ever*. I felt deeply contented about

that, which, along with the activity and noisiness of the room, caused me to be even more quiet and reflective than usual around everyone. I suspected I might be glowing.

Whatever had been observed at the dance and so far today, by the end of PE I had no doubts that I was public enemy number one. Again. I had purposely kept my gaze to myself and those closest to me at lunch—Robin, Tanner, Hannah, and Dave—but it was impossible now to not be aware of evil sidelong stares and looks of downright contempt from many of the girls.

I already felt almost overwhelmed by the noise during lunch, but now I was jostled on the way out of the changing room and nearly tripped, which didn't help. Then we were playing volleyball in the gym. Sharp sounds of impact as the balls hit the floor, nerve-rending screeches from court shoes, and loud voices all echoing in the vast room wore me down even further. I almost wished I'd decided on the quietness of the library at lunch.

When I get completely overwhelmed, it truly feels like I've reached a threshold of some sort. A capacity. Especially for noise. Any added sound is magnified and feels like it's physically hitting me, sometimes like a blow and sometimes like ocean waves to my face and body. I feel pulled thin and completely vulnerable, like a rubber band ready to snap. Or break. I become less aware of my surroundings and incapable of distinguishing one sound from another, especially voices.

Track team members were in the weight room, and the rest of us were playing volleyball with mixed teams. Hannah was chosen as one of the team captains and chose me first—the first time in my life I'd *ever* not been in the last few selected for any team. But I didn't hear her call my name, which meant she had to repeat it, making sure *everyone* was looking at me until I realized she had called me.

Things went sharply downhill from there. Not only was I unaware of most of the calls during play, I felt more and more disoriented. *That* began to affect my balance and spatial awareness. I'm very aware of my tendency to be clumsy, but it's accentuated when I'm tired or overwhelmed by other things. I tried to keep my eyes on the ball but missed completely several times and fell twice. I was able to deflect the ball before it hit my face a couple of times but then knocked it out of court. There was plenty of muttering about that, some of which I heard *very* clearly. But mostly there was shaking of heads and rolling of eyes.

I was trying to just hold myself together.

"Are you okay, Anderson?" Coach asked after the shower bell rang.

I was picking myself off the floor for the third time. Her tone was gruff, but she looked ready to help if needed. Hannah and Melanie ran over to me, but I didn't want any help. The extra attention was the last thing I needed. I would have preferred to find a dark, quiet hole in the ground.

"I'm fine," I said. "I . . . just need to take my time . . ."

They all looked unsure, but Coach hustled the others out. My head throbbed, my ears rang loudly, and I felt even more brittle than before. For added effect, I was pretty sure I'd have bruises. But I'd make it through today. The sensory overload was something I'd dealt with all my life. There were no feelings involved this time. *They* were intact. I could often hold it together if my emotions weren't rubbed raw too. Just knowing Dave was somewhere close by, might even be thinking of me, and would definitely find a way to talk to me soon, gave me the impetus I needed to get moving.

I took my time, avoided the other girls, and showered and dressed slowly. The passing bell rang and everyone left. Hannah and Melanie both made sure I was okay, but I assured them I was. There was no class coming in as it was study hall, and the bell rang again. I sat in the quiet locker room, eyes closed, hugging my backpack, rocking slightly.

"Anderson," Coach barked, and I froze, extremely embarrassed. I hadn't meant to rock. I never did it in front of people or where anyone could possibly see me. Not anymore. But then she said, in a softer tone, "Allison." I don't think I'd ever heard her call anyone by their first name before. She frowned deeply and I thought she might be angry.

"Are you going to be all right? You're late for your next class."

Much as I hated being late, I wasn't too worried. It was only study hall, and all I cared about right now was making it through the day. I didn't know why I felt the way I did, but at least it was purely physical and sensory. I felt relatively calm inside, though now I was trembling.

"Do you want to go see the nurse?"

"No!" That wouldn't help me at all.

"Stay there a minute," said Coach. "I'll write you an excuse for your next class."

Mrs. Ochoa being one of my most lenient teachers, I didn't think I'd need one, but I was grateful to be able to sit still and quiet for a few moments more.

Coach returned with a pad of paper and a pen and began writing. "I know you had a rough time out there today, but you've improved this year. I see you really trying, and your fitness level is definitely better. Are you exercising at home?"

I smiled, glad that she had noticed and wasn't mad about my blunders today.

"I ride," I said. "Horses. A lot. And I walk more, sometimes even run. And just taking care of my horse is good exercise." I was afraid she might think I was bragging but thought, under the circumstances, it would be all right. "My trainers say I'm doing really well. Getting better all the time."

Coach gave me one of her rare smiles. "Good for you. Is everything else okay?"

I had no idea what "everything" referred to, so just said, "Yes."

"Well," she said, holding out a slip of paper, "just keep doing your best. Take it easy today. Okay?"

I nodded and left for study hall. I was already feeling more my usual self by the time I got there. Mrs. Ochoa simply smiled and took my note. I could tell Ben was curious, but I got my geometry out and was glad to have a relatively quiet time to myself.

The bell startled me awake. I had fallen asleep with my head on my arms over my geometry book. Disoriented and supremely embarrassed, I looked around quickly. Scornful looks from the girls in the back; a couple of them were in my PE class. I heard some of what they said, too: *weirdo, faker,* even *spaz.* I tried not to care but felt sick anyway. Ben came over and squatted next to me.

"Are you okay?" He looked genuinely concerned. "You've never done *that* before."

Feeling numb, I wanted to rub my eyes but remembered the mascara and decided it probably wasn't a good idea. "I'm fine. Just tired."

"Come on. I'll carry your backpack." And he did, which was sweet but unnecessary.

Mom was waiting in the parking lot, and I was relieved to sink into the seat of the car and close my eyes again. As he often seemed to do, Ben kept a conversation going with Mom until we dropped him off, and I felt much better by the time we got home.

That's when I thought of Dave. It wasn't that I hadn't *thought* of him—he hadn't been completely out of my thoughts all day except perhaps when I'd fallen asleep. But I hadn't thought of *him*. I'd only thought about how I felt about him and how happy I was. I got my phone out and found two texts.

'*Locker?*' and then, '*?*'

I texted back, '*Sorry. No locker.*' I was wondering if I should explain when the doorbell rang.

Mom and I were both in the kitchen, but I was sitting at the table so Mom answered the door.

"Dave!" she said, sounding happy to see him. My heart did a somersault. Then I had a stab of fear. I hoped he hadn't heard about PE.

I heard him say, "Hey," to Isabel in the living room then he followed Mom into the kitchen.

He smiled softly at me, no hint of concern. I was immensely relieved until he said, "Is Mr. Anderson here?" It was my stomach that somersaulted this time, but not for joy.

I tried to glare at him.

He looked back, his eyes twinkling.

Mischief.

Mom said, "No, he's out of town for a few days." I could tell she was trying to seem neutral, but she was clearly curious. "Did you need to talk to him?"

Dave hesitated for a few moments—purposely letting me squirm, I was sure—then said, "I wanted to get started on that fencing. You know, for Allison's arena. Would it be okay if I measure and stake it out?"

Mom's reaction was kind of weird. I couldn't tell if she was glad or disappointed that his purpose here was apparently business. "Oh . . . um . . . sure? Yes, I'm sure that would be fine. Would you like a sandwich first? Why don't you sit down?"

He smiled broadly and said, "Thanks," then proceeded to investigate the homework I was working on—Spanish.

Dave ate a sandwich and I let him "help" me conjugate verbs, though I was actually pretty good at it. When I was done with Spanish, we headed outside. Remmy often whickers softly when he sees me, but he whinnied loudly today when he saw us both.

"Hey buddy!" laughed Dave, immediately stepping through the paddock rails, embracing Remmy and patting him heartily. He ran his hand down

all four of his legs and checked him over carefully. "Looks like you're taking great care of him. Is he being good for you?"

"Yes!" I said, happily. "He's wonderful, of course. I'll be glad to have a real work area for him, though. And it'll be nice to have a bigger place to turn him out in."

Dave nodded and looked thoughtful. "You know, we could probably rig something up so that the stall runs lead straight into the arena. I'll think about it and work something up with Tom. Then we'll show it to your dad." His smile slid sideways and he said, "I take it you haven't told your parents?"

I put my chin up a little and said, "No," though I still kind of wanted to tell my mom.

"Well, I guess they'll figure it out when I'm hanging out here all the time."

Delighted at the prospect, I laughed and said, "I'll tell them if they ask, but . . ."

I didn't finish the thought as Isabel had come out. Not sure where I stood with her as far as disclosure went, or whether they had even been properly introduced, I said, "Dave, this is my Aunt Isabel." Then I realized that I hadn't really told him anything about her. It just hadn't come up. "She has a stables and farm in Colorado and has been staying with us . . ." Then I wasn't sure what to say again.

Isabel, pragmatic as always, jumped in and said, "I had a heart attack and then had surgery. My family don't trust me to take it easy at home, so they took me as far away as they could." She smiled slightly and held her hand out toward Dave. "That happens to be here. It's nice to meet ya." Dave shook hands with her vigorously, smiling widely, eyes laughing.

"It's nice to meet you, too," he said.

"So yer the one that gave Allison this pony."

"Uh, yeah." He looked sideways at me, as if for direction, but I had none to give.

"Well, he's a good 'un. Seems perfect fer her. Shame he doesn't have a buddy though. He probably gets lonely. Yer gonna treat'er right, aren't ya?"

Her abrupt leap to personal matters floored me, and I'm sure I turned scarlet. Dave's brows had risen slightly in surprise too, but a slow smile spread across his face.

"Yeah." He looked at me and said, "Always."

Somersaults doesn't begin to describe what was going on inside me now; more like a whole gymnastics routine. With streamers and fireworks. It had been too rough a day for this.

"Good man," said Isabel. "Well, I'll leave ya to it."

With that, she headed back to the house, leaving me to wonder what she was thinking, what "it" was, and especially wondering what Dave thought. I'd once thought that *his* family would be the end of me, but now I thought *mine* would, too.

"That was . . . interesting."

"I'm sorry," I said. "I didn't—"

"It's okay. I like her. I like it when people say what they think. Mostly." He smiled and really didn't seem to mind the charge Isabel had laid on him.

I was just happy having him here, being able to talk to him, knowing he liked me and, especially, that apparently he liked me as *more* than just a friend. That's all I could think of right now. I certainly wouldn't dream of holding him to more than that.

"I'm gonna go get the truck," he said, then walked away.

I gave Remmy a quick brush around his head and then bridled him, thinking about what Isabel had said about him being lonely. I hadn't really considered it before and felt bad. When the truck appeared, I was riding him around the arena area.

Dave smiled widely. "Look at you all bareback."

I smiled happily at the note of pride I thought I heard in his voice. "I've been practicing. Just around here."

"Hnh. We need to go for a ride together."

That idea thrilled me even more. "Yes!"

He walked toward me saying, "We could ride together right now."

"What? How? Oh!" I said, as his meaning sank in. My cheeks felt warm just imagining that. "Um . . ." I loved the idea, but the thought that Mom might see us from the kitchen window tempered what would have been enthusiasm.

Dave looked over his shoulder toward the house. "Oh. Yeah. I guess not. Not . . . yet."

I loved it when the things he said held promise. I smiled widely back, incredibly happy.

Remmy and I followed Dave around as he paced out a rough arena area, staking the four corners. Then we helped him measure by holding the end of the tape, using our sidestepping skills to find the right alignment.

He nodded. "Very impressive." I couldn't tell if he was serious, but it didn't really matter. When we were done, he said, "This is the rough area. Now we'll have to wait for Tom to survey it."

I led Remmy back into his stall and took his bridle off. Dave walked around the other way, through the back door of the stall, then caught my hand and pulled me toward him.

My poor heart.

"Practice session?" I said, almost a whisper, his face close to mine.

"Yeah."

And he kissed me. I thought he was getting pretty good at it. I hoped I was too. This made up for everything rotten about today.

He let me go when we heard the kitchen door. By the time Mom got to the stall, Dave was innocently picking out Remmy's feet.

"Would you like to stay for dinner, Dave? We've got plenty."

"Oh, thanks, Mrs. Anderson, but I've got chores to do. Better get home."

"Oh," she said, but I still couldn't tell how she felt.

Dave walked off, and I heard the truck start up and leave.

"That was nice having him over, wasn't it? Did he get done what he wanted to?"

I could feel a blush threatening but tried to appear stoic. "Yes, I think so."

"Do you think we might be seeing more of him now?"

"Yes," I said firmly. "Yes, we will."

Chapter Twenty-Eight

On Tuesday morning, it occurred to me that I might not see Dave at all until English, but there was no angst attached to the realization. I knew I'd see him. And I knew he cared. He *liked* me. No amount of harsh glances or verbal slurs from others could diminish that. The main reason I cared at all for the opinions of others right now was for his sake. I thought it was a good thing to keep our relationship to ourselves. Who knows what everyone would say, think, or do if they found out. If not *used* to the harsh judgments, I was at least familiar with them. I couldn't imagine Dave had ever had to suffer the kind of humiliation I had over the years. I'd rather die than be the cause of that for him.

Morning classes passed uneventfully enough. Matthew seemed a bit more distant than he'd been lately, but that was actually a relief—less to worry about and less I had to act like everything was the same as before the dance. Because it wasn't.

I met Melanie for lunch.

"Are you doing better today?" she said gently. "You seemed a little out of it yesterday."

I realized I'd barely spoken to her the day before and had already almost forgotten how stressful the day had been.

"Oh . . . yes! Much better. I guess I was just tired." Not exactly the truth but as close as I could get considering *I* didn't even understand. "Oh! I need to give your dress back."

"Don't worry about it. There's no rush. I won't be using it." She smiled and we ate in silence for a while. Finally, she said, "It looks like Dave is warming up to you again." I must have looked startled as she clarified, "At the dance. I saw him with you quite a bit. You both looked happy."

I searched her face wondering exactly how much she was aware of. "Was it very obvious?"

She tipped her head slightly. "Judging by the behavior of certain other people yesterday, I'd say I wasn't the only one who noticed." She was quiet for a moment, then said, "I hope you won't let them affect how you feel. You should like who you want to like. It's none of their business."

This was oddly similar to what Isabel had said, and I started to wonder if *"Doesn't know her own mind"* was visible across my forehead, like the moving LCD notices at the front of the school. I was grateful for the added encouragement though.

"I won't," I said. Then I added, "They can't."

She raised her brows and I smiled, feeling slightly embarrassed but extremely happy. No one sat nearby, but she lowered her voice even more anyway. "You're going out with him?"

I felt color rising to my cheeks and nodded. "But . . ." I said, then wasn't sure how to finish.

"You're keeping it quiet?" Melanie didn't look surprised or perturbed.

I nodded again. She nodded too, and I was so glad she knew. *One less person to be careful around.*

I wondered if Dave would return to his original seat at the back of the classroom in English. I wouldn't have blamed him if he did. I wouldn't even have minded—it was going to be even more difficult to concentrate now with him in the room.

But he didn't. And he didn't ignore me either. I got there before him and he came in with a crowd—Hannah, Kyle, Roberta, and others—but he smiled when he saw me and came to sit in front of me, as he had lately. I tried not to smile too widely in response or look too pleased, but I have no idea how successful I was.

We walked out together with Hannah and Kyle—they were talking and laughing, and I was swept along with them, just happy to feel so restored. Since our next classes were all out in the back portables, we walked together.

Dave bumped against me, purposely, before heading off with Kyle. I floated the rest of the way to Art.

Melanie took one look at me and raised her brows again, smiling. "It looks like you're having a *much* better day than yesterday."

I smiled and nodded. Indeed I was.

I half expected Dave to meet me after school, but he texted instead.

'Choir?'

'Yes.'

'I'm working. Can I come over later?'

'Yes!'

I was barely aware of anything else for the rest of the afternoon but the expectation of seeing him later. Mom, Isabel, and I were sitting down to dinner when the doorbell rang. Mom answered it.

"Oh . . . Dave! Come in," she said.

"Sorry, I didn't mean to interrupt your dinner," he said, not looking sorry at all.

"Have you eaten? We've got plenty if you'd like to join us," said Mom, though she sounded uncertain, as if not sure whether inviting him was okay with me.

"Uh . . . no. I mean, I haven't eaten. Thanks," he said, and came to sit next to me, across from Isabel.

Mom went out to the kitchen and brought an extra plate and silverware. *If she had any doubts, she probably doesn't now.* Isabel was already eating, but I thought she looked pleased.

"Tom was wondering if Mr. Anderson would be back by Friday. He said he could come over in the afternoon to make sure I staked out the arena right, and we could maybe start leveling on Saturday if it doesn't rain." He glanced at me.

"Greg should be home on Thursday," said Mom. "I'm sure it would be fine."

I caught Dave's glance at me, mischief in his eyes, and I thought I knew what he was thinking—*one more day without my dad around.* I tried to smother a smile and concentrated on my spaghetti.

Dave talked comfortably with Mom and Isabel throughout dinner, several times trying to pull me into the conversation. But I was happy just *being*.

Dave. Having dinner. Being here just for me.

I was in heaven.

We started to help clear the table, but Isabel insisted she'd help Mom and shooed us away. Once they were both in the kitchen, Dave and I slipped out the front door. It was dark and a light rain was falling.

"Oh! I forgot something! I'll be right back, okay?"

Dave looked amused and nodded. I went back into the house and up to my room. Back outside, I gave him the gift I'd gotten him.

He grinned and held it up slightly. "Christmas wrapping."

"Yes. It was supposed to be for Christmas." I sat on the top step near him.

He moved closer and opened the gift slowly. I'd gotten him a black T-shirt with a silver Chevy logo on the front.

He laughed. "Perfect! This is great!" He took his jacket off and slipped the T-shirt over the thermal he was already wearing. I was relieved that it seemed to be the right size. Then a little more seriously, he said, "Thank you. But I didn't get you anything."

"You took me to Winter Formal! It was a wonderful gift!"

He smiled and took my hand in his. After a moment he said, "So, after tomorrow your Dad's home. It might be more . . . awkward . . . to hang out like this."

I thought he was probably right, but I wasn't unhappy about it. "I don't care," I said. Not petulant, honest. "He'll have to get used to it."

Dave was quiet, then said, "I agree with you, but I don't want to be a problem. I don't want to, you know . . . push your dad too far."

I had no idea what he meant. "Push him? How are you pushing him? He doesn't get to decide who I like or who I want to spend time with." Now I was shaking a little—both from nerves and cold.

Dave took his jacket off again and put it around my shoulders, effectively wrapping me in his warmth.

"Don't worry," he said. "Nothing's gonna stop me from being with you. *Nothing.* Okay? But I don't want any kind of trouble with your family. I want your dad to trust me, even if he doesn't *like* me."

I felt indignant. I wanted to say that I didn't care if my dad liked him or trusted him, but I couldn't. It wasn't true. I realized that I very much wanted my dad to both trust *and* like Dave. To accept him, even as Dave's family accepted me. Isabel certainly seemed to approve, and I was pretty sure Mom was more than halfway there in spite of recent reserve.

Reluctantly, I nodded again. "Okay."

He gently bumped shoulders with me a couple of times. "I should probably go. Hey, what if I come over early tomorrow and we take Remmy out for a while?" His head close to mine, he added, "We can explore."

This sounded highly enjoyable, whatever he meant by "explore," and my heart thumped a little harder. *That* would be something to look forward to. Then I remembered: Northfield.

I needed to tell him about it sooner or later, but I dreaded his reaction. He'd disapprove; he'd made it clear that he didn't want me going there. And I wasn't sure how I'd react to *his* reaction. Would I cave? I hated conflict, and I certainly didn't want to have a fight. I couldn't bear the thought of doing anything that would come between us—not after everything. But I'd fought too hard to gain my independence from him—even if he hadn't been actively involved. I didn't want to give up Melanie, Kitty, and my new-found interest.

"Um . . . I can't . . . tomorrow. I hang out with my friend Melanie on Wednesdays."

"Hnh," he said. "Okay. Choir on Tuesdays and Thursdays. Melanie on Wednesdays. Right?" I nodded, glad he didn't ask what we were doing. "You're very busy all of a sudden. Anything else I should know about? You know, so I can scheme around it?"

It was too dark to see his face clearly, and I *almost* wished the porch light was on, but his voice was soft. He sounded more amused than anything else. I considered teasing him that my new activity level was his own fault. But his positive attitude and my intrigue at the word *scheme* tempered the impulse. Besides, this was one of those situations where I wasn't sure how it would sound.

Then I remembered something else. "Babysitting," I said. "For Cheryl. Usually a couple of times a month. And lessons with her. It's usually on Saturdays."

"I think I'll like babysitting. I can be very . . . helpful."

That made me smile.

"I'm gonna go," he said softly, leaning his head closer to mine. "But I'll see you tomorrow."

I turned toward him and he kissed me, as I'd hoped he would. For those moments, I felt wholly wrapped in him. His fragrance was just *him* again—plain soap, wide open spaces, and sunshine, even on this dark night—which

made me even happier. I felt his lips tighten against mine in a smile, and he kissed me lightly once more before standing up and walking away.

"Wait!" I said. He stopped abruptly, turning back. "Your jacket!"

I stood and held it out to him. He took two steps toward me, took the jacket, then walked backward in the drizzle. He was still smiling. My heart overflowed.

Wednesday I got slammed. Literally. I'd managed to stay reasonably focused in my early classes, though my thoughts were dominated by my source of happiness. It was raining, so at lunch I went with Robin to the Ag Science room with similar results to Monday. I'd picked up on what felt like simmering aggression all morning. It reminded me of the way static electricity feels—a force I didn't want to push back against. By the time I got to PE, I felt it even more, my nerves instead of my hair straining out in all directions.

Before going out to the gym, I used the restroom. Someone—I think some*ones*—must have been looking for the opportunity and followed me. As I released the stall lock to exit, the door was slammed back in on me, hard, straight into the right side of my face and nose. I fell backward, almost into the still flushing toilet. There was a brief snorting laugh and the sound of running feet.

I steadied myself, shaking violently and trying not to whimper. Feeling light-headed, I cautiously opened the door again. There was no one there.

My nose was bleeding slightly, and the mirror confirmed a long red welt, darkening even as I watched. It started between my eyebrows and continued across my cheek. My nose hurt so severely it added tears to those already standing in my eyes from the shock. All I wanted was to sit down somewhere quiet. Alone.

It was Hannah that found me a few minutes later. "Coach was wondering where—" She stopped when she saw my face. "What *happened?*" she cried.

"The door," I said without thinking. "It hit my face."

"What door?" Hannah frowned. "How?"

I couldn't, *wouldn't* tell her the truth, so I said the only thing I thought made sense. "I fell." Everyone had witnessed my clumsiness. I doubted anyone would be suspicious.

Though I tried to extricate myself, Hannah insisted on steering me toward Coach, who took one look at me and told Hannah, "Help her get some ice on that."

I knew we were being watched. It made me angry and anxious. And sad. Why couldn't they just leave me alone? A new worry struck me. What would Dave do? He was probably in the weight room.

"Don't tell Dave," I said as Hannah guided me back into the changing room. I still wasn't sure if she knew about us, but if I didn't ask her not to tell, I was sure she would.

She didn't say anything, and it occurred to me there were others out there who might tell him. But I couldn't do anything about that.

Hannah got an ice pack from Coach's freezer for me to hold across my face, but it just hurt worse. She wanted to stay with me, but I thanked her profusely and insisted I'd like to be alone. Coach came in soon after, looking closely at my face—especially my nose, which was still bleeding—and wanting to "get to the bottom of this."

"I just fell," I repeated.

"How? Against what?" she asked.

I didn't know what else to say and had started shaking again.

"Are you being bullied?"

I desperately wanted to be tough and brave and stronger than the girls who hated me, but I'd reached my limit. Completely overwhelmed, I dissolved into tears.

Coach rubbed my back. I knew she meant well, but it exacerbated my already straining senses. When I was a little calmer, she said, "Who did this to you?"

Still shaking, I shook my head. "I fell," I insisted.

This was awful. And I was *still* thinking more about Dave than what had actually happened to me. He mustn't know. And I certainly didn't want him to see me like this. I needed to get a grip.

"I don't think your nose is broken, but you'd better go to the nurse's office," said Coach.

I wanted to object—the nurse's office was figuratively one step away from the principal's and counselor's offices, as far as places I *didn't* want to be—but I didn't want to wait here for the girls to return, either.

"Please . . . can I just go early to study hall?"

"No. I'll send someone with you, though. Hannah?"

I didn't want anyone to go with me. The bigger the fuss, the more people involved, the worse it would be. But Coach looked resolute.

"Can Melanie go with me?" Hannah was nice, but too close to Dave.

"All right. Get your things. You can change at the nurse's office. But I'm going to be watching, Allison. Don't you dare let anyone get away with hurting you. Do you understand?"

I nodded but was thinking of what had happened between Dave—and Cris—and the Northfield boys. There was no way I could let him find out and get in trouble again. I already felt sick with dread, both at the necessary lie and the thought of what Dave would do if he found out. I was convinced from past experience that he'd react badly. And I'd be no less of a target.

Melanie walked with me and asked a few questions that I refused to answer. I just shook my head to everything she said and held tissues to my nose. We walked slowly to the office, and she left me there to be inspected and questioned some more. I repeated the lie, feeling worse and worse about it and starting to get a headache. The nurse declared there was no lasting damage done, gave me a fresh ice pack, and insisted I lay down. I just as firmly insisted I was fine, wanted to change my clothes, and asked to go to my study hall class early. She agreed to give me a pass five minutes before the passing bell if I'd lay down until then.

I stopped at my locker so I wouldn't have to after school. The halls were quiet and the classroom empty when I got there. I sat at my desk and put my head down, glad of the respite. When Mrs. Ochoa came in and asked what had happened, as I assumed she would, I gave her the note from the nurse and repeated that I'd fallen.

The unfriendly elements in the class were strangely subdued as they entered the room. Ben blurted, "What happened to your *face?*" as soon as he saw me, then seemed to immediately regret it. I didn't say anything and felt like sinking into the floor.

Worried Dave might have heard all about it and dreading having to explain anything to him, I left as quickly as I could when the bell rang, going straight to where Roger's car was parked. He got there before Melanie and let me into the back seat.

"What happened?" he asked, looking at me in the rearview mirror.

I told him the lie. It wasn't getting any easier. He frowned and turned all the way around to look at me properly.

Melanie appeared, obviously rushing from her last class. As she got in, she looked at me and said, "Are you all right?"

I nodded but didn't want to meet her eyes.

Uncharacteristically, she persisted. "What really happened?"

"Nothing," I said. "I'm okay."

I could tell she wasn't buying it. She said, "Coach made the girls stop early and gave us a locker room lecture on bullying. Please tell me what *really* happened."

Roger was frowning and glancing at me in the rearview again as he drove.

She'd *lectured* them? I very much doubted it would diminish the target on my back, and it was probably all over the school by now. I felt nauseated at the thought of everyone talking about it, and that made me relive it. Every time someone asked me what happened, I physically felt the blow again. My heart beat faster. I felt dizzy and shook. I wanted to curl up in a ball or rock to ease the pressure, to focus on the movement and try to get my mind and body back in sync. But I wouldn't. Not around others. I jiggled my foot so the others couldn't see. It helped a little.

The lie was repeated to Tatiana. She suggested I take my time changing and maybe sit in the office for a little while, which I did. When the shaking had ceased and I felt more in control, I still had time to groom Kitty. Brushing her soon had me feeling more normal, and it occurred to me how many people were concerned about me; how many seemed to really care.

It was annoying to process that in hindsight, but it also made me feel better. Not so long ago, Brenda was the only one who cared enough to stand by me and, when pushed, intervene.

Unfortunately, knowing people cared didn't change my situation or the way I physically or emotionally felt at that moment, but I clung to the knowledge. I wasn't alone. But right now was about horses and riding, even if I was still a little shaky and my face hurt.

I took my time getting Kitty ready. Lately, she had become much more attentive to me and less fussy. She seemed to enjoy me grooming her and talking to her, and I felt much more confident around her both in and out of the saddle. When she was ready, I led her out to where the younger girls were having their lesson.

Melanie approached with a piece of paper in her hand. "I had planned to have you working over higher *cavaletti*, but I think maybe we should take it easy today. You know all those circles you've done?" She handed the paper to me. I stared at it, uncomprehending for a few moments. Then the letters and directions made sense.

"A dressage test!"

"It's an old pre-test. We'll work in the covered court near the show arena since it's raining." I knew where she meant. "Study the test and the markers. If you feel up to it, you could try walking the test. Just follow the directions on foot."

She smiled and left me to it, and I did as she said. The test was just walk, trot, and halt. At first I felt silly walking—sometimes pretending to trot—the course, but it really helped me visualize and understand what I would be doing on horseback.

Later Melanie brought Kitty over and read the test aloud as I rode through the movements. She didn't say much else the first time through; she let me stop and start and falter and retry until the final halt. She showed me how to do the salute properly, then let me rest as she gave me feedback on my ride. Then we did it again. And again. She was more critical now, but I was ready for it. By the time we stopped, I was tired but flushed with a sense of accomplishment, in spite of my headache. I dismounted, ran the stirrups up, and loosened Kitty's girth.

"There's a dressage show this weekend," said Melanie as we walked back toward the barns. "I thought, if you wanted to come out and ride Kitty, you'd be interested in watching a little."

"Yes!" I said. "My dad will be home on Friday. I'll ask."

We hadn't quite worked out the logistics of my leasing Kitty or getting me out to Northfield more often, but I hadn't had much opportunity to even think about it. I realized Dad and I might be talking about *other* things, too, but I didn't want to think about that now.

When my mother came to pick me up, she took one look at me and cried out, "Allison! What happened? Your face!"

Immediate anxiety attack. I felt the force of the blow again and began shaking. I'd almost forgotten about it. Almost. I didn't want to explain, to lie, in front of anyone else and waited until we were in the car. On the drive home, when Mom's questions were exhausted and so was I, it occurred to me to check my phone. A call from Robin and three texts from Dave.

The first had been right after school. *'Are you okay?'*

Darn. He must have heard something.

Then, *'Can I come over?'* Mixed feelings about that. I wanted to see *him*, but I didn't want him to see *me*.

Lastly, about an hour ago, *'Where are you?'*

This one I answered with, *'Going home now.'*

Almost immediately, he replied, *'Can you talk?'*

'Not yet.'

'Call me when you can.'

My anxiety was almost overwhelming again, and Mom looked very interested in who I was texting. It was nice to know that Dave was concerned. I just wished it wasn't about something like this. I didn't want to talk to him right now either, but if I didn't call him, he was likely to turn up on my doorstep. Which both added to my anxiety and made me ridiculously happy.

When we got home, I went straight out to feed Remmy. I brushed him and talked to him while he ate, and some measure of calm returned. Then I went upstairs to examine the damage to my face in the bathroom mirror. An angry-looking red welt started from above my eyebrow and made my cheek look inflamed. My nose was very sore, too. I sighed. There would probably be bruising by tomorrow. It seemed like I'd had bruises somewhere on my body all my life, but they were usually the result of my own inattention or miscalculations. And I'd been tripped and pushed and hit with projectiles, but I'd never been purposely struck in the face. I wondered if that had really been their intention or if they'd just meant to scare me. I guessed it didn't matter; the result was the same.

I changed my clothes and called Dave.

"You fell?" was the first thing he said.

"Yes."

"You didn't have any *help* falling?"

I didn't want to talk about it anymore and told him so.

He was quiet then, but I could practically hear him thinking. Finally he said, "I want to see you."

"Um . . . I'm *really* tired. And I have a headache. I think—" How could I tell Dave I didn't want him to come over when I was scared of discouraging him and wanted to see him so badly?

There was a long silence. He finally said, "I guess I'll see you tomorrow."

"Yes," I said, hoping he wasn't offended.

I startled awake several times that night—heart racing, stomach painfully tense, every sense straining—reliving the impact of the bathroom stall door hitting my face and then falling, almost into the toilet. Each time it took me longer to fall back to sleep, my mind launching into suppositions of possible causes and projections of probable outcomes. None of them made me feel any better, and none of them changed my resolve to keep Dave as unaffected as possible.

When my alarm went off, my stomach involuntarily tensed again; this time a slower, creepy feeling I was all too familiar with—massive dread.

I was extremely conscious all day of the darkening line across my face. I had tried to minimize it—and hopefully any comments on it—by wearing makeup and my black-rimmed glasses. They at least partially covered it, but I still felt watched and whispered about. I tried to ignore it but couldn't.

Dave met me at my locker and studied my face intently, tight-lipped. But, "Accident, huh?" was all he said. I was glad. I didn't see him again until English and, although he sat mostly sideways, as he usually did, he paid no more attention to me than to anyone else.

At the end of class, he got up quickly to talk to Kyle, and I slipped away. But he sent me a text before I got to Art.

'I'm coming over later.'

That made me smile. I thought I could look forward to the rest of the day, but an office aid came during Art. He gave Miss Laski a note and left again, but not before giving me a sidelong look that made my stomach clench hard like it had that morning.

It was the same boy that had brought a note for me at the beginning of the year. I'd also seen him training with Cris in the gym and now recognized him as one of the boys I'd seen Matthew with at Northfield. He must be on a swim team there with him since swim season hadn't started yet at school. He made me feel nervous but I didn't know why.

Miss Laski came over and said, quietly, "Allison, Ms. Woolton would like to see you right now."

My stomach tightened more and began to writhe. My counselor had said she wanted to see me again, but I had assumed she'd give me more notice. I left my things and walked to the office.

"Allison," said Ms. Woolton warmly. "Please come in."

I entered her office and sat down.

She went to the door and called to the boy who'd brought the summons. "Please take this to Mr. Payne." She gave him a note. He gave me another sidelong look before leaving. I thought it strange that he kept looking at me like that and immediately began thinking of all the reasons it could be. *Is it the mark on my face? Does it have something to do with that time in the gym? Does he just do it to everyone?*

Ms. Woolton closed the door and sat across from me, smiling.

"How is your year going so far?" she asked lightly.

This had such a complicated answer, I didn't know where to start. I still doubted she'd be satisfied with the socially standard "Fine," but I didn't know what specific aspect of the year she was asking about.

"Fine."

She didn't respond right away. I could tell she was staring at my face even though I wasn't looking directly at her.

"Are you happy in your classes?"

"Yes."

She examined the papers in the folder open in front of her. "You've received good grades so far this year, so it looks like you're doing well academically. Your elective teachers, especially, are very pleased with your work. As is Miss Sanders. And I see you're taking an extra period choir class. How do you like it?"

I thought about how reluctant I'd been at first, and how much I now looked forward to Choir. "I like it. A lot," I said, still not sure what else to say.

"You're earning extra credit with it too. That's always good, right?"

I hadn't even thought of that, but I supposed it was.

"And friends?" she prompted. I had a feeling this was much more the reason I was here. "Do you have friends in your classes?"

I thought specifically of each class I had and realized I did. Most of my classes included Robin, Melanie, or Ben, my closest friends. Dave was in

English, as well as Hannah and Kyle. Matthew was in Chemistry. Paola was also in choir. That was a lot of people. "Yes!" I said, and smiled for the first time at her. "*All* my classes."

"That's wonderful," she said. She became quiet and looked very serious before saying, "Allison, there's still concern from some of your teachers. They suspect you're being picked on. Bullied. Your accident yesterday . . . could you explain to me how it happened?"

"I . . . I was in the restroom, in the gym, and I tripped. The door hit my face."

"Which door?"

"The stall door."

"And you were going in, or coming out?"

I was no good at this. I'd always been amazed, in a very uncomfortable way, how easily some people made things up. For me, it only got harder and harder to lie.

"Allison?"

I tried not to show how much I was squirming inside, but my hands were fists in my lap, and my stomach felt like a similar shape. "Coming out."

She was quiet for another few moments. I didn't want to look at her face, even though she was looking down at the papers in front of her.

"Okay," she finally said. She was smiling, but I felt like I'd disappointed her somehow. "I just wanted to check in with you. But I'd like to have a conversation with at least one of your parents. We'll try to set something up for next week."

I didn't know what to make of that. "Am I in trouble?"

"No, no, not at all. You have nothing to worry about, Allison. But if any-body . . . *anybody* . . . is bullying you, in *any* way, I want you to tell an adult; a parent, a teacher, or me. Someone you trust. Will you promise me that?"

Promising something I wasn't sure I could do just felt like more lying, so I didn't answer. She smiled again and said I could go back to my class.

I was horribly distracted for the rest of the day.

"Something's wrong," said Dave. He'd come over after school, as he'd said he would.

"What?"

"You tell me."

I didn't know how to explain my nebulous fears about the projected meeting between Ms. Woolton and my parents. And along with those fears was guilt that a meeting was even necessary, as if I'd done something wrong. Secondary to that were other nagging but more familiar fears surrounding everything else to do with school; people in general and unknown assailants in particular. How could I explain *any* of that, especially to Dave? In spite of his obvious concern and protective nature, I hated the helpless feeling I sometimes had. I couldn't control other people's actions or thoughts toward me. I often barely understood my own. Even more, I hated the thought of him thinking me weak or pathetic in any way. It wasn't the way I wanted to be perceived, even if it was true.

"Sorry," I said. "I just have a lot on my mind."

"Hnh," he said. "Like what?"

I tried to think of viable yet innocuous thought-filling things. "My dad's coming home tomorrow. And Aunt Isabel's leaving on Monday. And I've been thinking about what classes I should enter Remmy in at the Bar 8 schooling show." This was partially true; the show was next weekend. But in remembering all these things, I began to feel even more overwhelmed than I already did. I didn't need more to think about!

He watched me closely for a moment, not looking at all convinced. "I've been thinking. I don't want to keep pretending we're not, you know, together. It's too difficult. Maybe it'll be better," his eyes searched mine and I tried not to avoid them, "better for *you* if everyone knows. Even Cris thinks so."

I needed to think that through. I'd come to have a healthy regard for Cris' opinions, but I wasn't at all convinced it was best for either of us. But guessing how other people would react or what they would think had always been problematic for me, often failing both my logic and my emotions. I just didn't seem to think or feel the same way about some things as others did.

I responded with a question. "Remember last year when you said I might not see you much? It was the day you and Cris brought hay over for Gold."

He looked uncertain.

"You told me not to worry about it, but I didn't know why you'd said it, so it was kind of hard not to."

He frowned and nodded slightly.

"Was it just because of soccer? Things keeping you busy? Or was there another reason?"

He was still frowning. "I guess we were practicing a lot. You know. Plus games."

"It was right after Labor Day . . . after the play day. And people . . . *some* people . . . seemed to really hate me after that."

At the time, it had seemed like both he and Cris were purposely distancing themselves from me. Whether for their own sakes or for mine hadn't been clear. But I hoped he'd remember what led up to it. From the look on his face, he did.

He picked up my hand and appeared to examine my fingers, still frowning. I was embarrassed that there was dirt under my nails from Remmy, but I didn't want to pull away. His fingers felt nice on mine.

I was sure that letting the school at large know our relationship status wouldn't improve anyone's opinion of me or cause them to leave me alone. High school, against all my hopes, seemed to be continuing much like elementary and middle school in that regard. But Dave didn't have to be subjected to it too. I was convinced the general knowledge of our, for want of a better word, *dating*, could only damage Dave's quality of life—at least at school. He was such a social person, it was the last thing I wanted to do. I dreaded people knowing—for *both* our sakes.

"I'd rather not tell them," I said. "I think it's easier this way. Please?"

I could tell he wasn't happy about it, but he nodded. Then he drew me behind Remmy's stall, holding me quietly for a while, and then kissed me. In those moments I was sure everything would be all right. But my sleep was disturbed for over a week by violent dreams that woke me, each time my heart throbbing, my stomach a hard knot.

I muddled through Friday, keeping my head down, literally, until school was over. I was happy that Dad was home. Mom fixed a special dinner and there was a lot to talk about during it. Dad told us about his trip, but I was barely listening, too busy rehearsing all the things I wanted, *needed*, to say.

The conversation turned to Isabel, and she talked at length about everything her manager had been relaying to her since Dad had been gone.

"You must be very anxious to get home," said Mom.

Isabel appeared to give this some thought, then said, "No, I'm not anxious 'bout anythin'. Joe's a good man 'n knows what he's doin'. I'll be glad t' get home, though." She seemed to think again and added, "Not that it hasn't been real nice stayin' with ya. And especially gettin' t' know my niece."

She looked at me and surprised me with one of her rare smiles. A second surprise was the strength of my reaction—a warm glow and stab of regret. I was going to miss her.

"Y'all have an open invitation t' come out 'n visit if ya can. I got plenty of room. Can always use more help with chores." She gave a bark of laughter, then concentrated on her dinner again.

Dad looked at me and said, "What have you—" He looked more intently at my face and frowned. "Is that a black eye?"

I adjusted my unnecessary glasses and squirmed.

"I . . . fell."

"Riding?" Dad looked intently at me.

"No. At school." Now I was thinking again of the incident and the upcoming meeting with Ms. Woolton, and my stomach was tying in knots. Not conducive to having the conversation I wanted to have. I pressed on. "But I'm learning a dressage test. Melanie says I'm doing really well and wants me to show soon. So does Tatty." Everyone said encouraging things. "There's a show . . . this weekend . . . at Northfield. I'm not ready to ride in it, but Melanie said I might want to go and watch. And I can ride Kitty. And I do. Want to go, that is."

Dad nodded his head. It looked like *that* wasn't going to be a problem.

"I'd like to go tomorrow if that's all right."

More nodding.

"I wouldn't mind a round of golf," said Dad. "I can take you. I'll call James and see if he wants to join me."

"I'd like to go," said Isabel, and Mom and Dad both looked surprised. She stared blankly at them for a moment then gave another explosive laugh. "T' the show," she clarified. "With Allison."

Dad looked to me, I guess to see my reaction, but I was already smiling.

"Well, let's all go," said Mom. "I wouldn't mind a day out somewhere. I might go into Lowell for a while."

Plans for the different aspects of tomorrow's activities were discussed, mostly by Mom and Dad, but my anxiety grew. I still hadn't broached the subject I was determined to.

Mom said, "Don't forget, Tom is coming over in the morning to start on the arena. We'd better wait until you've had a chance to speak to him."

That was my opportunity. "And Dave," I said, my heart beating fast. Dad looked confused.

"Dave is coming over too. He works with Tom. Remember?" I wasn't sure if it was important that Dave actually had a paying job on top of everything else we knew he did, but it couldn't hurt to remind Dad of his responsible character. "And I wanted to tell you . . ." I took a deep breath and announced, "I'm Dave's girlfriend."

It came out sounding even weirder than I'd thought it would, and it occurred to me it might have been better to say *he* was my *boyfriend*. But that sounded so possessive in my head. He wasn't *mine*.

These thoughts, along with many tangential ideas, raced through my mind as I processed the expressions around the table. Dad looked—I'm not sure. I guess *surprised* covered it, though what his underlying emotion was I could only imagine. He stopped in mid-chew for a moment, then looked at his plate as he continued to eat. Mom looked surprised, too, though it was harder to understand why. Surely she'd guessed by now.

They exchanged glances and seemed to be holding first opinions in check. That was probably a good thing. I was hoping this could be accomplished without adding too much more to my current anxiety level.

Isabel didn't look surprised one bit and helped herself to more mashed potatoes.

"Well," said Mom, "I expect we'll be seeing more of him again. That's nice."

She smiled at me and got up to go to the kitchen, but she squeezed Dad's shoulder as she passed him.

A little while later, I got a text from Dave. *'I'll see you in the morning.'*

'Yes!' I responded.

I went to bed with a completely clear conscience and only woke up once from a nightmare: practice-driving with Dad and somehow getting hit in the face with a stop sign.

The meeting between Tom and Dad was uneventful. Tom beamed at me when he arrived, and I assumed Dave had told him about us. I probably blushed, but I was so happy that he was pleased and hoped Cheryl would feel the same way. I had reason to suspect she would.

Dave and I followed them around and listened, I think both of us consciously on best behavior. Tom had drawn out the plans for the arena with a section connecting to permanent stall runs, making sure that Dave got the credit for the design. Dad said it was a great idea and actually smiled at Dave. I saw that as progress.

As the two men moved away, now discussing materials for both footing and fences, Dave said, "Are you going to hang out today?"

I'd been expecting that and was getting ready to tell him the truth about Northfield, but I still didn't want to unless asked a direct question. Things seemed so perfect right now—I didn't want to do anything to change it.

"I'm going to go watch a horse show with Isabel. We'll be home later. I'll be home all day tomorrow though."

He didn't seem disappointed and I was glad. "Okay. I'll take Remmy down to the old corral while we're digging. We'll move the pipe paddock nearby, but you'll have to move him in and out. It shouldn't be for too long if the rain holds off."

I nodded.

He reached for my fingers right in front of Tom and my dad. "See you later." His mischievous smile set me up to have a great day.

Mom drove us all to Northfield, and Melanie and Tatty met us there. There was a short discussion about the terms of Kitty's lease, already drawn up by Tatty, and making me an official member of the Northfield Equestrian Center, which meant I could come and go and ride whenever and wherever I wanted—within the Center's rules, of course.

I felt elated but wondered if this new status would somehow be evident to others. I had a brief flash of a newspaper article announcing, "Allison Anderson newest member of Northfield," accompanied by a deer-in-the-headlights photo of me. That was silly, of course, but it diminished the elation a bit.

Mom said she'd find us later and drove Dad to the golf club to meet up with Dr. James. Melanie left to help some of her other students who were showing. Isabel made friends with other horses as I groomed and saddled Kitty, then observed and commented as I warmed her up in one of the barn paddocks.

The weather was gray and drizzly, but it wasn't supposed to really rain. Other people, mostly female, also exercised in the paddock we were in, as well as in others nearby. Most were dressed to show. I thought I might be picking up on a little disdain from some of the other young riders, but I couldn't imagine why. I concentrated on riding and tried to block them out.

I worked Kitty for about thirty minutes until she felt relaxed and supple, then attempted to ride the dressage test I was working on. Isabel occasionally gave me feedback, and I was thankful for it. We eventually left the barn area to look for Melanie and watch some of the classes. She had said she would be helping at one of the dressage courts all morning and would be riding later in the day.

We found her at the covered court I'd ridden in earlier in the week. She was opening and closing the courts as each rider entered and exited. In between, she came over to talk to us. I loved being able to remain mounted on Kitty while watching others ride their tests. She was very used to this environment and remained calm, and I felt confident and happy. I couldn't wait to ride my first test and told Melanie so.

"There's another show here next month. I think you'll be ready and so does Tatty."

Isabel agreed too.

"Yes!" I was very excited at the prospect. Anxiety crept in too, but not about the show. I really needed to tell Dave about this.

After a while, I left Melanie and Isabel talking and rode Kitty back to the barn to get her settled in her stall. Then I rejoined the others. We enjoyed a light lunch together then Isabel and I went into the huge indoor arena. A dressage court was set up within the larger arena, decorated with greenery on all sides.

After I'd learned that Gold had been trained in dressage, and especially after he'd left, I'd hungrily watched everything I could find on video, from other teens at their local shows to Prix St. George Olympic rides. But I'd never watched any upper level tests in person. Isabel was extremely knowledgeable and explained the movements I didn't know.

"I hope I can ride like that one day," I said, half to myself.

"No reason ya can't," said Isabel. "No reason at all. As long as yer willin' t' put in the time 'n hard work."

We watched mostly in silence broken only by starting bells and the occasional comment from Isabel or question from me. When Mom texted me, we met her outside.

"Melanie's riding soon. I'd like to stay and watch."

"Of course," she said. She hadn't heard from Dad yet anyway.

Melanie rode Digs, warming him up in a nearby paddock. She was very focused on riding, but after crossing the paddock one more time, she looked around, letting Digs walk on a long rein. I waved and she waved back, then pointed beyond us to another dressage court. I assumed that was where her test would be and I led the way to find a place to sit out of the drizzle. Tests were already in progress. There were two more before Melanie entered on Digs.

I didn't know what level she was riding, but it included collected, extended, and lateral movements. Melanie and Digs together were the personification of beauty, strength, and elegance to me. Though I was still learning, I could recognize the control and ease demonstrated in every movement and transition the duo performed. I felt full to bursting with pride for my friend *and* Digs. They made an amazing team. I hoped one day I could achieve the same with a cherished equine partner.

When Mom got a call from Dad, it was time to go. We said goodbye to Melanie—and Digs, of course—and left to pick Dad up at the golf club. Mom told him about her trip to Lowell and what she'd seen at the dressage show. I watched out my window, thoughts already far away in my hopefully horsey future and racing ahead today, picturing Dave at my house, half-hoping he'd still be there. But only half. I dreaded questions I didn't want to deal with right now. Besides, he was coming over tomorrow, too.

It took a while for me to realize that we were headed toward Lowell and not Douglas. When I asked, Mom just said, "We're picking something up in Lowell before heading home."

Then we pulled into the tack store parking lot.

"Seemed like a good time to find a saddle fer ya," said Isabel.

This time we spent all our time looking at the used saddles. The store lady measured me for seat length, and Isabel and Dad both looked at the stock of saddles critically. In the end, we chose a couple of general purpose saddles to try, and Isabel found Remmy a beautiful new bridle. She had measured my

bit at home and found a suitable plain snaffle for it too. We also got another saddle rack. I planned on keeping it and the new tack in my room for now.

I needn't have worried about talking to Dave. Dad wanted to stay in Lowell for dinner—a last meal out together before Isabel left on Monday. I was so excited about the new tack I could barely sit still through dinner and all the way home. Remmy was already back in his stall when we got there. Tom and Dave had left.

I texted Dave, *'Thank you!'*

Immediate reply, *'You're welcome. Can you hang out tomorrow?'*

'Yes!'

Sunday was pretty much a perfect day in every way. I got up early to feed Remmy and tried the saddles out on him as soon as he was done eating. They both fit him well and I liked both; it was going to be difficult to make a decision. Then, with Isabel's help, I adjusted the bridle and bit to fit him. Afterward, I took both saddles and the bridle up to my room.

Dave arrived around eleven and walked Remmy down to the corral with me. We lingered down there a few minutes talking—and *not* talking—but Dave seemed as aware of appearances as I was and we returned to the house soon after. Tom had just arrived.

It was a gorgeous day, sunnier and warmer than it had been for a while, but a chilly breeze called for a sweater. The sky was the bluest I could ever remember, and a few fluffy white clouds hung over the sparkling green hillsides. It seemed like someone had painted the most perfect landscape just for me. Every fear and worry seemed far away like a distant memory, and I clung to the feeling—the *lack* of anxiety.

And watched Dave. *My boyfriend.*

Yesterday he and Tom had made a start on digging out and reshaping the arena area. Today, Dave mostly helped from the ground—running, fetching, and checking levels—but occasionally he took a turn driving the backhoe or roller, giving Tom a break. When he wasn't needed, he was sitting next to me on the porch, distracting me from the homework I was half-heartedly doing.

"Tom's not going to need me much after today until the base is done. Then I'll help with the fencing. But I could probably find other reasons for being here."

I looked at him, trying to decipher his tone. He laughed and bumped shoulders with me.

Mom insisted Tom and Dave eat lunch with us, so they left their boots on the back porch and washed up in the kitchen. Isabel was fascinated by Tom's family's business, the Bar 8 Ranch, and the conversation revolved primarily around that. I was a little on edge, expecting Northfield to be mentioned, but it never was. I was also nervous in case something was said about the English tack, but it didn't come up either.

At the end of the day, both Tom and Dave bid farewell to Isabel, saying they hoped they'd see her again someday. Tom left, then Dave walked back down to the corral with me to bring Remmy back up. This time we lingered longer in the lengthening shadows.

As we returned to the stable, Mom came out and, a bit hesitantly, invited Dave to stay for dinner. But he declined

"I've got homework I should probably get done," he said.

I walked with him out to his truck. He'd parked at the back corner of the house and, out of sight of the kitchen, he kissed me again. He examined my face and lightly brushed his thumb across my brow where the bruise was already starting to fade.

"I'll see you tomorrow," he said, his voice very soft. "Take care of you."

I nodded and said, "I'll try." That's the best I could do. Most of the time it seemed entirely out of my control.

He got in his truck, turned it around, and drove away.

I returned to the house, focused on everything that had happened this weekend and refusing to worry about anything else. Including tomorrow.

Chapter Twenty-Nine

Monday was rough.

Isabel made one last big breakfast for everyone. I got ready quickly so that I'd have time to actually sit down and spend this last morning with her. And that's when it really sank in; she wouldn't be here after today.

She was so unassuming most of the time that she'd blended into the background of my life in the way that many things, even people, often did. She was so quirky and outspoken at other times that I was constantly re-evaluating how I felt and what I thought about her. But speaking or not, she'd become a real presence in my life.

She had challenged the way I thought about some things, especially how I thought about myself. She'd also made me more confident in some ways. Watching her now, holding Violet on her lap with one hand while she ate with the other, I realized I loved her. I really did. She wasn't just a name now—she was truly a part of my family and a person that I valued highly. I'd miss her and I had no way of knowing when I'd see her again.

It made me sad to think of her traveling all by herself and going back to an isolated place where, at least for part of the year, she lived alone. I suddenly realized with a stab of fear that *that* was what I feared more than anything else, one of the things I couldn't think about my own future—not just being completely alone; being truly *lonely*.

There had been some heated discussions between Isabel and Dad about her geographical isolation and other related topics. Dad thought she should sell the farm and move to town. Or maybe she should relocate all the way to Denver, closer to Dan. His reasons were many and seemed logical. The farm was too big for her to manage on her own. The students and clients she had couldn't possibly provide enough income to keep the whole place going. And what if she had another heart attack and nobody was there?

Her responses had been equally logical and surprisingly passionate. She wasn't budging.

At the moment she was perusing an itinerary of her trip. She was going back to Colorado by train as she couldn't stand the thought of flying, and she recounted every stop the train would make and how long each leg of the journey would be.

When I got up to leave with Mom, I said, "Goodbye, Aunt Isabel. I hope you have a nice trip home."

She surprised me again by putting Violet down and standing up, then opening her arms; an invitation to hug.

We embraced each other tightly and she said, "Hope ya come and visit real soon. Summer, winter, whenever ya want. I'll put ya to work."

"I'd like that," I said, and meant it. I was already wondering if I'd have to fly or maybe I could go by train, too. I liked that idea.

At school, in Chemistry and World History, it felt like something was wrong. Both Robin and Matthew seemed a little chilly. I wondered if I'd completely ignored them for the past week. I hadn't meant to, I was just so preoccupied what with one thing and another. And Ben! Except for rides home together, it seemed like a long time since we'd hung out, even at school.

Robin and Matthew both sat at the tables near Dave during lunch but there was no room for me, so I sat with Ben and Hannah on the grass. I wondered if I was being excluded—punished—or not. I'd never been sure in these situations unless people actually told me to go away, and I'd actively avoided *those* situations since middle school.

After school was the worst. Mom picked me up, as usual for a Monday, but she seemed unusually preoccupied. Maybe worried. I thought of Isabel.

"Is everything all right?"

Mom seemed startled and looked searchingly at me for a moment, then glanced in the rearview mirror.

"Is Isabel okay?" Now *I* was beginning to worry.

"Yes, she's fine. She seemed very happy to be going home and excited about the train ride. She promised to call when she gets back to the farm."

Mom smiled but still looked pensive. Clearly something else was on her mind. My stomach tightened and I felt sick. *Was it about Dave? Are my parents unhappy with him? Have we spent too much time together? Are they going to forbid me to see him?*

Mom looked in the rearview mirror again and seemed to be extra conscious of Ben's presence. When we'd dropped him off, she drove back down the street very slowly.

"I got a call from the school today," she said. "From your counselor."

My mind cast about, trying to remember what had been said, what had been talked about.

Teachers suspicious? About what? Oh yeah, bruises. Had she said she was going to call my parents? I felt angry and very betrayed. This was *not* the kind of attention I felt I needed right now. But I was relieved, too. At least it wasn't directly about Dave.

"You never said anything about meeting with her . . . or that something had happened," said Mom.

I thought she sounded hurt. Fear of disappointing my parents, disappointing *anyone*, was one of the main reasons I *didn't* talk about these things.

"Daddy's very . . . unhappy," she said. I had another stab of fear until she clarified, "Not with you. But we're concerned. We need to talk as soon as we get home. Dad saw Isabel off at the station in Sacramento then went to work, but he's home already."

Anxiety spiking, I went into the house and straight upstairs. I set my backpack down and changed my clothes. Then I picked Violet up—she'd been asleep on my bed—and slowly walked back downstairs.

Dad sat at the kitchen table. Mom stood near the sink.

"Do you want something to eat?" she asked me. "Or a drink?"

My stomach felt shriveled small and hard as a golfball, but not from hunger. I shook my head.

Dad stared at me. I wasn't used to such focused scrutiny from him. Not that he didn't look at me, especially if we were actually talking, but not this intensely. Last year there had been a couple of times—when he first learned about Gold and the Calderas, and after my accident—but that had seemed like eons ago. Now it felt like yesterday. And I had been trying to be so careful.

"Sit down, Allison," said Dad. I couldn't tell if he sounded angry or just worried.

Mom brought him a cup of coffee and sat down across from him with a cup of her own. She looked at Dad then back to me and said, "Ms. Woolton called because she and some of your other teachers are concerned. They believe you're being bullied . . . that your fall last week wasn't an accident. Is that true, sweetheart?"

Mom's voice was kind and reassuring. Her face just looked concerned. But I still couldn't admit to it. There was too much involved—too much history. Too much fear of personal safety. Too much anxiety about what people thought, the people I cared about. And Dave—how any of it would affect him. Him *and* me. *Us.*

I couldn't articulate any of those things, nor the myriad other thoughts and feelings this questioning stirred up. My fingers were busy in Violet's fur. She began purring loudly.

"It's not the first time they've been concerned," said Mom softly.

Dad finally spoke again. His voice was even, calm, reasonable, but he still *looked* angry. "This isn't something you should keep to yourself, Allie. If you're being made unhappy by people purposely being mean, it's *not* okay. If you are physically hurt by those people, it *has* to stop. *Now.*"

It wasn't that I wanted to lie to them. I didn't. But this was similar to grade school and the beginning of middle school, when I was teased and sometimes even physically hurt by classmates for no reason I could ever discern. I supposed I just seemed different to them. Either I did things differently or *didn't* do things I was expected to. They were aware of it, and I was sometimes aware of their awareness; they just always seemed to have much more of a handle on what those differences were. And only they knew why they didn't like them.

I had tried so hard to fit in back then, but that *striving* sometimes just got me into deeper trouble. I talked too much. I didn't talk enough. I said the wrong things when I did venture to speak. I insisted on keeping game rules. I had severe trouble with rules that made no sense. I often physically couldn't keep up with games anyway. I was too good at certain subjects. They'd called me a "know-it-all." I was woefully slow in other things. There were a million other differences. I could just never understand what they wanted from me.

That's when I began to disappear. Trying to fit in was exhausting. Keeping to myself was easier in some ways and much harder in others. And then later I had Brenda. She became something of a guard, a buffer between me and others, and life became a little easier, though later I realized what it cost her socially. I still felt I owed her a lot.

These days it was different. I still kept mostly to myself; it was just easier that way. After all, even Brenda used to get annoyed with me all the time. But I wasn't invisible anymore. I had friends, *real* friends, who liked me as I was.

Even so, I was beginning to realize I still wasn't completely myself with them. I felt most at ease with Melanie. She never seemed put out or annoyed with me at all, and I'd never heard her say anything judgmental about anybody. Even Robin got frustrated with me sometimes. And Dave. . . .

I couldn't help remembering the things Matthew had said at the river. It's true I was *most* careful around Dave. Could it be true that he only liked me because he perceived me as quiet? Possibly compliant? And if so, what did that mean? Matthew had implied it was because he thought me weak-willed; I had a feeling it was what Grandma meant by "easy." I hated thinking along those lines and felt mad at Matthew for saying it.

Every possible negative thought about my life was pushing to the forefront of my mind, and I could *feel* depression crawling around behind them, gnashing its teeth and smacking its lips. And it felt like my parents were egging it on!

I was shaking now and felt sick but couldn't answer. I couldn't even remember the exact question. One part of my brain was screaming, *You're in trouble!* Another part screamed back, *But I didn't do anything!*

Violet purred very loudly and kneaded my leg so fiercely her claws pricked my skin through my jeans. I let go of her and she jumped to the floor, immediately grooming herself. Lacking occupation for my hands, I stuck them under my legs.

"Allison," Mom's voice was very soft but cut through my continued abstraction. "Do you remember when you were younger, about seven, and we went to a doctor who asked us a lot of questions?"

I had fractured memories of this. We never talked about it afterward, and the memories were vague and muddled. It was a clinic attached to a hospital, and I could still remember the smell of the place. It had made me feel sick. I remembered disembodied voices booming over a speaker system as we walked into the hospital, and other sounds that seemed disconnected, echoing, and too loud. There were a lot of people in white coats and strange uniforms—scrubs I suppose, but I'd never seen anyone dressed that way before. I'd found the place overwhelming, and that's about all I could remember. It was my main reason for hating hospitals.

The doctor himself had kind of scared me too. I couldn't picture him clearly, but he had seemed *very* old. He had asked if I could look at his eyes, so I did, though I didn't want to. It was one of the few things I now remembered. I think it took so much of my concentration that it distracted me from anything else that happened. I vaguely remembered being asked to do things with toys and dolls, and I tried my best to do what I thought he wanted.

Mom and Dad looked at each other. I wasn't sure exactly what they wanted from me now.

"I remember a little," I said, extremely uncomfortable.

Mom continued, her voice still soft. Not mad. "It was a screening. Your teacher at the time thought you might have a neurological disorder. You were having difficulties at school . . . trouble paying attention and following directions. You were very emotional, too, and she suspected the other children were teasing you. There were other things . . . things we weren't as aware of at home. . . ."

I was trying very hard to remember seven. I mostly recalled the even younger memories that had been triggered over the summer: going places with Grandma that sometimes overwhelmed me; playing word games with Grandpa and studying his butterfly collection for hours. I had the vaguest of memories about school at seven. It was definitely before Brenda. And what did it have to do with now? I looked at Mom.

"Ms. Woolton suggested you get rescreened. She . . . has experience with other girls similar to you. She knows someone who specializes in girls with . . . neurological differences."

I was trying to wrap my head around what she was saying. I was sure it was the first I'd ever heard of anything like this. I had no idea how to respond. *What am I supposed to say? To feel? To do?*

"It could be an important thing to know," said Dad. "It could help you—now and in the future."

What could help me? Knowing what?

"I've made an appointment, but they couldn't fit us in until next month. We'll go one time and see what the doctor says. Is that okay?"

Yes. No. I don't know! I was feeling railroaded. Mom didn't do that to me. She always gave me time to consider. Her urgency was frightening.

"Am I sick?" I asked. *Am I contagious? Is it like a tumor? Neurological—that has to do with the brain and nervous system, right? Did they think I might have some kind of cancer?*

"No, no, no sweetheart. You're not sick at all. It's just possible that your brain works differently from most people's. If we can find out for sure, it might make a difference to you. A *good* difference. I *promise* it's nothing bad. Nothing is *wrong.*"

I didn't find her insistence consoling at all but had nothing more to say on the subject. "Can I go out to Remmy now?"

"Of course," said Dad. I got up to leave and he continued, "But Allison, don't ever let anyone mistreat you." I had opened the back door when he added, "Not *anyone.*"

The emphasis wasn't lost on me, and I was glad Dave wouldn't be coming over to work for a while—not until the arena was ready for fencing. I didn't think I could sustain any kind of positive interaction right now.

I fled down to the corral where I could relax and be myself with Remmy.

Dave was even more careful how much attention he paid me at school, if any, and I watched my back and tried not to watch him. We both had slip-ups. It was hardest in English where he refused to sit with his back to me unless he absolutely had to, and I couldn't resist gazing at him. He could always tell when I was and seemed to have just as difficult a time not smiling. It's not like he's one of those people who smiles all the time for no reason, so it was probably noticeable to anyone paying attention.

I was extra careful in PE and anywhere that brought me into the vicinity of Roberta, Lori, or their friends. Avoiding just them would have been bad enough, but there were other random people, mostly girls, who made it clear they didn't like me. It felt like school had always been for me before Douglas, and I just kept my mouth shut and kept to myself unless my friends were nearby.

I also became more aware of Bradley. Since the Northfield show, when I'd seen him riding, it seemed like I saw him all the time. And when I noticed him, he regarded me in return. Sometimes he was alone, but sometimes he was with other guys, including Varsity Jacket.

It became *very* unnerving. The last thing I wanted was to tangle with those guys again in any way, but not just for my own sake. I didn't want to think of what would happen if Dave found out. In self-defense, my focus during passing periods became as narrow as it had ever been. I literally kept my head down and tried to be inconspicuous.

My after school activities provided respite and a chance to interact more naturally with people, at least physically, though I didn't speak any more than I needed to in choir. With Hannah, Paola, and Ben there, it was a relatively safe place where I felt I could let my guard down a little.

On the other hand, riding at Northfield was *all* good. I loved Wednesdays and felt I could get through just about anything at school on those days. Now I could saddle Kitty as soon as I wanted and ride until my lesson time. If the weather was nice, I walked her all around the arenas and paddocks. If it was too wet, I rode in one of the smaller covered arenas. Kitty became more and more responsive to me as my communication became clearer to her. It was very satisfying. And my troubles and concerns, if not completely erased, diminished significantly while I was at Northfield and especially while in the saddle.

The first Saturday of February was the workday at Bar 8. Unlike last year, it rained all day, but it was still fun. I got there early, mainly because I wanted to spend as much time as I could with Dave, but he had work at home and didn't get there until eleven. In the meantime, I helped Doris with deep-cleaning the kitchen.

Dave found me as soon as he arrived and we slipped away to the home barn until Tom came in and put us to work. As we couldn't paint outside and the guest barn was unoccupied, he set us painting the walls of the breezeway. Apparently they hadn't been painted in over ten years. The fresh coat of paint made everything brighter. A couple of wranglers helped too, which meant we didn't have any more alone time, but that was okay.

Robin arrived in her Mustang after she got off work at twelve. It seemed like we'd barely talked or spent any time together since Winter Formal, and I told her so.

"Oh yeah . . . I've got Melanie's dress in the car. Could you give it back for me? I don't see her very often."

"Of course," I said, then proceeded to ask as many questions as I could think of about her job. She brightened quite a bit while answering but otherwise seemed very preoccupied.

When she'd left us alone for a few minutes, I asked Dave, "Did you tell Robin about . . . you know . . . you and me?"

He frowned and shook his head. "I assumed she knew. I thought you'd tell her."

I felt guilty and weirdly incompetent. I supposed I should have told her. Most girls probably would have told their best friends something like that right away. But I was starting to understand that I didn't always do things like that—expected social things. Besides, it had barely occurred to me before now. Other concerns had kept my mind very occupied.

"Should we tell her? Now?" he asked.

I thought we probably should since she was best friends with both of us. So when she returned from the guest house, I did. As most things seemed to, it came out rather bluntly and awkwardly.

"Robin, Dave and me . . . I . . . we're," this is where terminology always tripped me up, "sort of going out. Together."

Robin stared at me and then at Dave. It reminded me of how my grandmother always looked to other people to corroborate anything I said.

Dave nodded and said, "Winter Formal was our first date . . . unofficially. I would have said something sooner, but I thought you knew."

Her response surprised me. She went very pale and looked sick as if she'd seen or heard something horrific. She just said, "Oh," before turning away to resume painting the tack room door.

I looked at Dave. He was frowning at Robin's back. Now *I* felt sick, enjoyment from being together with my two favorite people destroyed. Dave looked at me and shook his head slightly. I took it to mean I shouldn't say anything more about it.

I felt terrible. Leave it to me to say the wrong thing, or the right thing in the wrong way, or the right way at the wrong time. I hoped I could make it right—whatever was wrong.

She seemed to rebound soon after and, later in the day, even bantered with Dave as she used to, but it seemed forced, as did her smiles. Like she was being heroic but not wanting to appear to be so. Or I could have been oversensitive and read too much into it. Dave and I, by unspoken agreement, made sure we kept our distance from each other and focused on her.

By the time I had to go home, it seemed at least *some* balance had been restored. I hoped she and Dave could talk alone and reestablish whatever Robin needed from their relationship.

Robin's behavior throughout the following week was confusing and only added to the growing distractions in my life, especially at school. She seemed almost clingy during our classes together—very unlike her—yet even more distant outside of them. I tried to make sense of this but couldn't. At lunch, she gravitated to wherever Dave was but usually ended up talking to Tanner.

Ben seemed a little distant, too, but I was less concerned about that—mostly because I'd been too busy and distracted to think about him in any focused way except during choir and rides home. He seemed perfectly happy to bug other people instead of me and my feelings weren't hurt.

The following Saturday was the Bar 8 schooling show and the first day of a week-long break from school. Robin surprised me by begging me to spend the night at her house before the show, which I was more than happy to do. She'd been able to switch shifts with a co-worker so she could attend the show. But I still felt a tension between us. She was being almost *too* nice to me, which was worrying.

"You can sleep in my bed tonight," she said after she'd insisted I ride Gali most of the afternoon. And she hadn't become impatient with me at all, even when I tripped carrying Gali's supplement and spilled most of it on the ground. "I put clean sheets on and everything."

"You didn't have to do that," I said, feeling uncomfortable. "I don't mind sleeping on the floor." This, of course, was *not* exactly the truth as I knew I'd sleep very badly on the floor, but I didn't want to take her bed.

We seemed to have little to talk about once the lights were out, and I wracked my brain trying to think of what was wrong. There was only one thing I could think of.

"Does it bother you very much . . . about Dave and me?"

I had a sudden stab of fear. What if I lost my best friend over this? Why didn't it even occur to me before?

"It's . . . really weird," Robin said. "I guess I knew *you* liked *him*. I never would have guessed he'd ask you out though. I mean, not because you're not nice or anything. It's just not . . . you know . . . *obvious*."

I'd heard this before but wasn't sure what *obvious* meant in this instance. It seemed to me that Dave had been pretty obvious in his attentions—at least at times. It had been obvious enough to others to cause at least some of my problems at school for over a year now, even though I hadn't been aware of his true feelings.

"He said you're not telling people. I don't get why it matters."

And I couldn't explain. I wasn't entirely sure of the reasons myself except that he seemed to think it best for me and I thought it best for him. "But you don't mind?"

Her silence pressed down on me in the dark room. A light rain pattered on the roof and windows. Her clock, which never seemed to bother her but added to my difficulty in sleeping here, ticked off the seconds until she answered. In that space of time, my anxiety rose again. *What if she does? What if she says yes? What would I do? Give Dave up? Give her up? How could that choice even be made?*

My eyes were watering when she finally answered, "No. I don't mind . . . exactly."

I wiped my eyes and was glad the lights were off.

"I was just . . . worried, I guess."

"Worried?"

She was quiet again, then said softly, "You're my best friends. When you told me . . . it hurt that you didn't tell me sooner."

That stung. I just wasn't the type of person to communicate these kinds of things. Well, *any*thing, really. I didn't know why. Maybe because I'd never had anyone that was really interested in me or my life before. Even Brenda was rarely interested in things that affected or involved me. I thought I understood what she meant though.

"And I was scared that. . . ."

"What?"

"Scared that there wouldn't be room for me. That I'd still . . . *fit*. I don't know how to explain it, and it sounds stupid and selfish now."

"No, it doesn't," I said, starting to realize what she must have felt like. "I'm so sorry. I would *never* want to make you feel that way. You'll *always* be important to me, and Dave would never turn away from a real friend. You know that." Dave had told me that last year and I would never forget it. Yet until recently, I had begun to doubt him too. Now I believed him with all my heart.

"I know," she said softly. "I'll try not to mind. Just . . . no *kissing* in front of me, okay? Or I'll barf all over both of you."

I laughed. Now she sounded more herself. "I'll do my best, but I'm not making any promises. Dave has a mind of his own."

"Then you better not be near any water hoses. I won't be held responsible for anything I feel forced to do!"

The picture *that* conjured up made me laugh and she laughed too. It also made me think of Cris and then shudder. I'd barely thought of him in weeks, but I wondered what *his* reaction had been. He couldn't be happy about it unless his opinion of me had drastically changed.

"Allie?" Robin's voice pulled me back to the dark room.

"Mmm?"

"Do you ever get scared? So scared you can't sleep? Or eat? Or think?"

All the time. "Yes."

"What are you afraid of?"

This past couple of years I'd begun to realize just how much generalized anxiety I'd always lived with, yet I'd never asked myself that question. "I don't know. It's . . . it's hard to explain it. Sometimes I'm scared of something specific." I tried to think of examples. "Those guys last year. Especially the guy with the varsity jacket. But a lot of the time I just don't know. It feels like a huge, ugly bird hovering over me, but I don't know why it's there or what it is." I told her about the vultures I'd seen at the Calderas' ranch and how creepy it was. "Like one of those, but so big it almost blocks out everything

else. And I can *feel* it, just waiting for me to trip or do or say something wrong. And when I *do* make a mistake, it's ten times worse."

Robin was quiet for a moment, then said, "Wow. I didn't know."

"What are you afraid of?" I asked, hoping she'd really tell me. I wanted to know what had been affecting her since the start of school and, seemingly, again recently.

She was silent a few moments more, then said very softly, "I'm worried about the future. I'm scared of something bad happening to Gran." Her voice dropped so low I could barely hear her. "Sometimes I really hate my life."

That shocked me. I knew something had been bothering her, but she wasn't the kind of girl to become petulant just because things didn't go her way or because she didn't get something she wanted. And she'd been obviously depressed. Her hair had grown out a lot and now lay in soft curls around her face, but I could picture her on the first day of school—self-conscious and haunted.

I had to ask. "Robin, what happened to your parents?"

She was quiet so long this time, I thought she was either ignoring the question or had fallen asleep.

Finally, she almost whispered, "I don't like to talk about them. I don't want to think about what other people will think. And I don't want it to change *us*."

I didn't know what to say as I didn't understand. So I just said, "Okay," and assumed she wouldn't tell me.

Then she whispered, "My dad's in prison."

I still didn't know what to say. I had no points of reference. So I said, "Oh."

"Yeah. He's been there a long time, but he's supposed to get out next year."

I couldn't help being curious about why he was there but didn't want to ask. I wanted her to know I was listening though, so I asked, "Do you ever get to see him?"

"Mom used to take me once in a while when I was younger, but I haven't seen him in a really long time. He sometimes sends me letters. It's kind of weird, though. I don't feel like I know him. And that scares me too."

I was already processing hard, trying to understand what all this must be like for her, but it was going to take me longer than tonight to think it through. But at least she had finally mentioned her parents.

"Your mom?"

"Mom lives in Orange County. I spend a part of the summer with her."

This was news. "I thought you visited your aunt?"

"I do," she said.

I wished I could see her face as we talked. I was curious about her family but didn't want to inadvertently pry or cause her more pain.

"I don't want to talk about it anymore," she said.

"Okay."

"Goodnight."

"Goodnight."

But it wasn't. The floor was hard, the clock's tick resonated through the dark, and it was cold. And I couldn't help picturing a little red-haired girl led by the hand by a woman she didn't want to talk about into a dreary, gray prison with barbed-wire on top of the fences—the only kind I'd seen on TV—to visit a man she didn't feel she knew.

I didn't sleep well at all.

Cris and Dave arrived early to pick Gali up with Remmy already loaded in the trailer. The two horses called loudly back and forth to each other until they stood safely side by side.

To conserve her precious gasoline, Robin and I rode in Cris' truck. It had been such a long time since we had, and so much had changed! This time Robin moved as if to get into the cab next to Cris, but I beat her to it. Cris looked slightly alarmed, and Robin was forced to sit between Dave and me. I felt smug all the way to Bar 8 and didn't care what Cris thought.

It was a really fun day, even though it drizzled on and off for most of it. The turn out wasn't quite as large as it had been the year before, the weather probably dissuading quite a few, especially those who weren't local. But Tanner showed up to hang out, and Stacie and Jessie came later, too.

Dave didn't ride at all, but Miguel brought two young horses that Henry rode. Dave led Stevie through a trail class riding one of them. We cheered him on through every obstacle.

Robin rode Gali in a sorting class and did really well, and later rode a reining pattern she'd been working on with him. I was impressed and Dave seemed to be too.

Remmy and I entered the barrel racing and pole bending. Mom and Dad were there and knew I'd been working on it with Cheryl. Remmy still got worked up, but I was able to control him and rode as fast as I felt safe. We didn't have the worst times, and we didn't knock anything down. I was ecstatic and my cheering section—seemingly a growing population in spite of my detractors at school—yelled and whistled and generally caused a ruckus that would have alarmed me greatly under other circumstances. Most importantly, Dave seemed really proud of me, and that meant everything.

After a fabulous barbecue dinner, I went home with my parents. Cris and Dave gave Robin and Gali a ride home first, then brought Remmy home to me. Cris stayed in the truck reading a book, while Dave unloaded Remmy and I put his tack away. When we had Remmy settled in his stall, blanketed and munching on hay, Dave said, "It was a fun day."

I agreed wholeheartedly. He looked like he wanted to kiss me, and I certainly wouldn't have minded, but he glanced over his shoulder toward the truck. That made me look toward the house.

No kisses tonight.

"I won't be over tomorrow," he said, reaching inside his jacket, "but this is for you. Don't open it until the morning, okay?" He gave me a pink envelope and began to back away. "I'll call you tomorrow night."

I wanted to open the envelope as soon as he was gone—I *really* wanted to know what was inside—but that would be like opening presents before Christmas, something I'd never wanted to do.

I slept with the envelope under my pillow.

In the morning, I lay still a moment, trying to remember everything that had happened the day before. Then I remembered the card and retrieved it from under my pillow. There was nothing written on the envelope. I opened it carefully without tearing the flap and pulled out a pretty card—a few delicate pink and red flowers; a couple of hearts. The outside said, *"Will you be mine?"* I opened the card slowly. It was blank except for a few words written in Dave's uneven print.

"Wish I was with you right now."

Since I was still lying in bed, the image this conjured up was quite provocative. *On purpose?* It wouldn't have surprised me, but I wasn't even embarrassed. I liked the thought immensely.

I stood the card on my bedside table, thrilled to receive it and just as thrilled to not feel the need to hide it.

My first Valentine's Day card. Ever.

Presidents week held dry, mostly. Tom was waiting for more consistently dry weather before continuing with the arena. Dave was helping him at other jobs in the meantime, but he stopped by on Monday and Tuesday evenings early enough to play with Remmy and me for a little while before it got dark. And though Mom invited him to come in and have dinner with us, he declined, saying he still had work to do at home. He asked if I could go over and hang out sometime over the weekend at his house, at the ranch. But Dad asked who else would be there, and when Dave admitted he didn't know for sure, Dad said no.

And that was okay. I sometimes felt overwhelmed by my new status in Dave's life, and his in mine. I needed time and space and didn't mind not seeing him every day. In fact, I sometimes found I enjoyed just *thinking* about him, about *us*, almost as much—sometimes maybe more—than actually being with him. It was such a relief; no more angst or second-guessing. Mostly. For now, I was choosing to just go with the flow. If familiar concerns or doubts about Dave raised their heads, and they did, it wasn't too hard to channel my thoughts into more positive and *much* more pleasant paths.

On Wednesday morning, I called Brenda and talked to her for a while. I finally told her about Dave and me, and she had many questions, most of which I couldn't or didn't want to answer. I told her about Remmy and Kitty, but she wasn't interested in horses. And she was full of news about Trevor: sporting exploits, a new car, things he'd said and done. But there seemed to be a new wistfulness in the pauses between comments, as if she were forcing bravado for my sake. That was very unlike her and, later, thinking over our conversation, I wished I'd asked more questions. Maybe she would have told me more about *herself*. Still, she sounded much happier than the last time I'd talked to her at Christmas.

The rest of the holiday week passed quickly. Kitty and I concentrated on dressage on Wednesday. Robin had worked most of the rest of the week but came over and stayed the night on Thursday. Dave ended up going to a motocross event with Cris over the weekend, and I spent most of that time at Northfield with Kitty.

After President's week, school and time with Dave continued mostly the same as before it, except for my knowledge of the appointment to come and the new fear that something was wrong with me. But I tried not to think about it. It added nothing to my peace of mind and offered no solutions for the way other people thought of and treated me. I continued to be careful, to not stand out in any way, and to not provoke negative attention. *Any* attention, really.

The following weekend I attended another dressage show at Northfield that Melanie rode in. I especially loved watching her and Digs. Everything they did looked so perfect, a contained power both dynamic and relaxed. I gladly helped her with the horses in between classes and even got to be useful to Tatty, who was watching over several of her own students.

When the afternoon started winding down and people began leaving, I saddled Kitty and rode her around the show grounds. We eventually practiced a pre-test in an empty paddock. I felt very confident until I saw Bradley watching us. I'd never seen him actually around the barns, and I hadn't noticed him at the show today. I couldn't read his expression, but he stared a little too long for my comfort. I exited the paddock in the opposite direction and feigned nonchalance.

On Wednesday, I awoke in a foul mood—very unlike me—and I had a headache. I tried to keep my thoughts on riding Kitty later in the day, but I couldn't. The appointment loomed large and much too immediate, invading every corner of my imagination. I wanted to cry off, say I was sick and couldn't go, but that would just delay the inevitable and draw out my anxiety.

Mom said she would pick me up from school. We'd go to the appointment in Lowell, then get lunch, and then go to Northfield where I could ride and hang out until my lesson. She tried to make it sound like a fun day.

I only had the vague, childish memories of that similar appointment to go on as we drove to Lowell late in the morning. I dreaded it now. I'd already been to the hospital in Lowell, last year. I *really* didn't like hospitals.

We hadn't been to Lowell since Isabel was here. I watched out the window as we passed familiar fields and hillsides. Here and there spots of color could be seen—blue, white, yellow and, every so often, a shimmer of orange. They certainly hadn't been there before.

Mom didn't drive to the hospital. Instead, we pulled up at a long, low row of offices, similar to those of my dentist and ophthalmologist. That made me feel better, but I still felt anxious. I couldn't shake the feeling that they'd find something "wrong" with me, and that it was somehow my own fault.

I didn't remember anything specific from that initial screening, but people—adults—always said I was different. *"Too sensitive." "Keeps to herself." "Doesn't play well with other children."* These were comments I'd overheard or seen written on report cards. They all seemed immensely unfair when I had tried *so* hard to do the things the other kids did.

And then, sometime in middle school, I stopped trying. Then I *really* kept to myself, wanting to blend into the background without really connecting to anyone except Brenda. Even so, now I realized how mostly superficial that connection had been. That's when I started to feel invisible.

Until Douglas High. Until Dave and Robin and Melanie. Cris, too. Until horses and all of the people I felt a connection to now because of them. With the thought of all my friends on my side, human and otherwise, I felt some measure of confidence return as we entered the office.

The reception area was softly lit and decorated nicely, not sterile-looking. Very soft music played in the background—nothing I would have chosen to listen to but tolerable. And no overpowering smells to alarm or nauseate me. It was pleasant, and the receptionist was soft-spoken and seemed nice. I tried to relax and flipped through a magazine, but nothing caught my interest enough to completely distract me. By the time we were led down a corridor to an office, I was very nervous again.

The doctor—therapist, psychologist, psychiatrist; I wasn't sure exactly which—was a woman. Dr. Hanwell spoke clearly and not too fast, which I appreciated. She wore a pretty shirt and a rose-colored cardigan, not a white coat. Her office was bright but felt kind of cozy, with comfy chairs and no fluorescent lights. There was a large fish tank and bookshelves filled with

everything from medical books to complete sets of *Harry Potter, Chronicles of Narnia,* and *Anne of Green Gables.* I felt better and better but still very much on guard.

Dr. Hanwell just talked with us for a while, mostly with Mom. She didn't speak as if I weren't there, but the only direct questions she asked me were simple ones I mostly answered with nods or shakes of my head. Mom told her about the school I had gone to in Los Angeles and about our family.

I didn't pay very close attention most of the time. I scanned her bookshelves for more familiar friends—*Oz, Wonderland, Redwall*—and others I'd heard of but hadn't yet read. The fish tank was fascinating, too. Its lighting cast colorful prisms on the wall behind that shifted and changed with the movement of the fish.

Dr. Hanwell then said she would begin asking questions, and we should just answer them as honestly as we could. She asked Mom lots of questions about when I was younger. How I played. How I interacted with family, friends, other children. I was surprised by some of Mom's responses as I either didn't remember at all or remembered from a very different perspective. Some of the questions she asked me I couldn't answer. Some of them made me feel very uncomfortable, and I started feeling anxious again.

Why am I here? Does everyone have to do this in tenth grade? Or is it just me? Is there really something wrong with me? Will my friends find out? What will I tell them? Do I have to tell them? What will happen between Dave and me? Will I lose him again already?

That thought brought a thick, painful knot to my throat.

"There are some tests and questions we'll do another day, Allison. Just you and me. Would that be okay?"

I tried to focus on Dr. Hanwell's face, tried to read her intentions but couldn't. I listened harder when Mom mentioned Isabel. Dr. Hanwell had asked if she knew if there was autism in the family. I'd heard of autism but didn't really know what it was. It made me think of Stevey. *Had someone told me he was autistic?*

"My husband's older sister was diagnosed with Asperger Syndrome as a teenager," said Mom. "But I'm not aware of anyone else."

I looked at her in surprise but still wasn't sure what it meant.

"We're still learning about the nature of autism," said Dr. Hanwell. "Whether it has an environmental cause or is just a human variation. I tend to believe the latter, though it could sometimes be both. It does seem to be genetic in most cases. It's possible one of your husband's parents was on the autism spectrum but was never diagnosed."

"So," Mom said uncertainly, "you think that Allison is autistic?"

"As a preliminary diagnosis, yes. But I sense she's a little overwhelmed right now."

I was sitting on my hands and trying not to shiver.

She continued, "I'm going to give you some information to look over, and I have a list of websites you may find useful. We're still learning about how differently many if not most girls on the spectrum exhibit autistic traits, compared to what classic, mostly male diagnosis criteria dictates. It's not an exact science and probably never will be because everyone is different, autistic or not. But I hope you'll find the information helpful. Most of my patients find it helps them understand themselves better. There will always be challenges. Understanding those challenges can make specific situations and life in general easier."

I didn't know what to make of all that. I needed time to think. And I wanted to leave.

Mom thanked her and said she'd make the next appointment. I don't think I said anything. All I really remember was thinking, *praying*, over and over again, that I didn't want anything to be wrong with me.

Mom and I had lunch in Lowell and then she drove me to Northfield. She tried making conversation, but I was too busy—busy thinking, busy hoping, busy worrying. She seemed concerned and a little frustrated that I didn't want to tell her what I was thinking or how I felt, though I didn't know why. It was no different from how I usually acted. The truth was that both my thoughts and emotions were too complicated. *I* didn't even understand them. And the last thing I wanted to do right then was *talk* about them.

Mom offered to stay with me once we were at the stables—my lesson wasn't due to start for over an hour—but I wanted to be alone. Just me and Kitty. Mom said she'd do some grocery shopping and come back later. I nodded.

As soon as I had Kitty cross-tied and started to groom her, I felt better. I found it easy to transfer all my attention to her and avoid thinking of things that seemed less pleasant. The rhythmic exertion of brushing and

Kitty's warm smell and physical presence soothed me, but her temperament demanded my full attention. I was extremely grateful.

We warmed up in the *cavaletti* paddock, then I practiced jumping her over them. I didn't think of anything but gauging distances and staying with her. And then I realized I wasn't just *thinking* but *feeling*. It felt like a significant breakthrough and I was thrilled.

"It looks like you're ready for the next level." I hadn't realized Melanie was watching and was surprised at how much time had gone by.

We followed her over into another paddock where a few schooling jumps were set up. I let Kitty relax on a long rein while Melanie moved and reset a few of the jumps in low cross rails.

For the next hour, we trained over and around the jumps one at a time, then two, then all three, at a trot and finally a canter. Whether because she was already well warmed up when we started, or because I felt more confident, or because I was just more focused and attuned to her today, Kitty behaved perfectly, responding to my slightest cue. It felt like she almost read my mind. And jumping her was incredible. It felt like magic. It felt like *freedom*.

By the time Mom came back for me, Tatty had wandered over to watch.

"Allison's improving quickly. Kitty's an excellent partner for her," Tatty said to Mom. To me, she said, "You'll be ready for at least a schooling show soon, if you're interested in that."

Pleased, I nodded happily. Something else to look forward to and occupy my mind.

Chapter Thirty

"They're having tryouts on Monday. You'll go, won't you?"

It wasn't the first time Matthew had reminded me about the swim team over the past few weeks, but the idea hadn't taken root deeply enough for me to remember. I had too many other things on my mind, not the least of which was my relationship with Dave. Not that I was worried about it—exactly.

Dave still kept his distance at school, and I wasn't seeing him much outside of it, so anything even close to alone time with him was rare. He sometimes called but texted fairly often, mostly just letting me know what was going on in his world. I missed physical contact with him, but I wasn't worried. He was busy.

I was busy, too. I still had Choir and now went to Northfield two, sometimes three times a week—Wednesdays with Melanie and whenever else Mom or Dad could take me. I was working hard with Kitty for the upcoming schooling show. Remmy got all my other evenings and most of the weekend. And Dad and I continued our driving sessions, but driving myself around any time soon didn't seem likely.

Dave worked at home almost every weekend and worked with Tom after school when he didn't have track training. Cris was taking a "full load"—I wasn't sure exactly what that meant—at the college in Lowell and was hardly ever on our campus anymore. Apparently he was taking both day and night classes and wasn't home much either. That meant Dave and Henry were helping to pick up the slack at home from Cris being too busy, on top of

everything else. Dave said they needed to get used to it anyway since Cris would be gone in the summer. I couldn't imagine when Dave got his home-work done, except for the infrequent times he came over and did it with me.

"Come on. It'll be fun." My attention snapped back to Matthew, still waiting for an answer. "At least try out."

"I'm sorry," I said. "I don't think so. About trying out, I mean. I just have too much going on right now." It hadn't seemed urgent enough to re-ally consider before, but now I felt guilty for not making the decision sooner. I hated feeling guilty and resented it, but then felt doubly guilty for that.

I couldn't read Matthew's expression. He just said, "Okay," but I felt like I'd really let him down.

Though Dave came over that afternoon, he didn't stay long and was preoccupied with his own issues and upcoming events, which he told me all about. His preoccupation was a *good* thing. I was likewise preoccupied with lots of my own concerns but didn't want to tell him about *any* of them. There was no opportunity for a kiss goodnight, and I was surprisingly okay with it at the time, though while trying to fall asleep I worried a little about it. That and a million other things.

I decided that, if Dave asked me directly or said anything indicating he knew or suspected, I would tell him. *Everything.* I knew once I started, I wouldn't be able to hold anything back anyway. But until then I was still hanging on to—I wasn't sure what. It felt something like freedom; freedom to do what I wanted, where I wanted, without being too concerned about what someone else would think or say. Part of me worried that I was just cowardly, maybe even selfish, but I was protecting things that were impor-tant to me in the only way I knew how. The fact that I was protecting them from the person that mattered most in the world to me—well, I was trying not to dwell on that.

By the next Saturday I still hadn't looked up any of the websites Dr. Hanwell had given us. I didn't even want to read the information sheets she'd given me. This, in itself, was extremely unusual. My typical reaction to some-thing new and important that affected my life was to research the heck out of it at least until I felt somewhat comfortable with the subject. Familiarity was often enough to lessen anxiety and sometimes sparked intense interest.

That had been true with many things earlier in my life, more lately horses and rodeo in general, and barrel racing and dressage in particular. I'd also now done enough reading and video watching on motocross, skateboarding, and soccer to at least have an understanding of the basic terminology.

But I'd been avoiding *this* topic, worried about learning the worst. In this situation, I figured what I *didn't* know would cause me less anxiety and cost fewer sleepless nights. But Dave was out of town all weekend—state rodeo qualifying rounds—and by Sunday I'd finished all my homework and was looking for distraction beyond working with Remmy. Curiosity won out.

The pages mostly described what the medical profession knew and thought about autism and what the widely accepted traits were. At first I couldn't relate to most of them, not in the way they were presented anyway. But over the following days and even weeks, I explored more on my own online and began to recognize more and more of those traits in myself, especially those more attributed to girls. Most were things I had taken for granted—things I assumed everyone struggled with or were just quirks of my own: my lifelong difficulty with large motor skills and spatial perception, sensory issues, processing speed, and avoidance of eye contact to name a very few obvious ones. The *most* obvious was my confusion in social situations—difficulty reading people in general and social cues in particular, and not knowing how to fit in or do and say the right things in the right way.

Dr. Hanwell had said that most if not all of the traits were things a lot of people could relate to on some level. But it was the quantity and intensity of those traits and the severity of how a person's life was affected that indicated autism. That was harder for me to quantify. My life had always been like this. I didn't know anything else and had no way of comparing.

Beyond avoiding reproachful glances from Matthew on Monday—swim team tryout day—the next week continued much the same as before. Dave came over after school one evening for an hour or so, and we did math together, but that's all I saw of him outside of school. He asked again if I could come to his house sometime over the next weekend but still wasn't sure who else would be home. Dad said no. I figured it was just as well since the Northfield dressage schooling show was the same weekend. If Dad had said yes, I probably would have *had* to tell Dave about it. As it was, I was guiltily glad I didn't.

Dave had lowered his voice and said, "Looks like I'll have to organize something." But when I asked what he had in mind, he just smiled.

I spent Friday evening at Northfield riding and then bathing Kitty. I got up very early on Saturday to feed Remmy, then Mom drove me back to the stables. I was extremely nervous but excited, too.

I hung my show coat in the stable's lounge while I went to groom Kitty. When she was gleaming and virtually dust-free, I went in search of Melanie. She was helping several students today, and she'd be riding Beau in a first level class, but she took time to supervise my braiding of Kitty's mane and the applying of hoof oil. She also helped me secure my hair in a net at the nape of my neck, which I'd never done before. I went back to the lounge for my coat, then met Melanie and her other students in a paddock to warm up. Then I rode Kitty to the showgrounds.

I rode two tests at Introductory level. Melanie read the first test for me as I rode, like she'd done sometimes when we practiced during lessons. I had the A test memorized well, but riding before the judges, in front of *people*, felt so different from when it was just me and Kitty, or just Melanie or Tatty watching, that I had great difficulty concentrating on my riding; I was thinking too hard about the test itself and what came next. Still, nothing terribly wrong happened. Kitty behaved and responded well without taking advantage of my less than focused riding, and I was sure I'd do better on the next one.

Melanie read for me again on the second test and I did ride much better. After watching some of her other students in Training and First level classes, Melanie went over the judge's comments on my tests with me. They were pretty much what we'd expected—stay focused, look up, work on transitions, keep the horse moving forward—but also said "good developing seat" and "nice quiet hands." Individual element scores were mostly fives and sixes, but our circles all got 6.5. Melanie said she was proud of me and assured me I'd ridden very well for my first dressage show. That meant the world to me.

Monday was my second appointment with Dr. Hanwell. On the way, fields and hillsides that had hints of wildflower color before, were now broad brushstrokes; swathes of rich, vibrant color. I wished I could paint it. Especially striking was a vast ocean of California poppies. There hadn't been many the last time we'd driven here. The term *late bloomers* occurred to me. Grandma had once said it's what I probably was.

The bright reddish-orange made me think of Ben. Why had he dyed his hair? It was still orange, but his darker natural color was growing in. I wondered again if it was Robin that he liked, though he acted and reacted the same way about Dave. Had he dyed his hair trying to match hers? And Robin—she had seemed so uncomfortable that her hair was short when school started. Had they both just experimented with different hairstyles, like me? These musings kept me distracted the rest of the way to Lowell.

This appointment with Dr. Hanwell took a long time. Mom stayed in the waiting room while I was shown to a small quiet room to fill out a lengthy questionnaire. The room was pleasant enough: comfy chairs, pictures on the walls, a small table and chairs, and a toy bin in the corner. Dr. Hanwell explained the questionnaire but I had trouble focusing on what she actually said. She told me to let someone know when I was done and left the door slightly ajar on her way out.

I had a hard time settling into the new room. I studied the pictures—probably just cheap prints picked up somewhere, but pretty all the same—and wondered what was in the toy bin. My mind was still making copper-colored connections, too—Robin, Ben, Kitty, poppies. It's probably a good thing there weren't any bookshelves or fish.

A lot of the questions seemed repetitive and were confusing to me, and the whole thing was pretty stressful. I'm not a good test taker, and that's what it felt like. I panic when I feel pressured for time, and though Dr. Hanwell said there was no right or wrong answers and no time limit, I still felt rushed. And what if I *did* answer the questions wrong? What if I completely misunderstood the meaning and gave the opposite answer? What would the answers show her anyway? And I wanted the questions to be more specific. It seemed like many of them needed clarification. *What circumstances are involved? Who is involved? What else is going on at the same time? Why aren't there more choices?* I sometimes wanted a "none of the above" and once wanted "all of the above".

By the time I finished and told the receptionist I was done, I felt exhausted, had a headache, and was completely on edge. Mom made another appointment for the following week, which happened to be the day after Easter. Then we went to Northfield and I rode Kitty until my mind and heart were calm. Tatty was there, but I didn't see Melanie.

March turned into April. I still didn't spend much time around Dave at school, but he'd been over working with Tom on the arena. The fence was now done. Tom said we needed to wait until the ground was completely dry before putting the final footing in, so that might not get done until the beginning of May. In the meantime, I still enjoyed riding in it and was glad to have the bigger space for Remmy to play in.

It rained for a few days but most were dry. This meant Dave was usually down on the track at lunch. Robin and I, and sometimes combinations of other people including Ben, Hannah, and Paola, often ate in the bleachers nearby.

On the very few rainy days, the Ag. Science room was crowded and stuffy and incredibly noisy. I preferred the days I ate with Melanie, though the cafeteria was louder and more crowded on rainy days, too. Dave and Hannah seemed a lot closer again, but I was okay with that. Matthew often seemed to watch them with an expression I couldn't read. Except as my partner during Chemistry, he rarely talked to me.

I was sure Dave would have met me in the library if I'd asked him to, but I avoided that. It didn't occur to me at the time that I might be avoiding *him*. That wouldn't have made sense. I'd wanted to be close to him for so long, and now I preferred to keep my distance? No sense at all.

I *could* count on being physically close to him in English, which I anticipated with a quickened pulse as if he were still just a huge crush. I guess he was. He talked to me whenever class dynamics and assignments allowed, and sometimes lowered his voice enough for a few words only I could hear. It was enough to continue to feel accepted and safe in our new relationship. It was usually sufficient to keep me from worrying, too. I suspected that was his intention.

Some days I felt very confident, but on others, it was all I could do to not overthink everything. On those days, I kept my mouth shut and became very conscious of faking normal.

Of course "normal" now had all kinds of connotations attached. *Am I normal? What does normal look like? What does normal even mean?* I didn't like the thought of *not* being normal, but I liked the idea of being thought not normal by others even less. Especially by my friends. And *especially* by Dave.

And *normal* wasn't the only word tripping me up. There was a whole new vocabulary that I half wanted to learn and understand, and half wanted to ignore. *Aspergers. Autism. Spectrum.* We'd used that last one quite a bit in Art, and I was comfortable with applying it to my identity. It had sexual orientation application, too. But in spite of seeming to have little in common with most girls and feeling more comfortable interacting with guys in general, my feelings for Dave seemed to confirm my sexuality.

Other terms linked to autism—*proprioception, executive function, dyspraxia,* and a host of "disorders"—required looking up online. Many things were starting to make a lot more sense to me but were still very confusing.

Mom and I were invited to church with the Calderas and then to lunch at the ranch for Easter Sunday. Dad was away until the following Wednesday and Mom didn't want to go to church, but I was excited to be with Dave and his family under any circumstances. I couldn't help being curious, too. My understanding of and relationship with God was sketchy, to say the least, and after the first rush of heartfelt gratitude following Dave's admission of attachment to me, my attention heavenward had dwindled considerably. So far, I hadn't been aware of definitive reciprocal communication, but I somehow trusted its existence. I hoped for a more solid encounter. A religious service of some kind seemed like an opportunity for that.

I assumed it was an occasion for dressing up, so I wore a skirt and my best shoes—not what I normally would have worn for an invitation to Dave's house. Mr. Caldera, driving the big, dark gray SUV, came and picked me up Sunday morning. Except for Cris, the whole family was there. I got into the back seat with Dave. He smiled but it seemed strained, as if he were unhappy in some way.

Mr. Caldera and Angel, in the front seats, talked about family. Henry played his Game Boy in the third seat behind us while Stevey watched out the opposite window. Dave held my hand but didn't say much. That was fine with me.

I don't know why I was surprised when we pulled into the large parking lot of the Catholic Church in town. There were only two churches in Douglas that I was aware of: the Catholic Church in Old Town on the east side, and the Presbyterian Church on the west. Cris and Miguel were waiting at the steps with Robin with Fiona. Robin smiled at me, but the smile was quickly replaced with a grimace similar to the one Dave had worn.

The service itself was interesting, though ultimately unenlightening for me. The songs seemed simple, but I found them challenging to follow. The priest seemed nice, though, and I liked the artwork and details of the church itself. I spent most of the service focused on these with my mind wandering, though I tried to pay attention. Robin sat on Dave's other side and they had their phones out for most of the service. At the end, they had communion, which I didn't understand. When the family stood up, Dave said I could just wait for them to come back, so I did. I had a lot of questions, but with so many people around, I didn't ask any of them. I'd do research later.

It was a gorgeous day, and lunch at the Caldera's was a festive affair with tons of food. The dining room was filled with flowers, and the courtyard was bright with flowers too, mostly blooming on the fruit trees. Angel and Miguel put some things in the ovens to warm while we hung out in the courtyard: Mom and me, Hannah and her dad, Paola and her parents, Robin and Fiona, Tanner and his mom, and the rest of the Calderas. I'd never met Tanner's mom before. She seemed just like him: slightly disheveled and wiry-looking but very vibrant and friendly. I liked her.

After lunch, Dave and Henry led the way through the house to the garage where the wide exterior doors stood open. The garage looked big enough to house at least four vehicles, but there were just the two family cars: the big dark gray SUV and the smaller hybrid. The rest of the space was more of a work area with tool cabinets, spare tires, and a workbench. And motorcycles.

Dave grabbed a helmet off a shelf and threw it to Tanner. "Ride the two-fifty out for me."

Tanner grinned and said, "Sure!"

Robin, Hannah, and Paola followed Tanner outside to where a relatively new bike stood, the one I'd seen Dave ride at the freestyle demo last year.

"Come on," said Robin to no one in particular. "We'd better get a head start."

The other girls followed her and so did I. But Dave said, "Allie," softly, and I assumed he wanted me to hang back with him. I hesitated, not wanting to get too far behind the others but not wanting to say no to him either.

Robin looked back at me, causing the others to as well. She grimaced slightly and waved the others forward. She probably rolled her eyes.

Henry had already taken off on his smaller bike. Cris put soft plugs in Stevey's ears before placing a small helmet on him. Then he lifted him onto the seat of his silver bike before putting his own helmet on. Tanner kept pace with the girls until Cris zoomed past him with what seemed like excessive revving. Then Tanner took off too.

Dave stood at his older bike, the green one he'd ridden the very first time I saw him. He held a black helmet out to me, but I didn't reach for it.

"If you don't wear it, you're not riding with me. You can walk with the others."

"But you should wear it," I argued.

He took a step closer and lifted the helmet gently onto my head. "I'll wear it when we get there," he said.

"Get where?"

"You'll see." He walked the bike out of the garage, mounted, and started it. He smiled that smile—half tender, half smirk. "You're not exactly dressed for this, but you sure look cute." His grin widened and my cheeks started to tingle. "Get on behind me. Be careful of the exhaust pipe, though. It'll burn your skin off."

He showed me the passenger peg and told me to hold onto his shoulders. I mounted as best I could, sure I'd burn myself just because he'd told me not to, and trying to figure out how to sit on my skirt so it wouldn't blow up as soon as we moved.

"Now hold on," he said, reaching back for my hands.

I did as he said but still felt precarious on the narrow seat. I'd never ridden on a motorcycle before. And wasn't this a little too much focused attention in present company? *Or do they all already know? Does it even matter anymore?*

He pressed my hands to his sides and said, "Hold on tight!" And I did.

It wasn't a long ride, and Dave drove slowly and carefully. I felt safe but a little too busy hanging on to completely enjoy it. I liked having an excuse to hold on tightly though, just wishing the helmet didn't prevent me from

crossing my arms all the way around him. Still, the *feel* of him so close—it was worth any temporary discomfort.

We rode through the open gate at the end of the driveway behind the house. There the road narrowed and continued unpaved through pasture-land to the west, though no animals were visible. We turned left off that road onto a wide track heading south and soon passed the other girls. Robin yelled something and I think Dave laughed, but between the helmet and the engine noise, I didn't catch what she said.

The trail rose and I could see we were on the other side of the orchard at the back of the house. Here was a broad area covered in solar panels. I couldn't help saying, "Wow," but I don't think Dave heard me.

Over another rise and through some trees Dave stopped, bike idling. What looked like a barren wasteland lay before us; dirt for acres. Well-worn paths crisscrossed the ground, and small hills, mounds, and large rocks were everywhere. In roughly the center were two hills, each with opposite long sides with a wide gap between.

Ramps. Oh boy.

"Welcome to our track," said Dave.

He drove slowly over to some large, flat-topped rocks shaded by trees. The rocks were perfect for sitting on, but there was an old redwood picnic table nearby too.

Tanner and Henry were out of sight, the sound of their motorcycles rising and falling like angry monster bees. Cris sat on his bike with Stevey under the trees near the rocks. I couldn't tell if he was watching for the other boys or just lost in thought.

I would have loved to stay as I was, on the bike with Dave, but the other girls would reach us any moment, and I didn't want Robin annoyed with me. The helmet was still in the way anyway. I reluctantly loosened my hands on Dave's sides.

His right hand caught and covered my left for a moment, pressing it against the edge of his ribcage. "Careful getting off. Remember the pipe . . ."

I dismounted a little awkwardly—*Note to self: don't wear skirts to Dave's house. Ever*—then took the helmet off and handed it to him.

As he strapped it on his own head, he said, "There's a cooler by the table." He indicated over by Cris. "We brought it out earlier. There's soda and water inside."

I nodded and stepped away as the other girls walked through the trees and joined us.

"Oh!" Paola said, her smile and eyes wide. "Your own race track?"

"Just a practice track," said Dave. "We don't race much. Just freestyle."

"I have never ridden a motorcycle," she said, watching the boys on the track. "*¿Es divertido?*"

"*¡Es muy divertido!*" said Dave, his smile wide.

Cris helped Stevey dismount and take his helmet off, setting it on the table. He pulled a few small toy cars out of his pockets and gave them to Stevie, speaking to him softly. Then he rolled his bike away, started it, and rode toward the track. Dave restarted his, too, and said, "Be back in a bit," and rode after him.

We sat under the trees. The guys appeared to be having a conference out on the track near the ramps. Dave and Tanner switched bikes, Dave now riding the newer, bigger one.

Paola asked Robin and Hannah if they'd ever ridden on a motorcycle. They both described instances of riding with Dave similar to my brief ride, comparing experiences, which I figured was a good thing. Letting me ride with him today should appear to be nothing special.

The girls talked about many things, and I smiled and nodded a couple of times when spoken to, but I was thinking more about earlier in the morning, the church service.

I'd been a little disappointed that I'd felt no different afterward, no more enlightened or closer to understanding God. But now, enjoying our surroundings—the cool breeze on my face, the feeling of inclusion with friends—was more inspiring. Mingled with this was the recent physical memory of holding Dave so close, the warmth of him, the feeling of my hands against his sides. *Does he like feeling me close as much as I like feeling close to him?*

A sense of complete contentment, more blissful than I'd ever felt before, made me want time to freeze just so I could enjoy it longer. I was glad the other girls didn't ask me any more questions.

The boys rode around for a while but then came together near one of the ramps to talk. One by one they sped up one side and flew over the edge to land on the opposite side. They continued this for several turns before conferring again.

Then Cris raced up the ramp and did a handstand, one hand on the handlebar and the other on the gas tank. He regained his seat and landed safely on the other side. Dave took off and accomplished basically the same move. Tanner followed after but didn't attempt the trick. Dave took off again, this time kicking his feet out behind him as the bike left the ramp, his body twisting sideways before regaining his seat just before the motorcycle touched down again. The bike wobbled on impact.

He returned to confer with Cris and Tanner. Cris was very animated, using his whole body, apparently giving advice. I'd never seen him so physically expressive. It made me smile and wish I were close enough to hear their voices. The other girls immediately wanted to know why I was smiling. I wasn't sure myself.

"They're so *into* it," I said. They nodded but obviously weren't as fascinated as I was.

The girls went back to their conversation about a television show I didn't watch. The older boys continued taking turns doing jumps, though only Dave and Cris did the more advanced tricks. They consulted with each other after each set, I supposed for critique and advice.

In spite of my apparel, I joined Stevey on the ground. He was engineering a track of his own for the little cars. He graciously showed me how to bulldoze with a thick piece of tree bark and gave me small rocks to landscape with.

I'd noticed a few vultures wheeling and gliding in the general vicinity and was intrigued by them. After the work day earlier in the year, I had looked them up on the internet: so ugly up close, with a distasteful purpose in life, yet so graceful in their element. And their purpose *was* important. They couldn't help it if their practical design was repelling to most humans. I supposed they found each other attractive though, and that's all that mattered. That reminded me of something Brenda had said last year, about me finding people like myself. And the design concept made me ponder God again.

I realized I was smiling once more and became self-conscious. If the others asked me why again, I wouldn't know what to say. "*Contemplating the mutual attraction and dating potential between vultures.*" No, definitely not.

The presence of the vultures also reminded me of the last time I'd seen them around here. How uncomfortable I'd felt, not knowing how or even *if* I still fit into Dave's world. How devastated I was, overhearing his conversation with Cris. I still didn't know what that was really about. And after that, how much more miserable I'd become, spiraling down into a vortex of jealousy and the accompanying guilt and depression. How I'd cried out to a God I didn't know for help. How I'd begged for Dave and me to just be friends again. *That* had made me feel closer to God.

At that moment, the contentment almost exploded in a new feeling. It was very close to the acceptance I'd experienced for the first time last year—the incredible feeling of having real friends—but this was so much deeper and more pervasive. A *bigger* feeling. *Joy?* They had talked about joy this morning, but I hadn't understood the context. Before that, I'd never heard the word used beyond a simple synonym for happiness or a word in a Christmas song. This feeling was so much more than that. Whatever it was, I was deeply thankful. I sat very still, praying, but also soaking the moments in, memorizing and storing it up.

Grateful.

I was grateful to be with Robin, Hannah, and Paola—my *friends*—listening to them talk and laugh. They included me, but I didn't feel pressured to speak or be something I wasn't. I didn't feel awkward around them in any way. At least not most of the time and, so far, not at all today.

I was grateful to be here, watching some of my favorite guy friends race up the ramp and seem to fly. I imagined the weightless feeling, hanging in the air for a few crazy moments trying to get the perfect lift, the perfect twist, the ideal angle of their bodies or combination of moves before coming back to earth. I could also almost feel the impact when they landed, my body involuntarily jolting each time they did.

I was even grateful for the vultures—watching them ride the thermals, circling ever higher as if exulting in their freedom, unencumbered by earthly troubles and other people's opinions.

It was an absolutely perfect day, and I reveled in it.

Then I saw the hybrid coming through the trees along the trail toward us. Miguel was driving, but it was seeing Roberta in the passenger seat that threatened my contentment. Miguel stopped the car nearby, and Roberta got out without a word or glance at him, focused on the boys. She seemed surprised when she turned toward us. I wondered if it was the sight of me there, or one of the other girls, or both.

She recovered quickly and smiled, greeting us with a chirpy, "Hey!" Miguel began backing the car out of the trees but noticed me watching. He

looked directly at me and straightened the fingers of one hand just before he turned around. The acknowledgment made me smile. I straightened fingers back at him.

Hannah and Paola had responded, "Hey," back to Roberta. But Robin voiced what I was trying not to think, "What are *you* doing here?"

Roberta laughed as if Robin had said something funny, her expression betraying no waver in confidence. "Dad was bored and called to see what these guys were doing today. Alex said everybody was just hanging out and to come on over."

This produced a variety of thoughts simultaneously, from wondering how often this kind of impromptu visit happened, to what Roberta imagined "everybody" and "just hanging out" encompassed. She obviously wasn't expecting to see all of *us* here. My feelings were relatively benign, though. I wasn't happy to see her but realized, with a certain amount of satisfaction, that her presence wasn't necessarily a threat to my current happiness. Or a threat at all to my relationship with Dave. That made me smile too.

Conversation among the girls now turned to even less interesting topics than before and I tuned out completely. Stevey had moved off a little way by himself, still extending his roadway. I focused on the other boys, tensing and holding my breath at each jump, relaxing and breathing again on each landing. I enjoyed watching their expressive interactions in-between jumps, trying to imagine what they were saying.

Then I heard Roberta say, "I'm surprised *she's* here," in a whisper plenty loud enough for me to hear.

There was a beat or two before Robin said, in nothing close to a whisper, "She's sitting right there. She's not deaf, you know."

In an only slightly softer voice, Roberta countered, "Yeah, but she's so *weird.*"

"*She* was invited."

I could tell Robin was nearing a limit and appreciated her obvious disgust and, for her, tempered responses. It would have been unbearable if she'd made a bigger deal about it. But the exchange effectively sucked all the elation out of me. In spite of everything good about today, I was back to being the outsider. The interloper. The misfit. The *weird* one.

Still sitting on the ground, I pulled my knees in tight, tucking my skirt up between my legs as modestly as I could, then rested my forehead on my knees. I closed my eyes and searched for the previous feeling. I even imagined invisible hands reaching out from all over my body. *Palms open, seeking joy.* I enjoyed the feeling. The arms the hands were attached to grew longer and longer, changed shape and color. *Feelers. No, antennae. Sky blue antennae, almost invisible against—*

"Allison . . . are you okay?" Robin's voice.

I nodded without looking up. "I'm fine."

"Why don't you come and sit with us?" Hannah's voice. I imagined a look of concern on her face.

The antennae disappeared. I angled my head sideways, forced myself to look in their general direction and smile. "I'm fine," I repeated. "I just . . . feel a little tired." That wasn't exactly right, but I didn't know how to explain how I felt at that moment and probably wouldn't have tried anyway. I turned back to my knees and shut my eyes, my hair falling forward, a flimsy curtain between us. I tried to focus on the drone of the motorcycles, contemplating.

Weird is one of those words that carries different weights and meanings depending on context and who is using it. Sort of like *love*. Or *like*. I used the word *weird* all the time, at least in my head. I'd always known that I was different and had become used to the word. I even used it in thinking of myself sometimes. I didn't see it as a bad thing. Robin and Brenda called me weird and I didn't mind one bit. But they *knew* me. I wouldn't have cared if Dave called me weird. He'd used the word *idiot* at least a couple of times in regards to me, which was probably far worse, but I hadn't doubted his affection and concern. And I was pretty sure he didn't really think I was an idiot.

But having someone describe me as *weird* who not only didn't know me but obviously didn't *like* me prompted all kinds of memories and emotions not as deeply buried as I'd thought.

I didn't want to let Roberta's presence or attitude affect me, but as the minutes passed, the whine and revving of the motorcycles began to wear me down, and the voices of the girls seemed to pierce my head, though I knew they weren't talking any louder than before. Every laugh made me wince, especially Roberta's. She was just a loud person. I pushed my fingers against my ears as inconspicuously as I could and started humming. I might have been rocking. Very slightly.

A soft patting on my back alerted me to Stevey's attention just as I heard a motorcycle approach. Then the engine cut off but the sound of the tires continued closer. I assumed it was Dave and looked up trying to force a smile.

Cris regarded me solemnly, expressionless. Extremely embarrassed, I got up carefully, dusted off the back of my skirt, and sat on the rocks nearby. Cris's gaze shifted to the girls at the picnic table. Dave rode up next with Tanner following. Henry remained by the ramps, riding tight doughnuts noisily and sending up rooster tails of loose dirt.

Dave said, "Hey," to Roberta, and she responded with a flirty, "Hey yourself."

Henry rode up right next to Dave and looked almost just like his brother but more calculating, his sharp eyes regarding everyone in turn, summing them up. *Like a Jedi. Anakin Skywalker. That would make Dave Obi Wan....*

I was considering whether Cris was at all like Qui-Gon Jinn when Henry's eyes fell on me. I blushed and squirmed. His eyes narrowed slightly.

Dave addressed all of us. "I promised Dad we wouldn't ride for more than an hour today, so we're heading back to the house. We'll meet you there."

"Can I get a ride?" said Roberta. "I've always wanted to ride on a motorcycle."

Dave said, without hesitation and regarding her steadily, "These bikes aren't built for passengers. Besides, I don't have a spare helmet."

This simple response caused several observations in me. First and foremost, Roberta couldn't know Dave well at all if she believed either of those things would stop him from doing whatever he wanted. I considered whether I would have believed him before he'd given me a ride. I certainly wouldn't have believed about the helmet.

And I wondered what the other girls were thinking, especially Hannah and Paola. Robin knew about Dave and me, of course, but I suspected Hannah and Paola did too—if not before today, they probably did now. Also, it must be why he'd ridden the older bike first. It had a longer seat and footpegs.

Robin had snorted when Dave finished speaking. Now she smirked and didn't bother to disguise it. Hannah smiled complacently. Paola looked from Dave to Roberta a couple of times but didn't say anything.

Henry took off, apparently bored, distracting Roberta. Dave glanced sideways at me, a conspiratorial glint in his eye. I met his gaze fully and tried not to smile.

"See you in a minute," he said.

"Want us to bring the cooler?" asked Robin.

He shrugged. "You can leave it. We can get it later."

He, Cris and Stevey, and Tanner rode off. Robin and Hannah each took a handle of the cooler and began walking. Roberta walked beside Hannah, and Paola and I followed. I struggled to find a topic to talk about then remembered something.

"You did gymnastics in Cuba?"

"Yes! I miss it very much. We hoped I can continue here, but there is no place near. Have you done *gymnasia?*"

The idea made me laugh. "No, but I love watching it on TV, like in the Olympics. I don't think I could do it. I have weak wrists and ankles. And I'm very . . . clumsy."

"You are not clumsy when you ride though. *¿Verdad?*"

Her smile and words warmed me through and through.

We took over the cooler about halfway. By the time the house was in view, the cloud of oppressive assumption that had arrived with Roberta had dissipated a little.

Coming back toward the house, I saw a stairway behind the north wall leading to a door above the garage. I hadn't noticed it on the way out. *Cris' bedroom? That would explain a few things.* It distracted me for a while, imagining the benefits of having an external door to your room. *You could come and go whenever you wanted without disturbing anyone else. You could also effectively avoid others if you wanted to. I bet Cris likes that.* I pictured a door and stairway leading outside from my room. *It would make it easy to sneak out to visit Remmy when I can't sleep. Or to see Ben. Or—*

"You brought it anyway," Dave observed, looking at the cooler and then smiling warmly at Paola and me. "Thanks. You can just leave it there." He indicated a spot near where Cris was making an adjustment to his bike. "I'm starving again. Let's see what's left in the kitchen."

Dave let Paola and Hannah lead the way. I thought he might be hanging back for me, so I planned to hang back too.

Roberta had other ideas. For whatever reason, she turned directly toward me and said, "Come on, Allison! Let's go inside."

I was perplexed, her sudden, smiling attention as unwanted as it was unbelievable. Her words were, I assumed, meant to be friendly. But her tone was more modulated to encourage a dog or small child. She surprised me again by taking my arm, the way Robin sometimes did. I allowed myself to be led into the house. I didn't want to cause a problem, so I quietly but unhappily went along with her. Inside, I disengaged from her as soon as I could.

Cris was the only one who didn't come back into the house with us, and I wondered if he was still working on his bike. Or one of the other bikes. *Or had he just avoided us and gone to his room using the back stairs?*

Leftovers from lunch were dug out of the refrigerator, and paper plates were distributed. The adults were all out in the courtyard. Mom looked happy, engrossed in conversation, and I was glad.

Stevey picked up a stuffed toy, then put it under his arm and climbed up on one of the stools.

Roberta went straight over to him and said, loudly and condescendingly, "Hello, Stevey! What do you have there?" She took the toy from him, and I was touched to see it was the Lady dog I'd given him for Christmas.

Stevey didn't say anything, which wasn't unusual, but he looked shocked, his eyes wide, his body tense. *That* was unusual.

Dave took the toy gently from Roberta and calmly gave it back to Stevey. "That's your favorite. Right, Stevey?" But he wasn't looking at Stevey or Roberta. He was looking at me. I probably blushed but didn't care; the acknowledgment made me so happy.

We ate for a while in and around the kitchen, then headed upstairs to watch a movie. The others—mainly Roberta and Robin—argued over which movie to watch. Roberta, Tanner, and Hannah wanted something scary. But Dave said it had to be something Stevey could watch and I was glad. They settled on *The Incredibles* and I was glad again. I'd never seen it.

I sat in the wide, comfy chair on the off-chance that Dave, Robin, or even Stevey would share it with me. But it was Paola that came and sat with me, and that was really nice too. Tanner pulled the heavy drapes closed, and we settled into the darkened room.

I don't know how Dave would have acted around me if Roberta hadn't been there, but her presence definitely affected further interaction between us—at least consciously on my part. She changed her position right away, leaving the couch to sit right next to him on the floor. I was surprised that it didn't bother me. Dave got up soon after and collected empty paper plates to take downstairs with his own. When he came back, he sat next to Hannah on the couch. I pretended not to notice.

About an hour later, Cris appeared at the room's opening and got my attention. I got up and went to him. "Your mom wants to talk to you," he said quietly.

I nodded and went downstairs and out to the courtyard. It wasn't until then that I realized Cris had changed his clothes. I wondered if he'd been hanging out with the adults all this time or staying in his room. Then I wondered why I was even wondering.

Mom said, "I'm heading home, Allison. I'm taking Fiona home too. Do you want to come now or do you want to stay? They'll bring Robin home later and said they could drop you off too."

"I'll stay," I said.

She said her goodbyes to everyone there, waved at me, and left with Fiona through the dining room. I went back upstairs.

When the movie was over, we hung out for another hour or so until Paola and Hannah left with their parents. Soon after that, Robin wanted to go too, to make sure Fiona was okay. She hadn't said anything lately, but she was obviously still very concerned about her grandmother. I told her that if she was leaving, I'd get a ride home too.

We all followed Dave downstairs. The adults were still out in the courtyard. Cris was there too, Merle at his feet.

"We need to take Allison and Robin home," said Dave.

"Can I get a ride too?" asked Tanner. His mother must also have left earlier.

Angel started to get up, but Cris stood up faster and said, "I've got it."

Roberta immediately said, "I want to go!"

I was relieved when her dad intervened with, "We should probably get going too."

Roberta looked petulant for a moment, then said to Dave with her sweetest smile, "Oh well, I'm sure we can come over *next* weekend sometime."

Robin turned toward me, rolling her eyes and pretending to gag. So when Roberta looked at me, I was trying not to smile. Apparently, I wasn't successful.

Roberta smiled at me and said, loudly and in that patronizing tone that made my skin crawl, "It was great getting to know you better, Allie."

I had no clue how to respond unless it was to say that she knew absolutely nothing about me. So I kept my mouth shut. It just wasn't worth it. I didn't think anything she could ever do or say would really bother me again. But I was wrong about that.

In the end, Roberta and her dad left before we did. Angel gave Robin a large plate with foil over it to take home with her and gave us both warm hugs. She hadn't hugged Roberta. I hadn't seen Roberta even acknowledge Angel.

Cris drove us in the hybrid to Robin's house. She agreed we'd try to spend some time together during the holiday week, but she was working as much as she could. Tanner got out of the car with her. Dave got out too and talked to him for a minute before Tanner waved and started up the street. Cris had gone into the house with Robin, and I wondered if I should follow, but he was back within moments. I assumed everything was fine.

Sitting by myself felt a little odd, and I wondered if Dave had even considered getting in the back with me, now that the others were gone. But that would have felt weird too. I wondered if it would have made Cris feel weird. *Am I the only one who thinks about these things?*

When we got to my house, Dave wanted to see Remmy. The guys came in and said hi to Mom again. Cris scooped Violet up on the way through the house and brought her outside with him. He inspected the arena and seemed to approve.

"I think we'll be over during the week to finish the footing," said Dave. Remmy had come straight over to him, and Dave scratched around his ears. "So I'll see you then, okay? We're kind of busy the next couple of weekends . . . shows and stuff."

I looked past him toward Cris. He turned away and walked back toward the kitchen.

"Yes."

Dave stepped close enough to kiss me softly and said, "Thanks for today."

Perplexed, I said, "For what?"

But he just smiled, *my* smile, and followed Cris.

Chapter Thirty-One

The next day was my last appointment with Dr. Hanwell, and she spoke to me alone for most of the appointment. I thought I was coming to terms much better with the experience and information gained from these visits. I still didn't want to go, but I liked the doctor's office—the aquarium, the prism rainbow against the wall, the comfy chairs, the mostly natural lighting, and the books. And Dr. Hanwell was very considerate, even seeming to anticipate some of my feelings and questions before I'd processed them properly myself.

The previous visits had focused more on what my mother could tell her about when I was very young, and me taking some tests. Now she asked me what I could remember from when I was younger. It didn't seem like much; snapshot memories at best, a few painful incidences in slightly more detail. I didn't want to share those.

"Did you have many friends?"

I thought about the kids who had wandered in, through, and back out of my extremely limited range of orbit in elementary and middle school. Sometimes we just didn't seem to speak the same language. Sometimes we didn't seem to belong to the same species. Other times they seemed to like me at first but eventually succumbed to the influence of others' opinions. Then I'd find myself ostracized and alone again. It always left me mystified and hurting. I thought I just wasn't cool enough for them. In spite of my

close observation of others, I'd never figured out how to be like them. And I'd never had the ambition to be popular, but I was often very lonely.

I was sure I'd already answered that specific question at least once but answered it again anyway. "Mostly just Brenda."

"And now? Are you and Brenda still friends?"

"Yes. But we moved and she still lives in Los Angeles. I spent some time with her last summer."

"Do you talk to her on the phone?"

"Sometimes," I said. I realized it had been a while again since we'd talked. I assumed she must be happy and too busy with her other friends. And Trevor, of course. Again. That was okay, though. I had plenty of my own distractions.

"Do you *like* talking on the phone?"

This seemed like a strange question. I hadn't thought much about it but realized I didn't. I shook my head.

Dr. Hanwell looked like she wanted to ask why but didn't. That was just as well as I didn't have a ready answer. I'd need to think about it.

"And what about friends now? You said you have a friend who's giving you riding lessons. Tell me about it."

This I was very happy to do, but I wasn't sure where to start. So I started at the very beginning. I told her about Gold, about Dave and Robin teaching me to ride at Bar 8, and the lessons with Cheryl. I told her about getting Remmy for my birthday and finally about taking lessons with Melanie and Kitty.

It took a lot longer than I'd thought it would, but once I started talking I couldn't stop. I felt embarrassed, sure I'd included way too much detail, and I caught myself spinning off on tangents quite a few times—the kind of thing that used to cause me trouble and perhaps made people avoid me. It was one of the reasons I often kept everything to myself now. I usually ended up feeling like I was testing people's patience, often too late. But Dr. Hanwell listened, only occasionally asking a question or writing something down. She didn't seem mad or bored, and I felt a little more comfortable with her.

"You've mentioned Dave several times. He sounds like someone special."

"Yes."

She smiled. "Boyfriend?"

"Yes." No blush. *Progress!*

She nodded. I was relieved when she didn't ask more about him.

"Do you have any questions for me?" she asked.

I was sure I should, but none leaped to mind.

"Let's ask your mom to come in again. Okay?"

When Mom was sitting in the chair next to me, Dr. Hanwell said, "I'm confirming that Allison is on the autism spectrum. Let's talk for a minute about what the diagnosis means for you, Allison, and also to you as her parent." Speaking directly to me, she said, "First of all, it's important that you know there's nothing you shouldn't do if you want to. Some things may not happen as quickly or easily for you as for other people you know. You may need modifications for physical, social, and intellectual aspects of your life. Unfortunately, not everyone will understand or accept that, but it's essential that *you* do. You'll find your strengths—the things you're most interested in and the things you're best at—and it's okay to focus on those. They could lead to an interesting and fulfilling career. It's the same as for everyone, really. It's just that with autism, things often happen differently, at a different pace, and may not look or seem the way other people expect. You may need accommodations and support in some areas of your life.

"You also need to know that the difference in the way you think and experience the world is due, at least in large part, to a difference in the way your brain works. The way you process everything—from language to emotions, to social interaction, even how things look, taste, feel, smell, and sound—might be very different from other people, even other autistic people. But I want to emphasize *different*. There is nothing *wrong* with you."

There were suddenly tears in my eyes. It was too much to take in, and my emotions were a huge blurry mess. I'd have to sort it out later. A part of me was severely alarmed. I didn't want to be different, even though I'd always known I was. I had sometimes been bullied and treated as if I were trying to be unique or quirky, when I'd actually worked so hard to blend in, especially since middle school. I'd striven for it, often at great mental and emotional expense. Being different certainly wasn't something I was *trying* to do.

But another part of me was relieved. *So* many things were starting to make sense. My sensory issues, especially sound and smell, and some of my physical traits that I'd always blamed myself for and had caused such disdain in my classmates. The diagnosis explained an awful lot.

"There are many things—disorders, syndromes, physical and psychological issues—that are often found in autistic populations to a greater degree than nonautistic. They may cause one person to be considered disabled while another might not. And some disabilities are invisible like autism usually is."

Disabled?

Mom and Dr. Hanwell continued to talk, but I was barely paying attention anymore. I'd never thought much about disability. I never would have thought about applying the word to myself. I'd been aware of a boy at my old school who used a wheelchair, but he hadn't been in my grade, and I didn't know him at all. I hadn't thought of him as disabled then, though now I realized he was. Is that how my friends saw me? How much did they know? And now I was worried again about how Dave perceived me.

I didn't even know what to think of myself. *Autistic? Disabled?* How did I feel about that? There were other words that Dr. Hanwell had used, naming some conditions she thought might apply to me. Some would need diagnosis by a different doctor. I'd recognized a couple from the reading I'd done, but I didn't grasp hold of them. They whizzed by, and I was too overwhelmed to reach out and grab them to examine them closer. I supposed they'd be written down somewhere. She said we could meet again if I wanted more specific diagnoses, or just to talk further about anything.

She said a copy of my diagnosis would be mailed to us and we could use it, or not, at our discretion. If we felt I needed modifications at school, even in college, we could give them a copy of the diagnosis and ask for them. But it was up to us. Up to *me*.

I liked that.

The rest of that week, Spring break, Dave often texted me during the day and called some evenings, but the calls weren't long. And that was okay. They were long enough to connect with him, and his voice was sometimes the last thing I heard before falling asleep. I *loved* listening to his voice.

Since Dr. Hanwell's question, I realized I *didn't* like to talk on the phone and tried to analyze why. I'd never been good at conversation. I wasn't good at making things up to talk about—social chit-chat, I guess. Talking just for the sake of talking had never interested me. I also realized I had a harder time processing language over the phone, especially if the other person talked fast. The context was often confusing and visual clues were missing. I guess I needed those. I always tried to picture the other person's face and what their expressions might be, but it was challenging. And I was never sure when I was supposed to talk. It was difficult enough face to face, but over the phone was far worse. At least now I knew why I was okay with getting mostly just texts from Dave, in spite of loving the sound of his voice.

No, I'd never liked talking on the phone.

On Wednesday night, Dave called. I was listening to him talk about how his track meet had gone, but my mind wasn't really registering most of it. I wondered if he usually texted me because he realized I didn't like talking on the phone much. Had we ever discussed it? I couldn't remember. Then I wondered if it was because he knew *why* I didn't like talking on the phone.

Tell him! Just tell him!

He diverted me completely instead. "Oh hey, we've got motocross and demos on the twenty-fourth. I want you to come again. You know . . . *picnic*." I could practically feel him smiling. "I'm not sure if Robin can come. Seems like she's working on the weekends all the time. But Angel'll be there. Ask if you can go, okay?"

His comment about Robin was valid. Except at school, I barely saw her these days either. And his oblique reference to my dad's possible objection wasn't lost on me.

I agreed but later thought it through more carefully. Although I'd enjoyed watching the boys on Easter, I also remembered last year's motocross event vividly. It had been hot and dusty and incredibly noisy. And watching Dave and Cris racing around the track and then defying gravity in the demos had been exciting but extremely nerve-wracking. Just thinking about it made my stomach churn. I tried to remember if I'd actually *enjoyed* that day but couldn't.

But Dave had asked me to go. I wasn't going to say no.

I thought more and more about telling Dave about everything—the things I was involved in and that concerned me. I needed to tell him about Northfield and about jumping and dressage. But for some reason, I clung even tighter to keeping it to myself. I just didn't want to deal with his opinion on it, positive or negative. It would affect me too much. And that made me feel guilty, as if I were being selfish. I wouldn't have been able to explain that to anyone, but it made sense to me.

And that's why I couldn't bear the thought of telling him about my—I didn't even know what to call it. *Condition? That sounds like I have a bad heart or I'm pregnant or something.*

Doctor Hanwell said autism was still designated a disorder by most of the medical world. But I didn't *feel* disordered and didn't want to call it that either. Did I find it hard to fit in with others? Difficult to communicate with and understand them? Were there other things—sensory issues, my clumsiness, my thought processes—that seemed different from all my friends? Yes, undeniably. But that was it—*different.* I wasn't sick. I didn't feel disordered and I didn't need fixing. I wasn't *wrong.*

And I didn't think I could talk to Dave about it. Not now. *Not yet.*

I tried not to think about all the things he might think or say about it, but that was wasted effort. But the *not* telling and worrying what he would think if he knew made me feel guilty and miserable. I had many imaginary conversations with him, exploring all the scenarios I could think of, even talking to myself in the mirror at home. But that made me feel silly, even guilty as well. I much preferred talking it out with Remmy, always a gentle and supportive listener.

I had questions that were starting to bother me—questions about my relationship with Dave—but asking them could, probably *would,* lead to other questions, and I'd feel compelled to confess everything. For the most part, I continued to be content with the status quo and didn't want to do or say anything that might upset it.

By the middle of April, daily life at school felt pretty weird. Almost everyone close to me was involved in after school sports. And most people were driving now too, so they disappeared as soon as the last bell rang. Some—like Robin, Melanie, and Dave—had real jobs as well. Even Choir was affected by how busy everyone was. Sometimes there was less than half our number there, but I didn't mind that. Ben, Hannah, and Paola were always there. It became even more of a haven. But apart from those times, I felt more isolated than I had in over a year.

I was still aware—sometimes hyper-aware—of negative attitudes, but there'd been a noticeable shift in behaviors around me. No one seemed out to get me anymore; no veiled threats, extended legs, or purposeful assaults.

In fact, it seemed the complete opposite. Of course, I'd never been popular. Outside my now more extensive but still limited circle of friends, I had remained mostly invisible. But now people seemed to actively avoid me, moving away from an area if I entered it. Conversations ceased if I got too close. They even avoided looking at me, which I guess was better than the glares I'd become almost used to, but it made me feel weird all the same.

Had I done something new and heinous? Was I suddenly looking weird? Weirder than usual? Did I smell bad? I couldn't think of anything different. Unless they *knew*.

I had tried to be so careful at school. I thought I'd been much more cautious than Dave had. He hadn't done anything to overtly indicate we were more than friends. No whispered conversations except those few words in English. He never touched me in any way, unlike last year when he'd seemed to find excuses for physical contact. He didn't gaze into my eyes the way I still tended to do to him. Even imagining him doing that made me laugh. But he was around me much more and, even to me, seemed less accessible to other girls than he was a short time ago. To those who seemed to monitor his every movement, it had to be noticeable.

But if they knew, I was surprised they avoided me. Experience indicated they'd be more aggressive, not less. I tried not to worry about it, but it became hard to ignore.

At the same time, I had a growing need to confide in *someone* about my new neurological status. I finally decided to tell Brenda. She was my oldest friend, and I figured if she hadn't turned her back on me after all this time, she probably wouldn't now.

"What's that mean?" she said. I'd told her I'd been to a doctor and was diagnosed as autistic. "You're not going to die, are you?"

"No. It means my brain works differently than most people's."

"Oh," she said. She was quiet for a moment, then said, "I guess that makes sense."

And that was that. She went on to tell me of Trevor's latest exploits and even asked about Dave without adding innuendo to everything I said. All in all, the conversation left me feeling validated and glad I'd told her.

Around midnight that same night, still awake and endlessly hashing out imaginary conversations in my head, I felt in desperate need of downloading, verbally, everything stuck there. Another confession seemed in order.

Pulling on sweats and thick socks, I prepared to go and talk to Remmy, my favorite confidante. But I stopped and picked up my phone, pulled up Ben's number, and texted, *'Are you awake?'*

'Yep.'

'Can you talk?'

'Sure. Come on over.'

That wasn't exactly what I had in mind.

A second later, *'Joking. BTIAM.'*

Shaking my head and smiling, I went quietly down the stairs, out the back door, put my rubber boots on, and went over to the stable. Still keeping my thoughts to myself, I continued to go over what I thought I'd say as I pet Remmy. When I heard Ben say my name in a harsh whisper, I left the stall.

"It's cold!" he said, rubbing his arms. He hadn't worn a coat.

"Let's go in here," I said, opening the third stall door.

Ben followed me into my tack and feed room. I handed him a saddle blanket that wasn't too dirty, and he wrapped it around his shoulders.

"Thanks."

I sat on a bale of shavings, he on a bale of hay. There was no electric light in the stall, but moonlight streamed in through the top half of the door.

"What's up? Changed your mind about dating me?" His eyes were wide, his straight eyebrows raised impossibly high.

That made me laugh. "No. Sorry. Actually, I wanted to tell you something. A couple of somethings."

"A couple of somethings," he repeated, now looking skeptical or worried, but sort of smiling, too.

"You know Dave? Dave Caldera?"

"Of course."

"Well . . . we're going out. I mean, he's my boyfriend."

I watched Ben's face for signs of pain, but apart from a considering look, his expression didn't change much.

"Really."

"Yes."

"It's not obvious," he said.

"That's good."

"Why good?"

I wasn't prepared to explain that. *Moving on.*

"Do you mind?"

"Mind? Why should I mind? I told you I was just joking about stuff before. You didn't think I was serious, did you?"

"No. But I thought you might . . ." Now I felt uncomfortable. I didn't care one way or the other, but he might not like me thinking he had feelings for Dave.

"I think he's a great guy. I mean, *really* great. I really . . . admire him." He smiled slightly, but I couldn't read anything into it.

"Also, I'm autistic."

Now he looked perturbed, but perhaps more by my sudden change of subject than by the revelation itself.

"Okay," he said.

"I just wanted you to know. I . . . I'm not used to knowing about it myself yet. I've only told one other person. No one around here. I'm not sure whether to or not."

Ben didn't give his opinion but nodded his head.

"I have ADHD," he said. "I used to have to take medication all the time when I was younger, but I don't like the way it makes me feel and the way it makes my brain work—or *not* work. So I don't take it much anymore. That's one of the things that makes Vivian unhappy."

I considered what he'd said. My doctor had mentioned ADHD but hadn't recommended medication. Maybe I didn't actually have ADHD, or it was less severe than Ben's. "My doctor said I might be affected by it, too. I'm still learning about it." I frowned. "Is that why you told people you do drugs?"

He snorted. "Yeah, when I first moved here. Just to get a rise out them. Funny how stuff like that gets passed around and blown out of proportion, right? I guess I shouldn't have."

His confession only confirmed my reasons for being reluctant to share personal information. One part of me wanted to completely own my diagnosis. The other part was more determined than ever to be careful and keep the information from those who might somehow use it against me.

"I mean, I've tried a couple of things . . . before I came here. But I hate anything messing with my head. So, I don't anymore."

I nodded, mostly to acknowledge what he'd said, but I guess I approved, too. "So you don't think that it's weird? That I'm autistic?"

He shook his head. "It doesn't change who you are. You're my friend. It's just a word."

It's just a word. I smiled. "Thanks. And . . . I'd still be your friend if it *were* true, but I'm glad you don't do drugs."

He gave me his leprechaun grin, and I was happy I'd told him everything.

"Tell me a story," I said.

"Have I ever told you about Finland?"

The story had more fantastic elements than usual, and I was sure it couldn't be true. But I loved the way he told it, acting out parts and describing things in such detail I could almost see and feel and smell it.

I slept very well for the rest of the night.

On Wednesday, Roger had a baseball game, so Melanie had driven her mom's car to school. She said she could drive me home, too, so I could stay at Northfield later. Dave had a track meet somewhere near Chico and wouldn't be home until late, so I knew I wouldn't be seeing him. It seemed like the perfect opportunity to see what Melanie's reaction would be, if any.

"I went to a psychologist," I said as she drove. "She says I'm autistic."

She completely surprised me by saying, very calmly, "I thought so."

"You did?"

She smiled gently but didn't say anything more. My mind was running down well-worn paths: *Is it obvious?* I remembered something Henry had said, or almost said. *Do I look a certain way? Is it the way I talk? The way I don't talk?* I thought of Isabel. *Is it the way I walk? The way I move?* I wasn't aware of moving in any particular fashion, but I'd been more self-conscious about it since Isabel's visit.

There seemed to be a million things—traits, characteristics—that I was learning I shared with other autistic people. But not all of the characteristics. And I'd apparently repressed some things, but I hadn't been aware of it until now. I'd certainly learned to avoid betraying many of them—I just wasn't always conscious of doing it.

"How?" I finally asked.

"Eva, the Farrington's daughter, was diagnosed a few years ago. You're not really that much like her, but you remind me of each other sometimes.

And I have an autistic student. But she's quite different from you—she doesn't communicate verbally and has physical disabilities."

I looked out the window and thought about that. One of the things I recognized in myself was how much less I talked than what appeared to be average. Apart from language just failing me sometimes, especially in times of stress, I didn't often have much I wanted to talk about—unless it was something I was vitally interested in.

I thought about it the rest of the way to Northfield. And I thought about it during my lesson, allowing Kitty to take shameless advantage of me. And I thought about it when Dave called later that evening to say hi and tell me how the track team had done.

He said that he'd won two out of three races and achieved the third highest jump. I tried to make the right responses, mostly "Wow"s and too-stuffy "Congratulations." I was worried about not sounding excited enough but just wasn't sure what to say. And the whole time he was talking, I was thinking, *"You need to tell him. Tell him now! Just tell him!"* but an easy opportunity didn't present itself.

When he asked, "What have you been doing all afternoon?" I almost said, "Riding."

But he answered his own question with, "Oh yeah . . . you hang out with that girl, Melanie, huh."

Tell him about Northfield!

But he changed the subject right away, and I didn't tell him. It was easier, *safer*, to say nothing.

Before going to bed, I checked my email and found that Estephanie had sent one at the beginning of the month. It was accompanied by photos of three foals: a dark colt—Estephanie said he would turn gray like his mother—and two palominos, a colt and a filly. She said they were very pleased with Gold's ability to pass his color on and that the two colts were already spoken for. They were keeping the filly. The foals were so adorable, and I studied them carefully. How I wished I could see them in person! I sent her a short reply and printed the pictures to show my friends.

Robin agreed to meet me early in Geometry on Friday. "What's up? You're going to motocross with Dave tomorrow, right?" she asked.

"Yes. You're working?"

She looked dissatisfied but said, "Yeah. I want to go with you guys, but I don't want to turn work down. I've saved almost five hundred dollars already. I hope I can save a thousand before. . . ." She didn't finish, but I supposed she meant before summer.

"That's a lot!" I said, trying to sound encouraging. I'd never even seen that much money.

"Yeah." She frowned though, as if she didn't think it was much at all. "Is that what you wanted to talk about?"

"Oh, no. I'm still working through it myself, so I'd rather you didn't tell anyone. I haven't said anything to Dave."

Robin looked serious, maybe even worried, but nodded her head. I never would have trusted her with the information before, but I did now.

"I recently was diagnosed as autistic. I just wanted to tell you."

Robin frowned. "Are you sure? Stevey's autistic and you're not at all like him."

That had stumbled me too, but I *did* relate to him. I certainly didn't feel separated from him by language—or lack of it.

I smiled. "Yes, I'm sure."

"Huh." She shrugged. "Okay."

Then I showed her the pictures of Gold's babies and we talked about them, speculating on their futures. She said it reminded her that she'd lost my school picture again and asked if she could have another. We laughed about that, but I was relieved, too. She acted like I'd never mentioned autism.

The motocross meet was everything I'd remembered from the year before, only without Robin there for support and distraction. I'd brought my backpack with pencils and sketchbook and even some homework, but I was too preoccupied to do the homework and once I'd sketched the surrounding landscape, Angel reading a magazine in the shade of a canopy, and some quick, very imperfect sketches of motorcycles, there didn't seem to be much else to draw. I did do a quick study of Stevie. I asked him if I could draw him and he smiled, looked away toward the track, and sat very still for quite a long time. His only movement was twirling one of the wheels of a Hot Wheels car with his fingers. I showed him the drawing when I'd done all I could to it. He looked at it for a long time, wiggling his foot. I hoped he liked it.

Later, I walked to where the SUV and trailer were parked, hoping to see Dave alone for even a few moments. Instead, I found Cris. He looked at me briefly as he rolled his silver motorcycle off the trailer. I suddenly remembered something important.

"I forgot to tell you . . . at Christmas. I'm sorry."

Now he looked at me steadily, his brows raised.

"About last summer. My dad . . . I know he blamed you and Dave, which he shouldn't have done. I explained that neither of you had anything to do with my decision. But I'm sorry. *Really.*"

He looked up again, a strange expression on his face. He nodded slightly and I thought he looked wary, though I couldn't imagine why.

I blushed—the first time in a long while—at the memory of last year when I'd made a similar apology. It suddenly felt like all I ever did was say I was sorry to him. Or berate him. No wonder he didn't like me much. Still, his family liked me, for whatever reason, so he probably tolerated me for their sake.

I leaned against the edge of the trailer as he made some adjustments to the motorcycle. Then he picked up his helmet and sat on the bike, but didn't seem in a hurry to leave, his helmet resting in front of him.

I felt no need to fill the silence between us, but he seemed to feel uncomfortable. He frowned again, then asked, "How's it going at Northfield?"

I perked up immediately. "Great! Melanie and Tatty both say I'm doing really well. I rode in my first dressage schooling show. I think I did pretty well. And I'm jumping! Well . . . starting to jump. . . ." I babbled on about how fantastic Kitty was and how well we seemed to get along now, at least most of the time, and how Remmy was doing with English tack, and how much I enjoyed going to Northfield but how great it was having our own arena, too.

I finally realized I'd been talking too long. Extremely embarrassed, I wondered if I was keeping him from something important.

"Sorry. I don't mean to make you late for a race or anything."

He shrugged slightly. "I have no more heats today. I'll do the demo later. That'll probably be the last time I ride."

Not sure what he meant, I frowned.

"Here. Motorcycles. I'll be in LA and won't have time anymore."

Right. University. "Will you miss it?" For some reason, I was trying to have a normal conversation with Cris. This seemed like a reasonable question to ask.

He looked at me as if he knew exactly what I was doing—*annoying girl trying to get on the good side of Dave's brother.* That's not exactly what I was doing, but close enough.

He shrugged again. "Maybe. Life's going to be different. I'm hoping I'll be able to surf more. It's a trade-off I can live with."

That seemed like a reasonable answer, and I was happy he seemed willing to talk. This was nice. Angst-free. I tested the boundaries of his goodwill with a more personal question.

"Why didn't you want your family to know you were at Northfield?"

This elicited a more surprised look. "That's . . . complicated."

"Because of the trouble last year?" Feeling guilty, I added, "Because of me?"

He still looked surprised. "No. It's got nothing to do with you. Technically, Dave and I aren't supposed to hang out at the community center, but there's nothing stopping us from being at the equestrian center."

This was news to me but was not a satisfying answer.

"*Technically,*" he continued, "it's James that's not supposed to be at the equestrian center."

"But he's a vet. Why wouldn't he be allowed there?"

"He's allowed," said Cris, "but he also works for Dr. Simons. Dr. Simons refuses to work out there because of the ongoing problems between the developers of Northfield and the agricultural community. Purely politics. But James plans to start his own practice as soon as he can, and he'll go anywhere he's needed."

I was still frowning. "So you don't want your family to know Dr. James is willing to work out there?"

Cris frowned back at me. "They don't care where he works. Though," he said, looking away as if thinking, "I guess it's possible my dad might say something if the subject came up."

I was more confused than ever but didn't want to push my luck. I didn't want to annoy him *too* much. A change of topic seemed in order. There was only one other thing that popped into my head; a question that was becoming more and more philosophical—at least on my part—the more I asked it.

"Do you believe in God?"

This time he looked more than surprised. *Startled.* I thought it was an odd reaction and he looked like he'd say something immediately, but stopped. He looked off into the distance again.

After a few moments, he said, "That's complicated, too." He paused again and I waited for an explanation, but he put his helmet on and started his bike. "I need to go," he said.

"Okay," I said, wondering if I'd crossed a line. As he backed his motorcycle away, I called out "Cris!"

He stopped and looked back at me.

"Be safe!" I said, hoping I was loud enough over the bike's engine.

He nodded slightly, turned the bike, and took off.

I walked to where the family was gathering to watch the demos, questions remaining from talking with Cris almost a buffer against the stress of watching him and Dave flying through the air doing crazy things with motorcycles.

Later, back at the house, Dave and I went upstairs with Henry and Stevie to watch a movie. I'd been invited to stay for dinner, and my dad had actually said I could. I saw this as a huge step forward, not so much in my relationship with Dave, as in my relationship with and independence from my parents.

While the boys decided on a movie, I went back downstairs to go to the bathroom. Coming back, before I got halfway up the stairs, I became aware of Cris coming down, but I couldn't really look at him. Stairs demand my complete attention. I stopped and moved more to my right to make room for him to pass me, but he didn't.

I looked up, still holding the railing. He looked down at me and I made my eyes meet his. His searched mine in return for a heartbeat or two. I'd always thought his eyes looked like Dave's, and I guess like Henry's too—their dad's eyes. But now I didn't think they were so much alike. Maybe it was because I knew Dave better.

Cris looked uncomfortable and broke eye-contact first, now looking out toward the family room. I felt awkward, too, but kept looking at him, waiting.

After another moment, he said, "Do you. . . ." He looked back at me again. "Thanks for not saying anything about seeing me at Northfield."

"You're welcome. And, same."

He frowned and nodded. The exchange felt weird; I guess we were back to awkward again. He stood aside and I continued up the stairs.

What was that about? Is that what he was really going to say? And if not, what?

I tried not to overthink it. I didn't see him again until dinner. The family was joined in the dining room by Miguel, but Cris disappeared again. After dinner, Angel and Dave drove me home.

Chapter Thirty-Two

The last week of April was sunny and dry. According to Dave, we hadn't received as much rain as local agriculture needed, though it had rained sporadically through the winter and spring. We were still in what was considered a drought and ranchers and farmers in southern California had even fewer water resources.

But the dry weather certainly made riding and taking care of the horses easier, and I enjoyed our new finished arena at home. So did Remmy. Dad had liked and approved Dave's design for connecting the new stall runs to the arena. I loved being able to let Remmy loose in it, knowing he could retreat back to his paddock and stall if he wanted to. It was especially useful for the days I didn't ride him.

At school, there was some conversation, at least among any older kids present, revolved around the senior camping trip starting on Thursday and the hope that it wouldn't be rained out. Every year before finals and graduation, the seniors went on a long weekend camping trip, a bonding experience before everyone went their separate ways to college or whatever. I'd heard about the trip last year but hadn't known any seniors, and I'd barely noticed when they all went missing.

I wouldn't have cared or thought about it at all except for Cris and our odd conversations. I rarely saw him at school and apparently he'd hardly been on campus since the middle of March. Dave said he was taking as

many classes as he could at Lowell College before transferring to UCLA. So I wondered if he'd be able to go on the camping trip, or if he even wanted to.

That Thursday and Friday were strange days at school, not just because a quarter of the school's population was missing along with about half the cars in the parking lot, but there felt like a significant shift in the atmosphere on campus.

Summer was coming. Nights were still often cold enough for winter coats, but nuances in day to day living—warmer days, longer daylight, signs around town—heralded the even warmer temperatures and school-free days to come.

I was trying not to think about them and succeeding pretty well, very content with the current status quo. My days were mostly predictable and manageable. Roberta's pointed patronizing continued, but only when Dave was nearby. It might have been funny if it didn't always set my teeth on edge.

But I felt like I knew where I stood with everyone important in my life.

A recent phone call from Brenda also confirmed the encroaching season. She was ecstatic about joining her parents in Cabo this year but full of sighs for the concurrent separation from Trevor. Both moods sounded forced somehow, as if she were trying to convince herself of how she felt.

Though I hadn't met Trevor, I didn't think very highly of him. I knew a part of that prejudice was due to what Brenda's friends had said about him last summer, but nothing Brenda had ever said had altered that opinion. So it was difficult to feel empathy for her. Before I could try to imagine myself and Dave in a similar scenario, she changed the subject.

"What are *you* doing this summer? Hanging out with your cowboy?" Her taunting tone had no power over me now, and I accepted the implied ownership of Dave, even if I didn't perceive my relationship with him that way. I supposed he was "mine" from an emotional point of view, but no more in physical reality than the things I'd claimed when Brenda and I played "Mine" in grade school.

"I don't know yet. Dad's talking about a trip to South America, but I don't know if Mom's going as well."

I hadn't asked Dave about his summer plans, and he hadn't offered any information. I was very much living in the moment. If Dad went to South America and Mom went with him, I supposed I'd be staying in Los Angeles again. I doubted they'd be able to take me too. I wasn't sure I'd want to go even if they could. Too many unknowns. So I just wasn't dealing with it; not until I had to.

"So have you and Dave done it yet?"

It took a moment before I understood the question. I shouldn't have been surprised that she'd ask this, but I was unprepared all the same. Trying to formulate an appropriate response took too long. She felt the need to clarify.

"*You* know . . . have you had sex?"

Had I thought about it? Yes, but in vague, cuddly, rose-tinted vignettes. I wasn't in any hurry. Dave had never brought the subject up and, apart from kissing and embracing in few and far between moments of privacy, he'd made no moves to make me think he was in a hurry either. Another area of status quo that I was content with. I kind of dreaded anything disrupting it.

"No," I said and then changed the subject.

Dave still came over once or twice a week on the days he didn't have track meets or extra work with Tom or at home. I felt bad that I'd never seen him compete at track, but the home meets were always on Wednesdays. I couldn't bear the thought of missing a riding lesson. They were the highlight of my week and I looked forward to them so much. But he never seemed to expect me to be there, so I didn't worry about it too much.

When he could come over, I appreciated his help with geometry the most, though I found it much easier than algebra. Still, I might not have done as well in the class if not for him. I was doing okay on my own account in Spanish, but he obviously enjoyed helping me, and I loved hearing him speak it. So he usually "helped" me with that too.

Sometimes he said things that I was sure had nothing to do with the homework, but were beyond my ability to translate. It was a little frustrating, and embarrassing too. I wondered what he was saying and worried about whether my parents could understand if they overheard, though such phrases and words were usually uttered in a softened voice a little too close to my ear for comfort. My expressions at such times only earned mischievous grins or laughs from him.

"One day I'll be able to understand, you know," I said once.

"I look forward to it," he said, eyes glittering, eyebrow slightly raised, but his smile as soft as ever.

Apart from that, his behavior around my parents was exemplary. This actually made me more nervous than if he hadn't been so careful. It didn't

seem quite like him, I guess, and I mistrusted it. Then I felt guilty, of course. Dad seemed, for the most part, resigned to Dave's presence in my life. He even thanked him a couple of times for helping me with homework.

Mom was quietly reserved around him, which was a little harder to figure out. I knew she liked him. I think she even thought he was a good influence on me in some way. But there was still something not completely accepting about her. Something watchful. And it wasn't necessarily *him* she was watching.

Our only real alone time was out with Remmy, down by the stream or while Remmy played in the old corral, or a few stolen moments in Remmy's stall or the feed room. Except for the day Gold left last year, Dave had never been in my room. I'd never invited him, mostly because my English tack was there. I still wasn't dealing with him knowing about that.

There were still so many questions I had about him—questions about the distant past, the recent past, and the immediate future—but any of those questions could open topics that might turn back on me. I just wasn't ready to go there. So conversations with him still often felt weird to me. Not being completely alone with him usually avoided those situations. He didn't seem to mind, though he sometimes looked slightly puzzled. And *that* was still one of my favorite expressions.

I loved feeling important to him, though. I tried not to let doubts sneak in, but they did, sometimes accompanied by memories of things Matthew had said or implied, as well as guilt over the things I still hadn't told him. I just didn't want anything to affect our relationship. I had lost too many people in the past—people who might have been, *could* have been friends—through not being careful enough. At least, that's what I assumed. I'd never understood what I'd done or hadn't done to change people's attitudes toward me. It hurt way too much to think that my relationship with Dave might be that fragile, so I tried not to consciously think about it at all.

So I *was* still careful, *very* careful, and it often made me feel exhausted by the time we parted. I adored his attention, even craved it sometimes, but I couldn't help or explain the sense of relief I sometimes felt when he'd left. This was also much too confusing to dwell on. So I didn't. It was much easier at school where there was more distraction and his attention wasn't focused on me.

Purposefully avoiding even *thinking* about the things I hadn't told him, while actually *with* him, was also exhausting. It made conversation even more awkward and sometimes downright weird.

"What are you doing tomorrow?" he sometimes asked.

My response depended on the truth. If the next day was a Wednesday, I avoided the question altogether and would say something completely unrelated, as if I hadn't heard him. I was sure if he thought about it he'd remember I spent Wednesday afternoons with Melanie, but I didn't want to give him a chance to ask what we did. He never forced the issue, and I couldn't tell how he felt about my prevarication. I'm sure eventually it was obvious.

If the next day was Tuesday or Thursday, I could just say, "I have Choir." This often sparked a relatively short, safe, and enjoyable conversation about music. He preferred classic and heavy rock, metal, and rap. I preferred alternative and indie rock and pop and pretty much anything that made it impossible to stay still. I spent hours listening to the bands he suggested. He always forgot what bands I'd talked about, but I didn't mind and wasn't too surprised. I was busy, but he was even busier.

He sometimes asked about what we were singing in Choir, but I got the feeling it was just to keep me talking. I didn't mind. I loved explaining the songs—what they were about, when were written, who the composers were, and anything else I thought relevant.

Sometimes Dave's face remained placid but his eyes would dance, and I felt he was laughing inside. I didn't mind that too much either. And sometimes those conversations went in directions I didn't want them to.

One day he said, "Yeah, but what does it *sound* like?"

My mood abruptly changed. "You heard us sing earlier in the year at our first concert."

"I didn't hear *you* sing."

Panic.

"Sing something for me."

Every thought in my head scattered to the four corners of the earth. "What?"

He laughed out loud but spoke softly. *Too* softly. "I want to hear *you* sing."

The first time he asked, I was too shy. The second time, too.

"I'm never going to stop asking you. You've heard *me* sing."

That made me laugh. I remembered that conversation. It occurred to me I hadn't been exactly complimentary. *All the more reason to not open myself to return criticism!*

I began imagining I was singing for him when I was at choir practice sometimes, or practicing the songs down by the creek or old corral where no one but Remmy could hear.

Dave's persistence eventually wore me down. We were sitting down by the stream while Remmy grazed on a long line. I sang some phrases from one of my favorite choir songs, very softly and self-consciously.

He smiled. "Latin, right?"

"Yes."

"Do you know what it means?"

I did and recited the English translation. It was a hymn, the ancient text set to a Baroque composition.

"Hnh," he said. "I understood some of the words. They still say some things in Latin at church. But I don't go very often."

My heart beat a little faster. It felt, just for a moment, like we could be on the edge of discussing more serious things. Things I'd wanted to talk about but hadn't known how to approach him with. And those kinds of topics could lead to a more revealing conversation; maybe confessions. I tried to mentally steel myself to disclose *everything* and asked a recent question still very much on my mind.

"Do you believe in God?"

I expected him to take at least a few moments to think about it, hoping there would be an opportunity to discuss the answer. But a shrug and, "I don't know. I don't think about it," was all he offered before saying he should probably be getting home.

We kissed and held each other for a minute before returning to the house, and I'm sure he acted no differently than usual, but my mind was in turmoil. I concentrated so hard on also acting "normal" that everything in those minutes felt surreal, weirdly outside myself.

It wasn't the first time I'd felt like that with him, where I was so conscious of every little thing within my focus—every word, action, and expression—that everything else disappeared and became immaterial. After he'd said goodbye to my parents and left, I agonized over those previous few words.

He hadn't seemed angry or defensive—no, I was quite sure he hadn't. But would he have shown me if he was? I didn't know. It was probably nothing. He probably just didn't want to get into trouble with my parents for staying too long away from the house, though that didn't sit right either. It wasn't that I desperately needed an answer to that particular question, but I suddenly realized we never really talked about anything beyond day-to-day happenings, horse-related topics and, very occasionally, stories from his past.

The latter I always listened to with rapt attention, trying to picture him in whatever situation he was relating, along with whoever else was involved. His life seemed so rich, so cram-packed with activity and people and animals. But he still never mentioned his mother. There was never even a gap in his narration where she might have been. It was just another unanswered question.

By the first week of May, Dad's trip to South America had been confirmed. He'd be visiting several companies in different countries. I never heard my parents discuss what Mom and I would be doing, and I didn't ask. I vaguely hoped we'd just stay here in Douglas, but I mostly just didn't think about it.

There were plenty of other topics to direct my thoughts onto: our final choir performance, attending a horse show with Cheryl and Remmy, another schooling show, and the first big USEF dressage show of the year at Northfield. I was extremely excited about all of these things, and when topics around me became boring or too stressful, I'd retreat inside my head to mentally practice my dressage tests or choir songs or review recent jumping lessons.

I still hoped to slide through the last weeks of school relatively unremarked and unnoticed except by my close friends. But it was not to be.

On the Monday after Mother's Day I was called into the councilor's office during Art. I didn't want to go. Not only did I *not* want to listen to or discuss whatever Mrs. Woolton had on her mind, I also resented being pulled away from Melanie and the one class I unreservedly enjoyed. Miss Laski assured me I wouldn't miss much and could get any information I needed from herself or Melanie. For me, that wasn't the point.

"Oh, Allison," added Miss Laski as I reached the door. "While you're there you should pick up your still life from the office." She turned back and

addressed the class. "If you had art on display in the office, it's all been taken down and is ready for you to pick up."

I left and walked as slowly as I could to the front of the school. I hadn't seen Mrs. Woolton since before I'd begun seeing Dr. Hanwell, and I wondered what she wanted to talk about. I still didn't feel ready to talk to anyone about my diagnosis, besides the few people I'd told. I especially didn't want to talk to any adults at school about something this personal and confusing.

Mrs. Woolton's door was open and she called me right in. "Hello, Allison. Sit down." I sat. "I just wanted to see you once more before the end of the school year. How has your year been? Any problems since our last meeting?"

Her reference to problems suddenly brought up sharp memories of things over the last year. I had not exactly forgotten them but had avoided thinking about them. The run-in with Lori and the others at Dave's soccer game. The tripping and jostling incidences at the beginning of the year. Getting slammed in the gym bathroom; that had been the worst. The general hostility and disdain I was still aware of in English, Spanish, PE, at lunch, and at other more random times.

Dave's presence had been more than adequate insulation during English. I didn't know whether he was aware of the animosity or not, but for the past couple of months he and Kyle had stood talking outside the Language Arts building until I arrived, and then followed me into the building, up the stairs, and into the classroom—not too close, but close enough.

Dave didn't pay *too* much attention to me during class, of course, which was a good thing for several reasons, not least of which was my ability to concentrate. He always made a point of walking out with me, usually accompanied by Hannah or Kyle, and sometimes Roberta too, though the latter probably not by design. I wasn't curious enough to ask about reasons for his actions.

No, things had been pretty much okay for a while.

"Allison?"

"Oh . . . yes. I mean, no. No problems."

"Well, that's good. I thought we should have a look at your schedule for next year and make sure it's still what you'd like to do."

I nodded, trying to remember what my choices had been.

"Algebra II, US History . . ." She listed off more required classes. "Those are your core classes. Spanish II . . . do you want to continue with Spanish?"

"Yes!" I blurted a little too passionately. I hoped she wouldn't ask why.

She looked at me longer than I thought necessary, then said, "I assume you're also continuing with Art? I saw your work here in the office. It's excellent."

"Thank you. And yes, I'm continuing."

"Is art something you're thinking of continuing in college?"

College seemed a hundred years away. I really hadn't thought of it at all. The only connection I felt to college was through Cris, and that was minimal.

"I . . . don't know."

"I'd like you to start seriously thinking about college, Allison. Your grades are quite good, especially Art and English. So far straight "A"s for the past two years. What do you see yourself doing after school?"

It was Monday. I thought it a strange question, but I could picture my immediate, predictable future quite clearly. "I'm walking to the pool with a friend. We do homework and then ride home with my mom. I'll probably ride my horse before or after dinner and then finish my homework."

Mrs. Woolton smiled. "I really meant after high school and college." I sank a little in my chair. *Duh.* "What kind of career would you like to have?"

Career? I was trying not to imagine one month ahead to June. I didn't *want* to think that far ahead. If I thought about the future, I just assumed it would be like now. Horses and Dave. What more could I need or want?

"I don't know," I said, feeling guilty for not having an appropriate life plan in place.

"Try to think about it over the summer. Talk to your parents about it. If you can come up with some options, I can help you with finding colleges and programs that might be a good fit for you. You should start planning that by the beginning of next year. Okay?"

I pictured trying on colleges as if they were coats or shoes. Since trying things on wasn't something I particularly liked to do, the idea hardly excited me. Mrs. Woolton seemed to be waiting for an answer, so I nodded.

"Just one more thing, Allison. Finals are coming up and I wondered if you had any concerns? Are there any modifications that you'd like to have?"

Modifications was a word Dr. Hanwell had used and I understood its intent, but I had no idea what it actually alluded to or what they looked like. Apart from not having to take exams at all—and I doubted I'd get away with that—I couldn't think of anything.

"There's a group of students that will be taking their exams in the library. Some people have difficulty concentrating in a normal test setting. Some people just need a little extra time. Do you feel that might help you?"

What she'd said, the difficulty concentrating and time constraints, were always problems for me. But didn't most people have similar challenges? I had no idea what the repercussions of being singled out like that would be, if any. So I said nothing.

"If you think it would, just let me know and I'll arrange it."

I nodded.

"Are you doing anything special this summer?"

As I still had no idea but didn't want to seem rude, I said the only thing that popped into my head. "I might be visiting family."

She smiled and said, "That sounds nice. Well, I'll see you next year if not before."

I said goodbye and left her office. Not far away was one of the girls I sometimes saw hanging out with Lori and Roberta and she looked at me weirdly. I hurried back to Art.

It wasn't until later, when I was sitting with Ben at the pool doing homework, that I remembered my still life.

Oh well, I'll get it tomorrow. . . .

There was a lot of whispering in the back of the room in Spanish on Tuesday. I tried to ignore it and not be paranoid, but it was difficult. I hoped to feel more at ease in Geometry with Robin, but she had seemed more and more distracted lately, sometimes even distant. And she didn't seem happy today. I was worried that it was because of something I'd done or said—or *hadn't* done or said. I knew she was working at the bakery a lot, which was great for her. But between that and my schedule, I hadn't seen her outside of school in over a month.

"Is everything all right?" I asked as I sat down near her.

"Hmm?" She was frowning over what appeared to be her homework, as if she hadn't finished it. That wasn't like her at all. "Oh . . . I just need to do this. . . ."

I left her alone and hoped to speak to her after class. When the bell rang, I asked her again.

"Yeah. Mostly, I guess." She said nothing more and I was still scared that she was somehow mad at me.

"Can we hang out sometime? Maybe on one of your days off?" At this point I would have skipped choir, riding lessons, *anything* just to feel everything was right again.

"Oh . . . yeah . . . sure. That'd be great."

This was such an odd response from her that I started to feel panicky. I was going to walk with her to the tables, even though I'd planned to eat with Melanie as usual. But I stopped at my locker first and became completely distracted.

A folded note lay on top of my books inside. It was impossible to tell whether it had been placed there by someone who knew my combination or had been slipped through the vents and just happened to land that way. Inside in an uneven boyish print, it said: *Library. You know where. D.*

By the time I exchanged my books for my PE bag, Robin had gone. I felt an urgent need to speak to her again, to make sure we were okay, but if Dave was waiting for me in the library, I'd go there first. The request was so unusual, I assumed it was important.

There were a few kids there but I didn't notice who. I walked straight back to the table we'd often sat at last year. On it was a small stack of books with another note: *For A. Your summer reading. It's like they know you. LOL*

The only book I'd heard of was *Of Mice and Men*. I didn't recognize any of the other titles but turned the first few over to read the backs. A theme quickly became apparent—multiple personalities, schizophrenia, psychosis. I put the books back down slowly and stared at the stack, my mind spinning, trying to understand the meaning of what was happening. I felt slightly sick, as if a dangerous secret had suddenly been made public. Was this supposed to be a joke? Something was very wrong. I looked more closely at both notes.

It wasn't Dave's writing. It was close; an uneven print similar to his. But we'd been working together in English and at home for months now. I *knew* his writing and this wasn't it. But whoever was responsible for this prank—and I assumed more than one person was involved—wouldn't be aware of that.

I probably stood too still for too long, confused and searching for something in my experience to relate the situation to. Anyone watching me—and I also assumed someone was—probably felt justified in their opinion of me. There had been some situations in elementary and early middle school, before I'd learned to be more suspicious and careful of others' intentions, but I couldn't remember anything quite like this. The only vivid memory triggered in my mind was a relatively recent one: overheard words about girls who look different from the majority of kids here.

Still confused and now extremely self-conscious, I turned to walk away without expression as calmly as I could. But then I stopped and turned back. I'm not sure why—whether it had to do with trying to erase the evidence of the incident or just a more inherent tendency. I picked up the small stack of books and carried them toward the front of the library. Finding a returns cart, I set them on it very slowly, methodically, careful not to betray any emotion. They were probably excellent books with great stories and inter-esting characters. Books I might want to read one day. But not today, and not to give any ill-intentioned morons satisfaction. I crumpled up the notes and threw them in the trash before leaving the library.

I joined Melanie in the cafeteria and tried not to dwell on the episode.

During PE, Dave's group were out on the track while mine was in the gym playing badminton. I focused very hard on not tripping or bumping into anyone and not noticing if anyone was watching me. After school, Dave was working with Tom and I had Choir, so I didn't see him at all. He texted briefly later that night but didn't call. By then the protection of my earlier pretense had worn off and anxiety kicked in full force.

What was being said of me? Why was it such an issue? Why couldn't they just let me be? It's not like I'd ever asked anything of them. Did Dave know about what they thought? Did he know the truth? Would it matter?

By dinner time, I felt so nauseated I couldn't eat, and it took forever to fall asleep. In the middle of the night, I woke up with my heart pounding and felt immediately oppressed by a sense of imminent doom; completely overwhelmed.

Why hadn't I just told Dave everything when it was on *my* terms? I couldn't bear the thought of losing his good opinion and affection after ev-erything that had already happened.

I didn't want to go to school on Wednesday. I sat on the edge of my bed hugging Violet for a long time, playing through scenario after scenario in my head—what *might* happen if I went. A day at home might restore some equilibrium. Or it could make it even harder to go the following day. Plus, finals were starting next week. I had Chemistry and History today and we were doing a lot of reviewing. I needed that, especially for Chemistry. I wasn't too worried about English.

And if I didn't go to school today, I wouldn't be able to go to Northfield later. That thought was enough to get me moving again.

I prayed everything would be okay, put my newest Converse on in spite of wearing a skirt, shouldered my backpack, and picked up the bag with my riding clothes before going downstairs. I still couldn't eat anything, but Mom insisted on making me a sandwich.

"Is everything all right?" she asked on the way to school.

Ben had texted earlier to let me know he'd gotten a ride to school with his uncle. He was with us so much of the time, at least going and coming back from school, that Mom and I rarely had conversations about anything personal in the car. She had tried for a while now to get me to express my thoughts and feelings about my diagnosis, but those were still confused and fragmentary—I was never sure what to say.

"Of course," I said, the standard reply, wondering what specifically had made her ask.

"You've seemed withdrawn since you came home from school yesterday. And you haven't eaten. *Please* tell me if anything is going on."

"I'm fine," I said. But I wasn't.

The evil intent of whoever had left those books hit me again like a physical blow. My stomach tightened painfully.

"Is Dave coming over this week?"

Her tone had lightened—it wasn't a prying question, just making conversation. Unfortunately, it set in motion a host of doubts and worries.

"I don't know. I think he has a track meet today after school."

Mom was quiet, then said, smiling, "I'm glad he feels comfortable enough to come over. It's nice to have him around."

I looked out the window, tears threatening to spill over. "Yes, it is." *For how much longer?* The same thoughts as last night assailed me again. *Did he know what other people thought about me? Would it matter to him?*

I wanted to give him the benefit of the doubt, of course, but history is a harsh teacher. Too many past experiences had taught me that friendship is a fragile thing, prone to fracture and shatter with seemingly little provocation except that I hadn't met expectations somehow. There was some unwritten, invisible test that, more often than not, I failed.

Brenda, Melanie, Dave, and Ben had seemed to be the great exceptions to this rule. So far. Robin, the *best* of my best friends, might not have become my friend at all if not for Dave. And she seemed withdrawn lately, not like herself. I hadn't figured it out and it worried me.

I wasn't entirely sure about Brenda, but our relationship, lopsided though it sometimes felt, seemed to be stable enough to weather just about anything. Melanie? She had experience with autistic people and was steadfastly patient with me. And beyond that, she seemed to like me for who I was. I felt pretty secure with and extremely thankful for her.

And Dave. His littlest brother was autistic. Did that mean he'd be more accepting? Or possibly the opposite? Matthew's insinuations had been intruding into my thoughts again. *Why exactly* did *Dave like me?* And Matthew himself was now acting differently toward me too. He'd been talking with Hannah a lot, which didn't bother me. It obviously made her happy but seemed to make Dave *un*happy. In fact, Dave had seemed to prefer Hannah's company to anyone else's at school for quite a while now.

But Matthew had been, not cold exactly, but distant toward me. I was trying not to worry about it, but it felt like a losing battle. It *did* bother me that the boy that brought the summons from Mrs. Woolton was on his swim team, and I'd seen them hanging out together at school. That boy also hung out with Roberta and Lori and looked at me in a way that made me uncomfortable.

I tried to mentally shake it all off as we pulled into the school parking lot. There was no point dwelling on things I didn't know or understand. I had one firm resolution, however: I must explain everything to Dave as soon as possible.

As if to make a lie of my previous ruminations, Matthew was attentive and helpful in Chemistry, and Robin seemed talkative in History and almost clingy again. Confusion temporarily replaced worry and distracted me enough to be able to concentrate on finals review.

When the bell rang, I started to walk out to the tables with them, wondering what the best way of getting Dave's attention would be, and how to talk to him alone, hopefully before my current resolve weakened.

Then I remembered my still life. I'd forgotten about it yesterday and was likely to forget again if I didn't go get it immediately.

"I need to go to the office for a minute," I told Robin.

She stopped with me at my locker. Matthew looked our way but kept walking.

"Want me to go with you?"

"No, it's okay. I'll just be a minute."

She shrugged and continued over to her own locker while I exchanged books at mine. I grabbed my sandwich bag, though my stomach was starting to clench and churn at the thought of going to the tables.

I went to the office and picked up my artwork. Someone had carefully rolled it up and put rubber bands on either end. As I left the office, I took my phone out to text Dave.

What to say? Although I usually didn't talk much, when I *did* talk I sometimes avoided brevity for fear of sounding rude, or because more explanation seemed necessary to avoid being misunderstood, or to make sure the person I was speaking to had all the essential facts. Which is why I didn't text much either. But by the time I'd decided that straight-to-the-point was best, I was already crossing the quad.

I would spend a great deal of time replaying what happened next over and over and over again in my head, for various reasons. I eventually pieced together a relatively cohesive scene in my mind, but at the time, it was disjointed and surreal—quick impressions that felt like they were happening to someone else.

I was trying to text Dave while walking—a dangerous feat for me—and had gotten as far as, *'Can we—'* when I almost collided with a girl crossing the far end of the quad. She looked annoyed. I dropped my rolled-up still life and it rolled to the edge of the grass. Already feeling more exposed and awkward than usual, I stooped to pick up the drawing and glanced at my phone. Somehow I'd sent the incomplete text. Not the end of the world, but annoying. I stood up, wrote the message again correctly, and sent it. Then I looked toward the tables, just down the hill.

The last time I'd looked in that direction, Dave had been sitting, but he was now on his feet, looking at his phone—I assumed at my text. There were a lot of people in the table area—not unusual for this time of year—and a lot of them were looking at their phones. I didn't think too much of it at that

exact moment but later realized how weird it was and that some people were laughing and showing others.

Apart from Dave, I guess Matthew and Robin stood out because I'd been with them most of the morning. Matthew had been looking my way before, but was now turned away. Robin looked confused. Then there was more laughing and a lot of people looking in my direction. Unbearable. I didn't know what to do except to keep walking, but I felt shaky.

And then Dave was walking toward me and I stopped, just at the edge of the grass. My heart leaped, as it usually did when he approached, but his expression alarmed me. It was one I was unfamiliar with. I couldn't tell if he was angry, worried, or just upset. A sickening dread washed over me. *Have I done something? Was this the end?* In an instant, all the guilt I'd experienced earlier in the year hit me like a huge wave. *Has he discovered what an awful person I really am? He's finally realized the mistake he's made?*

His steps slowed slightly as he neared me and my heart thudded heavily. He wasn't frowning but still looked so serious, his eyes never leaving my face.

Without pause or word, he walked right up to me and folded me into his arms, crushing me against himself tightly as if he'd never let me go. He'd never hugged me like that before. I dropped my still life again and almost dropped my phone, too, but willingly embraced him in return.

Time stood still. It really did. I could have sworn the quad, buildings, and people disappeared except for a long gasp that seemed to surround us. Then, for a moment, there was no sound but the beating of my heart, loud in my ears, and the sound of Dave's soft breath against my hair.

"I'm *so* sorry," he said softly, roughly. "I've been such a jerk. I didn't understand." He pulled back to look earnestly into my eyes.

I gazed back, completely confused, but I could see he really meant it.

"Forgive me . . . please. . . ."

"What—"

My question was interrupted by his lips on mine. The kiss was long. Soft. Almost unbearably gentle. My heart and mind were racing again, but the rest of me melted completely. Any shred of resistance to him fell as he continued to hold and kiss me so tenderly in front of the whole world. At least, *our* world.

He finally drew back. I became aware of a rush of sound—laughing, swearing, even cheering—as if everyone in the whole school were talking at once. I felt a little dizzy, like after I'd passed out last year. I might have forgotten to breathe while he kissed me.

"Let's get out of here," Dave said softly, his cheek against mine and still holding me tight. "Do you trust me?"

Usually a question I had difficulty with, but in this circumstance, I had no doubts. "Yes."

He stooped to pick up my drawing with one hand and took my hand with the other, then began leading me away from both the quad and the tables toward the parking lot. I tried to stay focused on just following Dave, but Roberta ran a few steps toward us.

"Dave!" she shouted. "What are you *doing?* Don't you know? She's *retarded!*"

He stopped abruptly and I bumped into him. His hand tightened on mine, his face expressionless but his eyes intense.

"She's not retarded. I'm not sure about a lot of other people around here, though." His voice was steady, normal-sounding, but from the tightness of his grip on my hand and the tension radiating from him, he was holding himself on a very tight rein.

Roberta looked confused, then her face turned bright red. But Dave was already moving again and I focused on keeping up. He led me to his truck and opened the passenger door for me, then went around and got in the other side. I'd never been in the Beast. The novelty distracted me just enough to keep me from completely processing what had just happened.

Dave rolled his window down and laid his arm along it. It was like a furnace inside so I rolled mine down too.

"We need to talk," he said, still looking straight ahead.

"Yes." I was relieved. I would finally say all the things I'd bottled up for so long. But his tone worried me, and my mind leaped to the most apparent cause of it—Roberta's last word. It was still ringing in my ears.

"I'm sorry—" we both started at once.

"Allie, you've got nothing to be sorry about. *Nothing.*"

I disagreed but was still too confused and overwhelmed by what had just happened to verbalize it.

"I'm sorry 'cause I should have done that a long time ago. We just weren't sure what would be the best thing to do, you know, once we'd started going out. We thought it might be better for you if we made it look like nothing had changed."

There were so many questions clamoring to be asked, and I felt relieved and excited that he was finally, *really* talking to me about this. But one immediate question stood out.

"We?"

He was quiet for a moment, frowning. He picked up my hand and gently played with my fingers. Finally, he said, "Robin and I have been best friends a long time. Everything was cool until middle school, especially seventh grade. We had most of our classes together and hung out all the time at school. I used to walk home with her a lot, too, and then someone would pick me up from her house.

"Well, a bunch of girls got really jealous. I wasn't aware how much they liked me. They tried to bully her—treating her meanly, sometimes actually pushing her around."

"What did she do?" I asked.

He grinned. "She pushed back. But you know Robin. Now she doesn't take shit from anybody."

I could picture her standing up to Varsity Jacket last year and knew it to be true. It seemed we'd got off track though. "So, you and Robin made that decision? About me?"

He looked confused for a moment.

"You said, 'We.'"

"Oh . . . yeah. I mean, no. Me and Cris. Remember back when we first met? About the time you caught Gold? You asked me about it before."

I remembered it clearly. It was one of the conversations that had stuck. "You said I might not see you so much. You said you didn't want me to worry. But I did."

He nodded and frowned. "Yeah, I know. I'm sorry about that, too. Cris had noticed some things and we got worried that you might be bullied too, like Robin used to be. Except you aren't like Robin, and we agreed you probably wouldn't cope the same way with that kind of negative attention. It seemed like the best thing to do was not to appear to be too close, as friends, at least at school. You know . . . to back off a little. Then that other stuff happened—"

"The guys?"

"Yeah. And then there were crazy rumors about you and Cris. . . ."

I'd almost forgotten about that.

"It seemed like we were always getting you in one kind of trouble or another."

"What?" I was completely surprised by this. "I always felt it was *me* getting *you* in trouble."

He laughed softly. "Nobody gets me in trouble except me." He looked at my hand again, now gently threading and unthreading his fingers with mine. "Your dad was worried about stuff, too, though. I didn't think it was any big deal . . . was sure things would just blow over, you know? Then you got hurt."

"That was *my* fault, not yours."

"Mmm . . . another matter of opinion."

"Is that why you stopped talking to me? Over the summer and when we came back to school? I missed you *so* much. I couldn't wait to see you when school started. But you seemed so changed. You didn't want to be around me at all. I . . . I thought I'd imagined our friendship. Or that you were just bored with me."

He frowned deeply, looking at my hand again, now holding it in both of his. "It was almost impossible . . . trying not to pay too much attention, but not wanting to encourage you either. Not wanting to hurt you further. And all the time it felt like something inside was curling up and dying more and more, but I couldn't figure it out. I was too busy . . . too *stupid* to realize that *I* missed *you*. And even when I did start to figure that out, it took even longer to understand why."

"Why?"

He regarded me silently for a moment, and I was content to regard him right back. His gaze dropped to my lips and he kissed me, long and warm and slightly invasive.

My mind went completely blank. That certainly had never happened before. It felt like I could float away, just Dave and me, the world falling away below us—inconsequential, unimportant. My head was swimming again when he finally pulled away.

"Does that answer your question?" His face was still close, his eyes watching my lips as if he'd kiss me again if I answered incorrectly.

I remembered the question but not the reason I'd asked it. I frowned, struggling to reorder my thoughts. *These* were the answers I'd wanted for so long! *Concentrate!*

The bell rang then, signaling the end of lunch, and Dave sat back.

No! We didn't have enough time! There's too much more to be said!

There were so many reasons I didn't want to leave. I wanted to stay here forever with him. Okay, maybe not *forever.* The truck seat was comfortable but very hot right now and somewhat movement constricting. But I didn't want to return to earth just yet either. To reality. That thought reminded me of what had happened on the way to the truck in the first place. I didn't want to face anyone else. Not now. Not yet. I didn't want to think about anyone else's opinions or motives at all.

I still wasn't *used* to Dave, by any means, but I certainly felt more comfortable and less awkward around him. Especially right now when he seemed open to talking about these things—things that had perplexed me for so long.

He watched the rearview mirror. I turned to look out the back window. I couldn't see the tables clearly, but people were generally moving away in the opposite direction.

"Do you trust me?" Dave asked, his eyes still on the mirror.

There's that question again. I hated that the answer always seemed dependent on circumstances and context. This was not as resoundingly affirmative in my mind as before, but right now I trusted being with Dave far more than being without him.

"Yes."

"Good," he said, and started the truck.

We didn't speak as we drove out of the parking lot and south, away from town, toward the main entrance to Bar 8. I was thinking about all the things wrong with this. We'd miss English, our next class. With both of us missing, and who knows how many in the class witness to what had happened near the quad, there'd be little doubt we were together. This would be far worse than last year when Cris took off with me. But at this moment I didn't really care about what most people thought.

I *did* care about what Miss Sanders might think. And would anyone enlighten her about what had happened and why we were both absent from her class? I also cared that we were breaking a school rule. Juniors and seniors were allowed to leave campus for lunch and work experience or, like Cris, to attend classes at Lowell College. But freshmen and sophomores weren't allowed to leave school for any reason without a parent. *And if my parents find out that I cut class to drive around with Dave?*

I couldn't help considering all these things, but I doubted I would have gone to class anyway. Left to my own devices, I would have hidden somewhere until school was over. Escaping with Dave was definitely a much more enjoyable alternative.

Relegating thoughts of potential consequences to the back of my mind, I said, "How . . . *when* did you figure it out?"

"What?"

Now I was confused too. *What exactly had he said before kissing me?* "You said it took a long time to figure out that you missed me. And that it took even longer to figure out why. Because you liked me?"

"*More* than liked."

"Well, I hope you don't go around kissing people you only *like*."

He laughed. "I promise not to."

My thoughts began to rabbit trail on that—*Dave likes an awful lot of people*—but I forced them back in the first direction. "How?"

He frowned and looked at me as he drove. "How what?"

He wasn't getting out of this—I wanted to know and understand too badly. "*How* did you figure it out? How you felt about me? When? I've *always* known how I've felt about you. Well," I amended, always conscious of accuracy, "at least since the end of the second week of school *last* year."

"Wow," said Dave, glancing at me again several times as he drove. "That's . . . specific. And a really long time ago."

I could recall every detail of certain scenes from back then, and *exactly* how I'd felt. I still wasn't letting him off the hook. "You don't remember when?"

He was quiet, frowning at the road ahead. "You stopped looking at me the way you used to. It should have been a relief. You were *supposed* to not like me as much. I think I started noticing it on Labor Day. Every time I looked at you, you looked away. You didn't use to do that. At least, not in that way. Then it was the same at school. It really bugged me 'cause it felt like I was losing your friendship. And I'd never wanted that. I guess," he frowned deeply at the road ahead and his jaw tightened slightly, "one day it hit me . . . that it would kill me if you ever looked into another guy's eyes the way you *used* to look into mine."

We'd just passed the entrance to Bar 8, and he was still focused on the road ahead. He found my hand and held it again. I imagined scenes his last words conjured up.

"You were hanging out with Ben a lot, and you seemed so chummy. It took a while to realize how jealous I was. I'd never felt like that before."

My heart beat faster. *He'd felt like I had?* "I was really jealous too. It was . . . horrible."

He pulled the back of my hand to his lips and kissed it, then murmured, "I'm sorry. I really am."

"You certainly don't have anything to be sorry about. You didn't do anything to make me jealous. I just was. I'd never felt like that either."

"I wish I'd known. By the time I fully realized how I felt about you, you seemed to have moved on. Which you were supposed to do. That killed me too, but it didn't seem like I could, or *should*, do anything about it. The plan had worked, and I was miserable. And everything was so much more complicated. Because I'd promised."

"Promised?"

"Before summer, I'd promised to back off. To let you get closer to other friends. To be careful not to encourage you to . . . like me too much. Or depend on me. And I'd thought I'd be okay with it. I figured we'd still be friends. Back then, I hadn't thought about you being my girlfriend. You know . . . like *this*." He held my hand tight against his chest. "So it had seemed reasonable at the time. Except, I wasn't sure how to go about it. You know, distancing myself. Summer vacation was the most obvious opportunity.

"Then when school started, when I first saw you, you looked so different. And for the first time, I really wondered what you'd been doing all summer. But I thought, 'Good. She's figured things out. She's doing her own thing.' And I told myself that I was glad, and I didn't want to get in the way. Cris kind of warned me about being careful, too. But there was a part of me that was disappointed."

"Disappointed?"

He shrugged. "It hadn't occurred to me that anything would really change . . . you know, on your side of things. It was confusing. But I had other things on my mind too. I kind of thought, 'This'll be easier than I expected.' Because I didn't want to hurt your feelings. I was. . . ."

He was oddly at a loss for words. I'd been trying to follow his train of thought and match it to my own memories, but I was still sorting it all out. But his last sentences reminded me of a conversation with Cris earlier in the year that finally made some sense to me. "You were interested in other girls."

His face screwed up slightly. *Embarrassed?* "That sounds fu . . . messed up. But, yeah. Just in general. You know." He shrugged.

I nodded, not exactly sure I understood, but willing to accept it. Back then, I suppose Cris had been warning me, too.

Dave pulled the truck over to the side of the road and stopped near a long gate, but left the engine running.

"Hold on," he said. He got out of the truck, opened the gate, got back in, and drove through. Then he stopped again and closed the gate behind us.

"Short cut?" I asked as he got back in the truck.

"Not so much short cut as stealth route. It probably takes just as long, but we're less likely to be seen."

These last words were followed by his most dangerous smile, but I wasn't ready to be diverted from the subject at hand.

"So . . . you and Hannah?"

The rutted dirt road made us proceed more slowly and carefully, and Dave was frowning deeply. I didn't know whether the road demanded such concentration or if he was confused.

I tried to clarify. "You seemed . . . *very* close . . . when we came back from summer vacation. Especially on the first day of school. And then you were both missing at lunch for a while. I. . . ." It felt awkward to confess my doubts, but now that I'd brought the subject up, it was one of the questions I'd had for a long time. "I wondered if she'd been in Hawaii too."

"Hannah? Naw, we're just good friends. I've known her since kindergarten, like Robin. I definitely had a crush on her when we were little, but we didn't really hang out until freshman year. Her mom had died right after school started. Our dads have known each other for a long time, mostly through school events, I guess. So, when we heard about Hannah's mom, Dad was there for her dad. And Angel helped too, making meals and stuff for a while. Hannah was pretty subdued most of last year, but she seemed happier by the end of it."

He frowned, obviously thinking. "This year. . . ." Deeper frown, then his brow cleared. "Oh yeah. She had cheerleader tryouts on the second day and wanted me to go with her. Moral support. After that, I was training with one of the coaches. They insisted on it if I was going to play Varsity. Hannah was still probably doing cheerleader stuff. I don't know."

So much I didn't know! "I just hadn't been aware of her before. At least, not until. . . ." I felt suddenly embarrassed, remembering how desperately I'd wanted Dave to dance with me in PE last year. How disappointed I'd been that he'd danced with Hannah instead. It made me feel so selfish, not realizing that he was just friends with her the same way he'd been friends with me. That she had needed him too. Probably much more.

He was watching me closely; watching me think. I hated myself a little for it, but now seemed as good a time as any, and for peace of mind, I needed to know. "Roberta?"

He shrugged a shoulder. "We've known her family for a while, too. You know, through the show circuit. But last year Carl, her dad, started doing more training for us. With Cris being so busy and since he'll be going away, we need extra help starting the young horses. When they're old enough, they stay at the Fletcher's place for a while, just getting used to being handled every day, doing groundwork, and stuff like that. He's really great with the young ones. Then they come back to us for training under saddle. It's usually just one or two horses at a time. We don't actually raise a lot of horses. And when Carl picks the horses up or brings them back, Roberta usually comes along." His mouth tightened and he frowned slightly. "I've tried not to, you know, *encourage* her. But I can't be too rude to her. Hopefully after today it won't be an issue."

I hoped so too, but wouldn't have bet on it.

We had reached the back of his house and pulled up next to the basketball court, facing the stairs that I assumed led up to Cris' room. Dave turned the engine off and sat back, watching me again.

I was thinking over everything he'd said, trying to remember, picturing everything I could from the past year—no, *two* years—and trying to piece it all together. Randomly, one question popped out.

"Did your mom die of cancer? Is that why the Labor Day rodeo raises money for research?"

His eyes narrowed and he looked perplexed. "My mom's not dead."

Chapter Thirty-Three

My turn to be perplexed.

"Come on," he said, opening his door and jumping out.

I opened mine too, leaving my backpack in the truck. Dave was at my door before I had a chance to close it, so he did it for me. Then he retook my hand and we walked toward the garage.

"There shouldn't be anyone home right now, but I'm not sure. Dad's almost never in the house before dinner. Angel's usually out in the afternoons, at least until she picks Henry and Stevey up. Cris and I used to pick them up whenever we could, but Cris isn't around most of the time now."

The garage doors were open and both family vehicles were gone. I was surprised when Dave led me straight to the elegant sitting room, opened the door, and turned the light on. I assumed we'd go through the closed outer doors to the courtyard, but he drew me through the door on the far wall instead. Pulling me gently through a dark room that appeared to be a small office, we continued to the adjoining room. Here he also turned on the light.

The first thing I noticed was a stunning portrait on the far wall facing us—a woman in a long sapphire blue dress. She had dark golden hair braided and coiled on top of her head and striking, light-colored eyes, and she sat in a gilded and beautifully upholstered chair. The background was less detailed, a pastoral scene with columns draped with vines in the near distance. It could almost have been a fantasy scene and reminded me very much of artists we'd studied this year; Gainsborough with the more modern palette and sensibility of Waterhouse. Her smile was slight, yet she looked kind. There was something familiar about her, too. It was a beautiful portrait in a heavy gold frame and appeared to be finely painted with exceptional sensitivity.

"Cris' mom, Daniela. She was sick for a long time. That's when Angel came to live here, to take care of her and Ric and Cris. She died of breast cancer." I wanted to look more closely at the portrait to see if her eyes were indeed the same color as mine and to examine the brush strokes and the details. I was sure it must have been painted with small brushes in spite of the portrait's size. But Dave pulled me farther into the room and then pointed behind me. "*That's* my mom."

I'd already started to turn, quickly taking in the other features of the enormous room. Double doors, paned with glass and curtained, obviously led out to the courtyard. An entrance into another darkened room—I assumed a bathroom or closet; maybe both. A massive bed with ornate wooden headboard and matching furniture, very masculine. A well-stocked bookcase. But facing Cris' beautiful mother was another portrait about the same size in an equally elegant golden frame, though much less ornate.

This one dazzled me, and I whispered, "She's . . . gorgeous!"

She was. She was also almost Daniela's opposite. Glowing brown complexion, dark brown hair falling around her shoulders in luxurious waves, a slight sultry look in her dark brown eyes, and dressed in a far less demure gown than Daniela's: a form-fitting fiery red dress matching her hint-of-mischief smile. If she'd appeared older, I would have been a little shocked. But this woman was obviously very young, perhaps barely out of her teens.

Recovering from the first visual impact, I tried to see Dave in her, but the resemblance wasn't striking. Perhaps his mouth—fuller and more finely shaped than his dad's. Definitely his skin tone—much darker than Cris', at least for most of the year. That mischievous sparkle in his eyes—there was just a hint of it in the portrait—though otherwise he definitely had his father's eyes, as did all his brothers. Stevey looked the most like her.

"Yeah. She's still beautiful," Dave said, but there was no warmth in his voice.

"What—" I stopped, worried about asking the wrong thing. But I wanted so much to know about this mysterious woman no one would talk about. "She looks so young." This seemed a safe observation.

He frowned slightly. "She was. I think this was painted not too long after I was born. Definitely before Henry. She's a lot younger than my dad."

"Where is she now?" I asked softly, watching his face closely. I didn't want to ask anything that would hurt him, but it seemed important to know.

He continued gazing at the portrait as if it wasn't something he did very often, his expression inscrutable. "San Diego. Los Angeles. Miami. Vegas. Who knows? Miguel keeps track of her. Maybe Dad, too. Not me."

This last comment held an icy edge. I thought it might be dangerous to keep the topic open, but I was so curious. "Miguel?" I pictured the tall, kindly man who helped run the ranch.

"They're cousins. He came to work here after she married my dad. She left. Miguel stayed."

My emotions were conflicted following his last words: hurt and sad for him about his mother, but extremely happy about Miguel. "So, Miguel's a part of your family!"

Dave finally smiled warmly again and laughed a little, as if my happiness at the thought amused him. "Yeah, Miguel's great. He's family, but I don't think of him as my mom's cousin. More like my grandmother's nephew."

I realized I was frowning, working through the relationship, when Dave laughed again and said, "Yeah, I know. It's complicated. Him and Angel, I think of them more like my own cousins, but closer. And older, of course. Almost like an uncle and aunt."

Now I wanted to ask about Angel—another Caldera woman of mystery— but Dave squeezed my hand and said, "Come on. I'm starving! Are you?"

I nodded, though I hadn't thought of food at all. I took last looks at both portraits, storing up details for later contemplation as he drew me back toward the door.

"I left my lunch in the truck," I said.

"I'm sure we can find something here, unless you'd rather have whatever's in your lunch bag." He was laughing, but I didn't know why.

"I . . . I don't really care."

We moved back through the rooms and into the hallway, Dave turning lights off as we went, and then past the front entryway and dining room. The only light now came from the large window in the kitchen and light filtering down from the French doors above in the game room. It felt bizarre to be here right now.

With Dave. In his house. Alone. . . .

I'd daydreamed so many times, for so long, about being in a situation just like this. And here we were! I felt suddenly shy. Dave flipped on one of the kitchen lights and didn't seem to feel shy at all.

He opened the fridge. "Mmm. Enchiladas from last night. Miguel made those and they're delicious. Or there's some soup Angel made. It's good too. Or we could make sandwiches . . . beef, ham, tuna. . . ."

"I'll have whatever you have," I said softly. I wasn't really hungry. I just wanted to relish every moment of this time with him.

"Enchiladas it is."

He pulled out a long casserole dish, only about a quarter full, then got two plates and cut portions for us.

"Here you go," he said, putting plate and fork on the counter.

I sat down on one of the high stools and he came around and sat next to me. He started eating immediately, apparently as ravenous as he'd claimed. I took my time, cutting a small piece and chewing slowly. Dave had already eaten about half of his. He frowned at my plate.

"You like enchiladas, don't you?"

"Yes! They're really good."

He continued to frown, watching me cut another piece.

"Want me to heat it up?"

"Oh . . . um . . . yes, please!"

He frowned deeply at me again, as if disapproving. I started to feel bad about bothering him—was it rude to want my food warm? But he took my plate and put it in the microwave. When he set the plate back down in front of me, he leaned in very close over the counter, his gaze holding mine.

"You need to ask for what you want," he said, firmly but softly. "Never be afraid to ask me for anything. Okay? *Anything.* And if I ever do something, or try to get *you* to do something you don't want to do, you've got to tell me. Just say no. I mean it. Don't ever be afraid to do that, okay? I can be stubborn. Or sometimes just get carried away and don't think."

My heart skipped around like mad, and all I could think of was kissing him. I looked at his mouth, then *he* was kissing *me*. Nothing else existed for a few moments.

He broke the kiss suddenly and looked toward the entryway, leaning away as we heard the front door close. Merle came trotting straight to me, bottom wagging. A moment later, Miguel walked toward us.

"Hey," he said, not seeming as surprised to see us as I would have thought.

"Hey, Miguel," said Dave. "We're just eating lunch."

"I can see that. I saw your truck parked out back. *¿Por qué no estás en la escuela?*"

Ignoring Miguel's question, Dave countered, "Do you know where my mom is right now?"

Miguel looked from Dave to me then back to Dave. "She's still in San Diego."

"That's what I thought," said Dave, as if this not only answered his question but Miguel's as well. To me, he said, "Eat! I'll be right back," and walked toward and then past his mother's cousin.

Miguel smiled at me calmly and followed Dave. I heard the front door open and close again. Then quiet except for the sound of Merle lapping water in the mudroom.

I forced myself to eat but just wasn't hungry. Alone without distraction, my mind was overrun with more questions. Questions about Dave's family. Questions about what Dave was telling Miguel right now, and what Miguel would say in reply. Questions about what was happening back at school. Questions about what would happen next. I hoped Dave wouldn't be gone long; my mind was circling closer and closer to the ugly, specific thing I didn't want to think about right now.

Dave came back and frowned at my plate. "If you don't eat, I'm going to tell Miguel you don't like his cooking."

"But I love his cooking!" I said, only half believing him. "What did Miguel say? What did you tell him?"

"The truth, mostly. He said he wouldn't say anything about seeing us unless someone asks." He smirked and I got the feeling he wasn't telling me everything. He sat down and continued eating.

"Is that all he said?"

Dave looked at me, mischief in his eyes. "He said, *"Pórtate bien."*"

It wasn't a word I knew so I just stared at him.

He laughed. "He told me to behave myself." I felt a blush starting but still thought he wasn't telling me everything.

He'd finished eating already. I cut a piece of enchilada and said, "Tell me about Angel," before putting it in my mouth.

He nodded. "Angel is family, too, but I forget exactly how. She's Dad's second or third cousin or cousin twice removed or something like that. Her close family all live in Spain. Dad met Daniela when he was pretty young. Maybe on a visit to Spain or when he studied there, I forget. He went to high school and some college there until he came home and went to UCLA.

"Anyway, they eventually got married back in Spain because most of both families are there, and then they came home here. It was a while before Ric was born, and then Cris. And then Daniela got really sick and couldn't take care of them and the house and everything. So Dad wrote to one of his sisters, and she sent word to the whole family, asking if anyone could come and help.

"Dad hadn't seen Angel since they were kids. She came from a large family in a small rural town. She's told us lots of stories about growing up there. She had never gone to college, had no profession, and wasn't married. But she'd taken care of her parents when they were still alive, and she was used to helping her brothers and sisters with their children. She wanted to come. She's been a member of *our* family ever since."

I thought it through, thinking it a wonderful though sad story, and said, "So, she was here before you were born. You've known her all your life."

He nodded. "Angel's closer to me than my own aunts." He frowned and I wondered if he was thinking what seemed likely—that she was closer to him than his own mother.

I thought about how pronounced Angel's accent was and how she still sometimes stumbled over English, but I was afraid it might be rude to mention it. Instead, I said, "She speaks English very well."

The corners of Dave's eyes crinkled slightly. "Yeah, I tease her about it though, and she makes fun of my Spanish. Apparently she hardly knew any English when she first came here. Dad thought it was good for us all to speak Spanish at home. You know, so we don't forget our heritage and language. Daniela was Spanish too, of course, but I guess they'd mostly spoken English once they moved here. My mom's Mexican, so when Dad married her later on, it was easy for everyone to keep speaking Spanish, though she speaks English just as well as Miguel does. They were born in Mexico but have lived in the United States most of their lives."

"San Diego?" I asked.

"Yeah, mostly. My mom moves around a lot, but my *abuela's* there."

He suddenly pulled his phone from his back pocket and looked at it. The text message obviously amused him, but he didn't say anything. I realized I'd left my phone in my backpack in the truck but didn't really care.

I took one more bite of the enchilada—it really was delicious—then pushed my plate toward Dave. I had more questions—like, why were there no photographs of either of their mothers on the mantel or anywhere else that I'd seen—but figured they'd keep. I was mostly wondering what we'd do next.

Dave finished my enchilada then took both our plates to the sink. "I'll wash them later," he said. Standing on the other side of the counter again, he asked, "How're you doing?"

His gaze was intense; this wasn't small talk. I was immediately back near the quad, feeling clumsy, overcome by Dave's very public display, then devastated by one word and the mentality behind it.

"Okay," I said, but I knew the response lacked conviction.

"Do you want to head back to school?" He looked at the kitchen clock. "We can still make it back for most of study hall."

It didn't bear thinking about. I shook my head.

"Okay," he said softly. "But we'd better go outside or Miguel'll come back. Besides, I want to introduce you to some guys you haven't met yet."

I almost shook my head again, alarmed. I didn't want to meet anyone new or deal with *anyone* I didn't have to. Not right now.

Dave appeared to understand my hesitation. "No, trust me. Come on."

He moved toward the hallway and I got off my stool to follow him.

"Come on, Merle," he called.

Merle's nails clicked on the tile floor as she ran ahead toward the front door.

As we walked out past the statue, I looked up into her face. It definitely looked like Daniela. I looked at Dave and wondered if it was okay to ask about it, but he seemed to understand again.

"It's Cris' mom . . . well, a statue that looks like her, obviously. It used to be just a fountain, but Dad had the statue made to resemble her."

More thoughts and questions whirled in my mind. I wasn't sure about voicing *any* of them but was relieved by the distraction.

The open space that served as a plaza on Labor Day was completely deserted. The only people I could see were a couple of men on the hill in the distance, unloading bales from a big truck into an enormous open-sided shed—apparently the main hay barn. We walked past the small barns, one of which I'd been in before, and up a slight hill toward another small barn with turnouts near a long low building that looked like small apartments.

The closest turnout was occupied by a magnificent horse. At first I thought it was Dave's horse, Tee. But this horse reminded me strongly of Gold: thick, high-crested neck, long wavy mane and tail, powerfully muscled body. Instead of golden palomino, this horse was a solid, inky black except for some dusty patches. He was also quite a bit smaller.

"Def," said Dave, walking up to the fence and running his hand down the horse's face when he moved close enough. The horse threw his head slightly. "Barbed Defender, Dad's horse and our top stock stallion. He's the sire of Remmy, Tee, and Gali, and a lot of the cutting horses we train and sell. He's Spanish Barb and Dad's very selective who he's bred with."

Def wasn't content to stay near us but walked off, head and tail high, and rumbling as he moved. He came to a stop and neighed loudly. An answering neigh floated up from somewhere down the hill.

"There's a new girl in town," Dave said with a slight smirk. "He thinks all the girls are for him, but she's not." He looked like he'd say more but changed his mind. "Come on and meet the others guys."

"Spanish Barb?" I'd never heard of this breed, in spite of all the reading I'd done.

"He's descended from the first Barb horses the Spaniards brought to North America. They're originally from North Africa and eventually became the Iberian breeds. Spanish Barbs aren't purebred, of course. Def's parents were mustangs, but his DNA proves his ancestry. That's why we're careful about who he's bred with. Most of our own horses are his offspring. They're fantastic work horses, but they're not breeding stock. Dad's interested in Aztecas, though. That's one of the reasons. . . ."

I wondered what he was going to say, but he shook his head and said, "Never mind."

We walked into the relative cool of the small barn and Dave introduced me to the other occupants: two beautiful quarter horse stallions, a gleaming dark chestnut and a buckskin. These horses seemed more even-tempered.

The chestnut was in his stall nibbling at hay but came over to visit with us. He was tall, densely muscled, and seemed calm and friendly. The buckskin stood outside but turned toward us as we looked over the stall door. He swished his tail languidly, content to remain where he was.

There was an empty stall next to Def and another across from the chestnut, but the sixth stall's occupant, next to the buckskin and right across from Def, was Sam, the brown and white paint I'd ridden last year. He was also out in his paddock but came into his stall to greet us when Dave called him. Dave opened the stall door, picking up a dandy brush before we both slipped inside. Dave moved to the off side, his arm resting along Sam's back as he watched me. I stroked Sam's neck. I hadn't seen him since that first Labor Day here.

As if reading my mind, Dave said, "You need to come over and ride with me." His mouth twisted and he added, "When your dad'll let you."

I nodded, knowing that was indeed an obstacle, but it also reminded me of something. "You said you'd promised . . . to try to get me to not like you as much?"

He frowned, but I didn't know if he was annoyed or just trying to remember. He didn't respond right away and seemed to be concentrating on brushing Sam's shoulder. But I wasn't willing to let this one go. It would keep me awake at night if I didn't get to the bottom of it.

"You promised who?"

He frowned more deeply. "I wasn't supposed to say anything; I messed up again. You can't let on that you know, or he won't *ever* trust me—"

"My dad." The confirmation left me feeling sad, disappointed, guilty, angry, embarrassed—too many emotions at once. I suddenly felt a little shaky.

"Yeah. But I don't blame him." He laughed and his eyes twinkled at me over Sam's back. "After all, I just kidnapped you. See? Not to be trusted at all. Who knows what I'm capable of?"

I was still trying to process and also trying not to feel overwhelmed with all this sudden knowledge. There were too many things to think through, and my emotions were completely scrambled.

Dave frowned deeply again. "But do *you* trust me?"

"That's the third time you've asked me today."

"It's important to me. I'd never do anything to purposely hurt you. You know that, don't you?"

I nodded and looked deeply into his eyes. Whatever other reservations I might have, I trusted him enough to let him in this way. And that's what it felt like, making eye contact for so long, so deeply. I felt pulled in, too, almost like falling, surrounded by him, embraced though he wasn't even touching me. I could have remained that way for hours if Sam had obliged by standing still.

"So . . . do you trust me?"

I nodded again but found I couldn't reply out loud. I looked away and combed Sam's mane with my fingers. I could still feel Dave watching me but didn't want to connect too deeply again with his eyes.

His phone buzzed and this time he looked annoyed. Looking at it briefly, he tensed, but his expression didn't really change.

"Do you need to go back to school for anything? Books? Homework?"

I actually did, but there was no way I was stepping foot on campus again today. I shook my head.

"I should probably take you home. Or do you want me to take you into town? Were you going to the pool after school?"

I wasn't thinking about town or the pool. "I wish I didn't have to go back to school at all. Ever," I said quietly, still not looking at him.

He ducked under Sam's neck, folded me into his arms, and just held me. I closed my eyes and absorbed the moments—the feeling of Dave's arms wrapped protectively around me; breathing in his comforting scent; feelings growing that seemed to have little to do with anything that had happened today.

He leaned back to kiss me, but I held him away gently, already flushed and fighting against inclination. "I . . . I have to tell you something. *Things.*"

It wasn't going to get any easier than now, and I wanted everything out in the open. Sam had moved outside; we were still in his stall. It seemed both a very odd and completely appropriate place to make confessions.

"I'm autistic."

"Yeah."

"You *knew?*"

"It came up, sometime or other. I think when your dad first came to talk to us last year. Remember? That specific word wasn't used, but your dad had a lot of concerns. He talked about how you were different and might not understand things or act the way other girls do. And last year it occurred to me that I sometimes felt the same way about you as I feel about Stevey. You're not the same at all, but there was something . . . I don't know. A gentle spirit, like . . . a kind of innocence. The way you respond to things. Or don't. The things you say sometimes. And the things you *don't* say."

I needed to correct him. My previous thoughts and feelings toward Roberta, Paola, Hannah and Ben still tormented me. "I'm not innocent," I said softly. "I've had terrible feelings about people. I guess I hated them. And I feel so bad about it."

"Yeah," said Dave, taking me into his arms again. "You feel bad about it. I bet you beat yourself up about a lot of stuff, don't you." It wasn't a question. I didn't respond. "Who do you hate right now?"

I searched for any scraps of anger or ire. "No one."

"See? A lot of people hate other people for no good reason at all and never feel bad about it one bit."

I suddenly remembered, again, things Matthew had said at the river. "I . . . I don't feel right letting you think I'm better than I know I am. I need to be completely honest with you right now. I can't . . . I can't stand the thought of you liking me for something I'm not. Something I don't want to be to you."

He leaned away and smiled but looked confused. "I didn't say you weren't human. Nobody's perfect. But I can't imagine you'd ever purposely do something mean to someone else."

"But I have! I've thought *horrible* things!"

"You've thought of doing horrible things to other people? All the time? And how many of those horrible things have you actually done? How many would you ever do?"

Now I felt confused. I couldn't remember thinking of actually *doing* anything against anyone, even if I had bad feelings toward them. "I wanted to pull Roberta out of your truck once."

He laughed loudly. "I would have let you!"

I smiled then shuddered. "I worry that if you *really* knew what I was thinking most of the time, you wouldn't like me as much. Maybe not at all."

He held me at arm's-length and tried to keep eye contact with me, but now I felt exposed and uncomfortable. "I can't imagine there's *anything* you could do or say or even *think* that would cause me to stop caring for you. You make me . . . you bring a . . . a . . . I don't even know how to describe it. It's like . . . contentment, I guess. You bring a sense of peace into my life. I've only ever felt that sometimes with Stevey, when it's just me and him and he's calm and happy."

"Quiet? You like me because I don't talk too much?" I was still hearing Matthew's voice.

"No, not exactly. I sometimes wish you'd talk to me more, though I like that you're not constantly pestering me or trying to make me do stuff I don't care about. I really *hate* feeling nagged or manipulated. I like that you're talking so much to me right now. You usually don't, and that's okay, too. I sometimes feel like I can almost hear what you're thinking. Though," he frowned and paused for a moment, "sometimes it was Cris who told me stuff he thought was going on with you. Anyway, I get tired of the same old bullshit most of my friends talk about every day. I actually *like* being quiet sometimes. You let me do that. You're not demanding."

I thought about that. "I sometimes *feel* like demanding," I admitted. It felt like a terrible flaw. "I sometimes feel like I need your attention, but I try not to. I've never wanted to be like that."

He smiled. "I hate to think of you ever *not* wanting my attention."

"So you don't mind . . . that I'm autistic?"

"Why would I mind? It's just a part of what makes you who you are. Stevey's autistic and he's one of the smartest, gentlest people I know. He's different and he has a lot of struggles I don't have, but I love him. I'll always love him. I'd never want him to be someone he's not, though I'd love for some things to be easier for him. My family always works on communicating with him better. We have to take into account his sensitivities and a hundred other things. We have to live around him, but he has to live around us, too. We find ways to make our family work. It's an ongoing process. But I'd never *change* him. Any change will be because *he* wants to and is able to. Just like anybody else." He frowned. "I guess I feel the same way about you."

I felt tears threatening, completely overwhelmed by what he'd said, by my fantastic good fortune to be in Dave's life this way. *No, not good fortune. Blessed!* A prayer more than answered. I breathed out slowly, trying to hold myself together. "There's something else."

He waited.

"I've been learning how to ride English." I watched his face for any change of expression. "Dressage," I added. "And I've started jumping, too. I really love it."

He seemed to be processing this, but he didn't look mad. "Okay," he said. Then he frowned slightly. "You have English tack?"

I nodded.

He frowned again. "How come I've never seen it?"

This now seemed so silly, and I was embarrassed. "I kept it in my room. I was afraid for you to see it.

His frown deepened. "Why? What did you think I'd do?"

"I didn't know. But I cared too much about your opinion and didn't want to deal with it."

I thought he looked annoyed, but he said, "How does Remmy like being ridden English?"

"He's wonderful! We're still working on the jointed snaffle and reining difference, but we're taking it slow and he's doing great. But . . . well, I ride another horse, too. We're leasing a horse from my friend, Melanie."

The frown was back. I figured I'd best come out with all of it at once.

"She's from Northfield. She trains and teaches at the equestrian center. That's where Kitty is."

"Kitty," he said. He still didn't look precisely mad. Concerned?

"The horse. Her name is Copper Copycat, but her barn name is Kitty. She's lovely. It took a while for us to get used to each other, but we work really well together now. But I still ride Remmy all the time," I said, afraid he might think I was now neglecting him. "I only get to ride Kitty two, sometimes three times a week. I usually ride Remmy more than that. I practice almost everything I learn with him, too. He's doing great!"

The frown had disappeared but Dave's expression wasn't happy. He seemed tense.

"I really like it there . . . at Northfield." I felt guilty about that and resented it. "Why don't you like it?"

He didn't answer right away. He was holding my hands and looking at them, still frowning.

"It's complicated. I'm not sure how to explain it completely. I don't even know when it started. But there's ongoing . . . animosity, I guess . . . between the developers there and a lot of the ranchers and farmers in this county. Water is always an issue. When there's a drought, like there's been on and off for a long time, the state regulates how much water we can use. *We* don't

waste water. It's used for irrigation of crops for both people and stock, and water for that stock too.

"Northfield uses hundreds of thousands of gallons of water every week just to keep their grounds green. The worst is the golf course. All that water just to keep the grass green for a relatively few people. It's not even as if it were used by the public. Not everyone can afford to play golf. But somehow they're regulated differently and not as affected by rationing in dry years. The Rancher's Association has been fighting it ever since plans were submitted for Northfield. That was before I was born.

"Then a few years back they submitted plans for another community west of Northfield. *And* another golf course. That's going to at least double the water use. The ranchers and farmers began lobbying state legislature about it. That's when bad stuff started to happen."

I'd been listening hard, trying to follow and understand the conflict. I remembered something Robin had told me last year. "The cattle," I murmured.

"Yeah," he said, his mouth a hard line. "Among other things."

Robin had told me that some cattle had been brutally killed, years ago, at several of the bigger ranches. Just the memory of her words made me shudder, and I struggled to not picture the events. "Why?"

He shrugged. "It probably wasn't adults. They suspected it was kids of prominent Northfield community members, but there was no way to prove anything. And all it did was make the agricultural community even angrier."

"So those boys . . . the ones last year. The boy in the varsity jacket. . . ."

"Dillon Pryce." Dave's expression was unreadable. "At least one of the people involved in killing the livestock must have been older. They would've had to drive to get to the locations and to get to as many as they did in one night. Unless there were a lot more people involved, which doesn't seem likely or someone would have talked by now. But Dillon's got an older brother who's just like him. Probably worse. He's not around anymore, I assume at college."

I was processing all this as he stepped closer and pressed both my hands between his. "Can you understand why I don't want you at Northfield? It's not a safe place for you. Especially now. They hate me for other reasons, too."

His eyes searched mine. This time it felt invading —though willingly on my part—and as if I could embrace him with my whole being. It was an overwhelming sensation that made my brain and entire body hum. But it scared me, too. How easy it would be to simply agree with him and give in, to go along with whatever he thought best. And that's exactly what I'd been afraid of before. Everything in me wanted to make him happy.

Almost everything.

"I *have* to go to Northfield," I said. "It's where Melanie is. And Kitty. And Tatiana." He looked confused—I hadn't mentioned who Tatty was, but her presence in my life was significant, too. "It's really important to me. I've learned so much, but I have so much more to learn!"

I looked away and slowly pulled my hands from his; a wrenching feeling.

We were quiet for a few moments. I watched Sam, out in his paddock. I didn't know where Dave was looking. Maybe he was watching me. I didn't feel I could afford to get locked into his gaze again right then. His will seemed so much stronger than mine.

Finally, he said, "I don't want you getting hurt. In any way."

I nodded, not as thrilled by his words as I once would have been. As I probably *should* have been. "Nothing's happened so far. Not at Northfield."

"Yeah . . . but things are going to be different now."

I was still watching Sam, now down on one knee next to the fence and trying to nibble on some grass just out of reach. It took a few moments for me to come back from the theoretical future to the immediate present.

Dave kissed me, really kissed me, in front of the whole school, more or less. Anyone who hadn't seen it would certainly hear about it. I wondered how much bigger the target on my back had become. And did I care?

Dave continued, "I'm not supposed to go near Northfield. Cris either. So I can't protect you there."

Mention of Cris distracted me. *He's certainly been at the equestrian center. Is that why he didn't want me saying I'd seen him there? Well, at least I can keep his secret.*

"I'll be fine," I said. "I've been going there for months and nothing's happened. I don't think that will change."

I actually wasn't sure about that at all. I'd already wondered about Bradley and whether he'd told Varsity Jacket—Dillon Pryce—and the others that he'd seen me at the stables there. But I certainly wasn't going to say anything to Dave about that. Maybe it was a *good* thing that he felt he couldn't go there.

"I'd better take you back," he said, reaching for my hand again.

I nodded and let him lead me out of the stall, down the hill, and back toward the truck. Neither of us spoke, and I was preoccupied with too many of my own thoughts to wonder what his were.

When we reached the truck, he slowed, then gently pulled me toward him. "I can't bear the thought of something happening to you," he said.

"I can't bear the thought of anything happening to you, either." He looked surprised. I'd been thinking of all the crazy things *he* did, yet he didn't want me going to Northfield? It seemed hypocritical, but I didn't want to say so. "You should wear a helmet more often."

He smiled slowly, his face softening. He kissed me—the *new* kiss that seemed to, at least momentarily, wipe everything else out of existence. "Okay," he said, a little huskily, his lips still near mine. "Just for you."

We stood like that a few moments more before he reached behind me to open the truck door. I got in feeling like we'd arrived at some new level in our relationship, but unsure why. It would take some mulling over.

Chapter Thirty-Four

There was immediate fallout, of course, but it could have been a lot worse.

It didn't occur to me until Dave was dropping me off at the pool that it might have been better to have gone straight home. I didn't want him getting in any more trouble than he might already be in, but it would have bought me a little more time to think about possible repercussions. But, all things considered, it was probably for the best that he didn't. Suppositions were probably running rampant enough already.

I could see my mother through the chain link fence when we got there. She was standing and talking on her phone. She turned and saw us, obviously hugely relieved to see me. My stomach churned.

"Should I go say hi to your mom?" asked Dave.

I considered for a moment. He'd once borne the brunt of my parents' anger for me. I didn't want that to happen again. I shook my head.

"Okay." He didn't sound sure. "Tell your parents what happened. If they want to talk to me, let me know. And call me later. Okay?"

I nodded but didn't look at him until he squeezed my hand. His gaze was intense, and I nodded again before getting out of the truck. He waited until I'd joined my mom inside the pool area, then he drove away. Mom was still on the phone and I didn't want to hear the conversation, so I went and sat in the shade where I usually did my homework.

I vaguely remembered that Dave had a track meet but didn't know where. I hoped it was at our school so he wouldn't be too much later than he already was. As well as feeling like a horrible girlfriend for not remembering about it earlier, not knowing where it was, and not considering that he might get in trouble for being late, I was trying to formulate what to say to my mom. But that just brought up the scene at school again. It also finally occurred to me that I didn't know why Dave had walked up and kissed me when and how he did.

Mom put her phone away and came and sat near me. "Allison, where have you been?" she said softly but earnestly. "That was the school saying you hadn't gone to your afternoon classes and they had reason to believe you were with Dave. I'd actually have been more worried if they hadn't said you were probably with him. But *why?* Why did you leave school?"

I didn't know what to tell her. I hadn't wanted to think it through before. I'd been very happy to let Dave distract me with portraits and enchiladas and beautiful horses. But now I tried to make sense of the sequence of events.

I was walking out to the tables, trying to text Dave. I wanted to talk to him during lunch, to tell him everything I'd been keeping to myself before I talked myself out of it again. He walked toward me and inexplicably hugged me, then kissed me. Really kissed *me. Purposefully. In front of everyone. And then he wanted to leave, I guess. He didn't want me to go to the tables. But why? And then Roberta. . . .*

It wasn't just that she'd called me retarded. It was the whole situation and the *way* she'd said it—so seriously. The implication of it. Something must have happened before I got there. *What?*

"Allison?"

Mom was frowning and trying to lock eyes with me, but I just couldn't. I was desperately looking for the right words to make her understand, and eye contact wouldn't have helped at all. The words just weren't there. Nothing made sense.

Mom looked even more worried and her voice dropped to barely more than a whisper. "Did he *force* you to go with him?"

"No! No, of course not." I was finally able to look her in the eyes, but only for a moment before her intensity and the strain in her expression made me look away again to try to keep my thoughts from scattering. "Something . . . something happened. At school. At lunch. We went and sat in his truck, just to talk. Then I didn't want to go back. I would have hidden in the bathroom or something all afternoon. We went to his house. He gave me lunch and showed me some of their horses. Miguel knew we were there." It seemed a good idea to mention this. "Then Dave brought me here."

This account sounded unacceptable, even to my own ears, and very juvenile compared to actual events and the emotions involved. But it was all I could manage.

Somebody in the pool climbed on the dividing rope which distracted Mom. She blew her whistle—which startled me badly—and walked over to talk to the kids involved. I looked in my backpack for something to do. That's when I realized I hadn't seen Ben. I looked around but he definitely wasn't there. And *that's* when I remembered what day it was. Ben always found his own way home on Wednesdays. I was supposed to be at Northfield. Even talking to Dave about it earlier hadn't reminded me.

I dug my phone out of my backpack. Four text messages, three missed calls, and two voice mails. Two calls were from Melanie with the two voice mails from her number, which I listened to first.

"Allison, we're wondering where you are. Give me a call back." The call was at three fifteen. They'd waited for me.

The second was ten minutes later. "It's me again. We have to leave. Sorry. Roger's got work and I teach at four. Call me later, okay?"

I felt awful for making them wait. And Melanie was probably worried, too. But she'd given no indication of knowing anything unusual had happened. That was good.

The other call and first text message were from Ben, probably right after Dave and I left. *'That was awesome! You should have seen everyone's faces! LOL.'*

Three texts were from Robin. The first one said, *'What the hell was that about? *Getting hose ready.*'* It was timed just after Ben's.

The second was about an hour later, probably between classes. *'Crap. I saw the video. Don't pay any attention to it. Where are you right now?'*

The third was sent just after school. *'Okay—now I'm officially freaking. Where are you guys? Call me!'*

I wanted to call her right then, but Mom was heading back in my direction. I texted her back, *'I'm fine. I'll call you later.'* Then I frowned and sent another. *'What video?'*

"Allison," Mom started, but her phone rang. After frowningly looking to see who the caller was, she answered it. "Hello? . . . Yes, Mrs. Powell . . ."

The principal. This can't be good.

"I see," said Mom. Then she was quiet so long I thought she'd been put on hold. Finally she said, "Of course . . . Yes, that would be . . . Yes, before noon, if possible . . . Thank you."

Mom looked at me, still frowning. I was trying to figure out both how I *actually* felt—still wrapped in Dave's affection and slightly guilty for breaking a school rule and cutting classes, but not overwhelmingly so—and how I was probably *supposed* to feel. For the latter, I didn't have a clue.

Mom started to speak but then pressed her lips firmly together and sat down, watching the pool. I waited for her to say something, but she didn't. She looked sad and worried. At one point she wiped her eyes. Now I felt genuinely guilty, feeling she must be unhappy about what I'd done. That made me feel sad, too, and my eyes started burning.

After what felt like minutes of silence between us but probably wasn't that long, I said, "I'm sorry. I didn't mean to make anyone unhappy or worried."

Mom turned and looked at me, but I couldn't read her expression. *Still sad? Mad? Confused?*

"Am I going to be grounded?" I asked, this new fear suddenly taking hold. My mind immediately started spinning off along all the parts of my life being grounded would affect—mostly time with Dave and going to Northfield.

Mom's face crumpled a little, but then she pulled herself together as if she wouldn't let me see her really upset. She managed to smile and said softly, "No, Allison. You've done nothing wrong and will *not* be grounded."

Much later I realized that she was simply being strong for me and didn't ask me anything or tell me what the last phone call was about so I wouldn't worry even more. I loved her so much for that.

There was nobody I knew at the pool and nothing more happened there. I'd started to worry about what Dad was going to say and do by the time we got home, but he was his usual happy self, mostly interested in what was for dinner and then unwinding with television.

I fed Remmy as soon as I got home but went back into the house right away, expecting that some kind of critical discussion would take place and wanting to get it over with—and to learn the worst—as soon as possible. But though Mom tried to appear upbeat and extremely interested in everything Dad said, she didn't contribute much to the conversation, and I could tell she was still unhappy. I worked on homework until dinner was ready, feeling like an axe was suspended over my head and just waiting for it to fall.

After dinner, I wanted to help with dishes but Mom said I should go spend time with Remmy or finish homework. I escaped the imaginary but palpable dangling axe and went outside to call Robin.

"Hey, are you okay?" Hearing her voice was both reassuring and unnerving.

"Of course. Why wouldn't I be?"

"Oh, nothing."

This unacceptable response reminded me of her text. "What video were you talking about?"

Quiet on the other end of the phone. I could practically hear her thinking. "Nothing. Really. It's just . . . stupid. Don't worry about it."

She must have already talked to Dave. I was torn between wanting to know the truth and not wanting to get upset for any reason. I felt relatively calm and happy right now and chose to not pursue it.

Next I called Melanie, apologizing for not letting her know I wouldn't be going to Northfield.

"Are you okay?" she asked.

"Yes, I'm fine. It's just been a really weird day. I was—" I was going to say that I was upset about something, but then she'd ask why, and I was having too much difficulty sorting through everything to explain. She still hadn't indicated that she knew anything, so I said, "I just completely forgot what day it was." Which was true.

She forgave me, of course, and asked if I'd be going out there the next day or Friday. But I had no idea. I still didn't know what the actual fallout of today's events would be. I didn't want to think about tomorrow at all.

Lastly, I called Dave. We didn't talk for long or refer at all to what had happened earlier in the day, but it was calming just to hear his voice. He seemed to feel the same way and I remembered what he'd said before, about how I made him feel. That made me much happier.

I rode Remmy bareback around the property until almost dark. Then I went in to take a shower and afterward retreated to my room with Violet.

The only other thing that happened was after I'd gone into my room; my dad shouted, "*What?*" loud enough to startle me and make Violet dig her

claws into my leg. I waited, holding my breath and listening hard, expecting at any moment to be summoned downstairs. I never was.

I awoke around midnight to the rattle of gravel against my window. *Ben.* I pulled on sweats and silently went downstairs and out the back door. There was no moonlight, but I could see Ben standing an arm's length away from Remmy, just barely touching his nose.

"Couldn't sleep," he said. "I thought maybe you'd want to talk."

I walked over to Remmy and stroked his cheek. I wasn't sure I wanted to talk, but I didn't mind the company.

"Did I wake you up?"

"Yes, but that's okay."

We were quiet for a few moments. I couldn't imagine what he was thinking. I was trying to decide if I wanted to talk about what had happened at school or not. Then I remembered again.

"Robin mentioned a video. Do you know what she's talking about? She wouldn't tell me."

He'd been watching me but now looked away. I thought he was going to deny it, but after another moment he took out his phone. "I'm only showing you because, if it were me, I'd want to know."

I had a sudden sick feeling and almost told him to put the phone away. He handed it to me, open to someone's Facebook page. A video was playing.

It took a moment to recognize myself walking across the quad. It was weird to see myself on a video. Except for a few taken when I was much younger, the only one I'd seen was the one that Cris had made of me riding Gold last year. I liked that one a lot and watched it often.

This was very different.

The video showed me looking at my phone and almost walking into someone. I'd forgotten that. You could hear someone—maybe more than one person—quietly laughing then saying something that induced more laughing. Then I tripped slightly and dropped my scrolled artwork. I'd forgotten that too. I didn't remember tripping at all. The worst part was that I'd worn a skirt. I had tried to be careful when I picked the scroll up, but a breeze apparently caught the edge of my skirt, flipping it up just enough that my underwear could be seen for a fraction of a second.

It probably would have been barely noticeable and wouldn't have been too bad, but whoever had edited this video had slowed those frames down, zoomed it in, and looped it a few times before panning back out and resuming normal speed.

It was juvenile, bizarre, and obscene to me. I felt like all the blood was draining from my body. How could someone do something like this?

The video continued with me standing back up and looking toward the tables. A girl's voice—obviously someone at the tables close to whoever took the video—said, "*So* retarded." Then words scrolled across the bottom, "Retard alert!"

I was now shaking and tears rolled down my cheeks. I wasn't sure how I felt—upset, obviously—but I mostly just couldn't wrap my head around why anyone would be so mean. *What did they get out of it? How could they sleep at night? How could they even live with themselves?* I took a deep breath and tried to calm myself.

"Shit, I'm sorry," said Ben and pulled me into a hug. I might normally have resisted but didn't now. "Some people got the original in a text immediately. Somebody showed me right after lunch. This edited one was made later. Maybe I shouldn't have shown you, but it would have been much worse if you hadn't known about it and then seen it tomorrow at school. Trust me, I know."

I nodded but had only processed a part of what he'd said.

"I wanted to make sure you remember that there are people that like and love you," he said. "Tons of people."

I nodded again against his shoulder but couldn't speak. Right now, I couldn't think of tons of people.

"Think about all the people who really like you. They're the people who've taken the time to get to know you. The others, they don't matter. They probably don't even like themselves. I've had to deal with their kind all my life, too."

I'd now pretty much stopped processing altogether, but I remembered some of his words later. I pulled away from him and wiped my face. "Thanks," I whispered. "I need to . . . go . . ." I began to walk back to the house.

"You're going to school tomorrow, aren't you? You need to go. Don't let them change anything. Are you listening?"

I was but I wasn't. I heard his voice, but the words weren't really sinking in. I just wanted to get back to my room.

I couldn't sleep, the video repeating endlessly in my head. I held Violet close and her steady purr soothed me. I tried to do the one thing I remembered Ben saying: *think about all of the people you know really like you.*

Robin, Melanie, Matthew, Brenda; I felt pretty confident these people wouldn't turn on me. Melanie and Brenda, though polar opposites in temperament, had never given me any cause to doubt them at all. Both, in their own way, had remained constant friends. Robin was the most important to me, but I had a slight fear. Things had been kind of weird this year. I didn't feel like I was in her confidence a lot of the time and didn't know what that meant. And Matthew ran a little hot and cold toward me for no apparent reason. Still, I didn't think either of them would abandon me. I hoped not.

Tanner, Kyle, Hannah, and Paola, even Stacie and Jessie; I didn't feel quite as close or at ease with them, but I didn't think they'd treat me any differently. In fact, I had a feeling they'd already known I was really different somehow and accepted me anyway. It had never seemed to affect our interactions. That was even more comforting.

Ben had already proven himself my friend over and over. He not only accepted me, I felt he *understood*—at least as much as anyone could.

Dave—

I knew Dave cared, probably more than any of the others. I was fairly convinced that nothing—not parents, not teachers, not my own idiosyncrasies, not friends, not even his own brother—could turn him against me. He'd made that very clear. He'd said it last year and now more than followed through.

I was glad I'd left school with him today. And I now realized why it had felt like we'd reached a new place in our relationship; it was the most we'd ever talked about serious topics. Spending that time with him and *really* talking was worth any disciplinary action I might have to face. Then I realized I wasn't the only one likely to face those actions. Now that was something else to worry about. I hoped he felt it was worth it too.

Angel, Cheryl and Tom, Gloria and Phyllis, Tatiana, Dr. James. They were adults, but they were important friends too.

Cris.

My heart suddenly thudded hard, filled with dread and confusion. What would *he* think of all this? Would he see the video? Did he *know* about me? I hadn't seen him since the motocross event. *Why am I thinking of him now?*

All these things, including the video itself, raced through my mind and continued to cause stabs of panic as I contemplated the impact of everything over and over with varying outcomes.

It was about three o'clock when I finally gave up, the candles Robin had given me last year, and sketched while listening to music through my headphones. Violet opened her eyes and yawned once, then moved next to me and fell asleep again.

When my alarm went off, I was lying on top of my bed, sketchbook leaning against me, earbuds on my chest. Thoughts of Dave were foremost in my mind on waking. The candles were almost completely melted and I felt ashamed, both because I'd wasted them and obviously it wasn't safe to fall asleep with candles burning. I'd learned that from *Jane Eyre*, even though that's not really what had happened in the story. I sat up long enough to blow them out then fell back against my pillow.

Then the previous day's events and thoughts and emotions crashed in. I remembered Roberta and everything that followed and pulled my pillow over my face. I needed to get up to feed Remmy, but I didn't want to even think about school. I wanted to stay at home. To sleep. To hide. To pretend nothing had happened. I'd play with Remmy and sketch and read and watch Animal Planet on TV and music videos on YouTube.

My phone buzzed next to the melted candles on my nightstand. *Dave.* "You need to go to school."

I said nothing for a moment, then, "I don't want to."

"I don't blame you. I really don't. But you need to go anyway. It'll only get harder if you don't. You can't let the assholes win. You should go and try to act like nothing's different. Except it *will* be different. I promise. You won't be alone for a second. I promise that too. Go. Go for me."

Well, if you put it like that. . . .

"No more hiding, Allie. We can avoid people if you want to, but we're not hiding. Okay?"

"Yes," was all I could say. But his voice, as always, had given me strength and set my mind *and* heart more at ease. I got up, fed Remmy, took a shower, then dressed with care, trying to look my best for Dave's sake.

When I came downstairs again, I was surprised to see both Mom and Dad sitting at the table. Dad was dressed as he usually was for work—neat but casual—but Mom seemed to be very over-dressed for the pool.

"Sit down, Allison," she said.

My stomach flopped and my mind raced. Were my parents going to tell me how disappointed they were with me? Were they going to describe what my punishment would be? Would they try to keep me from being with Dave?

That thought caused a stab of despair and the feeling like I was sinking into the floor. I felt slightly dizzy and suddenly exhausted. Less than three hours of sleep probably didn't help. Overwrought, I couldn't hold it together anymore.

"I'm sorry!" I gasped, my whole body shaking. Tears ran freely down my face. I wiped my eyes then remembered the light coat of mascara I'd put on. *So much for trying to look my best.* "*Please* don't blame Dave. . . ."

Both my parents frowned but I didn't know exactly why. My mind was still racing, this new worry added to all the others.

"Allie, please sit down. Let's talk," said Dad, his voice gentle.

So we talked. Well, *they* talked. I had a hard time processing a lot of what they said. But the one thing that stood out and that I clung to was Mom saying, "We don't blame Dave for anything. He was protecting you in what we're sure seemed like the best option at the time. He removed you from the situation and didn't make it worse by retaliating. It sounds like he just wanted to distract you from dwelling on what happened. So we're thankful. But. . . ."

They were concerned about what had happened at school. They were concerned about the video. They wanted to know how extensive the harassment was but didn't specifically ask me, which I was grateful for. They were mostly concerned that I hadn't told anyone.

That made me feel even more useless and was pretty much all I could handle. My own thoughts were too loud for the rest. *How can I tell anyone about things I'm not aware of? I didn't know they'd made a video. I'm not always sure what's going on. I can't afford to start* looking *for hurt.*

The only other thing that really registered was Mom saying, "We're not taking you to school right away. We're meeting with the principal and your counselor at nine o'clock. We didn't tell you last night because we didn't want you worrying about it.

Ha! It certainly wouldn't have helped.

Mom insisted I eat something, but my stomach immediately retaliated. I ran to the kitchen sink and threw up.

"Okay . . . let's forget about eating." Mom's head tilted to one side, and she looked sympathetic. "You'd better wash your face though. Would you like some help?"

I shook my head and, balance severely compromised, carefully made my way up to my bathroom. I brushed my teeth again and scrubbed my face, deciding makeup probably wasn't a good idea at all today.

I tried to focus during the meeting at school, but it was difficult. I couldn't shake an oppressive sense of guilt and my mind raced down familiar paths. I came back to awareness periodically wondering what I'd missed.

The gist was, they were trying to track down who had actually taken the video, and then who had edited it and posted it to social media. The first video had been sent within seconds of taking it and had quickly been further passed around to an extensive list of people. But they were confident they would find that person. The second video was more troubling as it could be the same person, but anonymous accounts were involved, and it had already spread so far they didn't have the resources to track the origin. The police were involved and there would be a thorough investigation. There would be an assembly during Study Hall today. I didn't have to go.

I was shuddering uncontrollably and just wanted to go home.

They'd already talked to Dave and his dad about the inappropriateness of his actions, both kissing me at school and then leaving with me. But they understood his motives and wouldn't punish him for them. I was embarrassed—I hadn't thought about it before now, but my parents probably didn't know about the kiss. But I was immensely relieved Dave wasn't in trouble again. Dad looked stern and uncomfortable but didn't say anything. Mom just looked sad.

It was impressed on me to seek adult help and tell them if anything, anything at all, ever happened again. I wished I could explain how difficult, sometimes impossible, that was. I didn't say anything throughout the whole meeting. I couldn't.

The last thing Mrs. Powell said was that they had some safe places for me to go if I ever felt overwhelmed or in danger of any kind. Some of my teachers—Miss Laski, Mrs. Ochoa, Miss Sanders, Mr. Tanaka, and even Mr. Payne, who wasn't even my teacher this year—had gotten together earlier that morning and made a schedule of when they would be in their classrooms, whether teaching or not. I was to go to one of them if I ever felt threatened or if I was overwhelmed and just needed a quiet place. There were only a few more weeks of school left. I hoped I wouldn't feel the need.

After my parents left, I waited in the office until the bell rang. I was surprised when Robin and Tanner arrived to escort me to my locker and then to Geometry. Tanner seemed his usual self, but Robin was very quiet and looked pale, as if this whole thing were affecting her as deeply as it was me.

The rest of that day was really weird. Just as my favorite teachers—well, except maybe for Mr. Payne, though I was touched that he was concerned—had rallied around me, so too did my friends. I didn't know until lunchtime that Dave had texted everyone—except Melanie and Ben because he didn't have their numbers—to meet him at school early. They agreed to be extra watchful on my behalf, and I wasn't to be left alone on campus. Ever. This was embarrassing and didn't help the guilt and oppression, but I was very grateful, too.

I wanted to see Melanie at lunch, but Dave intercepted me right after Geometry and wanted me to eat with him in his truck. How could I say no? As soon as we were in The Beast, he asked, "Okay?" An all-encompassing question.

I nodded. I still didn't feel like talking or eating, but I enjoyed just sitting with him and listening to the radio.

When the bell rang, he walked me all the way to the girl's locker room door. Melanie and Hannah were waiting for me. Melanie said nothing but wrapped her arms around me in a warm hug. I assumed Hannah had filled her in on the Allison protection plan. Neither of them left my side for the whole period, and I wasn't aware of much else. I refused to look at anyone but them.

After PE, Dave was waiting outside and, though no one actually touched me, I felt handed off like some kind of baton. I also felt protected and grateful for it, but I was unhappy about the necessity and that all my friends were affected.

Dave walked with me up to the school office; everyone else, students and teachers alike, would be gathered in the gym. Under normal circumstances, I'd be pretty happy to skip an assembly. But right now I was too overwhelmed feeling that I was the *cause* of it. Mrs. Powell had said that other people had been bullied and called names lately, so the assembly wasn't just because of me. But she said it a little too pointedly, which assured me I *was* the main reason. *Just one more thing to live down.*

Hannah, Paola, and Ben all picked me up from the office to take me to Choir. We were rehearsing for our last concert in two weeks, but I didn't even want to think about that. I wasn't sure I'd be able to stand in front of people ever again, let alone sing as well. But it felt good to sing today.

After, I was surprised that Dave met me at the choir room door—he'd never waited for me after Choir before—and walked with Ben and me to where my mom was parked. He looked like he wanted to talk to me, but he didn't say much with Ben there. Mom had taken the whole day off just so she could pick me up. That didn't make me feel any better.

Dave seemed reluctant to part, but I was relieved to get in the car. I couldn't wait to get home and just be alone. I was utterly exhausted, which seemed strange. I'd been "protected" all day and had barely spoken a word. Where had my energy gone?

I spent the evening with Remmy, grooming him and practicing my dressage test. Being with him and focusing on my riding helped my anxiety a lot, but I was still far from feeling anything like normal—*my* normal.

Other repercussions, I assumed due both to my disappearance with Dave on Wednesday and whatever had been said at the assembly yesterday, started on Friday and lasted pretty much through the last weeks of school. Having endured the assumptions of the previous year—when I'd been seen arguing with Cris, was carried by him to his truck and driven away with, then didn't return to school for days—I was at least partially prepared. I was surprised by some of it, though. Not only was I shunned by what felt like almost the entire school body, but I was also perplexed by the behavior of some of the people I considered friends.

Kyle acted the same as he always had, and it was a relief to be around him. But Stacie and Jessie and even Tanner seemed on edge around me, as if afraid of betraying the wrong emotion or saying the wrong thing. Maybe they were experiencing a measure of what I felt like *all* the time. With *everyone.*

Paola went out of her way to be near me and include me in conversation, which was very sweet but only served to highlight everyone else's discomfort.

Matthew barely looked at me, and when he did, I didn't recognize his expressions. I certainly couldn't read them. He wasn't mean or rude at all, but our few brief interactions felt cold. *So* cold. I half expected him to change his seat in chemistry—there was a girl without a regular partner who'd been joining other students all year—but he remained with me, though our interactions were stiff and confined to the subject at hand. It made me uncomfortable around him. It was a good thing the year was almost over; I doubted his help and patience would be offered as freely as before.

I wished it didn't bother me, but it really did. Was it because my relationship with Dave was now out in the open? Was he hurt? Angry? Or was this a reaction to the label Roberta had applied to me? If so, it looked like he believed it. That alone would keep me from trying to talk to him about it. But even if it were the former, what could I say?

As uncomfortable as Matthew's behavior made me feel, it was nothing compared to the growing dread I felt because of Robin. She seemed increasingly distant, or at least preoccupied, and noticeably paler and more depressed, yet she almost clung to me whenever we were together. It was very confusing. I tried asking her about it a couple of times, but she just acted like she didn't know what I was talking about. In spite of her seeming physically attached to me, I feared for our friendship. She never laughed anymore. Even Dave started to notice.

He now spent every moment he could with me at school, I'm sure leaving no one in any doubt of his sincerity. But it didn't make me happy. I was too aware of the underlying reason for his now constant attention. It began to feel like the label I'd been given was engraved across my forehead or something. I was sure that's what people thought whenever they looked at me. Could my friends really be unaffected by it? Could Dave? I rarely looked around at people in general at school now and could barely make eye contact with my real friends.

I missed eating lunch with just Melanie, but Dave wouldn't hear of me eating in the cafeteria. We had started eating farther out in the field, avoiding the tables. I knew we weren't really supposed to be there, but so far no one had bothered us about moving. Just our closest friends joined us there. It was kind of nice but felt weird too. And I was still too aware of the reason.

"Why doesn't Melanie come and eat outside with us?" he asked.

I still wasn't entirely sure about this. "I think it has something to do with her asthma. Her mom makes her stay inside at school as much as possible."

"Hnh," he said. He didn't ask about it again.

Later the next week, he met me after History and, after walking with Robin and me to my locker, said, "I need to talk to you. Let's eat in the truck."

We hadn't been completely alone together since last week. I hoped his needing to talk to me actually meant something else—something a little more physical that would take my mind elsewhere or perhaps make it go blank completely. But he really did just want to talk.

It was a pleasant day, and once we'd rolled the windows down and let the breeze flow through the truck, it felt good to just sit there with him.

"Sorry I haven't been able to come over. Between track and work . . . and stuff going on at home. . . ."

I searched his face, feeling ashamed. I'd been so overwhelmed with my own issues all week—and to an almost equal degree, worries about Robin—that I hadn't thought about what his day to day life had been like lately.

"What stuff?" I asked, startled at the sound of my own voice. I hadn't spoken at all yet today. Had I talked yesterday? *The day before that?*

"It's a busy time for us. We just finished harvesting spring hay. Stock inoculations. Track finals. I've got a rodeo this weekend."

"You do?" I felt as out of touch with him as I ever had earlier in the school year, even though he'd recently been staying so close to me on campus. "I'm sorry!" I said, feeling awful.

He frowned deeply but smiled at the same time. "What on earth are you sorry for?"

"I . . . I don't think I've been a good girlfriend. I haven't even been a good *friend* friend. I haven't been supportive at all. I . . . I don't know what's going on in your life right now."

His face relaxed in a soft smile; *my* smile. His gaze caressed me and I felt the stirrings of a blush—a sensation I hadn't felt for quite a while. The breeze had blown a few strands of hair into my eyelashes, and he gently pulled them away.

"I don't want you to feel like that," he said. "You've had enough on your mind. This weekend's the final qualifier or I'd skip it. But I need to let you know about this summer."

Summer vacation started in a few weeks. I'd only thought about it when others brought it to my attention.

"We're going to Spain," he said. "Most of my dad's family and Cris' mom's family are there. Angel's too, of course. We go every three or four years."

I nodded but couldn't think of anything to say. I wasn't exactly surprised. He and Robin had mentioned it last year.

"We'll be gone about four weeks. We're leaving the Monday after school gets out."

He earnestly watched my face, I guess to gauge my reaction. I couldn't even fake one.

"Okay," I said.

Several expressions crossed his face in rapid succession—so fast I couldn't begin to read them. The final one was clearly amusement.

"So, are you gonna miss me?"

I studied his face for a few long moments. He studied mine back. I surprised him by leaning forward and kissing him. *Really* kissing him. It was all I'd really wanted to do since we'd gotten in the truck. He responded with a gratifying amount of enthusiasm.

When we came up for air, I laid my head against his shoulder and sighed deeply. His arms encircled me and I felt content, at least for the moment. *This* is what I would miss most of all—just *being* with him quietly like this. I wished we didn't have to return to classes.

"What about you?" he murmured against the top of my head.

"Me?"

"Does your family have plans? Are you going to Los Angeles?"

I supposed this was the main reason I wasn't thinking about summer vacation. "My dad's going to South America, so . . . I don't know."

"Hnh," was all he said.

The bell rang and we walked together to English, but our conversation had given me an idea. For the rest of the afternoon, I thought of nothing *but* summer vacation. I was so distracted by the idea and the rabbit trails it led me down that I could barely pay attention in class, earning me curious and amused looks from Dave and exasperated ones from Miss Sanders.

When I got home, I wrote an e-mail.

The next day, Friday, was something of a red-letter day; Cris was back, at least in the morning. His semester at Lowell was over and he'd be around a little more.

I was so happy to see him that I almost cried, which was ridiculous and confused me greatly. *Exactly how much has Dave told him about recent events? What has he heard from others, and what does he think about it? Are things okay between us?* I suddenly realized—more than anyone else except maybe Dave—I cared what he thought about me. I couldn't bear for him to think of me as less than I was, intellectually inferior or damaged, whatever my social or physical shortcomings might be.

He didn't talk to me directly or even look at me during lunch that I was aware of, but I was distracted for most of that time, wondering.

The tables had become very crowded, and more and more people began sitting with us out in the field. Some of them I didn't know at all, but some, like Roberta and Lori, I knew as much as I ever wanted to.

I wasn't aware of any discussion about it, but an alternate lunch spot had been looked for. I got the feeling that Ben had been the primary instigator of this, but he wouldn't admit to it. He did make himself responsible for keeping track of where we'd eat every day though, which surprised me. He had such a hard time remembering things. I was kind of proud of him for it, and thankful too, and told him so. I certainly wouldn't have been able to remember.

He also gave the new core group a name: Allie's Posse. I wasn't sure how I felt about that. I would rather it had been called Dave's Posse or even Ben's Posse. But after a few days, it didn't seem to matter. The name got reduced to AP and was only used to communicate lunch locations.

The days were becoming increasingly warm, and Mr. Tanaka and Miss Laski both said we could eat in their rooms until the end of the school year. The choir room was more comfortable to lounge in so it became the primary destination. It was weird to see Dave in the choir room but even stranger to have Cris there.

Tanner, a percussionist in the advanced band, surprised almost everyone by asking for permission to play the piano, and playing very well. Ben, Hannah, and Paola took advantage of that, getting him to play popular songs they could sing along with. A closer friendship seemed to be developing between Ben and Tanner, and I was glad.

Conversations were much the same as they'd always been—sports, cars, upcoming events, and summer vacation. It made me happy that the new group, now including Melanie, was everyone that had come to my birthday party.

Everyone except Matthew. He didn't hang out with us at lunch, and I didn't know if it was because he didn't know about it or because he didn't want to be there. And if he hadn't been told, why not? And if he didn't want to join us, why not? I struggled a lot with whether to ask him about it, but I now only had close contact with him during Chemistry.

As the days passed, it ate at me—I hated the feeling of distance between us—but I also wondered if it was for the best. I tried to imagine how I'd feel in the same circumstances, even tapped into memories of how I'd felt earlier in the school year with Dave. Had that been the same? I wasn't sure. If Matthew had really liked me—and I'd certainly suspected he might—perhaps it was better to leave things like this, at least for a while. But, truth be told, I had no real idea of what was best in this kind of situation. It had never come up before. My standard protocol, if-in-doubt-do-nothing, seemed safest.

Dave was gone the whole weekend after Cris came back to school; he and Kyle had both made it into the state high school rodeo finals. He'd wanted me to go with them and seemed willing to do or say anything if my parents would allow it, which was both extremely flattering and rather alarming. My parents both said no, of course. I loved Dave so much but, probably because of everything that had happened recently and the currently unstable nature of my life, I felt relieved the decision wasn't up to me.

I actually looked forward to just being at home. I never seemed to have a moment to myself anymore. I convinced Dave that I had too much to do anyway—an art project I pretended hadn't been finished two weeks previously and a lesson with Cheryl. We were working on agility and speed. I finally had everyone's permission to enter the pole-bending as well as some other gymkhana games at the Memorial Day show.

I also wanted to go out to Northfield and practice my dressage test with Kitty, but I didn't mention that.

Those last weeks before summer vacation were unnervingly strange, probably because of all the abrupt changes in my school life and the constant attention I now got, and they seemed to fly by impossibly fast. Three things helped me hold myself together somewhat and served as a mental escape when approaching maximum overwhelm.

The first had to do with the e-mail I'd sent. I was still waiting for a reply, but that wasn't unusual and in itself wasn't a huge concern. The *potential* outcome was intriguing enough to provide distraction and a safe place to mentally retreat to whenever I needed it most.

The second were the upcoming dressage shows which I was extremely nervous about but excited, too. The first was another schooling show. Melanie said there would probably be people from the Valley—maybe as far away as Chico and Stockton—but still relatively local. The second was the first major Northfield show of the season, and there would be riders from all over the country, probably even some international competitors. There were so many classes it was spread out over three days. Just participating in it would be an enormous accomplishment for me. I made cardboard signs for court letters and stapled them to posts in my arena, so I could more easily practice at home.

Mentally practicing my tests also provided needed escape from daily stresses at school, and I carried my test notebook with me everywhere. I didn't really need to consult it anymore, but it gave me a sense of security, and I sometimes outlined the test on clean pages. I'm sure anyone watching me would have no clue what the circles and arrows meant, and I could imagine what they'd think, though I tried not to.

The third thing was more immediate but took even less mental and emotional energy: the show at the county fairgrounds. Last year had been a disaster, but I felt confident about my ambitions for this year. The organizers of the show had moved the date to Memorial Day, and I was glad. It gave most of my friends and me a focus away from looming finals. It dominated conversations and didn't make me or the people around me feel awkward.

Well, except for Tanner's comment. He jokingly said, "Are you entering the barrel racing, Allie?"

That made me laugh, but everyone else immediately fell silent and seemed to feel uncomfortable. So then I felt uncomfortable, too, but wasn't sure why. Tanner looked extremely embarrassed. Dave frowned and changed the subject.

"Dad and I are taking Tee and two other horses and need to get there really early, or I'd take Remmy for you. Maybe Tom can trailer him there."

"I'll take him," offered Cris, surprising everyone. While he definitely wasn't as broody as he'd been last year, he rarely contributed to general conversation.

"Could you take Gali, too?" asked Robin.

We all looked at her, surprised again. Before now, every time the show was mentioned, she'd said she'd be working.

She shrugged. "I changed my mind. I want to ride."

There were spots of color in her cheeks as if *she* were embarrassed, though I couldn't imagine why. I was just glad she was showing an interest in *something*. Cris said it wouldn't be a problem.

That gave me another idea. When I explained to my parents, Dad agreed without thinking too hard and Mom seemed thrilled. It had been a while since we'd had company and a very long time since she'd seen Robin.

Robin's hesitation in accepting my invitation troubled me, but I resisted questioning her. I wanted so badly to know what was bothering her but was too afraid it was something about me. Something I had no control over.

That week was our final choir performance, but I didn't enjoy it. I felt so nervous about it that I skipped going to Northfield and was even more self-conscious than usual, my mind wandering so badly I forgot some of the lyrics. Not like me at all. Maybe no one else noticed but I was mortified.

Dave was at his last track meet and I was glad he wasn't there. It probably would have been even worse. I couldn't help looking for Cris, but he wasn't there either. Which, of course, was a good thing.

Definitely.

By Memorial Day weekend, Robin still hadn't confided in me, and Dave said he wasn't aware of anything amiss. I was sure she was still acting weird, though I suspected my sense of reality was very unreliable right now.

I often felt overwhelmed at school and close to shutting down for no apparent or immediate reason, and I wasn't fighting it. I just didn't have the energy. Better to shut down than unexpectedly dissolve into tears or run screaming from a room. I doubt I ever would have actually done the latter, but I felt like it a couple of times. I still wasn't talking much either, but sometimes caught myself angrily chanting in my head, "I'm *not* retarded. I'm *not* retarded. I'm *not* retarded."

Yes, it bothered me that much.

Chapter Thirty-Five

On Saturday morning I received an affirmative answer to the e-mail I'd sent. I wanted to tell my parents about it immediately but decided to wait until after the show. If I discussed it now, I'd be even more distracted by the idea. It would keep.

I spent most of the morning getting the spare stall ready for Gali and the spare bedroom ready for Robin. When she'd slept over before, she'd chosen to sleep on my floor, but I wanted to be prepared. I was happy she'd agreed to spend the night at all and was trying very hard not to assume anything.

On Sunday, Dave did his weekend morning chores—the ones Miguel did the rest of the week—then picked Gali up and brought him to my house. Together we settled him into the spare stall and unloaded Robin's tack. Gali went straight out into his paddock to greet Remmy, and it was fun to watch the brothers reconnect. They play-fought for a short while through the fence before settling down.

Robin had worked in the morning then drove over to my house in the early afternoon. Dave stayed after Robin arrived, which was nice but also a little awkward. I still wondered if my relationship with him had anything to do with why Robin was acting differently.

We spent most of the afternoon riding and then bathing the horses. Dave kept his distance from me and by late afternoon things felt more normal between the three of us, which was a huge relief. Mom invited Dave to stay for dinner, but he declined, saying he had his own preparing to do for the next day. He left soon after.

Robin had put her things in the spare bedroom, which was what I had planned for, of course, but I became worried as we got ready for bed. Not staying up late talking was a good idea as we had to get up extra early. But with so many things changing and summer coming, I was very concerned. I hated feeling insecure in our friendship.

I took a shower and then sat on my bed playing with Violet while Robin took hers. As she left the bathroom—dressed in the cute pony pajamas I'd given her for Christmas—I called to her. I wasn't sure what to say but seeing the pajamas gave me courage. They already looked soft and slightly faded as if they'd been worn and washed many times. Delighted, I said, "Those look adorable on you."

She smiled almost shyly as she sat next to me but also looked a little agitated. Had I said the wrong thing?

She wrapped her arms around herself as if holding the pajamas closer. "They're my favorite."

That made me happy, too, but I frowned. I didn't know how to open the subject that troubled me, so I just said, "Something's wrong."

I was shocked by Robin's response; not just curiosity or surprise, but something much stronger. *Fear?*

"What?" she almost whispered, as if afraid to learn the answer.

"I don't know," I said. I struggled to properly communicate my fears without sounding accusatory or petulant. I wasn't trying to blame *her* for anything. At the same time, trying to interpret her reactions and silences was too much for me. I just had to express myself in any way I could. I *had* to get to the bottom of this. "I'm worried. I feel . . . you seem . . . different. To me. I mean, things just feel different between us."

She went suddenly pale and I realized it wasn't just that. She'd been acting strangely almost all year. I remembered the first day of school, how different she'd seemed. Her hair had now grown out quite a bit—an unruly mass of copper curls almost brushing her shoulders again. She *looked* more like my confident friend of last year. But she didn't *act* like her. I'd been so worried that it was because of Dave, or maybe knowing about my diagnosis. But those hadn't been issues at the beginning of the school year.

"Something's making you unhappy." *And nervous. And depressed. And maybe even afraid.*

The look of shock, perhaps fear, appeared again. I hated seeing it and hurried on. "I thought maybe it was because of Dave and me. And then I thought. . . ." This unfinished last thought now seemed ridiculous, and I felt ashamed I'd even considered it for a moment.

"Allie," Robin whispered. The fear in her eyes dissolved into tiny drops that slid down her cheeks. "God . . . don't *ever* think that. You're the closest friend I've ever had. I'm *so* sorry!" She suddenly and fiercely hugged me.

I gratefully hugged her back, intensely relieved but even more worried. "Then what is it?"

She released me and sat back, wiping at her eyes. Then she reached over to stroke Violet, now curled up in the middle of my bed. "It's just . . . family stuff. I don't want to talk about it now."

"Okay," I said, frowning again. But I couldn't help asking, "Is Fiona all right?"

Robin stared at me as if my train of thought had surprised her. She appeared to think for another few seconds before answering. "She has diabetes. They're worried about her kidneys and her heart. But she's doing better right now."

I nodded and believed her, but I also got the feeling I'd provided her with a convenient ploy to avoid telling me the truth. Still, she'd said she didn't want to talk about it, and I could understand that.

We said goodnight and she went to the guest room. I shoved Violet over, which caused her to start purring loudly, then turned the light out and got into bed. Immediately my brain crisscrossed well-worn paths of my own concerns tangled with continuing worries about Robin. Knowing these thoughts would rob me of much-needed sleep, I got up to take action against them. I opened my laptop and sent another e-mail. Then I went back to bed, pulled Violet close, curled into a favorite position—imagining myself snuggled against Remmy—and quickly fell asleep.

Robin emerged from her room looking refreshed and happy, whatever was bedeviling her temporarily subdued if not forgotten. I determined to emulate her and pretend I wasn't worried about anything, too. With the excitement of the day's events ahead, it wasn't too hard to do.

Cris arrived at seven o'clock with the tandem trailer to pick Remmy and Gali up, and we all followed him in Dad's car through town and then northeast. It was the fourth time I'd been to the fairgrounds, so it was starting to feel familiar.

Robin had entered a few advanced rider classes, including poles and barrels, and one amateur reining class. I'd entered a novice poles class along with a couple of gymkhana events and an equitation class. None of our classes were the same but weren't held at the same time either. So we spent the whole day going from one arena to the other watching each other.

Some of our friends were there—Jessie, Tanner, Stacie, and Kyle—though Kyle was obviously there in a purely supportive role. Stacie still had the big thoroughbred she'd been rehabilitating last year. Apparently she'd fallen in love with him and decided to keep him. Jessie was there on a new horse and wearing more bling than anyone I'd ever seen.

Cheryl was there with a couple of her other students and cheered for me in my timed events. Dr. James came by to say hello, too.

Dave found us when we got there to say hi, but then he was too busy with his own horses and classes to hang out much with us. Cris hung around more than Dave, which was simultaneously nice and unnerving. He wasn't riding in any events and Henry didn't need much help. I often saw Cris nearby, watching us, but he never sought our attention. I hoped he wasn't only there in case I did something stupid like last year. That would be really annoying. But otherwise, I decided I liked the fact that he was there. For some odd reason, I felt more confident and relaxed, and I think Robin enjoyed his quiet presence too.

Remmy and I didn't embarrass ourselves in any of the classes and took a fourth in the big equitation class which I was thrilled about. By the end of the day I felt better—happier and more relaxed—than I had in almost a month. But I wished the next day were the beginning of summer vacation already. I didn't want to return to school.

Dave appeared when we were packing up. He helped us briefly but had to get back to his own horses. We didn't really need his help since Cris was there, silently stowing our gear in the trailer's compartment, but he found an opportunity to give me a quick embrace. I felt terrible that it made me feel uncomfortable, hoping no one was watching. When he'd left, I tried to recapture the elation I'd felt before those moments, but it was elusive.

We drove to Robin's house, with Cris following, and unloaded Gali and her gear while Mom went in to say hello to Fiona. Robin ran into the house for a moment, too, but I went back to the car where Dad waited. Mom appeared very preoccupied when she came back to the car. Then we all headed back to my house.

Mom invited both Cris, who I'd barely heard say a word all day, and Robin to stay for dinner, but both thanked her and declined. Robin wanted to get home to Fiona. Cris didn't give a reason.

I was actually glad it was just my parents and me. I had a partially formed plan beginning to occupy every unguarded thought, and I wanted to see if it could fly. And if it could, I was going to need a lot of help getting it off the ground.

"I've been thinking a lot about summer," I said, when there was a lull in my parents' conversation. I'm sure it seemed to come out of nowhere, but they had no idea how long and how *much* I'd been thinking about it.

They looked at me with interest.

"I don't want to go to Los Angeles."

I don't know what they thought I was going to say, but that obviously wasn't it.

Dad frowned.

I could tell that Mom was exercising patience. "We already have plans to go while Dad's in South America. It's just a few weeks. I really would like to spend time with Grandma and everyone. I haven't seen them much since we moved. It'll be fun. I've been talking with Audrey and Kate about us all going to Disneyland."

I actually loved Disneyland most of the time, in spite of the crowds and noise, but said, "I think you should go, Mom. But I'd like to stay with Isabel in Colorado."

My parents looked surprised again.

"She invited me when she was here, and I e-mailed her to find out if I could. She said she'd love to have me stay as long as I want. She said she'd put me to work. And she'll coach me, too. She says she has the perfect horse for me to ride. Can I go? Please?"

Mom and Dad looked stunned. I think they were amazed that I'd taken the initiative to come up with an alternate plan, complete with communication and everything. I had to admit it was certainly unusual for me.

"And I'd like to invite Robin to come. She's been really depressed. It would be fun, and I think it would be good for her. I'd like to have someone to travel with, too."

I hadn't thought through that last part until just now, but realized it was also true. I'd never traveled by myself and had only flown once when I was very young. Though I couldn't remember much about it, it wasn't something I looked forward to. I hadn't put much thought into *how* I'd get out there, but having someone to travel with seemed like an excellent idea.

"Fiona was just telling me about how Robin spends time with her mother every summer. Something about the terms of Fiona's guardianship. I don't know, it sounded a bit vague and strange to me. But apparently it's not something Robin looks forward to." Mom looked concerned.

"So maybe she could spend a week or two with me first." If there was any way to make it happen, I was going to try.

Mom and Dad looked at each other. Mom seemed very uncertain and Dad was still frowning, but neither seemed inclined to immediately shut the idea down. That was encouraging.

"We'll need to talk about it and talk to Isabel and Fiona." Then Mom's expression softened and she said, "We'll see what we can do."

Finals and my projected scheme of spending the summer in Colorado with Isabel kept my mind occupied the next day and beyond, though the same concerns that had plagued me before still crept through too. I remained purposely aloof at school and acutely conscious of *not* making eye contact with anyone, even Robin and Dave.

Dave stayed close. *Too* close. I wouldn't have minded except that he seemed concerned all the time. I didn't want to be the cause of that concern and didn't want to be reminded about the incidents I was trying to forget. It just made my existence that much harder. Was I ever going to be allowed to just *be?*

Dave mentioned Senior graduation and said he and his family would be going on Thursday. He asked if I wanted to go with them. I didn't immediately make the connection that it was Cris, of course, that they were going for. I only remembered what eighth-grade graduation was like and wasn't sure I wanted to go. I told him I didn't know. He didn't ask again.

The highlight of that week was my lesson with Melanie. As well as just working on my basic seat and aids for my upcoming tests, we worked on lateral movement and Kitty was so responsive it made me feel extremely successful. We were doing shoulder-ins, which Kitty was an old pro at, of course, but Melanie said my hands were perfect and my seat and legs very good. Kitty understood what I was asking for and obliged without much misunderstanding.

By Thursday evening, my parents had discussed my request between themselves and then with Isabel. They still hadn't agreed, but they were looking into the logistics of it. They said I could mention it to Robin and see how she felt but not to set my heart on it. I was trying not to, but it was really too late for that.

On Friday morning Dave was waiting for me at school, as had become usual. He waved to my dad. I didn't see if Dad waved back, but there seemed to be tolerance there if not enthusiastic friendliness and trust.

I tried my news out on Dave. I wasn't sure how Robin would respond.

"I think I'm going to stay with Isabel this summer."

Dave searched my face. He also now held my hand. "You *want* to do that, right?"

"Yes! Dad's going to South America. Mom wants to go to Los Angeles, but I don't."

"Maybe you should come to Spain with me instead." He squeezed my hand and his playful expression should have been enough to make me blush, but it didn't.

"I really want to visit Isabel and help her. And she'll coach me, especially with jumping. That's what I really want to do." It felt so good to tell him the truth about everything.

Dave nodded but didn't say anything as we reached my Chemistry classroom. I suddenly remembered about Cris and gasped.

"What?" said Dave, frowning.

"Last night. Graduation. I forgot!" I felt a sense of loss I couldn't explain. *I should have gone!*

"It's okay. It was pretty boring, except for Cris' speech."

"Speech?"

"Yeah. He was one of the Valedictorians, you know, with the highest GPA, and he had to give a speech."

"Oh," I said, feeling even worse. "I would have liked to hear it."

"It was good. You know, 'Work hard. Play harder. Don't give up on your dreams. Find people that make you a better person.' That kind of stuff."

Matthew approached at that moment from the opposite direction. The guys said, "Hey," to each other, but it didn't feel as friendly as it should have. I still didn't know if the tension between them was because of Dave's now public relationship with me or just because of me, but it made me feel horrible.

I'm not retarded!

Matthew glanced at me before walking into the room. I gently pulled my hand free of Dave's.

"Part one of Chem final," I said.

He tried to look sympathetic but failed. "You'll do great!"

Very sweet. Totally unrealistic.

"See you at lunch," he said.

I nodded and went into the room.

I had spent quite a bit of time copying out the periodic table with color codes and everything—if I could picture something, notice patterns, and make associations, I could usually remember it—so I probably did pretty well on that. But I still didn't understand most chemical properties, and formulas were as abstract and elusive to me as those of algebra. I wasn't going to worry about that, though.

Matthew wasn't close enough to talk to today, but once I'd entered the classroom he seemed to completely ignore me anyway. I was mostly worried about Robin. Would she like my plan? My trip didn't depend on her coming, but now I really wanted her to.

I couldn't talk to her in History—I had to concentrate on remembering dates and names, one of the hardest things for me—and I didn't want to distract her either. But as we walked toward the choir room at lunch, I said, "I think I'm going to Colorado this summer."

I watched her closely, but she didn't betray any strong emotion.

"That's where Isabel lives, right?"

"Yes. She invited me when she was here, and I really want to go. Mom's going to LA, but I don't want to."

This time there was a definite change in her expression and even the color of her face. She looked a little sick. "I don't want to go there either," she said softly.

"So you should come with me! Even if it's just for a week. Isabel wants you to come. My parents are talking about it. What do you think?"

Robin had stopped, now staring at me and looking even paler. "I can't go, Allie. I just *can't*."

She looked stricken and I felt terrible, as if I'd asked her to do something critical but impossible for *my* sake. That certainly wasn't my intention.

"Can't go?" Dave said. He joined us in the corridor.

"I was hoping Robin could go to Colorado with me for at least a week." Dave looked at her.

"I . . . I *have* to go to Santa Ana. You *know* that," she said, looking back at Dave. Her tone was pleading and it hurt to hear it. "And I can't . . . *won't* leave Gran any longer than necessary. I can't bear to."

This hurt even more. I felt so bad; she was obviously worried about so much. I wished I'd never thought of it. I wanted to say I understood, but I knew I didn't. I did feel for her, though, and my eyes burned.

Dave didn't say anything more about it but looked thoughtful throughout lunch.

Dave said he wanted to come over on the weekend, but he was very busy and so was I—he with work at home and with Tom, and me riding Kitty at Northfield both days. We only had one more week of school, then he'd be leaving for Spain the following Monday. I wasn't sure how I felt about that and wasn't allowing myself to think about it too much. But apparently Mom was. She suggested I invite him to dinner on Sunday. So I did.

He'd eaten with us many times before, of course, but this was different. I didn't realize *how* different until he came over, a little earlier than I expected. He'd obviously showered and was, for him, dressed up. I was out riding Remmy in the arena, practicing my tests. Again. I'd been to Northfield in the morning and hadn't bothered to change yet. I certainly hadn't showered.

I assumed he'd parked in the driveway, too. He usually parked down by the side of the house. Now he came through the back door from the kitchen looking so handsome I halted Remmy and just watched him walk toward the fence. I walked Remmy over to meet him.

"Hi," I said, feeling suddenly shy and a little embarrassed. I guessed an advance invitation for dinner on Sunday was different than impromptu midweek ones. "You look nice."

His smile slid sideways. "So do you."

"Um . . . I wasn't . . . I didn't . . ."

The truth was, I hadn't been thinking about his coming over at all. *Bad girlfriend!*

He frowned, probably trying to figure out what I wasn't saying.

"I'd better get cleaned up," I said, beginning to dismount.

"Don't," he said.

I searched his face, looking for any trace of disappointment or aversion. But he still had that crooked smile. And his eyes. . . . No, it wasn't disappointment.

"Show me," he said.

I nodded and pointed to my clipboard on a nearby post. "We're practicing Test 2 right now."

He reached for the clipboard and nodded.

I circled Remmy once around the arena at a trot before coming down centerline. For the next few minutes, I focused on Remmy and the memorized diagram and movement order.

When we finished, halting and saluting Dave as if he were a judge, he whistled and clapped enthusiastically. My cheeks burned but I was thrilled too. Not only had Remmy and I performed the test extremely well, I hadn't cared that someone—especially someone as important to me as Dave—had been watching. It just wasn't an issue. That was an incredibly liberating and empowering feeling.

I walked Remmy back to Dave on a long rein, patting his neck. Dave opened the gate and watched as I dismounted.

"That was terrific," he said softly. "I never would have thought of Remmy doing a dressage test."

"I think he likes it. He likes being made to think," I said.

We got Remmy unsaddled, brushed, and settled with his dinner. Then we both took our boots off at the back door and went to the kitchen sink to wash up. Dave's new black jeans were dusty and there was a tell-tale streak of slobber on his nice striped shirt. That made me smile.

"What?" he asked suspiciously.

"Nothing," I said, not trying to conceal that there *was* something. But I figured I now didn't have to worry too much about my own appearance.

"So, how's work with Tom going?" Dad asked when we'd sat down and started dinner. "Is he keeping you busy?"

Dad's tone was light and didn't sound forced or fake *or* patronizing. He appeared to be genuinely interested. *More progress!*

Dave smiled widely. "Yeah, he keeps me pretty busy. But with Cris leaving in a few weeks, I'll be doing a lot more at home. So I'm hoping I can still work for Tom next year . . . that I won't be too busy. He's really taught me a lot."

Dad nodded and seemed very satisfied with his reply and the work ethic it reflected. He asked what kinds of things they'd worked on, which Dave enthusiastically described.

Mom and I listened with interest and it occurred to me that this meal, conversation, and general atmosphere of acceptance seemed to confirm another new status between Dave and me. I just wasn't exactly sure what it was.

And I only partly listened, thinking about many other things. Primary among them was worry about Robin. A very close second was still wondering whether Dave secretly thought I was less capable than I was.

Time crawled by during the last week of school, every moment there dragging out and seeming an eternity. I felt worn thin from trying so hard to approximate normal for the sake of my friends and trying to be invisible to everyone else. It felt like I spent every day laying low, refusing to speak or make eye contact at all. I was just so tired of the whole struggle. It hurt that people—at least, people in general—thought I was in some way *less* than them. It made me sad and even angry that I was made to feel this way. Unacceptable. Alien. Even stupid.

But I knew I wasn't. I might struggle with remembering how to do some things that weren't vital to me—dates and formulas and information that didn't take root deeply enough—but I was great at other things. Patterns and puzzles. Words. Art. Music. And, apparently, animals. Although my grade in Biology had been mediocre last year, I'd actually aced most of the animal components. I just wasn't interested in plants and found it more challenging to retain that information.

These were thoughts that prevailed and confused me most of the week and during my remaining exams. I hadn't requested to take my exams in the library, but I was always one of the last still working on them.

The time outside of school went by satisfyingly fast. Choir was over, so there was no need to stay after school anymore. I was a little relieved. Although I'd mostly enjoyed the class, it was that much less time I had to force normal now, and one less thing on my schedule. That gave me more time to ride Kitty at Northfield as well as Remmy at home. I now actually felt more at home on horseback than off.

Roger had bought a brand new truck and gave Melanie the old blue Mercedes, so she was able to drive herself to school, and I rode back to Northfield with her more often. Dad detoured to pick me up on his way home from work and always seemed happy for me to be there. I tried not to think too deeply about why. I was just glad to stay busy with the horses. Dad was working late most of the time, but I didn't mind at all.

Paola came out with us a couple of times, too, just to hang out.

At first I wasn't sure how I felt about that. I had loved the relatively calm, quiet drives to Northfield with just Roger, Melanie, and me. But I didn't feel under any pressure to talk or act in any specific way around either Melanie or Paola, and once at Northfield, I could get lost in the peaceful rhythm of the barns and grounds.

Just being on Kitty's back was therapeutic, and the physical and mental exertion of practicing my tests and sometimes working over *cavaletti* and very low cross rails helped even more. By the end of the week, Paola had her first riding lesson. It was fun to watch her learn and have that to share with her now. I usually went home feeling exhausted but happy and peaceful.

The rest of my time was spent with Remmy and Violet. The evenings were long, so I usually rode Remmy after dinner. I mixed things up, riding English and practicing dressage tests one day, then riding Western and setting poles out on the ground in various configurations the next. Sometimes I just rode him bareback around the property, hopping over fallen branches and the stream, which was only a couple of feet wide now.

At school, I had gathered signatures in my yearbook—not as many as last year, perhaps, but each one counted as a real friend and important to

me. That's all I really cared about. I made Dave promise not to deface his picture like he did last year. He said he'd write in it later, after everyone else.

He still stayed close—meeting me in the mornings, at lunch and, however briefly, after school. Many evenings he turned up at my house, though he usually didn't stay long. I wasn't sure what to think. *Is this normal boyfriend behavior?* I had no way of knowing.

It almost felt like he was hovering, worse than my parents ever had, and I had very mixed feelings about it. On the one hand, it left me with no doubts about whether he really cared about me, though I hadn't doubted for quite a while now. And I always loved seeing him, of course. But on the other, it didn't help my feelings of separation from what felt "normal" to me. It also didn't help that he seemed unusually moody—not quite his carefree, confident self. In fact, it had been more and more noticeable as the week progressed. I wasn't even sure when it started. A week ago? Two? More?

There was only one thing I could think of that had changed in that time. The thought left me sad and a little anxious.

I'm not *retarded!*

After school on the last day, instead of hanging out as I'd hoped, everyone went their separate ways. Robin, Dave, and Tanner had work. Robin had driven her car to school because she'd be working late. I had no clue what Matthew was doing; he didn't talk to me much these days. I didn't even have the option of going to Northfield since I'd told Melanie I was probably hanging out and she'd already left. I was so rarely completely alone these days, I should have been glad, but I felt oddly forlorn and extremely exposed walking toward the pool.

"Hey!" I heard behind me. Ben ran to catch up. "I haven't seen you all week," he said. "Except, you know, at school."

I tried to smile as we continued together. "Oh . . . I've been going with Melanie a lot . . . Northfield . . ."

"Riding," he finished the sequence.

"Yes. I have a big show in a week. It's really important to me."

"Yeah, I think I heard you talking about that. Can I go?"

"*You* want to go? To a *horse* show? You do realize there are *horses* at horse shows? Lots of them?"

He shrugged. "It'll beat sitting around being bored. Besides," he frowned, "I'm gonna miss you. You're going away one way or another. Right?"

I nodded but was diverted. "You'll miss me?"

"Of course. Won't you miss me?" He looked comically dismayed and overdramatically clutched his chest. "You are such a cruel lover."

"And you've been *very* fickle. You never even come over anymore." I hadn't really thought about it before now, but it was true.

"Yeah, well, you have company a lot these days." He shook his head with a resigned expression. "I'm being the better man by not getting in the way."

"Right," I said, laughing. "And what happened to all those phone numbers you got at the dance?"

He grinned impishly. "I saved them, of course. I always have someone to at least *talk* to now. I bet I could tell you every piece of gossip at our school: who's going with who, who *wants* to go with who, the best place to get your nails done—you know, *important* stuff."

I laughed then frowned. I wasn't sure I really wanted to know but couldn't stop myself. "Do you hear anything about me? You know, about what happened . . . before?"

He was quiet for a moment, then said, "You're my friend. And Dave is, well, *Dave*. I don't talk about you guys, except maybe to agree that Dave's ho—" he comically cleared his throat and lowered the pitch of his voice, "a great guy. But if I ever hear something I think you should know, I'll tell you. Okay?"

That was hardly comforting, but maybe he was right. Not knowing was safer.

It was a hot day and we decided to go to the coffee shop for iced drinks. We left our backpacks with Mom at the pool and took her order for a mocha *frappuccino*. It felt good to keep moving, and Ben's company was just what I needed to keep from moping and overanalyzing current concerns. I was thrilled that school was now officially out but felt uneasy and moody too. I just didn't know why.

Mom invited Ben to stay for dinner. He looked at me, seeking permission, I suppose. I nodded but felt sorry again that he thought it necessary. When we got back to my house, Ben and I went straight out to the stable. I fed Remmy first, then went to grab brushes.

"When did you get those?" called Ben.

Curious, I joined him by the arena. The difference didn't strike me at first, and I wondered if he meant my cardboard signs. Then I saw them.

Just under the fence, beneath each of my makeshift signs, were wooden squares painted white on all four sides with neat black letters large enough to be seen easily from anywhere in the arena. *Real dressage court letters!*

I opened the arena gate and walked into the center, turning to look at each one. "I don't know," I breathed. *Were they here yesterday?* I couldn't be sure. Remmy and I hadn't gone into the arena. More importantly, who put them there? *Dad? Dave?*

I gave Remmy a good brush and we returned to the kitchen. I said to Mom, "There are court letters in the arena. *Real* ones. Who put them there?"

Mom looked confused. She knew what court letters were as she'd helped me staple my cardboard signs to the fence posts, but she obviously didn't know where these had come from. She wiped her hands on a towel and went outside. We followed.

"I have no idea," she said. "They're very nice, aren't they? It looks like someone made them for you."

Indeed it did.

Chapter Thirty-Six

On Saturday morning it hit me hard that, not only was it finally summer vacation, but Dave would be leaving. *Soon!* My feelings were very complicated concerning that: uneasy about the long separation from him but unsure why. Would I miss him? *Of course!* At least, I assumed I would. I'd missed him last summer.

And yet I was looking forward to getting away from everybody too, including Dave. That made me feel a little guilty and unhappy. I wanted to be the girlfriend Dave needed and wanted me to be. I just really didn't understand what that entailed.

Part of me wanted to go to Northfield today, as much to practice in the actual dressage courts as to ride Kitty. Familiarity with my surroundings usually mitigated anxiety. I wasn't feeling anxious yet, but I knew that could change, especially on the day of the show.

But I hadn't heard from Dave since the day before, at school. I didn't want to miss any chance I had of seeing him before he and his family left for Spain.

I had also hoped for a last minute beach trip, like last year; a chance to relax and just enjoy being together, especially with his whole family. After all his hovering, it felt weird that he hadn't come over. I wasn't sure whether to call or text. Even though he really was my boyfriend now, I still didn't want to bug him. I didn't want to seem needy.

Late Saturday afternoon, he called.

"Sorry I didn't call before. We've been pretty busy here, making sure the house is clean and ready to be locked up while we're all gone. Tomorrow we've got a lot of stuff to do, too."

He was quiet for a moment and I wasn't sure what to say. I half hoped I'd be invited over to help with the "stuff" and half hoped I wouldn't. "So, you'll be busy all day?" I hoped it wasn't the wrong thing to ask and tried to say it without strong inflection.

"Yeah. Maybe. I don't know. I think most things are taken care of around the place, but we want to make sure Miguel doesn't have too much to worry about while we're gone. Just the horses and taking care of any emergencies that come up. Brad and the other guys'll take care of everything else. They're all gonna keep an eye on Fiona while Robin's gone.

"Hey, I wanted to thank you . . . for inviting Robin to go with you. I think we've convinced her that Fiona will be all right for the extra week. I know she hates leaving her. But I think you're right, too. I guess she really hasn't been herself lately, so I'm glad she can take the trip with you. I hope it does her good."

"I hope so, too."

"I'll come over later if I can. Okay?"

"Okay," I said, trying to sound positive and happy but, honestly, I didn't have a clue how I felt about anything lately. "Oh! I almost forgot to ask . . . did you bring over court letters for my arena?"

"Court letters?"

"You know . . . the markers for dressage."

"Yeah, I know what you mean but . . ." He paused, then said, "Cris must have brought them."

"Cris?" I was flabbergasted. "*Cris* made them?"

"We both worked on them. I told him about your cardboard signs, and he said the same thing I'd thought—that they'd be ruined as soon as it rained. So he suggested we make you some. He must have finished them and brought them over so we wouldn't forget. Like I said, it's been a little crazy over here."

These statements seemed strange to me, and I felt like saying, "*Cris?*" again but didn't. Instead I just said, "Thank you," with as much feeling as I could. Unfortunately, it came out sounding rather husky.

"Are you all right?"

"Yes." I tried to sound bright and positive again, but that's not how I felt.

"They're all right, aren't they? We didn't have a lot of time, so we can probably make them better later."

"No, they're fine . . . they're wonderful! Thank you so much!"

"You're welcome. I'll try to see you later, but I'll definitely see you tomorrow. Okay?"

"Yes!" I replied, still trying to sound upbeat because I knew he'd want me to be.

Later that day, Mom asked about Dave. She knew they were leaving on Monday and seemed surprised he hadn't been over since Thursday. I told her what he'd said, and she suggested I invite him to dinner again on Sunday. So I called him back and did.

"Yeah, that'd be great," he said. But I couldn't tell how he really felt about it.

Shortly after calling him, I got a call from Robin. "I think I can go . . . to Colorado." I couldn't tell how she really felt about this either. She didn't sound despondent, but hardly excited.

"Really? That's great!" I didn't hide my true feelings at all.

"Yeah, just for a week. Gali'll go to the Caldera's like he usually does. He'll just get a longer vacation. Miguel says he'll put a little cow work on him. Gali'll like that. And Cris said he and Miguel and Brad will make sure Gran is okay."

It didn't strike me as odd until later that she'd mentioned Cris. I was too excited about the proposed trip. *We're both going to Colorado!* "I'm so happy! I can't wait!"

"Do you know when we're going exactly?"

I confessed I didn't. We'd been waiting to see if she could come and hadn't made firm plans.

"It's just . . . I'll have to go straight from there to LA. I'll need to arrange for that."

"To your . . . aunt's?" I asked, hoping she'd explain.

"Yeah," she said, but hesitantly, as if not sure whether to tell me more. She might not know that I'd heard her mom mentioned. "Yeah, anyway . . . Gran's going to work all that out with your parents, I guess. The Calderas said they'd help with the ticket."

I knew even saying that had cost Robin something. I really hadn't thought about the extra expenses, though I was sure my parents would have paid her way.

On Sunday I stayed home. I figured Kitty deserved a real break from me, and my parents deserved a break from driving me all the way out to Northfield. I also wanted to make sure I had plenty of time to clean up and dress decently for dinner. It would be the last time I'd see Dave for a long while and I didn't want to get caught wearing barn clothes and smelling of horses again. I was a bit nervous, and left myself tons of time to shower and get ready as if it were some big important date like Winter Formal.

But earlier in the day I relaxed with Remmy. We spent part of it playing at liberty inside the arena; not doing anything specific but enjoying each other's company. Later I rode him bareback down to the stream and let him splash to his heart's content. It was an absolutely gorgeous day, and I felt happier and more hopeful in general than I had for months.

I was glad I'd taken time to bathe and dress up a little bit as Dave had again, too. My nervousness was back, and I felt unaccountably shy as he sat down to watch TV with Dad. I said I'd be right back and started up the stairs to my room in search of Violet. I figured holding her would make me feel less nervous.

Then I heard someone behind me. *Dave.*

He followed me into my room and immediately reached for Violet in the middle of my bed, just where I thought she'd be. He sat down, lifting her into his lap, and looked around as if seeing my room for the first time. He'd only been in it once before, and that had been a terrible day. Perhaps he'd been as preoccupied as I had. His presence there now didn't help me feel any less shy, but he seemed supremely unconscious of any awkwardness, as usual. It was one of the things I liked most about him.

"Is your room always this neat?" he asked, frowning slightly. "Where's all your stuff?"

That made me squirm. The reasons I kept my room so neat were complicated. I certainly didn't want to own up to anything I perceived as a weakness right now, so I kept the answer simple. "I just prefer it this way. There's stuff in my closet—"

He narrowed his eyes at me and got up right away to verify my words. That gave me a stab of panic, wondering what would meet his eyes when he opened the door. It was my habit to shove things in there until I couldn't close it. My closet is wide with two sliding doors; luckily he chose the side that stays relatively neat, the clothes side. He stuck his head in and looked toward the unopened side but thankfully didn't open that door.

"Hnh," seemed to sum up his feelings about that. "Where's your yearbook?"

I looked around my room, trying to remember where I'd last had it. Then I remembered. Trying not to blush, I reached for it under the far side of my bed. The only decent pictures I had of him were in that book and, yes, maybe I sometimes gazed at them before falling asleep. I certainly wasn't going to admit that to him, though. He traded Violet for the yearbook and sat back down on my bed.

"Hey, do you still have any pictures? The one I had disappeared."

That struck me as strange, but I couldn't immediately decide why. I opened a drawer in my desk and gave him one of the many remaining photos.

"Pen?" he asked.

I found him one.

"This is going to take a minute."

"Do you want me to leave?"

He shrugged and acted as if he was thinking about what to write in the back of the book. I felt awkward again and oddly unnecessary, so I left him there and carried Violet back downstairs with me. Dave rejoined us after barely a minute, completely unperturbed, but I felt Dad watching us both more closely than usual. I kept my hands busy in Violet's fur.

Conversation at dinner was mostly about our various projected trips: Dad to several South American countries, Dave to Spain, me to Colorado, and Mom to Los Angeles. Mom stated she was going to fly with us to Colorado first, spend a week at Isabel's, and then go on to Los Angeles with Robin. That was news to me but didn't concern me too much. I wasn't yet thinking about details.

Dave would be away for about four weeks, and that's what my plan was, too, though I'd be home a week later than him. It would still leave us a little vacation time together before school started.

Mom planned to be gone for a maximum of three weeks, one way or another. Though I knew she wouldn't be looking forward to being at home alone after that, she had previously declared her intention of spending time with Fiona, which I was sure swayed Robin's decision to go with me. She said she could also fill in at the pool if they needed her.

Cris wasn't going to Spain, which should have occurred to me earlier due to things I'd heard but not fully comprehended. He'd remain in Douglas for the first week and a half after his family left, then he'd go to Los Angeles, settling into his dorm and athletic program at UCLA.

Dave didn't stay long after dinner as they were leaving early in the morning. It was still light and we went outside so that he could "say goodbye to Remmy," but he didn't pay much attention to Remmy at all. Remmy was still eating when we entered his stall. Dave immediately pulled me into a close embrace and I completely relaxed into it, shyness and awkwardness temporarily forgotten. He held me like that for what seemed a lovely long time. Remmy's munching, his occasional movement, and birds calling to each other outside were the only sounds.

After a while, Dave said softly against my hair, "I'm going to miss you," and held me a little tighter.

I held him tighter back but didn't reply. Part of me just didn't want to talk, completely wrapped up in the delicious feeling of holding and being held by him. And, while it had briefly occurred to me before now that of course I would miss him, I hadn't spent much time actually thinking about that particular aspect of our separate trips. Right now, it was easy to imagine missing the *feel* of him, the warm comfort of the way he felt and smelled, and the sound of his voice. But it was also easy to imagine remaining in his arms like this forever, so I couldn't feel sad.

Eventually, Dave pulled away slightly to look into my eyes. I looked back and fell easily into him again when he kissed me; a long, lingering kiss. What a different parting to the much more platonic goodbye we'd shared last year. There was nothing platonic about this one.

He finally broke the kiss, hugged me again, and said, "I'd better go. I should help get Stevie and Henry packed and ready too. I'll try to be in touch, though, if I can."

I smiled and nodded, still warm and tingly.

"Try to send me pictures . . . show me what's going on. Okay? I'll try to send some too, but I'm not sure if I can."

I nodded again.

He backed slowly away from me and left the stall. I listened to his retreating footsteps and heard him reenter the house, probably to say goodbye to my parents. But I stayed with Remmy, replacing one embrace for another less physically reciprocated one. I was sure to miss Dave—how could I not? But I *knew* I'd miss Remmy.

When I went back to my room, I found my yearbook resting upright against my pillow. I got ready for bed quickly, then lit what remained of one of my candles and turned the book to the back page. A folded piece of paper fell out. My heart beat a little faster on seeing a note written in Dave's uneven print on the back inside cover.

Can't wait to spend Junior year with you!

Dave

I opened the folded paper. I read the paragraph once, then read it again. Then I realized he must have written it before even coming tonight, so I read it another couple of times, marveling more each time.

Thrilled, embarrassed, guilty, and very moved in about equal measure, I doubted I'd be able to sleep at all, but I must have.

Monday morning, I awoke late and felt a stab, no, more like a slash of anxiety until I remembered there was no school. The relief was immense. Then I also remembered Dave was leaving today, was probably already in the air. I reached for my phone and saw he'd sent a picture: him, Henry, and Stevie sitting together on a plane. Dave was smiling widely. Henry was making a monster face. Stevie, sitting between them, smiled slightly, his gaze low, his hand raised and blurry.

I smiled hugely and jumped out of bed, disturbing Violet who wasn't as excited to start her day. I grabbed my yearbook from where it had fallen to the floor and reread Dave's note. Then I replaced it in the book, made my bed, and stuffed the book under my pillow. I began to throw on barn-dirty clothes but stopped and found a clean shirt. I washed my face and brushed my teeth and hair, then ran down the stairs and out to Remmy with my phone. He was anxious for his breakfast, of course, but I managed to get him to pose with me before feeding him. I sent the picture in reply to Dave's.

I fed Remmy and hung around outside for quite a while hoping for—no, *expecting*—a response. I finally gave up and went in to change again. Mom was going to drive me out to Northfield before she went to work, and Melanie said she could drive me back to Douglas before Mom was done.

I had hoped to have a text back from Dave, but there was nothing. Maybe he couldn't text from Spain.

I still tried to text him, but didn't have much to text about as my daily life was pretty much the same. I was either at home with Remmy and Violet, or riding at Northfield. I had Melanie take a cute picture of Paola and me, both on horseback, and sent it, hoping that he'd get it. But I was hesitant to send more from Northfield knowing his feelings about the place.

Melanie suggested I spend the night on Friday, the day before the big dressage show, and I gladly accepted. We stayed rather late at the stables. I'd ridden Kitty, of course, then bathed her and walked her until she was dry. Then I wrapped her legs lightly to keep her pretty white socks clean. Melanie had given lessons all afternoon and early evening, so when she was done, I helped by getting Digs ready for the next day while she worked on Beau.

We were both famished by the time all three horses were dry and wrapped and tucked into their stalls with full hay racks for the night. Melanie drove us over to the shopping center to get sandwiches, and we got back to her home around nine o'clock.

We needed to go to sleep right away because we'd be getting up early, and I assumed there wouldn't be time for much talking. Mrs. Teodorescu brought out a comforter, a sheet, and a pillow and asked if I wanted her to make the couch up, but I said that I could do it. She retired for the night and I assumed we would too, but Melanie lingered, sitting nearby, watching me spread the sheet on the sofa then cover it with the comforter.

"Are you excited about going to Colorado?" she asked, her voice lowered.

I considered that. I wasn't sure *excited* was the right word. I was *happy* about it. "I'm looking forward to it," I answered, matching her quiet tone. "But I'm trying not to think about it too much. Kind of like this show. I really want to do it, but if I think too much about it, I get really nervous and start doubting if it's a good idea."

Melanie smiled. "I guess I can understand that. I've never been to Colorado, but I used to want to go. I've hardly ever been out of California. Just a couple of times with Roger and his family for shows in Nevada, but other than that. . . ." She shook her head. "We don't travel. Mom doesn't like to take time off and she hates to spend money." Melanie frowned and looked concerned. "Not that she's stingy or anything. She just saves as much as she can. She doesn't want to live and work here forever."

I remembered her mentioning something about it before and nodded. Since she seemed to be in the mood for confidences, I dared to ask something I'd wondered about for a long time. "Why are you a sophomore instead of a junior?"

Melanie looked surprised, I suppose at the change in subject, though in my mind everything about Melanie was interconnected. "Did I tell you I almost died when I was eight? I was in the hospital for two months in an oxygen tent. My lungs were so weak, they were afraid I'd get pneumonia, which would have killed me. When I was released, I did school at home for most of the rest of that year to avoid infections. Besides my parents and my doctor, Roger was the only other person I saw.

"Then in seventh grade, I contracted mono . . . I have no idea how . . . but my asthma flared up at the same time and I got extremely sick again. This time I was so sick for so long that I just couldn't catch up when I returned to school. So I was held back a year. That's all."

I'd heard of mono before but wasn't sure what it was. But the way she'd said, "That's all," *didn't* sound like it was all. But it was apparently all she was going to say about it.

She asked about Dave and I showed her the picture he'd sent me. "I'm glad you two are together," she said. "He seems like a genuinely great guy."

"He is," I said.

She said goodnight and went to her room, but I lay thinking about everything she'd said, wondering, for quite a while.

I slept surprisingly well—the couch was comfortable, the room quiet, and I guess I was tired enough—and was woken by Melanie shaking my shoulder gently, finger to lips. I'd been dreaming about Gold and Dave and Brenda, but couldn't quite piece it back together enough to remember details

on waking. I got quietly and quickly into my barn clothes, used the bathroom after her, then followed her silently out into the big kitchen.

She grabbed toaster pastries and a few apples on our way through the storage room, which also served as a kind of pantry. Then I followed her out to the car.

The streets were mostly deserted as we drove back through the residential area. In no time we were at the stables, and they weren't deserted at all.

People had begun arriving the night before, but I'd been preoccupied with our own horses and hadn't paid too much attention. Now even more people had come, either later last night or very early this morning. All of the barn areas were full of horses being groomed, lunged, and otherwise readied for the day. The long rows of visitor stalls, usually empty, now had trunks, grooming caddies, and other equine accouterments outside each one that I could see. Every paddock was in use, and there was a growing stream of riders and horses walking back and forth between the barns and show areas.

I tried to concentrate on grooming Kitty, but she was distracted and being difficult. She pawed the ground as I brushed her and was very fussy about her feet. By the time I started plaiting her mane the way Melanie had taught me, I felt a little frazzled, worried about being ready in time to warm her up properly. I had separated her mane into sections the night before, so all I had to do was actually braid and secure them, but with Kitty restless and me seeming extra clumsy, it was taking longer than it should have.

I had finally gotten the hardest ones done, the ones nearest her poll, and was removing the band from the next section when somehow it shot over her neck and into the breezeway beyond. Wondering which would be faster, searching the hay-littered breezeway for it or tracking down Melanie's bag of hairbands, I ducked under Kitty's neck and was brought up short by the sight of a boy bending down to pick something up near his booted foot.

He was dressed for competition, but I recognized him from his unhelmeted blond curls.

Bradley.

"You *almost* got me," he said lightly, as if that had been my intent. "Your aim was just a little off." He had a slight Southern accent.

"I didn't . . . I wouldn't. . . ."

He wasn't smiling—I'd actually never seen him smile—but he didn't look angry either, and I couldn't tell if he was joking or not. The fact that he'd been approaching me, that he was *talking* to me, threw me into something close to panic. I returned to the other side of Kitty, away from him, and struggled to organize my thoughts.

I couldn't help associating him with Dillon Pryce, the boy I still thought of as Varsity Jacket. But Bradley himself, apart from gently pushing me into Dillon's arms that one day, had never done anything to harm me. Still, I certainly didn't trust him.

"You know, the needle and thread method is much better. Makes them more stable and look neater." He walked around Kitty and examined my handiwork so far. He held the tiny hair elastic out to me. "I could show you sometime. If you want."

What the heck is this? His voice was soft and expressive in spite of his bland facial expression. But I wasn't buying it.

"That's okay. My friend can show me."

"Mel," he said, nodding his head. "She's a great trainer. You're lucky to have her."

"I know," I said, wishing he'd go away.

"Have some great rides today," he said, and walked away.

Relieved but shaking slightly, I finished braiding Kitty's mane, put polish on her hooves, then tied her back in her stall while I went to change. I tried to recapture the confidence I'd felt earlier; I had felt *good* about this and looked forward to my parents seeing me ride Kitty in a competition, especially my dad.

I warmed Kitty up in one of the paddocks and then rode toward the showgrounds, watching for my parents and Ben. I found them and directed them to the court I'd be riding in, then waited to be called.

My first test didn't go terribly well. I had so much on my mind and still felt a little frazzled after the interaction with Bradley. Plus, I knew I'd been tense while warming Kitty up and she was very sensitive to that. So I didn't ride as well as I could have—bouncing unbecomingly during the change of rein and forgetting to keep my eyes up; rookie mistakes—and Kitty responded accordingly, I'm sure just to teach me a lesson. I didn't even want to know what my score was and hoped the judges would be different for my second test. I felt terrible that my parents and Ben had come all the way out there to see me ride so badly.

I walked Kitty straight back toward the barns and entered one of the paddocks, the one with the fewest other riders in it. I walked her on a long rein for quite a while, letting her relax and stretch as I ordered my mind, trying to forget about Bradley and whatever his motives were, and even to avoid, at least for now, thinking about Dave.

After a while, I gathered the reins and rode Kitty into the paddock with *cavaletti*, jumping her slowly until it felt like we both were more relaxed and happy. Then I walked her back to the barn, wiped her face, neck, and legs with a towel, then mounted and walked her back to the arenas to wait for our next test.

This time I stayed calm and focused, not looking at anything but the direction we were going, and concentrating on Kitty's movement beneath me and communicating with her clearly. She remained calm and steady, her responses immediate and her movements smooth. After the final salute, I walked her out on a long rein, stroking her neck and thanking her.

Melanie waited beyond the court exit and she was beaming. "Allison! Well done!"

Her praise meant everything to me, and I know I blushed but it was okay. I swung my leg over Kitty's back and hopped down.

"I did much better this time," I said, as I knew she'd watched the first test.

Tatty walked nearby on her way somewhere. She winked at me and nodded. That meant almost as much to me as Melanie's approval.

"We'll start work on your 'C' test next, but you'll do fine with it. We can start dressage training level in the fall," said Melanie.

I just nodded. I couldn't think beyond this moment: the sun shining, the gaily colored flags nearby flipping and flapping in the breeze, one of the people I admired most so pleased with me, my parents and Ben walking toward me with smiles on their faces. And somewhere in southern Spain, the boy I loved. I wondered if he was having a good day too, with the sun shining and the breeze blowing.

"Ben, do you have your phone?" I asked him.

He dug it out of his pocket and held it up.

"Take a picture of Kitty and me?"

He grinned and obliged. "You need to smile," he said.

I wished he hadn't said that as it just made it more difficult.

"Never mind," he said, waving a hand. "Just be you."

"Thank you," I said. But the picture he took captured a smile anyway. The kind that Dave said he liked.

I wanted to stay and watch the upper-level tests, especially Melanie riding Digs, so Mom gave Ben and me some money for lunch. My parents were going to get lunch nearby and then come back for us. Ben walked with Kitty and me to the barn and watched as I unsaddled and settled her in her stall. I took my jacket and helmet off and left them in the office. Then we walked back to get something to eat and watch the more experienced riders.

Melanie and Digs were inspiring, as were the other riders. They made every movement look so effortless—the extended and collected trots, the changing leads, the lateral movements. I loved it. I don't think Ben understood the complexity or difficulty of what we watched, but he seemed to enjoy just being there immensely.

Later, Ben sent the picture he'd taken to my phone and I sent it to Dave. 'We did really well in our second test. Second out of twelve!' Our first score had been abysmal, but I didn't want to say that.

Confidence restored, future accomplishments within sight, and physically exhausted, I slept like a log.

In the morning I checked my phone, but the text and photo had not been able to send. Then I noticed the other pictures and texts I thought had sent also hadn't been successful. It looked like it would be a while until I could communicate with Dave again.

The following week was quiet but busy. I went to Northfield four times, sneaking in two lessons with Melanie. I remained watchful for Bradley, but I didn't see him. I also had two lessons with Cheryl at Bar 8 working on improving transitions for western pleasure classes. I babysat for her on Friday night and had hoped Robin could join me, but she was working very early the next morning. In fact, I didn't see her all week. She'd been able to pick up some extra shifts at the bakery, and we never seemed to be at home at the same time.

Ben came out to Northfield with me on one of the days I didn't have a lesson and came over for a couple of evenings. Dad hired him to water the back lawn and flower beds, and to weed while we were gone.

The only other friend I saw before leaving for Colorado was Paola, having her lesson with Melanie. She rode a bay lesson horse and looked so cute in riding clothes. I mentioned something about needing to find a place for Violet while I was on vacation, and she lit up, asking if she could keep her for me. That seemed the perfect solution and made me extremely happy.

I had texted Dave every day but only heard from him twice during the week. Once was a short phone call and then three short texts that might have been sent on different days but all arrived at once.

The Saturday night before we left there was a full moon, and since the skies had been clear for weeks, I remained dressed and expected the gravel against my window.

"So, you're not going anywhere this summer?" I was pretty sure we'd covered this topic, but I felt suddenly awkward and didn't know what else to say.

"No. Bill's not taking any time off. I'm going to try to get a job in town, though. I'm not sure how I'll get there, but I'll never be able to get a car if I don't get a real job. And I think Vivian'll be a lot happier if I get a job."

"Why?"

He shrugged. "She's always nagging me that I'm lazy and pretty soon I'll have to make my own way in the world. I think Bill likes me around, but I'm pretty sure Vivian expects me to move out as soon as I graduate."

"Why?" I asked again, though I suppose if I'd taken the time to think about it, I probably could have guessed.

He shrugged again. "She scolds me in Korean and I don't understand it. I think she'll be a lot happier if I'm working and not at home so much anyway."

I just nodded, scratching around Remmy's ears as we leaned on the paddock fence.

The stable area looked so nice now, even in the moonlight; all proper white fences, giving each stall its own paddock. Those were attached to a common run with a gate that opened into the arena; Dave's clever design.

We talked about unimportant things for a while and then said goodnight. We promised to text during the summer.

Sunday was tranquil, just my parents and me. All three of us used the day to pack for our trips, though I spent most of the morning with Remmy. Mom and I were leaving the next morning. Dad would leave on Tuesday. Tom came over in the afternoon to pick Remmy up for his own little vacation. Tom promised to take great care of him, and I knew he would. After he'd left,

I became restless and a little anxious, and couldn't settle on doing any one thing. So I emptied my suitcase and backpack. And then I packed them again.

Then I called Brenda. I hadn't told her about my trip, so I did.

"Well I guess that sounds . . . great," she said but she obviously didn't think it did.

"When do you leave for Cabo?" I asked.

"Next week," she said, but she didn't sound as excited about it.

"Is everything okay?"

"Yeah," she said, unconvincingly. "My dad's not going though. I was really looking forward to us *all* going. You know?"

"Sure," I said. I could imagine wanting to go somewhere like Cabo with both my mom and dad, but my parents didn't fight like hers did. "I hope you still have a wonderful time," I said sincerely.

"Thanks. You too."

We agreed to catch up later in the summer and said good night.

Our flight was out of Sacramento and it was a long drive, so we were all up very early so Dad could drive us to the airport. Mom had suggested Robin spend the night with us to save a little time, but when I asked her, she looked stricken. I understood and said no more about it.

My growing anxiety was tempered by excitement once she was in the car with us. It seemed like such a huge adventure, to be going on a plane and taking the trip with Robin, even if Mom was coming along. And I was secretly glad she was.

The airport was loud and bright and busy and almost immediately overwhelming. I don't remember saying goodbye to my dad, though I'm sure I must have. I hated the long line to go through security, and then it seemed like we had to wait forever before we could board the plane.

Boarding was a whole other experience. Robin said I should sit next to the window since I hadn't flown before, so I did. But the entire process of boarding and people struggling to get past each other and stowing their stuff overhead and talking and a baby screaming and someone smelling of cigarettes and the weird smell of the plane itself all had my nerves jangling before the engine even started.

I thought the noise of the engines and the air blowers was bad, but when the air pressure started changing I wasn't sure if I could make it. It felt so uncomfortable, though Robin didn't seem affected. She tried to distract me and gave me gum to chew, but it was no good. The flight was something I was just going to have to endure. I was surprised the actual take-off didn't bother me more than it did, but once we were airborne, looking out the window triggered vertigo, so when the seatbelt lights went off, I switched places with Robin.

I might have been second-guessing our mode of transportation, but I was so looking forward to getting away to a place where no one knew me or any of the things that had happened this year. A place where I hoped I could just be myself without worrying about what anyone else thought. A place where I wouldn't be expected to act like someone I wasn't, or think a particular way just because everyone else did.

An hour and a half into the flight—well over halfway—and sharing earbuds with Robin, I sat with eyes closed. We'd been looking through my yearbook, but turbulence caused me to close my eyes and just grit my teeth. I'd been careful to keep the note from Dave hidden in my backpack, but now I held the book close, picturing what he'd written. I'd read it so many times I had it memorized:

> There are so many things I want to say to you, and I don't want you to ever worry about them or forget, so I'm writing them down.
> Never be afraid to ask me for anything or tell me anything.
> Never be afraid to be who you really are around me or my family.
> Never be afraid to say no, to me or anyone else.
> Never doubt how important you are to me. I'd do anything for you.
> Like I told you last year, I will always watch out for you and care for you.
> Always.
> Knowing you and being with you is the best thing that's ever happened to me.
> Dave

The plane continued to buck like one of Dave's broncs. I prayed for safety, and for the turbulence to end soon, but I also prayed my thanks. For everything.

"Are you okay, Allie?" Mom asked.

"Mmmhmm," was all I could say. I wasn't, but I was trying very hard to be.

A little while later, the captain came on the speaker and asked everyone to remain seated as the plane would begin descending. On top of the turbulence, gravity and atmosphere shifted again. Robin was looking out the window and suddenly grabbed my arm.

"Allie, look!" she said, her eyes alight.

I leaned over to look out the window. Through breaks in the clouds, I could see black streaked and blotched with white. Then I realized they were mountains—the Rockies—streaked with snow. Immediate vertigo again. I leaned back in my seat and closed my eyes once more, still holding my yearbook tightly. But I was smiling and excited.

Colorado!

Next in
The Glister Journals
Series

Book 3

*Visit theglisterjournals.com or follow B B Shepherd
for news and updates.*